THE SHEPHERD

BOOK I: IDENTITY

DEVIN ANAVITARTE
STEPHANIE WILCZYNSKI

-God bless you!

Printed in the United States of America

First Printing, 2015

Edited by Gerald Wheeler
Cover art by Makala James
Map by Matthew House

ISBN-13: 978-0-69246-028-3
ISBN-10: 0-692460-28-4

DEDICATION

To Jonny, whose support and encouragement gave a soldier his purpose, a Shepherd her dreams, a Warden his forgiveness, and a farmer his love.

Thank you, Pooter.

AKCNOWLEDGEMENTS

To our families, David and Kathy Anavitarte, Donielle Halvorsen, Lee and Laura Rudisaile, Ray and Brenda Wilczynski, and John Barroso for the love and support, dedication and faithfulness they have provided us since the days we entered this world. For hours reading and loving every word we've written.

To our students Sarah Mizher, John Paul Calixto, and Noah Bishop for living in Oldaem with us for the duration of two school years.

To our friends Nikki Facundo, Ryan Songy, Chantal Williams, and April Chisholm for reading the manuscript in its entirety and begging for more and more.

To Jonathen Blue for the hours he spent helping with the final edit.

To Makala James and Matthew House for their beautiful artwork.

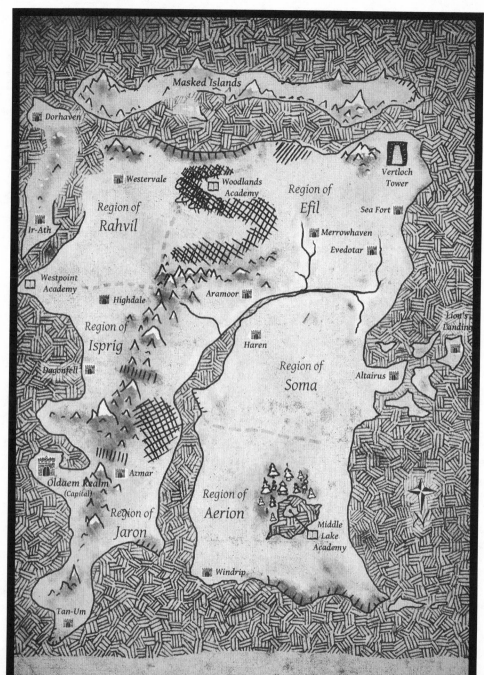

OLDAEM

"Someday Esis will be made whole. Someday we can change. Someday we can be forgiven. Someday we can be together. . . "

-the silver-eyed maiden

PROLOGUE

Their footsteps crunched on the dead leaves scattered across the forest floor. The strong, steady steps came from the older, tallest boy--the one in the lead. Quicker ones that erratically bounced all over the place belonged to the young girl who couldn't wait to find what they were looking for, even though they weren't really searching for anything at all. The final pair of footsteps were somewhat slower and had started to lag behind the farther they travelled into the forest. Those came from the boy who was starting to regret some of the more impulsive decisions he had made in the past few days.

At first it had sounded like a great idea. Get out of the boring town. Go on a real adventure with his two best friends. He and the girl had slipped out of their houses in the middle of the night and into the storage wagon of a caravan that the older boy was leaving with early in the morning. Even when someone caught him the next day suspiciously sneaking food into the storage wagon, their adventure did not get cut short. Because the caravan had travelled far enough that turning around would have created an inconvenient loss of time, those in charge wrote a letter to the worried parents and allowed them to continue on, provided that they didn't cause any trouble. They didn't even have to sleep in the storage wagon anymore. Leaving the town had turned out better than expected.

It was after they had left the caravan that the boy started to have misgivings. He felt that he and his friends were probably testing their luck a little bit too much. And yet, there he was. Aimlessly trekking through a forest that led who knew where, in an area he had never been to, with a guide only two years older than himself.

"Are you sure you know where you're going?" he ventured to ask the boy in the lead.

"Yep," the taller youth smiled without slowing his pace. "Forward."

Somehow that wasn't very reassuring.

He tried again. "It's just, I think it's getting dark, and your dad will probably start wondering where we are ..."

The girl jumped in front of him before he could finish. "It's not getting dark yet, silly! Well at least not because the sun is going down." She looked up. "It's more like the trees are getting closer and closer together the farther we go into the forest and are blocking out more sunlight. In a few more minutes, we probably won't even be able to see each other!" she exclaimed happily and turned around, skipping.

"Is that supposed to sound better? Well, it doesn't." But the boy was mumbling to himself.

The girl had caught up to the leader. "You *do* see how the trees are getting thicker, don't you? It almost looks as if they're all leaning in to tell each other a secret. Or keep a secret. Do you think they're keeping a secret?" Her eyes were full of wonder.

The tall boy smiled down at her. He held her hand as they continued walking. "Of course they are. There are all kinds of secrets in the world. And it's up to us to find them. Out here, who knows? There's probably a secret treasure chest buried in the ground, or the ruins of a lost city, or …"

That's when they ran face-first into the wall.

The younger boy, who had been a few steps behind but lost in thought, was startled to see his two friends bounce off the wall and land on the forest floor. "Ow!" the older boy exclaimed.

The girl was too preoccupied with the fact that there was actually a wall in front of her to acknowledge that she had also run into it. Her eyes were practically popping out of her face. "What is that?" she asked. The wall was high. The younger boy guessed it was probably at least three times taller than his older friend, and it stretched as far as he could see on both sides. Vines grew twisted and tangled all along it. It was unlike any wall the boy had ever seen before. Although it appeared to be made out of stone, instead of one rock piled upon another, it just seemed one solid mass. For a moment, they all just stared. With his former doubts pushed to the back of his mind, the boy was the first to touch the wall. It felt cold and smooth beneath his hand. And somehow old. Very old.

He turned to the older boy. "I guess you weren't kidding about those secrets."

The older boy got up and put his hand on the wall too. "I knew there was something out here," he said in awe. "I could feel it. Couldn't you?"

What the younger boy felt at that moment was an overwhelming curiosity to find out what was behind that wall.

He wasn't the only one. "I bet it's not a wall at all." The young girl led the way as they walked single file, youngest to oldest, left hands on the wall. "I bet that it's a stepping stool for giants!"

The boy in the middle rolled his eyes. "Why would giants need a stepping stool? They're already, uh, giant."

10

"Everyone needs a stepping stool when they're trying to reach the cookie jar their mother placed purposefully on the highest shelf," she scoffed.

"Doesn't explain why they left it outside away from any shelves."

"Well then, what do you think is inside?"

The boy looked thoughtful. "I think it's a prison."

"A prison?" the girl in front and the boy behind said in unison.

"Not just any prison. A prison where they keep all the horrible people, you know, the worst of the worst."

"Any possibility in the world and the best you can come up with is 'prison'?" The girl looked skeptical. "Where's your imagination? We have those at home."

"Well, why else would you need such a big wall other than to keep people in?"

"I think it really is a lost city," the boy behind him said. "But—like--one that's not in ruins, just one that the world's forgot about. Maybe there's a whole civilization of people in there that nobody knows exists."

The girl shook her head. "I don't think it's very easy to lose a whole city. I mean the world is big and all, but there are people all over Oldaem. It's not that easy to hide anywhere."

"Yeah," the younger boy added, "and why build a wall if you're just gonna be stuck behind it forever?"

"Because"--the boy in the back looked at his friends--"a wall like this doesn't get built to keep people in. It gets built to keep them out."

They followed along the wall until their legs started to ache and their stomachs began to growl, but they never found a gate or an entrance or any sign that one might be somewhere up ahead. Finally, the younger boy observed that it was getting dark, and unless they wanted to be stuck there all night, the three of them had better head back to the campsite.

"Wait," said the oldest boy as they were about to turn away from the wall. "We should do something. To prove we've been here. A wall like this, it isn't going anywhere. And if I ever come back here someday, I want to be able to see something I left here."

"Like what?" the girl wondered.

"Let's carve our names into the wall, right here!" It sounded like a splendid idea to the younger explorers, so the oldest boy used his pocketknife to engrave each of their names into the hard surface of

11

the stone wall. As the boy watched, he was certain that their friendship would last as long as the stone wall did.

A few minutes later, as they were walking up a steep hill on the way back to the campsite, the girl lost her balance and tumbled back a few feet. The two boys stopped and looked back at her. "Are you okay?" But the young girl didn't answer. She was staring at something off in the distance. The boys followed her gaze. They couldn't see the wall anymore, but behind it, partially illuminated by the moon, rose a tall Tower.

CHAPTER 1: COLE

Maybe today will be the day. He heard laughter in the dusty street below him. Three little girls were skipping along the pathway, kicking rocks as they went. They didn't even look up at him. Why would they? He was nothing special.

"What are you doing on the roof?"

The question startled him. "Huh?"

"What are you doing on the roof?" the youngest girl said slowly and deliberately.

"Just looking."

"Looking at what?"

"Come on, Edith!"

"Well, I wanna know what he's lookin' at!" Edith said as her companions dragged her away.

"He's weird." They giggled as they disappeared down the hill, and Cole kept staring at the road stretching beneath him. *Maybe today will be the day.*

The breeze stirred around him. The lake always made the wind pick up at this time of morning, right when the sun seemed to settle in for the day. How long had he been up here? His gaze shifted from beyond the road and down the hill to the lake. Along one end was The City of Flowers, his town, the place he had grown up in and had never left except for the couple times he went with his brother Fenris to Windrip. Fenris was a man now. Sixteen years old. Brave, strong, smart, like his dad. The City of Flowers wasn't a big town, but the people in it always seemed busy, and it was all he knew. Everything about it was familiar. When he glanced up into the sky, not a cloud was up there. Perfect blue. The roof was as close to the sky as he could get. *Maybe today will be the day.* Staring across the lake, he could see a boat docking not too far from the hill where his house sat. Probably it was some Shepherd Instructors loading up to go to Middle Lake Academy, located on an island in the middle of the lake. *What a perfect name*, he thought. Perhaps they were returning after a night of some important business he wouldn't understand, or wouldn't be allowed to know about. Shepherds always had secrets like that.

His dad was a Shepherd, a Shepherd of Mind, so he was really smart, not like baby Belen. Belen was just a child, so he was really dumb. It was even dumber that they had to share a room. Fenris had his own room, but his bed was always empty, because his older

13

brother was always gone to Windrip making money for his family since his father had left. Sometimes Cole slept in Fenris' bed, but only sometimes. Fenris would return after being gone for several days telling stories about all the ships he would see coming in from the coast. Cole loved hearing those stories. His brother got to meet amazing people like Shepherds and sailors and priestesses and merchants. But Cole never got to see anyone--only Belen, Arissa, and Lily. Cole watched five people crammed into the one boat and started sailing toward Middle Lake Academy, a small dot he could see far in the center of the lake. The boy felt sorry for the guy stuck in the middle. That was him, the one stuck in the middle--crammed between amazing Fenris, crazy Arissa, annoying Lily, and stupid Belen. No one ever really noticed him up here on his roof. But *he* got to see everyone and everything around him. And he almost felt safe up here. Safe from what? He wasn't sure. Maybe safe from his mother's sobs every night and day, or Arissa trying to put her to sleep, only to hear his sister sobbing later on at night and Lily trying to put her to sleep. Safe from Lily throwing things at him, or Belen always wanting to play with him.

Noticing a huge duck paddling around the lake, he couldn't help but think of Belen at bathtime making a mess everywhere and Arissa screaming at him and Lily cleaning up all the water. *Wait a minute that's not a duck.* Although he couldn't really tell what it was, he saw some people gathering by the water in confusion. He could hear some shouts and even some laughter. *That's a lady. Is she swimming?* Cole stood up to get a better angle. Squinting his eyes and shading them with his hand, he could see what looked like a fully clothed redheaded woman swimming around in a silver evening dress. *Mom.* He watched as what seemed to be Arissa wading in after her and escorting her back to shore as some fat village women wrapped a towel and some blankets around her and sat her down on the rocky shore. Just as Cole shook his head in confusion, an acorn hit him right in the face.

"Hey! Dumb baby! Time for school!"

Cole rubbed his cheek. "Lily, that hurt!"

"We're gonna be late." She bounced up and down. Baby Belen stood by her side, his hand in hers, trying to keep up with his sister.

"I'm coming." He had lost track of time. Cole hated school. It was always the same. Sit. Listen. Sit. Listen. Get yelled at. Play with annoying kids. Sit and listen some more. Heading over to the huge maple tree that grew by the house, he stepped onto the huge branch

14

that spread over his rooftop. It was his favorite tree, perhaps one of the only consistent things in his life. Besides getting hit in the face with things thrown by Lily.

"Gaaaaa looop hi Gaaaaa loop hi!"

"Yes, Belen!" Lily said. "Cole is selfish for making us late! I agree!"

"Lily, Belen isn't talking. He's dumb. He doesn't know how to yet." Cole dropped down from the tree, skinning his knee in the process. "Ouch!" He could feel his sister eying him.

"Are you going to go to school like that?"

"Like what?" He looked down at himself covered in dirt, blood dripping from his knee.

"Never mind."

"I don't care, Lily."

"Yah. I noticed. You look like a frog in a bog."

"Froggy boggy goggy goooo!"

"You tell him, Belen. Come on!" She pulled him up from the dirt he had been digging in and skipped ahead toward the schoolhouse as Belen laughed. Walking to school always felt *so* much farther than coming home, probably because he would run home excited to be free, instead of walking slowly toward his imprisonment. "See anything awesome from the roof today?"

"Not really."

"Awesome." Lily scratched her cheek and tugged at her two braids. "I saw a ladybug today. Belen smashed it."

"Belen smash! Pow! Glaa booo teee!"

"Poor bug." Lily shook her head. Cole kept on walking, watching Lily and Belen just a few steps in front of him. Then he noticed some kids playing in the grass off to his left and some women working in their gardens. He hadn't seen his mom ever work a day in his life.

"Arissa had to get Mom from the lake."

"Belen, stand up!"

"She was swimming."

"Yeah?" Lily looked back at him and then to her younger brother. "Belen, today I'm going to tell you a very important story," she smiled gently.

Cole didn't understand why the younger child even came to school with them anyway. Probably because Mom was too tired every day to help out, and Arissa had to work in the bakery. So they were in charge of Belen, and one way to calm him down was to tell him

15

stories. And here it came, Lily's favorite thing to talk about, the Old Order.

"In the beginning there was the Creator. Can you say 'Creator'?"

"Gaaaaaaa."

"Good, Belen!" Cole rolled his eyes. A raven squawked above his head. *Stupid raven.* "There was also the Liberator and the Comforter, and everything was perfect in Aael." She stopped and pointed up into the sky. "Aael is *way* up there. But you can't see it, Belen, so don't bother trying."

"Boo ko bleh blah!"

"You're the smartest Belen there ever was." Cole watched as the child smeared dirt on his face.

"Anyway, the Creator, the Liberator, and the Comforter called themselves 'The Order,' and they decided they wanted to create another world. Esis. That's where we live." Lily poked Belen in the stomach as they walked. The child laughed.

Although Cole had heard the story practically every time Belen acted up, something about it would calm him down, too. Maybe it was because it was a story his father used to tell him. The three children started up the hill that led to their schoolhouse. *Longest hill ever.* The sun seemed hotter than usual.

"The Order made four Shepherds. A Shepherd of Spirit to watch over everything "spirity" . . . a Shepherd of Defense to make sure everyone was safe, a Shepherd of State to run things, and a Shepherd of Mind to keep everyone smart–like Dad."

Cole looked around. "Lily, I don't see anyone else. Are we late?"

"Don't interrupt!" Lily snapped.

"But there's no one here." He looked back and forth along the path, then suddenly remembered the kids he had seen playing along the road. "Do we even have school today?"

"Of course we have school today! What a silly question."

"Then what is that piece of paper hanging off the schoolhouse door?"

"Go check." Lily sat down among some daisies as Belen attempted to put one up his nose. "Isn't he cute?" Speechless, Cole stared at them. "What are you waiting for? I'm not getting' any younger!" she continued. With a groan, Cole slowly headed up to the schoolhouse.

"Lily, it says 'No School. Holiday. Enjoy your break.'" Cole frowned. "Why didn't Mom tell us?"

"Who knows?"

"So now what?"

"We go home."

Returning to his brother and sister, Cole felt relief at not having school, but not any happiness or joy. He hadn't felt that since Fenris came home. And that had been a long time ago. "Well, should we go get some food?"

"I bet Arissa brings something back from the bakery."

They continued in silence for most of the way home. Cole noticed how happy people seemed. Everyone had so many reasons to be happy in the City of Flowers. Nothing bad ever really happened there, it seemed. Everyone's lives were perfect. Belen seemed the happiest of all. Sometimes, though, a blank or confused expression would fill his eyes, and he would look up at Lily and ask, "Daddy?" She would always give him different answers, and always with a huge smile.

"He's sailing on a boat, saving the world."

"He's fighting a war overseas. The biggest war ever!"

"He's working at an orphanage healing sick babies."

"He's telling the world about the Old Order and the return of the Liberator!"

"He's finding a cure to heal Mommy!"

Cole knew none of it was true. He wondered if Lily believed any of it. She was only 9. He was 12. But sometimes it seemed as if she was older than him. Or at least she thought she was.

When they got back home, his mom was in her bedroom with the door closed as usual, and Arissa still had not returned. Belen collapsed by the fireplace, where Lily liked to sleep when it was lit, and passed out from exhaustion. Cole found himself once again on top of his roof, surprised to find Lily sitting beside him. The sun shone brightly, but it felt cooler on the roof.

"I'm hungry."

"Arissa should be home soon."

"I hope so. Fenris too."

"I hope so too." Cole wondered what time it was.

"I'm glad we don't have school."

"Me, too."

"I miss Dad."

"Me, too."

Lily looked up into the sky. "I miss Mom."

I'm afraid of her. He hesitated. "I do too, Lilly." And he did.

17

Although Cole didn't know how long they sat on the roof, it really didn't matter. Honestly, he liked having her up there, though he would never tell her that. Sure she may have been sometimes annoying, but out of all of his siblings, she understood what he couldn't explain. They had each other. And perhaps that would be enough. And Fenris would be home soon. Cole knew she was on the roof waiting for their brother to return. But as for Cole, he was waiting for his father. *He'll come back. I know he will. Maybe today will be the day.*

CHAPTER 2: IAN

Never swallow saltwater, Aupaipaupy always warned him, "Always shut your mouth when you're talking with a woman and when you're surfing." If only he'd followed the advice. Ian tumbled upside-down with the surf, the waves smashing him against more waves. Fish dodged out of his way, some eying him with annoyance and others judging his belly as it created massive whirlpools along the surface. The saltwater burned his eyes, his throat, and his confidence. But Bumo? Bumo sailed above the waves like a golden god. Perfect hair, perfect teeth, perfect tan, perfect body. That was Bumo. Perfect. Bumo probably didn't even need the surfboard to stay on top of the water, unlike Ian who required it just to keep himself from drowning, although, his chubby arms would probably keep him afloat like little life rafts. His lungs began to burn. *May I please stop spinning?* Paddling against the current, Ian struggled to reach the surface. Above him he could see the bottom of Bumo's board, gently floating above the wave as if it was a cloud. Finally Ian reached the surface in a gasp of desperation, water and spit spraying out in a fountain of relief, exhaustion, and quick embarrassment, as he noticed two brunette surfer girls nearby giggling at his epic failure. To his right he could see Bumo's wave ending and him entering the water like a perfect feather floating gently upon the surface.

"Wasn't that awesome, Ian?" Bumo glowed in the sunlight.

"Yeah. So fun." Ian's nose bubbled with snot.

"Told ya! Told ya!" Bumo side-stroked next to Ian, his teeth shining like white sand reflecting in the sun.

"Bumo," Ian still gasped, "that was really hard."

"What? You rocked it!"

18

"Bumo, I almost died."

"Nah, I would have saved you immediately!" Ian glared as Bumo flexed his arms. He wondered if Bumo did it on purpose or if it just happened naturally. "Wanna go again?" His friend's eyes twinkled with excitement and adventure. Ian sighed from fatigue and resentment. He was Ian, the extremely tall, fat boy who smelled like seaweed and fish guts, someone accustomed to being jeered at. The boy whose parents were known for being loud, obnoxious, and often screaming:

"Fresh fish! Get your fresh fish here! Buy two, get three for free!"

"No, I don't want to go again. Please, let's go back to shore. And let's get some food. I'm starving!"

"You *would* want food, Fatty Mcpatty!"

"Fatty Mcpatty?"

"She wants me." Bumo pointed to the shoreline at the girl who had been recently giggling at Ian. "Hey, wanna see me go again?"

"Huh?" the girl shouted from afar. "I can't hear you!"

"I'll come to you!" Ian watched as Bumo swam toward the shoreline, every stroke perfection, as if he had been swimming since birth. Ian had lived in Lion's Landing his entire life. By all accounts he should be a fish himself, but he was more like a beluga whale, or even a beached whale. He wasn't huge. But, then maybe he was. He wasn't really sure. Sure, he knew he was overweight, but it was impossible to be a part of his family and not be bulky. His father was large. His mother was massive. And Aupainana, his grandmother, was bigger than both combined. Well, perhaps not. But she was always huge and terrifying to him.

Ian surveyed the beach from offshore as the waves raised and dropped him with each passing current. Lion's Landing was beautiful. As he thought about it, he knew he was fortunate, blessed. He couldn't help but smile. Lion's Landing was an amazing place. Every passing ship had to stop by when sailing by Oldaem on the Eastern Seas. People from nations as far as Sther to Kaya frequented Lion's Landing. Everyone looked different. The architecture was diverse, flags of many colors flew high above the towering arches, stonework met brick, and stucco was set against pure gold. Different smells, languages, skin colors, and foods filled the city. As for the foods, praise the Tide and the Rock for the foods. Ian smiled with the thought of stuffed sea clams. Sea clams were a delicacy from Beelz, the country his parents had been born in. Although he himself had been born in Oldaem, his parents were immigrants. Their thick

19

accents alerted everyone to that fact. That was his favorite thing about Lion's Landing—the different people. Ian loved watching them. And he loved helping people. Being one person in a sea of many made him feel as if maybe being fat and not very talented and ordinary . . . maybe it was okay to be those things. Maybe it was okay to just be Ian—and maybe not. He sighed. Lion's Landing was the place to be. And Bumo was the guy to be. Ian watched as Bumo flirted with a blonde girl sitting on the beach. *She wasn't even who he was talking to before.* His stomach growling, Ian started slowly making his way to the shoreline. *Salt water. Disgusting.* Feeling something nibbling on his toe, he kicked at it, and in the process hit a sharp rock. *Ouch. I hope that wasn't a tooth.* He froze. *Oh no. Quiana.*

There she sat on the sand, eyes glued to him. Quiana: the 11-year-old girl who always stared at him for some reason. And she was doing what she did best: staring. *Why is she staring at me?* Suddenly Ian felt 90 pounds heavier. As Quiana smiled a gap-toothed grin at him, he could imagine her familiar snort in the process.

"She likes you." Bumo appeared out of nowhere.

"Shut up, Bumo."

"She snorts with love for you."

"I'm going to sit on you."

"You have to catch me first." They both looked at the girl as she waved nervously. Bumo gave her a nod and smiled. "You're 14, Ian, the time has come."

"What time?"

"Love time. Kiss time."

"She's 11. And she's ugly."

"And you're quite the looker?"

"She works for my mom."

"Good point." Bumo looked back at Quiana who was still waving. "So what time tonight do you want to have our *final* training session before we leave?"

"I don't know if I can. Family dinner." Ian hesitated. "And I still have to ask permission . . . for tomorrow."

"You still haven't asked?" his friend asked, flabbergasted.

"Nope. But I believe it's gonna be okay."

"And why's that?"

Ian smiled a hopeful grin. "Because it's what I was born to do." Bumo looked at him as if he was crazy.

"Whatever you say man. My parents have been drilling me themselves. They are fully behind me. I'm totally ready."

"I wouldn't expect anything else." Ian patted Bumo's back. Because they were polar opposites, he didn't know how or why they were friends. But even though Bumo was vain and conceited and already completely absorbed with himself at the age of 14, Ian knew Bumo cared for him like a brother, and would do practically anything for him. The realization that he had a brother, even if he never would be as good as him, made Ian smile to himself.

"See you tomorrow? At the pier? What if your parents say no?" Bumo started walking away, a somewhat worried expression on his face.

"They won't. I feel it in the Rock." After splashing water toward Bumo and shaking his head, Ian headed for shore.

"AUPAINO! STOP PLAYING IN THE WATER! AUPAINO! YOU HAVE TO GUT FISH! AUPAINO! STOP PLAYING IN THE WATER! THERE'S WORK TO BE DONE AUPAINO!"

Mom.

"Coming, Mom." Ian swam toward her. A really great person and mother, she had a large heart and even larger hands—at least that was always how he heard people of the market speaking about her. His parents owned a fish market right on the central street in Lion's Landing. People said it was one of the best in the region of Soma. His father caught the fish, his mother sold them, and Ian gutted them. That's how the process went. Quiana helped at the front desk. Even now he could see his mother, Quiana, and his little brother, Talo, walking along the surf. Talo at the age of 3 was splashing in the water and laughing hysterically. He was a happy child. Ian always sang to him and fed him extra sea clams when no one was looking in the hope that Ian wouldn't be the fattest kid in the family. *I'll make you fatter than me, Talo.* Just then he noticed his mother holding a bag, one definitely full of fish.

"It's gutting time," his mother said with a smile as she held up the bag.

Finding his footing on the slimy surface beneath him, Ian started walking toward the shoreline, water dripping from his torso. He could hear Talo singing at the top of his lungs.

"Aupaino, why are you wasting your time playing in the water?"

"Bumo was teaching me how to surf."

"What a lucky friend you've found in him. His skin is white, but his heart is good. Tell him to come for dinner."

21

"Mom, he's already gone."

"Hi, Ian." Quiana blushed as she spoke. Her voice was deeper than Ian's. Even lower than his mother's and possibly even his Aupainana, his grandmother. And that was deep.

"Hi, Quiana."

She snorted with glee.

"Quiana asked to help you gut fish today. Wasn't that nice of her?"

"So, so nice." Ian had reached the shore by now. Retrieving his shirt, he struggled to pull it over his wet body.

"Aupaino, you're getting black in this eastern sun. Almost like our people in Beelz. I'm so proud of you." His mother smiled as they all three started up the beach toward the rocky road full of foot traffic and carts and wagons. It was a busy day in Lion's Landing.

Ian hesitated as he noticed a group of Shepherds in their dark tunics walking intently in front of them. "Mom?'"

"Yes, my boy."

"I have something I need to talk to you and Aupaipaupy about tonight."

"Aupaitalo, keep up!" Ian turned to see his brother chasing some seagulls by the sand. Quiana rushed to his side and took his hand.

"Do I have permission to discuss something on my mind tonight?"

"I shall have to see what mood your Aupaipaupy is in. It might be a singing dinner only."

"I see."

Many people in Oldaem didn't understand the customs of Beelzians. Bumo, for one, didn't. But that was what was perfect about living in Lion's Landing: diversity of customs. Ian's family was strict in their Beelzian practices. Dinner was a sacred time. It was up to the Patriarch what was discussed and what was best left unsaid. Most dinners consisted of songs and folklore and praises to the Tide or the Rock. Tonight Ian hoped would be different. He had something on his heart that had been weighing heavily upon him. Something he needed to explore. His hopes and childhood dreams might finally come true. Tomorrow. It could be tomorrow.

They finally approached Fishgutz, the store his family had owned since his parents got off the ship from Beelz. They opened the wooden door, and the musk of fish hit Ian in the face. Most of the structure was wooden. Rows of giant fish lay upon huge ice blocks for display. The counter to purchase the fish sat by the door, and a huge window lined the street so that passers-by could view the many different options available. A large staircase at the back of the store led to their apartment, the place where he had been born.

"Here"–his mother handed him the large bag–"get started." She took Talo by the hand and dragged him upstairs. "Bath time for you, my little Blubber fish."

"Bum Bum!" Talo chirped.

And fish gutting with Quiana for me. Perfect. Ian watched his mother and brother disappear upstairs and his attention drifted over to Quiana whose eyes were glued to his.

"I'll use this corner of the store"–he walked over to the opposite table and dumped out half of the fish–"and you can use this corner."

"Okay." Her voice sagged in disappointment.

Ian returned to his corner and sat down. The remainder of his afternoon he spent doing what he had done every night since he could figure out how to gut a fish. As he avoided the stares of Quiana, his hands were quickly at work, and his mind took him to the exciting world of "someday." He dreamed of the day he would be a fully realized Shepherd of Defense. A faint smile on his face, he imagined the medallion that would one day adorn his neck, the sword by his side, the adventures he would have, the people he would save, and the weight he would lose. When he realized that perhaps Quiana might think he was smiling at her, he began to frown, but his mind kept racing with the places he would visit, the lessons he would learn, the friends he would make, and the lives he would possibly change. Ian never really asked for much, but he wanted to make a difference. His passion was to matter somehow, to be able to brighten up other people's days. *Maybe he should smile at Quiana.* Okay, maybe everyone's day except for Quiana. That made him smile again. Sometimes he couldn't help but smile. Feeling incredibly blessed, deep down in his heart he *knew* he was going to be a Shepherd. While he didn't know how he *knew,* he just did. Someday he would be important, and not just for its own sake, but because deep in his heart he realized that everyone was important for some reason or another. And it would all start tomorrow.

Tomorrow was the Shepherd Interview. If he passed successfully, it would send Ian and Bumo to the Shepherd Tournament in the Capital. Held once a year, it determined which 15-year-old potential Shepherds would make it into one of the three Shepherd Academies in Oldaem. His parents *had* to say yes. Tomorrow, he and Bumo would journey to Altairus, the capital of Soma, by ferry, where they would face the STC: The Shepherd Tournament Committee. The STC was a group of seven retired Shepherds who made a circuit of the country to find worthy 14 and 15-year-olds to compete. They only selected eight applicants from each of the seven regions every year to participate in the tournament. Fifty-six applicants would compete against each other in the tournament, and Ian was determined to be one of them. But first he had to convince his parents. *Why did I wait until tonight?* For weeks now he had been putting it off. He knew his parents were content with him settling down in Lion's Landing, possibly with Quiana, and taking over Fishgutz after they died. Ian realized that was enough for them. But it wasn't for him. This was his chance. *Please, let them see I want to do more. Let them understand that I'll still love them.*

CHAPTER 3: SAYLA

Sayla couldn't figure out where she was. It felt cold, and she couldn't see anything, but somehow she sensed that the space she was standing in was not very big.

"Hello?" she called out, but the only answer she got was her echo repeated again and again. *How can that be when I'm in a small room?*

Suddenly a scream coming from somewhere behind her jolted her around. Frantically, she reached for her sword only to find that it wasn't there. Great, the one time she needed it. The screaming continued. She held her head in her hands.

"Get it together, woman, you're almost a Shepherd of Defense!" Taking a deep breath, Sayla tried to reassure herself. Suddenly a blinding light momentarily flashed and everything became quiet. Without any weapon, she balled her hands into fists, ready to face some unseen attacker, but quickly she saw that she was alone in what was now a dark hallway. Directly across from her was a barred cell. Somehow she knew that that was where the screaming had originated.

"May the One help me," she muttered as she raced toward the bars. Sometimes Sayla wondered if she was too curious for her own good. Instead of stopping at the iron bars, she found that she could run right through them, and there, in the far corner of the small cell, sat a man. Unsure what to do, she inched forward. Was he even alive?

His eyes closed, the man looked in pain. He appeared to be middle-aged, tall, and muscular. A soldier, she figured, or a Shepherd. Somehow she knew he shouldn't be there. That he must be needed somewhere else.

Sayla jumped when she heard voices coming from down the hall. Quickly she sat next to the unmoving man and pressed herself up against the wall, her heart racing. While she waited for the voices to stop, Sayla couldn't help but glance at her motionless companion. The man had shadows under his eyes, cuts and bruises all over his face. His dark hair was matted and blood tangled his beard. Or was it blood? She leaned closer. It was not easy to see, but Sayla could have sworn that the cut on his cheek bled … purple. Just as quickly as it registered in her mind, a new cut opened on his forehead, this one bleeding red. At least it was the right color. But then more and more cuts opened up all over the man, bleeding purple and red but mostly yellow. Yellow was everywhere. And yet still the man did not move.

Her hand shaking, Sayla tentatively reached out to touch the golden blood. Then the injured man suddenly grabbed her arm and shot forward. This time Sayla recognized the scream as coming from herself. "It's all a distraction!" he shrieked. The wild-eyed man pulled her to her knees. She tried to fight but he was stronger. "You have to stop it! You, Sayla!"

For a split second she ceased struggling.

"Stop what? What are you talking about?"

But the man's face was becoming blurry and distorted. With one final shove she broke free of his grip but found herself falling past the floor in the same way she had gone through the bars before.

Thankfully she didn't have far to fall. Suddenly she was outside. The light was so much brighter now. She landed on her back next to a large stone wall. Sitting up, she looked at it in awe. *Stop what?* she wondered to herself.

"What do I do?"

Jerking her head to the left, she saw a little boy with bright eyes and a face full of indecision. "What do I do?" he asked again, this time looking straight at her.

"I … I don't know." Sayla shook her head. "Do I know you?"

The boy turned to face the wall. "Maybe today will be the day." Tears started flowing from his eyes.

Sorrow filled her mind as well, though she couldn't quite figure out why. The boy looked so sad, so lost. She knew what it felt like to be lost. As she stood up to go over to him, the world suddenly tilted sideways and a river of purple, red, and yellow flowed through the trees, sweeping up her and the boy. Sayla saw him go under. But because she was a Shepherd of Defense, she couldn't let a child drown in front of her. Reaching down, she found his shirt and pulled him up. But when his face came out of the water, it was not the little boy's face at all, but that of someone she hadn't seen in a very long time.

"Protect them," he whispered, "They can't protect themselves." Then a strong current tore them apart. Sayla couldn't breathe as the river of purple, red, and yellow swept over her. Suddenly she couldn't move her legs anymore. Something was wrapped around them.

In desperation, she lashed out her arms ... and hit someone in the face. Sayla hadn't realized that her eyes were closed, but she opened them as she bolted upright. Something wasn't right. She ... she was in a tent with the rest of the female apprentice Shepherds of Defense. It was the middle of the night and she could hear the crickets chirping outside. Glancing down at her feet, she realized that she couldn't move her legs because she was so tangled in her bedroll. It occurred to her that it was just a dream. A very unsettling one. And it had felt so real.

Especially the part where she had ... Suddenly it dawned on her. Sheepishly she turned to her right to see Tali, the youngest Defense apprentice, staring at her with astonished eyes and holding her nose. "Did I hit you?" Sayla asked tentatively. Tali was not only the youngest first-year student, but also the smallest. It still confused her how out of all the well-qualified 14-year-olds in Oldaem, Tali had managed to grab a winning place in the previous year's tournament. Sayla knew some big strong guys who hadn't even come close to winning. Of course, last year's tournament had ended in disaster, something she didn't enjoy thinking about.

"Sayla?"

Shaking her head, she looked back at Tali. "Sorry, what did you say?"

Tali rubbed the sleep from her eyes and sat up. "You asked me if you hit me, and I said yes, and then I asked if you were okay." She paused. "Which I still want to know, mainly because you stared off

26

into space there for a solid 10 seconds. And when I woke up, but before you did, you were making these nightmarish noises."

"Nightmarish noises?" How embarrassing. "Did … did I say anything?" Sayla glanced around at the other girl in the tent. Aveline was the only other fourth-year Defense apprentice from Woodlands Academy. A tall and strong 19-year-old with a bright red curly head of hair, she definitely appeared to be a threat. At this moment, she also seemed to be fast asleep, something Sayla was intensely grateful for. At least she didn't have to explain her strange dream to her closest friend and greatest rival.

"Nope." Tali shook her head. "Just weird little noises. It's possible you snorted, can't be sure." She leaned close to Sayla. "I bet I know what you dreamed about."

Sayla's heart started racing. "You do?"

"Yep." Tali leaned even closer, her voice getting quieter and quieter as she kept talking. "Was it that you were facing examination day … in front of all the Shepherds… and you weren't wearing any pants?"

"Yes," she nodded solemnly, feeling her heartbeat slow down. "That was it."

The other girl leaned back and let her breath out. "I am so sorry. That happens to me all the time! I am so glad I'm not the only one." Concern filled her eyes. "May I get you some water or an extra blanket—or a hug?"

Sayla rolled her eyes. She needed to think. "I'm fine. I think I'm just gonna go for a walk." Slipping on her boots, she left the tent.

Their small camp was next to a ridge overlooking the city of Sea Fort, their destination in the morning. Sayla had never been there herself, but from what she knew it was a rather large city. She assumed that was because Sea Fort not only was a center for trade as it sat on the eastern edge of the country, but also that it was home to one of the largest military bases in Oldaem.

Sitting on the ledge, she dangled her feet over the edge. She could just barely see Sea Fort off in the distance. The distant ships in the harbor reminded her of insects crawling across the water. Sayla wondered what they looked like up close. The already bustling city had grown massively in the past year alone. So much had changed since the war started.

It had been almost a year ago. Sayla remembered she had been at the annual Shepherd Tournament in the Capital. Shepherd apprentices were required to be there. Everything had been going well until near the end when news had reached the city that Oldaem's colony in the neighboring country, Leoj, had fallen under attack, the four Shepherds stationed there murdered. It had come as a shock to her at first--to everyone really. Oldaem and Leoj had been strong allies, and even though Oldaem had been in plenty of wars, they were usually the ones starting them.

Sayla had no doubt that Oldaem would prevail in the end. It had been 15 years since the conflict with Kaya, the nation to the south of Oldaem, but the situation had been very similar to what was happening now. When the people of Kaya had rejected the New Order religion that the Oldaem colony presented to them, they rebelled. Oldaem had rather quickly squashed the revolt, and now Kaya was a territory of Oldaem. Sayla had been just a child when that happened, but even then she knew Oldaem was a force to be reckoned with. Besides, with the One on their side, how could they not be the victors?

She looked back over to Sea Fort. Still, though, fighting a war was different when she was almost a full Shepherd of Defense. And it was different when she knew someone in the army.

"I don't know if you ever noticed this, but people usually sleep during the night." Glancing behind her, Sayla found Shale, the fifth-year Shepherd apprentice standing behind her, his muscular shape outlined in the moonlight.

At first she felt comforted to see him until a brief moment of panic when she realized that she probably had a massive case of bedhead. She quickly swept her loose, light brown curls into a messy bun and tried to keep calm. "Shale, what are you doing up?"

He sat down beside her. "It's my turn to keep watch." *Wow, he had a great reason.* "So it seems to me, that I should be asking you that question." He playfully poked her shoulder, and she thought her arm went numb.

"I ... had a weird dream," she answered bashfully. The horrors of the night sounded really silly when she said it out loud. Running from a rainbow river. Who does that?

"I told you not to eat those berries."

"For your information, that was Oghren who ate the berries."

"Oh, really."

"I'll have you know I finished Wilderness Survival Plants top of my class and everybody knows that the first rule ..." Shale put a finger to her lips and she went silent. She also stopped breathing.

"You talk too much," he told her in the most attractive way possible. Then he leaned closer. "It's late. Go get some sleep. You need your rest for tomorrow."

Sayla looked back toward the sleeping city. "What exactly are we doing tomorrow, anyway?" She knew the basic plan, but Shale didn't like to give details.

"Well, we'll take a tour of the military base. Oh, and you know Royal Shepherd of Defense Demas will be there?" She nodded. Shepherd Demas had come all the way from the Capital to show his support for the troops about to ship out to Leoj.

"What about him?"

"I guess he heard that the Defense students from Woodlands Academy were coming to hear him speak, and he actually wants to meet us tomorrow," Shale said with a hint of excitement.

She was astounded. "The Royal Shepherd of Defense? He wants to meet us?" In all her years of watching tournaments and attending the oldest of the three Shepherd academies, she had only seen the Royal Shepherds from a distance. As one of the four Royal Shepherds, Shepherd Demas was in charge of the entire military. Still, it was highly unusual for him to come as far east as Sea Fort. Although Sayla had lived in the region of Efil her entire life, she had never even seen the man.

"Yeah! I guess he probably heard about how awesome I am ... I mean ... we are," he answered smugly.

She laughed. Shale had such a great sense of humor. "You haven't even finished your training yet. Probably, you still have a lot to learn."

When he put his arm around her, she wanted to squeal with glee, but she refrained. "Let me give you some advice, Sayla." Her name sounded so great when he said it. "You're a fourth-year. And you just might make it to five." He believed in her. "Unless Aveline totally destroys you." Well, there was that possibility. "But if some miracle happens and you do become the fifth-year student, just remember, it's not about what you know. It's about what you can do." With that, he winked at her and got up to resume his guard duty.

Sayla thought about what she knew. She knew that Shale was hopelessly adorable, whether he had a brain or not. And she knew that she probably should go to sleep if she ever wanted to get up in the morning. But the thought of going back to sleep frightened her since she was still unsure what to think about her dream. Hopefully she would make it to be a fifth-year Shepherd. And most of all, she hoped that she would be able to see her old friend who was stationed in Sea Fort. She hadn't realized how much she missed him until she had seen his face in her dream.

CHAPTER 4: DAKU

The lights of Lion's Landing flickered over the water. A thick and heavy mist floated over the quiet waves as the ship drifted toward shore. First stop, Lion's Landing: an island city of trade and commerce off the eastern shores of Oldaem, and then on to Vertloch Tower. *Almost home.* Daku peered into the misty waters. He couldn't even see his reflection. Not a star to be seen. It had been a sunny day, but the night brought with it a dense fog that made it difficult to steer the vessel they sailed on. His back ached, his muscles were tense, and his head throbbed. It had been a long day. But then it had been a long month and a long year. Daku looked down at his hands. Strong and rugged, they had endured much.

The ship floated quietly as it gently made its way through the water. As silent as a spider. Images flashed through his mind. Of blood. Screaming. Fire. A dark room. A sword drawn. And more blood. *Golden eyes. Golden hair. Golden skin. Malvina. Beautiful.* But he was safe now. Daku took a deep breath. He was on a ship and almost home. When he tried to clear his head, it seemed a nearly impossible task. His mind was always racing. Daku stared harder into the water, yearning to see *something* of clarity within it. But all he saw were golden eyes. A golden smile.

"Yeah, it doesn't look as if Oldaem is interested in negotiation. This is full-out war," a voice said from somewhere on deck.

"I'm surprised Leoj broke the truce. We're going to crush them."

"Their military is stronger than you might think. Word is that Royal Shepherd of Defense Demas is coming to rally the troops. Oldaem is angry."

"We have reason to be, murdering our Shepherds, there is nothing worse."

"Hemia and Remia are staying neutral. I wonder what other countries will intervene?"

Daku listened to the soldiers' conversation as they walked by him. They didn't notice him. He could blend into the night as easily as a shadow. It was the Warden's way, what he was trained to do. People

30

often had conversations in front of him without being aware of his presence. *I wonder where Malvina is?* he thought as the soldiers wandered out of earshot.

Their voyage from Leoj had been uneventful at first--smooth sailing, few conversations with the passengers on board. He hadn't seen Malvina since the storm. A huge tempest had blown up two nights before, the wind whipping the ship back and forth. The waves crashed down upon the wooden vessel and shattered its masts. Three passengers vanished into the depths of the Eastern Ocean forever. There had been screaming and terror. But Malvina wasn't afraid. She didn't fear anything. *Golden eyes.* When he looked around again, he saw that he was alone. Daku liked being by himself. Bitter experience had taught him that people couldn't be trusted. They should be avoided. The mission was all that mattered. Accomplish the mission. Stay focused on the task. That was the Warden's way, and he was a Warden for the Golden Priestess Malvina. His most recent mission now accomplished, his mind was a blank. It was always during such times that Daku didn't know what was next. But he didn't care.

You are mine.

You belong to me.

You love me.

You serve me.

It's the way.

Forsake them.

Forsake them all.

Malvina's voice rang strongly within him. Her words penetrated his inner being. He couldn't shake them. But then he didn't want to. Out of the corner of his eye he caught the glimpse of another shadow--Jorn. Jorn was the other Warden to the Golden Priestess Malvina. An older man--a hard man--he had been her Warden longer. But after Malvina's original Warden fell into the sleep of death, Daku had been chosen in the Tower. She preferred him to Jorn, that he, Daku, was *hers.* Now he watched as the man leaned over the railing. The Warden had two long scars etched vertically across his eyes. Daku didn't know where or how he got them, and he had never asked. Jorn was a mystery. Always serious, he rarely spoke and never made eye contact. His movements were slow and calculating. Daku didn't trust him, aware that he would kill him in a second if it served his purpose. The feeling was mutual. Daku himself would have no problem eliminating Jorn, especially if he got in between him and Malvina. Often he watched Jorn in action: how

31

he observed his surroundings and ruthlessly swung a sword, how mercy was a foreign word to him and compassion a waste of effort. It was the Warden's way. And it was also Daku's way. He respected Jorn, feared Jorn--he *was* Jorn. Daku paused.

But sometimes . . . yes only sometimes, he would wonder what Jorn was like . . . before he was a Warden . . . before Malvina. Did he have a family? Children? Did he ever . . . love anyone? Daku loved someone. *Golden eyes.* At least, he thought he did. Shifting his gaze from Jorn, he stared at the foggy sky. *It can't be.* It seemed as if the fog was . . . parting, as if there was some . . . color up there besides black, gray, and despair. *Light?* Through the hazy fog, through the confusion, and fear, and distortion, Daku could see what he thought could be a star . . . *Beautiful.* He sighed. *Aelwynne, I'm almost home.*

You are mine.
You belong to me.
You love me.
You serve me.
It's the way.
Forsake them.
Forsake them all.

The fog returned. Jorn no longer leaned against the rail. Daku was alone. *Golden hair.* Returning to Vertloch Tower, he would wait until his next assignment. From now on he would assist Malvina in whatever she needed, would breathe a word to *no one* about what they had just done, and would further the work of The Three in turning hearts and minds to Golden, Crimson, and Amethyst glory. *Golden eyes. A secret.* He would be a Warden. Nothing would stop or sway him. And nothing would deter him. It didn't matter who he used to be, what caused him to do this, or what he left behind. All that was important was Malvina. Her voice. Her face. Her eyes.

But it did matter more than that. Somewhere deep inside, in a place he was forced to forget. In a place he initially fought to protect.

You are mine.
It *did* matter.
Eyes.
Aelwynne mattered.
Skin.
She always will.

Daku shook his head to clear away the cobwebs within. But they wouldn't disappear. They wouldn't . . . wouldn't . . .

Forsake them.

"Soon, Aelwynne, I'll be home . . ."

Forsake them all.

"My love."

You serve me.

He couldn't speak. Couldn't think. Couldn't remember.

Golden eyes.

His lips moved but no sound came from them. And his brain fought to form thoughts but none did. As he struggled the mental fog swirled slowly around and around. He fought it. Where was he? What was he doing? Slowly thoughts did emerge He was on a ship. *Light? Clarity!* A heavy sigh. *My wife.*

Relief.

Darkness.

Golden eyes.

The lights of Lion's Landing flickered across the waters.

CHAPTER 5: KAYT

And then the Liberator rebelled and betrayed the Comforter and the Creator. They were once one, once united, once family. Jealousy stirred within the Liberator's heart. Power. Intrigue. He wanted what they built for himself. And so he came to the Creator and the Comforter under the veil of love and companionship, only to do away with them under the cover of the darkness of his own rage. The merciful, faithful One attempted to come to their defense, yet it was too late. They fought a fierce battle over Esis, and Esis never before witnessed such destruction. The One was victorious and cast the Liberator down to Esis where he continues to roam and force his destruction and dark terror across the land. Here he is now known as "The Betrayer." The One is forever. The One is power. The One is hope. He will come again (Tales of the One, Prologue, Book XIII. Author: Xilia Thomaston).

Kayt's eyes felt heavy. It had been a long day. Every prologue read the same in every one of the books she had been leafing through, volumes that shaped her religion. Her heart surged with loyalty to the One as she scanned the tales of victory, despair, and rich culture. Oldaem had come so far. She'd learned so much. Then she noticed the Keeper of Books approaching. *Just leave me alone, you old hag.*

"Magnificent series, isn't it?"

"Oh, it's grand."

The old woman had graying hair and crooked teeth. "Every word, the truth." She stood as upright as her twisted back would allow and raised a pointed finger to the domed ceilings of the library. "The One forever."

"The One forever." Kayt echoed and arched her back. It ached. *How long have I been sitting here?* Annoyance swept through her. *Is she still talking?* The woman's black eyes kindly scanned Kayt's weary face.

"It is a high honor to have a Shepherd of State here in Westervale." *Here it comes.* The Keeper approached her closely, her breath smelling of mint and crackers. "I'm *so* sorry for what happened to you." She rested her bony hand upon Kayt's shoulder. "Vengeance will be His. May the One give you peace."

"He has." With a sigh Kayt gave the most vulnerable, soul-torn expression she could muster.

"It's not right." Once again that bony finger pointed into the air as the Keeper hobbled away. "It's not right." Her voice faded as she disappeared behind the high shelves of the old ancient manuscripts and tomes.

Shaking her head, Kayt stared out the window. Darkness. *I've sat in here all day. Better than being out there.* She could see remnants of the lights of Westervale shining from the bottom of the hill, through the slight fog creeping up to the slope where the library sat. Her gaze rose up the high glass windows. Then she looked straight above her at the huge light fixtures hanging on a golden chain. Kayt loved ornate things. *I could get used to this.* Perhaps it's why she had stayed for six months. They treated her like a Shepherd of State *should* be honored here. More than just respecting her, they actually revered her. And they felt sorry for her, which was better than the alterative. She was alone. *Finally.* Scooting her bronze chair away from the old polished wooden table, she stood to her feet. Suddenly she realized that she hadn't moved in hours. But she didn't care. It was why she had come—to get lost in a world of books and theory and knowledge. The hours she spent bettering herself she would put to practical use once she had figured out a way to climb back up, to actually be a Shepherd of State in a region somewhere, or perhaps the Capital itself. *They can't keep me down.* The high arches and vaults were mesmerizing. The carvings etched in gilded panels and the classic works of art surrounding her took her to a different world.

34

One where *she* was in control. Where everyone did what *she* wanted them to do and she didn't fail, wasn't disgraced. There she could have the best of *both* worlds. She didn't have time for sentiment, for people's feelings, and for tiptoeing around how *they* felt. *If you want to make something of yourself, you have to push, and fight, and claw, and scream to be noticed.* That was what growing up in a family of eight children had taught her. Whoever runs fastest to the table gets the most food, whoever screams the loudest gets noticed first, and whoever is the strongest will receive the most attention. *They can't keep me down.*

She started walking, tired of studying, of sitting--of everything. Glancing into the Keeper's office, she noticed six or seven record-keepers writing feverishly with their quills. They all stared at her with that hint of *pity* in their eyes that she had endured the past six months. Kayt *hated* that look. *Better than the alternative.* Her pace increased. *I need some air.*

"Leaving already?" *Blast it. The Keeper again.*

"Yes. I have exhausted this room for the day."

"May I direct you to this section." The woman had a twinkle in her eyes. "I don't believe you've seen it yet?"

"No, thanks." Kayt swept by her. *Crazy loon. Leave me alone.*

"How much the staff respects you!"

"I'll have my bath drawn for me. I'm out to get some air." Her voice was cool.

"Of course, Shepherd."

"And some food. And not the same *slop* you gave me last time." *Get me out of here.*

"Sorry, Shepherd."

Kayt turned. "I expected more from the chefs at Westervale Library." Her green eyes penetrated into the Keeper's.

"Of course, Shepherd." She hobbled toward her. "It will get better. The One will preserve you."

"*Stop* following me." Kayt towered above the Keeper.

"I only meant . . ."

"And tell your cronies to stop staring at me." The record-keepers were all standing, watching Kayt head toward the library's exit.

"Back to work," the Keeper told the others. Then, glancing at Kayt, she said, "They only stare because they want to show sympathy for the pain you've experienced."

"Do I look an invalid? Do I look incapable of defending myself? What happened happened! I've *moved* on. The One has given me

35

the strength I needed. What I *don't* require are some old, shriveled hags reminding me *every* day that I live and breathe of what I went through." She was getting heated. "I came here to escape the pain and the shame, and your staff have made me relive it every minute! "

"Shepherd . . ."

"I'm *done.*" Now she was shouting. Usually Kayt did not lose her composure, but now she didn't care. She'd had enough. *Get me out of here.* Her footsteps seemed to thunder on the marble flooring of the foyer.

"Have a good night, Shepherd," a young, smiling, pretty record-keeper sitting at the front desk chirped.

"Shut up." The door slammed behind her as she found herself standing outside of the library on the stony path. A cool breeze swept her blonde hair around her face. Kayt should have felt chilled, but her blood was boiling. She leaned her back against the door. *Why can't they leave me alone?* She sighed. She was 25 but felt 45. *What is wrong with me?* The door bumped her forward.

"Oh, Kayt! I'm sorry"

For a second she stumbled. *Composure.* "Think nothing of it." Her body stiffened.

A tall, aging man with reddish hair stood in front of her, tomes in his arms.

"Have you been here since this morning?"

"Yes. Just studying up." She averted her face. "I've had a lot of time as of late."

"I'm sorry." He gently approached her. "Just know, everyone still backs you, Kayt. You are *greatly* respected. What he did was wrong."

"Thank you. How were your lectures today, Brulis?" His Shepherd Medallion of Mind reflected the library's lights, as he shifted his body.

"The students of Westpoint Academy have been very receptive."

"You're lecturing the first-year students who are touring the library, right?"

"Yes, that's right." He rubbed his head.

Kayt noticed that he sounded tired, fatigued. And she knew how that felt. Being a Shepherd was very demanding, especially a Shepherd of Mind. She respected him, something she did of few. Her mind raced back to the day she graduated as a Shepherd of State, such a high honor. It was every graduate's dream to be selected by a Regent and rule by their side. Each Regent had four Shepherds to assist him or her: Defense, Spirit, Mind, and State. Every five years

36

elections took place in Oldaem. All of the seven regions would vote between their current Regent, with his or her established Shepherds, or would choose the opposing Regent and a new crop of Shepherds. In some cases, regions would continually select the current reigning Regent. That would allow a Regent and their Shepherds to rule for possibly 30 or more years. In other cases, or when regions were dissatisfied with their leadership, they would select a new Regent with new Shepherds. The losing Regent would be a Regent no longer, and his or her Shepherds would find themselves back in the pool of other unemployed Shepherds, seeking work in either one of the three Academies as professors, as tournament facilitators, in the military, or on the STC. In some cases displaced or never-hired Shepherds returned to the work force as normal citizens. They got married and watched their dreams of being successful, honored Shepherds fade away.

"I'm sure they enjoy your lectures. You are a very prolific speaker."

"Thank you, Kayt. I return to Dorhaven tomorrow."

"How often do you go out?"

"As often as I'm needed. I travel a lot." Brulis' eyes seemed far away. Regents would often send their Shepherds of Mind across the region to speak at events, educate citizens, and especially make appearances at their Academy.

"Well, know you're making a difference."

"Thank you, Kayt. I'm sure you'll be back in the game soon enough."

"Soon enough." She hurried off the path and up the hill behind the library, leaving Brulis standing on the pathway. But she didn't care. He was successful, he was an acting Shepherd, and she was not. The man was revered, and not because people thought he had experienced something terrible, but because of his accomplishments--something Kayt coveted. Something she wanted more than anything. As she walked up the steep hill, she kicked her shoes off in the grass. The terrain was rocky and anything but soft, but she loved it. It reminded her of Highdale, the capital of Isprig, hill country, where she had once almost ruled as Shepherd of State. And it reminded her of Silas. She had never known the joys of being an established Shepherd working for a Regent. At the top of her class, she had won her tournament with high honors. And she had won his heart with even greater effort. Everyone knew who she was, but not for the reason she wanted. Silas, her "Regent," had been defeated, and she left Highdale. *Don't start, Kayt. It's not worth dwelling on. What's done is done. You did what you had to. Now here you are.* Determinedly she pushed the painful thoughts to the back of her mind.

A few minutes later she stood at the top of a cliff, overlooking the library, and further down, the city of Westervale itself. Old in architecture, and being so near the Limestone Cliffs, it had been built to withstand even the deadliest natural disaster. But it wasn't her home. *Silas.* Rahvil wasn't her home. *Silas. Stop, Kayt.* Nor was Highdale her home. Her real home was in Dagonfell, far to the south, near the Capital, in the region of Jaron. A wealthy region nestled between the Barisan Mountains and the Western Seas. That was where her *family* was—her *children.* And her *husband—Arnand.*

"I hope I didn't offend you."

"What?" Brulis' voice made her nearly stumble off the cliff. "What are you doing up here?"

"I hope I didn't offend you." The man no longer held his books, but rather a cape that he had draped around himself. "With what I said, about getting back in the game—I shouldn't have said that. I know you care more about your situation than just the station you didn't get to fill."

"You didn't have to come all the way up here just to say that." Kayt looked uncomfortably at him. *What is he doing?*

"No, I know." He paused to catch his breath.

"It's fine." Her emerald eyes were impenetrable. She had learned how to prevent anyone from peering into her heart.

"Are you okay?"

"What?"

"Kayt, I'm a Shepherd of Mind. I've been trained."

"I *know* what you've been trained to do."

An uncomfortable silence settled between them. However much she hid her feelings, Kayt realized that a Shepherd of Mind could see right through her. She hated that. But she also knew there was no way of him knowing the truth of what had really happened—the truth about who she was, what she was capable of.

"I know you have a family, Kayt."

She looked at him in surprise.

"I have one too. I know that Shepherds are discouraged from marrying, and even more so from having children." His eyes looked further away than before. "But sometimes, life happens." He turned to her. "Doesn't it?"

"We control what happens in our lives." Her voice didn't even flinch.

"Yes, I guess that's true."

Suddenly she wondered about Brulis' history as she stared at the redheaded, tired man. Who his family was. What brought him here, as a Shepherd of Mind? Did he miss his family? What was *he* capable of?

Brulis stared into space. "I guess, my purpose for coming up here was to say, we all make sacrifices for our country, it's the Shepherd's way, and I have no regrets for that. What you're going through . . . it's for a reason you won't see today. But the Liberator knows. And he's with you."

She stared at him with shock. "You're . . . a believe of the Old Order? Why? Are you crazy?"

"I'm not crazy." Suddenly he sounded wiser than he ever had before. "And I have the freedom to believe what I will."

"Brave of you," she scoffed.

"Just because it's not what you believe, doesn't make me wrong, you know. I am a Shepherd of Mind. I have put my time in the libraries as well."

"Old Order Mythology has been disproven."

The man smiled slightly. "Has it?"

"Yes," she said curtly.

"If you say so." He started to go. "Just wanted to offer you some encouragement. Shepherd to Shepherd."

She turned her back to him. "I told you I'm fine." *Leave me alone.*

"If you say so."

As he descended the mountain, she could hear his footsteps soften as he went. Something from the pits of her stomach started rising up, and before she could stop it, she blurted out, "Do you miss them?" She knew he stopped, but she didn't look at him.

His voice sadly echoed, "Ussa . . . Fenris . . . Arissa . . . Lily . . . Belen . . . Cole . . . their names are engraved on my heart. I miss them every day. But I do it for Oldaem. Keep the Faith, Kayt." Then he was gone. She realized then, possibly for the first time, how different they truly were. For her, her country never came first, but neither did her family. It was *her. She* always came first.

A single tear trickled down her cheek. She didn't know why. Perhaps it was the wind, the cold, or even sheer exhaustion. *Bayln . . . Lei . . . Arnand . . .* she missed them too. After she whispered a

39

prayer to the One for strength, for the first time in her life she wondered whether or not the One was real. *Doubt is a dangerous thing.* As she pushed the thought away--a practice she had perfected—she stared off into the dark, foggy horizon, wondering what her children were doing. How they were faring. Did they think about her? Did they remember her? Did they resent her? Did they love her? *Arnand.* He was always so simple, so kind, so loyal. *My children.*

As she headed down the hill she realized how empty she had been in the library. It didn't fulfill her. The knowledge didn't satisfy. The gilt and the bronze and the vaults and arches and isolation . . . none of it fulfilled her . . . *neither had Silas.* Only her kids. Only they made her feel she had worth, that she was needed. *Just them.* When she reached her shoes again, her eyes were clear and her head determined. *No more reading. No more libraries. No more being nothing. No more pity. I'm going home.*

CHAPTER 6: IAN

The fog had become thicker as the night wore on. Ian's hands were rubbed raw from gutting the fish, and he stunk as usual. Even after bathing, it was impossible to remove the stench of fish. Perhaps it was embedded within the wooden structure of his room. As he peered out his window, barely a wisp of breeze stirred, yet it was a cool night. As he watched the increasingly obscured lights of ships arriving in the port, Ian knew he was lucky. He had an incredible view. Most houses were blocked from seeing any of the ocean by the massive walls and high towers surrounding Lion's Landing. But his room faced the street, and beyond it lay the ocean and a partial view of the port. Somehow the weather seemed to reflect how he felt inside.

A dog barked somewhere, but he couldn't see it. Tonight could go two ways for him: either his parents would be behind him completely, and at this time tomorrow he would be sailing toward his Shepherd Interview, his life completely changed and full of potential and possibilities, or they would say no, and his life would be full of Quiana. The barking continued, and Ian peered through the fog. *Nothing.* Ian had always loved the little awkward critters. He was the one who when running through the streets with his friends would pause for the random turtle or other creature. Ian would spot the bird flying at the back of the pack, high up in the clouds, or the deformed mutt in one of the marketplaces of Lion's Landing. Always he noticed the odd and the deformed--the misshapen and the different. *Maybe one day someone will notice me.* But he thought it with hope, not with bitterness, despair, or self pity. That wasn't Ian. He believed in change, in the possibility of tomorrow. And he believed in peering through the fog to notice the abandoned dog.

"Aupaino! It's time to eat!"

"Coming, Mother." *It's time.* Closing his window, he started toward his bedroom door. The barking continued but was muffled. Then on sudden impulse he went back and swung open the window once again. *I hear you, little guy.*

Then Ian clomped down the stairs, halfway down already out of breath, his belly flapping up and down. "I'm so excited to share dinner with you both." He smiled at both his parents, sitting at opposite ends of the table.

"Baaaaa Blooooh."

"With you too, Talo."

"Come, sit. Your mother has made more than she should have." His father's large warm eyes had invited him to share the table at many a dinner. And his father's large hands gently rested on the table's surface. Only "large" could describe his father. Ian's parents looked like two wide, tall towers sitting at opposite ends of a long wooden boardwalk. The boy couldn't help but smile. He loved them. Ian's father was a highly respected man in the Beelzian community. Everyone knew him. And everyone could hear him when he spoke or could pick him out in a crowd. "Stop staring at us, son," his deep voice rumbled. "We are waiting for you."

"Sorry, Father." Talo bounced up and down in his seat, clutching giant spoons tightly in chubby hands. Ian nervously walked to the table and took his seat opposite Talo. He swallowed. *Steady, Ian. It's just a question. You'll be okay.* He could still hear the barking.

"Let us give our blessing." His father stretched his long arms across the table to his two sons. Talo stood in his chair so that he could reach. As Ian took his parents' hands he knew his palms were sweaty. "Praise be to the Tide for ever-flowing waters. Praise be to the Rock for our foundation. Praise be to the Source for life. *Amenaino,*" his father breathed in reverence.

"*Amenaino,*" the family repeated, Ian a bit delayed, still trying to figure out how he would formulate the question in his mind. He looked up at his father who slowly took back his large hands, his eyes closed deeply in thought. *Now we wait.* The barking continued. Ian knew he couldn't breach the topic unless his father opened up "free conversation time." Beelzian customs were quite clear on the events of Dinner, the culture's most sacred time. If Father's eyes were closed in silence, the family's eyes were closed in silence. No one ate until the father did. They only ate the courses he ate. If Father didn't feel like Starfish Rolls, no one ate Starfish Rolls, even though Mother had gone through the trouble of making them. That rarely happened in Ian's house though. Looking at the bellies of both Mother and Father, he was sure that like at every other meal, no course would go uneaten. And glancing around, Ian noticed many, many courses: Lobster Bisque, Crab Cakes with Herb Salad, Oven-Roasted Dungeness Crab, Shrimp and Mango Skewers with Guava-Lime Glaze, Old-Fashioned Crawfish Boil, Sea Bass with Citrus and Soy, and Ian's favorite: Starfish Rolls. He had smelled them all afternoon. The Beelzian's ate heartily and well. The Beelzian's laughed, raised families, and protected the gifts of the Source. Thus they honored the creatures of the Tide by eating them, the creatures of the Rock by giving them attention. And they stayed home and became helpful members of society. One did not interrupt dinner with announcements of joining the Shepherd society of a foreign nation and no longer contribute to household duties, to make a name for *self,* to move far, far away, to become possibly warlike in nature. To take part in political issues, possibly stress-inducing. Beelzian's lived simple, stress-free lives, full of light and love and food. *This isn't going to be easy.*

His father's eyes were still closed. Ian wondered if Mother had fallen asleep. Talo peeked and noticed his brother's eyes open. His little jaw dropped in shock, and he quickly closed his eyes again. *Talo is more obedient than I am.* Ian sighed, but a quiet sigh. Sometimes Dinner could last for two to three hours, depending on Father's mood. He needed to get a good night's rest for tomorrow. As if in response to Ian's thoughts, his father's eyes snapped open and his hands reached for the Starfish Rolls. Ian couldn't hold back his smile. *Maybe tonight will be my night after all.*

The Starfish tasted better than ever before. The focus of the conversation changed several times. It shifted from surfing to the marketplace beggars to the future of Fishgutz to the taste of the Sea Bass to the weather and back to surfing and to Talo's weight to Mother's hair to the beauty of Quiana (*gag me*) to the increase in population of Lion's Landing (*one hour gone*), to Quiana's beauty again, to Fishgutz, to the Motherland, to the Tide, the Rock, the Source, the Moon, Talo's schooling, (*barking*), and Quiana again. *Two hours gone.* The eating continued. Ian sat silently through most of the bellowing laughter, his Father pulling out the lyre and singing Beelizian songs through stuffed mouths of prawn, and a short nap, and more singing, and a little bit of dancing, which Ian usually enjoyed watching. The sight of his huge parents dancing around the room often reminded him of the sea lions rolling around the rocks during low tide.

"Ian, you've been awfully quiet tonight. Is something on your mind?" His father's words jolted him to reality--the reality that the time was now. He had been asked a question, one that would link him to the question he had been waiting to raise for years now.

"Quiana's on your mind, isn't she?"

His mother beamed a huge toothy grin. "Ah, love is important."

"No!" Ian nearly spat out. "It's not her."

"Don't be shy," his mother leaned against the table. "She's a beautiful girl."

"Please, let's not talk about Quiana's beauty anymore." *She's always looked like a giant toad to me.*

"Aupaiano, always the ladies' man. Like his father," his dad commented.

"It's *really* not about her."

"Speak, son." At last he had his father's full attention. His mother seemed to be occupied with wiping Talo's double chin.

Here we go. "Tomorrow is an important day for Oldaem." He found himself saying the exact words he had rehearsed for days now, hesitantly, yet they were coming out of his mouth. "Tomorrow in Altairus the STC, the Shepherd Tournament Committee, will be conducting interviews to find the best Shepherd Candidates across Oldaem." Ian swallowed. Both of his parents' eyes were glued to him, his mother's mouth half open in shock. Even Talo's open mouth was frozen in mid bite, a giant spoon stuck against his tongue. *This is it.* "I would . . . like to go."

"No. You're too fat." His mother's words struck him like a wooden paddle across the face.

"But . . ."

"They'll never let you in." Her words continued like more and more slaps. "You can barely run up the stairs, Aupaino. What makes Beelzian people strong the people of Oldaem condemn. Our weight,

43

our strength, our fortitude, our song, our smiles. Shepherd Academy will take that away from you. What about Quaina? What about Fishgutz?" She looked horrified, but the worst was yet to come: "What if you . . . *lose* weight?"

"Faaat faaaaat," Talo added.

Ian couldn't get a word in. "But . . ."

"You're Beelzian! They won't let you be a Shepherd! It's too dangerous!"

"No! I'm from Oldaem!" Ian spoke more harshly than he had intended. But he couldn't stop himself. His words tumbled out like lava from an erupting volcano. "I was born and raised here. My friends aren't Beelzian. *You* came here that I might be raised in a better country, with opportunities. *This* is my opportunity! I feel it in the Tide and the Rock." He spoke with passion he didn't know he had. "This is what I need to do. It's tomorrow . . . or never. I'm 15. This is the only year I can do this."

His father's eyes stood unwavering, his face hard to read. But his mother continued, "And you wait until tonight to ask?"

Silence filled the room. Talo played with his food. Ian's eyes studied the wood of the table. Then his voice filled the silence, nearly breaking. "I want to help. I want to do *something* with my life that . . . helps people."

"Mother, why don't you and Talo clean up? There are many dishes to wash. My son and I will go to the Tide. He needs some fresh air, and some clarity of thought." His father was already standing. Quickly and angrily his Mother pushed her chair back and strode into the kitchen, Talo waddling behind. Ian sat there, his father towering above him at the end of the table. "Come, Aupaino."

Before Ian realized it, he sat in the room alone. *What just happened?* The front door stood open, the foggy night beyond it. He knew what was waiting out there with his father: rejection, discouragement, more of the same, Fishgutz, family dinners, a life with Quiana, the Tide, the Rock, a silent dog. *Better get this over with.* As Ian stepped out into the dense fog, he could barely see the sand of the shore beyond the dark street. He knew his father was already by the ebbing waves–Father always went there to think. So did he. And so did every Beelzian. He could see a giant form sitting in the sand a ways down the beach. As Ian walked on the cool sand, every step took him away from becoming a Shepherd. Every step led toward a life of self-indulgence. That is what he realized he hated the most about being Beelzian. They rarely paid attention to anyone but

44

themselves, their eating habits being a reflection of that. Their focus was only on themselves and their families. Maybe he was being selfish too. Maybe he couldn't escape who he was. And maybe being Ian *wasn't* okay after all.

"The Tide is uncertain tonight." His father's voice sounded strained and tired. Ian plopped down beside him. "It roars and crashes with strength I haven't seen in years. Something is wrong on Esis."

"Things are changing." Ian's voice felt tinier than a single grain of sand.

"Yes, Son. You're right."

His father's words surprised him. Ian sat quietly, slowly gazing over to his Father's large face with its big sad eyes. Those eyes showed shadows of something he had never seen in his life: fear.

"Why do you want to be a Shepherd?"

Ian was thunderstruck. No one had ever asked him that question. He wasn't sure he had ever been allowed to entertain the thought. Another chance to speak his mind--another chance to bark. "People need help, Father." His thoughts gained clarity, and once again he spoke with passion. "That's what I think. I think the Tide and the Rock agree. We spend so much of our lives focusing on what we want and what we need and what we like. But what about those people who need help? What about the people who don't live as blessed lives as we do? The Shepherds bring hope to people, they make a difference, they help so many." His voice picked up speed. "And I'm not saying that what you and Mother do isn't important, that you're not making a difference, because you are, especially to me, and you do it in the best way that you know how. Well, this is my way. This is me. And I believe in a better Oldaem, a better Esis. I believe in no more war or murder or death or sadness. I believe in an Esis where people can live together in peace and love, like Lion's Landing, except that the Beelzians love the people of Oldaem, and the Lameans aren't pushed aside, and the Leojians are welcomed, and all can laugh and swim and run, and it doesn't matter if you're thin or fat or loud or soft or tall or short or married or . . . single. I believe in that Esis." Silence. *Did I say too much?* Ian was almost dumbfounded at his own words. They were words he hadn't necessarily processed in his mind, but ones that had lived deep within him as he observed the world around him. He felt more confident than he ever had before. Perhaps he would go to Altairus tomorrow, no matter what his parents said.

"Aupaino, look at the stars."

Ian glanced up, not even realizing the fog had started to break up, especially above him.

"There are so many, son, each with a story of its own. Each one holding its place in the sky, each one important in its own way. Some shine brighter with more intensity, while others are so dim that they don't seem to make a difference"--his kind eyes twinkled back the reflection of the bright ones--"but each one does. And I notice them. I notice you."

"Father . . ."

"I love you, son."

"I'm sorry, Father. I didn't mean to upset you and Mother so much." A tear fell down his cheek.

"I know you're different. I always have. I know you believe differently and that you think differently. You love differently, and that's what I like about you."

"Father, I *have* to go."

"I know you do," his father cut him off, not with anger, but with understanding. "So did we, your mother and I. I had a very different conversation with my own father on a beach in Beelz. I told him we needed to come to Oldaem, to break Beelzian customs, to find our own way"--his large hand brought Ian closer to him--"for you."

"For me?" Ian's father had never spoken of such a thing before.

"Your mother was to have a child . . . you, and we wanted to give you the best life. Oldaem was the best life. We left our friends and family and beliefs and faith to make new friends and family and beliefs and faith. Yet we found that our faith stayed the same."

"I'll never make a new family!"

"Yes, you will. It's what time does to you. It's how the Tide ebbs and flows, and so does family and friends. People will flow in and out of your life. But remember the Rock. The Rock will keep you grounded in what you know to be true."

"I don't know . . . what is true. Only what you've told me." *Where did that come from?*

Ian's father's face grew into a wide smile for the first time since he had reached for the Starfish Rolls at dinner. He hugged Ian with a passion and intensity he had never displayed before. His low voice rumbled, "Then you're ready to go."

Ian rubbed his tears away on the rough fabric of his father's shirt. *What if I find something different to believe in? What if my truth changes? What if it needs to? What if I am too fat? What if I do find*

46

*new family? What if I stay? Is Quiana that bad? YES SHE IS. What if
. . . I never make a family of my own?*

They sat on the shore, just holding each other. The stars were
visible, but nothing else around them was. Fear struck Ian–fear and
comfort, which can be a confusing thing to feel. Perhaps it should be
defined as *life*. There were so many things that words could say, but
sometimes a hug said it better: *I'm proud of you. I'll never let you go.
Go with an open mind. Guard your heart. Guard your body. Guard
your soul. This hug is long because I know you're good enough to
become a Shepherd, and therefore this hug is goodbye.* That was
what his father's hug was saying. Ian hugged his father even more.

"You should go to bed," his mother's warm voice broke up their
hug, or maybe it was Talo's giggling. Then he saw them standing
there, a basket of food in hand. "You have a very busy day tomorrow."
Her words could only mean one thing: *Mother heard everything, and
she had changed her mind.* "Starry snack?" she asked, holding out
the basket. "I'll pack another basket for you tomorrow. You're going
to need to eat a big breakfast, because if you're nervous in your
interview on an empty stomach you might vomit up all your nerves
all over the STC, and they'll never choose you." She grinned.
"Maybe I shouldn't feed you after all." Ian's heart filled with
adoration for his parents. Following Mother and Talo was perhaps
the ugliest dog he had ever seen. It had no tail, only one eye, and was
black and yellow and brown and fat and awkward. It was beautiful. It
was him. And it was barking.

The stars both bright and dim watched a Beelzian family dance
around an awkward dog that could barely move, barking in freedom
and love. They laughed and sang and ate some more, spoke freely,
then swam and talked and sang deep into the night. The Tide rose
and fell while the Rock stood still. *Maybe it's okay to be Ian after all.*

CHAPTER 7: SAYLA

After her disturbing dreams the night before, Sayla felt as if she
hadn't slept at all. But she tried not to show it. A Shepherd of
Defense is always strong, she reminded herself. Still, she couldn't
keep from yawning as she cleared away the remains of breakfast from
the makeshift campfire.

All around her the small camp was bustling with activity. Aveline and Zayeed, the second-year student, were supposed to pack up the tents.

"Get up, you wimp!" Sayla noticed that Aveline was seemingly taking down the tent by herself while Zayeed was moping on the ground.

"I told you, I slept on a rock and now my back is all full of knots," he answered crossly.

"Full of knots?" Aveline apparently wasn't buying it. "Do you hear this guy?"

Sayla turned toward Zayeed. "If you're not strong enough to pick up the tent, just say so."

His face reddened. "That's not why … I already told you." He looked at Sayla and Aveline who were smirking at him. "Never mind." Grabbing the tent material from Aveline, he started storing it away.

Smiling to herself, Sayla resumed packing their leftover food. She loved how she and Aveline made such a great team. Back home, Sayla had always been sort of a misfit. Her best friends had always been boys. Both of her sisters were so much older than her that it had been as if she grew up with three mothers. *And I'm a disappointment to all three.* Her father might have been proud of her, but he was so soft-spoken that she could never really tell where he stood on anything. Her whole family had not even been that impressed when she actually got into the Shepherd Academy, a high honor. She had been the only one of her siblings even to try. The rest of her family had all reasoned that they were well enough off with their fabric business that they didn't need anything else.

But when Sayla had gone to Woodlands Academy, her whole life had changed, and a lot of that was because of Aveline. Aveline was the first girl who really understood her. Like Sayla, she was also a Defense student.

Sayla looked over at Zayeed who was sulking behind her, and then at Oghren, the third-year student who seemed to be having trouble tying the laces of his boots. It wasn't fair. The system wasn't fair. Sayla and Aveline were leagues ahead of what Oghren and Zayeed would ever be, and yet they both were almost assured the title of Shepherd of Defense once they graduated. And out of Sayla and Aveline, there could just be one. Only one would graduate and become a Shepherd.

Each academy only held 30 students every year. There were a total of eight first-year students: two for Mind, two for State, two for Spirit, and two for Defense. On Examination Day, at the end of every year, one student would get eliminated from each class so that by the fifth year there would be just one student for each section. It just so happened that among the fourth-year students, the Defense spot was the only one left to be filled. Sayla hated it. She felt as if she could never relax and let her guard down. Constantly she had to compete against Aveline, and the best-case scenario was that Sayla would graduate and destroy her friend's dreams of ever becoming a Shepherd. Zayeed and Oghren were lucky that their competition had already been eliminated. Shale was assured the title at the end of this year's tournament, as long as he followed all the guidelines.

Sayla sighed. Well, she could do nothing about it. Rules were rules. She just had to make sure that she seized every opportunity to prove her worth so that she would be the one to earn that Shepherd of Defense medallion.

The apprentices made their way down the hill and into the town. Shale and Tali were already ahead of them, renting a stable to board their horses for the duration of their stay.

When they caught up with the rest of the group, Shale gathered them in the square. "Alright, listen up," he said in his most stern voice. Sayla thought he was trying to mimic one of their professors. "This meeting is very important. You aren't just responsible for yourselves--you are representing Woodlands Academy. Be professional. And especially be respectful of Shepherd Demas."

Grunt, the other first-year student, raised his hand. He seemed like a nice kid, but because he always looked at Sayla strangely, she politely tried to avoid him as much as possible.

"No questions!" Shale glared. Grunt timidly lowered his hand. "Where was I? Oh, yes. No talking unless you are spoken to first. Avoid contact with citizens. We're Defense Shepherds, not Spirit Shepherds." The small group chuckled. "Pay attention to everything you see on this tour of the military base. This is your inside look at how Oldaem's military facilities are run, something, assuming you graduate, you might be in charge of someday. Make me proud!"

They started toward the base. Grunt walked next to Sayla. "Do you think it will be dangerous?" he asked hesitantly.

Sayla looked down at him. "Why would it be dangerous? It's a military base, not a war zone."

"I know. But we're about as close to Leoj as we can get, and that is a war zone. What if they … I don't know … attack Sea Fort or something?"

Sayla's green eyes twinkled in the sunlight. "Then we all die slow and violent deaths at their hands." Her answer seemed to disturb him.

Oghren, who had been listening, shoved Grunt from behind. "Shut up, you big baby. We're Shepherds of Defense, we'll be fine."

For once, Sayla agreed. She was really excited to see the base. Well, she was actually excited to see *someone* in the base. She patted her pocket to make sure the letter she had written was still in it and smiled.

The town of Sea Fort looked as if it had once been quaint and rustic, but was now overrun with people. On the walk through it she spotted more Stherians than she would have preferred, but that was probably because Vertloch Tower, their colony, was just a little to the north. Sayla was not sure how she felt about Sea Fort. It had the hustle and bustle of a big city like Evedotar, the capital of the region of Efil, but also the small-town feel of Sayla's hometown. She wondered if her friend had felt the same way when he first came here. Hopefully, she would get to ask him in person.

As soon as they arrived at the military base, they received a tour by a bald, gruff-looking general named Zevran, who did not seem particularly pleased about being relegated to tour guide. Sayla figured it was probably difficult to spend your whole life working to be a general just to know that any one of these Defense students could outrank you immediately upon graduation. While the things Zevran showed them were relatively interesting, she couldn't help but look down every hallway and into every room, hoping to see a familiar face.

The last stop on the tour was the armory, something Sayla was very excited to see. However, as they were walking through the door, she spotted the main office right next door. *Maybe I can leave my message there*, she figured.

"Cover for me," she whispered to Aveline who gave her a questioning look but nodded as Sayla silently and briskly walked toward the office. She ran up the steps and just as she was about to open the door it swung open by itself, knocking her off balance. Sayla felt a rush of cold water as she fell to the ground. Trying to remember if she had ever learned in class about a tactical response to a flooded office building, she looked up and saw a young girl about her age staring down at her in horror.

"I'm so sorry!" It only took a moment for Sayla to see the girl's terrified expression, the clothes she was wearing that identified her as a Lamean slave, and that she was holding a mop and an empty bucket that had been full of soapy water a few seconds ago. Sayla didn't know how strict they were with their slaves in Sea Fort, but she could certainly see the fear in the girl's dark-brown eyes. Undoubtedly, spilling dirty water on a guest, let alone a Shepherd of Defense apprentice, would call for some dire form of punishment.

"It's fine, really," Sayla said as she quickly got up and started to wring out her shirt. At least it was black and the water stains were not obvious. "It's hot outside anyway," she said with a smile.

A glimmer of surprise spread over the slave's face. "Are you sure?"

Sayla nodded. "Don't worry about it."

The girl smiled in relief. "Thank you. May I get you anything?"

Sayla bit her lip. "Actually, I was wondering where I could leave a message for my friend. He's a soldier here."

"Right inside and to the left is the record-keeper's office. Someone in there will be able to deliver the message."

"Thank you." Sayla smiled once more. The slave nodded respectfully and they parted. Before she went inside, Sayla redid the twist in her hair so that it would look less as if she had just gone swimming or was really sweaty.

Quickly she found the record-keeper's office. It had glass doors at the entrance, and she was about to open them when once again they opened themselves. This time she was prepared, though, since she could see that someone was exiting. Stepping to the side, she let the young soldier pass by. Sayla remembered a professor telling her once that she could be as nimble as a deer if she wanted to, but she always had the tendency to look to the side instead of seeing what was right in front of her.

The soldier paused as she was about to walk in. "I don't think I've seen you around here before."

The young man certainly did not look like Sayla's concept of an ideal soldier. He did look intimidating, though. He resembled a square wearing a uniform. Well, you probably don't need brains to be brute force. "I'm visiting from Woodlands Academy."

"A Shepherd? Well, isn't that exciting." The recruit started to lean against the wall, but noticing that it was further away than he thought, changed his mind at the last minute. "I'm Adar, by the way."

"Right, well have a nice day." Sayla started through the door.

"I don't believe I caught your name."

"Didn't give it to you."

"Well, if you're …"

"I'm not." And with that she walked into the office.

Hurriedly she left her message with the person on duty and ran out to join her group. Shale looked at her a bit quizzically, but thankfully did not comment on her absence. Tali nudged up to her. "Sayla! You should have seen the armory! There were so very many weapons that I thought I'd have a heart attack! Also, you smell like dish soap."

"You kind of do," Aveline added. The others agreed.

"I may have had an encounter with a bucket of water," Sayla admitted.

"Were you meeting that boy you know here?" Tali wondered.

Sayla looked uneasily at Shale. He caught her eye, so she looked away quickly. "No. Uh, I was just leaving him a message." She looked back up at Shale. "I won't leave the group again. Sorry."

Shale stopped everyone as they started to head out of the gate. "Actually, we can all split up now. The rest of the day is free, so take this time to wander about the city. Make sure you don't get lost or be an embarrassment of any kind. You are still Shepherds in training after all."

Grunt raised his hand again. Grimacing, Shale looked at him. "Um, where are we staying?"

"I was about to mention that. We'll be at the Sea Side Inn. Don't be too late getting back there--we have an early morning tomorrow. Sayla, since you're so eager to separate from the group, why don't you go check us into the inn instead of exploring the city?"

She looked up. What was his problem? He had never singled her out like that before, unless it was to compliment her.

"Okay, fine." Was he jealous that she had left her friend a note? But then, she had never mentioned her friend was male.

"I'll go with her," Grunt volunteered. "I'm kind of tired anyway."

"Whatever," Oghren snickered. "You're probably just afraid the Leojians will attack or something."

"I am not! I'm just tired!"

Shale raised his hands. "Fine, fine. Do what you want, Grunt. Now if anyone needs me, I'll be at the market picking up ladies." Winking, he left.

Sayla pursed her lips. "Well, come on then, Grunt."

They walked on in silence for the next few minutes. Sayla pretended that she was alone, but the sound of Grunt's breathing got in the way of that. She tried to think of her friend, but it had been so long since she had seen him that it was difficult to picture his face. Probably he looked different now anyway.

"He was right, you know." Grunt broke her concentration.

"Huh?"

"Oghren." Grunt looked at his feet as they walked on the cobblestone pavement. "I feel really uncomfortable here."

Sayla sighed. *I suppose I should play the caring friend here.* But the truth was, she just really didn't care. The Shepherd Academy had no room for weak people. Grunt would either have to man up, or find another way to make a living.

"You mean about the whole war thing?"

He nodded.

"You realize you have, like, nothing to worry about, right? Leoj will never attack us here. We would obliterate them immediately."

"But ... what if we didn't?"

She rolled her eyes. "Look, Grunt, it's ridiculous to think that way. We have the One protecting us, and he has blessed Oldaem with a fantastic military. Don't you believe in the New Order?"

"Well, of course, but I don't think we're invulnerable. Especially not here." Grunt looked unsure.

Sayla stopped and turned to him. "Look, I'm gonna give you some advice." She lowered her voice. "You need to get it together. You're a Shepherd of Defense in training, and if you have any hope, any hope at all, of making it all the way, you better keep your doubts to yourself."

The boy looked at her intently. "I wanted to be a Shepherd, because I always felt as if it was here I could make a difference. Defense is what I always wanted, too. And when I got it, I was so excited. But then, almost immediately after I learned I won a place in the tournament, we found out we were going to war. And suddenly everything changed."

Sayla remembered the announcement the king had made that day. She had been in the crowd, watching the tournament. But her reaction had been different than Grunt's. Instead, she had felt a surge

53

of excitement at the prospect of defending what she believed in. Still though, she could see what he meant. Her tone softened. "If you want to help people, then war is a prime opportunity. You get to be right in the center of everything."

But he shook his head. "It's different for me, Sayla. You're brave. You're popular. I don't have what you have."

It was true, Sayla had found everything she was looking for when she joined the academy. Friendship. Acceptance. Faith. Family. She was good at being a Shepherd.

That night, as Sayla lay on her bed, she thought about her conversation with Grunt. What would it have been like for her if her dream had not turned out the way she hoped? It was even hard to imagine. She smiled as she heard Aveline and Tali talking about the boys they had seen in the town and how they all fell short compared to Shale. This was her family, where she belonged. She watched a bug crawl across the ceiling. If Aveline noticed it, the beetle would be dead before it hit the ground. But Sayla didn't mind. As she watched it scuttle along, it reminded her of someone else she knew long ago.

CHAPTER 8: COLE

"Cole?"

The voice seemed far away–farther away than usual. And weak. "Cole? Wake up."

Darkness filled his mind. *Just let me sleep.* He was dreaming of a picnic, one he'd never had before, one in which his father and Fenris and Arissa and Lily and Belen and his mother were all together. His mother was serving food while his dad had him on his knee. Fenris was smiling at him, giving him two thumbs up. They were on an island, surrounded by water, and his mother was soaking wet, yet smiling–a bigger smile than he had ever seen on anyone. Water dripped from her face as she breathed, "Cole. I love you."

"Cole, wake up."

I don't want to wake up. I never want to wake up. Dad? Fenris? Come home. Maybe today will be the day.

"Cole, I really need your help."

His eyes flickered open to see pale gray ones, a tired face looking older than it should, and red hair tightly pulled back into a bun. He rubbed the sleep out of his eyes and tried to sit up. It still seemed as if it was too early to awaken.

"Cole, Mom doesn't feel well today"--Arissa hesitated--"worse than usual. I have to go in to work."

As he sat up, he could tell that his sister didn't really feel well either. "I have to go into work--can you watch her?"

He stared at her. "What do you want me to do?" His voice felt deeper so early in the morning. As deep as a 12-year-old boy who just wanted to be left alone could sound.

Arissa flinched, her voice jagged. "Just . . . watch her?" She looked pained. "Please?"

"Okay, Arissa." He wasn't sure what he was supposed to do. It wasn't the first time she had asked him to do this, but he still had the same questions about what his role should be while his mother locked herself in her room. *What can I really do?*

His sister was already at the door. "Keep giving her water. Make sure she stays down."

"And if she cries?"

Her pale hand on the door, Arissa paused. "*When* she cries, it's okay to go upstairs and play so you don't have to hear." Then she was gone.

It always made him feel uncomfortable. Every time Fenris left someone would tell Cole to be the "man-of-the-house," Arissa was basically saying the same thing once again. *I don't remember a time I wasn't the man of the house.*

Cole stretched his arms above his head and arched his back. He was stiff after sleeping so hard and his eyes had not yet fully adjusted to the dark morning. Barely any sunlight yet reached his small room. He noticed Belen's little bed was empty. When Cole stood to his feet, the wooden floor was cool this early. *What time is it?* His feet made faint thudding noises as he crossed the room. Pushing open his door, he glanced around the hallway. Empty. He could see his mother's room a few paces to his right. The door was closed. Then he glanced off to his left and up the stairs. *I wonder if Lily and Belen are upstairs.* Not wanting to call their names lest he awaken his mother, he stepped softly across the floor. The house had little furniture and few pictures. It was practically empty. When he passed the kitchen he saw no breakfast or anything on the table. His stomach grumbled, a familiar feeling. Reaching the staircase, he started ascending one step at a time. The creaking steps seemed to echo across the house. No matter how carefully he put his feet down, the boards groaned and moaned. Fenris' and the girls' rooms were upstairs, one to his left and the other to his right. He headed to the one on the left and knocked. No answer. *Where is everyone?* Pushing open the door, he saw two empty beds neatly made. No sign of Lily, and he knew where Arissa was. *They wouldn't be in Fenris' room. No one goes in there but me.*

Fenris' room had something special about it. It was the only place he could be alone, the only place that seemed bigger than everywhere else, and the only place he felt safe. He didn't go in there a lot, usually just when he was sad, or when he had had a bad day. On a day like that he would crawl underneath Fenris' thin blanket and dream the world away. He liked the scent Fenris had left in the bed. His brother smelled strong and brave and important. But now he didn't go near Fenris' door, rather headed back down the steps.

When he reached the bottom he eyed his mother's room once again. No indication that she had awakened yet. Going to the front door, he pulled it open. It was a very cloudy morning, the sun giving barely any warmth or light. *No sign of them.* Probably Lily had left early with their sister to hunt frogs or turtles. Sometimes she would take Belen with her, especially on holidays. Cole usually just sat on the roof when they would go, watching them run around the bog or the base of the hill, other times pestering merchants or performing in the square. Lily was usually a hit with her funny words, and everyone loved Belen. *Stupid Belen.* He didn't understand the reaction to the child. *What's so great about being a fat stupid baby anyway?* All he could do was waddle around. *Give him a prize for having chubby legs.*

He didn't see them in the bog or by the hill. But then he didn't see much of anyone. The lake was completely still and nothing appeared to be happening at Middle Lake Academy either. It seemed to be a lazy day, but he figured there was more life going on in the village—probably anywhere except where he was. *I'm going to the roof.* Retreating back into the house, he softly closed the door. Gently passing his mother's room once again he climbed the steps and went to the easiest way to get on to the roof: through his sisters' window. Slipping through the window, he pulled himself around, his back facing the open air. Then he put his hands and feet on the roof tiles, scrambled up to the top, and sat down. He didn't know how long he might stay there. Eventually he lay on his back and watched the morning clouds as his stomach grumbled. The clouds barely moved at all, each taking its time, in no rush at all. They had nowhere to go.

But he knew what that felt like. *I'm hungry.* Standing up, he studied the island that held Middle Lake Academy. Always he wondered what being a Shepherd was like and what his father did every day. *Brulis is one of the best Shepherd of Minds in all of Oldaem.* Cole had heard merchants sometimes say that near the docks to the Academy. While he wasn't sure how his dad was so famous, the fact that people spoke about him had to mean he was. No one ever talked about him. People loved Fenris too. Fenris had a way of making people feel secure when he was around. His brother was possibly Cole's favorite person on all of Esis--him and his dad.

Cole now noticed more people coming and going in the village. Their earlier absence had, he guessed, been because he had been up really early. Now as people were waking up they were starting their day again. He watched merchants and vendors, farmers and fishermen. Girls giggled among themselves and boys played with wooden swords. Adults had intense conversations and old people walked slowly, and no one really noticed. Crowds wandered up and down the streets, and the hours went by. The sun had moved higher up into the sky. *Time to eat.*

Pulling himself back through the window and into the hallway, he quietly went down the steps again and started toward the kitchen. But he never made it there.

"Cole." A hushed whisper came through his mother's closed door. "Cole, come here, please." Although he shouldn't have been able to hear it, he did. He froze, and the hair stood up on the back of his neck. Motionless, he stared at the closed door. *Maybe I'm imagining things.* With a shrug he started toward the kitchen. Then it came again, louder this time. "Cole. Please." *Thud. Thud. Knock. Knock.* She was knocking now, and saying his name, louder and louder. "Cole. Cole." He couldn't move--couldn't go in there. The boy hated to enter her room. It was always hotter and darker and sadder than any other room in the house and filled him with fear. And it didn't even smell like his dad anymore. His sister's voice echoed in his mind: *"just . . . watch . . . her."*

Swallowing, he slowly approached the closed door. His hand shook as he twisted the knob and leaned his body up against it as it slowly slid open. The room was dark. Black, really. A strange smell hit him in the face. If despair was a scent, he would have smelled it. Cold and heat, loneliness and exhaustion all assaulted him. He knew all of those things weren't smells, but once again in his mother's room, he thought perhaps they were.

57

"Cole? Is that you?" Her voice cooed slowly as he stood in the open doorway. It was too dark to see inside. "Please come to me, Little One." He didn't know what to do. Usually she was never awake. When she was, Arissa was there to take care of her. While his sister wasn't the most helpful person, she knew how to handle their mother.

"It's me, Mom." His voice echoed as if from a distance.

"Come to me, please."

As he inched toward her bed, shapes and forms became visible from the light from the hallway. He noticed a small wooden chair next to her bed. A second later he found himself sitting in it.

"Don't leave me. Please, don't leave me."

"I won't, Mom."

Her voice was like a falling feather or a drop of rain. He couldn't describe it.

"I can't bear it. I can't do it without you." Her voice was stronger now, yet still barely audible.

"It's okay, Mom."

"Don't leave me, my love . . . I can't go on without you."

Cole didn't know what to say.

"Stay with me . . . stay with me."

When she slipped her weak hand in his, his fingers clasped around hers, fingers that once tucked him into bed, played with his red hair, wrapped about his body when he was cold or tired. Now they could barely move. He squeezed them harder.

"I will, Mommy."

"We need you . . . we need you . . . Brulis."

His dad's name jolted him.

"I love you . . . Brulis . . . please . . . stay with me."

Pine needles crunched under his feet as he hurried through the tiny forest near the back of his house. Besides the roof and Fenris' room, it was one of his other favorite places that he assumed no one knew about. Pausing, he looked around to find himself completely encircled by pine trees. It was as if he was in his own personal forest. Resting on the ground, he covered himself in needles. *She's just lying there anyway. She couldn't get up if she wanted to.* Cole peered up in to the sky. A ring of treetops circled white motionless clouds. *She's just lying there anyway.* Sleep hit him like a falling feather . . . or a drop of rain.

58

He wished he had dreamed of the picnic on the little island with his family. Although he tried with all of his might, he couldn't see their faces. None of them. Not his sisters or his brothers or his father . . . or his mother--only rain. Cole could only dream of rain. His eyes sprang open. It was dusk, the day gone. *How long did I sleep?* Quickly he stood and brushed the needles off of his body. Now starving, it dawned on him that he hadn't eaten all day. Pushing through the circle of trees, he saw the back of his house. It wasn't a big house, two stories, but only barely. It looked as if it was taller than it was wide, which didn't make sense, because it wasn't that tall. Suddenly he began running toward the door, though he wasn't sure why. Perhaps it was because he was supposed to be watching her, perhaps because he was hungry. *She's too weak to move.* Cole ran faster. Shoving the back door open, he paused, then quietly stepped toward her door. Shut, just as he had left it. She was probably asleep. Relief hit him, and once again, he wasn't sure why.

Arissa, Lily, and Belen came home after a while, Arissa entering the kitchen without a word. Belen jumped up and down in the sitting room, and Lily went straight to her room. Cole tried to find out where she had been, but she shrugged him off. *She wants to be alone.* It was unlike her, though. Usually his younger sister was bursting with energy and wouldn't leave him alone. *Not tonight.* He watched her disappear upstairs and close the door behind her. Now he could hear Belen in the kitchen, Arissa feeding him dinner. She would take food to Mother after everyone else. He couldn't even remember the last time his mother had joined them at the table. *I guess Arissa does do a lot.* As he watched her tenderly feed Belen, he realized that she was starting to look more and more like his mother. His older sister looked tired. Somehow he wasn't hungry anymore.

The day was gone, and although he had slept most of it away, fatigue now swept over him. But he had to go back to the roof. He did it every evening to watch. Although he knew his presence on the roof wouldn't be the reason they returned, he didn't want to miss a second of seeing them walk down the road toward the house. When it happened he knew he would literally jump off the roof onto the ground and roll on the soft patch of lilies and then race at full speed into Fenris' arms--maybe Dad's . . . maybe both. Not wanting to disturb Lily, he knew he would have to get on to the roof the hard way, climbing up the rough exterior stones of the chimney. Quietly he walked passed his mother's room once again and out the back door.

59

"Don't be out late," he heard Arissa instruct him, the tone in her voice revealing necessity rather than concern. It's what she had to say, because she was in charge again.

"I won't."

The sun was setting as he took his familiar place and scanned the horizon. He could see people packing up their things in the marketplace, fishermen setting aside their nets, men returning home to their wives and families, children going in for dinner, families eating together. Cole thought of how people would go to sleep and then happily repeat their days again and again, and wondered what that must be like. The colors of the sunset shimmered above the green of the darkening grass. He saw the Shepherd Academy in the distance closing down for the night, boats being tied to the docks, and conversations ending as bodies vanished into the fading day. Bodies once there . . . bodies now gone. A body. Suddenly Cole stood to get a better view. He heard screams and shrieks as several men and women seemed to struggle by the shores down near the village. He couldn't tell what was wrong. Then he saw, pulled from the darkening waters by horrified villagers, a lifeless red headed woman in a silver evening dress . . .

That night, Cole slept in Fenris' room.

CHAPTER 9: IAN

The sound of baby Talo's crying startled Ian so much that he bumped the wall next to his bed. Yawning, he rolled over as he rubbed his head. The sun was really shining brightly this morning. It would probably be a beautiful day to try surfing again. Except Ian couldn't shake the feeling that he already had plans. Then he jerked up in bed. "The interviews!" Hastily crawling over to the window at the edge of his bed, he threw open the curtains. The sun was already far above the ocean, meaning he had slept much longer than he had intended. Dressing hurriedly, he grabbed his satchel that he had packed the night before. As he stumbled down the stairs, he lost his balance on the loose step that he always forgot about, and landed sprawled on the kitchen floor right in front of his mother. She was humming an old Beelzian hymn while gutting a fish with baby Talo strapped to her back.

"Aupaiano, you know you should not run so quickly. Your belly will throw you off balance."

Ian scrambled to a standing position. "What time is it?"

"Oh, I imagine it's just about breakfast time." Baby Talo cooed as Mother turned her attention from the fish to the bread cooling by the window.

"No, I mean..." When he turned to ask his father, he saw him peacefully snoring at the table. "What time does the ferry leave?" he asked his mother instead.

"Why it runs all day, you know that."

"But if I don't leave on the first one, I won't be able to make it to Altairus on time!"

A slightly sad expression passed over her face for a moment, and her hands ceased their work. But immediately she smiled at him. "Then let the wind carry you quickly, my son."

With a nod Ian rushed out the door, but once he got to the porch, he hesitated, then ran back in. Grabbing one of his mother's thick, strong arms, he pulled her down into an embrace. With one last kiss on the cheek, he said goodbye to the only home he had ever known. It was exhilarating. And it was also terrifying.

Before he could head to the ferry, he had to see if Bumo had left yet. They had promised to wait for each other, but his friend sometimes had the attention span of a mosquito, and Ian worried that he had somehow gotten left behind. Bumo lived five houses down from Ian. Ian ran, jogged, then walked quickly across the beach to Bumo's house. Was he too late? Had Bumo left without him? The sound of laughter caught Ian's attention. A flood of relief washed over him as he spotted his friend in the water with four Lion's Landing girls surrounding him. At least he was pretty sure it was Bumo's feet sticking up out of the surf while he did a handstand. Breathlessly Ian ran up to the group. "Bumo! Bumo, come on, we need to leave!" Granted, he felt a little stupid speaking to someone's feet, but he didn't want to get all wet and sandy right before the big interview. The girls had stopped giggling and were staring at him as if he had a starfish stuck to his face. "Um, could you ..." he pointed to the feet. One of the girls tapped on Bumo's big toe. His legs disappeared and his head popped out of the water a moment later.

"Why yes, Irene? Do you want to play dolphin tag again?" Bumo shined his pearly smile. "Oh, hey, Ian! You can play too if you want."

"Um, first of all, no," Ian said over the annoying giggling. "Bumo, come on, we have to leave now or we're going to be late to the ferry!"

His friend's smile momentarily vanished. "Oh, right, that! If you'll excuse me, ladies, I have some very important Bumo Business to attend to." Ian was pretty sure he saw one of the girls swoon as he tossed on his t-shirt and shoes. Bumo patted him on the back. "Alright, let's do this!" And they were off.

They ran inland since the ferry dock was located on the other side of the island and facing Altairus, the capital city of the region of Soma. Ian wasn't sure if what he was doing was really considered running. More like wheezing and stumbling, he figured. He kept needing to stop and catch his breath. Bumo, on the other hand, ran circles around him. Literally. He kept getting really far ahead until Ian could barely see him and then doubling back. The kid had way too much energy. It couldn't be natural. Finally Bumo settled down at a leisurely pace next to Ian who was still jogging and sweating so hard that he might as well have jumped into the ocean earlier. They rounded a corner and Ian suddenly wished that Bumo had ran ahead and been able to warn him. There stood Quiana, dejectedly holding a bouquet of red flowers that matched her dress and the ribbons in her hair. Her face looked more wilted than the flowers ever could. The girl's eyes resembled large, dark sand dollars.

"I just knew you would come this way," she said in her most solemn tone. "Ian, I just couldn't let you go without telling you something first." She closed her eyes and took a long breath.

Now's my chance! If I leave real quietly she won't hear me.

But even as he contemplated escape, he heard his mother's overpowering voice booming in his head that he always needed to respect women. Well, he supposed Quiana sort of fit into that category. Besides, he needed to catch his breath anyway, and Bumo had already managed to find a new group of girls at the flower shop next door and was chatting with them. Finally Quiana opened her eyes.

"Ian. What we have ... it's electric. I know you feel it ... in here." He jumped as she placed her hand over his heart. "Believe me, I feel it too." But he was pretty sure they weren't feeling the same thing right now. "Which is why I must ask you not to do this! Not to leave Lion's Landing! I know you're meant for great things, Ian. But if you become a Shepherd then you can never have a family!" She took his hand in hers and dropped to the ground. "Please stay, Ian! I can't bear to live without you!"

Taking a gulp of air, he looked over to make sure Bumo was distracted by his lady friends. He was, so Ian turned his attention

62

back to Quiana. Hesitantly, he removed his hand from hers and patted her on the head. "Well ... that was ... nice ... to hear. I guess. But, um, Quiana I don't really ..." He must catch that ferry. "I mean I couldn't ever ..."—her eyes looked so hopeful—"...imagine a life without you," he sighed.

"Really?" Her face lit up.

What have I done? Did I just propose? "And I'll come back for you someday," he added in a monotone, now resigned to his fate.

Quiana bounced up and down, "Oh, that's what I wanted to hear!" She kissed him on the cheek and shoved the flowers into his hands. "Have fun in Altairus! Bye!" And then she skipped away.

Ian was still wiping his forehead when Bumo bounced back over to him. "So what was that all about?"

"I think I have a girlfriend," Ian responded, bewildered.

"I feel ya," Bumo added with a toothy grin and pointed toward the other girls walking away, "I think I have five." And with that they were on their way again.

The rest of their journey was uneventful, which was good since they were in a hurry. Despite the need to rush, however, Ian couldn't help but let his mind wander to what it would be like finally to become a Shepherd. He would certainly be selected as a Shepherd of Defense. Sure, he may not look the part now, but as the tournament began, and he was extremely far away from his mother's fried fish sticks, he knew he would drop that extra blubber on his stomach and become as ripped as Bumo. Maybe Bumo would even look up to him instead of the other way around. And with his newly toned muscles and prestigious status, he would be able to get himself five girlfriends instead of one Quiana.

By the time Ian and Bumo reached the docks on the other side of Lion's Landing, Ian was pretty sure he was going to have a heart attack right there on the pier. *Let's just call this good practice before the tournament.* As Ian imagined himself doing so well in the tournament that each of the three academies were fighting over him, he glanced at the faces passing him. One of the things Ian loved about Lion's Landing was its vibrant diversity. Immigrants mingled with native Oldaemites, and Ian was sure he recognized people from Kaya and Beelz, maybe even some travelers as far away as Hemia and Remia although he wasn't sure since the two countries to the northwest of Oldaem were engaged in their own war at the moment and mostly kept to themselves.

Ian wondered how many people from Beelz had ever become Shepherds. Would he be the first? *But I'm not from Beelz,* he corrected himself. *My heritage is there, but my history is here.* He was so proud to be native-born to Oldaem, the greatest and most powerful nation on Esis. It was such a wonderful place where people could believe whatever they wanted and still live together and get along. Sure, most Shepherds followed the Old Order or the New Order and Ian had grown up believing in the Wind and the Sea, but his parents had taught him to respect other religions, and Ian figured that if people believed in something that bettered them, then there was no reason not to try to coexist harmoniously with them.

Ian followed after Bumo as they turned the corner to where the ferry to Altairus was docked. He could just make it out at the end of the pier. *We made it! I'm actually gonna be a Shepherd, and make Mother and Father proud and...* Instantly, Ian put his hand around Bumo's shoulder. "Uh, is the ferry starting to move or is it just me?" The other boy's eyes widened. The ferry was beginning to pull out of the port. A short glance passed between them as if in silent agreement, and then they both bolted forward, determined to catch the departing ferry. Bumo immediately shot ahead, and Ian frantically tried to keep up. His eyes nearly crossed as he sought to keep track of both the departing ferry and Bumo. Trying to concentrate on each, he wasn't looking directly in front of him and, much to his surprise, Ian body slammed into a tall, dark-haired man. They both toppled over in shock, Ian crushing the muscular man underneath with the flowers Quiana had given him flying every which way. At first he thought he might have knocked over a soldier, but in a flash, Ian identified the tall man as a Stherian Warden accompanying a Golden Priestess. Instinctively, the Warden reached for his sword. Suddenly, hands gripped Ian's shoulders and he felt himself roughly yanked off the first Warden and thrown to the ground.

After his initial moment of surprise, Ian noticed the cold steel blade pointed at his throat. His heart began racing. *A Shepherd must be brave,* he reminded himself. Regardless, he threw his hands up in the air. "I am so, so, so sorry for running into you! It was a complete accident. You see, I'm on my way to the Shepherd interviews in Altairus, but I'm late, and I was trying to catch the ferry, and I didn't see you there..."

The younger Warden with the sword quickly lost interest. He lowered his sword and, almost mechanically, turned his attention to

64

someone else. Ian followed his gaze and saw the beautiful priestess that the two Wardens were clearly there to protect. At least he hadn't knocked her over. Otherwise, he might have showed up at the Shepherd interviews with a few less body parts. Cautiously, Ian stood. "Anyway, please accept my apology, and now if you don't mind, I'd love to continue running after my ferry."

The older Warden looked at him the way Ian sometimes did at the fish that enjoyed nibbling on him while he was trying to surf. "Watch where you're going next time, fatty."

"Yes, again let me say how very sorry I am about that."

The older Warden gazed at the priestess who gave a short nod, so small that Ian would have missed it if he hadn't been looking. With that, both Wardens resumed their stance behind the woman in gold. Shivering slightly, Ian felt as if he had just experienced what it must be like when a fly got caught in a spider web. Priestesses might be not as authoritative as Shepherds, but they were still intimidating.

The two boys dashed for the ferry. They were so close … if they could just hop on. Bumo reached the edge of the dock first. The vessel was only a few feet away, so without even a pause, he leapt across the gap of water, landing perfectly onto the deck without even breaking a sweat. A flock of girls who happened to be sitting on the ferry nearly swooned as Bumo's bleached hair waved in the breeze. Then it was Ian's turn to try it. Making sure his satchel was secured to his back, he leapt off the edge of the pier and sailed through the air. *I'm like a dove flying gracefully in the sky. The wind at my back, the sun in my face.* As he began his quick descent, Ian looked down at the ferry to make sure he would land correctly and was surprised to find water below him instead. Had he misjudged the distance? *Okay, maybe I was more like a flying turtle.* Thankfully, he was a strong swimmer. A few powerful strokes later, Ian caught up to the relatively slow craft. Bumo was at the railing and extended his bronze arm to assist him in climbing up. Seconds later, Ian stood on the deck, soaked. Graciously, Bumo offered him his shirt as a towel, which made the girls on the ferry swoon and blush once again. Ian accepted, although it did him little good, and when he finished wiping off his face a puddle spread around his feet. With a groan he realized the extra pairs of clothes that he had packed were probably soaked as well and therefore useless.

"Sir! Excuse me, sir!"

Turning, Ian saw a small man rushing toward him and wearing a green robe with the ferry line symbol across his chest. "Sir," the man continued, "as much as we are thrilled to have your business, I must inform you that water entrances are not allowed. Although we run a free service, there is no room for chaos here, and I must ask you to please clean up this mess you have created. Otherwise, I will have to ask you to leave this ferry."

Ian looked around at the water surrounding the vessel. The port at Lion's Landing was now a distant dot behind them. He decided he'd rather not disembark at this point. "Yes, of course. I'm so sorry for making a mess on your ferry. You see, I'm on my way to the Shepherd interviews in Altairus, and I was ..."

The man tossed Ian a towel and stalked away.

Cleaning up the puddle of water, along with the running through Lion's Landing, almost being killed by a Warden, and attempting to leap onto a ferry had left Ian exhausted. After collapsing onto one of the benches next to Bumo, he tried to catch up with his beating heart.

After they had listened to the waves sloshing against the hull of the ferry for a few minutes, Bumo broke the silence. "Can you believe it, Ian? We're on our way to the Shepherd interviews--the real Shepherd interviews. And after all we've done today, I feel like I can do anything. Like I can really become a Shepherd myself."

"Me too!" Ian eagerly leaned forward. "I know the Rock will give me the strength I need to become a Shepherd of Defense."

"Ha!" Bumo laughed good-naturedly. "A rock is just a rock. A warrior makes his own strength."

But Ian shook his head. "You can't make strength anymore than you can make the sun stand still. The power has to come from somewhere else." While Ian wasn't sure what exactly the source of strength was, he knew it wasn't him. The excitement and peace he felt had to have come from somewhere. One thing he was sure of, though: "Being a Shepherd is all about having faith." Bumo looked at him as if he had suddenly sprouted fins on his head. "You don't seriously believe any of that Old Order mumbo jumbo, right? That's not even our religion! All of that stuff, the Creator or whatever, is just an old story."

"But it's a nice old story, isn't it?" Ian shrugged. "Either way, faith is faith. People need something to believe in."

"Well, I believe in the power of my biceps to help me become a Shepherd of Defense." Bumo kissed one of them for good emphasis. "Hey, let's rank the Shepherds in order of prestige!" Although Ian rolled his eyes, he listened anyway. "Clearly Defense is number one.

66

I mean, come on." Ian agreed. Ever since he could remember, he had wanted to become a Shepherd of Defense. "What do you think is second?"

"I don't know. Mind?"

"Nah, I think State comes before Mind, because they actually do stuff. All Mind Shepherds do is just ... think." Bumo shuddered. "But it can go third, because clearly Spirit is last."

"Why is that last?" While Ian wasn't particularly interested in Shepherds of Spirit, he didn't have anything against them.

"Eh, I mean it's fine if you're a girl, I guess."

Ian looked across the sea. By now the dark shape of the city of Altairus was forming on the horizon. Suddenly, all of the nervousness that Ian had pushed down during the course of the day bubbled up all at once. "Bumo?"

"Yeah?"

"Can you explain how this whole thing works?"

"How what whole thing works?"

"The Shepherd system." It was as if all of his prior knowledge had done a great belly flop into the sea and vanished from his mind.

Bumo happily obliged. "Well, you know that all six regions of Oldaem have a Regent who's voted in every five years along with four Shepherds."

"Right. Defense works with the military and the mining industries, State does elections and politics and money and stuff, Mind directs schools and the Shepherd Academies."

"But they also have charge of media," Bumo reminded him.

"Oh, right! And Spirit does religion, music, history, agriculture, stuff like that."

"The three Shepherd Academies only accept eight new students every year, two for each category of Shepherd, but a whole lot more than that try to get in."

"Which is why they have the tournament."

"Right. Those happen every year, and any 16-year-old can apply. Even strange little Beelzians like you."

Ian sighed. "I was born in Oldaem, thank you very much. And just you wait. I'm gonna make it all five years in the Academy."

"Ooh, I like the confidence! But first you gotta survive the interview, and then if you make it through that, then you gotta get past the tournament, and there are only 24 spots for winners. And with me for competition, you better watch out!" Bumo lightly punched him on the arm. Ian hoped that somehow they would both be selected to participate in the tournament. He knew there were only eight spots available for the region of Soma, but it would be such a relief to have a friend on the journey that he felt sure awaited him.

Soon the ferry docked and Ian found himself in the busy capital city of Altairus. Ian had been on the mainland a few times with his parents, but it never ceased to amaze him. He always felt a little uneasy without having the water surround him on all sides. *Better get used to it, unless I end up at Middle Lake Academy.* Maybe his nervousness just came from being someplace unfamiliar.

Altairus was the only city he had ever been to outside of Lion's Landing, but even he could tell that it was pretty dilapidated. The territory of Soma was not one of the wealthier regions, and its capital city reflected that. Ian knew that Lion's Landing did not have very much either and was much smaller, but it was generally relatively clean and safe. Here, however, he felt as though he would get grime on him just by bumping into any building or person. Either that or he would get kidnapped by one of the numerous suspicious-looking characters roaming the streets. At least everyone looked as if they had something to do, some purpose. He was used to laid-back fishermen and their families. Even at the port, where people were always going somewhere, an incident like what had happened between Ian and the Stherian Warden was rare. But in Altairus, Bumo and Ian had to sidestep several times to avoid hurrying carriages and scurrying people.

Bumo and Ian easily located the capital building. It was a large, tall, white stone complex in the middle of the city. Its whiteness alone made it stand out from the brown, moldy feel of the rest of the city. Ian wondered who had erected such a magnificent structure in the middle of such ruin. Endless rows of steps led up to the columned front and door. Taking a deep breath, then whispering a silent prayer to whoever might be listening, he climbed the steps.

CHAPTER 10: DAKU

Golden light hit his eyes through the tiny slit in the side of the ship. His head was pounding. He heard voices above him, footsteps sounding on the deck. *They must be ready to disembark.* Daku hated when he overslept. It was unlike a Warden to be unprepared.

Hearing Jorn's voice giving instructions to the deckhands, Daku leapt from his bed and put on his simple gray tunic. During the night he had slept restlessly--always did. While he knew he dreamed, he could never recall them. Somehow, though, he sensed that he ran and fought and bled and screamed endlessly through them, but he didn't know what he was fighting or if it was his blood he dreamt of or that of those around him. That's how it was every night. He always heard *her* voice in his dreams. Every time he drifted off into sleep, she would call him back to the world of chaos where she seemed to dwell. What she spoke, he did not know, but it held him powerless.

Light. Something had happened the previous night on the deck. Something different. He seemed almost to remember . . .

Golden eyes . . . he was needed on deck. Malvina would be waiting for him to disembark, and he didn't want to fail her--would not fail her. *Jorn is probably already by her side.* Pulling his britches up, he buckled his belt around his waist, then slid his hands through his sweaty hair. It had been an intense night of dreaming. *Just like every other night.* Daku found himself pulling the blanket over the rough pillow of his hard bed and tucking it neatly on each side. He had to leave the room he wouldn't return to without blemish. It was not to be polite or clean--rather it was to be efficient and spotless. Daku never left a blemish behind. Not when he slept and not when he killed. It was the Warden's way.

After pulling on his leather gloves, he approached the rickety door. The voices on deck were muffled but he made something out along the lines of "the port being busy today" and "a plethora of fish were to be had down under." Daku turned the handle and more golden sunlight hit his face as he headed toward the wooden stairs. With each step he took he dreaded facing those around him more and more. Nothing any longer motivated him except satisfying her every desire. Without her he felt meaningless, wanting nothing except to return to the Tower and perhaps get some much needed dreamless sleep. *Maybe she'll give me at least that.* He paused. *Forgive me, I'm grateful for all you give, my Lady.* "Jorn never complains," he mumbled under his breath. He couldn't even remember the last time he had seen the man sleep.

Daku took the stairs two at a time and sucked in a big gulp of sea air once he reached the top of the deck. It had a different taste and scent now that they'd docked at Lion's Landing. The sounds of city life murmured below the starboard bow. A Warden's ear could discern farther and clearer than most, and Daku could hear

69

conversations in various languages. The crew around him were scurrying and fastening ropes and scrubbing the deck beneath him. Oblivious to the clean patch of deck as his dirty boots stomped along the planks, he also ignored the glares of the cabin boy as he continued along the ship. Gulls flew above him and called out their joyful shrieks of hunger. The waves of the bay gently rocked the ship back and forth. Most of the ship hands stayed out of his way. They had learned not to tussle with a Warden. Jorn had thrown one overboard after a lingering stare back in Leoj. Looking down at his own hands, he could not shake off the memory of the lives they had taken. But he felt no guilt. In fact, he felt nothing at all. He looked around at the busy port of Lion's Landing--so many people coming and going. But he didn't care about them at all. They were either in his way, or they were useful to him. It all depended on what Malvina wanted.

Malvina. She stood before him, Jorn by her side, her hands gently folded in front of her, her face unreadable like the ocean stretching out before a sailing vessel on a calm day. She was tall, her cheekbones high beneath her piercing golden eyes. He remembered a pout always seemed to cling to her red lips. Her shimmering hair cascaded down her back like a golden rain shower. As her intense gaze froze him in his tracks, he immediately found himself kneeling before her, the heat of Jorn's gaze upon him as well.

"Need more sleep?" Jorn's voice was like a low rumble.

"Silence." The Golden Priestess' voice was calm, yet capable of stopping a stampede of charging beasts in their tracks.

"Forgive me, Malvina." A lump formed in his throat. It was almost hard to breathe.

"We disembark. We have transport to catch." She swept by him and toward the gangplank that led to the wooden pier the ship had docked against. Everyone moved aside for her, Jorn practically glued to her right side. Drawing his weapon, Daku quickly took up position on her left. *Soon I'll be at her right.* Neither side of Malvina was actually vulnerable, yet tradition stated the older Warden took the place of the priestess' right, the honored position.

As they advanced through Lion's Landing, people stared. It wasn't that the people seldom saw a Priestess of the Three, rather that Malvina's beauty was stunning. She demanded attention simply with her presence. Daku marched with pride beside her. There was nowhere else he would rather be. His heart raced at the thought of assisting Malvina to accomplish whatever task the High Priestess of

Vertloch Tower would next assign her. He imagined them kneeling before her, her shawl swathed around her head, looking upon them with approval of their success in Leoj, and then bestowing upon Malvina yet another responsibility to complete, in order to bring further glory to the Three and to establish greater Stherian power within the world of Esis. Nothing else mattered.

Once on shore the murmur of countless voices greeted him. Everywhere he looked he saw children playing and merchants selling. Flags flapped and snapped in the breeze, and carts rattled along the roads. Lion's Landing was a busy port with towering stucco walls. While not the largest that he had seen, it still was certainly a major center of trade and commerce for Oldaem. The variety of cultures were astounding, almost enough to remind him of earlier days in the Trade Nation of Najoh. *Najoh.* That country was important to him, but he wasn't sure why. The sky seemed a bit bluer now that he had Najoh on his mind. It made him sigh in quick relief. Daku had loved it there, and he wanted to go back. Even now he could see in his mind's eye the white sands and the crystal blue waters. Suddenly, everything around him seemed to get clearer, the people more in focus, a golden haze seemed to temporarily lift as he remembered Najoh . . . the palm trees and the food and the smells and the sun and the clouds and her laugh and her kiss and her smile and . . .

"Keep walking."

Malvina's sharp voice propelled him back into Lion's Landing. Swallowing, he hurried to catch up to her and Jorn again, just as he did every other day. He noticed the ferry port up ahead and heard the sounds of the horn blown to announce its departure. Ferries left the island of Lion's Landing and sailed south to Aerion, west to Soma, and north to Efil. That's where they were heading. Vertloch Tower stood in Efil, the farthest northeastern corner of Oldaem, Vertloch even further east than Seafort. The Tower being somewhat inland, a special port stood to the east of the Tower and accepted ferries only from Lion's Landing. Up ahead a group of people waved goodbye to the passengers on the ferry. It looked as if it was departing toward Soma, probably Altarius.

Suddenly, an obese boy barreled stupidly towards Malvina, flowers in his hand, not looking where he was going. Instantly Daku stepped in between them and allowed the boy to crash right into and topple on top of him, the flowers scattering all around him. The entire thing happened in the split of a second, but Daku had enough

71

time to react. Malvina must not be touched. His hand reached for his sword, his face as emotionless as Malvina's. Jorn had already thrown the boy to the ground. Daku held the sword to the lad's throat.

Hands flailing in the air, the boy chattered, "I am so, so, so sorry for running into you! It was a complete accident. You see, I'm on my way to the Shepherd interviews in Altairus, but I'm late, and I was trying to catch the ferry, and I didn't see you there ..."

Realizing that the lad presented no apparent threat, Daku lowered his sword. *Stupid boy.* He glanced at Malvina who stood taller than he had seen her before. Unshaken, she glowered at the boy as if he were an insect. The lad's eyes widened as he stared at her, mouth ajar.

"Anyway," the boy continued, voice shaking, "please accept apology, and now if you don't mind, I'd love to continue running after my ferry."

"Watch where you're going, Fatty," Daku heard Jorn snap.

"Yes, again let me say how very sorry I am about that."

As Daku watched Malvina nod her head slightly, examining the boy up and down, he wondered what was going through her fascinating mind. Before he knew it, she resumed her journey. Daku and Jorn followed her without looking back.

He kept pace with Malvina as his mind wandered to his own Shepherd interview years ago. It had gone well. Daku was the ideal candidate. His answers were concise and well thought out, his body in perfect shape, and his head clear and ready to be filled with knowledge. The STC immediately selected him to represent Efil in the tournament. The odds were on him to win the entire thing. Now he often wondered what would have become of him had he become a Shepherd–if he had continued down that path and had stayed in touch with his friends. That is, if he hadn't been thrown out of the tournament. What would have happened if he had never got on his father's merchant ship and spent that year stranded in Najoh? *Aelwynne, I'm almost home.* Fear. *She's not going to be happy with me for what I've done.* Should he feel regret for his actions in Leoj? Would Aelwynne understand and forgive him?

Glancing up, he saw Malvina and Jorn staring at him. His mind had wandered and he had again stopped. Suddenly he realized that she was glaring at him. *What is happening to me?* In her eyes he saw a glimmer of something he hadn't seen before. Although he couldn't place the emotion lurking behind her perfect eyes, he recognized it had to do with him, with his wandering mind. *Stay focused on Malvina. She is all that matters.*

You are mine.
You belong to me.
You love me.
You serve me.
It's the way.
Forsake them.
Forsake them all.

The sky was overcast as they boarded their ferry to Efil. They hadn't stopped to eat, buy anything, or to speak to anyone. Daku recognized Malvina's need to return to the Tower. Timing was always important to her. Later he realized he couldn't really remember anything that happened that day after the fat boy crashed into him. It was a blur. But that was as Malvina liked it to be. *It's how I like it to be.* As they sat upon the ferry as it drifted north toward Vertloch Tower, Daku noticed a small insect crawling across the deck. His heart caught in his throat, and tears flooded his eyes. *Bug.* Visions flashed before his mind of his childhood. *Don't, Daku. She'll know. You're not supposed to. You can't go there.* But he couldn't help but go there in his mind. A forbidden place. He went to Aramoor, where he grew up, with *Bug*, along the shores, within the mountains, a promise, his friends, dreams of becoming a Shepherd, innocent, a little girl with big eyes, "I love you, Bug." A voyage to Najoh, beautiful, perfect Aelwynne, a kiss at the beach, vows, perfection, never want to leave, you're happy, you're okay, you're free, *sail away with me, be who you want to be, stay with me,* "I love you, Bug." *Golden eyes.*

As Malvina's eyes met his, he swallowed uncomfortably. Gray water surrounded them. The sun couldn't possibly shine. She shook her head slowly, her eyes unwavering. He was unable to look away from the golden pools of eternity before him. But then he didn't want to look away. Jorn smirked a half smile. Daku watched her eyes drift downward toward the approaching, tiny, perfect, innocent bug. Then she crushed it beneath her heel. Golden blood oozed out of it and stained the wooden deck.

CHAPTER 11: IAN

The hot sun reflected off the white steps leading up to the capital building. Ian squinted in the bright light, carefully putting one still slightly damp sandal after the other. *How embarrassing if right before my big interview I*--suddenly his big toe caught, and he fell--*tripped*. With a sigh he untangled his legs out from under him and got up to inspect the damage. His blue pants had a hole in them and his left knee was scratched and bleeding. *Great, add that to the fact that I'm still damp from the ferry ride.* Although he hadn't looked in a mirror, he feared that his hair was probably sticking out at various angles as well, not to mention the squishing sound he made every time he took a step. While he would have preferred a more presentable appearance for his interview, hopefully the Shepherd Training Committee would see that what was on the inside was much more impressive than the sweaty, round, bleeding 15-year-old before them.

Ian wasn't really sure what to expect from the STC at all. All he knew was that they were a group of seven retired Shepherds who convened every year in the Capital and then made a circuit of the six regions. In each region they would interview countless 15-year-olds-- anyone born in Oldaem and wanted to apply--in search of eight applicants to represent their region in the tournament that would take place in the Capital in six months. The eight applicants from each region combined with eight from the Capital itself meant that 56 eager teenagers would be able to compete for a spot at one of the three Shepherd academies. And Ian fully intended to be one of those 56, bloody knee or not.

Bumo waited for him at the top of the stairs, not having gone in yet. Ian noticed that tense shoulders had replaced his friend's normally naturally relaxed posture, and his face was a little pale. Although Ian had always considered Bumo as brave and strong, suddenly he wondered if perhaps his friend was just as nervous as he was. *Maybe he's just better at hiding it.*

In silent agreement they each grabbed a handle and pushed back the solid oak doors. Together, they stepped inside. The beautiful architecture on the outside of the building continued on the inside. High windows flooded the interior with sunlight. The floors consisted of black and white tiles, and columns that matched the ones outside were lined all along the room. Strung across the two center columns was a bright yellow banner with green letters that shouted WELCOME FUTURE SHEPHERDS! The room was crowded with young people and their parents, all waiting to get an interview.

As Ian pushed through the throng of people, he quickly lost Bumo. He didn't even know where he was supposed to go, but it seemed as if everyone was facing something under the banner in the middle of the room, so he decided that was a good place to start.

The enormity of the room echoed each voice and amplified the noise in it, making Ian's ears hurt. As he waded farther into the middle of the crowd, he was jostled from every which way. He concentrated on not tripping lest he get trampled. Ian tried to see over the crowd, but just as he was getting a good angle, a very tall girl with fluffy red hair stepped in front of him, blocking his view.

"I can lift you up on my shoulders if that would help." As Ian turned to see Bumo's toothy grin and blond hair to his left, he immediately felt relieved. He was glad they had found each other again.

"I'll pass, but thanks." Instead, Ian tried to shoulder his way past the people in front of him. However, he misjudged the space and accidentally bumped into the tall girl with red hair.

In a flash she turned her intimidating green eyes upon him and shoved him back. "Watch it!"

Not wanting to challenge her, he threw his hands up in defeat and backed away slowly as far as he could. It was only about three inches, but it was better than nothing. "Bumo," Ian turned to his laughing friend, "how about you quit just standing around and help me out here."

With Bumo in the lead, they finally made it to the center of the room after a couple unpleasant encounters between Ian, who became even more drenched in sweat, and a very angry mom who didn't appreciate being bumped into. The point of attraction turned out to be the location of the registration desk where a very skinny woman with glasses and a pointed nose was handing out folders to applicants. Bumo and Ian added their hands to the ones reaching toward her, and Bumo received a folder almost immediately. Ian was just touching one with the tip of his fingers when the woman he had bumped into earlier snatched it out of his hands.

"I'm gonna go start filling this out. Meet me at that table." Bumo indicated a cluster of tables scattered about in a room off to the left.

"Ok, I'll be there in a sec." Again Ian tried to grab a folder, but the crowd kept pushing him away from the table. After a few unsuccessful attempts, he finally got his hands on one and yanked it

75

away from the table. Unfortunately, he pulled his arm away at the same moment a father was reaching his arm out, and they collided. The papers in Ian's folder flew out of his hands and scattered themselves on the black and white tiles where they immediately got trampled.

With a groan Ian turned back to the table to try again. Just as he did, the woman behind it announced, "Ladies and Gentlemen! I apologize, but there are no more applications. We apologize for this oversight. If you do not have one, we will allow you to come back tomorrow, but that is it for today. Thank you." She sat back down. A murmur of complaint ran throughout the crowd, but the people without applications started making their way to the doors. Ian glanced at the scattered sheets he had dropped a few moments ago. *That's my only chance.* Somehow he managed to avoid getting trampled while he picked them up and stuffed them back into the purple folder.

He could see Bumo sitting at a table with a few blonde girls. When he started over to them, he quickly realized that there were no available seats. Bumo saw him and said, "Sorry, I had this seat saved for you, but Jessica here didn't have anywhere to sit, and I didn't want her to be alone, ya know?" The girl waved, and Ian rolled his eyes.

"That's fine. I'll just ..." But he couldn't find any empty spots at any other table. "I'll just lean here." Ian leaned against one corner of the square table as he opened his purple folder. Some of the papers were upside down, others quite crumpled, but all appeared to still be legible.

The first document was a brief history of the Shepherds of Oldaem and what they stood for. *Protect the regions, stand up for truth, blah blah blah, skip to the next part.* There were instructions on how to fill out the waiver form, a complimentary pencil with the Shepherds' seal on it, a discount for the inn down the street, and ... *Wait, a waiver form?* Ian dug through the folder until he found the one titled "Waiver." "The STC (Shepherd Training Committee) will not be held accountable if in the course of the tournament the applicant is maimed, decapitated, drowned, exploded, or otherwise injured."

Ian's eyes widened as he continued reading. He did not like any of those options. Soon he felt the urge to throw the papers again and just storm out of the building. Nothing had gone right today. In fact, everything had gone wrong. *Maybe I should just take that as a sign that I'm not meant to be here.* Suddenly he wanted to just forget it all, to go back to the ocean where he belonged. *I'm fat, I'm scared, I'm not strong. I have nothing to offer the people of Oldaem. I'll never be Bumo ... What am I doing here, anyway?*

Closing his eyes, he imagined that the pounding in his ears was the sound of the waves crashing on the shore. He could almost feel the sand under his feet. Just a couple days ago he had been there, not a care in the world, searching the tidal pools for hermit crabs. It was one of his favorite activities. They were all over the place if he looked hard enough. At first it would appear to be any normal shell, but scurrying in the sand would inform Ian of a hermit crab's presence. There they were, just going about their business, obliviously stuck in the tidal pool, unaware of the great expanse of the ocean that lay just beyond it.

Bumo always liked to pick up the hermit crabs and toss them into the ocean, although Ian had always felt sort of uncomfortable with that. *Why not let the hermit crab decide for itself?* For the first time, Ian was starting to think that getting hurled out into the ocean might not be such a bad idea. He didn't want to get stuck like those hermit crabs, shoved around by every wave. Maybe it would be a constant struggle, and he realized it would be dangerous for a little hermit crab like him to be out in the open water. But Ian knew that he was meant for something greater than tidal pools. *And,* he resolved, *I won't give up right at the beginning.*

With his mind made up and before the rational part of his brain talked him out of it, Ian filled out and signed the waiver and handed it in to the woman at the registration desk.

It was three days later when Ian had his interview. After he had turned in his paperwork, he had received a yellow slip of paper with the date and time printed on it. It had been a difficult few days of waiting, but he and Bumo had survived. With the double discount they had on the Portside Inn, they were able to stay quite comfortably in Altairus while they anticipated the interviews. They had debated going home, but after a long conversation they had both agreed that having to say goodbye again wouldn't help anyone.

Finally, the day arrived. Ian's interview was in the morning while Bumo's was not until the afternoon, so Ian had walked into the capital all by himself. Nervously, he tugged at his white cotton shirt and tried to adjust so as to hide his belly. He was fully aware of his wrinkled khakis and dusty sandals, but there was nothing to do about it now. At least he had tried to tame his unruly dark curls.

Now he sat on one of the wooden benches that lined a corridor full of closed offices. On either side of him were other people waiting for their interviews. Ian counted seven individuals including himself. Already, two people had come and gone to their interviews, and the girl who had been sitting next to him was in her's.

Ian wiped away the sweat that had begun beading on his forehead. *Almost there, just stay calm. It can't be that bad, right?* Before he had finished his thought, the door swung open and the girl he had been sitting next to ran out shrieking and with tears flying down her face. His eyes widened as he stared in her direction.

The same woman who had been at the registration table before came out wearing a brown cloak and her hair tied up in a bun, making her features seem even more severe. But this time Ian could clearly see the bronze medallion around her neck with a scale on it that labeled her as a Shepherd of Mind. Clearing her throat, she pulled up her clipboard. Before she could open her mouth, an expression of confusion crossed her face. After rereading the list, she hastily raised her head and resumed her confident posture. "Appanow."

Ian looked around. No one got up. The Shepherd tried again. "Uh ... Applenote?" No response. "Owpayno?" Nothing. Then Ian realized what was happening.

"It's Ow-pie-ee-no," he said hesitantly. "Aupaiano. But you can call me Ian."

The Shepherd nodded. "Right this way."

This was it--his moment. Despite having just seen a very nice-seeming girl leave the room in tears, Ian put on his most confident smile and got up from the seat. Suddenly, the sweat marks he left on the seat didn't matter. The fact that he bumped into the doorpost with his shoulder and almost lost his balance didn't matter. All that did were the people in the room in front of him.

The room was certainly not as magnificent as he had imagined. It was a simple study with bookcases lining the walls and a window directly across from him. For the first time, he looked into the eyes of the seven Shepherds that made up the Shepherd Training Committee. They were all sitting in chairs scattered about the room, and all of them strictly business. He knew there was one Shepherd from each of the regions, including the Capital. As he studied their faces he noticed a reassuring variety. There were three women including the one who had let him in. *She must be the Shepherd of Mind for the region of Soma. That's why she is in charge while they are here.* Out of the seven there was also a range of skin colors, one almost ivory, and two with skin even darker than Ian's. Tall, skinny, fat, thin, external features apparently did not matter when it came to being a Shepherd. Which was exactly what Ian was hoping for.

The Shepherd of Mind gestured to a chair directly to the left of him. Hastily, Ian sat down and looked expectantly at the members of the STC.

A man with short-cropped gray hair and a yellow and white robe cleared his throat. "Please be advised that any and all conversations that take place in this interview must never be shared with another person. Will you adhere to these rules?" Ian nodded. "Very well. Please state your name."

"Aupaino. But you can just call me Ian."

The Shepherds glanced at each other. The man continued. "And where are you from, Ian?"

"Lion's Landing …"

"No," a broad shouldered, plain-looking woman Shepherd interrupted him, "where are you originally from?"

Ian was confused. "Well, my family immigrated from Beelz, but that was before I was born."

The man in the yellow and white robe leaned to the Shepherd next to him and said quietly, "We need to verify that." To Ian he asked, "You were born in the region of Soma, correct?"

Ian nodded. "In Lion's Landing. My family still lives there."

A dark-skinned young woman smiled. "Good, then your birth records should be easy to locate in this building."

The Shepherd who was sitting in the corner sighed. "Look, you seem like a nice kid, but honestly, you don't look like a Shepherd." Ian stared at the variety of faces in the room. *What does that even look like?*

"You don't fit the bill," the broad-shouldered woman added.

The man in the corner continued, "So thank you for your time, but I'm going to have to ask you to leave now."

"What?" Ian felt a surge of anger that gave him unexpected confidence. "But you don't even know anything about me. I've been in here for, like five seconds!"

"Boy!" The man in yellow and white stood up, eyes flaring. "We conduct thousands upon thousands of interviews every year! We have

79

some of the sharpest minds in the country. We have seen enough applicants come and go to understand *exactly* what we are looking for. Do not *presume* that we do not know what we are looking for!"

"Well, you don't *know* me!" Ian stood up without a thought of anything except that he had to make them understand. "I may not look like it, but I have a lot to offer. I grew up by the ocean, and one thing I've learned is that even the tiniest fish in the sea is important. It has a purpose. It might not seem like it, but every single creature that lives in the huge ocean has a reason for being there, and the whole world would be different without it. So don't presume that because I'm fat, or brown-skinned, or the son of immigrants, or whatever excuse you're trying to use on me, that I'm not fit to be a Shepherd. Maybe I don't look like a hero right now. Maybe I never will. But I have a heart full of courage and determination like you wouldn't believe." Ian stood a little taller. "And if you can't see that, then I feel sorry for you. And if all Shepherds are as judgmental as you, then maybe I don't want to be one at all."

The room was silent. Ian had even shocked himself, but he certainly did not regret anything he had just said. He was only sorry that the interview had gone so sour. "Thank you for your time." With a blank expression, he turned his back to them and walked out of the room.

The next couple of days were torture for him. All of his dreams had been crushed, and he felt so disappointed by the people who had been his heroes. *It's like thinking you're swimming with a dolphin and then finding out it's a shark instead.* He wanted to just go home, but he wasn't allowed to tell Bumo what had happened in his interview, so he had no viable way to leave Altairus without the letter of rejection he knew was coming.

So he reluctantly stayed at the inn with Bumo who, even though he didn't give details, alluded to the fact that the STC had practically worshipped the ground he walked on during the entire interview. *Typical.*

One morning, a couple days later, Ian and Bumo were sitting in their room after eating breakfast. Bumo was tossing an apple up and down while laying on his bed, and Ian was trying in vain to fix the hole ripped in his blue pants from when he stumbled on the capital stairs. Then a knock at the door made both of them jump. "This is it!" Bumo cried as he bolted to the door. He flung it open, but no one was there. Instead, on the floor in front were two white envelopes sitting neatly on top of each other. Quickly, Bumo grabbed the one labeled "Bumo of Lion's Landing" and tossed to Ian the one that contained an interesting misspelling of Ian's name.

Ripping open his letter, Bumo scanned it and immediately screamed louder than Ian had ever heard him. "I made it! I made it, I can't believe it!" With Bumo's luck, Ian could certainly believe it.

His heart sank as he slowly opened the letter. *How am I going to tell Bumo?* But then his heart leapt as he read its contents.

"Congratulations! You have been chosen along with seven others to represent the region of Soma at the Shepherd Tournament this year. Please report to the Capital immediately."

CHAPTER 12: GALEN

The fire made a loud popping sound as it took out another support beam. Even the rain drizzling from the sky could not slow it down. Galen watched in horror as the angry flames consumed his home, the only place he'd ever known. It had been a small, bare, one-room building, but it had also been cozy and warm and safe. His coat was too small for the freezing air, and he couldn't do anything to help his mom or the other villagers who were frantically scattering around.

His mom had set him by the tree a safe distance away and told him not to move a muscle until she came back for him. She had wrapped a wool blanket around him and pushed him into the shadows of the branches. That had been several minutes ago, yet Galen was still alone. He turned his gaze back toward the inferno that was destroying where he had been asleep just a few hours ago. The scorching heat from the inferno overwhelmed the cold winter air. Galen wondered if his favorite toy boat would survive the fire. Maybe there was a chance that the rain would somehow put the flames out.

The boy sat down on a big rock beside the tree. Although he was perched on a low hill, close to his village, the tree cast a shadow over him so that he could watch without being seen. His heart racing, he worried about his mother, his home–and himself. *The fire can't get to me here. Can it?* Screaming came from somewhere ... maybe from everywhere. Perhaps even from himself. Galen felt as if a whirlwind swirled around him. He couldn't figure out exactly what was going on other than the fact that flames were swallowing the only place he'd ever known as home, and he knew that there was something he was missing. Something else was going on that his young mind could not grasp. But he did know that whatever it was, it was wrong.

Desperately, Galen looked down the hill to the villagers racing around. He could not see his mom. *Where is she?* he wondered as he pushed his straight brown hair out of his eyes. *She said she would come back for me.* Unconsciously, he reached up to his left collarbone and traced the top of the jagged scar that went diagonally down to the middle of the right side of his rib cage. Galen scanned the faces of the crowd, searching for anyone that he recognized. What would he do if she didn't come back?

Fortunately, he did not have long to wonder. He heard a noise coming from behind the tree. Still clinging to his blanket, he quietly shifted around the trunk to see where the sound was coming from. Outlined against the moonlight, Galen saw the silhouette that he recognized to be his mother's. A wave of relief washed through him. *If she's alright, then everything else will be too.* His mother was talking to a man in a big coat, gesturing wildly and pointing toward the tree where Galen was hiding. When she saw him watching her, she gently gestured for him to come over to her, and then she continued talking.

Hastily wadding the blanket under his arm, he ran over to his mother, hugging her waist tightly. She hugged him back with her right arm, her left hand clutching a large traveling bag. Her brown coat and coarse green dress smelled like pine needles and soap and safety. Galen squeezed her small frame even tighter.

His mother dropped her bag and knelt down in front of her young son. "Galen," she said as she placed her warm hands on his shivering shoulders. "Do you trust me?"

He nodded.

"Good." Her bright brown eyes looked unusually worn and lines of worry etched her face. "Then trust me when I tell you that no matter what happens tonight, you have nothing to worry about. You and me, we'll be okay." She gave him a small reassuring smile and patted his cheek.

The man in the big coat cleared his throat. "Meira, you need to go."

His mother nodded and stood. Picking up her traveling bag in one hand, she held his in the other. The two of them began to walk away. One last time Galen looked back at the only home he'd ever known. Every step was taking him farther away from the fiery destruction and the frantic villagers and toward something new, something he did not understand. *We're probably just going away for a little while. I'm sure we'll be back soon ...*

Galen jolted awake. *Where am I?* For a moment he thought he was in that small house in that village that he had lived in long ago. But why would he think that? That had been years ago. *My dream,* he suddenly remembered, *I had that dream again.* He had been so small when the fire happened that he barely even remembered it. Rarely even thought about it. But then a few nights ago he had begun having a recurring dream about that night, and he couldn't figure out why. Because he had been so busy at the military base he hadn't seen his mother in months, so that couldn't be why. Galen absentmindedly rubbed the scar on his chest. The details of that night were blurry, but the fear and confusion he had felt when they were leaving the village always came back in a flash, drenching him in a cold sweat.

Leaving his bunk, he walked across the cold stone floor of the barracks to the window. The moonlight lit up the Sea Fort military base. It was still an hour or so before daylight, but he was wide-awake. Galen ran his hand through his hair. *Well, I'm up now. Might as well get some practice in.*

Noiselessly, he walked back to his bunk and tossed on his military-grade green training shirt, pants, and leather boots. He headed out the door, careful not to wake Adar, his bunkmate or any of the other soldiers in the room. Jogging down the steps of the barracks, he headed to the training grounds. Sea Fort got quite hot and muggy during the day, but thankfully the nights were cool.

The training area was one of his favorite places in the whole base. It was where he could go when he needed to think. There he could avoid people by looking busy as he ran around the track or practiced on the obstacle course. Galen began taking his usual circuit around the track. He had no patience for stupidity, and the majority of the soldiers were rejects of the Shepherd Tournament like himself. They were annoying outcasts who weren't good at anything but following orders. *Maybe that's why I should feel like I belong here.* But if he was really honest with himself, he didn't feel that he really did. Or anywhere, for that matter. He hadn't felt worthwhile since ...

Stop it, Galen, he reprimanded himself. *Concentrate on your running.* But his mind continued to wander, though he refused to think of the friends who had abandoned him for a better life. Instead he thought of his mother. He wondered if she was doing okay. Up until a couple years ago, they had always been together. Many years earlier, his mother had found a job in an inn and they had settled in Aramoor, a city in the region of Efil. She was still there now. At first he had felt guilty for leaving her, but he saw no future for himself in the city, especially after his friends had left. Needing to get out of there, he had joined the Oldaem army almost exactly one year before the war had begun. Galen grimaced at the thought.

He had come here to get away, but after Leoj had attacked Oldaem's colony, suddenly Sea Fort had become the center of the war effort. The town had become overrun with people, and the base was nearly bursting at the seams since they were the easternmost military base and just across the sea from Leoj. More and more troops were training to be sent out every day. Galen knew it wouldn't be long before his unit would receive orders to join the fight, and he hoped he would be ready. *I don't want to go.*

Just as the sun rose above the horizon, Galen started getting tired. Slowing to a stop, he sat down in the field to catch his breath as he watched the sunrise paint vivid colors across the sky. *I don't want to go to Leoj, but it's not as if I want to stay here. Or go home. What do I want then?* He wanted to be left alone. *I wonder if they're watching the sunrise too.*

"What do you think you're doing out here?" a voice demanded from behind him. Galen turned to see Zevran, his commanding officer standing behind him with his arms folded. Bolting upright, Galen put his hand over his heart in salute.

"I'm sorry sir. I couldn't sleep."

"Oh, and that makes you think you can just leave your barracks in the middle of the night? You're not some green recruit, soldier, you've been here for two years."

"It won't happen again, sir," he sighed. Galen would have rolled his eyes if he wasn't being reprimanded.

"You better put that attitude in check, boy. This isn't the first time I've caught you sneaking out." Galen gave up being polite and was about to reply, but he didn't get the chance to.

A Lamean slave tentatively approached them and bowed his head hesitantly. A feeling of repulsion swept through Galen. Unwelcome memories flooded his mind as his hand curled into a fist at the sight of the slave. "What do you want?" he asked darkly.

The slave looked at Commander Zevran for permission to speak. "I was instructed to give you a message from the Record Keeper's office. It apparently was supposed to be delivered to you yesterday afternoon. My deepest apologies for the delay and for the earliness of the hour." Galen grinded his teeth as he stared at the slave. "I was going to leave it at your barracks but I saw you out here." The slave looked down and held out the letter.

With a snarl Galen grabbed the letter. Without a word he began walking back to the barracks. "Galen!" He stopped and turned to face Zevran. "I catch you out here again, you're out."

"Yes sir." *Guess I won't let you catch me then.* Galen paused on the steps outside his room to read the letter. Probably it was from his mother. He had not heard from her in a while, and it was like her to send a letter every so often. However, as he looked at it closer, he realized that the "Galen" written on the front of the envelope was not in his mother's handwriting. In fact, it looked kind of like ... he tore open the letter.

While it was not from his mother and just a short note, the words on the page gave him more joy than he had felt in months. He read it again.

"Hey! Hope you're doing well. Turns out I'll be in Sea Fort to hear Shepherd Demas speak. It's been ages since we saw each other last. Meet me at the Northern Pier tomorrow night around sunset? It would be great to catch up.

Your friend,
Sayla"

CHAPTER 13: DAKU

The ferry ride to Efil was a silent one. Oddly enough only the three of them were on the vessel. The captain spoke not a word as he maneuvered the vessel along the rocky coast of Evodotar's port shoreline, then still farther north. The journey took the entire day, and Daku's thoughts drifted aimlessly. He looked around at all the empty seats and watched as Malvina sat in deep meditation. He wondered if she had used the Golden Power to convince possible passengers to wait for a different ferry, or to change their travel plans as she simply strolled by them on the pier. He knew she was powerful, but the extent of her power, he imagined, he had never truly witnessed. Jorn couldn't keep his eyes off her. Probably the other Warden never doubted, never let his mind roam into forbidden places. Jorn never wavered. *I'll never waver. Forgive me, Malvina.*

The sun had all but set as the ferry docked at Evodotar's port town. Exhaustion swept over Daku. It came not from the events of the day, but rather from those of the past few months, from his time spent in Leoj. They had left him physically and mentally drained. Evodotar lay several miles inland, and Daku's eyes scanned the stony shore before him. The port town was a small, under-developed village with only a few little buildings lining the coastline. A few fishing vendors had closed up shop for the night, and the sound of music and laughter came from a shabby tavern built up against a tall cliff face. Daku watched as Jorn helped Malvina from her place on the boat and onto the wooden dock. Since no one was about, he no longer stood by her left side, his Warden's senses not alert in the slightest. Instead he walked behind them, often turning behind him to stare out into the dark waters of the sea. He was nearly home. Home had become such a foreign concept to him that he wasn't sure of what its reality would be anymore.

"She doesn't matter." Glancing up, he could see Malvina staring at him. Daku could hear her voice inside of his head: *"she doesn't matter."* Reluctantly he shook the previous thought from his mind. *Malvina's right, she doesn't matter.*

He continued walking behind her and Jorn up the stone steps, Malvina gracefully lifting her golden dress above her ankles as they climbed. Except for them, the steps were deserted. They ascended toward The Rocky Solitude, the inn they would stay in for the night. It was too far to walk to Vertloch Tower. Attempting to travel through the rocky terrain at this hour would be unwise. Malvina was never unwise.

They entered the inn to find a broad-shouldered woman in brown linens behind a counter with her back to the door. Malvina stopped as the door closed behind her, and her eyes drifted downward. Jorn took a seat on a nearby bench. Daku knew what that meant. It was his turn.

"I need two rooms please." He approached the counter wearily.

"Oh my goodness. I didn't even hear anyone come in. You startled me." The woman gasped, her cheeks flushed and round.

"Two rooms." he repeated.

"Yes, of course." Daku watched her eye Malvina nervously. It wasn't out of the ordinary for priestesses to frequent this inn, especially with its location being so near the Tower, but that never put people at ease. Priestesses were capable of anything. Malvina was capable of anything. "Few are in port this time of year. Where are you traveling from?" The woman swallowed nervously.

Daku thought the woman should know better than to ask a priestess about her journey. Could Malvina had so unnerved her that she asked exactly what she knew she shouldn't? Undisturbed, Malvina continued to look down.

"Keys?" Daku could hear his voice demand--he couldn't prevent it, nor did he want to. Without another word the woman hurriedly grabbed two metal keys from the wall of the strangely colored array and held them out toward him. Grabbing them both in his fists, he turned from the counter. He could hear the woman swallow as she faced away from him. Malvina's eyes met him as she approached. Slowly he displayed the keys in his palm, and she gracefully accepted one, her touch lingering, then swept past him toward the stairwell. Jorn continued to stay seated on the bench. Daku's gaze followed her as she ascended the steps. It was as if she was floating upward into the Tower itself.

"Come to me."

He didn't know if she spoke those words audibly or inside his head, but he knew what was next.

"What's your name?"
"Daku."
"What do you do?"
"I'm a Warden."
"What do you believe in?"
"The Three."
"Whom do you love?"
Aelwynne. "Malvina."
Her voice shook with power. "Whom do you love?"
Daku swallowed, a bead of sweat dripped down his forehead. The room was dark and musty. A single candle stood between them on a small oaken table, which sat low to the floor. Two poorly stuffed pillows draped in dark fabric served as seats. Low hanging beams struck out above them. Cobwebs adorned the corners of the ceiling and dust hovered over the floor. The air was thick with smoke, smelling of wax and mildew. Silence whirled around them. Their

87

giant shadows danced along the wall: a dangerous dance, a forbidden dance, a dance he grew tired of performing. But a dance he didn't want to stop. They faced each other, legs crossed beneath them. Her eyes did not waver. He wanted to say Malvina--yearned to say it--but he knew it wasn't true. His heart and his head refused to agree. Every inch of him demanded that he say the priestess' name. He knew that it would be dangerous if he didn't, that punishment would be a reality and Jorn would have the upper hand. Yet his gut screamed for Aelwynne--for freedom.

"Malvina."

"What will you do?" Contentment and interest dripped from her lips.

"Whatever you say." His answers came instantly. He didn't need to think of them--knew them from deep within the confines of his soul.

"Where will you go?"

"Wherever you go."

"Whom will you serve?"

"Only you, Mistress."

"Whom will you obey?"

"You, Mistress."

Her eyes showed no hint of satisfaction or relief. Nor did her intensity let up. She was searching his soul, flipping through the pages of his mind with every blink and every breath, looking for things that did not belong, and discarding every forbidden thought and longing he had within him. Daku both gave them up freely and held on to them fiercely. He loved Malvina, yearned for her touch. Most of all he wanted her approval, needed it, and lived for it.

"Daku, I am everything. I am forever. I am your tomorrow."

"You are my everything. You are my forever. You are my tomorrow."

She leaned forward slightly. "Shut your eyes."

He did.

"The swiftest river joins the sea, carrying unwanted debris." *Golden lips.* "Strong currents bring with them the carcasses of the dead, rubbish, and waste, things that do not belong. It makes irrational and erratic turns, going right too fast, left too fast, down too fast, washing away rocks and plants and earth. It can't be faithful, can't be consistent. It splashes and sprays without thought. It has and serves no master."

She's beautiful.

"It cannot be trusted."

She's perfect. Golden eyes.

"You are not a swift river."

I am not a swift river.

"The still pond also joins the sea."

I am yours, Malvina. She was all he saw. All he wanted.

"It brings with it what is stable. It makes intentional turns, going when it needs to, and staying still when it must. It is always faithful and consistent. It serves its master, the sea, giving more than the swiftest river, because the amount it gives doesn't depend on the flow of rain or the degree of the slope. Little bits at a time. They are one. They are forever. It is deeper. It is fuller. It is eternal."

We are forever.

"Stay with me."

I choose you, Malvina.

"It can drown and submerge and sink anything upon it."

I'm sorry for failing you, Malvina.

"Thrust the swiftest river upon a pond, and a pond remains. Thrust a pond upon the swiftest river, a pond will remain."

Golden hair. Master and pupil, hearts beating as one, eyes blinking at the same time. There was nowhere else he would rather be.

"You must be still and listen with me. You must be quiet and wait for me. You must not let your mind wander like the swiftest river. Danger lurks in intense drops and sharp turns. Float towards me." She was whispering now, as he felt himself leaning forward. "Drift with me."

Drifting now in a misty sky, all he saw were her eyes. He was aware of a large pool of golden water all around him. Still as glass it lay, above and beneath him. The flames of the candle were to his left and his right, reaching and grabbing toward him with their golden fingers. He didn't move. He was still. He was silent. He was numb. And he was in pain.

"You are mine. You belong to me. You love me. You serve me. It's the way. Forsake them. Forsake them all."

Daku's eyes opened to darkness, his mouth dry, feeling numb, and sweating profusely. He didn't even remember leaving her chamber and walking lifelessly down the dank hallway to his own.

There he must have lain upon his bed and shut out the world he feared to exist in. The horrendous nightmares, the blood and murder and death and screams and running and crying—he didn't remember that all the things that happened in his dream had been caused by him. The only thoughts that lingered were images of golden pools of water and a candle and a beam and fear and terror and intense loyalty. Jorn's even breathing came from the bed adjacent to his. Even, like ripples in a pond. Slowly he sat up, because he couldn't have gotten up quickly even if he had chosen to. Through the window he could see it was a moonless night, or at least from his position in bed, little light was peeking through. The world was sleeping, and he was awake. *Why am I awake?* His bare feet hit the hard wooden floor. It was cold beneath him, the first true sensation he had felt in hours. His head told him to lie back down. It screamed and pulled at him, the weight of his existence slamming him down into a bed of terror and stillness and defeat.

But his heart . . . his heart told him to stand, to gently close the door behind him, to walk down the stairs past the woman asleep behind the counter. It led him to open the door to the dark outside world and allow the breeze to blow upon his face, to stir his closely cropped hair. Walk past the rocky coast to the section of dark sand, it urged him. His heart commanded him to stand in the surf, as the freezing water washed over his fatigued feet. Acknowledge the cold, it said. But above all, it pled for him to remember Aelwynne and Najoh and the white sandy shores of the warm southern ocean.

And he did remember. He could see her. Could feel her soft white hand clinging tightly to his. Could hear the sounds of Najoh behind them, the laughing and the murmur of trade and commerce. The warm sun beat down and the salty breeze whispered freedom and bright futures. He could hear her breathing beside him, but not close enough. As he drew her nearer, his touch squeezed a pleasant laugh from her lips.

"Daku, what's next?" Aelwynne's bright gray eyes looked at him questioningly. Not with a motive or an agenda, but from hope and assurance of already knowing the answer.

"What do you want to be next?" Gently he pushed a single strand of black hair away from her eyes.

As she looked down, he wondered what she was thinking. He knew what he thought: that he loved her, that she was perfect, that he never wanted to leave the shores of Najoh without her.

90

"I want to stay." Her voice didn't crack or falter. It sounded resolved.

"But your father . . ."

She didn't let him finish. "I don't care." Her voice snapped like a whip. Then she smiled. "This could be perfect for us."

"You know he's going to want to go back."

"It's simpler here. It's easier here."

Daku couldn't disagree. "You're right." He kissed her forehead. "If only..."

"Why not?" Standing on her tiptoes, she stretched her arms into the air. She looked like a tiny white bird about to take flight.

"We have to be realistic. My father, your family . . . we're not the only people on Esis."

"I wish we were." She looked up as a seagull cawed above.

He wished that too, but he knew that if he never came back, he would disappoint them--his friends, especially Bug, who would be waiting for him, who would be looking for him. Daku inhaled a deep breath of sea air. "We can go and come back. We can always come back here. Wouldn't this place be more special if we weren't always here?" He watched her as she looked around. Aelwynne was quite a bit shorter than him, lithe and limber, tiny, but not weak. No, she was strong and firm and resilient. Quiet, soft-spoken, reserved, she spoke only when she had something to say, not all the time, and he knew if she chose the words to speak, they must be important ones. The girl had been through too much in her life, more than anyone as sweet as her should have to endure. *I will protect her.*

"*You* can go and come back." She smiled innocently. "I'll wait for you."

"It's not that easy, Wynnie."

"I wish it were," she said after a pause.

He sighed. "Your dad is slated to return to the Tower soon."

"I don't want to return to the Tower."

"What your dad does there is important."

She swallowed and shut her eyes. "I know." Again she paused, as if she were contemplating and solving all the problems of Oldaem. "So, my question stands. Daku, what's next?" Her eyes opened again.

If only he knew the answer. He wished he could build her a sand hut and live out the remainder of their days on the white, windy shores of Najoh. He wished that his friends would move there too. He wished he could measure up to the man Vorran wanted him to be. Oh, he wished a lot of things. But he knew it started with her father, Vorran. However strong and determined Aelwynne was, he realized that all paths and solutions went through him. *Be patient with me, Wynnie. I do this for you.* He couldn't look away from her; from the silver pools of her eyes.

As they stood side by side on the white shores of Najoh, he put his arm around her, and she leaned her head into the hollow of his arm. He couldn't answer her question with anything but a kiss. She accepted it, because she trusted him. And he gave it because he loved her. Hopefully that would be enough for now. But would it be enough for eternity?

Daku remembered all these things as he stood alone on the rocky shores near the inn. It was still a dark night. But there are times, even during the blackest nights, when one must choose the screaming heart over the screaming head. The heart doesn't always choose wisely, but then again, neither does the head. Each must discern for himself or herself which is better. And when one doesn't know, when a person can't discern between the choices before them, they must make one anyway, because that's what being human is all about. He wasn't free, but then he wasn't trapped. He was Daku. Gold or silver? He would stand here till morning if life allowed. *Aelwynne, I'll be home soon.* But life makes choices too. He swallowed. *Golden eyes.* The struggle continues. *Forsake them all.* Maybe it always would.

For he knew not how long he stood there in the surf, feeling and ignoring the cold washing over his feet. *Soon, Aelwynne.* Finally, he turned and faced the steps leading back to the inn. Jorn, a black shadow, loomed in front of him. They were face to face. Daku's heart raced, then stopped. Silver or gold. *You are mine.*

Chapter 14: Galen

By the time Galen returned to the barracks and back into his bunk, it was almost time for everyone to get up anyway. Instead of going back to sleep, he lay awake in his bed, listening to Adar snore in the bunk below him and thinking about the last time he had seen Sayla. It had been years. They had grown up together, just like siblings. He had always felt as if he knew her better than anyone else.

But when she was 16 she had won the Shepherd Tournament and been selected to attend Woodlands Academy to train as a Shepherd of Defense, the only one to do so out of his friends. Galen had not really been surprised--he had seen her inner strength and courage time and again. But he had been jealous of that, though.

By the time she won the tournament, the two of them had been the only ones left in Aramoor out of their group of friends. Galen had been alright with that, because they had each other, but then she left as well. Everyone had departed to start a new life except for him. He had been 18 years old, still stuck in his hometown and longing for something more. After spending a year working in the inn with his mother, trying to get his life together, he also left to join the army where he had not yet quenched his thirst for a purpose in life. *Two years ago, then. I saw her just before I left for Sea Fort.* How much, he wondered, had she changed?

The last time he had seen her had been Winter Break two years ago. She had only come, because he told her he was leaving for the army. Even as a Defense student, she had still been as scrawny as ever, tall but skinny. He remembered the loose curls of her hair and how they always tumbled around her face so perfectly even though she always tried to push them back. *I wonder how much I've changed.* Two years was a long time, after all.

Galen shrugged it off. He would find out soon enough.

He spent a few more minutes in silence thought until he heard the morning reveille. Although he was already completely awake, Galen stayed in bed, facing the wall with his eyes closed while the rest of his company got ready. *If they think I'm asleep then I won't have to talk to them.*

"Hey, Galen and Adar are still asleep. Do you want me to wake them?" he heard someone ask.

"No, leave them. Let them face the consequences." Galen pursed his lips as he heard the voice of his company leader, Gadiel. Even his voice grinded on Galen's nerves. As much as he wanted to reply, he stayed still until the last of his company had left. Then he hopped off his top bunk and landed lightly onto the cold floor. Sure enough, Adar was still soundly sleeping, oblivious to the world.

After tossing on a clean army issue green shirt identical to the one he had worn earlier, Galen ran his fingers through his brown hair. He needed to trim it. It was starting to curl around his ears. Leaning over, he shook Adar on the shoulder to wake him up. "Mmmmmm, hey there beautiful," the soldier mumbled.

Galen made a face. "Adar, wake up. We gotta go to breakfast."

"Why, yes … I am a daring soldier …. And you are the most …. attractive … Shepherd of Defense I have ever seen…" The man never opened his eyes, but he was smiling in a way that made Galen cringe. *Maybe I'll just let him wake up on his own …*

Leaving the barracks, Galen headed over to the mess hall. After grabbing a tray of food he made his way down the rows of tables and benches. Off to the left he heard someone break into obnoxious laughter and turned to see Gadiel sitting at a table with some of the higher-ranking officers. *Kiss up,* he thought as he plopped down at an empty table. It wasn't just the fact that Gadiel was his company leader and he had only just turned 19. Rather, it was that he had clearly not gotten it by his own merit. He was too busy flaunting his heritage and groveling at the feet of his instructors. It was not as if Gadiel was that special, though he was the son of a Royal Shepherd. *Good for him. He's still a tournament reject like the rest of us.*

"Attention!" A general whose name Galen always kept forgetting stood on a raised platform at the end of the mess hall. The room quickly became silent as everyone stood up, hands on their hearts. *Mindless monkeys,* Galen thought as he followed suit. "As you all know, Royal Shepherd Demas has come to Sea Fort military base to speak with us today. In fact, he has just arrived." Galen stole a glance at Gadiel who was obnoxiously grinning from ear to ear. He wondered what it felt like to have a father to be so proud of. "This is a high honor. Shepherd Demas does not often make this sort of trip, and with the war effort going on, he must be very busy which is why full attendance is required at the auditorium tonight to hear him speak. We want to make Shepherd Demas particularly proud of this base." He paused. "Now, Gadiel, please go make your father feel welcome. You are relieved from your duties for the rest of the day." Galen almost gagged on the food he had just eaten. *That kid always gets special privileges.* "As you were," the general finished. The usual rumble of talking resumed.

Disposing of his tray, Galen headed back outside. He wanted to get some more running in before he had to report for training. Just as he was exiting the mess hall, he ran into Commander Zevran who was walking with a distraught looking Adar. "Ah, Galen, just the man I was looking for."

Well, this can't be good. Galen saluted. "Yes, sir?"

"Since you decided to sneak out last night, and you," he pointed at Adar, "decided to skip breakfast, the two of you have been honored with kitchen duty today."

Galen groaned. "Seriously?" Zevran bristled. "I mean, seriously, *sir?*"

"Galen, you watch that tone of yours before I decide to move you to the kitchen permanently," Zevran said, emphasizing each word. Galen remained silent. He knew exactly how far he could push Zevran, and that the officer liked him more than he would ever let on. Otherwise, Galen would have been kicked out long ago. "Now," Zevran resumed his formality, "any questions?"

"No sir," Adar said.

Galen echoed, "No sir."

"Good. Report back to your unit one hour before the meeting this evening in the auditorium." Then he was gone.

They went to the kitchen. The cook was thrilled to see them. He enthusiastically handed them an exorbitantly long list of items and instructed them to go into the town's market to pick up the needed food supplies. *Maybe kitchen duty won't be so bad after all. I like going into town.*

Adar and Galen headed into Sea Fort. It always surprised Galen how much the place had grown in the past year since war had broken out. When he had first arrived, he had enjoyed the small town feel that reminded him so much of Aramoor. Now, it was overcrowded with a lot more businesses than when he had first arrived. Galen did not really mind, though. *A lot has changed since the war started.*

Nor did Galen mind Adar's company, something he could say of few people back at the base. They weren't exactly close friends, but they got along if only because they were the only two in their unit who regularly got called out for doing something wrong. Galen only half listened as Adar recounted his experiences of the day before.

"Oh, man, I met this unbelievably attractive girl yesterday. And she was *totally* into me."

Galen smirked, "It's not that one-eyed girl again is it?"

"No, no, no." Adar shook his head. "She wasn't in the army! She was a Shepherd trainee. I don't know what she was doing there, but she had these, like intense emerald eyes that made me a little terrified for my life!" He sighed. "It was great."

Stopping in his tracks, Galen stared at him. "Wait, a Shepherd trainee?" He felt for the message he had kept in his pocket. "What was her name?"

"Oh, uh, well… I don't *exactly* remember. I mean, she definitely told me, it just slipped my mind, that's all."

"Defense? From Woodlands?"

"Yeah, that's her! Did you see her, too?"

Galen's jaw dropped. "No, but I think I know her. At least… well, I have this friend who said she was coming to hear Shepherd Demas speak but I didn't know she was already here." *Why didn't she look for me yesterday?*

It was Adar's turn to be surprised. "You *know* her? Why have you never told me about her? I would definitely have remembered you mentioning a gorgeous Shepherd trainee friend."

"Because she's like my sister." *But she is beautiful, though.* "Besides, we're not that close anymore. We were just childhood friends. She's only here to hear the Shepherd speak."

"Oh. Well, there's probably a lot of people that are going to want to see him. He usually just stays around the Capital. I mean, his oldest kid lives in the same room as us, and we've never even met the father."

"Yeah, well I could do without his oldest son living in the same room as us."

Adar snickered. "I guess if Gadiel was my son, I'd stay away too."

Galen nodded. "Shepherd Demas probably wouldn't even be here now if Leoj hadn't attacked our colony last year."

"Can you believe it's almost been a year? We should have squashed them by now, the way we did when Kaya tried to attack us."

"I guess they're putting up quite a fight. I've heard even the royal family is trained in combat." Galen had definitely become a little concerned about being shipped over there. "But Oldaem will prevail as it always does."

"Maybe by this time next year Leoj will be a territory of Oldaem, too," Adar said hopefully.

"That's what they get for killing the Shepherd of Spirit living in the colony."

"It's not as if the whole country planned it though, right? Just that group of radicals?"

"Yeah, radical followers of the Old Order. But it's the King of Leoj's fault for allowing those kind of people to roam free. At least here, the Lameans are under control and paying for their primitive beliefs." *Not enough,* Galen reminded himself, *never enough.*

Adar held his hands up. "Whoa, okay. The Lameans aren't the only ones who believe in the Old Order, and that's not why they're slaves. What did they ever do to you, anyway?"

"Nothing good," Galen snapped, glaring at his friend. *Sayla would understand.* He was glad to be meeting her tonight. His outburst effectively ended the conversation with Adar and left Galen in a bad mood. He didn't like to think of his childhood very often, but lately it was as if all he was doing was living in the past. His recurring dream was dredging up memories he preferred to leave buried.

In near silence, Adar and Galen bought the items on their list and instructed each store owner to have the food delivered to the base by evening. It was early afternoon by the time they finished, but Galen and Adar agreed to walk back slowly so as to avoid getting handed any more mundane tasks by the overeager cook. As they meandered back, a spark of movement in a back alley caught Galen's attention. *Did I just see someone run back there?* A familiar sound caused an unwelcome memory to flash before his eyes, and he dashed into the alley.

"What are you doing?" Adar asked, following him.

As they rounded the corner, the shouts became louder. Then Galen saw the source of the noise. Behind a trash pile, a group of boys, maybe ages 10 or 12, were crowded around something, laughing and snarling all at once. At the center Galen could just make out a much smaller boy cowering as the crowd kicked and hit him. He was yelling, begging for them to stop, but the bigger boys just laughed.

"Hey! Break it up!" Galen shouted, but they ignored him the way they did the boy's pleas. "*Hey!*" With a shout, he pushed his way into their circle. "I said stop!" Galen yelled as he shoved one boy into another, effectively knocking them over. Then he elbowed one bully in the back, kicked another in the knee, and made his way into the middle of the circle where the younger boy cowered. Identifying one tall kid as the ringleader, Galen pounced on him. His fist connected with the ringleader's mouth, again and again. The boy instantly started crying and tried to back away in shock, but Galen pulled him down. As he lifted his bloodied fist again, he was surprised to feel his right arm forced backward.

"Galen, stop! They're just kids!" Although Galen tried to fight Adar, as his friend pulled him away from the group of kids, Adar was stronger. The bullies saw their opportunity and frantically ran away from the furious soldier who had attacked them. Shaking from tension, Galen sank to the ground.

Only the small little boy remained. As he leaned against the wall of the alley, his lips were bleeding and his eyes were wide. Galen started to get up to see if the boy was alright, but his movement brought the little boy out of his shock, and the child leapt up fearfully and ran out of the alley.

Galen sighed. "You're welcome!" he shouted at the retreating figure.

"What in the world was that?" Adar threw his hands up. "You're a trained fighter. Those were just little kids!"

His heart racing, Galen closed his eyes. He had not seen *just little kids*. In fact, he had not really seen anything. Instead, he had only felt the fear of being pushed into a back alley, the pain of being punched and hit by those bigger than him, the humiliation that came with not being able to do anything about it. Just like that he had been thrust back in Aramoor, small and vulnerable and unable to protect himself and no father to teach him how. And then one day his tormenters had stopped because of someone who had come to his aid. *No,* Galen thought, *those kids deserved worse. Not enough,* he reminded himself. *Never enough.*

CHAPTER 15: SAYLA

As the late morning sunlight trickled in through the open window, a cool breeze also drifted in and gave Sayla a chill. Although it was the beginning of summer, the air coming from the sea created the semblance of a cool spring day. Putting the last hair pin in place, she looked at her reflection in the mirror. Her light brown curls had an annoying habit of poking out in ways she didn't want them too, and Sayla was getting frustrated as it was taking longer than anticipated to get her hair in place. She, Aveline, and Tali were getting ready in the room they shared at the Seaside Inn. Today Shepherd Demas would give his speech to the troops. It was also the day she would see Galen. After patting down one particularly unruly spot above her left ear, she decided it was good enough.

"Oh no. Oh, no, no, no!" Tali's distraught face was staring at her from the mirror.

"What?"

"You're not going like that are you?"

Sayla looked at herself. She was wearing the standard Defense Shepherd trainee uniform: a long black cotton shirt tied at the waist, black leggings, and boots. "Well, considering I didn't have a lot of clothing options ..."

"I mean your hair, silly! It always looks like that."

Sayla glanced back at her own reflection. "What? No, it doesn't."

Her friend rolled her eyes, "Oh, just because you used hair pins instead of a ribbon doesn't mean the result is different. It's still a boring old bun." *Sounds just like my sisters,* Sayla thought.

Tali had her hair in two long brown braids that neatly fell down her back. "Here, let me help you." Without warning, she started pulling the pins out of Sayla's hair.

"Hey!" Sayla tried to bat her hands away. "Don't mess with my hair! I like it up so it doesn't get in my face. Imagine suddenly having to enter a fight, but you lose because the bangs in your face block the sight of your opponent swinging at you."

The other girl stared blankly at her. "Okay," Sayla reluctantly added, "that argument sounded better in my head. But still."

"Don't worry, I happen to be an expert at doing hair, and I assure you that I will give you the prettiest, fanciest, most beautiful hairstyle that won't interfere with your fighting abilities."

Sayla sighed. "Fine." She leaned back into the chair as Tali expertly began repining Sayla's curls. It probably couldn't hurt to look a littler nicer than usual. After all, the Defense Shepherd students from Woodlands Academy had a private meeting with Shepherd Demas at the military base in just an hour or so. She wanted to make a good impression. *Maybe someday I'll take his place.*

Aveline glanced over from a chair where she was lacing up her boots. Her hair was still loose. "Tali, how is it that you got selected as a Shepherd of Defense candidate?" Aveline pointed at Sayla and then to herself, "We don't usually go for the whole glamour thing."

"Oh, you two are just so silly! Anyone knows that you can look like a lady on the outside and still be a terrifying warrior on the inside!" Tali giggled.

Sayla wasn't sure what she thought about that. It wasn't that she didn't care at all how she looked--it just wasn't at the top of her priorities. After all, an assassin coming to attack you would hardly care whether you looked presentable or not. And despite her lack of trying, she still had no shortage of boys noticing her. Maybe Shale would be one of them.

Her thoughts went back to a time when she was still in Aramoor. She had been 15 when one of her classmates, Bryce, had told her of his undying affections for her. Mortified, Sayla had run to Galen and told him everything.

He had laughed so hard that he almost fell out of the low tree branch they had been sitting on. "He what?"

"Kissed me ..." Sayla's face was beet red.

"And then told you he was in love with you?"

"Yes ..."

"No, but what were his words exactly?" Galen's deep blue eyes sparkled with amusement.

Sayla was beginning to think that telling him had not been such a great idea. "That he would love me for eternity, and did I love him back?" she said flatly.

"And what did you do?"

She hesitated. "Punched him in the face." Galen's laughter practically shook the leaves off of the tree.

"Guess I don't need to offer to do that then."

"I'm gonna punch you in the face if you don't stop enjoying this so much!"

He wiped the tears from his eyes. "Worth it." She could never really stay mad at him, and he knew it.

They had sat in pleasant silence for a while, just watching the nature around them. But Sayla had something else on her mind, and after a couple minutes, she asked, "What do you think he's doing right now?"

"Who?"

"You know who." *The other person that I would have told about Bryce kissing me.*

Galen's demeanor changed. "I don't know," he said to his shoes.

"But," she persisted, "don't you ever wonder?"

He swallowed as he gathered his thoughts. "Do you remember how we used to play war when we were little, and I would always pretend that my dad was the king or a Shepherd, or some noble warrior?"

She remembered those days fondly. *It was during those games that I realized I was meant to be a Shepherd.* "Of course."

"I did that because I thought that if he had some honorable cause, some important reason to be gone, it would explain why he never

100

tried to look for me. But … even that didn't make sense enough. Every explanation I could come up with, it never justified why he abandoned my mom and me, or why he's never contacted me. So, finally, I realized that it's just better not to think about it." Galen held her hand in his. "This is the same kind of situation. He chose to leave us. He chose to start a new life. So it's better for us not to wonder about him and just move on."

Sayla had tried to do that. She had mostly succeeded, but she still thought about him from time to time, and she figured Galen did too since she knew he was not one to let go of a grudge easily.

Tali tugged on Sayla's hair. "Ow!"

"Oh, sorry! But I was just locking the last piece into place. What do you think? Ta da!" Once more Sayla looked into the mirror. Her friend had actually done a good job. Tali had left her hair still up and out of her eyes, but it was braided along the base of her skull and came to a twist behind her ear.

"Huh." *Maybe she's not completely useless.*

"I'll take that as 'Tali, you are the most amazing hair-doing person ever!'" She jumped up and down and clapped her hands.

Aveline laughed, "I'm sure Shepherd Demas will be very impressed."

Tali gasped, "Oh, I'm so nervous--stop reminding me!"

"He's just a person," the ever practical Aveline commented.

"Not just any person, he's a Royal Shepherd! There's only four of them!"

"True, and one of them is going to be me someday." Aveline awkwardly glanced at Sayla. "Well, if I become a Shepherd."

"What I don't understand is how he can be so high up in the chain of command and not follow the New Order." Tali's eyes were huge and wondering.

"What?" Sayla said as she began to put on her boots. "That's ridiculous. Of course, he's a follower of the New Order. Practically everyone in the government is."

Tali shook her head. "Maybe he's a little more neutral than he was before, but I think he was even Old Order at one point."

"How would you even know that?" Aveline asked, a question that was on Sayla's mind as well.

"I'm from Isprig, the region he was a Shepherd of before he became a Royal Shepherd. I mean, not that I remember any of that, I'm not that old! My mom told me."

A Royal Shepherd a follower of the Old Order? Impossible, Sayla thought. *He would get booted out immediately. There was no room for the old beliefs among the leaders of Oldaem. Then again, maybe he changed his beliefs in order to get such a powerful position. Wouldn't be the first person to do it.*

"If what you're saying is true, that totally ruins my opinion of him," Aveline commented. "Thanks."

Tali ran over to her. "That's not what I meant at all! If anything, it's good that he stopped believing in those Old Order myths and is open to the One and the New Order now."

"They're not myths," Sayla blurted out before she could stop herself. *Oops. Where did that come from?* Saying things impulsively was unlike her. *Tali must be rubbing off on me.*

Aveline and Tali looked at her, surprise on their faces. She corrected herself, "I mean, they used to be true. The Older Order used to be right." They still looked skeptical. "Like a long time ago. A really long time ago."

"How would you know," Aveline asked her quizzically, "You weren't there."

"Because … I just do," Sayla answered reservedly. "Of course," she added, "the New Order is correct now. Only Lameans and uneducated people think differently." And she meant what she said. *I don't know what I would do without my belief in the One. Who I would be?* He had saved her.

"We better get going," she said, standing. "The others will wonder where we are."

After they had eaten in the tavern below the inn, the group of Defense apprentices departed for the military base. Sayla tried to strike up a conversation with Shale, but he brushed her off and started talking with Zayeed about everything that was wrong with his swordsmanship technique. Unfortunately, that left the door wide open for Grunt, her apparent shadow, to walk beside her.

"Hey," he said.

"Hello."

"How'd you sleep?"

"Fine." *Take the hint. Go away.*

"Me, too, surprisingly." He smiled. "And it was all thanks to you." He had piqued her interest but she tried not to show it. "What are you talking about?"

"What you said yesterday. About war being the perfect time to help people. Well, it helped me." Then he added quietly, "Not that

102

I'm sure I'd have the courage when it actually comes down to it, but I think I'm willing to try."

Sayla rolled her eyes and looked at him. "Okay, what did I tell you about saying stuff like that? You can't just try, Grunt. Make it happen or go home."

The boy nodded. "Right. Make it happen. Thanks again." She nodded back.

Soon they arrived at the military base. Shale stopped them at the entrance once again. "Okay, just like last time, remember to hold your tongue, be respectful, and ..."–he glared at Sayla–"stay with the group." *Guess he's still upset about that.*

As they walked across the base to the meeting hall, Sayla once again glanced around, hoping to get a glimpse of her friend. At one point, she thought she saw him leaving the meeting hall as they headed toward it, but it turned out to be some other soldier who resembled Galen a little as she had last seen him. *He might look different now. I guess I'll find out tonight after Shepherd Demas' speech.*

As they approached the doors to the hall, Sayla became a little more nervous than she expected. She was confident that while she could remain calm during the heat of battle, she had never met someone so powerful as Demas, and she didn't know what to expect. *He's just a person*, she reminded herself.

She was in the front next to Shale when they entered. The light had been so bright outside, that at first all she could see were silhouettes of people, one tall one in particular that she guessed was Shepherd Demas by his stance and placement in the room. Shale led the group up to the bald shadow of Zevran who, in turn, escorted them to the Shepherd. Sayla squinted, trying to get her eyes to adjust faster. "Shepherd Defense students of the Woodlands Academy, meet Royal Shepherd of Defense Demas."

The man stepped forward and offered his hand to Sayla. "It's an honor to meet you." She reached for his hand. It was warm and calloused, but for some reason sent a shock through her that gave her the sensation of falling through the floor. Just as her eyes adjusted, she looked up into his welcoming eyes and ... froze. Standing before her, real flesh and blood and not a figment of her imagination, shaking her hand, was the tortured prisoner in her dream from two nights before.

CHAPTER 16: GALEN

Galen's knuckles hurt. It had been a while since he had been in a real fight, and even though what had happened in the alleyway an hour before could hardly constitute as a legitimate brawl, it had been enough to break the skin around his knuckles and leave them bloody and raw. But somehow he kind of liked the feeling. Running or sparring never gave him that sort of adrenaline rush. In those few moments, he had felt alive in a way he hadn't experienced in … he couldn't remember the last time. *Okay, maybe I overdid it a little,* he allowed himself to think as he made his way to the kitchen with the receipts for the orders that would arrive today. Adar had gone to the storage room to make sure there was room for all of it. *I mean, they were just little punks.* But little punks like that would grow up to be even bigger, more unmanageable ones if they got away with that sort of trouble when they were young. *Like Gadiel. I bet he got away with all kinds of things being the son of a Royal Shepherd.* Galen decided that he wasn't that sorry after all. People like that needed to be put in their place. Then he wondered if Sayla would ask about the battered state of his hands this evening when he saw her. For the first time it dawned on him that she might already be here on base. *Of all the days to be stuck on kitchen duty.*

As he approached the mess hall, to Galen's surprised he found it still crowded with soldiers. Although he had missed lunch, people still milled around. Lunch usually happened in shifts, and this would be the last one. His stomach growled as he smelled the food coming from the kitchen. He would have to grab something before the kitchen staff sent him on his next task. Pushing past the trashcans and into the back where the kitchen workers were busily tidying up, he quickly found the cook.

"Hey, I got the food supplies you asked for."

The cook looked up with a smile that quickly disappeared. "Oh, uh, thank you. Just set the orders down over there." He gestured to an office off to the left of the kitchen.

"Sure." Galen left the papers and wandered back into the kitchen. "So … what am I supposed to do next?" The cook was back busily chopping an onion.

"Actually, nothing. You're relieved of kitchen duty."

Galen wasn't sure he had heard right. Wasn't this some sort of punishment for Galen being a freethinking individual who refused to hand over his brain while wearing his uniform? Zevran had said he wasn't supposed to be able to rejoin his unit until shortly before the speech. *But I'm not going to question it.* He nodded to the cook, and then went through the swinging door and back into the mess hall where he grabbed a tray of food. *For smelling so good, it looks disgusting.* Galen scanned the room for a free spot. Although he saw a few members of his unit grouped together, they were Gadiel's friends, but Gadiel was nowhere to be seen. *Oh yeah, he's probably off being pampered somewhere with his father.* Finally, Galen decided to sit in the same spot he had chosen at breakfast. Plopping down on the bench, he began to eat the gruel.

"Galen," a booming voice broke his train of thought. Galen turned to see Zevran's intimidating form advancing through the crowd. The man looked angry. *Well, more angry than usual.*

"Sir? Would you like to join me?" Galen asked with a grin, gesturing to the open space around him.

"Pack your bags."

Galen stared at him. What was he talking about? Had he misunderstood when the cook told him he was relieved of kitchen duty? Had he unintentionally not followed orders? "Excuse me?"

"Pack. Your. Bags. You're done."

Did he mean done as in done in the military? Surely mishearing his orders didn't constitute that. Plus, he hadn't been sitting down for more than five minutes. It wasn't as if he had been avoiding duty all day.

"What?"

Zevran shook his head, a vein on his thick neck pulsing. "I've given you too many chances, kid. But enough is enough. You've gone too far this time."

Conversations around the room tapered off and Galen could feel the heat of multiple stares aimed at him. Rising to his feet, he backed away from the bench. "What are you talking about?" He was pretty sure he hadn't done anything that bad.

Zevran snatched the tray of food out of Galen's hands and slammed it on the table. "Go immediately back to your quarters, pack up your belongings, and speak to absolutely no one. You are to leave immediately."

Galen had had enough. *No one can speak to me that way, not even my commanding officer.* Having no idea what was going on, he couldn't own or deny what he was being accused of because he didn't know what it was. "No!" he shouted, "Not until you tell me what I did wrong!"

A flash of red passed through Zevran's eyes. "Soldier! It is not your job to question, it is your job to obey." He pointed toward the door. "Get. Out!"

As they stared at each other the room became silent. After what seemed like an eternity to Galen, but was probably only a few seconds, he heatedly shoved past Zevran and out of the mess hall.

Galen was furious. He hadn't even wanted to join this stupid army anyway, but once he had, they had been lucky to have him. And he did not deserve this sort of treatment. More than anything, he hated being pushed around. Sure, he had not been the most straight-laced recruit, but Zevran had always at least treated him with respect when he was being punished. *This was different. What had he done to deserve such treatment?*

Once he got to the barracks, he slammed the door shut behind him. But to his surprise he realized that he wasn't alone in the room. Adar jumped as the door shut. Momentarily, he turned away from the bedroll he was rolling up, but then wearily resumed it once he saw who was at the door. "You, too?" Galen hadn't considered that he wasn't the only one in trouble.

"I'm not supposed to talk to anyone," came the reply from the other side of the room.

Admittedly, Galen felt a little relieved. He was still enraged at how he had been treated and how ridiculous it all was, but whatever had happened, the blame wasn't solely on him. "What did he tell you?" Galen persisted.

Adar sighed, "To get out. It was awful. In front of everyone at the front gate."

"What does he think we did, anyway?" He grabbed his own bag and began stuffing his few belongings into it.

"Oh, I don't know—maybe beat up a few children?"

He hadn't thought about that. "But that just happened—there's no way Zevran would have found out about it that quickly."

"It's not as if it's that hard to identify us! We were in uniform. Your knuckles are all red. How else do you explain us getting immediately kicked out, no explanation whatsoever?"

Galen hopped onto his top bunk and began to roll up his own bedroll. "Don't pin this all on me."

The door opened and Zevran entered. Adar dropped what he was doing and stood at attention. Galen just crossed his arms from on top of his bunk. "Come with me." Then he turned and walked outside.

Adar scrambled to grab the last of his belongings while Galen watched him in silence. *Why do I have to go with him? I know my way out of here.* As he was almost to the door, Adar quietly urged, "Come on, Galen."

Halfheartedly, Galen shouldered his duffel bag and hopped down from the bunk. He didn't look back as he walked out the door.

They followed Zevran across the training field. Galen quietly seethed at the general's back as he trudged along behind him. He had looked up to Zevran. The officer was one of the few people on the base who actually had a spine. And a personality. He had always been honest and ... trustworthy. Galen glanced up as they arrived at the turn for the front gate. Zevran kept walking. Confused, Galen looked around. *Do we have to stop somewhere first?* He had a long journey back to Aramoor, and if he had to go, then he wanted to get started as soon as possible. *At least Sayla won't be there to see me come home disgraced. A reject once again.* "Where are we going?" Galen asked, his brows furrowed.

Without looking back, Zevran grunted, "The boat dock."

The answer only confused him more. He halted. "But, I live in Aramoor." Zevran slowed to a stop, but kept his back to him.

"So?" Adar asked.

"So it's landlocked. You don't go there by the ocean."

Without so much as a glance at Galen, Zevran began walking again. "You aren't going home."

Clearly. "Then where am I going?" Adar picked up his pace with Zevran, but Galen remained motionless, planting his feet in the dirt and crossing his arms.

Zevran only went a few more paces before sighing and turning to face Galen. They were about 15 feet apart, but Galen could still make out the strained look on Zevran's face that he had seen so many times before. "You're going to the boat dock. Now shut up, and keep walking. That's an order." He started forward again. "We don't have time for this," Galen heard him mutter under his breath.

"Huh, seems to me that being kicked out of the army means I don't have to listen to your *orders* anymore."

For such a big man, Zevran seemed to cross the distance between them in a heartbeat, grabbing the front of Galen's green shirt and pulling him uncomfortably close. "You're not kicked out, you insolent fool," Zevran whispered huskily, "Now shut your mouth, go to the boat dock, and *maybe* I'll feel like answering your questions." Then the man shoved him backwards. Galen wanted to punch him in the face, but didn't because his curiosity got the better of him. *And my knuckles are already sore.* Instead, he nodded curtly and they resumed their brisk walk in silence.

Soon they reached the small dock area used for relatively local traveling and fishing. The navy portion of Sea Fort was another mile or two away. That port was much busier, especially with waves of soldiers constantly either shipping out or returning from Leoj. Reinforcements and weapons all left that port. This dock was much smaller and did not house any of the massive ships. Instead, it had only five or six smaller, but sturdy vessels. It was to one of them that Zevran led Adar and Galen. Brown, it had a sturdy mast and a dragon carved on the prow. "Now what?" Adar wondered out loud.

"Now you get aboard the boat," Zevran answered dryly. He gestured for them to board it. Adar and Galen looked at each other questioningly. Adar's face reflected the uncertainty that Galen himself was feeling. But, despite all his current anger toward Zevran, Galen had to admit that he trusted him. Taking a breath, he went up the gangplank.

Adar was close behind him. "Is he going to kill us?" he asked, only half-jokingly.

"Guess we'll find out soon enough," Galen shrugged. The ship seemed deserted. Actually, Galen hadn't noticed it before, but the whole dock was empty. Not a soul was in sight, and the Limestone Cliffs on either side of them made it seem as if they were isolated from the rest of the world.

Zevran led them down into the captain's quarters below deck. There, Galen faced Zevran. "Now are you going to tell us what this is all about?" It was dark, but Zevran lit a candle and indicated for them to sit around a small wooden table near the door where sunlight mixed with the light of the candle to create strange shadows on the wall.

"We don't have much time." Zevran sighed as he took a seat as well. "But you need to know. Something … has happened." He licked his lips and cleared his throat. "Royal Shepherd Demas … has disappeared."

Galen's blood seemed to freeze and drain out of his face. "What?"

Zevran's strained voice continued, "We have reason to believe he was taken by the Leojians."

"But how is that even possible?" Adar interrupted, "He was right here in Sea Fort this morning surrounded by thousands of Oldaem soldiers! It's the safest place he could be!" Galen was wondering the same thing. Of all the times to kidnap someone, why wait until he was in the most secure place imaginable? *Unless ...*

"Because someone involved had to have been on the inside." Suddenly Galen understood the tension in Zevran's voice and the strangeness of his actions in the past hour. "You think someone in the base was a part of it." He was still having trouble wrapping his mind around the thought that Shepherd Demas had just vanished. Countless questions filled his thoughts.

The general nodded and added gruffly, "Which is what brings you two here."

Adar's eyes widened, "You want us to go on a rescue mission to find him?"

Galen paled at the thought of it. *But that doesn't make sense. Why us? We're not even trained in covert missions. We're just foot soldiers. And we're not even that great at marching.*

"Don't flatter yourself," Zevran smirked. But the smile didn't quite reach his eyes. "As of now, only a handful of people know about what has taken place. We believe it just happened a few hours ago, which means we need to act quickly if we want to catch the trail of the ship they took him on. His disappearance will remain a secret until tonight at the speech when it will be revealed. That way, the traitor among us will not believe we have already gone into action, and we will, hopefully gain the element of surprise."

"So if we're not doing the rescuing, then why are we here?"

Zevran shrugged. "There is an elite team being assembled by Seff, the Defense Shepherd of Efil. They will arrive soon. I have been trained as a ship captain, but in a delicate situation like this, I need a crew I can trust."

"You're kidding." Galen had never even been on a watercraft for more than an hour. He had a friend who used to tell him about his experiences on the sea, but that was as close as Galen had come, and the stories had faded in his memory.

Zevran hesitated. "Part of the reason I picked you two was because you were both on probation this morning. It wouldn't be too far of a stretch to believe that either of you had done something inexcusable."

Galen grimaced and leaned back in his chair. "Thanks for that."

"But it was also because I knew I could trust you," the officer added, ignoring his comment. "I knew you could handle something like this. You're both smart and fast learners." Zevran turned to

Galen. "Now do you see why I had to make such a show of kicking you both out? There had to be a plausible explanation for your sudden disappearance."

"I get it." Galen crossed his arms. *That's about all I get.* "But what I want to know is how you're so sure that there was a Leojian spy in the midst of our very secure base. Especially since this 'disappearance,' as you're calling it, was witnessed by no one."

Zevran knit his eyebrows together. "I never said ..."

"Because I was there." A familiar voice came from the top of the ladder to the deck. Galen and Adar both looked up in surprise. Galen had thought they had been alone on the vessel. Wearily, Gadiel descended the ladder and turned to face them. He looked haggard, a shell of the annoyingly person Galen had glared at just this morning. His eyes were bloodshot, and he winced with every step as he joined the three men at the table.

"You were there?" Adar's jaw dropped. "What happened?"

After he turned a questioning glace toward Zevran who nodded slightly, Gadiel closed his eyes for a moment. Although Galen couldn't help but feel a small sense of elation at Gadiel being knocked down a peg, he kept his expression a mask. The room was dead silent. "I wasn't there exactly when it happened. Well I was, but I don't ..." Gadiel paused, then started again. "I was with ... him all morning until he sent me out of the meeting room when he was going to meet the Shepherd apprentices from Woodlands." *Sayla!* Because of all that had happened, Galen had completely forgotten about their planned meeting that night. Well, it wouldn't be happening now. When they were little they had always joked that they could read each other's thoughts. A small part of him wanted to believe that was still true. *I hope you understand why I won't be there.* Gadiel had resumed his narrative. "... but instead I went back to his quarters and decided to wait there for his meeting to be over. When I got there, there was a Lamean slave cleaning. Well, at least he was dressed like one." He shook his head desolately. "I thought it was odd because the room had already been cleaned, so I asked him what he was doing." Gadiel shuddered. "The man didn't even answer. He just had this terrible smile. And then ... and then someone hit me on the back of the head."

When Adar gasped, it broke Gadiel's concentration, and he looked down at his hands. *Not so high and mighty now, are you?* "When I woke up, I was tied to the bed post ... with a splitting headache. The room was destroyed ... it looked as if there had been a fight or something ... but I was alone. I called for help, but no one heard me." He stole a quick glance at Zevran, then stared back down at the table. "A couple hours later, Zevran came to escort my father and me to lunch. He found me ..." Gadiel's face crumpled and his voice shrunk to barely above a whisper. "But he didn't find *him*. He and his guards ... just ... gone." Gadiel stared off into space. Clearly he was shaken. *Welcome to the missing father's club. How's it feel?*

Zevran broke in. "Gadiel is the only one who can identify one of the kidnappers. From what he described, we have reason to believe that the person he saw was not a Lamean, but, in fact, a Leojian. That is why Gadiel is coming with us, too." *Finally, I get to do something exciting, and the spoiled brat is coming along.* "But he, too, will be working as a crew member until we find the people responsible for this." Zevran looked somberly at the three in front of him. "With Royal Shepherd Demas' knowledge at their disposal ... this could change the tide of the whole war. We will leave as soon as Seff's special team arrives."

"What happens if we say no?" Galen interrupted.

"Then I really will kill you," Zevran retorted. Galen didn't want to find out if he was joking. But he didn't have to think about his answer. "I'm in."

"Me too," Adar added. Gadiel nodded.

"Good." Zevran stood. "We have about an hour to teach you how to man a ship. Let's begin."

CHAPTER 17: SAYLA

It had to be a coincidence--it just had to be. Sayla kept replaying the past four years of her life at Woodlands Academy, trying to recall when she had seen a painting of Royal Shepherd Demas. She supposed he could have even visited Aramoor when she was little. Or maybe she had seen him at one of the several tournaments she had attended. *Yes, that's probably it.* For some reason her mind had found the memory of a face she had not even been aware of. She sat leaning against the outer wall of the practice armory in the center of the Sea Fort base, her arms curled around her legs. The meeting with Royal Shepherd Demas had gone quite well, although Sayla feared she hadn't heard a word he had said. She was too busy trying to figure out where she had seen him before. The man had been cordial enough. She knew he had given some advice to the future Shepherds and gotten to know them a bit on a personal level.

"Sayla," he had asked her, "how do you enjoy your training?"

Still lost in thought she had mumbled something along the lines of, "It's great, I love it."

And he had responded with something like, "Stay dedicated, and you'll go far." No, it had not been that generic. Even in her distracted state, she could tell that the individual standing before her was intelligent and good at reaching people on a personal level. Having never really considered it a useful trait in her future occupation, Sayla had not become good at it. Maybe she'd have to reassess that, but right now she had other things on her mind.

After the meeting had ended, the trainees had some free time until the speech. Shale decided that they would have some sparring practice. Explaining that she didn't feel well, which really wasn't a lie, she declined. She watched as Shale instructed Tali, his bronze muscles rippling with every swing. Zayeed lost to Aveline, and Grunt and Oghren made mistake after mistake, both of them so bad that neither one could beat the other. She wasn't really watching them, though. As much as she wanted too, she couldn't shake the feeling of dread that had been forming in her stomach ever since she had put a name to the face in her dream. *Leave it alone,* she kept telling herself, *it's nothing. Why are you making it such a big deal?*

Maybe she could mention it to Galen tonight when they met. She used to always tell him everything. But would he still care now? Maybe it was too insignificant of a problem, and maybe it had been too long since they had seen each other. *I hope you understand.* She stared unblinkingly into the distance.

Oghren and Grunt pushed away from each other, exhausted and frustrated. "I'm going for water," Oghren shouted toward Shale.

Grunt wiped his forehead with the back of his hand and panted over in Sayla's direction. *Don't sit down, don't sit down,* she silently pleaded. He sat down. "How's your stomach?"

"What?"

"Your stomach"--he pointed at it as if he was making sure she remembered where it was. "You told Shale your stomach hurt."

"Oh, right. No, it's still bothering me."

Grunt looked at her for a moment, confused. Sayla didn't really care. She didn't have to explain herself to him. "Well, I hope it feels better soon. It's not like you to turn down a sparring match."

She shrugged, "It would have made the matches uneven, anyway. Someone would have had to sit it out. Might as well be me."

Leaning against the wall, too, he sighed tiredly. "Maybe I should have done the same. I keep trying, but I can never beat Oghren."

Sayla gave him a quick glance. "You realize Oghren is two years older than you, right? Trust me when I say it's more embarrassing for him that he can't seem to beat *you.*"

He smiled at that thought. "Yeah, maybe."

Sayla rolled her head to the left and looked at him more intently. "Hey, can I ask you something?" *Might as well.*

"Sure," he answered, perhaps a little too enthusiastically.

How do I approach this? "This might sound stupid, but … do you remember ever seeing any paintings of Royal Shepherd Demas at Woodlands, or I guess, anywhere?"

"Hmm, no not that I can think of. I don't think I even saw him at the tournaments. I mean he was probably there somewhere … but there's always such a crowd."

Turning away, she bit her bottom lip. *That's what I thought, too. Then where have I seen him?* She briefly wondered if she had seen the boy in her dream somewhere, too.

"Why do you ask?"

"Just wondering." When Grunt didn't pursue the issue, it made her opinion of him grow ever so slightly. He was still annoying, though.

The rest of the day trickled by. They ate supper in the mess hall. Sayla hoped to catch a glance of Galen, but the dining area was huge and filled with people, and she didn't see him anywhere. The bald-headed guide they had before had been replaced by a mousy young man who kept stuttering nervously when he was around the soon-to-be Shepherds.

Immediately after supper, everyone was directed to the huge auditorium where the speech would take place. Sayla had been excited with anticipation before, but now she didn't know if she could sit through it. She didn't want to see the Royal Shepherd's face again. Just thinking about her dream made her shudder. *It was just a dream, stupid. Just get through this speech, and you can meet Galen on the pier. Hopefully he'll just tell you you're being overly dramatic and to get over it.* It's what she needed to hear since she couldn't seem to convince herself.

As the Woodlands Academy students arrived at the auditorium, their guide led them to special seats reserved for them near the front left. Sayla felt cramped and claustrophobic as the huge room rapidly filled with people. The majority, of course, were soldiers from the base, but some local townspeople were there too, and somewhere in the huge crowd was most likely the Regent of Efil and his four Shepherds. She didn't bother to look for them. The only face she cared to seek out belonged to her childhood friend. But there were so many people. Chances were better that he would observe her in her reserved seat than she would spot him, just another soldier in a crowd of them.

The audience settled down to wait for the speech to begin. Waited and waited. People conversed with friends and family next to them. Sayla, who was sandwiched between Shale and Aveline, a place she normally would have been ecstatic about, brushed aside each of their attempts at conversation. She didn't feel like talking to anyone, not even Shale.

However, even she was starting to get bored. *What is taking so long? He probably would have finished by now if we had started on time.* The rest of the audience was getting restless, too; especially the people who had come too late to get a seat and were standing in the back and along the sides.

Finally, a hush swept across the crowd as someone walked onto the platform. Being close to it, Sayla immediately recognized him, not as Royal Shepherd Demas, but as Shepherd Seff. He was a round man who seemed to have lost his prowess as a fighter years ago. His dark hair had thinned on the top of his head, but he had a thick mustache. The black uniform and medallion of crossed swords he wore identified him as a Shepherd of Defense. Seff was a friendly man. She had spoken with him many times when he visited the academy. *He must be here to introduce Royal Shepherd Demas.* Sweating profusely, he kept dabbing at his forehead with a handkerchief as he waited for the room to quiet. *Maybe he gets nervous speaking in front of people.* Then a strange though struck her. *He looks as if he's going to be sick.*

"Troops of Sea Fort, and ladies and gentlemen," he began, "First of all, I want to thank you all for coming tonight to hear Royal Shepherd Demas speak." The room broke out into applause. Shepherd Seff nodded quickly. "Yes, well, I fear that I must share with you some terrible news. Royal Shepherd Demas will not be speaking here tonight." Sayla sat up in her seat, almost forgetting to breathe. The man cleared his throat. "I'm afraid he has been … I'm afraid he has disappeared." The crowd erupted into a murmur, but

114

Sayla only heard the ringing in her ears, the screaming coming from the jail cell in her nightmare, now issuing from Shepherd Demas' throat. In her mind she saw him chained and beaten bloody, frantically grabbing her arm and pulling her down. She felt like she was falling through the floorboards again. *The prisoner. The captive.*

"He has been taken captive by Leoj," the Shepherd echoed her thoughts. *No. It's impossible. It's a coincidence. It has to be.* But Sayla couldn't convince her heart what she kept telling her head. She didn't hear anything else Shepherd Seff said. Instead, she bolted upright out of her seat. Shale and Aveline called after her, but she ignored them. Some began rushing for the door, and they provided the perfect cover for her as she slipped away from her group.

Desperately, she ran to the Northern Pier. She had to talk to someone, she needed someone to tell her that she was being silly, that she was overreacting, that it was just a coincidence. Hopefully, Galen would arrive soon. If he had been among the people who had left immediately as she had, he might already be there. Sayla waited for hours. It grew dark and the moon rose above the water. But he never showed. Somehow, she had always known he wouldn't.

At last, Shale found her there, staring blankly at the expanse of the ocean. He sat with her in silence, even put his arm around her. *At least I'm not alone.* But she couldn't bring herself to tell him her terrible secret. Eventually, he sat up and told her that everyone Shepherd Demas had spoken with today was being questioned. Just as a precaution, he assured her, to try to figure out what had happened.

Shepherd Seff conducted the interviews. He had assured her that they were a formality. Was Shepherd Demas acting strange? "No," she answered. Did she see anything unusual during the course of the day? "No," she replied again. Did she have any prior knowledge of a plan to kidnap the Royal Shepherd? "No," she answered once more, but this time she was lying. She had known he would be taken as a prisoner--had known for two days.

That night, Sayla had the dream again.

CHAPTER 18: COLE

Lanterns blazed all around the lake. He didn't know where they came from, or who had lit them. By now it was early morning--dawn. People in black lined the shores. He heard some women crying and some mumbling as the priest droned on. But he paid no attention to a word the man said. Cole couldn't. All he could do was stare at the water and think about how he hadn't gotten to say goodbye to his mother. The lake water was still as a mirror, as if nothing had ever disturbed it. As he looked around at all the faces mourning his mother, it dawned upon him that he only recognized a few people. Hardly anyone had ever come to see her when she was alive. Why did they now that she was dead? She wouldn't even know. What good would it do? Do they suddenly care now? He watched the white-haired-priest continue to speak about his mother. Wrinkles lined the man's withered cheek, his hands looked as if they were soft puffy clouds. The priest spoke slowly. A woman coughed in the background. Belen, who was standing in front of Cole, turned around and looked at her. *Does he even know what is happening?* He felt Belen's chubby hand grab hold of his. When Cole pulled away, Belen went back to focusing on the worm wriggling along the ground, seemingly oblivious to anything else.

Strong hands firmly squeezed Cole's shoulders. *Safety.* That's what he felt when Fenris was around. He looked up into his brother's green eyes. Fenris winked quickly at him and continued to watch and listen to the priest as he spoke. *Fenris is home.* Although he wished it could have been for different reasons, he was so glad he was there. His brother brought strength and wisdom and warmth and courage and fun and laughter and love with him every time he returned home. He became the man of the house, and Cole could finally just be a kid. The boy remembered when he saw Fenris running up the path toward the door. Cole had practically jumped off the roof to meet him in the middle of the road. Fenris had held him and cried and cried. But Cole didn't cry, though he was surprised to see his brother cry--he never had before. Fenris had told him it was going to be okay, that he was home now, that they would figure it out together. His brother had been everything for everyone that day. He helped Arissa clean up, and Cole had heard their hushed whispers in the kitchen. Then Fenris had held Lily while she cried, refusing to let him go until she fell asleep. Finally, Fenris had tucked Belen into bed, singing Mom's lullaby from years past. Fenris was home. *But he isn't Dad.*

"Ussa was a beloved wife and friend to all around her. But more importantly, a devoted mother to her five children, whom she leaves behind to traverse the perils of this world."

Cole stared at the priest he had never once seen visit his mother. *Devoted mother?* Cole wondered why the priest didn't mention how she never left her room. Why he didn't mention how she stopped preparing food or talking to them or laughing with them or buying clothes for them, or cleaning the house, or getting out of bed, tucking them in at night, kissing their foreheads. Nor did the priest tell how she cared more about her own tears than Belen or Lily's. Assuming the role of their mom, Arissa never got to be the youth she still was. He had nothing to say about how their mother had stopped loving them and selfishly killed herself. No, all this fake priest did was make people believe his mother was something she wasn't, and Cole was furious. Although he wanted to flee, he just stood there until the man finished talking. Then he remained motionless until all the people he didn't know stopped hugging him and telling him it was going to be okay. In silence he listened to them as they told him how brave he was, how they would be there for him, and how much he was loved, but all he could think about was how afraid he was, how no one had been there for him before, and how alone he felt. Fenris would have to go back to work. Then it would just be him, Arissa, Lily, and Belen, and he knew his Dad probably had no idea what had happened.

The five of them were the last ones sitting on the shoreline. The sun was up, and everyone went back to his or her daily routine, as Cole knew they would. Some did eventually visit during the course of the next few days. A few brought food and pitiful flowers that Arissa took and pretended to enjoy. Most, though, just seemed to avoid him. They would look at him with distant stares and pitiful glances. He figured people just didn't know what to say. His brothers and sisters didn't really talk about it, either. Fenris worked around the house for a while, repairing the door and patching up the roof. Arissa worked more now in the bakery, and he, Lily, and Belen went back to school. Lily seemed very different. Her eyes became cold, empty, like two black bottomless pits. No longer did she tell Belen the stories about the Old Order as much. Perhaps it was because the priest of the Old Order had made them so angry by what he said about their mom. Maybe the whole Old Order was bad. Or perhaps people themselves were just bad. Cole didn't know. He just knew he would rather stay away from them.

117

The boy kept wondering how and when and if their dad would ever find out about their mother's death and return. For that matter, why hadn't he come home already? Also what might happen next to his little family? One day he and Lily and Belen walked home from school and found Fenris and Arissa sitting at opposite ends of the kitchen table, staring at each other. Cole knew they were talking about important things. He could see the veins bulge on Fenris' forehead, and Arissa's tired eyes intensely focused on him. Lily sent Belen upstairs to play and took her place at the table too, always trying to be a grown-up. Cole stood at the edge of the room, leaning against the doorframe. He could feel the tension in the room.

"You have to go for him." Arissa's voice sounded as if it were going to break, with tears soon to follow.

"I don't even know where he is, Arissa." Fenris calmly replied.

"We know he is stationed in Rahvil."

"They send him away from there all the time--he could be *anywhere!*"

"So you're not even going to try?" Clearly, she was frustrated.

"Arissa, we sent a letter, what more can I do? You don't bring in enough at the bakery. If I don't go back to Windrip, you will all starve."

"I can get more hours!"

Fenris rubbed the sides of his head, trying to stay calm. Even more than that, he had been attempting to keep everything together—to be a man. "You can't, Arissa," he swallowed. "They need you here."

Cole could tell she knew Fenris was right, but the question that he could feel floating around the room was, *what if Dad doesn't come home?*

Arissa drummed the table with her fingers, her auburn hair tied up sloppily in a bun. "So you're just going to leave us again?"

"I have to, Arissa."

"And I'm supposed to . . ."

"Really, nothing has changed," he interrupted.

Cole knew Fenris said what everyone was thinking. Arissa stood up from the table and formally pushed her chair in. Then she turned her back on everyone. "It's too much," she whispered.

"I know," Fenris replied, his voice a low rumble.

"I can't be their mother, Fenris."

That was enough for Cole. Leaving the kitchen, he walked back up the stairs, listening to the hushed voices continue. He didn't want

Arissa to be his mother--hadn't asked her to be. Nor had Lily and Belen. Furthermore, he hadn't asked to be born into this family, to have a father who was always gone, a mother who was dead, and a brother and a sister who had to be grown-ups now. Maybe that was what was wrong with all of Esis. It just wasn't fair. Perhaps his mother had gotten the best end of the deal.

Silently Cole lay beneath his thin blanket, his mind numb, tears flowing constantly. It felt as if he lay there for hours, tossing and turning and unable to get comfortable. He couldn't remember the last time he had been comfortable. Rising, he stepped out onto the roof. The sun was setting over the shore. *I hate the water.* He thought of his father. *If Dad knew, he would come running home.* Before his dad had left, one thing he had been sure of was how much his dad loved his mom. He remembered sitting on this very roof, watching him push her in the old rope swing, back and forth, when Belen was even more of a baby than he was now. His father had done the same when Lily was an infant. And Cole remembered being pushed himself as a baby, his mother's faint laughter in the back of his mind. Cole could still see his dad's smile. Hot tears started to form even though he thought he had already cried every tear he owned away underneath his blankets. But he was wrong.

The world was a blurred view of orange and yellow and red and pink and tears when Fenris sat next to him.

"You okay, Cole?"

No. "Yes."

"Are you sure?" Compassion filled his voice.

No. "Yes."

"I'm not." As Fenris stared straight ahead, Cole looked up at his strong face. His brother was always honest, even about not being brave. Cole's heart swelled with love for him, but he couldn't tell him that *he* was falling apart and was scared about tomorrow and the rest of his life if he had to grow up in a place like Oldaem. It was a place where no one cared, where everyone lied, and where everyone who was supposed to love you . . . didn't. Knowing that Fenris had to go away to earn money, he wanted his brother to think he was leaving his family in good hands--in Cole's hands.

"Dad's gonna come back, Fenris. It's going to be okay."

Fenris' eyes met his. "You're so brave, Cole."

No, I'm not. "As soon as Dad comes back, everything will go back to how it was. I promise." *You're going to get your own life, a wife, a family. Arissa will be able to stop being a mom, Belen will have a*

119

better role model than me, and Lily can smile again. Dad will come back. He has to. It's not fair to you.

"Please listen to Arissa. She needs . . ."

"I won't be a problem," he interrupted.

"You're never a problem, Cole." Fenris looked older than he ever had. Cole wanted to reach out and hug him, to lay his head on Fenris' shoulder and feel his big strong arms hold him like the tiny baby he felt he was inside. But instead he kept his back straight and swallowed.

I won't be a problem. I'm going to end this.

"Cole, promise me something?" Fenris' voice jolted Cole to attention by its seriousness.

"Yes?" His voice felt as if it had to struggle through a wall of water to reach the surface.

"Don't blame them."

Who?

"Don't blame the Old Order: the Creator, the Comforter, the Liberator," Fenris continued gently but firmly. "They didn't do this. They are not to blame."

Yes they are. But Cole kept listening.

"It's going to feel sometimes as if Esis is against you. That everyone has abandoned you, and you're the most insignificant thing in Oldaem. Often it will seem as if you don't matter and that there's no point in trying anymore." Fenris leaned in closer. "It's a lie, Cole. You are *loved. You matter. You have a purpose.*"

Somehow Cole held back the tears.

"It's not *their* fault. Nor is it *your* fault. Or even *Mom's.* It's the Betrayer's fault. He's the reason these things happen. Always remember that. You're not safe unless you rest in the arms of the Old Order. If Dad were here" –Fenris now looked as if he was 4 years old, fear in his eyes–"he would say the same thing."

Cole couldn't meet his eyes. Although he greatly respected his brother, what he said didn't make sense. If the Old Order was in complete control of Esis, how could they completely neglect his family? How could they allow people who were so fake and constantly lying, like the priest, serve them? And why were they doing nothing to stop the pain that Fenris was feeling? Cole would do *anything* to heal his family. *Anything.*

"I won't." Cole lied. He didn't want to lie, but he didn't believe what his brother was trying to tell him. But he knew Fenris would feel more pain if he told him the truth. *Sometimes lying to stop someone hurting is better than telling the truth to cause pain.*

With a look of relief, Fenris wrapped his strong arms tightly around his brother. Cole felt relief at Fenris' warm touch. As he squeezed him tightly a familiar song came from his brother's lips. The familiar words and tune triggered memories in Cole: his mother's face, her smile, her laugh, her bravery, her cooking, her gentle caresses, her rolling in the leaves and swinging on the swing. The boy remembered picnics beside the shore, family dinners with warm fires in the hearth, his dad's soothing voice, Lily's obnoxious laugh, Belen's soft cries soothed by his mother's gentle touch, stories of the Old Order, lazy days on the rug beside his father, wrestling with Fenris. Cole wondered when he would see his brother again.

After Fenris left for Windrip, Cole put his plan into motion. First, he had to figure out exactly which way they would to have to travel and how much food and money he would have to have for the trip. He would need to write a note so that Arissa wouldn't be worried, and he would have to leave at just the right time. While he realized that, as Fenris had said, *his dad could be anywhere,* Dorhaven was as good a place as any to start, and it was where he was supposed to be. *Dorhaven is far away.* It sat upon the far northwestern shore of Oldaem with the City of Flowers in the southeastern corner. He imagined mountains and rivers and dangers and cold hungry nights lay between them and their father, but he knew he had to tell him about Mom, or things would never be the same again.

The next several days he would tuck away the food Arissa gave him and would work cleaning houses and straightening up yards. People seemed to give him more money now that his mother was dead, though it left him feeling annoyed, because his family had needed it just as much when she had been alive. For every five pieces of gold he earned, he put one away for Arissa and Belen. He knew she could handle *just* Belen for a while, but not Belen, himself, *and Lily.* It was time to talk to Lily.

It was the weekend, and he had made all the preparations to leave as he approached her with his travel gear. He found her sitting against a tree, throwing acorns at some ravens perched along the fence. She had terrible aim. *Just like a stupid girl.*

"Lily?"

"What?"

"I need your help?"

"With what?" She sounded uninterested. Come to think of it, he hadn't talked to her the past several days.

He swallowed. "Finding Dad."

Her eyes met his. "You're crazy." She threw another acorn, pretending not to notice the things he had piled beside him.

"Seriously, Lily. We can't make Arissa keep taking care of us. We need to do *something* to help too. Fenris is working. So is Arissa. But *you're* just pestering birds. Let's do something *useful.*"

"How are *we* going to find Dad?" She sounded angry as she chucked an acorn at Cole's head. He swerved to dodge it.

"Hey!"

"You're just a stupid little boy. You'll die after two days."

"No I won't!"

"Yes, you will!" She threw another.

"Stop that!" he shouted.

"Besides, you don't even know where to go."

"Yes I do! Every time I go into town for Arissa, I stop by the library and study the huge map of Oldaem. I know *exactly* where Dorhaven is."

"Yeah, right. It's a lot farther away than it looks on the map."

"I know that, Lily. I'm not stupid."

"Yes, you are."

"Fine." Angry, Cole's face reddened. "I'll go without you!"

"Bye!" Throwing herself on the ground, she stared up at the tree branches. He stood there, listening to her breathing.

"Why won't you help me?" he asked, his voice strained. He *needed* Lily to go with him. Cole hated that he somehow looked up to his younger sister.

"I couldn't help nobody." She sounded sad now, and distant.

Her answer surprised him. "Huh?"

Then she sat up, her tone changing, "What do you want me to do? Fight off the lions?"

"There are lions?" His eyes widened.

"Dummy. There are lions and deer and foxes and monsters all over Oldaem. What do you have to fight off the monsters?" She stared at him as if he was a little worm.

She wants me to beg her. This is a game to her. "I was hoping to have you."

"No."

"Please?"

"No."

"But everyone will be really sad if I die."

"We're used to it."

"Lily! Come on!" By now he was becoming annoyed. She would be going with him even if he had to drag her body all the way across the mountains.

She laid back down. "Let me think about it."

As he watched she closed her eyes and began humming a song that she knew he hated. Cole glanced again at the supplies he had collected for the trip. He had everything ready for their journey and had even left a note for Arissa. It read:

"Arissa,

"Lily and I are going to find Dad. Don't worry, we brought food and money with us. I left some money for you and Belen, too. We'll be back with Dad, so don't try to follow us, it's a waste of time. Keep singing Mom's song to Belen. He likes it. He likes blueberry pudding too. I realized that yesterday."

Patiently Cole waited for Lily to finish her song. When she kept adding verses and pretending to forget words, he wanted to swing her by her red braids against the tree. Suddenly she sat up.

"I have decided."

"You have, huh?"

"Yes." She stared back at him and smiled.

"What did you decide?"

"That I don't want you to die."

"Well, thanks."

Rising to her feet, she dusted herself off. "So I am going to take you to find Dad."

"Wait, you're going to take *me?*"

"Do you have dust in your ears? We have to go before it gets dark." And she started down the hill.

What a great idea, Lily.

"Keep up, Babyface!"

"Don't call me that!"

"Monsters always eat the slowest babies." She waved him to her.

Suddenly it dawned upon Cole what a long journey it was going to be. But finally he had *something* to do, something that mattered. For the first time in days Cole smiled. He smiled because he wasn't

123

alone, because he knew he was going to find his dad, and most of all, because deep inside he believed his father would be proud of him, if he only knew. But his mom never would.

"We aren't going to be crossing any water . . . are we?" Lily stopped, worry in her eyes.

"I . . . I don't know." Her question confused him. *She's probably just trying to make things more difficult.* But the fear in her eyes revealed that she really was afraid. "We'll be okay." He forced a smile.

"Of course we will!" She darted off toward the sun sitting motionless in the sky. As he walked, all he could think of was Fenris' voice ringing in his ears: *Don't blame them.* Cole didn't know what to believe. Maybe it mattered and perhaps it didn't. But one thing he did know was that he wouldn't be motionless like that sun. He was going to do *something.* Hopefully that *something* wouldn't turn him into his mother . . . sinking beneath the water.

CHAPTER 19: KAYT

A light rain fell upon her as she studied the sign on the wooden post that read "Highdale." The people of Highdale were scurrying to get out of the rain as thunder boomed overhead. But she ignored them, her attention focused on the words above her. Then, when she did glance around, she realized the city looked just as it had a year ago. The same blue rooftops still adorned the stone structures. Tall green grass still bordered the gravel roads along with masses of wildflowers and rocky outcroppings of granite and sandstone. No one seemed to notice her. Everyone was only aware of the rain. She felt in no hurry. The warm rain was a nice change to the piercing cold of the mountains in Westervale. Taking off her black gloves, she let the droplets of water pool in her palms as the rain came down harder. Her blonde hair started to become matted to the purple hood that concealed her face. Her travel bag protected her few belongings and now her gloves as she tucked them away.

Lifting her skirts away from the puddles, she slowly walked into the city, hoping no one would recognize her. *That's the last thing I'd need.* Her feet crunched on the gravel beneath her. It had not been her plan to enter Highdale--she had been hoping to avoid it--but the sound of the approaching thunder and the hour of day drove her to seek the shelter of the city. Highdale sloped upward as the road penetrated into the city center. Buildings of various heights lined the street. Shops and carts crammed between the larger buildings, and some even jutted out into the rocky road itself.

She could hear voices up in the second story of the building to her right. Two women, it seemed, were talking and laughing. As she passed by, their voices became hushed. Slowly she pulled the cowl of her hood farther down her face, as water dripped upon her nose. She had hoped no one had recognized her. Maybe she had only imagined their voices had changed when she passed by. *Not everything is about you, Kayt.* Glancing down at her feet, she saw that a red flower had grown from between the stones--at least until she had squashed it under her heel. She stopped, her heart racing, probably from all the exertion of walking up hills and slopes.

Together, we can do anything. His voice rang in her head. She shook it away, sending more water racing down her face, her cowl slipping off her hair. Quickly she pushed it back into place, her eyes glued to the flower. *Together we can do anything.*

"Together we can do anything."

"Of course, Silas." She blushed. It was what he wanted her to do. Kayt had become a master at doing or saying whatever he desired. She had learned to play the role that would get her everything she had ever sought. *Finally, a Shepherd.*

"This way." He reached for her hand. Bashfully she took it and giggled—another art she had mastered.

"What a beautiful city," she breathed. She looked up at the blue-colored buildings. Children played along the street, banners hung high overhead, and people stared in awe at her and waved. Kayt could hear them whispering about her-- her hair, her emerald eyes, her soft lavender gown. *I can get used to this.* Gripping Silas' arm, she continued walking up into the city of Highdale.

"It's where I grew up." He smiled gently.

Kayt had grown accustomed to that smile. He really was attractive--if she could look past the ignorance he wallowed in, his clueless nature, and how easily someone could manipulate him. She could never truly respect him, truly defer to him, or truly love him. "I love you," she breathed. Leaning toward him, she kissed him on the cheek. Women cooed when she did.

"I love you too, Kayt." Waving his arm around him, he exclaimed, "They love you already. How could they not? We are going to *win*."

"Your people seem so supportive and loving. It's a very different environment than Dagonfell," she lied. The truth was that she never really paid attention to the people in Dagonfell, just as she didn't those of Highdale either.

"They will need your leadership. The current Regent has been driving Highdale into ruin."

"They will need *our* leadership."

She gazed deeply into his chocolate eyes. He looked at her with such hope and admiration. Glancing away, she smiled to an elderly couple making their way slowly into a bakery.

"Kayt, whom do you have in mind for Defense? Is there anyone you gradated with?"

Her mind raced back to her class at the academy. It seemed so long ago, though she could still see their faces and hear their voices. "No. I want *you* to pick someone you trust. My opinion doesn't really matter."

"Oh, Kayt." He stopped them in their tracks. "You don't really believe that, do you? There is no one I trust more with my life or my resources or my future than you. In Highdale the Shepherd of State will be second in command to the Regent. Your opinion means *everything* to me."

Arnand is not so easily swayed. Why are you thinking of him? Feeling a tinge of guilt, she shifted her attention to a flock of ravens flying overhead. Occasionally she did feel a trace of guilt, but rarely. This was the path she had chosen--what being a Shepherd of State was all about. Sometimes you had to make sacrifices and compromises that hurt people. Even if those people were your family or even your children. She noticed a young mother kissing her baby's forehead. Kayt forced herself to a smile, but only externally. Inside she was seething.

"My manor is up this way. You'll love it. Our gardens are the finest in the city." When he hurried their pace, she had to struggle to keep up. She was tired of being dragged across the city. Her mind raced to all that had brought her there, to all the people they had encountered, all those she had trampled upon and lied to. But again it had been what she had chosen, had wanted in life. As they neared the manor, more and more people kept stopping and staring at them. The city didn't appear to be in shambles as he had told her, nor did the people seem to be struggling. For the first time since she had signed up to do this she began to wonder about the certainty of their victory in the approaching election.

They stood before a massive golden gate with Silas' family-name engraved upon it. All the houses around it were also fenced in and large. Kayt noticed the city hall sat just a few staircases above his neighborhood. *Well, that will be convenient--if we win.* The gate slowly swung open toward the towering manor. It was snug in the shadow of the hill above them. Servants bustled about the grounds, some raking leaves, others weeding the beds of gorgeous red flowers, and several pushing wheelbarrows of dirt to someplace seemingly important. She could hear the sound of rushing waterfalls on the side of the hill. Although she noticed that Silas did not take his eyes off of her, she continued to act oblivious to his attention.

"Oh, Silas. It's beautiful."

"You're beautiful." He stopped her. They were face to face, almost nose to nose. Kayt could feel the eyes of his staff upon them. She kissed him passionately, leaning in vulnerable and available. His arms wrapped around her, bringing her in closer. A voice broke their kiss.

"It seems you're here early."

Pulling himself away, he looked toward the house and smiled. "Melnora!"

As Kayt watched, Silas ran up the three steps and laughingly hugged the woman in pale green. The woman laughed as well. *Who is Melnora?*

"What brings you early?" The woman was all smiles, glowing under the sun, radiating kindness and friendliness. Kayt didn't trust her.

"I wanted to show Kayt around Highdale before the debates begin."

"What a wonderful idea." The woman's voice had a gentle tone that Kayt sensed could be quite persuasive.

Melnora has to go.

The green-dressed woman gently smiled as she eyed Kayt up and down, apparently not out of judgment, but out of curiosity. "I've heard *so* much about you, Kayt. Come." Her arms extended in a generous hug, her smile wider than before.

Before Kayt knew it she found herself in Melnora's arms, the hug neither too intense nor too limp. *This woman is calculating.*

"Strange . . . Silas has never mentioned a . . . Melnora," Kayt cooed innocently.

127

The woman gently laughed. "He doesn't like to brag about his family."

Brag?

"I'm sure he wanted to keep the focus on you. He's written so many letters about you, Kayt. You must be exhausted from your journey. Come inside. I'll have the servants prepare a bath for you."

Before she could even respond, Melnora floated up the stairs and into the manor. Once again, Silas' arms surrounded Kayt.

"She's my sister. She's also who I'm considering to be my Shepherd of Spirit. What do you think?" His grin widened.

No. "Wonderful!"

"I knew you'd love her." He looked deeply into her eyes. "So what do you think? Do you like it here?"

"Silas. No matter where you are . . . no matter where we are. As long as we're together, I'll love it. Yes. I love it here." The words came so easily out of her mouth. Kayt didn't even have to think about what to say. She knew what he wanted to hear. But then she had known what Arnand had hoped she would say. But she had begun to feel a sense of unease after seeing Highdale and the luxury Silas and his family resided in. She worried that he was out of touch with the people and what they needed. It very well could be that they might not win after all. As they kissed she felt herself holding back a little bit of herself. It was something that she'd never given to anyone, a part of herself that she would reserve until she felt perfectly secure in its receiver's care. Silas wasn't the individual . . . at least not until they won. And now that Melnora was in the picture, winning might be a bit more difficult. She would need to figure out a way to dispose of the woman without alerting Silas of her intentions. If she could come up with some way to make him think it was his own idea, that would be ideal.

"Come." Silas released her hand and led her toward the manor. As they walked she looked around the estate. She could definitely get used to the lavish surroundings she would soon call home. Surrounding her were beds of deep-red flowers. Picking one, she smelled it. It had a sweet scent. When she touched the petal, the pollen from its stamens clung to her skin. Then she crumpled the blossom in her hand, the pale-green stem and all, and smiled. *Melnora will be the first to fall.* In a perfect world, all a Regent would need would be a Shepherd of State. What did Defense, Spirit, and Mind do anyway? She could fulfill all those roles for Silas–*would* fulfill them.

"You coming?"

"Right behind you, Darling." She went up the steps toward the manor, toward her dream of *finally* becoming a fully realized Shepherd of State.

Together we can do anything.

Stepping past the crushed flower, Kayt headed to the older part of town, shaking the memories from her head. She figured less people would recognize her in the poorer district of Highdale. If only the weather and hour would permit her to continue her journey away from Highdale, but she was not about to get stranded out in the wilderness, or catch her death because of the freezing rain. A chill shivered through her as she pulled her traveling cloak tighter around her head. *Don't let anyone see you. Don't let anyone know.*

Thunder boomed above her. It was getting worse. As the rain poured down harder, her steps quickened. She was alone on the streets, save for a few children laughing and splashing in puddles, their mothers unamused, calling them back in. Her breathing became heavier as she continued to walk briskly, her thoughts raced before her. Was it guilt? Surely not--probably just exhaustion. But as she continued on she couldn't help but remember his eyes when Silas realized what she had done to him. The way Melnora looked at her, with disgust and outrage. How his own people sided against him . . . how they turned on him so quickly once her story got out and spread across the region. Kayt could not forget how they pitied her, how they grieved with her, how they looked at her now as someone who needed help instead of someone empowered to help others. It made her sick. *Guilt? No. Regret? Maybe. Exhaustion from running through this One-Forsaken-Town? Absolutely.*

The sign caught her attention: "Foothills Tavern and Inn." But she didn't recognize the name. Perhaps it was a new establishment, or more likely it had never served her purpose to notice its existence previously. Either way, she pushed her way inside, keeping her head down, and headed for the registration desk.

"Room, please."

The thin woman seemed incredibly busy—didn't even make eye contact with her. "Fifteen gold."

Kayt reached into her purse and set the payment down on the counter, the woman fumbling through parchment and documents.

Kayt huffed so as to hurry the woman, but it didn't seem to make a difference in her pace. *Patience, Kayt, don't draw attention to yourself.*

"No, it's a great change! The golden era!" loud, boisterous voices exclaimed behind her, followed by laughter and the clinking of glasses together. Although she kept her head down, she listened intently.

"Highdale is in its prime!"

"Best leadership we've ever seen!"

"We should never vote out this Regent!"

"Best crop of Shepherds ever to graduate from any academy!"

"If only Shepherd Kayt were still with us."

"If only Silas hadn't shamed himself."

"If only Esis were a fair and honest place."

"Poor Kayt. She was just a helpless woman."

"She didn't deserve what he did to her."

"She deserved better!"

"Women are *always* taken advantage of!"

"Here is your key." The innkeeper still didn't look at Kayt as she slid her her key. Mumbling a quick thank you under her breath, Kayt hurried up the staircase. *I can't believe they are still talking about it. Or that they are still talking about me.* Although her lie had successfully shielded her from the shame of losing the election with Silas, it hadn't brought her any joy or satisfaction. It hadn't surprised her that her plan had worked and that she had gotten what she wanted. She usually did, if she worked hard enough. But still, something was unsettling to her. Perhaps it was what drove her home back toward Arnand and her children and had led her to enter Highdale in the first place.

Kayt turned the key to her dimly-lit room and closed the door behind her. With a heavy sigh she leaned her back up against the door. Rainwater dripped from her cloak and created a small pool beneath her feet. She kicked off her wet shoes and shoved them aside, then removed her heavy cloak and let it sink to the floor. Across the room from the door stood a small table and chair. As she wearily sat down in it, she found a deep-red flower in a lonely vase upon the wooden table.

"Why, Kayt? Why did you do this to me?"

Whipping about, she saw the shadow of Silas standing by the door.

"You know why," she replied, turning away from him, staring again at the flower.

"Why did you tell the people what you did about me? Why did you fabricate a story so terrible as to ruin me? Would losing with me have been so bad? Wasn't not loving me enough?"

"Why are you here?" Her voice grew more agitated.

"Do you really think your family will take you back after abandoning them?'

"Go away!"

"They know the truth about you. They can see right through you." He paused. "I wish I could have had the foresight to see through you."

"Go away, Silas. Just . . . go."

"I loved you, Kayt."

"I didn't," she snapped. "I didn't love you. I never did." She swallowed. "I don't know how."

"I loved you, Kayt."

She turned back toward the door and the shadow of Silas vanished. Maybe he had never really been there . . . the conversation had played in her mind before . . . and she knew it would again. Had she loved him? *Perhaps.* Did she love her family? The realization that the *perhaps* was the same made her heart skip a beat. *I can't stay here.*

Refastening her boots, she snatched her cloak. The laughing voices greeted her as she stumbled down the stairs, tossing the key back to the woman, still fumbling with her documents. The voices followed her out of the tavern:

"Poor Kayt."

"Slimy Silas."

"Never a Shepherd of State as great . . ."

"Got what he deserved."

"Women should stay out of politics."

"Men are pigs."

"She couldn't defend herself."

"Couldn't keep his hands to himself."

"She deserved better."

"Poor Kayt."

Soaked to the bone, she soon found herself on the outskirts of Highdale. Her teeth chattering and her body shivering, she felt about to collapse from exhaustion as she stood before a small, humble chapel to the One. *Sanctuary.* When she pushed her way inside; candles softly gleamed in its six windows. A statue of the One rested on the platform behind a pulpit, and beyond it a giant candelabra with every candle lit. A kneeling platform with a cushioned bar fronted 14 unlit candlesticks. When Kayt knelt on it, she could feel moisture from her soaked cloak puddling around her knees. As she wearily rested her elbows on the cushioned bar, her gaze drifted to her cherished deity staring back at her. Her heart racing, she had never felt more unhappy and unsure of herself.

Please great One . . . let them forgive me. Let them love me. Let them remember me. Her thoughts drifted to her children, to Arnand, to the people she had let down, destroyed, and ran from. She thought of Silas, the man she had betrayed her family for, then had betrayed for herself. So many betrayals. *It was all for me.* The shadow of Silas knelt beside her.

"I'll never forgive you, Kayt," he whispered.

I would do it all over again, Silas.

As she glanced around the chapel at the six windows, they each suddenly became a scene from her past. The first when she had begun to lust after Silas instead of her own husband. The second when she realized Silas' potential power meant more to her than her own family. The third when she decided to run in the election with him, and leave her family behind potentially forever. The fourth when she realized the election was unwinnable. The fifth when she falsely accused Silas of physical misconduct. The final when she left Highdale, Silas' reputation shamed and ruined for a crime against her he did not commit, and all so she wouldn't have to lose the election with him. Each episode seemed to come to life in all its misery, shame, and reality. She could hear the voices from her past, see the pained faces of those who once loved her, feel the pity that nearly crushed her beneath its weight. *Please, One, let me forget, cleanse me of my memory, cleanse me of my past, make me new, make me whole, make me strong.*

Kayt lit a candle for Silas that night. It was not one seeking redemption for her sins, but rather a plea for wisdom never to fall for a foolish man again and to escape the shadow of Silas.

CHAPTER 20: GALEN

Three days. It had been three impossibly long days out on the horrendous sea. Never in his friend's stories of sea voyages had he ever mentioned the incessant rocking of a ship on the waves. Galen heaved once more over the railing. *There goes lunch.* Once again he felt as if he was about to die. Any of his delusions of grandeur about being part of a rescue mission had been quickly swept into the sea along with the contents of his stomach. And it had been like that since the first day.

Zevran had barely had time to show them anything before the team assembled by Seff had noiselessly boarded the vessel. It consisted of three men and two women. Galen had not caught all of their names yet, but since they were not the least bit interested in him, because they thought of him not so much as "soldier" but rather as "crew," Galen had decided that he would not pay the least attention to them. In overhearing their conversations, he had learned that one woman, slim and muscular with ebony skin and a shaved head, was their leader. Her name was Veroma. He had observed that she did not speak much, but when she did, it was loud, clear, and met with respect.

He had heard them call the oldest man, thin and serious, Endcer. His hair was graying in a salt and pepper way that reminded him of Shepherd Demas, but it could have been his commanding presence that connected the two in Galen's mind. *I wonder if Gadiel sees it, too.* Demas's son had been much quieter than Galen had ever seen him. The confident smirk was gone. All that remained was a constant expression of misery, and he wasn't even trying to hide it. He rarely spoke unless someone else addressed him first, and every evening he just came back to the tiny crowded room he, Galen, and Adar shared and fell asleep in his bunk. It kind of pleased Galen, although he would never admit it to anyone. He realized that he probably shouldn't feel that way, and that if he told Adar, his friend would probably point out that Galen should be feeling pity for Gadiel and not be gloating over his misery. *I mean I guess I can identify with not having a parent.* But the situations were quite different, and Galen had never really cared about pitying people, especially rich sons of Royal Shepherds who, up until a few days ago, had never known what it was to feel deep pain. *The kind I have lived with every day of my life.*

133

Absentmindedly, Galen stroked the puckered skin on his chest where the jagged scar met his collarbone. His stomach was not protesting as fiercely for the time being, and he tried to get his bearings again. He had been so seasick that he had been virtually no help to Zevran. *Well, it's not my fault we're on a stupid boat.* One could barely classify the vessel as a ship at all. Galen had thought it was on the small side when he had first climbed aboard, but crowded with Gadiel, Adar, Zevran, the five special force team members, and their three Lamean slaves, there was virtually no privacy. Even now, the two male specialists whose names Galen had not figured out yet were sitting just a few feet away from him playing cards. They had politely ignored his unpleasant retching over the side of the boat, and he politely pretended he had never made those noises to begin with.

It was just kind of an understood thing that Seff's team kept to themselves and the makeshift crew to themselves. That irked Galen a little. He could see why they did not interact with the three Lamean slaves–they were there only to serve. In fact, they were doing the cooking and cleaning. But Galen was a soldier of the Oldaem army. He was not a cabin boy, and he did not want to be treated as such. Of course, he was not quite sure how to communicate that to the men in front of him who had just seen him puking his guts out.

Hesitantly, Galen stood on his feet. *Good. The world isn't spinning anymore.* He figured he better go report for duty again. Zevran was getting pretty frustrated at his constant seasickness.

The officer glanced up from the helm as Galen entered the tiny bridge. "You ran out pretty quickly. Still seasick?"

Galen nodded, his green complexion answering for him.

"Don't worry, you'll get your sea legs soon enough," Zevran chuckled. "Please tell me you're ready to get back to work."

"I'm ready." Galen straightened. "What am I supposed to do?"

The captain quickly ran over some instructions with Galen and sent him on his way. From what Galen had understood, he was supposed to tie some knot to another rope for some purpose that involved something attached to the rigging. *Something like that.* He was still unfamiliar with nautical terminology, but he got the gist of what he was supposed to do. *Look at me being a good little unquestioning slave.*

And he really did feel a little guilty about having been so useless the past few days. Several times he had felt recovered enough to start working on something, only to feel his stomach rebel, and he would have to abandon his post. Gadiel or Adar would have to be pulled from whatever they were working on to complete his task.

Galen sighed as he pulled up the rope and began tying it to the other one. After carefully making a loop, he connected the two. He was thankful he wouldn't have to do this forever. He had always imagined the sea as full of adventure, including beautiful princesses and vicious pirates. Vaguely he remembered a time when his friend had been on his father's merchant ship and had been shipwrecked for a time in another country. That seemed a lot more adventurous than being seasick. But he supposed it would probably get exciting as soon as they got to Leoj. The team had hoped to overtake the vessel carrying Royal Shepherd Demas before it reached Leoj, but considering they had no idea what it looked like or exactly when it had left, the chances of that were pretty slim. Now, Galen knew that they would travel to Leoj, but what would happen once they got there was a closely guarded secret. He figured they would probably try to get to one of the Oldaem bases in the war-torn country and plan an extraction operation once they located the Shepherd. However, he had no idea how long they would actually be there. Part of him was terrified, but going to Leoj in this situation certainly beat being shipped there to fight on the front lines.

Gadiel joined Galen next to the rigging he was working on. "You're looking a lot less sick now," he commented as he dropped the rope he had been carrying next to Galen's.

"How did you ..."

"It's a pretty small boat. I, uh, heard you."

Galen sighed. "Right." *Well then everyone else did, too.* He went back to his knot. Gadiel set down some tools and started working on his own section of the sail, mending a section that had torn loose from the mast. As they worked in silence, Galen wondered what Gadiel thought of the whole situation. At the same time he considered how he would feel if the purpose of their mission had been to rescue his missing father. Glancing up at Gadiel who had climbed above him, he saw the kid's mouth set in grim determination, focusing only on the task at hand. He guessed Gadiel was handling everything pretty well, considering. *At least he knows the general area where his father is. And that he didn't leave intentionally.* That was more than he could say for his own father, whom Galen could only assume was drunk in a tavern somewhere. Or dead. Or living a very successful life with another family. Long ago he had given up trying to guess. Nobody had ever bothered to send a search party for him.

"It's not gonna stay if you knot it like that."

Galen glanced up to see Gadiel gesturing at his newly tied rope.

"Excuse me?" He inspected his rope. It looked perfectly fine.

Gadiel hopped down next to him. "See, you're supposed to loop it near the end so that when you run it back through, the loop is large enough to go around the pole." Then he started to untie the rope. Galen pushed his hands away.

"There's nothing wrong with it." *Thinks he knows everything.*

But Gadiel persisted. "Trust me, I know about rigging and sails." Pausing for a second, he then took a breath. "My father used to take me when he would go on special journeys with the king. It's not going to stay if you leave it loose like that."

He was just looking for a reason to tell that story. Galen pushed him to the side. "Going on yacht adventures does not count as learning how to sail. Stop acting as if you know more than I do."

Gadiel threw up his hands. "I'm just trying to help! But if you don't want my advice, fine. Do it your way. Don't come crying to me when Zevran corrects you."

"You're not the leader anymore, Gadiel, you're just like everybody else, so stop acting as if you're so special." It felt so good to finally put him in his place. Gadiel certainly needed to hear it.

"What are you talking about?" Gadiel's deep blue eyes flashed, and Galen recognized the look.

But it was too late to stop and Galen was on a roll. "Company leader at 19? Come on, Gadiel, we all know how that happened."

The other soldier's eyebrows raised. "Is that why you hate me so much? Because I've been trying to figure it out for years." He crossed his arms.

Galen rolled his eyes. "You act as if I'm the only one."

"I have been living with people judging me because of my father my whole life. Believe me, I know what it looks like. But you," he pointed at Galen, "you are the only person at the base that I haven't been able to convince. You still … look at me that way." His jaw clenched. "Why?"

"Because I have no respect for people who ride their father's coattails to the top." Gadiel's face grew stony. "Well, guess what? He's not *here anymore.* So you better get used to being treated like the rest of us."

Without a word, Gadiel smashed his fist hard into Galen's cheek.

Galen would have dodged it, but he had been caught off guard, and the full force of Gadiel's blow landed on his face. Knocked off balance, he crashed into the maste. Galen snarled and swung, but Gadiel was prepared and pushed him to the deck. Ready this time, Galen grabbed Gadiel's legs as he was on his way down, toppling them both.

"Stop!" Zevran's voice boomed from a distance. Neither of them did. Galen never got a solid hit before Zevran seized Gadiel and a Lamean slave yanked Galen away. Instant flashbacks of his time as a child on the streets of Aramoor shifted his anger from Gadiel toward the Lamean slave restraining him. Sickened, Galen shoved the man aside. "What is going on?" Zevran demanded in exasperation. Gadiel wrestled himself free of Zevran's grip and stalked off toward the cabin.

Galen glared at the Lamean and gingerly touched his cheek. "He just flew at me out of nowhere."

Zevran rolled his eyes. "Yeah, I'm sure that's what happened." Glancing at the rigging, his eyes narrowed. "Were you even listening when I gave you those instructions? Your knot is all wrong." Untying the rope, Galen threw it at him. "Then you do it!" Swinging around, he stomped off.

But he didn't know where to go. He couldn't return to the cramped cabin. Gadiel had already claimed that area. Nor did he want to stay up on deck where there was no privacy. *Well, I am kind of hungry.* Then he remembered that he hadn't held down his meals for a while, and even though he had a headache now, his stomach was still behaving itself. *Better eat before the next wave of nausea.* On impulse he headed to the kitchen.

Unfortunately, he found it occupied by the other male Lamean and the only female one. As much as he didn't want to talk to them, he figured he had to if he wanted any food, and approached the young girl. She had dark brown straight hair tied back with a ribbon and was wearing a homespun pink dress. To his surprise, she was well kept.

"May I help you with something?" she said, facing him and wiping her hands on her apron.

"Um, do you have anything I can eat?"

Realization dawned on her face. "Oh, you're the one who's been sick the whole trip." His eyebrow raised. *She's a talkative one.*

"Can I just have some food?"

"Sure!" she smiled. Galen stared. "Let me see what I can find you. The name's Leilani, by the way."

"Nobody asked." *Someone trained her wrong.*

Her smile went away, but she didn't lower her eyes when she talked to him. "I apologize. It will just be a moment."

"Yeah, well, make it quick. I don't have all day to chit-chat with you," he sighed.

She went off without another word. He hated having to talk to Lameans. It was bad enough that he had to say anything to them, but when they were overly chatty like this girl, it was even worse. Someone had to put them in their place, just as someone needed to put Gadiel in his place, too. Galen didn't understand why he was the only one with the courage to speak his mind, but he was more than willing to be the one to do the job.

After a few minutes, the Lamean returned with a box of food and a wrapped bag of ice. She handed him the box. "Left over from lunch." Taking it, he started to leave. "Wait!" she called after him.

She seriously needs to remember who she is. He was about to tell her so, when she continued. "This is ice." She offered it to him. He looked confused. "For your cheek. It's swollen."

After staring at her in surprise for a moment, he accepted the ice and left without another word.

CHAPTER 21: KAYT

It was dawn when Kayt finished with her prayers to the One. She had spent the night in deep meditation to cleanse her spirit and renew her soul. And he did not let her down, just as she knew he wouldn't. Kayt left the little chapel in better spirits. True, she had hurt her family and those she cared about in ways unimaginable, but they would forgive her. They would take her back. *If you set your mind to something, you will always succeed.*

Kayt had always succeeded, and this situation would be no different. Part of her mind brought her back to her biggest failure and unrealized dream—that of becoming a fully recognized Shepherd of State to a Regent. She could never become a Royal Shepherd without that stepping stone first.

No, she reminded herself, *the only mistake I made was thinking that Silas had what it took to become a Regent.* But all hope was not lost. Maybe someday she could move to a region far to the east such as Efil or Soma where no one had ever heard of her. Where no one would look at her with eyes full of pity. There she could start over.

It sounded like a good plan, but at the moment it completely disinterested her. Right now she wanted her family. Fame and glory could wait. Kayt wanted to feel her little boy's chubby arms wrapped around her, to have her daughter to fall asleep in her lap. And she wanted to embrace her husband. *Arnand.*

As she made her way out of Highdale, she told herself that what had happened there was in the past and that she never planned to come back. Instead, she thought of her husband. She had not allowed herself to think of him in a long time. *I never thought of Silas the way I think of you.* Kayt was sure of that now.

Marrying Arnand had made sense at the time. She knew he had always loved her, and she regarded him highly. They had grown up together in Dagonfell, a wealthy city in the region of Jaron. Even when they had been children, Arnand had made his love for her clear. She had never led him on--she respected him too much.

At the time she had told him point-blank that she had every intention of becoming a Shepherd and leaving, never to come back. Nevertheless he said he would support her in anything she did. He even travelled the short distance to the Capital to watch her participate in the tournament.

She had succeeded, of course, just as everyone knew she would. Westpoint Academy, the nearest Shepherd training school, had even selected her. Arnand promised he would visit, but she told him not to. Kayt wanted nothing to distract her from her studies. Having never been that close to her own large family, she had nothing to tie her down.

For five years she had studied diligently. As Kayt crossed the long distance of the region of Isprig and into Jaron, she could still hear the voices of her professors ringing in her ears. "Fantastic." "Brilliant." "Cunning." Straight away she had knocked out her opponent, the other Shepherd of State candidate, and had slithered her way to graduation day.

Arnand had been there with flowers in his hand to see her graduate. She had been surprised to see him.

"Kayt, I'm so glad to see you," he had said, starting to hug her, but she pushed him away, not unkindly, but just unsure. Undeterred, he reached out his hand to tuck her straight blond hair behind her ear. "I'm proud of you. And I missed you."

Arnand was not handsome. In fact, he was rather plain looking with light-brown, close-cropped hair that was the same color as his sun-tanned skin. While he was not short, Kayt was rather tall, so they were around the same height.

Other than his family wealth, nothing really stuck out about him, but for some reason, Kayt felt something stirring that day that she had pushed aside for as long as she could remember. "I missed you, too."

"I know you told me to stay away," he began hesitantly, "And I did, for as long as I could. But Kayt … I had to see you again." Gently he took her hand in his. This time, she didn't pull away.

But she didn't shy away from the truth either. "I'm a Shepherd of State now, Arnand. They don't have families."

"I know, Kayt. I know." His brown eyes darkened. "But I've been thinking a lot about this, and I have a proposition. I want you to make me a promise."

Kayt never did that lightly. "What's your idea?"

"I want to marry you."

Her mouth dropped opened, and she took a step back. *Was he not listening to what I just said? I can't have a family if I want to have a successful career. Maybe once I become a Royal Shepherd … but that could be years from now.* "Arnand, I've already told you …"

"That you're a Shepherd of State," he interrupted. "I know. I just saw you graduate. That you can't have a family. I know. You've been saying that for years. But I also know that what I feel about you … is real. And I know you feel something too. You pretend and pretend that all you care about is self-advancement, but I can see right through it." *He's wrong. He doesn't know the first thing about what I'm after.*

"I know you feel something toward me as well, and you're afraid to admit it. So here's my proposition. The next election for the regions isn't for three more years which means you'll have to find work at an academy or in the government."

"What's your point?" It had not concerned her that she would not immediately be able to run in the elections and become Shepherd of State for a region. In reality, she had planned to spend the next few years making contacts in the Shepherd community.

"So take six months. Look for work. I'll help you in any way you can. But if you don't find anything by the end of those six months"– he knelt on one knee in front of her–"then promise me you'll accept my hand in marriage." He held his hand out to her.

Kayt touched the newly acquired Shepherd of State medallion that hung around her neck. Arnand looked almost pathetic, just kneeling there in front of her with a goofy grin on his face. *Six months.*

Still though, it was kind of nice to see him offering everything he had, every part of himself to her. She could use that kind of devotion, and with his family backing her along with Kayt's own family money, she might become a candidate for Royal Shepherd even sooner than expected.

However, marrying Arnand would come with a risk—it might prevent her from being selected to run with any prospective Regents when election year did come around. It was a gamble. *Am I willing to take it?*

Kayt looked back at Arnand, who knelt expectantly, although his knees were becoming a bit wobbly since she had kept him waiting on her answer. For a moment she was tempted to ask him to give her time to decide, but in her heart she already knew what she was going to say. The potential for success was too great. And if she was going to marry anyone, Arnand was logically the best match.

"What are you thinking?" he asked her.

For a moment Kayt swallowed, and then with resolve, looked him in the eyes. "If I don't find work in six months, I *promise* to become your wife."

The dry grass crunched under her feet as she walked along the well-trodden path. It appeared as if this part of Jaron was going through a drought. So far Kayt had been up in the mountains of Westervale where it was still cool even in the summer.

Now she approached the familiar bend in the path with a bit of trepidation. *I wonder what he'll say. Will Balyn and Lei even remember me?* She wondered how long it would take for things to go back to normal. It was close now, her former home.

Arnand's parents had given them a large cottage just outside of the main part of Dorhaven. It had been the perfect place to raise a family. Kayt wondered if he was teaching Lei how to grow flowers in the garden. She was 2 now. *Can she say "Mama"?* Hopefully he had taught her.

Finally, after days and days of journeying, she could see the white cottage in the distance. Nothing about it looked different, and that

gave Kayt hope. *Maybe not much has changed at all.* The lawn
looked well-kept, even green despite the drought around it. Since it
didn't matter who recognized her now, she took off her purple hood.
She was home.

Walking up the three steps that led to the wooden door, she took a
deep breath and reassured herself, *He said he would always love me.*
Then, knocking confidently on the door, she waited impatiently.
Adjusting her medallion, she fluffed her hair and looked around
aimlessly. For a few moments she sat on the steps. Finally she
knocked again and looked in the window. No one appeared to be
home.

Deciding at last to get a room in an inn farther into town and
return in the morning, she started one final time to make sure no one
was home.

"They aren't there," a voice behind her startled Kate. She turned
to see an elderly woman walking up the path from the road. Her gray
hair was pulled back stylishly in a bun and expensive jewels adorned
her red dress. Resentment filled the strong features of her face.

"Hello, Martha."

"You have a lot of nerve just showing up here like this, Kayt."
Placing the basket she had been carrying on the ground next to the
flower garden, she wiped her hands. "After what you did to him--to
them."

"Where are they?" *Maybe they are staying with her.*

"They're gone," Martha said bitingly. "Did you really think they
would stick around? That he would wait for you to come back?"

"He did it once." Kayt's eyes flashed.

"A mistake," Arnand's mother threw back. "One he will not make
again. Why are you here, anyway? I had hoped never to see you
again."

"You know why I am here, Martha. Now tell me where they are."

"They *left.* After you did. *"* Clearly she was enjoying this
confrontation. *I never liked her. Even when I pretended to.* "What
kind of woman leaves her husband with a toddler and a newborn
baby?"

Kayt stiffened. Martha had no right to judge her. Everything she
had done had been justified. "I'm back now." Above all else, she
must remain calm. After all, she was a Shepherd of State, trained to
handle any crisis. She just had to find a way to get from Martha the
information she needed.

"Two years too late! You should feel ashamed of yourself."
Arnand's mother raised herself to her full height. "But do you know
what I see when I look in your eyes?"

Confidence.

"Selfishness. You don't regret leaving, do you?"

Kayt raised an eyebrow. "I would do it again."

Martha pursed her lips. "I know you would. Arnand had no idea
what he was getting into when he married you. Just like that poor
man whose reputation you destroyed. They're both your victims."
Does she mean Silas? He did that to himself. "You think we couldn't
figure out what you did to him? You may have fooled the rest of the
region, but I know better. Because that's what you do, Kayt. My son
may not have seen it, nor Silas, but I do. I can see right through you."

"You know nothing about me."

"You use people. You do whatever it takes to get ahead, regardless
of the victims you leave in your wake. Is that the real reason you
came back? Because you got *bored* wherever you went after you lost
the election? Well, I won't let my innocent grandchildren be your
next victims." Martha started to push past her, but Kayt held her
ground. *Don't let her leave without telling you their location.*

"They're *my* children. I deserve to see them."

"You know what you deserve." The older woman's eyes were ice-
cold. "You stay away from them." Then Kayt's mother-in-law walked
around her as if touching Kayt would give her a disease and vanished
into the house.

Kayt felt at a loss. She had not considered that Arnand would have
moved away and taken her children. Having grown up in Dagonfell,
he'd never shown any intention of leaving. *I guess he changed his
mind.* Maybe she had been wrong to assume that he would be
waiting for her just like last time.

When she gone to join Silas, her husband had accused her of
breaking her promise to him. Now it appeared that he had broken his
promise that he would always wait for her, always love her. *He is not
devoted to me anymore.* That was probably for the best. Arnand had
always gotten in the way, anyway.

Now the problem was what to do. While Kayt always had a plan,
this time it had fallen through, and she did not have a contingency
one. *Where should I go now?* She did not want to stay in Dagonfell.
Now that Martha knew she was here, it was only a matter of time
before her parents or siblings found out. And if they knew the truth
about her messy end with Silas, there would be no welcoming arms

143

to greet her. Her family had known Silas' for years. The only choice she had was to leave.

Had she been elected as the Shepherd of State for the region, she would be going to the Capital now to watch the upcoming tournament. *If everything had gone according to plan, who knows how different things would be?* Now that Kayt thought about it, the Capital was not too far away. Two days on foot at the most. When she had been young she had it visited many times. Her family line had ancient roots, and her parents knew many of the well-known figures in the government.

Gragor. She had not seen her childhood friend in years. While she wasn't sure why she thought of him now, he did live in the Capital and was not married yet. *Maybe I will go see him and watch the tournament.* Yes, the Capital sounded like a good idea. Everyone who was anyone would be there. *It is the perfect place to start over.*

Taking a deep breath and turning her heels, Kayt headed south.

CHAPTER 22: COLE

Don't blame them, Cole. He could hear Fenris' voice in his dreams. Sometimes. Most of his dreams, though, involved water. He couldn't escape it. Most mornings he would wake up in a pool of sweat. Strangely, he didn't scream in his dreams. Instead, he would silently sit before a still lake without even a ripple. There was no way to know what was beneath its surface. But then he didn't want to know. Sometimes in his dreams he would try to jump in, but every time he did, the water turned into a cloudy and glassy surface. Although he strained to see into the murky substance, he never succeeded. At times he would hear crying in his dreams and knew it was Lily. And other times he realized that he was awake when he heard her crying. Once he dreamed of a giant wall, and like the water, he couldn't look beyond it. A faceless girl wandered near the wall. *Maybe today will be the day.* Unsure who she might be, he wondered if she was his mother at a young age, but her hair was brown and curly. Always he saw faceless people in his dreams. There was no detail, sometimes there was no color, and always there was no joy. After a while he began to wonder if possibly he had dreamed about the wall much earlier, before his mother's death, and perhaps often. That for some reason he was just now remembering it.

Cole lay on his back on top of a high field on a hill, several hilltops away from the City of Flowers. He wasn't sure just where they were. Their journey had led them through forests and glades and over hills and across fields. They passed farmers and merchants and Lameans and nobles and Shepherds as they walked. Surprisingly, nobody stopped them. Sometimes Lily would want to talk to passing travelers but Cole always pulled her away and made her hide by the side of the road until they were out of sight. He was determined to let nothing stop them or delay them from finding their father. But sometimes it seemed as if something or someone was following them. Maybe it was in his mind--he couldn't be sure--but occasionally when he looked behind him, he imagined a shadow dodging behind a tree or a rock or dropping into tall grass. While he didn't tell Lily about it, because he didn't want her to be afraid, he couldn't shake the feeling they were indeed being followed.

Dorhaven was far. And Cole knew from looking at that library map that they had mountains to cross and a very long bridge. He also understood they would continue to need to find food. They took turns leading and made a pretty good team. As he looked over at his sister and heard her snoring lightly, he also noticed she was shivering a little. *Of course, now I have to be cold.* Sitting up, he took the small blanket off of himself and gently laid it on her. Then resting with his elbows on his knees, he shivered softly while studying the dimly-lit sleeping village below. *Maybe there's food down there. Or lions. Lily and her lions. And maybe there's a shadow.* Briefly he glanced around. Nothing.

He wondered what his father would think when he found out Mom had died. Surely he would immediately drop everything Shepherd-related and take them the swiftest route back home so that Arissa and Fenris could just be the kids they never were able to be. His dad was a good man, even if he had gone away. Somehow he knew he had left them because he loved them. It didn't make sense when he thought about it too hard, but deep inside he understood how. Sometimes the heart grasps things the head couldn't possibly figure out. His sister began shaking again. *How could she still be cold?* After all, she had his blanket. *Lily always gets everything.* Then he realized she wasn't shivering--she was crying softly in her sleep. Cole quietly scooted over next to her and gently placed her head in his lap. Still she cried and still she slept. Slowly he rubbed her arm, trying to calm her down. It was what Arissa always did for Belen when he cried. *If she's too loud, someone may hear us.*

145

For the first time since they left home, Cole realized that maybe Esis was a lot bigger than he had imagined it would be. The world had more people than he realized, more pain, more danger, more death. Perhaps they would need more help than he had originally anticipated. He didn't regret the trip to find their Dad--he knew it was important--but perhaps for the first time he was genuinely worried they may never make it. After all, he didn't really know the way. Fenris had taught him how to tell north from south and east from west. Cole knew he needed to chase the sunset until they reached the water, and then keep it to the left until they passed out of Aerion and into Soma and came to the bridge that crossed the great expanse. After that, it would be very hard to figure out the way to Dorhaven without some more help. Now Cole found himself praying, something he was hesitant to do. Perhaps he only did it because he knew Fenris would be proud of him, because he begged him not to blame the Old Order for everything that had happened. But deep inside he did blame them anyway. Yet still he prayed. Because he knew, even though sometimes he and Lily fought, at the end of the day, they still loved each other. Maybe this was kind of the same thing with the Three of the Old Order. He was mad at them today, but maybe, they still loved him anyway, and, maybe, he could still believe in them as Lily and Fenris did. So he prayed for his dad and for their safety, for Lily, Arissa, Fenris, and Belen, and for the courage he would need to face tomorrow. The courage he must have to endure the pain and the danger and the death that filled Esis. Finally he fell asleep.

"Mable, they aren't fawns, they're kids."

"What in tarnation are two little kids doin' out here on top of this hill?"

"I don't know," the old man whispered, "but here they are."

"Well, are you gonna wake them up?"

"Should we?"

"Would you want to be left alone if you were two little kids sleeping out in the middle of nowhere?"

"Mable, I don't rightly know." He sounded frustrated. "It's been a long time since I was a little kid in the middle of nowhere."

"Wilber, wake them up." She sounded resolved, even though her voice was shaky, old, and very, very heavy. Cole kept his eyes closed.

"Well, how do I wake them up?"

"I don't know, Wilber. Shake them a little."

"You want me to shake them a little?"

"Yes, Wilber, I want you to shake them a little." She sounded far away, and up higher, as if she sat on a cart or something. Cole was *not* happy they had been discovered. He had warned Lily earlier that night, before they stopped, that they needed to sleep somewhere less exposed, but she had convinced him that no one would bother to climb to the very top of this hill. *Stupid Lily.* His sister still snored on his lap.

"Maybe I could just tap them a little with my walking stick."

"Whatever you want to do, Wilber."

Cole felt something poking him in the side.

"Wake up, kid, you're in the middle of nowhere."

"They know that, Wilber. People just don't fall asleep in the middle of nowhere."

Though Cole felt Lily sit up, he continued to lay on his back with his eyes closed. *Maybe they will just go away.*

"Hey!" he could hear Lily's voice still scratchy from just waking up. "Can't a girl get any sleep around here?"

The old man spoke again. "Well, you're sleeping on a hill."

"I know." Lily sounded the way she did when she loved being right.

"Why are you sleeping on a hill?" the man asked.

"Why are you standing on a hill?" she quipped back.

"Lots of people stand on hills, Dearie," Mable said.

Cole suddenly felt himself being shoved roughly by his sister. Instinctively he pushed back.

"Get up, you stupid baby, we've been found! I told you this was a bad place! I told you, and you *never* listen to me." She was screaming now. *You told me? Are you kidding? Guess it's time to get up.*

"Lily, they are 452 years old, they won't hurt us." Cole rubbed his eyes as he sat up. It was bright outside. *Too bright.* He wished it were cloudy.

"I woke them up, Mable."

"I see that, Wilber."

"Wilber and Mable?" Lily's big eyes laughed with her voice. "What old people names!" Again she laughed and rolled on the grass.

147

"My grandma's name was Lily," Mable said gently. That instantly stopped Lily from laughing and made Cole chuckle.

"I'm a grandma?" Lily said, shocked.

"She's dead now." Wilber triumphantly smiled.

"Wilber! Don't talk to the kids about death."

We're used to death.

"Why are you out here, where are you headed?" Wilber asked, leaning on his staff.

Cole could tell the old man was getting winded and wondered if Wilber should sit down. When he glanced behind him, he saw Mable sitting on an old wooden cart with two ancient horses hitched to it. Their clothes looked old too, as did their eyes and their hair and their skin. They smelled old too. *Gross.* Lily gave Cole a guarded stare in response to Wilber's question. He decided he would let her answer this one.

The girl stood up, trying to look taller than she actually was, and replied in a much more adult tone. "We are heading to the sea," she said quickly. "There is a little beach town our parents are at. It's called . . . uh . . . Beach Town . . . We got separated in that bad, bad storm the other night, and they always told us if we get separated to meet up there. A huge wind and thunderbolt struck the ground and started a really big fire. Our sister got burned and Daddy had to rush her to the village. Mom was already sick to begin with, and she ran away to get out of the rain. She's sick in the head. It was raining so badly that I took my baby brother Cole here to get out of the rain so we wouldn't get sick too. We fell asleep in a cave but a bear was in there so we went to another cave, and when the storm was over and the sun came back up, we couldn't find any of them. We *hope,* no, we *know* they will be at our beach town. So we are on our way there, and we would very much like to ride in your cart. Cole, get on the cart!"

She spoke with such authority it was hard to dispute her words. He could tell the old couple was just as shocked as he was as she started climbing up the back of the cart, her little legs attempting to swing onto its load of hay. Unfortunately not getting very far, she started huffing and puffing as she struggled. *I better help her.* Cole pushed her up and over into the bed of the cart.

"Yeah, we need ride," Cole heard himself say. "May we get a ride?" *What am I doing?*

"Looks like Lily isn't waiting for an answer," Mable said with a smile in her voice.

"Come on, Cole."

Tossing their pack of supplies ahead of him, he found himself following his sister onto the wagon. Before he knew it they were bouncing up and down as the cart took off down the hill. Lily looked content as they rode, as if she had accomplished some fantastic success. It was the happiest she had appeared since they left The City of Flowers. Mostly they listened to the elderly couple as they rode. They argued about what kind of birds were passing by, how hot it was, and whether Leoj would attack Oldaem or not. Several times they stopped to ask someone whether they were actually heading toward the sea or not. Cole and Lily would hide under the hay when they did. When they did he wondered if she thought it just an exciting game.

Cole grew tired of the arguing, and he almost preferred to stretch his legs and run alongside the wagon as the horses kicked up dust. But if he did that, the person tracking them would catch them. Hopefully, as a result of their ride they were sure to have lost their pursuer by now . . . if anyone was actually following them.

They passed a lot of animals, but Cole didn't really care about them--he just wanted to get there as fast as they could, although Lily kept talking about the different types and sizes. Her favorite were the fat cows. *Why does she love fat cows?* His only thoughts were about his father. His dad had to know the truth and as soon as possible. Cole wondered what Arissa and Belen and Fenris were doing. Were they out looking for them?

"Are you heading to the sea?" Lily's voice snapped Cole into realizing they had been riding for a while without either of them talking to the old, arguing couple.

"We're off to stop by my sister's before we go to Vertloch Tower." Mable coughed as dust swirled up around her.

"Her sister lives by the sea."

"I think they could figure that out, Wilber."

"Well, you didn't mention it."

"Why else would we be traveling to the sea?"

"I don't know Mable, I'm just makin' conversation."

"You've been makin' conversation since we left."

"Well, don't you like talkin' to me?"

"Yes, Wilber, sometimes I like talkin' to you."

Cole grew annoyed. "What's at Vertloch Tower?" He noticed Lily no longer paid any attention to the couple. Instead, she was silently gazing at the clouds.

"That one looks like a fat cow, Cole!" Lily happily exclaimed.

The old couple didn't say anything for a while, just staring at each other. It made Cole suspicious as the silence continued. "Hello?" he pressed.

"Sorry, Dearie, sometimes I'm hard of hearing. Our daughter has gone to priestess training."

"Mable! We aren't supposed to talk about it!" Wilber barked.

"Oh, calm down, Wilber, they're just kids. Who will they tell?"

Cole swallowed. "Did she *want* to become a priestess?" He watched them both sadly hang their heads.

"No." Wilber sighed.

"Oh." Cole could tell they were both uncomfortable.

"They came to our door," Mable continued, "soldiers of the Tower, said The Three had selected her to become a priestess. She had no choice. Then, she was gone." They didn't turn around as they spoke but kept their eyes on the road ahead and said nothing further for some time.

Wilber broke the silence. "We get to see her once a year"--he wiped sweat from his head--"it's been a year."

"What do you think you'll find?" Cole's curiosity had begun to grow.

"Hopefully her," Mable said with confidence. "She's always been strong. I hope they haven't been able to break her."

"Priestesses are crazy," Lily piped in. Cole hadn't even been aware she had been listening. "My brother says they spread lies and murder and violence. If I was a bad girl, I'd be a priestess"--mischief gleamed in her eyes--"and I'd be one tough priestess. HIYAA!" Lily chopped the side of the cart with her hand and laughed.

"All priestesses are bad?" Cole asked.

"Uh, duh!" Lily looked at him as if he was stupid for asking such a question.

"Serena isn't. She's still Serena." Lily watched Mable look up into the sunlight. "Please, Liberator, be with her."

That got Lily's attention as she stopped attacking the side of the cart with fast jabs of her hand. "You're Old Order?"

Wilber jerked around with fear in his eyes. "Well now you've gone and done it, Mable, just shout it to all of Esis. It's probably why the soldiers came to *our* door. If we had been New Order, they probably would have let us alone."

"I don't care!" Determination flashed in her eyes. "If we were younger, sweet Lily, this would be a rescue mission. But for now, just a visit has to be okay. And yes, we are Old Order."

"So are we!" Lily bolted toward the front of the wagon. "Our Daddy raised us to be!"

"We are few now, aren't we?" Cole heard Mable say with tears in her voice. The boy looked around as they rode, and saw some Lamean slaves working the fields. They appeared tired and worn out, sweating, slow, and sad. *They are probably still praising the Old Order.* Cole wondered what it would be like to be a slave. *If the Old Order is so great, how come most people who believe in them have to be slaves?*

Lily noticed the slaves too. "Are you Lameans?"

Wilber laughed. "Goodness no. Do you think we would own such a fancy cart as this if we were Lameans?"

"This is not a fancy cart," Cole muttered under his breath.

"No," Lily replied.

They probably would never admit if they were actually Lameans.

"But the Lameans are definitely not treated right. It's a shame Oldaem is slowly forcing people into New Order. When I was just a kid, we were allowed to worship whomever we want." *Mable sure does know a lot.*

"I didn't know Oldaem is *forcing* people." Lily said, curious.

"They aren't yet," Wilber coughed, "but that day is coming soon."

Cole could tell the old couple had been through a lot. In his mind he couldn't help but realize that all Old Order followers had to endure a lot and couldn't figure out why his father still believed in it. *It's just asking for trouble.*

It seemed as if they had ridden for several hours. The sun blazed overhead as they continued to pass by villages and Lameans working the fields. Cole had never seen so many slaves before. In the City of Flowers there hadn't been many of them. Some worked in shops here and there, but everyone was generally treated equal. And he knew there were slaves at the Shepherd Academy. He wondered if his dad ever helped the Lamean slaves. He knew his father was a Shepherd of Mind, though the Shepherds were now mostly New Order. How did his father maintain his faith in a place where a different one was so prominent? Off in the distance he thought he saw smoke, but he couldn't figure out why, unless people were having a bonfire for some reason. Lily continued to talk to Mable and Wilber about the Old Order. Her questions were continuous and

151

fast, and sometimes she would ask the same thing again and again. She would speak about the war long ago high above the sky in Aael, and how and why the Betrayer had turned against everyone. Then she would ask about the love the Comforter, the Liberator, and the Creator had for Esis. Next she inquired about what happens when people die, if they knew that they're dead, and about countless other things, Cole couldn't keep track of the answers. He drifted between being awake and asleep so frequently that he lost track of time.

The sun finally set, and they continued in the dark. Wilber lit a small lantern to light their path, and the old horses trudged on, having lost the race to catch the sunset. Mable and Lily sang a duet of an Old Order song his dad used to hum to them. He could tell Lily really liked them, but something about them made him not quite able to trust them. Perhaps it was because he knew they would part ways soon, so there really was no reason or use to get close to them. *People are people, which means people will leave and die and probably lie and turn out to be fake in the end.* He wondered what secrets they were hiding. Lily eventually moved up to the padded seat in between Wilber and Mable so that she could lie on Mable's lap and get better sleep. Cole decided to remain in the cart bed. He liked his space and his freedom. He also wanted to be able to jump off the back should anything suspicious happen. *There's that shadow again. How are they keeping up to this cart? Maybe I'm just seeing things.*

His eyes were heavy and he floated in and out of consciousness as he heard the hushed voices of the couple.

" . . . leave them there?"

"I don't know, Mable, what do you think?"

" . . . just children?"

" . . . is dangerous . . . better off . . than . . . Tower . . ."

"Older Order protect them."

Cole woke to the sound of the surf. He had been sleeping against a tree with Lily right beside him. Now he looked off in front of him past an overhang and into a vast ocean. They were on a cliff, and he knew that far down below the waves were crashing against the sand. Setting next to them was a basket full of food and water. *Mable and Wilber must have left us here.* He rose but left his sister sleeping against the tree. *We've reached the sea.* Cole starred out into the ocean, knowing that the other half of Oldaem lay across it. According to the library map, a large channel cut through the southern central portion of Oldaem, almost dividing the entire country in half. They needed to find the bridge between the two land masses. He remembered hearing about it in school. It was a large bridge, stretching across the channel. The farther north they went, the higher the elevation got. They wouldn't be able to find their way down to the ocean even if they wanted to. The bridge was the only way across, unless they went to Aramoor. He couldn't see the other shore of Oldaem from this cliff, which meant it had to be a very long bridge, and he guessed it was quite far away.

"Are you looking for the bridge too?"

Cole turned around to see a boy quite a bit taller than him.

"Who are you?"

"I'm looking for the bridge too." His clothes were more tattered than Cole's, his face more fierce, as if he had endured a lot in life. His arms were muscular, and he looked as if he might be a fast runner. But the eyes seemed distant, veiled. Somehow they reminded Cole of the lake of glass from his dreams.

"Who are you?" Cole pressed.

"The name's Zek." He stretched out his hand.

Cole looked at it, but didn't reach for it. "What do you want?"

"I just told you. I'm looking for the bridge." He sounded annoyed.

"Well, good luck." Cole turned away from him and headed back toward the tree.

"Hey, wait!" Zek followed and got in front of him, his arms outstretched to stop him. "Why are you out here all alone?"

"Why are *you* out here all alone?"

"My village got burned down."

"What?"

"Yeah, you might have seen the smoke. It was pretty bad."

Cole swallowed. "Did . . . people die?"

"Yeah. Lots."

More death.

But Zek's voice seemed unshaken.

Cole softened. "Your family?"

"Dead. But I got some family in the Capital. That's where I'm headed."

"I'm sorry." Cole hung his head. *I only lost my mom—I wonder what it would be like to lose my whole family.*

"Where are you headed?"

153

I might as well tell him. "Dorhaven."

"Why?"

"To find my Dad."

"Why?"

"My Mom died."

"Sucks, doesn't it?" Zek picked a blade of grass and stuck it into his mouth.

"Yeah."

"How old are you?"

"12. You?"

"14."

"You look dirty."

"I look better than you."

"Maybe. You're older, so you've had more time to grow."

"Clearly. You're like a shrimp."

"I'm only 12."

"You have a lot of freckles, too."

"You have a lot of dumb."

Zek laughed. "I like you."

"Bye." *Annoying.* Cole fully intended to wake up Lily and escape from this kid who just wouldn't go away. While he felt badly for him, there wasn't anything he could really do for him.

"Is that your sister?" Zek had followed him.

"Yes. Why?"

"It's just you two? And you really think you can make it all the way to Dorhaven by yourselves? You're crazy?"

"Well, at least I have *someone,*" Cole fired back. "You're going to the Capital alone."

He looked down sadly. "I don't really have a choice."

What a dumb thing to say, Cole. He just lost his whole family. "Sorry. I didn't mean that." *Fenris would be nice to this kid.*

Wearily, Zek sat down. "You're right, though. It is dumb for me to travel alone." After reaching into his brown bag, he tossed Cole a loaf of bread. "Here. It's for your sister. She looks hungry. I stole it from some dumb Lameans."

"Lameans aren't dumb." The girl stood up suddenly. *How like her to pretend to be asleep, snooping.* "I've been listening to your whole story, and I'm sorry your family is dead, but that doesn't give you the right to steal." Her cheeks were flushed. *She does not like him.*

"Well, how do you have all that food?" Zek asked, pointing down to the large basket.

"It was a gift," Lily answered defensively.

"From who?" he demanded.

"Mable and Wilber!"

"They sound dumb!"

"You look dumb!" Lily shouted.

"Lily, come on, let's go." Her brother led her away by the arm.

"Are you guys *Lameans* or something?" Zek followed them.

"What if we are?" Lily shouted again.

"Lily, don't yell at him. Just ignore him." *He's a lot bigger than us--we couldn't fight him if we tried.*

"Then you *burned* down my village and killed my family." Cole turned around to see tears streaming down Zek's face.

"Liar!" Lily quipped.

"What do you mean?" Cole stopped dead in his tracks and stared at the troubled boy.

"My village was New Order, and Old Order Lameans attacked and killed my whole family. We never even had slaves. We didn't deserve it!" Zek shouted.

Cole had never once in his life heard of Lameans attacking anyone. The news shocked him. Deep down inside his stomach he sensed that something about it rang true and made sense. Maybe because it agreed with the picture of an Order who consistently let him down, took his father away, and killed his mother--the Old Order.

"If you're Old Order, get out of here! Go away!" Zek shouted, hurling a stone over the cliff. He sat down along the edge and softly cried.

Cole and Lily looked at each other, knowing they had to make a choice. They could leave him here, or take him with them. Cole wondered what she would do. But he knew what he wanted. They *could* use a third and older person. Lily approached Zek and quietly sat down.

"My dad is a Shepherd of Mind," she said. "He's Old Order. I've never seen him once be mean to anyone in his life. He helps people. It's what he does. We are going to look for him because our Mommy died. I bet he could help you find your family too. Not all Old Order are bad. Let me show you the truth about us."

Lily sounded much older than she actually was, and Cole's jaw dropped. When she spoke it was like how he remembered his mom

155

before their dad left. Wise, loving, strong, courageous, bold, and determined. *She looks like Dad.*

Zek wiped his nose with his sleeve. "If your dad is a Shepherd of Mind, why are you going to Dorhaven?"

"It's where he lives."

"Yeah, but it's almost tournament time. Which means all Shepherds will be in the Capital. You guys need to be going to the Capital."

"Oh." Turning to Cole, she glared at him. "My dumb brother didn't think of that."

"I'm sorry!" he said defensively.

"It's not *his* fault," Zek said softly. "I shouldn't have yelled at you guys. New Order people usually have better manners. My mom did." Another tear began forming in his eyes.

"Do you want to come with us?" Cole heard himself asking.

"You guys really don't mind?"

"Not at all." Cole smiled. *Maybe I can have a friend.*

"I'll protect you. I have a knife." He pulled it out. "I'm good at stealing things too. Sometimes, it's necessary."

"I don't know about that." Lily stuck her nose in the air.

"Sometimes it is. Sometimes you gotta do things in order to make other things happen." He winked at Cole.

"My Daddy says stealing is never okay."

"My Dad did, too. And now he's dead." Zek stood and stretched his arms. Cole could see that he had muscles in them like Fenris. *He's strong for being only 14.* "Well, let's get going. We gotta travel through some farmland in Soma, which means we can get some more food, and then to the bridge. Come on, kid." With a wave he motioned Cole forward.

"Cole!'"

"Okay, Cole then." Zek smiled for the first time. His teeth were perfectly white and straight and his eyes had more life in them, but he still seemed somewhat reserved. Cole couldn't see beyond the veil that Zek hid behind. Perhaps it was so that people couldn't see his pain. What, Cole wondered, did *he* look like to others.

Zek took off ahead, encouraging them to keep up, telling them that he knew of places where they could sleep that weren't outside against trees and that he would be able to help them survive and find more food and fool people into aiding them, and that he knew this part of Oldaem like the back of his hand. Cole did his best to keep up, but he could tell that Lily was lagging behind although she smiled and mostly did what Zek told her to do. While her brother could tell she was being nice because she knew it was the right thing to do, he also sensed that she didn't trust Zek. Clearly something was deeply bothering her beyond just the death of her mother. But he didn't ask. To do that would have lifted the protective veil she hid behind. Sometimes it's easier to hide in the darkness of pain and the world of pretend. So Cole smiled at her and she smiled back and Zek smiled at them both. And so the veil remained . . . and so did the shadow in pursuit.

CHAPTER 23: DAKU

The buildings at the base of Vertloch Tower cowered in the presence of the foreboding structure that dwarfed them. It was the center of everything, stretching high into the sky, on certain days even amongst the clouds themselves. The Tower stood ominous and mysterious to the people living around it. Seldom allowed inside, they were ignorant to what happened within, yet they relied on it for protection, wisdom, and guidance. Most inhabitants of the city around the Tower had converted to the Order of the Three, after priestesses had settled it from Sther, per the agreement of the Esis Unity Pact that permitted them to construct and inhabit just one Tower in each and every country. Vertloch Tower was the only one in Oldaem. The Order of the Three used it to train and supply and house priestesses to further its mission of converting people and conducting research useful to the priestess sects. A'delath, High Priestess of Sther, supreme ruler in the motherland to the south, controlled everything. She remained in constant communication with each High Priestess in every Tower around Esis. Few had seen her, yet all felt her influence, even those not belonging to the Order of The Three. She wielded great power, and most countries and kings and Regents sought her approval and support. Of all the Order's three sects, Golden (psyche), Crimson (resistance), and Amethyst (jurisdiction), A'delath was a master of the functions of each. Her shawl bore all three colors, as did each and every High Priestess in every Tower among the nations. However unlike A'delath, each one still had one specialty above the rest, depicted by the color of the belt and veil. The High Priestess of Vertloch was a master of Psyche (Mind), like Malvina. Malvina was one of her

157

favored priestesses. As a result, Vertloch Tower was known to specialize in the development and training of the most elite Priestesses of the Gold or Psyche, although not limited to them, as the other two sects had sections of the Tower themselves. However, all were aware that the priestess focused her true preference and trust on Malvina.

Since A'delath had yet to visit Vertloch, some wondered if she found favor with Oldaem's Tower at all. However, the High Priestess of Vertloch swore that it was the most trusted Tower on Esis. Yet still, some priestesses whispered and wondered in dark hallways and corners as to what exactly was truth and what was fabricated. If their questioning ever became discovered, they knew they would face serious repercussions. The fear of such consequences kept most from going against Vertloch's High Priestess and formulated a rather loyal circle of priestesses and Wardens. Those outside the Tower, especially the ordinary people, had no idea of the malice, plotting, and political manipulations that went on within it walls. Even Daku didn't exactly know the true purpose of Sther. Sometimes he felt it was to convert all to the Order of the Three, sometimes that A'delath just sought political power, and other times he wondered if it was all motivated by the drive for wealth, seeing as the Tower's opulence had to be expensive to sustain.

Vorran, Aelwynne's father, was advisor to the High Priestess of Vertloch Tower, a high-profile position usually held by a female. Yet he was rarely seen within the Tower, which seemed to be a mystery. Few knew what he did, or his involvement with Tower affairs. Aelwynne, especially, was unaware of his exact duties. The fact that Vorran managed to obtain and survive in such a role spoke wanders to his political skills and maneuvering. It was also how Daku had secured a position as a Warden.

Now here they stood before the main gate of Vertloch, a Golden Priestess and her two Wardens. None had spoken on the foot journey to the Tower. After Jorn found Daku outside the inn standing in the surf on that cool night several evenings ago, not a word had passed between any of them. Jorn shifted between glares and watchful glances toward Daku, but Malvina refused to even meet his eye. He worried that perhaps she sought to replace him or dismiss him once they reached the Tower. Even though their mission in Leoj had been successful, he feared for his position and possibly even his life.

"Priestess Malvina, welcome back," a guard at the gate greeted them. Malvina was well-known to the people and wildly popular.

158

"It's good to be home, Sam." Her response was cool and measured. Daku could see chills go up and down the soldier's arms. He could tell Sam had no knowledge of how Malvina was able to decipher one of many soldier's name's so quickly. The vast majority of her skills were not understandable to most, sometimes Daku included.

"The people will be pleased to hear of your continued safety."

"Would they expect something less?"

He stuttered. "Um, no. That's not what I meant."

Her voice rose. "Do you mean to say I am capable of being overtaken?"

"No, of course not!"

"Then what a disappointing remark for you to make." She raised a white finger to his chin and circled up to his cheek. "Be intelligent, Sam. Intelligent men live longer. I want you to live. I'm sure you agree?"

He swallowed nervously. "Yes, Priestess."

"Good. Open the gate."

"Yes, Priestess."

The gate opened widely, and the rush of the city within almost forced the three of them back. Vertloch was an extremely busy city with people rushing to and fro. The main commerce involved foot merchants from all over Oldaem, excited to trade from Vertloch the expensive wares and merchandise of the massive country of Sther. Daku could see several priestesses headed toward the giant Tower rising before them. Priestesses seldom acknowledged each other in public. Malvina followed their example as she made her way past a Priestess of Crimson mediating a Lamean brawl. Oftentimes in crowded public rings, especially in the large cities in Oldaem, Lameans would square off in fights to the death, refereed by Crimson Priestesses who excelled in battle and tactics. Shouting men and women would bet on their favorites and afterward bestow money on the winners. The dead usually got thrown to the crimson Warder's watchdogs. It was something A'delath had thought up to continue to gather revenue for the Order of the Three. Malvina thought violence for money distasteful and beneath her--most Golden Priestesses did. They preferred to rely on the power of their minds instead of bloodied weapons. She did, however, nod slightly to the Crimson Priestess who was practically salivating at the funds she had taken in. Daku could tell Malvina was at least impressed with the piles of golden pieces strewn around the ring. Daku glanced to the right,

159

where a pathway led toward the garden section of Vertloch. A quieter, richer section of the city, it contained the residences of the elite, including Daku's flower-adorned cottage. Aelwynne would be there.

You are mine.

And as soon as Malvina stood before the High Priestess, he would secretly return home until he received word of his next assignment—that is, if he survived or lasted until then. He looked over at Jorn who was happily watching one Lamean bash another in the head with a rock. Daku could tell the man was happy, because for a second he wasn't scowling.

Malvina moved past the ring and farther along the main road leading to the Tower. Merchant stands and stores lined it, full of people talking and trading and shouting and laughing. When Malvina approached, most lowered their volume out of respect until she passed out of sight. The main street was not a place for children, and Daku didn't see any as they walked. Vertloch had a golden hue to it, perhaps because of the High Priestess' affinity for the color, and most buildings had a yellow tint to them. When the sun hit them they really shone and reflected across the cobblestone roads. It gave the appearance of an opulent city, even though most of the city buildings were built with limestone, not exactly an expensive material.

As they neared the Tower's entrance, the buildings seemed to shrink. They weren't actually smaller, but the presence of the giant structure dwarfed them. Guards stood at the entrance to the Tower. They didn't speak as Malvina and her Wardens passed by them. Every guard in the Tower itself was dressed in white armor with a golden hue to them. On sunny days they were almost blinding. A water garden was at the entrance, each pool one of three colors, yellow, purple, and red. The water shot and spewed over flowers and rocky surfaces. The garden was an architectural and horticultural masterpiece, unrivaled by any in Oldaem except perhaps by the Capital. The water created a rushing sound that almost drowned out all thought as they walked. That was its purpose--to cleanse all plans and plots from those who neared the entrance to the actual building which shot vertically many stories into the air. To gaze up the length of the Tower while standing at its base would create faintness and vertigo to the looker, the height overwhelming and its peak seemingly unreachable.

As they passed through the water garden several priestesses sat and meditated by their appropriate pools, some Wardens near them, other priestesses completely isolated. Wardens did not have to accompany priestesses at all times unless they were outside of the Tower or they otherwise requested their presence. Some glanced at Malvina as she passed, others ignored her completely, but all were aware of her presence, and all assumed that she had completed her assignment in Leoj. The favored Priestess of Vertloch could have received only one task. She *had* to have been successful as tensions between Leoj and Oldaem had escalated exponentially the year she had been away. Daku considered all these things as he watched the priestesses observe her passing. *You think you know what she's capable of, but you really could never possibly imagine the extent of her powers or her abilities or her beauty.*

They entered the domed entrance of the Tower itself, and lanterns lighted the windowless hallway before them. The narrow passageway was a giant painted tapestry above and around them, dedicated to the power of The Three. The series of pictures masterfully painted on all sides of it told the origin story of the Three and how they came to be.

The first scene portrayed four beautiful goddesses who lived up high in Aael. One was golden, one crimson, one amethyst, and final one ivory. They hovered over a giant pool of water, which Daku always assumed to house Esis beneath its waters, or the clouds. They all four had warm smiles and confidence that had obviously been passed down to each and every priestess who emerged in the Tower. The scene stretched from his left, above his head in an arched dome, and down to his right. The colors were vivid, the features detailed, the artwork lifelike in nature. Wardens and priestesses alike had walked this hall so many times Daku had it memorized.

Next came the scene of the great competition in which the people of Aael judged the goddesses to see who was the most beautiful. The scene showed each goddess painting the sky as a gift to the people once it was her time to perform. The Amethyst gave the dawn, the Golden noonday, and the Crimson dusk. Seeing as the sky was complete, the Ivory Goddess built a giant Tower, which stretched downward from Aael to Esis. The Tower would allow the people of Aael to climb down and explore the secret, new, and beautifully constructed world of Esis that the four of them had spent years in perfecting and building.

The next scene showed the anger of the other three, who had had no idea the Ivory planned to build a connective Tower between the two worlds. This violent painting depicted The Three deposing of the Ivory Goddess from the high world of Aael, casting her to the world of Esis as punishment for constructing the Tower.

The final scene presented The Three ruling on high as glorious as ever. However below, roaming the lands of Esis, the Ivory Sister was now broken and twisted. Her ivory hue gone, she was now black with revenge in her heart. Determined to reclaim her place above the Ivory Tower, the Goddess of Night roams Esis bent on destruction and chaos. Daku knew there was rumored to be a sect of The Order of the Three who were loyal to the Goddess of Night, though he had never seen a Dark Priestess or Warden--at least, he was unsure if he had. The Dark Order's motives were unknown, but he knew they did not have the best interest of The Order of the Three in mind and were probably bent on its destruction. More often than not, the Dark Order was not to be mentioned or spoken of, even though it was such an important part of the Order's theology. Dwelling on the Dark Order might drive a person insane. Some thought that any priestess could and might have ties to the Dark Order. Drawing attention to such suspicions, however, could lead to distrust and accusations among the different sects. It was best left untouched and ignored. Daku wondered how long it would be until members of the Dark Order might actually rear their destructive heads.

Malvina and her Wardens approached a winding staircase that opened into several hallways on multiple floors. Daku knew where they were heading to, the top of the Tower and the chambers of the High Priestess in order for Malvina to report her success in Leoj, and to receive her instructions for their next mission. Silence settled among them as they climbed. Daku could tell Malvina was focused on what she would say, probably making sure each of her sentences were perfectly constructed. Jorn was silent as usual, his footsteps not even producing a sound. As they went higher and higher Daku trained his thoughts toward complete and utter loyalty to the Golden Sect. He figured the High Priestess, who was a master of psychological manipulation, would be able to decipher any wavering on his part. Increasingly he focused on his breathing and on his Warden's training. His training had taught him not to reveal his thoughts on his face or in his eyes, to seem like a stone statue or a wall. No soul. No thoughts. No opinion. Complete loyalty to death. *You are mine.* "I am yours," he whispered.

162

They approached a long corridor, the one leading to her chambers, and continued to walk through it. A red carpet stretched the length of the room, and golden candlesticks sat upon oak tables along the sides of it. Lining the walls were portraits of previous High Priestesses from years past. Only one out of the 12 most recent previous priestesses had been from a different sect other than Golden. She didn't last long. Her fall from the Tower window had ended her rather short reign. Whether she had been pushed or fell accidentally had to this day remained unquestioned. Her eyes in the painting were a pale gray. *Aelwynne.* He wondered what his wife could be doing this very moment. Probably she was completely unaware he was even in the city. *Get it together Daku. Now is not the time to be thinking of Aelwynne.*

Few Wardens were married. Daku was one of the exceptions. Perhaps because Vorran was so tightly connected to the Tower no one questioned it. But regardless of his marital state, his loyalty had to continue to be fiercely devoted to no one but Malvina. The priestess' eyes in the portrait seemed to follow him as he passed. Malvina didn't look anywhere but forward. Although Daku could tell Jorn was watching him out of the corner of his eye, he ignored the other Warden.

"When we enter"--her voice like a small pool of water whirling in a circle, smooth, gentle, consistent--"think not of our success in Leoj. Think not of anything. Be a blank slate. Be calm. I don't need the High Priestess distracted with any nonsense that might be found within the confines of your minds."

"Yes Priestess," they said in perfect unison.

"We shall all present ourselves, and then you will both be dismissed for the time being. I shall remain here and get details on what is next. You both will get your much needed rest--at an inn, preferably."

Daku realized that she had directed the last at him. She didn't want him heading home to Aelwynne. *You are mine.*

"Yes Priestess," they chimed.

They approached a tall golden door. Sitting at either side were neophytes, women who were in the process of being raised up to be priestesses. They wore simple ivory gowns. Malvina paused before the door. They acknowledged her and spoke in perfect accord, "Enter Priestess, Mistress awaits."

"Thank you," Malvina said coolly. The doors swung inward, and she swept inside. Jorn and Daku followed her as the doors slowly

163

closed behind them. The room was mostly dark. A long golden table stretched in front of them. Multi-colored fabrics hung and were draped from the walls and across the ceiling, back and forth. A closed window sat on the back wall, letting in little light, and another door shut off the bedchamber to their left. Lit candles, books, and parchment sat upon the table and the High Priestess sat at its head staring them down. A blonde neophyte stood near the back window, head down, eyes closed. She looked as if she had been meditating. The High Priestess had a blank expression, her golden eyes calm and neutral. She wore a shawl of the three colors over her head, her tunic a pale white, wrapped with a golden belt. A golden veil hung across her face, masking her expression even more. Her age, Daku couldn't determine, but he remembered that she sounded somewhat youthful. He believed Golden Priestesses had the ability to fool the mind into believing pretty much whatever they wanted others to believe. He respected her. He feared her. He served her. He was hers. (He was Malvina's, actually.) Now he let his mind dwell on absolutely nothing until he was but a shadow.

"You've been successful," the Golden Priestess breathed.

"Yes, Mistress," Malvina answered.

"Kneel."

Daku found himself kneeling beside Jorn, Malvina in front.

"The plan has been set into motion."

"Yes, Mistress."

"The Three are pleased. You never fail me, Malvina."

"Never, Mistress."

"Leoj and Oldaem are at war. Royal Shepherd Demas has been captured. The Royals are desperately seeking to determine their next moves. The tournament is set to soon begin in the Capital. Malvina, your assistance is still greatly needed for Sther. A'delath has sent word of what she has planned next for you." Then her voice rose. "Wardens dismissed."

"Yes, Mistress."

The sun shone a little bit brighter outside. It seemed as if a veil had been lifted, a haze cleared. Voices were louder, laughs were fuller, colors were brighter, Esis was more alive. Daku always forgot that Oldaem was like this when he became separated from Malvina. It was the strangest thing to explain. He longed to run as far away as possible as he could from her, catch the first ship to Najoh, and spend out the remainder of his days upon the white sandy shores with his beautiful wife. Never again did he want to hear or speak of the Three. Yet he also wanted to race back into the Tower and beg Malvina's forgiveness for such traitorous thoughts. Part of him craved to run back to the inn he passed, the one he had seen Jorn enter, and lock himself in a room and pray to the Three until Malvina came for him, focusing on increasing and amplifying his deep loyalty and admiration for the perfect priestess. It seemed as the war between his heart and his head would never end. Parts of him sought to end it immediately while other parts found comfort in the struggle. At least it made him feel *something*. Feeling nothing was his greatest fear. Yet such numbness was also a comfort.

As he stood before his house, his heart in the pit of his stomach, he knew he shouldn't be there. It went against everything Malvina asked of him as well as his training as a Warden. But something about the love he bore Aelwynne occasionally overshadowed what he knew. Somehow he felt that what he *knew* wasn't always the right answer. Aelwynne should be there, watering the lilies that grew in the upstairs window box. Perhaps she was writing him another letter, which he knew he could never read. Maybe she was herself reading or sewing or baking. Possibly she was laughing with friends at the table. Daku hoped she was happy, living a full life without him. A part of him knew she was better off without him, and it crushed his already shattered heart.

It had been little more than a year since they had last spoken. She had begged him to drop it all and to run away with her. He couldn't. But he also could never explain to her why. It involved a promise he never could break and one perhaps more important than the vows he made to her on their wedding day. Only honoring that promise would keep them both alive.

He remembered the day he left. It had been raining, one of the fiercest storms Vertloch had ever seen. They had stood at opposite ends of the table, his one bag sitting against the door as the storm raged on outside of the little stone cottage they lived in. Aelwynne had positioned herself in front of the door as well, her white arms crossed in front of her, her hair tightly tied up into a bun, a scowl on her face, and tears in her eyes. He knew that her posture meant that he would have to move her forcibly away from the door if he was to get by. It would be an actual representation of him physically

165

choosing being a Warden over being a husband. But it was a choice he *had* to make, one that she would never understand.

"You have to choose, me . . . or Malvina."

"Aelwynne, don't do this."

"Choose!" A thunderbolt boomed as she shouted, but her voice was as powerful as the storm. She wouldn't be backing down--but neither would he. He couldn't. Though deep inside, a part of him knew he could.

"It's my job." His voice was also steady and firm.

"I don't care."

"Move."

"No."

"Move!" Daku spoke more forcefully than he had originally intended.

"No!" she fired back.

"Aelwynne, there are things in this world you can't control. You can't control *me.*"

"I guess that's Malvina's job."

"You don't understand!"

"What is your mission *this* time?" She was angry.

"I can't tell you." *Still as a pond.*

"Why?"

"*Because I can't.*" His shouts overtook the thunderclap.

She started talking faster and faster. "How can you do these things? How can you believe in the Three? How can you throw out your humanity? The killing, the violence, the chaos that the priestesses cause--I *know* what the Tower is responsible for. I know what *they're* capable of"--she paused, a tear running down her cheek--"I hope you're not capable of it too."

He rushed toward her. "Get out of my way."

Quickly she spread her arms across the door. "Please, Daku."

She will never understand. "I want to go. I *choose* Malvina."

"No you don't. There's something you're not telling me!"

Yes, there is. "No! I choose her!"

"Tell me the truth!"

"I am!"

"No you're not! I know the *real* you! The kind, caring, sweet, loving man I love. I know the *real* you."

"This is the real me--you've just been too ignorant to acknowledge me."

"No. Stop saying that!" Her crying got worse. The rain poured harder.

"This is *me,* Aelwynne"--he stretched his arms out--"it's what I've become. I get the job done. I do what they want, and I don't question. Now I'm asking you to do the same for me."

"Well, I won't. I won't do it." Again she crossed her arms in front of her.

"Fine." He picked up his bag. *I never want to leave you.*

"Look me in the eye and tell me you choose her!"

I love you. "Move out of my way!"

She was screaming now. "TELL ME YOU LOVE HER!"

I'm sorry, Aelwynne. Placing his hands firmly on her shoulders and looking deeply into her eyes, he said "I love her, Aelwynne."

Her knees buckled, and she fell to the floor, sobbing. She couldn't catch her breath as the wind picked up and the rain started beating against the door.

What have I done? Slipping past her, he opened the door. Water poured in. As he stepped past the threshold he remembered Najoh and her smile and her laugh and her touch and her love. Remembered their wedding and their kisses and their cozy cottage. The hope and joy and light she brought him. But he walked away anyway. Plunging into the storm, he could hear her voice behind him, pleading as he plowed through the mud, calling his name, begging him to stay, running after him, sopping wet in the streets. People looked down from their windows, then pulled shut their curtains. A wife of a Warden was a rarity, and this was the reason why.

"I love you, Daku," she cried out.

A thunderclap replied.

He had headed into the eye of the storm, got on to his ship, and sailed to Leoj with Malvina, the woman he *chose*, the woman he *loved*. It was just another choice in the darkness.

Now he stood inside the empty cottage a year later. Where flowers once bloomed in a vase on a dusted table, wilted pedals littered a cob-web-covered-table. Where delicious food once cooked upon a warm oven, dusty pots sat undisturbed. And where laughter and love and joy once permeated the bright sunny room, a chilling silence hovered over a darkened, curtain-closed dwelling. Aelwynne was gone, apparently for quite some time. As he walked through the empty house, looking anywhere for a note, a letter, her body, something that would bring him closure. But nothing was there. It

167

was as if she had vanished and left behind remnants of a broken house, symbols of a broken heart. A broken heart to match his own. As Malvina's voice rang within his being (*You belong to me*) Daku couldn't help but think, *perhaps I do.* He sat upon their bed and wept dry tears of loss, regret, and defeat. *She's gone ... gone ... gone.*

He didn't know how long he sat there. Daku felt nothing and was nothing. He was what he had chosen to be, which was the most painful part. Sometimes feeling nothing was the most excrutiating of all. A shadow passed behind him, and he slowly turned to see Jorn standing beside him, his eyes full of triumph.

"I should have known you would come here." To his right Malvina hovered over him. "You continually fail me, Daku."

He said nothing, his head pounding.

Slowly Malvina looked around the room, her head like an owl's almost making a complete circuit. "She's left you, hasn't she?"

Don't even speak her name, you . . .

"Don't presume that I don't know what you're thinking. Coming here makes you weak. Thinking against me makes you a traitorous snake." She knelt down to meet him at eye level. "Do you know what I do to traitorous snakes?"

Daku felt his head nod–he couldn't stop it.

"The same thing I do to bugs."

Bug.

"Come. Rise. We'll deal with this as we go. I don't have time to find *another* Warden. Jorn will protect me while you . . . *recover.* The High Priestess has given me our new task. We leave immediately." With that she and Jorn left the room. Daku found himself rising stiffly, then putting one foot in front of the other. As he walked out of the abandoned cottage, shutting the door behind him, there were no thunderclaps, no appeals from one who cared or who loved. No attempts to reclaim his soul or to wake him up. There was only silence. He clung to the silence as he followed Malvina and Jorn toward the western gate of Vertloch. They would be traveling on foot, with no guess as to where their next destination may be or to what their next mission may entail.

Daku was excited.

You are mine.

Daku had already forgotten.

You belong to me.

Daku was walking.

Forsake them.
Daku was following.
Forsake them all.
Daku was silent.
Golden eyes.
Daku was ready. *Forgive me, Malvina.*
You are mine.
Daku was soulless. Daku was a Warden.

CHAPTER 24: IAN

Ian awoke with a jolt. He wasn't used to sleeping at sea. Although he had lived beside it all his life, he had never spent so much time on it. One full day and one full night had been enough to make his stomach feel as if it was swimming on its own. Groaning as he rolled over, he eyed Bumo who was on a mound of hay a little bit closer than he had been when the night had first begun. As the ship rolled back and forth, so did everyone below deck. The space was packed with all the crew. Since they filled the bunks and cots, all that remained were piles of hay. Ian took one, Bumo another, and the lowest-level-Lamean crewmembers the others. The six girl Shepherd-Tournament-Recruits all slept soundly in a cabin above deck. *Lucky goldfish.* Smiling to himself, Ian rubbed his eyes. He could hear snoring and breathing. Bumo, however, slept silently. Even asleep he resembled a golden god. Every vein in the right place, his face was perfectly proportioned. Ian knew that when *he* slept he looked like a rolling blubber fish--drool, snores, the works. His head still swam as he sat up. *Well, at least Shepherds don't have to be sailors.* If he could help it, he had no intention of ever spending long periods of time on a ship again. Not sure what time it was, he reminded himself that they had spent one full day and one full night since they departed from the port of Altairus, on their way to the Capital to enter the tournament. Although it was in some ways almost a surreal feeling, Ian felt completely honored and excited.

He had hurried onto the ship, somewhat worried that they had made some mistake in their paperwork and selection. After his interview, after his screaming at seven strangers who awkwardly stared at him, Ian had been convinced he would be on the next ferry back to Lion's Landing. Yet here he was . . . sleeping in hay . . . next

169

to about 40 or so smelly, half-naked, drooling men. *I guess Soma isn't the richest region.* Perhaps the more wealthy regions sent their Shepherd Candidates in better style. Not Soma. But he was not complaining--the ship would have to do. Somehow he couldn't suppress his smile. *I made it.* Stinking men, roiling stomach, discomfort, stifling heat, and cramped quarters equaled the most exciting experience Ian had ever faced. *I wouldn't change a thing.*

When he got up, he felt his back in knots, sweat stained. Fanning the shirt he had slept in, he tried to dry it out. *I wonder if anyone is awake on deck.* Carefully stepping over sleeping Lamean crewmen, he made his way to the wooden stairway that led to the top of the deck. As he climbed, fresh air hit in him the face, and he was instantly very cold. Chill bumps raced up and down his body. It was dawn, and the sun was thinking about making its ascent into the sky. He couldn't wait until it did. No one seemed around except for a sleepy Lamean attending the helm. None of the girls were awake yet. Ian made his way to the starboard side of the ship. That he had recently learned that starboard meant right made him excited. *Maybe I could be a sailor.* But his stomach disagreed. As he headed toward the railing of the ship, he wished he could make time pass faster. Yet at the same time he wanted it to go as slowly as possible. Ian wanted to enjoy every second of this voyage even if it was making him sick, and every moment of his Shepherd experience. Then he would be able to tell his family back at home about every single detail. Reaching the railing, he peered down into the water. The waves were pretty still for being so far out into the middle of nowhere. Before, he had always imagined giant waves whenever he looked out into the ocean from the shores of Lion's Landing. Now it was almost like a sheet of glass. Nor did he see any leaping dolphins like they had as they were leaving Altairus. The ocean was free of ships in the distance or birds flying in the sky. *Everyone really is asleep. I'm glad I can be awake now.* It was just Ian and his ship. For a moment he imagined the day he would become a Shepherd of Defense, when he would send ships out to defend Lion's Landing from the evil attacking Leojians. But he wouldn't actually accompany them. Instead, he would remain on dry, safe, comfortable land. Still they would respect him, would look up to him. And they would admire his rippling muscles and quick wit and intellect. Everyone would say, *Ian is the most beautiful man in the world. He is the greatest Shepherd of Defense we've ever seen.* And women would name their boys "Ian", and their daughters Iana, out of respect for his heroic deeds. Yes, he would rescue women and babies and little dogs, but most importantly, he would truly stand for the defenseless and make a difference. Not only would he provide religious freedom for all and end slavery, he would help fat boys lose weight–once he actually learned the secret himself.

He was one of eight! Only seven others kids had been selected out of the entire region of Soma. *Why did they choose me?* Still, although he was thrilled to have been chosen, his gut kept screaming that there had been a mistake. *What did they see in me?* It couldn't have been his outburst. If anything, that should have counted against him. He wasn't attractive, strong, or very smart. Nor was he very spiritual, especially when it came to the New Order, the Shepherd's main theology. But they had clearly seen something, and that boosted his confidence. *Maybe it's okay to be Ian after all.*

He remembered when he had first met the other six Candidates. The morning after he and Bumo received their acceptance letters, they had to report back to the room with the bookcases where he had his interview. When he and Bumo first walked into the room, the tall redheaded girl with the fluffy hair was sitting in one of the nine chairs arranged into a circle. Bumo walked right up to her and extended his hand.

"Hi, I'm Bumo." She looked at his hand as if it had a disease on it.
"What of it?"

"Excuse me?" He didn't understand.

She's not interested, Bumo.

"What of it?" she said, raising her voice. Something was clearly bothering her.

Ian approached her. "Are you okay?"

"I'm fine! We're competition! There is *no* point in becoming friends. What do you want to do? Sit around a campfire and braid each other's hair?"

"Easy there, Red Lightning. We won't be competition for long. It's really unfair they would match *you* up with someone like *me.*" Flexing his muscles a little, Bumo smiled. Ian eyed the redhead.

I wouldn't count her out. Ian noticed her flexing muscles of her own.

"Don't call me Red Lightning." She looked away, clearly finished with their conversation.

Bumo sat across from her and stretched his arms above his head, then yawned. Ian had told him to go to bed earlier the night before, but Bumo had been so excited that he kept running circles around the Sea Port Inn. As for Ian, he had gone to sleep easily. Sleep always came easy for him.

An awkward silence filled the room. Ian decided to sit several chairs away from both of them. He realized the redhead was right about one thing: they were each other's competition. He needed to separate himself from his friend as much as possible.

"Bumo!" Jessica entered, bouncing up and down with excitement. She wore all orange, it almost clashing with her blonde hair.

"Jericha!" Bumo rose with a cocky smile.

"Jessica!" she corrected.

"Jessica!"

Before she could complain that he had forgotten her name, she was in his arms being spun around, laughing like Baby Talo. It was as if they were a long-lost but now reunited couple. But that was nothing new to Ian, and he rolled his eyes.

"I don't know why I'm surprised you're here," she smiled brightly. Her face was incredibly painted up, her voice extremely high. The orange dress she wore was a bit too tight.

I hope she doesn't suffocate.

"I don't know why either." He laughed. It was so effortless for him. She sat directly next to him, practically on his lap. The redhead was not impressed. Ian could tell she wanted to wipe the floor with both of them. Perhaps she would get her chance.

The room slowly filled up with the other Candidates. Alala and Erina came in next, two more blondes who already knew Jessica. The three of them laughed together and crowded around Bumo. The blonde reunion reminded him of the seagulls that wouldn't shut up outside his window. No one sat next to Ian yet. But he actually didn't mind. So far the count was four girls, one Bumo, and Ian. *Great.* The chattering around Bumo continued, each girl showering Bumo with compliments. They almost seemed brainless to Ian. *Is physical attraction so important to everyone? Does nothing else matter?* Next came a wall of a girl. Dark-skinned like Ian, she had long braids, swinging as she went. She was breathing quite heavily. Although she looked vaguely familiar to Ian, he couldn't place her. After greeting everyone loudly, without giving her name, she sat down between the redhead and Erina, who was chatting loudly with Alala. The redhead and Braids grunted at each other. Braids slapped the redhead on the back hard, who then slapped her back. *Perhaps it's a normal greeting between people of massive size. I should have understood it, I guess.* Still, Ian sat without a partner.

"Quiet down, please," an older woman announced as she entered slowly and closed the door behind her. Bumo was still talking loudly and Jessica was practically snorting with laughter. "Please, quiet down," the newcomer repeated as she took a place next to Ian. The room quieted. One candidate was still missing, as an empty seat to Ian's right remained vacant.

"Welcome to your first tournament orientation meeting. I am Celes, a retired Shepherd of Mind. The STC has appointed me as your guide to the Capital. We leave tomorrow morning. It's my job to make sure you all understand what it is you're getting into, as well as to provide counseling to ensure that you all are of a mindset to enter this tournament, and that you understand the ramifications and risks you are signing up for. You all remember the waiver you signed?"

The group nodded. The redhead grunted, Braids even louder. *Yeah I remember. The STC (Shepherd Training Committee) will not be held accountable if in the course of the tournament the applicant is maimed, decapitated, drowned, exploded, or otherwise injured.* How could Ian forget? *Exploded? Really?*

"Excellent." Celes had very kind and intelligent eyes. Instantly, Ian decided he liked her, although he could already hear Bumo complaining later about how it was a Shepherd of Mind that accompanied them and not a Shepherd of Defense. "Now, tomorrow we will set sail on *The Dolphin,* captained by Captain Cid and assisted by Helmswoman Terra. I've sailed with them before, and their ship runs like a well-oiled machine. It's not the nicest quarters you'll ever see, but it will get you there in one piece. And isn't that all that really matters?" Ian noticed she had a large gap between her teeth. It also made her "s's" not so "s-like."

The door opened and a very short girl with very short black hair entered meekly. Immediately, Ian noticed how piercingly blue her eyes were. "Sorry, I'm late. I . . . got lost," she stuttered.

"That's perfectly fine, dear. We're just glad you made it. Please have a seat." The woman continued to impress Ian. *I wonder if she used to surf.*

"Thank you." The blue-eyed-girl sat down in the only seat available--the one next to Ian, who felt his heart begin to race. *Those eyes. Pretty. Pretty girl indeed.*

"Now, as I was saying," Celes continued, "tomorrow we set sail, so I want to make sure you are all rested up as much as possible and that you write your family and loved ones tonight, seeing as any correspondence after we leave will take *much* longer, as you will be on the other side of the country once we reach the Capital. If you write them tonight, they will receive their letters tomorrow or the next day. Now, it's not my intention to keep you all up late tonight, but I did want you to come here tonight to pick up some packets to read that give detailed descriptions of the different events at the tournament and what expectations of you there will be. And before we go, I do want you to tell us a little bit about yourselves." She laughed lightly. "Although I know you will be spending *much* time together, it's good to know what to expect before you find yourselves cramped together on a floating vessel."

Everyone stared at each other. No one spoke.

"Well, not everyone all at once." Celes laughed again.

"I'll go first. I'm Bumo!"

Of course.

Bumo stood up and gave the pretense of a shy wave.

"Hello, Bumo," the group mumbled, Braids a little bit louder than the rest.

"I'm from Lion's Landing. I love the water. I love to surf. I like to make friends," and he winked at Jessica who giggled. Alala giggled too, perhaps thinking he had winked at her.

Good grief.

"Most importantly, I'm going to be the best Shepherd of Defense Oldaem has ever seen." He pointed his finger at the redhead. "So prepare yourself." With that, he sat down as the others clapped sparingly.

"You're so brave," Jessica cooed.

The redhead just glared at him, and then stood up immediately. "I'm Helen. I'm from here, Altairus. I grew up in the streets, and I've kicked the butts of punks every day of my life. My crew call me 'Defense,' cause it's just so obvious that's what I'm headed to be." She pointed at Bumo. "And I'm always ready." Then she sat down so hard her chair almost broke underneath her. Her hair seemed fluffier than ever.

The clapping continued, as did the introductions around the circle. Every time Ian was about to open his mouth and stand, someone else beat him to it. Alala talked about how she loved flowers and candles and dancing and frogs. *She doesn't seem very smart, but she sure is beautiful.* He figured she would be a Spirit Shepherd. Erina spoke about how she loved dancing and baking and studying

174

Oldaem history. Ian figured she lied about the last part, perhaps just to impress the Mind Shepherd. The girl seemed more interested in staring at Bumo. When Jessica had her turn, she kept flipping her hair back and forth while staring at Bumo the entire time. She didn't address anyone else in the circle. Her introduction felt to Ian more like a dating invitation than a Shepherd-to-be introduction. She mentioned how her favorite pastimes were long walks on the beach, watching surfers (*yeah, right*), taking care of her boyfriend, if she had one, and being in love--not the clingy type, but a love that lasts forever with the perfect-kind-of-blonde-muscular-surfer-boyfriend. He noticed Celes drifting off to sleep during some of their speeches. *I guess it's past her bedtime.*

"My name is Liarra," the blue-eyed-girl said quietly. "I am from a little village outside of Altairus. It's not really even on the map, there are only perhaps 50 people in it. I like reading a lot, and I love studying the different religions in Oldaem." She smiled. *Beautiful.* "And I love to eat." *Perfect.*

Ian found himself staring at her as she sat down. When she turned and faced him, he blinked rapidly and looked away. *She probably thinks I'm mental.* Now he felt all eyes on him. *Oh, I guess I should go.* He looked across at Braids and remembered that she hadn't spoken yet. But by the expression in her eye, she apparently thought it was Ian's turn as well. *Guess I have no choice.* He stood. "I'm Ian."

"Hello, Ian," the group mumbled again. Celes' eyes snapped open and she echoed the same, pretending to have been awake the entire time.

"I live in Lion's Landing." As he spoke Jessica leaned over to Bumo and they started whispering to each other. "I have a really loud family. My mom has big hands." He swallowed. *This is harder than I thought it would be. What do I say? There really isn't anything special about me. Might as well be honest.* "There really isn't anything special about me."

"Except that he's friends with *me!*" Bumo exclaimed as the blondes sighed dramatically.

"I'm really blessed to be considered to be a Shepherd." He looked down at Liarra who seemed so tiny in her chair, who gazed back up at him. "And I've lost two pounds already." Somehow he managed to smile broadly. *Idiot. Why draw attention to your weight.* "Thank you, and goodnight." *Why am I so awkward?* Sucking in his stomach, he took his seat as Bumo clapped. The others followed along hesitantly. Braids stared at him intensely. Slowly she rose.

"What your full name?" Her voice was deep and with a rumble.

He stared back. "Uh . . . Aupiano."

Suddenly he was on the floor, Braids on top of him. His head smacked the floor as she laughed and rolled off of him. Liarra shrieked and backed away as Braids climbed back on top of him, sitting on his legs, and holding him down by his wrists. Ian looked at her in shock. *What the . . .*

"Aupiano, don't you remember me?" Her eyes were bulging, yet she sounded friendlier than she had appeared all evening.

Celes stood. "Please, no sitting on each other." Jessica hopped off of Bumo's lap, not even realizing she wasn't being addressed.

"It's me! Aupaiwrexa! *Cousin Wrexa!*"

Suddenly Ian remembered. While he hadn't seen her in years, he hadn't recognized her, because she had probably lost close to 100 pounds. Although still a large girl, once she had been huge. The last time they had seen each other was perhaps five years ago when their mothers had gotten into a huge fight about how to cook sea clams. He wasn't sure if they were actually cousins, because all Beelzians were supposedly *family*. Nor did he understand how she hadn't recognized *him* until he spoke. Next, he felt himself being pulled up by her very strong grip before being smothered by her hug.

"I love you, cousin. I protect you from death!" She hugged him tighter. "You don't fear! You not allowed to fear! Wrexa is here!" Through the foggy haze of near death by suffocation he could hear slight clapping.

"Well, I'm so glad you are reunited. What are the odds?" Celes asked with a smile on her face. "Beelzian blood in Oldaem! I love our diversity!"

As Wrexa set Ian down on his feet, he suddenly realized she had lifted him off the ground, then she hit him on his back so hard that he plopped back down into his chair. Wrexa laughed loudly and took her place beside him, forcing everyone to scoot down a chair. Now she sat between him and Liarra. *Perfect.*

"Look at the time," Celes stated as she started to the door. "Be at Pier 5 no later than 6:30 tomorrow morning. Don't miss the boat! That would be most unfortunate. And don't forget to do your reading. See you tomorrow." With that Celes exited the room, taking her lisp with her. Wrexa immediately started asking Ian about his parents and food and other Beelzians. She was delighted to hear about Baby Talo. Ian was sad he really didn't get to talk to Liarra, who quietly left the room as the other girls swarmed Bumo. Helen also departed without saying a word. Wrexa was not only extremely chatty but also very loud. As he talked to her more and watched her behavior on the ship the next day, he realized that her eyesight wasn't the greatest. She bumped into things, ran into crew members on the deck, and knocked over buckets and barrels. He understood now how she hadn't recognized him. *She can barely see. I wonder how she got selected.*

Now, as he looked up from the water, he saw that the sun had decided to join him for the day. *Are all the girls still sleeping?* Then he heard laughter. When he glanced behind him to the port side of the ship, he saw Bumo and Jessica laughing together, his arm wrapped around her waist. She had her hands on his chest as she looked up into his eyes. Bumo kissed the tip of her nose. *Gross.* As he watched them kiss mouth to mouth, Ian wondered what it would be like to kiss a girl. *Maybe I'll never know.* The water was a deep blue. So blue, in fact, that it reminded him of Liarra's eyes.

When she and he first boarded the ship yesterday morning, Liarra had been extremely excited. He could tell she had never really been on a big adventure before. In that, they were the same. She held her tournament packet closely to her chest as she carefully walked up the gangplank onto the ship. At 6:30 it was relatively cool, the sun not up yet. The others had already boarded, and Ian quickly brought up the rear. They stood in a straight line, at attention, it being Celes' orders, as a tall, dark-haired woman shook Celes' hand, a buckler hanging at her waist.

"I'm glad it's you," the woman said with a smile as she firmly shook Celes' forearm. Ian couldn't place her accent.

"It's a mutual feeling, Terra." Recognizing that the women had worked together before, Ian wondered in what capacity.

"So these are the Candidates." Putting her arms behind her back, Terra slowly eyed them up and down as she paced past them. He noticed Helen stand straighter than she had before. Although he wasn't sure, he thought Bumo had winked at her. If she had seen it, she ignored it. "Raise your hand if any of you have sailed across the ocean before." Terra honed in on Ian as she asked the question, and he looked down. Only two hands shot up: Helen's and Wrexa's. He figured his cousin had been able to travel to Beelz at some point in her life. But he had never gotten the chance. "Interesting. Well, ship life is unlike anything you've ever experienced. No one is lazy on a ship. Everyone has a job. Everyone has a purpose. We are family. Follow orders, and Captain Cid won't throw you overboard."

177

Ian saw Liarra standing stone-faced. *I wonder what she's thinking?*

"Celes, the ladies will be staying in the cabin on deck, the two gentlemen will be down below with the men. Once you get everyone settled, come to my quarters so that we can catch up." With that, Terra the Helmswoman left them, barking out orders to her men to set sail. Captain Cid was asleep somewhere, Ian figured, or he would be joining them later . . . somehow. At this point Ian was too overwhelmed to ask any questions, as the ship seemed about to depart without him.

As the ship left the port, Terra kept everyone busy in some way. Some scrubbed the deck, while others tied ropes or polished the anchor, which didn't make any sense to Ian, seeing as it would spend some time deep under the water. But he did anything asked of him with sheer joy. Each got a turn at the helm, Wrexa most giddy about that job, though Ian feared she might crash the ship into a rock or something. Helen peppered Terra with questions. He could already sense a major rift developing between the two as they began to glare at each other. He didn't want to get in the middle of that showdown. The blondes seemed entirely worthless, spending a lot of time flirting with some of the cabin boys. Celes kept an eye on them, always kindly, of course. Jessica and Bumo often disappeared to the stern. *Oh, Bumo, you never change.*

The day flew by, and before he knew it, he and Bumo had gone below deck to prepare for bed. He hadn't gotten any time to talk to Liarra, nor did he even really see where she had been for the majority of the day. Bumo had his shirt off almost immediately. Ian assumed that he wanted to show off his body to the other men, but they didn't seem to care. All older than they were, though not by too many years, they basically ignored him or Bumo, but they were nice enough. As Ian closed his eyes to drift off to sleep, he listened to the men talk. Soon he realized that the entire crew was Lamean, Terra included. It shocked him. Everyone was so nice. Ian had seen Lameans in Lion's Landing, most of them slaves, but these Lameans seemed to be free men who had gotten paying jobs as crew of *The Dolphin.* They had a spiritual discussion about the Old Order. Several took turns praying to the Liberator to come down to Esis to set them free, to rescue them from the Betrayer and from religious discrimination. Ian had seen religious intolerance, but not until that night under the deck had he really been close in contact with it. *These are real people struggling with real issues.* As they prayed for their people in bondage, he felt their pain. The distress in their

178

voices and his sense of the faith in their hearts almost moved him to tears. Ian didn't necessarily believe in the Old Order, having honestly never thought about it. His family had taught him to believe in Esis itself--in The Tide and The Rock. However in those beliefs he had never seen such conviction among any Beelzian or any other person. Nor had he witnessed that much religious conviction among New Order believers either. While aware Shepherds were to follow the New Order, he now realized that for him, the perfect scenario, would be an Oldaem in which people and Shepherds could believe whatever they wanted . . . and in freedom. As he drifted to sleep he decided it was his goal to make Oldaem such a place. Becoming a Shepherd would put him in the perfect spot to do it. *Bless the Lameans, whoever is listening,* was his prayer.

The deck started to come to life on the second day aboard *The Dolphin.* Bumo and Jessica stopped kissing and went their separate ways for the time being. Terra barked out orders as Celes stood staring across the sea. As Ian scrubbed the floors with Erina, he noticed Celes didn't move from her spot by the railing. He realized that once a person reached a certain age, most others leave them alone. Wrexa was by Terra's side at the helm, her laugh distinguishable above all other sounds. Although Terra didn't usually smile much, Ian noted that she did have a smile when with Wrexa. He could tell she liked Wrexa's spirit. When it came time for breakfast, Wrexa's meal had to be rationed, or she would have eaten everything. As they ate, Ian spotted Liarra reading off by herself on some steps and made his way toward her. *Finally.*

"THEY MADE MY FOOD LITTLE!" Wrexa had her face pressed against his.

"I'm sorry, Cuz."

"Beelzian blood need many food!"

"I know, Wrexa. Do you want my food?"

"Cuz would sacrifice his own grub?" Her eyes showed intense excitement.

"What is family for?" When he handed her his bread, she immediately devoured it, crumbs dropping down her already stained white blouse.

"Love you much, Aupiano!" She started toward Terra but stopped dead in her tracks when she saw Helen talking to her. "Red Lightning is big mean girl."

"I know, Wrexa."

"Wrexa destroy Red Lightning!"

"I know."

"Aupiano believe in Wrexa! Wrexa protect Aupiano from death!"

"Why am I dying again?"

"Tournament make fat weak boys dead. I protect Aupiano from death!"

No one thinks I deserve to be here. Somehow he managed to smile as his back stung from the seventh slap from Wrexa that day. She disappeared into the cabin. As he glanced around the ship he smiled to himself again. He heard some Lameans singing old hymns, Bumo was telling a ridiculous tale to the blondes, and Helen and Terra continued their conversation. Celes must be asleep somewhere. Once again his gaze drifted towards Liarra who continued to read alone. *Now is the perfect time.* Sucking in his stomach, he approached her.

What do I say? "Lovely day!"

"Yes," she answered without looking up from her book.

He sat beside her. "Mind if I sit?"

"Sure."

This is hard. "What are you reading?"

"New Order versus the Old Order. The age-old debate."

"Oooooh! I'd really like to read that when you're finished."

"Okay."

Since she's really into her book, maybe I should leave her alone. "It's really good."

Ian brightened up. "Yeah?"

"Yeah."

"What's it about?" *Dumb question.*

She finally looked at him, almost incredulously. "Seriously?"

"I mean . . . yeah . . . I don't know." *Why even bother, Ian?*

Liarra laughed.

She laughed!

"You're a funny guy, Ian."

"Wait, you really think I'm funny?"

"Don't push it." Then she looked up and smiled at him. *Beautiful.*

He liked her. Liked that she was sarcastic, that she was who she was, no matter what anyone else thought. Ian liked that she was quiet. While Bumo was singing now at the top of his lungs, the blondes and crew alike clapping wildly for him, Liarra was content being on the sidelines. That was something Ian was familiar with. *Maybe we can be on the sidelines together.*

180

"Why do you want to be a Shepherd?" he asked her. *That's a good generic subject.*

She didn't even pause for a moment. Her answer came immediately as if she had been *waiting* for someone to ask her. "I want to help people."

"Me, too!" he exclaimed as she turned and looked at him. "Sorry. I'll let you finish."

Putting her book down, she sighed deeply. "My parents were killed, and I grew up in an orphanage. There are a lot of hurting kids out there, kids who don't really think that life can be good for them. I want to show people that there is always hope, and help create an Oldaem in which anyone can be okay, even if they're . . . not okay. Does that make sense?"

Ian realized that she had put so eloquently into words what he felt inside that he could only nod. Not only hadn't he grown up an orphan, he had had a great life. But perhaps by being content with what he had, he had abandoned people who needed help. Suddenly, he remembered the barking dog he had heard from his room. *I want to help them too.*

"Why are you friends with him?" Ian followed her gaze toward Bumo who was now walking arm in arm with Alala.

"I've known him forever."

"And that's enough reason to be friends with someone? Just because you knew them a long time?" She had caught him off guard.

"I . . . I don't know. I mean, I know Bumo can be . . . Bumo-like . . . but believe it or not, he has a big heart."

"I see."

"Yeah. He's like my brother."

Liarra looked at him, longer than she had yet. It made him nervous. "You're a good guy, Ian." Standing, she started down the steps toward the cabin.

"Wait!"

Pausing, she turned.

"Which one? New Order or Old Order?" As a Lamean walked by, he tried to say it not too loud.

"I haven't decided yet," she said with little emotion. "Either way, something is going on. People are suffering. Someone has some explaining to do."

Ian watched her walk away. *She is pondering the origin of evil, and what is to blame for it.* As for him, he usually just contemplated what his next meal would be. *She's out of your league, Ian.*

181

A burst of voices caught his attention. Captain Cid had arrived on a smaller vessel. All stood at attention as he boarded *The Dolphin.* Although a rather short man, Cid was well-built and athletic, hair graying slightly. Ian noticed that Terra, even with Cid aboard, didn't take a step back from her authority, and it seemed as if the captain felt just fine with it. The man seemed more interested in entertaining his crew and having a good time. He drank a lot of spiced cider and played his stringed musical instrument while Lameans danced and laughed. Bumo flocked to Cid's side, laughing and telling stories and singing off-key duets. But Cid barely talked to Ian, or rather, Ian didn't know what to say to the captain. All watched and cheered as Bumo and Cid arm-wrestled. Cid won every time, which made Bumo respect him even more. When Cid begged Terra to challenge him, she refused, and Ian wondered who would actually win such a contest. Celes was nowhere to be seen during the festivities, and Liarra had her nose buried in her book. Wrexa would hoard extra food, and Helen would often just try to emulate however Terra was acting. When Terra ordered people to return to work, Cid continued to provide music, his feet propped atop a barrel. Terra didn't seem to mind at all.

A couple nights later, Cid was telling tales about his younger days, the blondes listening intently, and the Lameans working at Terra's instruction. She manned the helm, as Wrexa and Helen also sat nearby listening to Cid, Liarra about halfway through her book. Then Cid offhandedly revealed that he didn't believe in any deity. The captain didn't believe in any Order, the Three, or in the Rock or Tide. Rather he felt that human beings created their own fate. Bumo nodded in agreement, while Ian disagreed inside. If people were in charge of their own fate, what would the point of life be? Why would some people suffer and others thrive if there wasn't a purpose or reason for good and evil? Why and how would people know the difference between the two? The more Cid talked, the more Ian wondered if perhaps the man had pushed his faith away as a means to protect himself from the pain. Ian realized that having faith and hope in something also made one very vulnerable. *Maybe old people don't want to be vulnerable anymore . . . being vulnerable means being hurt.* He remembered Celes' vacant eyes as she stared into sea. Excusing himself, he went to the bow of the ship, where no one seemed to be.

The stars were out bright, and Ian laid down, resting his head on his arms. For the first time since he had left Lion's Landing, he felt homesick. Boisterous laughter came from everyone. *Bumo probably said something hilarious again.* It all came so easily for him. *I'm fat, I'm scared, I'm not strong. I have nothing to offer the people of Oldaem. I'll never be Bumo… What am I doing here, anyway?* Then he wondered what his parents were doing, and how Baby Talo was. Was Quiana surviving without him? After all, he had proposed to her, kind of . . . Not knowing what was to come made him both very nervous and very excited at the same time. Something he didn't like feeling was sad, but tonight, that's exactly what he felt. *Come on, Ian, you wanted this! You fought for this! Don't beat yourself up! They chose you for a reason! You've dreamed of this! Count your blessings!* Then sitting up, he decided to be happy in that moment. Being happy, he realized, was a choice. He could be homesick and happy at the same time. *I'm thankful for The Dolphin which is taking me to Shepherd land. I'm thankful for Bumo, who is my brother. I'm thankful for Wrexa who is my cousin. I'm thankful for Liarra who is my friend. I'm thankful for the Shepherds. I'm thankful for faith. I'm thankful for the Orders. I'm thankful for the Lameans.*

"Are you all right?" Celes stared down at him.

Quickly he looked up at her. "Oh, yes. I'm just looking at the stars."

"Mind if I join you?"

"Not at all." *How is she still awake?*

"Are you happy to be here?"

"Very happy!" He smiled.

She smiled in return. "I believe you. It takes a rare person to smile in spite of being afraid or being homesick, and you, Ian, are always smiling. I admire that in you."

"Thank you, Celes."

"Terra and I were speaking about all of you Candidates, and we agree that there is something special about you."

She must be joking. "Really? Terra thinks that?"

"She does. She was mentioning how you've been incredibly kind to her Lamean crew. And she greatly appreciates that."

"Everyone has been very kind."

"Yes, Ian."

Then he studied her and the vacant expression in her eyes. "Are *you* okay?"

The woman looked at him in surprise. "Yes, why do you ask?"

"Well, your eyes look sad." *She did ask. I hope I'm not crossing the line.*

"Intuitive." The vacant looked continued. "They are sad because they are sad."

He nodded.

"My daughter was murdered last year . . . this week. It's been a hard week."

His heart sank. "I'm so sorry to hear that."

"Yes. She was a Shepherd of Mind for Oldaem. Stationed in Leoj."

She was one of the murdered Shepherds in Leoj. Her death triggered a war. For an instant he was speechless, then said the only thing that came to mind: the truth. "I bet every week is hard."

She answered, glassy-eyed, "It is."

Placing his arm on her shoulder, he heard her softly cry and whispered a prayer for her, to someone or something. *Be with Celes. Help her pain. Take her pain. Even if it means I share the pain, so she has less.*

They didn't talk about anything else that night. After a few more minutes of quiet stargazing and praying, Celes left him alone in the night. The wind had picked up, but Ian enjoyed it. It reminded him of late nights on the beach with his parents and brother--picnics and songs and laughs and dances. He had had such a happy childhood. *So many things to smile about. I will help people experience that joy. I will help them end the pain, even if it's one person at a time.* Then, with a smile, he turned around to make his way below deck to sleep for the night. But his smile didn't last long. His heart crashed against the deck as he saw Bumo and Liarra walking hand in hand.

CHAPTER 25: SAYLA

"You're beautiful, Sayla. Don't let your sisters ever tell you differently." His brown eyes were full of kindness and understanding as he gave her a reassuring hug. They were sitting in the grass outside of her house in Aramoor. He always knew just what to say. Brave and smart, he was everything Sayla aspired to be. The young man was her hero. While he knew that she was different, that she had never fit in at home or at school, he loved her anyway.

I miss you, she thought as she looked into his warm eyes. *Why am I thinking that?* she suddenly wondered. *You're sitting right in front of me.*

184

"Are you alright?" With a grin, he pulled her closer. For a moment in the sunlight his eyes flashed gold. "You looked a little disturbed there for a moment."

"I'm fine," she said, adjusting her dress. "Tell me something about the last time you traveled with your father."

He began a story about a storm that he had not been sure he would survive. As she heard his soothing voice she relaxed and watched his dark hair wave in the breeze. Suddenly, Sayla jerked upright. *That's funny, I don't remember his hair having gold tips.* As he continued talking, she watched the golden aura spread until it completely covered his face.

Although she tried to warn him, tried to get him to stop talking, he remained oblivious. As the golden glow covered his features, he stopped moving until he was completely frozen, like a statue. She shook him, screamed his name, but no matter how she tried to wake him, he did not respond.

I have to find Galen. He will know what to do! Leaping to her feet, she ran to the inn that Galen lived above. "Galen!" she screamed, "Galen! I need your help!" For some reason she had a growing fear that he would not be there when she needed him most.

He appeared at the door looking concerned. A wave of relief flooded over her. "Galen, thank goodness you're home! Something is wrong with …"

"Protect them," he interrupted her. "You have to protect them. They can't protect themselves."

Sayla had the strange feeling that she had heard that before, but she couldn't place where. "Galen, what are you talking about? We don't have time for this! Come on!" She tugged his sleeve and ran to where she thought was outside. To her surprise, Galen limped along behind her, clutching his side in pain. But she didn't have time to think about it. She must have gotten turned around, because now they were in a hall of some sort. Or a finely decorated room? Sayla did not know for sure since everything appeared to be blurry. Her eyes could not seem to focus.

Hearing a grunt behind her, she whirled around to see Galen fall unconscious to the ground. A girl stood behind him holding a fire poker. Using her training, Sayla rushed to Galen's aid, but the girl ran off into the darkness before she could reach her. Instead, Sayla knelt down and tried to shake Galen awake. At least she could see that he was still breathing.

A flash of movement in the corner of her eye caught her attention and she looked up just in time to see an older man in expensive looking robes staring up in horror at something on the ceiling. Although she could not see him clearly because he was too far away, she could sense the surprise and confusion on his face. Following his gaze up, she saw a grotesque mass of gold dripping down onto the man. It took the shape of someone that she almost recognized and pounced down on the individual wearing the fine robes. Letting loose a primal groan, the robed man struggled for a few moments before lying still.

Sayla tried to stand, to run and help the man, but somehow she knew it was too late. Regardless, she forced herself up quickly, only to become dizzy. The room began spinning faster and faster until finally it settled down. But it looked different now--darker and the walls now covered with stone. Was she in a cave of some sort? She saw the dark shadows the stalactites made on the ceiling. When she looked back down, Galen was gone.

"Sayla, there you are," Shale's confident voice rang in her head, but she could not see him. "Overslept again, I see."

"Shale? Where are you? I can't see you." Maybe he could help her out of this room. She could not seem to find a door or opening.

"We're going on a quest to the Limestone Cliffs."

"What are you talking about? Where are you?" she shouted frantically. "I think I'm trapped in here!"

Shale shouted a response, but she could not hear it over the loud rumbling. As she stared at the wall, a rock plummeted from the ceiling and almost crushed her. Her heart began racing as more and more rocks started falling and she desperately tried to dodge them. Finally, she had nowhere left to run and held up her hands protectively although she knew it wouldn't save her from the giant bolder plunging directly toward her.

Sayla jolted awake. *Where am I?* Looking around, everything she saw was familiar and safe. She was in her own bed in her own room at Woodlands Academy. The light peeking through the closed curtains of her window was enough to make out the room. She could see her dresser and mirror directly across from her. Her clothes were all strewn about the floor. A couple days ago, she and the other Defense students had arrived from their journey from Sea Fort.

After the announcement of Shepherd Demas' disappearance, chaos had broken out in the entire city. The news was still spreading across Oldaem, but Sayla knew it would not be much longer before everyone knew of the disaster that had occurred because she had not been smart enough to stop it.

As she leaned on the wall her bed was lined up against, she could see her tired reflection in the mirror. It revealed dark circles under her eyes and her curly brown hair was tangled. She had not slept soundly since before their trip to Sea Fort.

So far, she had had the same dream involving the Royal Shepherd twice since she had been able to put a name to his face. It was as if it was haunting her. Somehow, she had known for days what was going to happen, but had not realized that she did. *How did I know?* She was afraid to tell anyone or ask for advice. *They would probably think I was crazy anyway.*

Of course, the one person she would have told everything to had not been there the one time she had asked. Who was she kidding? He probably would never want to speak to her again if he knew that she was practically an accomplice to the Leojians who had kidnapped Royal Shepherd Demas.

She had been silly to think that he would meet her at the pier. It had been too long since they had relied on each other, and he most likely had moved on and did not need her anymore. Up until a couple weeks ago, Sayla had not felt as if she needed her friend anymore anyway. *I shouldn't have held him to a higher standard.*

Well, she would just have to solve it on her own. However, her last dream was a brand-new one and had left Sayla in a cold sweat as she sat in her darkened room. The now familiar feeling of dread swept over her as she contemplated what it could mean, and if she needed somehow to figure it out before something terrible happened again. Strangely enough, it was not the dreams themselves that filled her with a sense of foreboding, just their content.

Sayla wondered which aspects, if any, would come true. So far, only one part of her first dream had actually happened. Galen had never showed up to tell her to protect someone, she had not gone to any Tower, and she had not seen the little boy who apparently needed help. Of course, she had studied every person they had encountered on their way back, wondering in dread if she would see another face she recognized. *Maybe the rest was really just in response to what I ate before I went to bed.*

Now she had a new problem to deal with. She couldn't just ignore this dream, even if absolutely none of it really came to pass. Royal Shepherd Demas was either dead or chained up somewhere, because she had been too surprised and scared to do anything about it.

At the moment, though, there was nothing she could do but wait. She refused to think more than she had to about the horrifying images in her mind. *That old man's face when he was dying ...* Quickly she put her clothes on and fixed her hair. *Maybe this time it was just a dream.*

The small dorm where all of the female Shepherds in training lived was a clean three-story building of brown brick and green trim. Full of hallways, it had one large living room in the lower story. Woodlands was the oldest academy of the three, something its inhabitants took pride in. It was the original academy that the Shepherds built under the authority of the One ages and ages ago. Of course, almost all of the buildings had been replaced, but some of the original stones had been used to build the more modern structures. A museum held many of the ancient artifacts used through the years for Shepherd training.

The academy nestled high up in dense forest. Growing up in Aramoor, Sayla had not seen a lot of forest, but she had travelled to the woods when she was a child and still fondly remembered her experiences there. Now, after four years of living at the academy, she loved the forest, and it felt like home.

Sayla had relatively little interaction with the future Shepherds who were not in the Defense category, but she knew them each by name and often nodded and said "Hello" in passing. The school had only 30 students, so it was not as if any of them were strangers. She made her way to the ancient practice grounds where she was to meet the rest of her group. Yesterday had been a free day to regroup from the troubling events they had experienced, but it had not been very relaxing since they had been summoned into a meeting with their professors to discuss what happened at the military base.

Exhausted, Sayla didn't much feel like practicing. After her outburst at the meeting hall, she did not really know what to say or how to act around her friends. Nor did she speak much the entire trip back, and they had certainly noticed that something was wrong with her. *They have no idea how wrong.* As she approached the practice ground, she saw that everyone was sitting on the low wooden fence that surrounded it and listening to something one of their professors, Shepherd Albright, was saying.

Masking the turmoil she felt inside, she quietly climbed onto a fence post next to Aveline. "Sayla! There you are!" Shale, who was leaning against the fence nearby, punched her good-naturedly in the shoulder. Her stomach felt as if it had dropped into her shoes, but not because Shale had touched her. Instead it was because of what he was going to say.

"Overslept again, I see," he said as he smiled his toothy grin. *Well, that was fast,* the practical side of her thought as she tried to maintain her composure. She would have time to panic later—like when she actually found herself trapped in a cave with flying boulders. Which, apparently, was now more of a possibility than she had originally expected.

Sayla put up her hand. "If you were going to say something else, just don't. Don't talk anymore." If she knew she was living part of her dream, she could at least actively stop it. Maybe it would reset the whole thing. *Of course, it's not as if there's a manual on how to prevent your dreams from periodically coming true.*

Shale looked at her confused for a moment, before Shepherd Albright broke in. "Sayla, glad you could join us. Now that you're all here, I can give you the news. It has been requested that you, ah, be sent on a quest ..."

Oh no. "To the Limestone Cliffs?" Sayla asked.

Shepherd Albright stared at her in surprise for a moment. "Why, yes actually. How did you know?"

"Lucky guess," she said miserably.

"Anyway, yes, you are all to travel to Westervale and pick up a group of slaves that are to be taken to the Limestone Cliffs to mine them for the war effort."

"Hold on," Aveline interrupted. "Why are we doing this right now? Our training for the year is almost over. Shouldn't we be preparing for Examination Day right after tournament?"

"Yeah, and the tournament itself is coming up pretty soon, too!" Oghren added.

The older Shepherd sighed. "I realize this is unusual. But with the war still going strong and ... the recent incident in Sea Fort, troops are spread thin and the academies have been called on to assist where we are needed." He spread his arms. "This is one of those times. But you will be back in time for the ceremony."

Shale, ever the leader, asked, "When do we leave?"

"As soon as possible, preferably within the next week," came the reply. "In the meantime, you will each be expected to wrap up your training since you will not get another chance until Examination

Day. Your professors already know you will be leaving, but you must finish your training with them. Understood?"

They all nodded.

Sayla sighed. Not only was she tired, she was scared of something she didn't even understand. And she wasn't used to being frightened of things. She didn't feel like training, nor did she want to go back out into the world where, at any moment, she could run into someone whose fate could unknowingly be in her hands. Especially, she didn't want to fail again. In fact, all she really wanted to do was to crawl back into bed. *But not sleep.*

Climbing down from the fence, she decided to speak to her weapons' expert professor first. Shepherd Acele was a very driven woman, and Sayla admired her. Sayla headed off in the direction of the armory.

"Hey, are you okay?" Aveline matched pace with her.

Momentarily, Sayla glanced at her friend and rival. *Can I trust her?* Of course she could. *Should I tell her?* "I'm fine."

"Are you sure? Because you look really tired. Which is weird, 'cause when I came to see if you wanted to go to breakfast, you were dead asleep."

"I am tired," she admitted. "But we've been traveling a lot, and I just found out we have to again."

"I'm just a little worried about you." Aveline's gray eyes clouded with concern. "I've never seen you this unfocused before."

"Why do you care? That should be exactly what you want so close to Examination Day," Sayla said more bluntly than she meant to. Aveline stopped and just stared at her. "I'm sorry. That came out wrong." *What prompted that?* "Like I said. Kinda tired."

Thankfully, Aveline brushed if off and sat down on the cobblestone path. "Do you remember when we were younger how exciting the tournament and training and everything was?"

Sayla gave her a small grin and joined her on the pavement. "We would have killed for these 'adventures' we get to go on all the time now."

Aveline laughed. "Who would have thought the war would change things so much?"

"Honestly, I used to hope for a war so that I could become, like, a famous Shepherd." Sayla looked away. "Or, you know, you could."

"Are we ever going to talk about … that … or are we just planning on ignoring it forever?"

"I was sort of hoping we could ignore it forever," Sayla smiled sadly.

"Definitely, me too." Briefly, Aveline picked at a loose pebble on the path. Sayla understood. The other girl always had to be doing something. *I'm the same.* That was the problem.

"Would you hate me if I won?" Aveline asked quietly. Sayla had secretly wondered that, too. How would she feel if the basis of her life goals were taken away from her, because her friend succeeded?

"I think I would be sad," Sayla considered, "But I don't think I could hate you."

"Same."

"I'm sorry for what I said earlier."

"I know you didn't mean it." Aveline looked at her friend. "I really am concerned about you. If something's wrong, maybe I can help."

Standing, Sayla dusted off her pants. "I'm fine. Really." She had decided that, as much as she wanted to, she could not tell Aveline what was bothering her. As much as she liked her, they were still rivals, and Sayla was determined to win the Shepherd position.

Together, she and Aveline spoke to Shepherd Acele and arranged a time in the afternoon for them to wrap up their lessons for the year. Tired, Sayla made her way to the training field to seek out Shepherd Albright. He was the expert in combat. Not feeling aggressive at all, she hoped he wouldn't make her fight today.

As she entered the field, Grunt was just leaving. As they passed, Sayla nodded at him, and she noticed the worry etched on his face. *Please, just keep walking.* "May I talk to you for a second?" he asked cautiously. *Oh, here we go.*

"Just for a second." Sayla didn't have time for another session of raising his self-esteem.

"What do we do?"

"About what?" She had no idea what he meant.

"The mission we're about to go on! How do we get out of it?"

She shrugged. "We don't."

"But … it's wrong!"

"What are you talking about?" Maybe he thought it was wrong to leave so close to tournament time?

"Sayla, we're supposed to transport Lameans to work in the mines. You can't tell me that's okay?"

He's so ignorant. "Grunt, they're slaves. Working is what they do."

"They're people, Sayla. And I don't feel right about this. We aren't slave drivers. Shepherds are supposed to help people."

191

It wasn't as if she wanted to go either, but she understood the reasoning behind it and was not about to lose the chance to advance as the fifth-year Defense student. "And by taking them to the mines, we help the war effort."

"I don't know …" he said doubtfully.

"Grunt, stop being a baby about it. Stow your feelings. Get the job done, win the prize."

He was about to respond when Shale jogged up to them, glimmering with sweat. She had no idea how he looked so good after apparently working out in the heat of the day "Sayla, want to practice some hand-to-hand combat? I can teach you a few new things," he winked. Suddenly, she found energy she had not had earlier, and all she wanted to do was focus on her Defense training.

"Sure," she answered nonchalantly. They left Grunt behind and headed to the section of the field reserved for hand-to-hand combat.

"So, are you excited to go out on another mission?"

"Oh, totally," she smiled and laughed a bit too loud. "What about you?"

"Sayla, I'm so ready. I mean, after I graduate, I'm going to be doing exciting stuff like this all the time, so I'll pretty much be used to it by then." Sayla wasn't sure she considered transporting a bunch of slaves as something to get enthusiastic about, but if it turned out anything like Sea Fort … she didn't want to think about it. He flexed his biceps. "The world isn't ready for Shale the Shepherd!"

She looked at him and smiled. It wasn't quite genuine, but it was the closest she had come to one in weeks. Her heart still felt heavy, but the horrors of the night seemed to fade in the brightness of Shale's smile. *Maybe I could tell him. Maybe he would understand.* But as soon as she thought it, she immediately rejected the idea. Sayla could not tell him—or anyone. Letting Aveline know would give her friend an unwanted advantage. Should any of the other Defense students, such as Grunt, discover what she was struggling with, it would cause them to lose their respect for her. And should Shale find out, it would result in losing any chance she had with him, and he was the man of her dreams. *Well, the good ones anyway.* No, Sayla would just have to endure it. She needed to start taking her own advice. *Stop being a baby about it. Stow your feelings. Get the job done. Win the prize.*

CHAPTER 26: GALEN

They were almost there, though it had taken a lot of hard work and more seasick nights than Galen cared to think about. Captain Zevran, as they were now supposed to call him, had just spotted land on the horizon. It had been dusk and barely visible, but he swore he saw it, and nobody doubted him. He figured everyone else was as anxious to get off the claustrophobic vessel as he was and feel land under his feet.

By now, they were close to Leoj. Galen wasn't sure how he felt about that. On the one hand, he was ecstatic that their watery journey was over for now. He knew they would eventually have to sail back to Oldaem, but at least they would have a respite here. *Though not really a respite.* At least, maybe then, they could come back as heroes after saving Shepherd Demas.

Galen wondered if the Royal Shepherd was even still alive. He knew he wasn't supposed to think like that, that it was supposedly a rescue mission, but he couldn't help but wonder. Most likely the Leojians would keep him alive for a while—Demas knew a lot of information that they would want to learn. But what about after they got it? Or what if they had already extracted it?

Apparently, Veroma had just received a response to the messenger bird she had sent out as soon as they had sighted land. It came from one of the Shepherds stationed on the front lines. She had called a meeting to discuss its contents, but Galen had not been included. He did not think that was fair. Instead, he, Adar, and Gadiel had been assigned sentry duty since they were now in enemy waters. *That sounds a lot more exciting than it is.* As Galen stared out at the calm ocean, the only potential threat he saw were the dark clouds in the sky.

Galen looked longingly toward the mess hall where he knew the meeting was about to begin. Two hatches led to it, one on either side of the craft. They had entered by the one away from him. But he could see candlelight flickering through the little window in the nearest one. *Maybe if I just listen for a little ...* Kneeling by the hatch, he lifted it just a sliver. Although he knew he was disobeying orders, his curiosity still got the better of him. Besides, what was he supposed to do if Leojians did see their tiny craft and decide to attack? He'd probably be dead before he could warn anybody.

He could just make out the silhouettes of the five operatives and Captain Zevran. Veroma was closest to him. Hopefully, she wouldn't turn around and spot him. "I just got word from the front lines," she was saying. "According to the Shepherd of Defense who sent the message, they cannot confirm that Royal Shepherd Demas has arrived in Leoj. Many ships have sailed in and out, but they do not know of any coming from the direction of Oldaem. Nor have our spies received any rumors of where they might be keeping him."

The soldiers murmured among themselves. One of them, the youngest one who Galen had learned was named Fyn, asked, "So how do we find him, then?"

"I'm not sure that we do. However, with the blessing of the troops there, I have come up with an alternative plan."

"What is that?" Endcer, the most experienced man, inquired.

"The Oldaemite troops have laid siege to the palace where the royal family resides. According to the message, they have the palace surrounded." Veroma laid a map down on the table that Galen could not make out. "They are covering the entrances here, here, and here," she explained, pointing to certain points on the map. "There is a sewage tunnel that runs under the palace and lets out into the ocean here." Galen squinted, but the map was too far away. He could not see any part of it. *Maybe if I went to the other door.* But he didn't want to risk missing out on any important information. "That is where we will make our entrance."

"Well, if it's so easy to break into the royal palace, why haven't the Oldaem troops done that already?" Zevran questioned.

"They are planning too," Veroma acknowledged. "And when I notified them of our arrival, they worked us into their plan. Just as we are heavily guarding the outside of the fortress, Leojian troops are guarding the inside. Of course, they have much less manpower, and their supplies are running low. It is time for the Oldaem army to take action. They will attack early tomorrow morning from all sides. As they do so, it is their hope to draw attention away from the escape tunnel so that we will be able to quietly slip in."

"But what will we do once we get in?" the other woman in the group questioned. "Clearly Royal Shepherd Demas will not be in there if the castle has been under siege for so long. Are you proposing we kill the royal family?"

"Not kill," Veroma corrected, "kidnap. Killing them would just make them martyrs and would destroy any chance we have of finding Shepherd Demas. And if by chance he is being held in the castle, or wherever else, they will know how to find him."

"So we're proposing a trade?" Endcer said, nodding. "I see where you're going with this now."

"Yes. Once we have the royal family in custody, we will ship them back to Oldaem and attempt to negotiate an exchange. Them for Royal Shepherd Demas."

"And the troops know about this? They know we are coming?"

"I will immediately send a message detailing the plan. Is everyone clear?"

The others nodded solemnly. Zevran raised his hand. "What exactly are my crew and I supposed to do?" Galen had been wondering that as well. As much as it made him nervous, he longed to get in on the action. He had spent too long just sitting around while the war went on.

"Your job is to get us as close to the shore as possible, and to wait until we return. Sound simple enough?"

"Yes, ma'am. Mind showing me where that tunnel entrance is?"

Backing away from the hatch, Galen returned to his post and gazed across the sea. The plan was to capture the royal family? This mission was turning out more important than he had expected. To be part of the crew that singlehandedly ended the war with Leoj. Well, maybe he was getting a little ahead of himself, but it would certainly deliver a crushing blow to the enemy. Galen tried to imagine what would happen if they did seize the king and crown prince of Oldaem.

With so much at stake, he was a little irked that he would not be seeing any of the action. *Do they really think they're that much better than us, just because they've had a little more training?* At least they could have been invited along as backup. Galen rolled his eyes. *Such is life.*

The hours of the night dragged by as he uncomfortably manned his post. He had slept most of the day in preparation for the long hours he knew he would spend on guard. A couple hours before dawn he got a bit of excitement as he watched Seff's special forces team climb into one of the recue canoes and paddle silently toward shore. The ship was so close to shore now that Galen could see the outline of the beach.

The rescue team had not even acknowledged his presence, perhaps because they couldn't see him at his post between two barrels. But then he hadn't made any effort to be noticed. *I'd be invisible to them even if I wasn't hidden in the shadows.* He watched them head toward shore, but soon their outlines disappeared into the darkness.

Leaning back against the cabin wall behind him, Galen gazed up at the sky. He tried to make out the constellations, but it was difficult with the clouds out. He could only see a few stars here and there. It reminded him of those many nights he had camped out with his friends and they had made up names for the patterns they could see in the sky. Briefly he wondered if Sayla was looking at the same stars he was. It made him feel a little bit closer to her when he thought about it that way. The distance between them then seemed just a little bit less. *I'm sorry I didn't get to meet you out on the pier.*

A creak in the deck boards a few yards away caught his attention. He edged forward a bit to see past the barrel that was blocking his view of that section of the ship. As he did, he spotted a dark figure untying one of the ropes attached to the side of the ship. Soon he heard a *plop* as something dropped into the water. Galen reached for the knife he had tied around his waist. Had someone slipped aboard? Were soldiers about to overrun their ship? Galen shook his head. *But that doesn't make sense.* The noise had come from somewhere behind him, meaning that whoever had made it must have already been on the boat. Galen watched as the figure lifted a leg over the railing.

"Hey!" Galen got up from his spot on the floor as the figure he now recognized as Gadiel guiltily swung his leg back aboard. "What are you doing?"

Defensively Gadiel folded his arms. "What are *you* doing?"

"Well, I'm watching you steal the other rescue boat for starters."

"I don't know what you're talking about."

"Oh, really?"

"Yeah."

"Then what are you doing exactly?" Galen's eyebrows raised skeptically. What did this stupid kid think he was going to do?

"I'm ... *checking* the ropes on the rescue boat to make sure they don't come undone. And clearly you tied them since it just fell off when I touched it."

Although he had to admit that Gadiel certainly knew how to get under his skin, Galen wasn't about to fall for that one. "What do you think you're going to do with that, Gadiel? Singlehandedly take down the royal fortress?"

Looking down, Gadiel bit his lip. "I have to do this, Galen."

Galen rolled his eyes. "Trying to play the hero? Because usually I think heroes are a lot taller. And better looking."

"He's my father," Gadiel insisted, his eyes filled with pain. Galen felt for a second that he was looking in a mirror. "If there's any remote chance that he's in there … I have to look for him. I have to try."

"But they're not even going in there to rescue him. The plans changed."

"I know. They're going to kidnap the …" Realization dawned on both their faces.

"You left your post," Galen accused.

At the same time Gadiel said, "And you spied on their meeting!"

They stared at each other accusingly in silence.

Finally, Gadiel broke the silence. "So … what are you going to do?" Galen felt himself torn between amusement and anger at Gadiel. He was about to call Zevran and shove Gadiel back into their room. It would take care of the kid once and for all. And then the shadow of land caught the corner of his eye, and he made up his mind. "I'm going with you."

"What?" Gadiel demanded in surprise. "No, you're not."

"Yes, I am."

"You really think that's a good idea. You and me in a canoe together."

"I think it's a better idea than staying stuck on this stupid boat any longer."

Gadiel shook his head. "No way. This is *my* thing, Galen. He's *my* father. I don't want you getting in the way."

Galen shook his head in exasperation. "You should be grateful for me offering to cover your back! Have you even thought about what you're going to do when–or if--you actually get into the palace?"

"I … I'll figure out something!"

"Well, try this, Gadiel"–he poked his finger against Gadiel's chest-"you and I go together, or I pay you back for that shiner you gave me the by call Zevran tell him what I saw while I was *at my post.*"

Gadiel considered it for a moment. "Why do you want to help me?"

"Oh, stop being stupid. You're the last person I want to help." Galen looked down at him. *Why am I helping him?* It was a good question, being quite unlike him. Maybe he wanted to prove he could do something worthwhile, that he was more than just "the ship crew." Maybe some part of him empathized with what Gadiel was

197

feeling. "I just want to get off this boat." And then, perhaps it was simply that.

CHAPTER 27: KAYT

The Capital City was the center of Oldaem's culture and history. Formally named Oldaem Realm, it more commonly just went by the title the Capital. Situated in the far west in one of the most beautiful parts of the country, it was the perfect location for trade and commerce and government meetings and elections. At the moment, though, the entire city was primed for the beginning of the Shepherd Tournament. As Kayt walked the crowded streets, she could not help but remember her own experiences both participating in and attending the tournament. Despite the war, not a lot appeared to be different.

If anything, perhaps everyone was being a bit too cheery. Purple banners proclaiming "Welcome Future and Current Shepherds!" and "King Orcino is glad you're here!" with a sketch of the king, as well as "Don't be a sheep, become a Shepherd!" hung across the narrow streets. Every year people journeyed from all over the country to watch the games, attracting all kinds of street vendors. Kayt walked past vendors selling reproductions of Shepherd medallions and pins who encouraged her to "Collect all four!" Children carried balloons with the seal of Oldaem on them. Music played in the distance.

All the activity going on in the streets did not particularly impress her. She knew that even now those selected to participate in the tournament were either already training in one of the coliseums where the games would take place or still on their way. In the distance beyond the city's buildings Kayt could see the hill on which the royal palace stood. The sight of the palace made her feel a little more certainty about what she was about to do.

"Excuse me," she asked a nearby street vendor who was selling roasted turkey legs. "Is King Orcino in the Capital today?" Kayt knew that he was often called away, especially since the war had broken out.

"He certainly is," she replied. "Why he hasn't even left the palace since he received that terrible news about Royal Shepherd Demas." The large woman held up one of her products. "Turkey leg?"

Kayt looked at the woman quizzically and shook her head. "I'm sorry, what news about Royal Shepherd Demas?" She supposed most anything could have happened while she had been out of touch with the world for the past few months.

The vendor stared at her, surprised. "Oh, honey, you haven't heard? Why he was taken by Leoj!"

She hadn't expected that. "What do you mean?"

"Oh, it's a real shame! Plucked right off the shore in Sea Fort, the way I heard it. Out from under the noses of all those military generals. And these are the people who are protecting us?" She shook her heard. "I'm just glad Leoj isn't anywhere near here. It is a shame about that Shepherd, though. I saw him once here in the city. Seemed like a real upstanding man."

Without saying another word, Kayt walked away, lost in thought. *Shepherd Demas has been captured? Fascinating.* If that were true, it could put Oldaem in a difficult situation. The Royal Shepherd of State, Garrus, would have his work cut out for him. Should Leoj decide to negotiate, he would be at the center of everything. *It should be me.* She remembered meeting him when she was little, and she knew he was intelligent, though she doubted he had her cunning or shrewdness. *But he has the experience.* Once again Kayt scolded herself for throwing her lot in with Silas. It had been her worst miscalculation.

Her mind drifted to Royal Shepherd Demas. If he were alive, he would be tortured for the information everybody knew that he possessed. It was likely the reason for his abduction in the first place. *Maybe Royal Shepherd Garrus is past preventative measures and working on damage control instead.* He definitely would be busy for the foreseeable future. Probably he had not left the palace either.

Meanwhile, there Kayt was, drifting from town to town with no purpose. She hated not having a goal, no influence. *Maybe that's all about to change.* Before long she found a small café where she and Arnand used to go when their families would visit the Capital.

Kayt had always felt privileged to live so close to the city. It always came in handy to know people in high places. A member of one of the more influential and wealthy families in Oldaem, she had grown up visiting the palace and walking the Capital's streets. According to her family history, she was directly descended from the Jaron tribe, the group of people that had eventually made up the region of Jaron. Her family had lived there for centuries. So had Arnand's. And Silas's.

As she sat at a table by the window, memories of her childhood came flooding back along with the history lessons she had pored over for her training as a Shepherd of State. The stories were still fresh in her mind, because of her recent studies in the library at Westervale.

Long ago before there had been a king of Oldaem, the country had been divided into seven tribes: Jaron, Isprig, Rahvil, Efil, Soma, Aerion, and Lamea. During the time when the tribes ruled just themselves, chaos and violence had reigned throughout the land. It was unsafe to go anywhere without fear of bandits and thieves. In those ancient days, the rulers of the tribes had been protected by Shepherds, followed the Order, and worshipped the Creator, the Liberator, and the Comforter. *That was their first problem right there.* Eventually, the leaders and Shepherds of the tribes held a council to try to remedy the situation in Oldaem. That had been especially imperative since there loomed the constant threat of other countries challenging them in war. They would not stand a chance if their nation was not united.

The council decided that for the sake of their safety, Oldaem needed to establish a king to maintain order. Six of the tribes enthusiastically approved of this solution, but one tribe, Lamea, did not. It argued that the only king the tribes needed to follow was the Creator, and if they all would repent and worship Him the way they had in the old days, it would solve their problems.

That had certainly been wishful thinking on their part, but no matter how the other tribes tried to convince them, Lamea would not budge, and war broke out.

The Lameans quickly went down to defeat. As punishment for their insubordination, the other tribes, now called regions, enslaved the majority of the Lameans. Rahvil and Efil annexed their land, the boundary being some sort of ancient Tower with a wall around it. Kayt knew that the Tower was a part of early Old Order mythology and likely had never existed outside of stories. It certainly was not the dividing marker anymore.

The six newly established regions placed a king on the throne and created the Capital city. Of course, a royal line no longer existed like there had been in the old days. A new king could be elected after the death of the old one if the public was not happy with the royal family. Kayt looked out the window at the castle off in the distance. At the moment, people were very satisfied with King Orcino.

Glancing at the drink in her hand, Kayt wondered what it would have been like to live during the early days of Oldaem. Things must have been much simpler then. *I would have been bored to death.* Although the hustle and bustle of the city was something of an annoyance, she thrived on it. She couldn't imagine life any differently.

The sun had begun to set. Kayt figured she would finish up in the café and then head out. With any luck, she would not have to stay at an inn tonight. Leaning back in her chair, she watched the people passing by. When they had been children, she and Arnand would slip away from their families to explore the city. They had found this café one day when it had unexpectedly started raining and had rushed inside.

Kayt left her money on the table and stood to leave. As she did she took one last glance outside of the window … and wondered if she was daydreaming. A plain-looking man was crossing the busy street with a little boy holding his hand, his other arm carrying a little girl. Could she be mistaken? It had been two years since she had looked Arnand in the eyes and left their home. Was that him standing in front of her now, or had her imagination made him up? There was only one way to find out. She met him at the door.

"Arnand?"

The man had been looking down at the little boy, about to usher him inside, when the sound of his name forced him to look up, cold dread flooding his face. Kayt wasn't sure what she felt. Undoubtedly it was not the hurt and surprise so apparent on her husband's face.

Quickly he placed his daughter on the ground next to his son. *My daughter,* Kayt corrected herself. *And my son. Lei and Balyn.* But as she watched the little boy and girl in front of her, she saw no sign of recognition in their eyes. It was as if they stared right through her with nothing more than a mild curiosity about a stranger who knew their father's name.

"Go sit down," Arnand quietly told the children.

"But Dad …" Balyn protested.

"*Now.*"

Balyn took his sister's hand and ran over to a table.

Arnand straightened himself up to his full height and silently faced Kayt.

"The children have grown," she observed.

201

"Children do that," he answered flatly. "But I guess you wouldn't know since you no longer have any."

"I didn't expect to see you here."

He brushed his hands through his short, spiky brown hair. "Well, that makes two of us."

"I was looking for you. I went to Dagonfell, but you weren't there. Your mother wouldn't tell me how to contact you."

Kayt had always been able to read her husband so well, but now it was as if she was talking to a brick wall. "Then how did you find us? You just said you were surprised to see me."

I guess sometimes you find things when you stop looking for them. "I … I don't know. I suppose the One brought us back together." As she said it, she realized that could be the only answer. Maybe it was the One's will for her to bring their family back together after all.

Arnand exhaled. "Yeah, that or the fact that both of us were in the city and decided to eat at our favorite café."

For a moment, she regretted that she had had to hurt Arnand in order to fulfill her own goals. He had always been a valuable ally and a source of useful advice. Her husband had not deserved what had happened to him. It would take some time to heal that wound. But he had said "our." It was a start.

"Well, they do have the best pastries this side of Jaron." Kayt offered a tentative smile. He did not reciprocate.

"What do you want, Kayt?"

Her face sobered as she realized that he deserved a straight answer. "I've decided to come home. I know it must be difficult to raise two children on your own, and Balyn and Lei need a mother."

Arnand frowned. "What do you mean you've *decided* to come home?" His arms crossed. "You think that you can just … can just leave me with a newborn baby and a toddler for *two years* and then just *decide* to walk back into our lives?"

"I was hoping …"

"No!" he said a bit too loudly. A few diners nearby glanced up from their food. Her husband lowered his voice. "No. Let me finish. I loved you, Kayt. And seeing you today makes me think that maybe I still feel something toward you. But you have never quite loved me in the same way. I can see that now. It took you walking out on me for another man for me to understand it."

"I never felt the same about him the way I did you."

"I know that, Kayt. You did it for the job title, I get that. I know how you think, remember?" Tears began to brim in his eyes. *He's weak,* she thought, but she decided to ignore it. "We were going to be the unstoppable team, you and I. And then you left."

"I never deceived you, Arnand. I was always very clear about my goals. You married me *after* I was a Shepherd."

"Apparently that was my first mistake."

"Regardless, I am back now. I am willing to stay this time."

Stunned, he stared at her. "You know what? I really want to believe you're being genuine. When I look at my children sitting over there, I want to believe more than anything else that you want to be their mother again. But then you go and say something like that. Not once--not *once*--have you apologized for what you did. And it makes me realize that ... maybe you're not being genuine at all."

"I am being genuine, Arnand. I know this is what I want now. I ... made a mistake before. I can see that now."

"You only see it as a mistake, because you failed."

Maybe Arnand would not be as malleable as she had originally expected. Her husband had changed, hardened. "Then let me at least speak to the children."

The tears spilled over now. "I can't," he shook his head sadly. "I wish I could. But what happens when you get another job opportunity? Or when you get bored again? Are you going to just up and leave them with no word? I can't let that happen to them again."

An unexpected wave of relief washed over her. At least she could see them from a distance. Balyn was coloring on a piece of paper and kept pushing Lei away as she tried to color, too. Her children were healthy, and and her husband loved them. Somewhere deep down, in a place where Kayt did not go often, she knew that she could never give them the love and care they deserved. She was not cut out to be a mother.

"I understand. The offer is still open, Arnand. I will come back if you want me to."

"I do want you too," he answered quietly. "But I have more than me to think about now. Please leave. I ... I don't want to see you anymore."

She looked at him one last time as he stood there with his shoulders hunched in the café where they had together gone so many times. Kayt nodded to him, he nodded back, and then she left.

A feeling of exuberance filled her heart, and she realized that the One had not brought her and her family together in order to reunite them. Rather, he had crossed their paths to show her that they were not what she needed and she was not what they required. And now she knew exactly what she must find for her life.

Night had fallen, but Kayt walked confidently toward the palace on the hill, neither tired nor frightened by the darkness. She had a purpose now, and she knew how to achieve her goal. Soon she reached the gate that led to the palace. It was about to close for the night, but she walked through anyway. "Hey!" a guard shouted after her. "Hey, lady! We're closing!"

Ignoring him, she continued on. As she reached the great golden door that led into the castle, the guards caught up to her and pulled her back. "You have to leave. The king is no longer seeing anyone today."

"I'm not looking for the king," she responded. "Unhand me."

"I can't let you go in. You have to leave. Now go, before I throw you into the prison for the night."

"Is that any way to talk to a Shepherd?" a silky, confident voice behind them questioned.

The guards instantly let go of her arms and bowed before Prince Gragor. When he gestured for them to leave, they did not question him. Instead, they headed back to their posts. "I'm so sorry about that." The prince sped down the steps and grabbed Kayt in a friendly embrace. "But I was not expecting you! Kayt! It's been so long!"

"I wasn't sure you would remember me," she lied. *Everyone remembers me.*

"Why, of course! We had all those adventures when we were children. Come inside! My father will be thrilled to see you." As he led her up the stairs and into the richly adorned palace, Kayt looked around at the exorbitant furnishings, and for the first time in weeks, perhaps months, she smiled.

CHAPTER 28: COLE

"To whoever is listening . . . I guess I don't really know what to say." Cole sighed. "I guess keep protecting us." *Even though you didn't protect Mom.* Fenris had asked him not to blame the Old Order. Out of respect for his brother, he tried to pray every night, but memories of his mother's death made it very hard to do. "Help us to find Dad. Help Arissa to keep Belen safe. Help Fenris to be okay."

Crickets chirped around him. The wind began stirring, gently swaying the corn stalks he knelt among. The moon was full and bright. It was hard to stay focused on talking to someone he couldn't see. Someone he blamed for his misery even though it was someone he was supposed to love.

"Thanks for bringing Zek here, even if he doesn't believe in you. It's been nice to have a friend here." He thought about all that Zek had taught him in the short time they'd traveled together. The boy was a survivor in every sense of the word. Cole guessed that he, too, had become a survivor. Although Lily didn't like Zek, she had to admit that he had made traveling a lot easier. With him came knowledge, experience, safety, food, and constant humor. A trickster, he loved to tell jokes and stories and be the center of everything. But Lily didn't like the fact that Zek had taken charge of their journey. It bothered her that he stole food and made negative comments about the Old Order.

If You want me to love you, if You want me to forgive you, if You want me to believe in you, Cole thought to himself, *then You are going to have to do a better job at proving You're nice and real, and giving me another reason other than Fenris and Lily's suggestion to keep praying to you.*

"Who are you talking to?" Zek ripped off a corn stalk and smiled.

Startled, Cole turned around. "No one."

"Really?"

"You never talk to yourself?"

"I don't know." The older boy looked around. "Why are you out here? I woke up and you were gone."

"I was looking for food."

Zek appeared amused. "I see you found some."

"Should we take any of it?"

The boy's eyes glimmered in the moonlight. "Absolutely."

Silently they began to strip off ears of corn. Cole wasn't sure how long they remained out there, but after a while his arms began to tire. After they had filled a couple stolen baskets, Zek broke the silence.

"Tomorrow, we're going to go into the next village up ahead, and I'm going to teach you how to steal bread right out from under the baker's nose."

"Lily's not going to like that."

"Ah, don't worry about Lily. I'm going to send her to get water from the river or something."

They returned to their campsite, which consisted of a sleeping Lily next to their pile of food supplies. After Zek poked her with his foot a couple times, which she wasn't too happy about, they then continued on their way. The moon was still relatively high in the sky. Lightning bugs blinked off and on. Cole's mom had always said summer was when the insects had dancing parties. He imagined they were having one right now. *Guess Mom won't be seeing anymore of these.* Glancing over at his sister, he wondered if she was watching the dancing bugs, then realized she was practically sleepwalking. Zek kept whistling. Cole noticed that despite just losing his entire family, the older boy seemed pretty upbeat, something he didn't understand. Cole couldn't even remember the last time his own smile hadn't been forced.

They kept walking through fields and gardens. The region of Soma was an agricultural area. As they passed small farms and clusters of houses, Cole heard chickens clucking and cows mooing. Imagining people sleeping softly in their beds, he longed to join them. For a moment he wished that he could sleep in Fenris' bed. But that meant doing nothing. And walking for hours in the middle of the night was much better than doing nothing and watching his family slowly die away. Cole wasn't sure why Zek liked to travel at night. Maybe it was because it was cooler, possibly even safer, although Cole still felt as if they were being followed. He would often turn around and imagine a shadow darting behind a tree or bush. Not sure whether it was his imagination or not, he just kept going, eyes on Zek. The boy had surprisingly broad shoulders for someone only two years older than himself. Also he seemed to have dark circles under his eyes, and Cole wasn't sure if they were dirt smudges or from exhaustion.

"You doing okay, Lily?" Zek asked, though his tone didn't sound actually concerned.

"Why do we have to travel at night? Why can't we sleep at night?" Lily mechanically placed one foot in front of the other.

"Ah, you *are* awake," he chuckled. "Tomorrow I have a big job for you."

"I'm not going to distract people while you steal."

Cole could sense Zek smiling although he couldn't see his face. The older boy led the way, Cole was in the middle, and Lily brought up the rear. Zek bent down and picked up a large branch to use as a walking stick.

"I'm putting you on water duty."

"We *have* water."

"Yes, but we always need more."

"Then *you* go on water duty."

"I'm asking *you* to."

"I don't want to."

"Then I'll have you distract someone while we steal."

"Cole isn't stealing *anything*, right, Cole?" Her brother felt her catch up to him. Turning to her, he saw her bright green eyes gleaming in the moonlight.

"Lily, can't you just do what Zek says? So far he's gotten us fed."

"Really? Fenris would *not* be happy."

"Well, Fenris isn't here." Cole looked away.

"What's so great about Fenris anyway?" Zek asked, thumping his staff against the ground as he walked.

"Everything!" Lily said confidently. "He brings food home all the time. Food he's *earned,* not stolen!"

"He's also old enough to get paid," Zek calmly replied. "We have to do what we need to do in the meantime. Right, Cole?"

Tired of hearing them argue, Cole did not answer. That was one thing that did get annoying about having Zek around. But he figured it was better to have the other boy there so that Lily could argue with Zek, rather than her with him. They had fought mostly about the Old Order versus the New Older, though Cole wasn't really sure Zek even believed in the New Order. He knew Lameans had been responsible for his parents' deaths, so Cole understood that he had a reason to be angry with the Old Order. In that case, so did Cole. However, Lily was still fiercely loyal to them though he wasn't sure if it was because his father and Fenris were faithful, or perhaps it was just to annoy Zek, but whatever reasons either of them held, the arguments were consistent and mostly about the same things.

He remembered a certain discussion the day before when he had been standing on Zek's shoulders, reaching for apples in a tree. Lily had been stretched out on her back, watching, as the two of them argued.

"It doesn't make sense," Zek had chuckled.

"Just because you don't get it, doesn't mean it's wrong."

"Lily, followers of the Old Order killed my parents. They wiped out everyone in my village. How is that okay?"

"It's not okay. But not *all* followers of the Old Order are murderers." Sitting up, she smiled. "For example, I haven't killed you."

207

"Well, then, the Old Order let your mom die."

"New Order people die too."

"Barely anyone in Oldaem believes in it anymore."

"Most people in Oldaem are stupid."

"You have no reason to believe. Cole, get that big one above that branch."

Cole swung his fist, and the apple dropped.

"Hey! Watch where your stolen apples fall!" Lily glared. "Zek, you're dumb, you don't even know what you're talking about. Do you even know the *story* of the Old Order?"

"Doesn't matter. I don't need to hear lies to know they are lies."

"How do you know if something is a lie or not if you don't even know what it is?"

"Liberator, Comforter, Lover, or whatever threw down the 'Betrayer,' from Aael right? Sounds to me like when people leave others out of a game or ignore each other at school. An entire group of people believes in this? Come on." Zek moved to a different part of the tree. Cole hung on as he sat on the older boy's shoulders.

"The Betrayer is evil!" Lily declared.

"Why?" Zek looked uninterested.

"Because!"

"Because your Daddy said so?"

"Shut up, Zek!" She picked up a small pebble and threw it at him.

"Lily! I'm up here!" Cole shouted.

"He's evil because he tried to ruin a perfect place where people are all happy and no one dies or is killed or drowns or leaves their family or fights or gets sunburned or anything!"

"So if the Old Order are so great, why don't they just make Oldaem like Aael was? Why make everyone suffer?"

"I . . ."

"Sounds to me as if they enjoy watching everyone make each other miserable."

"The Liberator will come again and save everyone!" Lily shouted confidently.

Cole felt Zek shudder and sigh. "How? What does that even mean?"

"I don't know yet! But that's what believing is for. That's what faith is for!"

"So where's he at? Where is your awesome Liberator?"

"I . . . I don't know." Cole could hear discouragement in her voice.

"You know what I think?" Cole felt himself being lowered until he could look into Zek's eyes--cold, dark, and tired. "I think all of it is a lie. Old Order, New Order, all Orders. I think people just make up lies to feel better," Zek continued. "But people can never just feel better. They have to do things to make people hurt. All people do is hurt each other. You can't stop it. So you just have to make others hurt worse. I guess Old Order followers believe what I do deep in their hearts, or my family wouldn't be dead"--he looked at Lily--"and neither would your mom."

That shut Lily up for a while. And it really made Cole think, too, as they traveled on together. However, just because some kid whose family died didn't believe, it didn't mean that Cole would necessarily go against Fenris and his dad and his family. That's why he had prayed that night in the cornfield. He was still going to try, at least for now, until he gave the Old Order a chance to prove themselves once and for all. And they had a lot of proving to do. The more Zek talked, the more he made sense, the more he was annoyed with Lily, and the more he was irritated at himself for needing Fenris' approval, even if his brother was miles away. He longed for his dad's approval, too. Maybe it came down to just needing to feel loved. Cole was worried if he didn't believe what his loved one's believed, they would be disappointed in him. A dead mom and a disappointed family would be too much to bear. That's why he kept on his journey.

The days were hot and the nights were somewhat cool, especially among the hills. Summers in Oldaem were strange. Cole thought that because they were near the ocean, maybe it cooled things down a bit. Every day was similar to every other one. They walked and talked and argued and slept and stole and Lily was annoyed, and they walked some more. Cole spoke to his sister less and less, and she seemed uninterested in talking to him. He could tell she wanted Zek to leave them alone, but Cole realized their need for the boy outweighed her dislike of him. By now Cole had grown tired of sleeping outside, and finally he and Lily were able to convince Zek to bed down in a barn outside of a village. He was even happier that Zek agreed to let them sleep in the barn at *night* for once. *Finally, a good night's rest.*

They remained behind some bushes as Zek disappeared inside. Cole wasn't even sure why he worried that they might be caught. Perhaps it was because they had stolen so much the past several days that he was afraid some soldiers might have tracked them and would haul them to jail. Finally, Zek waved them in.

It wasn't a very big barn, and Cole was pleased to see that it didn't have any animals inside. It seemed as if it was just a storage place for hay, or perhaps the animals usually kept there were somewhere else. Zek climbed the ladder to the loft and made it quite clear that it was *his* sleeping quarters for the night, and that the Reds, which was what he had been calling them, were to sleep down in the dirt.

Cole watched as Lily dug in her bag and pulled out a dirty shirt, which she placed on the ground. *I guess that will be her pillow.* As he sat beside her he could tell that something bothered her. The two of them hadn't spoken alone since Zek had entered their lives. While his sister had never really opened up to him at home, he had felt as if they at least had an understanding. It was the reason he had asked her to come with him.

"I don't like him, Cole," she whispered. He glanced up into the loft to see if Zek was listening.

"I know." *What do you want me to do, Lily? I can't get us there on my own.*

"You know? That's it?" Her voice prickled with irritation.

"What do you want me to say?"

"That you're on my side!" Her whisper had grown louder.

"Don't wake him up," Cole hissed, then turned away. *I don't know whose side I'm on. I can't even keep up with all the sides.* Having realized during their journey that Oldaem was a much bigger place than he had expected, he now felt very insignificant.

"Cole, Dad and Fenris wouldn't like him either." She looked down and dug into the dirt with her finger. He guessed that she was probably right, but he didn't want to be alone with just her. Because he had little or no idea where to go, he would probably end up getting them both killed. At least Zek had a plan.

"Lily, you can't dislike everyone who doesn't believe the way you do."

"I don't! Just him!"

"He hasn't done anything bad to us."

"Cole! He taught you how to steal."

"I already knew how to steal."

"Yeah, but you didn't do it, 'til now."

"You ate some of those apples too, Lily."

"I know." She sounded sad.

"He's like us Lily--he doesn't have anyone."

210

"He *may* have lost people like we did . . . but he's *not* like us." As she looked at him, she became the spitting image of his father. "And don't act like *that's* why you let him travel with us. You *like* what he's getting you to become."

With that, Lily laid down and shut her eyes. Her words had struck him like a thunderbolt. *Do I like what Zek is? Do I like what I'm becoming?* Cole for one thing realized that at least the other boy was safe from people hurting him and being disappointed. Perhaps, Cole decided, it came down to a decision: did he choose to trust people and do what was right, only to be disappointed in them later, once they ended up leaving him? Or should he just shut himself off from everyone and be lonely and hurt now, never able to experience what being loved felt like? Sadly he realized that both roads ended in pain. *This is Oldaem? This is what the Orders provide? Isn't there another possibility?* Finally he drifted off to sleep, a tear trickling down his cheek.

"Get up, Red. It's time to hunt." Cole woke up to Zek's mischievous face.

"Where's Lily?"

"She went into town. Claimed she needed to buy some things. I said I could get them to her for free, and she make a face and left." He shrugged. "Just trying to help."

"Yeah, she's pretty stubborn." Rubbing his eyes, Cole sat up. "What's the plan?"

"This town is a trading center, and that means there will be a lot of carts with food and supplies. My goal is to get an entire cart for ourselves so we don't have to walk anymore."

"You're going to steal a cart?"

"Yup."

"Do you even know how to drive one?"

"What could be so hard about it? Just whip the oxen."

He's crazy. Cole smiled to himself as they left the barn.

The village didn't have many shops along the dusty main road, but Cole did notice a general store up a ways. Most of the villagers were either farmers or merchants, and children ran up and down the streets, playing with stray cats and dogs. Cole observed that most didn't pay attention to anything but themselves and their own business. *Am I like them?* Then he spotted Zek approaching a solitary grain cart parked next to a broken fountain in the square. Nobody was on it. A tired looking cow stood hithed to it, chewing her cud, flies buzzing around her ears.

"Cole, get on," Zek whispered as he swung himself up into the front.

"On back?"

"Wherever."

After glancing around to see if anyone was watching, Cole pulled himself up. Suddenly he remembered Mable and Wilber and wondered where their journey had led them. His attention shifted to Zek who grabbed the reins.

"Are we going to wait for Lily?"

"We'll drive it up to the store and act like it's ours. Otherwise, people will think we are stealing it."

"We *are* stealing it."

"Yeah, yeah."

The cart lunged forward, and its wooden wheels began to kick up dust. Cole tried to look as natural as possible. Once again, no one seemed to pay any attention. They got closer to the store as three little girls ran past, chasing each other and giggling. *I bet their mom didn't die. I bet their dad didn't leave them. I bet they haven't become thieves.*

Lily's eyes were huge as they pulled beside the store. She had a bundle of supplies in her hands as she shook her head. Then she angrily put it down and crossed her arms. "No, Zek. No way."

"Shut up and get on," he snapped.

"No!" she said, stamping her foot.

"Lily, don't make a scene," Cole urged.

"I won't do it. You can leave me here. I won't do it."

"Shut up, and get on," Zek snarled. Cole noticed his upper lip stretch upward and to the side.

"Please, Lily." When Cole looked around again, he saw that an old woman had stopped to watch. "We have to get to Dad," he said, lowering his voice.

"Thanks for pulling it forward. It will be easier to get my food on the back." A man with short dark hair smiled as he approached the cart.

"Uh . . ." Zek uncomfortably shifted in his seat as the man carried his sacks and set them gently on the back among the grain. His eyes met Cole for a second, and Cole looked away as he continued to make his way toward the front of the cart.

"Here you go, Odessa." The man fed the cow a carrot. The creature mixed the carrot with her cud. Then the owner of the cart petted the animal on her head as he looked up into Zek's eyes, a smile on his face.

He was neither handsome nor ugly–just a man. His clothes were brown and tattered, yet neat in appearance. Cole imagined he was somewhere in his twenties, and his gaze was calm. *He reminds me of Fenris, especially his eyes.*

"Scoot over," the light brown eyes of the man twinkled as he pulled himself up beside Zek.

"I uh . . ." Zek was without words.

Lily stood there dumbfounded. "We weren't going to take it!" she burst out.

"Where are you folks headed?" he asked, turning around to look at Cole, and give him a friendly nod.

"Get off his cart!" Lily demanded as Zek quickly hopped down.

"No! It's okay. The more the merrier. I would be happy to give you a ride, if we're going the same direction."

Cole heard himself speak up from the back of the cart. "We're heading to the Capital."

"I can take you as far as Azmar. Come along with me. There's plenty of room." He patted the seat next to him as Odessa the cow groaned.

"Are you sure?" Lily asked, kicking a stone with her foot.

"Absolutely." He smiled again, his teeth white and straight. Cole licked his own teeth, feeling how sticky they were. Lily pulled herself up next to the man as Cole glanced at Zek who kept staring at the ground.

"Come on, Zek. Get on," Cole urged. Zek joined him in the back of the cart. After a gentle snap of the reins and a clicking noise from the pale-eyed man, Odessa led the cart out of the town.

At first they rode in silence as the cart slowly made its way up a hill. Cole couldn't see the man's expression, but for the first time in a long while, he felt safe riding in the back of the cart. Scowling, Zek stared at the road behind him.

"You have nice eyes," Cole heard Lily say.

"Thank you. So do you."

"What's your name?"

"Sorry about that. I'm Azriel. And what are your names?"

"I'm Lily, the redheaded kid is Cole. He's my brother." Her hands covered her mouth as if she were telling a secret as she leaned toward

Azriel. "Sometimes he can be kind of grumpy, and the mean kid in the back is Zek."

"I'm sure he's nice." Azriel chuckled. Cole smirked as Zek rolled his eyes.

"Why are *you* heading to Azmar, Azmeral?"

He smiled, correcting her. "*Az-ree-el*. I'm delivering grain for the tournament. They'll transport it to the Capital once I drop it off. A lot of farmers from all around Oldaem will be traveling with their goods to provide enough food for the tournament attendees." With a wink, he added, "You picked a good time to travel."

"Well, thank you ever so much for taking us. Sorry about the whole cart thing. Like I said, Zek is a meanie."

"It's not a problem. I'm glad you pulled it forward."

Is this guy for real? So nice . . . all the time.

"Well, we're traveling to the Capital to find our dad."

"Oh, is he there?"

"We hope so. He's the greatest Shepherd of Mind there ever was! His name is Brulis. I'm sure you've heard of him," she exclaimed with pride and confidence.

"I have." Azriel smiled.

"Like I said, he's the best Shepherd on Esis. So, yeah, we're going to find him." Cole noticed that sadness tinged her voice for a second.

"You okay?" The man looked down at her.

"Yeah, our mom died. We're going to tell Dad." She didn't look at him, and Cole stared at the passing trees. *Mom is dead.* It still felt impossible to believe. A chill went up his spine. *Is that a shadow? I'm seeing things.* His gaze shifted back toward the front, and his eyes caught Azriel's. For the first time since they had met him, his expression harbored deep sorrow. *Could he really be so sad just because our mom is dead?* Quickly Cole glanced away.

"I'm so, so, sorry." Genuine sorrow filled the man's voice. Cole could tell he meant his words. It was something he had not yet seen in another human except his brother. *He reminds me so much of Fenris.* "My parents are dead, too. But they lived a long time. I grew up in Haran with them. They were farmers. Both of them. We used to make this journey together. I guess I still do it, because they loved to see the faces of all the tournament attendees, especially the kids. Kids love food."

"We sure do," Lily beamed.

"You're a Lamean," Zek snapped. It was the first words he had said since they encountered Azriel.

214

"I am."

"Lameans killed my entire family," Zek shouted angrily. "They attacked my village and destroyed my life."

Silence settled among them. Cole's heart started racing. *Will he throw us off now?* But Azriel kept looking straight ahead as he gently continued to guide the cart.

"I'm deeply sorry for the actions of my people." His head sank as he continued: "I wish they would love instead of hate. I wish they would forgive those who oppress them. I can't undo the pain they've caused you. But I can show you a Lamean who will try to do his best to help heal the wounds they've inflicted upon you--me." His words were soft, direct, and with a power in them unlike Zek's. It was a different type of power, one Cole couldn't identify, but he had a voice he wanted to listen to, one he wanted to believe.

"How old are you anyway?" Lily asked, quickly changing the subject.

"Seventeen."

"We have a brother who is 17. You kind of remind me of him."

"Is that so?" He smiled again.

"Yup." She was eating a slice of bread she must have bought from the store. The breeze had begun to pick up as they continued down the hill they had crossed over. More farms and houses stretched to each side as they drove. *I've never met a Lamean like him before.*

"So, Azriel, may I ask you something?" Zek asked with a note of irritation. The question surprised Cole.

"Of course."

"Do you believe in the *Old Order?*"

"Yes, I do."

"Why?" Zek sounded disgusted.

"You shouldn't have such distaste for something you don't understand, and haven't tried to." The directness of his answer startled Cole.

"What?" Zek seemed surprised, too.

"Since we left the village you've been scowling back there, glowering at everyone and everything we've passed. You were going to *steal* my cart, you harbor anger toward me for a crime against your family I personally did not even commit, and now your hatred for me grows, because I believe differently than you do. Zek, maybe you should consider changing some of your beliefs." Azriel smiled again. "I've seen the change the Old Order can make in a person's life."

"You know nothing about me."

215

"Perhaps. But I do know that your words and actions have incredible power and influence over those around you. Speak carefully and choose your actions wisely. You don't want to be responsible for someone else's downfall."

"Stop judging me!"

"*You* asked if I believed in the Old Order. My belief in them compels me to point out truth. Truth reveals, it shines light on the darkness. I'm sorry if truth has exposed you. Although, it *was* my intent." His voice softened. "I would like to get to know you, Zek. I hope with time, your opinion of me changes." For a moment he swiveled around, and Zek was unable to meet his gaze. Then the man faced forward and shook his head.

Lily's mouth had fallen wide open. "Mr. Azriel, you said what I've been wanting to say to meanie-head Zek for days!"

"Don't call him names, Lily."

"Sorry." Although her head sank, she smirked to herself.

Who does this guy think he is? Cole glanced at Zek who continued to scowl. Then he listened as Lily and Azriel discussed the Old Order. The way Azriel referred to it showed how much love and trust he placed in his beliefs. He spoke of the Creator with such respect and reverence, of how Esis was created and about the Tower that the Order built in order to connect the two worlds together. Then he sadly told of the Betrayer who had gone through Esis destroying the people and their beliefs and faith and twisting the truth of the Order. The deceit of the Betrayer had brought the New Order into being, and now people blindly followed it. One day it might become a national obligation to belong to it. Then he sadly described the oppression of his people and their bitterness and hatred. But at the same time it surprised Cole that he could also speak of lighter things. Azriel and Lily counted the animals they passed, and he laughed as Lily told silly stories. Then both sang Old Order Hymns, much like the ones Lily had sung with Mable. Finally, the child slept comfortably beside Azriel, obviously trusting him. Zek said not a word, although the Lamean tried to engage him in conversation. *Why didn't he get mad that we tried to steal his cart? Why did he speak so harshly to Zek? Why is he so nice to us? Or is he really that nice?* Questions flurried through Cole's mind as they rode in silence. He thought of the Old Order priest that did his mother's funeral--the one who seemed nice on the outside, but on the inside must have been faking it the whole time. *How do I know whom to trust?*

216

That night they stopped next to a grove of trees, the cart concealed so that passing travelers wouldn't be able to see it. Azriel lifted Lily off the front of the cart and laid her on some hay in the back. As he covered her with a blanket she didn't wake up at all. Zek had also fallen asleep. Cole watched the man as he covered him in a blanket as well, observing Azriel's eyes as he studied Zek. He couldn't find a hint of hatred or annoyance in the Lamean.

"Tired?"

"Not really."

"I sure am."

"Sleep then," Cole said, trying to sound indifferent. *I'm not gonna trust this guy so easily. He's going to have to prove himself to me.*

"I'm on my way." Azriel set a pack against the back right wheel of the cart and disappeared from sight as he lay down. Cole still sat upright in the rear of the wagon. "Do you need a blanket, Cole?"

"I'm fine."

"You sure?"

"Yes. I *said* I was fine." *Just leave me alone.*

"Okay, Cole," Azriel said, his voice fading into a whisper.

The boy's mind raced as he sat under the grove of trees, hidden in the darkness. Not sure what to think, he went around to the other side of the cart and rested his head against the spokes of the opposite wheel as Azriel had done. The leaves hid the stars. *What do I need to see to believe?* It was the question that had plagued Cole throughout the day as he heard Azriel and Lily talk. He had challenged the Old Oder to send him proof, to show itself to him, to give him a reason to believe, and Azriel had entered his life. *Could he be an answer to my prayers? Or is this just someone else to let me down? The priest lied. Mom died. Dad left. Fenris left. Arissa had to grow up. Belen doesn't understand. Who will take care of me?*

"I think you're brave." Azriel slumped down beside him. "Mind if I sit?"

"You just did."

The man laughed gently. "You're a tough kid, Cole."

"I have to be."

"I know."

"I thought you were going to sleep."

"Couldn't help but think you had something on your mind."

I do. "I don't."

"If you say so."

217

"You're weird." Cole shut his eyes.

"I guess we are all different from each other. Perhaps it's what the Creator had in mind."

"*If* he's real."

"True."

"We can't be sure."

"No"–he paused–"if we were sure, there would be no need for faith."

"*Is* there a need for faith? What does faith *really* do anyway?" *Why am I talking to him?*

"It's what got you out here in the first place. What made you search for your dad and what got you the courage to ask your sister to join you. It's the hope . . . no, the *belief* in something better. Faith is the energy to take another step through this dark forest."

Cole felt an unexpected sense of relief wash over him. Something in Azriel's voice rang true, something he couldn't name. But something else also rang false–experience, the dark of the forest, and the reality of rejection.

"It's knowing that soon the sun will come up and push the darkness of night and fear and uncertainty into nothingness. It always does, you know?"

"I hope so," the boy said faintly. He remembered his conversation with Fenris on the roof before he left:

"At times it feels as if Esis is against you. That everyone has abandoned you, and you're the smallest thing in Oldaem. It may seem as if you don't matter and that there's no point in trying anymore. But that's a lie, Cole. You are loved. You matter. And you have a purpose."

"Don't give up, Cole," Azriel said, staring up into the night sky. "I think you're really brave. I hope I can show you a new side to the Old Order. And I can't wait to get to know you better." Cole thought he could see Azriel's eyes smile as he watched the man lift himself off the ground and return to his side of the cart. "Good night."

Cole sighed deeply as he shut his eyes again. There came that decision again: did he choose to trust people and do what was right, only to be disappointed in them later, once they ended up leaving him? Or did he just shut himself off from everyone and be lonely and hurt now, never able to experience what being loved felt like? He shook his head. *I have to keep trying. Fenris says there's always a point in trying.*

Creator . . . Comforter . . . Liberator . . . to whoever is listening . . . I guess I still don't know what to say. I don't know if you can hear someone so small like me, or if my prayers get all the way up to Aael-- if it's real. I don't know whom to trust. I don't know if trusting myself is enough. I want to like Zek. I want to like Azriel. I want to be happy. But I'm afraid if I'm happy, I'll lose everything again, like when I was happy before Dad left and Mom died. There are so many things to ask for. I guess my request is simple. Opening his eyes, he saw the fireflies floating in the night. *I ask for one day when my whole family can watch those dancing bugs in the sky again . . . just one more time . . . together . . . just one more picnic . . .*

Just before he fell asleep he noticed a shadow disappear behind a tree.

CHAPTER 29: DAKU

When Daku had been a young boy, he had loved going on adventures. His father's job required his frequent absence, and Daku's mother had died giving birth to him. It left him with an entire world to explore--alone. And he took full advantage of it. He would go off into the woods or would sit upon the docks and watch ships pull in, imagining where they had just returned from. Other times he would run up and down the streets, pretending to save the passersby from danger. Like most boys his age, he dreamed of becoming a Shepherd. Recruiters would periodically come to promote the life of a Shepherd. He remembered the STC staying in the local inn on their way to some interview in some region's capital city. Then he would watch the older boys and girls as they shipped off to distant tournaments. But Daku was never a romantic, dreaming of having a wife and children. Because his father was constantly gone, Daku had little experience of family life. Instead, he wanted to have something that was solely his. But all that changed once he met Aelwynne. *Don't think about her, Daku.*

Since he had left Vertloch, color seemed to have vanished from the world. The days had been foggy as they traveled south toward Sea Fort. Daku still had no idea where they were going or why, and he didn't ask.

Anything to get away from here.

It hadn't surprised him when Aelwynne had left him, but he was angry just the same. His wife had forsaken her vow and thrown everything away. She couldn't—or wouldn't–understand why he did what he did. But then he never gave her any opportunity. Daku hated her—just as he hated himself.

The three of them traveled on horseback. Daku's black steed stood taller than the others. Jorn's stallion was a little bit smaller in stature, more nimble and quick, but Daku preferred his own. Malvina sat upon a small white gelding. She never once looked back as they traveled. Neither did Jorn. Daku didn't either. Something inside him led him to believe it would be quite some time before they returned to Vertloch. He wondered if he ever would. No one had spoken a word beyond what was necessary during the past several days. Somehow the mission felt different than the previous one. While the last one had been important, this one seemed as if it would be incredibly difficult and incredibly significant for the future of Oldaem. While he had no idea what it involved, he really didn't care. He would complete it. It was all he had left.

"Are you well?" Malvina's voice broke his concentration.

"Yes, Mistress," Jorn replied immediately.

"Daku?"

"Yes, Mistress," he answered just as confidently.

"I want to make sure you both have as much strength as necessary"–she looked down–"you'll need it. I haven't been pushing you too hard the past few days, have I?"

"No, Mistress," they answered in unison.

"Good."

She does care about me. Daku's heart fluttered as he thought of all he and Malvina had gone through together. Of the trust that a Warden and a priestess had to place in each other. The fact that she had *chosen* him. The bond they shared. She would be enough for him–she would have to be. *I never should have trusted Aelwynne.*

No breeze circulated as they rode. It had become a hot, muggy, sunless day. The terrain was mostly flat with occasional large outcroppings jutting out from the level plains that stretched endlessly before them. The rugged landscape made difficult going for the horses, yet still they pressed on. Sometimes they galloped, occasionally slowed to a walk, but most of the time they proceeded with a steady trot. The trio didn't pass too many other travelers. When they did, they kept to themselves. Daku didn't make eye

220

contact with anyone. He kept his mind focused. Losing that was what always got him into trouble.

No longer. I am yours, Malvina.

"Smoke." Jorn's words caused Daku to pull back on his reins. The three came to a halt as they saw the black cloud billowing up in front of them. "What do you think it could be, Mistress?"

"Smells like death." Malvina shut her perfect eyes.

They listened intently as they heard screams and wailing in the distance. The hero Daku would have galloped over there immediately to save the weak, but the Warden Daku eyed Malvina carefully.

"We keep moving." She kicked her mare, and they continued onward, the sounds and smells of destruction and chaos drifting toward them from the west. It had become an increasingly familiar experience.

They kept the smoke to their right as they made their way south. Eventually they merged with a caravan of other travelers. As they approached it, Daku realized they were prisoners chained together: children, old men, women of all ages, and young girls. But no young men. The prisoners' clothes were worn and torn, their faces gaunt, and they smelled of smoke. As he passed them, Daku could see the misery and fear on their faces. The Oldaem soldiers showed no mercy to the old, feeble, or young, often shoving them forward when they fell behind. The guards kept them moving at a quick and steady pace. Daku recognized one more thing about the prisoners: they were all Lameans. As the journey continued, he noticed more and more columns of smoke rising up around them and could see other imprisoned Lameans in the distance all making their way to Sea Fort, probably to be auctioned off as slaves.

The New Order is taking control.

Daku realized that New Order forces, under the watchful care of Shepherds, were now razing Old Order villages. While he had no idea whether the Lameans had rebelled first, he did know that they had lost their freedom. Malvina's face was completely impassive as they passed by. He recognized that they could have easily massacred the Oldaem soldiers and freed the Lameans if they wanted to, but followers of the Three cared nothing for either Order. It was not their fight. Ignoring everything else, they focused only on the mission at hand.

The eyes of a small girl looked up into Daku's. His heart froze in his chest. *Bug.* Curly-haired and with almond-shaped eyes, she held

221

a rag doll close to her chest. It was the first time he had made eye contact with anyone in days, and now he wished he hadn't. *She looks just like Bug.* Daku plodded forward, leaving the girl in his dust, Malvina turning her face just enough so that he could see her disapproving profile.

Focus Daku.

"Did that bother you?" Jorn settled in beside him, Malvina in front.

"What?" *Get away from me.*

"The caravan of death." Jorn smiled, his teeth gray and crooked.

"No."

"You sure? Are you growing soft?"

"No." Daku's voice was hard.

"You left the inn that night to get away from Malvina. You broke her orders to visit your little wife. Can you truly be a Warden?"

"Yes." Daku showed no emotion.

"Prove it." He revealed a sharp knife from his coat pocket. "Kill the little girl."

"Wardens don't kill without a purpose." *Steady, Daku.*

"Fine. I'll do it." Daku's breath caught in his throat.

"Wardens to me." Malvina ordered. The two men immediately kicked their horses and caught up to her.

"Do you realize what we just witnessed?"

Neither spoke.

"The New Order wishes to control all of Esis. They subjugate the Old Order followers under their control. Probably they want to do the same to followers of the Three."

"I'd like to see them try," Jorn snarled.

"Yes. But we work to prevent that. Let me ride in silence." With a dismissive gesture, she pulled forward as Jorn and Daku fell back.

As Daku eyed Jorn, questions began to form in his mind, ones he couldn't suppress. "What do you think our next mission is?"

The other Warden didn't meet his eye. "We change the game."

"What?"

Jorn faced him. "Wouldn't you like to know?" Then he smiled grimly.

"She told you?" Daku felt anger rising in his gut.

He showed his teeth again. "She prefers me to you."

"That's a lie!"

"Is it? I've been with her longer. I've never betrayed her. I never married. I never break her rules. Of *course* she told me."

222

"Jorn. With me," Malvina called out, turning around only slightly to reveal a faint pout.

With a look of pure satisfaction, Jorn pulled along beside her, as she leaned and whispered something in his ear. For perhaps one of the first times ever, Daku heard them both laugh together. Jealousy, anger, rage, regret, and despair all whirled inside him as he gripped his reins harder. *One day, I'll kill you, Jorn. I am a Warden. I am her Warden. I am Malvina's Warden.* His mind drifted to memories of his training.

"You are a Warden."

"I am a Warden."

"You only obey."

"I only obey."

"What would you do if a child was in danger at the same time your priestess was in danger?"

"I would save my priestess."

"Your sister or your priestess?"

"My priestess."

"Your *wife,* or your priestess?"

My wife. "My priestess."

Van stood there, eying him. Daku looked away, hoping not to reveal himself or his true thoughts. They stood on the Tower's training grounds. When he looked around, he saw several other Warden Masters training apprentices. It was a one-on-one experience. Warden Masters were Wardens who outlived their priestesses. There weren't many. An old, hard man, Van's hair was perfectly white, and not a wrinkle marred his tight face.

"Are you ready?"

Daku raised his sword. "I'm ready."

They sparred for hours. Every move Daku performed, Van deflected. Every thrust, the Master returned more powerfully. Daku spent quite a bit of the duel on the ground, but every time he got back up again. As Van taunted and threatened him, Daku would keep fighting back. He noticed other Masters allowing their apprentices to finish for the day, but not Van.

It was night now, and still they fought. Sweat dripped down his face, his muscles ached.

"You must always be prepared, Daku." Van paced around him as he lay on the ground, panting and heaving, blood dripping down his face. Daku felt bile rising in his gut. "No matter what happens, you *must* always choose her. It's the only purpose of a Warden. If you don't, you won't survive. If you do choose her, you probably won't survive either. But survival isn't what makes a Warden a Warden. It's *identity*. Not yours, but hers."

"Van."

Daku turned and looked at a tall, Golden Priestess standing before him, a dark, rugged man lurking behind her in the shadows.

"Yes, Malvina. I'm in the middle of training."

"I want *him.*" Her golden eyes penetrated into Daku's being. Immediately he felt a connection with her. Then massive guilt swept over him. *Aelwynne.*

Off in the distance the city of Sea Fort stretched before them. They had covered great distance in very little time. Daku's muscles ached with every step of his horse. Still Malvina and Jorn rode together as he brought up the rear. *You'll love me again, Malvina. I'm sorry for disappointing you.* His mind drifted once again.

"Where were you?" Aelwynne asked, wiping her hands on a towel, her back to him, as he entered the cottage. The sky was a clear blue outside.

"Training." His head hurt, and he wasn't in the mood for any interrogation. He just wanted sleep.

"Alone?"

"No."

"Was *she* there?"

Daku walked past her into the next room, then sensed her following him. "She will be, Aelwynne, all the time. You're going to have to get used to it. She chose me over all the other apprentices. I am her Warden now. Mission briefings begin soon. I passed the training weeks ago!"

"I don't trust her."

Facing her, he could see the stress and fear in her eyes. "You trust *me*, though, don't you?"

224

She nodded, as a tear trickled down her cheek. "Yes, and that's what scares me. Every night for hours and hours you're gone. Some nights you don't even come home. I just wait here for you. Daku, do you *have* to do this?"

I wish I could tell you why. "Aelwynne, as a Warden, I know who I am. I finally have *something* that is *mine.*"

"I'm yours." Love starred him back in the face, leaving him speechless for a moment. In his mind he saw them standing upon the shores of Najoh getting married. It had been the happiest day of his life.

"You know what I mean. I'm *good* at this. I have a clear purpose." *I do this for you.*

As she stood before him and looked deeply into his eyes, he somehow felt that in her eyes he saw reflected a loving husband, a protector . . . a hero. It was that hero mentality that had chosen this path for his life. He wished to save *her.* She leaned in and kissed him. "I trust you. Just . . . don't lose yourself, Daku."

But for Malvina he was untouchable, strong, a Warden. He *belonged.*

She's good for me, too. Malvina is good for me.

They reached the Sea Side Inn in Sea Fort while it was still black as night outside and had gotten two rooms. As they stood in the eating room, Daku heard whispers about the Royal Shepherd Demas' disappearance and stories of war and politics. Malvina went immediately to her room, and Daku and Jorn to theirs. Daku lay upon his bed in silence, staring up at the ceiling, feeling nothing. No longer did he feel any sadness for Aelwynne. Nor did he feel fatigue or annoyance or fear. In fact, he literally felt nothing. *I am a Warden.* He wasn't sure what that meant anymore. Had he lost himself? What had happened to the little boy who wanted to be a hero, who defended the bullied? *Bug.* And what about the man who had stood upon the shores of Najoh with his beautiful wife? Who was he? If he saw himself in a mirror, would he even recognize the heroic boy, or would he only see a golden Warden? Did he even have anything left of himself to lose anymore?

The door closed. As he sat up he realized that he hadn't even noticed the door had opened or that Jorn had gone. Silently he slipped out into the dark hallway and toward Malvina's room. He could hear hushed voices inside. No one else was in the hallway. He pressed his ear against the wooden door. *You shouldn't be here. You should trust her. You should go back.*

"What is your name?" she asked.

"Jorn."

"What are you?"

"I am a Warden."

"Whom do you love?"

"Malvina."

"You are mine. You belong to me. You love me. You serve me. It's the way. Forsake them. Forsake them all."

"Always, Mistress."

Daku felt chills race up and down his body.

"Whom will you follow?"

"Only you."

"Whom will you serve?"

"Only you."

"Kiss me, Jorn."

"Yes, Mistress."

Daku nearly broke down the door, but he managed to back away. He was hanging in the gap between two worlds that didn't want him, that didn't need him. No longer was he an explorer, a hero, a husband—he didn't belong anywhere. And it was his fault. That night, he didn't sleep.

One day, I'll kill you Jorn. I am a Warden. I am her Warden. I am Malvina's Warden.

CHAPTER 30: SAYLA

The constant traveling was getting tiresome. First, they had gone to Sea Fort and then back to Woodlands Academy. Now, they were on their way to Westervale, and Sayla knew that they were not anywhere near done once they got there. From Westervale, the Shepherd of Defense students would go to the Limestone Cliffs, drop off the slaves who were to work there, and then head straight to the Capital to see the games.

Sayla was spending long, hard, exhausting hours on a horse, a beautiful brown beast named Valor, her favorite among those in the stable at Woodlands Academy. It made the traveling a little bit better.

Truthfully, the journey itself was the least of her problems. She knew she was being paranoid, but she couldn't help it. Every village they passed through, every group they saw, she stared into strangers' faces, wondering yet dreading to see one she recognized from her dream. All she knew was that she couldn't let another person get hurt if she was able to stop it.

If I find the little boy, will I be able to aid him? Will I somehow run into Galen? Can I even stop that old man from being murdered? She had virtually nothing to go on. Sayla had done a lot of thinking during the past few days on horseback. Of course, she would occasionally speak to her companions, but often they would lapse into silence. She had had a lot of time to ponder those dreams. In fact, it was all she thought about lately.

While it seemed as if her dreams were little more than a difficult problem, just maybe they would prove to be a good thing if she could save those people. *Of course, the next question here is how I happened to dream them.* Not once, but twice, Sayla had dreamt of someone or some event that had come true. The first time she might have been able to write off as a coincidence if she had not so vividly seen Royal Shepherd Demas' face in the dream. But knowing exactly what Shale and Shepherd Albright were going to say about the mission they were currently on? Something was definitely wrong with her.

Sayla had been toying with an idea, but she hadn't decided if it made sense yet or not.

"Are any of you very familiar with the scriptures of the New Order?" It was a general question, but after a couple hours of silence, the group was ready to discuss anything.

"I know a little," Zayeed began. His scrawny legs barely seemed to reach the stirrups of the black and white horse he rode. "I've attended a few worship services, like on holidays and stuff."

"That doesn't mean you're very familiar with them, stupid," Aveline interjected. "It just means you know about as much as any New Order toddler."

"Oh, yeah and how much do you know?"

"I didn't claim to be an expert!" She pulled up beside Sayla. "But I know enough. It's not as if any of it really affects my life one-way or the other. After they created the Tower, the Liberator betrayed the Comforter and the Creator and killed them. The One, abhorred by the actions of the Liberator, battled him and cast him down the

Tower and into Esis. Now he roams the world wreaking havoc on the innocents, killing children, blah, blah, blah."

"You're such a devout follower," Shale snickered.

Aveline raised her hands in protest. "Hey, I don't waste my time on things that have little relevance for my day-to-day life. When the One descends the Tower and saves all humanity or whatever, well that's a battle I'll want to see. Until then, I'm not too worried. I got other things on my mind."

Sayla agreed with that to a point. She had never really thought of her deity as one who meddled in people's business, and she liked it that way just fine. Normally, she could take care of herself. On the other hand, she attributed her success as a Shepherd trainee to the One, and she could not imagine existence without him.

"Why do you wanna know, anyway?" Oghren shot an annoyed look at Sayla.

"I was just making conversation," she replied with a shrug. She brushed her hair out of her eyes. It had become damp and stringy from sweat. "What about, like, the ancient seers? Weren't there some people who, oh, I don't know, saw … things?"

"You mean, like, the future?" Zayeed asked.

"Something like that."

"That's sure some strange conversation you're making there, Sayla," Shale chuckled and winked at her.

"Ooh! Pick me, pick me!" Tali's horse almost bounced up and down with her. Grunt, who had been silent thus far, had to edge his horse away to avoid getting kicked by the girl's flailing feet. She began speaking as if she were reciting text from a book. "Every few generations, the One would bless an especially devout follower with the gift of prophecy. They would have visions and stuff and would advise the leaders. You're right, Sayla, they were called seers 'cause they could see things."

Aveline cracked a smile. "And how do you know that?"

"My dad's a priest for the New Order," Tali said simply.

Everyone stared at her, open-mouthed.

"And you waited until now to mention that?" Zayeed exclaimed.

"It's not something I just tell anybody, silly! Although my dad is the nicest guy ever. But still—not usually relevant."

"But," Sayla tried to sound casual, "do you think there are still any out there now?"

"If you wanna have your fortune read, you can probably find some strange woman to do it," Zayeed laughed, "but I don't think you need an actual prophet for that."

"That gift died out a long time ago," Tali answered confidently. "I guess the One hasn't found anyone amazing enough to receive it in a while."

Sayla wasn't so sure about the whole "amazing" thing. But if her dreams were a gift, or curse, or whatever, then they had to come from somewhere, and she figured a celestial being was a good place to start. *It's a theory, anyway.*

As they rode along, the scenery began to change. They had left the hill country behind, and the forest had begun to thin out. Now and then, they passed through little villages. Currently living near the border between Rahvil and Efil, Sayla had been to the region of Rahvil before. There wasn't much to say about it. Rahvil was not really known for any industry except for the mining in the Limestone Cliffs, but that was at the northern edge of the region.

The village they were passing through now looked more like a few ragged buildings strung together by an intersecting street. Children had been playing outside when they approached it, but the street all but cleared as they began to pass through. *This is not a place you stay overnight. They want you to move through as quickly as you can.* The town felt almost abandoned even though scattered faces peered through smudged windows, or laundry had been left to dry on a clothesline. It was almost worse than if the village had actually been deserted.

"Ugh, a Lamean village." Shale's comment confirmed what Sayla had suspected. It was a free Lamean village. Not many of them remained since most Lameans had been enslaved, but here, where Lamea used to be located before the civil war, there still existed a few scattered pockets of free, but poor Lameans. Sayla figured that would eventually disappear altogether.

Aveline took a swig out of her water canteen. "Have you ever thought about what you would do if someone actually did know your future? Would you really wanna know?"

"Who wouldn't?" Oghren replied. "Especially when your future is as bright as mine. All I need to know is which region will be lucky enough to have me as their Shepherd." His horse nickered as if amused.

"At least you *have* a future to look forward to," Grunt muttered, the first thing he had said in hours.

229

"What?" Oghren asked.

"Nothing." Shaking his head, Grunt looked into the windows of a closed shop as they rode by.

Oghren followed his gaze. "Oh, you mean these Lameans? Don't tell me you're pitying them." A frown crossed his face. "You are, aren't you? Lamean lover, Lamean lover!"

Grunt turned beet red and slumped against his saddle. "Never mind."

Oghren continued to berate him, but Sayla urged her horse ahead a little and ignored them both out. *If Grunt wants to let his emotions get in the way, who am I to stop him?* She felt as if she stayed too close to him, she might catch it like a disease. *I have enough to worry about as it is.*

Soon they left the village, and Sayla breathed a sigh of relief. She had not liked the oppressiveness that clung to it. Better not to think about such things, anyway.

Not much existed between Woodlands Academy and Westervale. Really, the only places to stop were the kind of small villages they had been through along the way. Now, they rode along a well-trodden road with large jagged rock outcroppings on their right and a forest of trees on their left. Unfortunately, the rocks did nothing to block the midday sun from roasting the back of Sayla's neck or making her constantly thirsty. *The glorious life of a Shepherd of Defense.* She was tired of feeling as if she was swimming in her own sweat. It didn't help that she had to wear black all the time.

Much to her surprise, Shale, who had been leading the group, pulled back a bit and began riding in line with her. She really hoped he couldn't smell her as well as she did herself.

"So do you wish you could?"

"I'm sorry?" *Just keep talking with that melodious voice of yours.*

"See the future."

"What? No, now who would want to do that? That would be ... weird ..." She busied herself by untying her hair and quickly retying it, praying the whole time that he was not looking at the perspiration pouring from her armpits. *Change the subject, change the subject.* "I was just trying to take a little boredom out of this long day of riding."

"Really? Well, it was an interesting conversation." Shale's dimples glistened in the sun. "I mean, I don't really care that much about religion stuff, but I liked thinking about who I'm going to be someday."

230

"I like to think about that, too," she admitted. It was what had gotten her through those lonely nights as a child when she felt like she didn't belong anywhere. "I used to always imagine myself as a Shepherd of Defense, going on adventures and saving people and stuff."

"And here you are. If you make it through next year, you'll become just that." There was always that "if," though. Sayla did not like to leave things up to chance. "You might even become as awesome as me."

Sayla tried to look at him without letting on that she was doing so. He was a handsome 20-year-old, tall, and muscular. About to graduate in just a few short weeks, he could see the finish line, and every bit of his confidence exuded that fact. "Maybe someday," she said finally.

Shale studied her and hesitated for a moment. His stormy gray eyes made Sayla's heart want to explode. "May I tell you a secret?"

"Of course." *Just don't ask me to do the same.*

"Well," he began somberly. Leaning in closely, he said in just above a whisper, "I wasn't always this awesome."

Impossible, Sayla thought, but she let him continue.

"See, I'm from this really big family, ancient roots in Dagonfell. Lots of important people. My great grandfather on my dad's side was the Regent of Jaron. My mother's brother was one of the generals responsible for the annexation of Kaya after that war 20 years ago. One of my sisters works in the king's palace, and the list just goes on and on. But no one ever thought I would amount to much."

Sayla definitely could identify with that. As the youngest of three daughters, she was always the odd one out. Both of her sisters were much older than her and had such different interests. Everyone ran the family fabric business. It was all they cared about. But Sayla had always been bored out of her mind even thinking about it.

She remembered the day she left for Woodlands Academy. Her parents had kissed her goodbye, but shed no tears. They treated her kindly enough, and she had been cordial in return, but nobody pretended that they would miss each other. Sayla had never been a good fit with the family she had been born into.

"But then," Shale continued, "I got accepted into the Shepherd academy." His eyes glittered with the memory. "Not just anyone can do that. I was the only one in my family in years. Well, I have a cousin who's also a Shepherd ... but she did some stuff ... we don't really talk about her anymore. So it doesn't count. And now my family is proud of me. Now they can tell me apart from all my other siblings. Now they see how great I am and always was."

Sayla bit her lip. That was what she wanted--to stand out, to be respected, to be understood. A thought rose like bile in the back of her throat, *Dreams that tell the future--that makes you stand out.* Quickly she squashed the thought like a pesky insect. *No, dreams that tell the future make you a freak.* "We have a lot in common, you and I." She offered a kind smile.

"Oh, I know." Shale beamed.

"So what is it you see in your future then?"

"Well, hopefully you."

Sayla giggled like a child.

The moment was short-lived, though, as the traveling party encountered a fallen tree blocking the road. Shale snapped back into his unbearably adorable leader persona.

"Okay, troops, we need to move this if want to continue on our way!" They had no choice. On the left the branches of the trees interlaced closely together and the dense underbrush would be impossible to get the horses through. On the right the rocks rose up into an impenetrable wall.

Everyone dismounted except for Sayla and Oghren, who were tasked with using their horses to haul the tree trunk out of the way once the time came. Sayla sat back in her saddle and held the reins of Tali's horse while the others tied ropes around the log in preparation of rigging a system to move it.

As she waited, Sayla tried to cover her yawn. Not wanting to seem bored while the others were working, she would have traded places with any of them in a heartbeat. But what she really wanted to do was continue her conversation with Shale. Sayla had had feelings for people before, one in particular that she was still having trouble getting over, but none of them had ever panned out. No boy had ever felt the same way toward her as she had toward him. Until now, apparently. *As soon as this stupid tree is out of the way, we're picking right up where we left off. I'm making sure of that.*

Unexpectedly, a few loose pebbles landed on top of her hair and shoulders. Sayla glanced up into the blazing sun. *Must have come from the rocks over there.*

And then everything became chaos.

Someone above her shouted, "Now!" and more and more pebbles bounced against Sayla's shoulders. The figures of men leaping down at them from the rock formations suddenly blotted out her view of the sun.

"It's a trap!" Shale shouted as he frantically ran for his saddlebag that held his sword.

Screaming came from somewhere, but Sayla couldn't identify who. She had no time to think. Instinct took over as she reached for the sword in her own saddlebag. Out of the corner of her eyes she saw Tali and Aveline wildly fighting two of the masked men who had seemingly appeared out of nowhere.

"You think you can persecute us?" one of them shouted. "Take our children? Kill our wives?"

Another yelled, "See how it feels to be the ones suffering!"

"For the Creator!"

Lameans, Sayla thought instantly, *we're being attacked by free Lameans.* The world was a frenzy. Although she had always been taught that in a battle everything would slow down, now she felt as if it had all sped up, as if there was not enough time to take everything in. Fighting spread all around her.

Thwack! Sayla turned as an arrow rooted itself into a tree trunk right behind her. Her horse reared, and too late she realized that the arrow had grazed Valor's hip. Flung out of the saddle, she landed painfully against the tree with the arrow in it.

Suddenly, the stars in her vision added to the confusion of the moment. Now everything slowed. She heard shouts from her friends as they saw her go down, but they seemed blurred and distant. No one had time to rush to her aid-- they were all too busy defending themselves.

A shriek came from Oghren as an arrow embedded itself into his shoulder, tossing him off his horse. Sayla wanted to help him. The closest to him, she was the only one not fighting off an attacker. But she could not make her limbs obey. Nor could she see clearly the faces of anyone. In fact, her vision was clouding. She needed to help her friends, but she couldn't remember exactly why.

For a fleeting moment, she thought sluggishly, *At least I didn't see this coming.* And then everything went black.

CHAPTER 31: COLE

Cole ached all over. He had many things to complain about. For one, his butt was numb from all the riding in the back of the cart. Lily had dominated the front seat, Zek had no interest in it, and Cole didn't feel like fighting her. As the cart traveled westward, the farmlands started turning more into rolling hills, and the bumps and turns and rumblings increased with each and every hilltop. Another thing that irritated him was the conversation. It was as if Lily couldn't get enough Old Order mythology. Every time Azriel presented another story, Zek and Cole would roll their eyes. Zek would sing old farming folk songs at the top of his lungs to drown out the stories. Usually once that happened, Azriel and Lily would join in, and Zek would then lay down, burying his head in the hay. The summer heat also bothered Cole, leaving him bathed in sweat. Then at night, it was cold. It made no sense. His clothes were dirty, he was always hungry, he never had enough sleep, he was getting annoyed with everyone, and he just wanted to find his father. Sometimes, after becoming tired of sitting, he would run along beside the cart. Whenever he did that, Zek jumped out too, and darted ahead of the cart, as if to show to Cole he was faster. Even the cow was annoying.

She just moos and moos.

Lily and Azriel had become inseparable. She became attached to him closer than he had ever seen her with anyone, even Belen.

He's not your dad, Lily. Nor is he Fenris. The man will just leave us like everyone else.

The hills seemed endless. Cole spent most of his time talking to Zek in the back of the cart. Azriel would try to engage Zek and him in conversation, but the older boy would usually answer in one or two word responses, and Cole would follow suit. Something about Azriel bothered Cole, though he couldn't quite put his finger on it. Perhaps it was the fact that he recognized if he opened up even a little, he would be as intrigued by Azriel as Lily was. That would be dangerous.

It's safer in the shadows. If he had learned anything from Zek, it was that truth.

After several days of more of the same, they reached the top of a hill, and the view was breathtaking. At the bottom of the valley lay a clear blue lake, one that reminded him of Middle Lake. Tall trees surrounded the water, and everything around and beside it glowed an emerald green. High green grass swayed as the wind from the ocean beyond whipped through it. They all recognized this would be a good place to stop for a while. Azriel unhitched Odessa from the cart, and the animal rested in the shade of a tree. Zek went off to one side of the lake and Azriel toward the other. They both acted as if they had something on their minds.

Cole approached the water and began to drink. As he gulped down the cool water, it soothed his throat. Lily carefully did the same beside him. Suddenly he realized they hadn't been alone together since their conversation in the barn.

"Why do you like him so much?" The question had been plaguing Cole since they had met Azriel.

She smiled. "He's like . . ."

"Fenris?"

"Yeah," she giggled.

"Besides that. I mean, I think we would both rather have Fenris actually here. There *has* to be another reason."

"He's positive. He's fun. He's happy. He's brave. He's nice."

"But is he *really?*"

"Yes!" she exclaimed confidently.

"But how can you know for sure?"

He knew her answer before she spat it out. "Faith."

"Faith. Of course."

"Why don't you like him?"

"I don't know if I *don't* like him and I don't know if I *do* like him."

"Well, what *do* you know?" she asked, her big eyes twinkling with relief.

"I don't know." He hung his head. Nothing had really made sense to him since he had watched them drag his mother's body from the lake. Things had been so much easier when he had been younger. He didn't feel like a kid anymore. It was as if Esis didn't allow children to be children.

It had to be someone's fault.

"You know, you should give him a chance. Go talk to him."

"I've talked to him."

"And you don't think he's smart?"

"I do think he's smart."

"Oh, do whatever you want. I'm done trying to force you to do things." Resting her head on the grass, she stared up at the clouds. Cole lay beside her.

235

There was so much he wanted to say to her. How brave he thought she was and how proud of her he was. He longed to tell her how happy he was that both Azriel and Zek were with them and that he was glad that he had asked her to go with him, especially since he was scared and felt alone and tiny all at the same time. But even more than those things, he wished he could explain that he *wanted* to believe in the Old Order even as he dreaded having anything to do with them. He still missed their mother every day, and wouldn't have been able to do the trip without her, his sister, because every time he looked at her he remembered a time that he had felt truly *loved* by his whole family. Lily was his hope. But instead he said nothing as he lay in the shadows while she rested in the sun.

I guess the light doesn't shine on everyone.

Cole slept for a few hours on the soft grass. When he woke up Lily was gone, and he noticed Azriel, eyes closed, sitting in shallow water in his pants. His shirt lay on the shore next to Cole.

"You're awake."

"Yeah. Where's everyone?" Cole asked.

"Lily went for a walk around the lake. I sent Zek to keep her safe."

"They usually avoid each other," Cole said with surprise.

"It's good for them to spend some time together." Azriel turned and looked at Cole. "Besides, I wanted to spend some time with *you.*"

"Why?" the boy asked suspiciously.

"Because I like you."

"You don't know me," he replied coolly.

"Sure I do. I know that you're 12 years old, that you're really stubborn, like me. And I know that you have a loving family."

Had.

"I know that you would do anything for Lily," the Lamean continued. "I know that you feel helpless, and that it's a very confusing thing to feel." He paused.

Cole stared at him, stunned. "How do you know those things?"

"Because I've felt the same way, too."

A silence settled among them as the sun started its descent for the day. Azriel pushed himself up from the water and dried himself off with his shirt. Then, after pulling it over his head, he took a seat beside Cole. "My mom loved watching the sunsets with me. After a

236

long day plowing the fields, she would take me out to the barn, and we'd climb on top of it and just watch the sun go down. I *loved* being up there."

Cole sighed and glanced at the man whose gaze seemed focused on something far away. It was as if he was on top of that barn right now. In his mind the boy returned to *his* own roof--*his* favorite spot. In his memory he could see Middle Lake Academy and the people of the City of the Flowers. He saw Fenris and his Father, then Belen, Arissa, and the priest, and finally his mother. "My mom loved fireflies."

Azriel glanced at him. "She did?"

"Yeah." Cole looked down.

"They are pretty."

"She always thought they danced at night."

"Your mother was pretty smart, huh? Did she have a big imagination?"

"Yeah. She used to."

"I'm really sorry about what happened to your mom, Cole. I wish I could take the pain away."

Cole studied his face, and it really did seem as if he meant it. "Well, you can't."

"I know." Azriel looked down at his hands and curled them into fists, not out of anger, but out of resignation.

After a second, Cole heard himself say, "I'm sorry you lost your parents, too."

"Thanks, Cole." Azriel put his arm around his shoulder, and a sense of safety and relief washed over the boy. He remembered the last time he had seen Fenris, feeling his strong arms around him, the promise that his brother had asked him to keep.

"Azriel, do you believe there will be a time, when . . . when someday, we won't lose people anymore? When everyone will be together again?" A lump formed in his throat.

His eyes twinkled. "I *know* there will be."

Momentarily resting his head on the man's shoulder, Cole tried hard to stop the tears from falling. "I *hope* you're right. Otherwise life is . . . just . . . too . . . hard." They sat there in silence for a few seconds, until Cole pulled away. "Why do you always gotta be such a sissy?" Standing, he announced, "I'm going for a walk." Without waiting for a response, he started around the lake, trying to get as much distance as he could between him and Azriel. Spotting something running and jumping at the opposite end of the lake, he assumed it was Lily and wondered what had become of Zek. Then he felt an acorn bounce off his head. Glancing up, he saw the boy smiling mischievously at him from the branches of a tall tree. The boy scurried down and hung from the bottom branch.

"I saw you snuggling with Azriel."

Cole was embarrassed. "He's such a sissy."

"Takes one to know one." Zek dropped down to the ground. "Wanna swim?"

"Okay."

With that Zek ripped off his shirt and raced into the lake, throwing himself beneath the surface. Cole struggled behind, self-consciously removing his shirt and noticing how pale his thin stomach was. He crossed his arms in front of his chest as he slowly waded into the water. It was freezing. They both held their shirts in their arms. Suddenly it didn't make sense to Cole as to why they had bothered to take them off, but he just shrugged. Now that the sun was setting, a cool breeze began to stir. Cole dove into the water to catch Zek who had already begun swimming across the expanse of the lake.

While Cole wasn't the strongest swimmer, living near a lake his entire life had made him used to it. Zek slowed down to allow him to catch up. They bobbed up and down, treading water.

"Feels good just to let go, right?"

"Yeah." Cole looked at Zek who spat water at him.

"Hey!" he splashed back, and for a while the two of them tussled in the lake. At times Zek would push him down, as Cole struggled to breathe, but he always pulled him back up. They splashed and laughed and dove down deep, trying to touch the muddy bottom, and were never able to. Then they attempted to catch fish with their hands and were also unsuccessful. Finally, tired, they floated on their backs, looking up at the stars about to fill the heavens.

"Do you miss your family?" Cole asked.

"Yeah. Do you?"

"Yeah."

"What were you and Azriel talking about?"

Cole swallowed. "He was blabbering about Old Order stuff, as usual." He didn't want Zek to be mad at him.

"It's all he ever talks about. I can't wait to get away from that guy."

Cole hesitated. "Yeah, me neither."

"We could run away from him tonight while he sleeps. Grab Odessa and get out of here."

"Lily would never go for it."

"Yeah."

Zek looked annoyed. Cole wondered if deep inside the boy wished it were just the two of them. But he would never leave his sister behind.

"Once we get to Azmar, Azriel will head back."

"Yeah. We're almost to that bridge, I think."

"Yeah."

"Cole, may I ask you something?"

"Sure." *He never usually is this talkative.*

"What . . . is your purpose?"

The question caught him off guard. "What do you mean?"

"Do you ever think about it? Like, what you're destined to do for Oldaem."

At first Cole decided that he hadn't ever really considered the idea. He was just trying to keep what was left of his family together. But then he realized that he had, up on his roof. Even he did have dreams, though mostly unspoken, dreams of being great like his father and even better than Fenris. "Yeah, I guess. I want to do something great."

"Why?"

The boy paused. "Because I've always been in the middle."

"You want to climb out?"

Cole nodded, a lot of questions racing through his mind. He wanted Zek to like him. Though he didn't know why, he yearned for his approval. And he realized that he had done a lot of things he never would have thought of doing just because Zek had done them. Never had he had a friend like Zek—but then he really hadn't ever had any friend. And it seemed as though Zek genuinely desired to be his friend. At the same time a deeper part of him wished that all three of them could all just get along.

"So, why don't you like Azriel?"

Zek sunk into the water, popped back up, and studied Cole. "Are you kidding me?"

"Well, like, just because he's Old Order?"

"No! Because he thinks he knows everything! He thinks he's *so* perfect. All he does is judge me and never wants to have any fun."

As Cole thought about all the time Azriel and Lily spent laughing together, it didn't seem to him as if the man refused to enjoy life. But he let Zek continue.

"He's a goodie-two-shoes. We could have had so much more stuff without him with us. I just don't trust him. No one is that nice all the time. He's hiding something. I can feel it."

"You really think so?"

"Absolutely. Just watch him for a while. You'll see what I mean."

Their eyes met. Zek seemed absolutely sure he knew what he was talking about. Cole liked that about him. The boy was confident. Also he had a way of making him feel safe. He realized Zek had gone through a lot and *had* to be tough to survive. So did he. They were more alike than Cole had originally thought. Maybe if Zek had lived such a great, comfortable life like Azriel, he would be soft and mushy too. Cole understood why Zek was the way he was. And Cole realized he would eventually have to make a choice as to whom to be like. However, it seemed as if Esis was making that decision for him. Soft people didn't survive in Oldaem. They got ripped apart and killed and stolen from and drowned and left behind. No, he wouldn't let that happen to him.

It's safer in the shadows.

"Come on, let's keep swimming."

Cole followed him as he quickly swam across the rest of the lake. They were out of breath by the time they reached the opposite shore. Lily looked at them wide-eyed as they emerged from the water.

"Come swimming with us, Lily!" Zek called out from the water.

"No, thank you." She sat, her knees tucked against her chest, arms wrapped around them.

"Come on, Lily, the water feels great!" her brother shouted. He had had a fun day.

"No."

"You're so *boring!*" Zek protested.

"Lily, you *love* swimming! And you need a bath, you stinky duck!"

"You're a stinky duck!" she fired back.

"Don't make me pull you in!"

The girl darted away from them both and toward Azriel who was a ways off and up the hill, the shadow of Odessa behind him. Cole had never seen her run so fast.

"Why doesn't she want to swim?" Cole looked at Zek.

"She seems scared."

Eventually, once they were dried off and settled in for the night, after having eaten fish caught by Azriel and listening to more Old Order tales while Zek built a mud castle, Azriel led them all in prayer. Cole kept his eyes open as he prayed. He noticed Azriel's eyes were closed reverently, as were Lily's. Zek was lying with his back on the grass, staring uncomfortably up at the sky.

I wonder what he's thinking.

That night Cole dreamed of his family and of a time when he was little. Lily had been just a baby and Belen hadn't even been born yet. They all sat at the kitchen table: Fenris, Arissa, his dad with Lily in his arms, and Cole. His mom stood making breakfast, her hair falling loosely around her shoulders. Laughter filled the house as his mother ruffled Cole's hair.

"What do you want to be when you grow up?" she asked, her beautiful eyes twinkling.

"I want to be just like Dad." Cole answered with full confidence.

"You'd be wise to be just like Mom," Brulis responded, a wide grin spreading across his face.

"Your father is right. I'm better." She smiled that sweet confident smile, the one that made Cole know everything would be okay. The smile that warmed up every room during the winter, made his knee hurt less when he fell and scratched it, that stopped Arissa and Fenris from fighting, and that made Cole know everything would turn out all right in the end.

He looked around the room and saw his family together, hugging and laughing and smiling and living happily. For an instant he felt as if it was really happening.

Then it changed, and he found himself standing in his house alone with his mother. Terror struck him as he saw her. A memory tugged at his consciousness, but he couldn't bring it to the front of his mind. Yet whatever it was it made him fear her. She started toward him, arms outstretched, an almost recognizable gleam in eyes. Screaming, he ran from her as fast as he could. But he couldn't escape. Her dead menacing eyes kept getting closer.

Suddenly, he looked at the doorway and saw Azriel sadly watching there. Blood dripped down his arm and pooled into his palms. Standing beside Azriel was Zek, anger in his face. Then Azriel walked out of the house and so did Zek. Cole followed them outside. They walked single file for a while until the road forked. Both paths were clouded and misty, a golden haze obscuring the paths' destinations. Zek stood on one path, Azriel on the other. Now safely away from his mother, Cole paused at the fork, contemplating the two paths before him. But when he looked behind him he saw with horror his house exploding in a giant ball of fire before crumbling to the ground in ashes, his mother's dead body lying on the ground. Both relief and regret filled him. Then he realized that another dead figure lay beside her, but Cole couldn't make out who it was.

"What do I do?"

They continued to travel, Cole forgetting his dream, unable to remember even the smallest detail. They left the lake behind them, and as they rattled along in the cart, the wind picked up and whipped around them, the grass along the road billowing back and forth. Odessa had seemed to find new energy after resting at the lake, and her pace increased. Azriel mentioned that they would be nearing the massive bridge soon, one that stretched across the ocean channel that nearly cut Oldaem in half. The bridge was well traveled. Usually Soma soldiers manned the east entrance, colleting a toll, and Isprig soldiers manned the west one. The tolls went to the Capital where Garrus, Royal Shepherd of State, would use it to repair roads and bridges all over Oldaem. Azriel mentioned that he had crossed the bridge many times. Zek said he did once when he was very little, but he didn't really remember it. Cole never had. As they neared the cliffs, the wind began to intensify. And with the wind came shouts and cries.

"What is going on?" Lily asked, a hint of fear in her eyes.

Azriel pulled on the reins as they sat and listened. The sound of shouting and swords clashing and men groaning filled their ears. "Get off the cart." he calmly told them.

"What's wrong?" Zek asked.

"*Get off the cart,*" Azriel repeated firmly. Lily hopped off, her legs wobbly. Cole and Zek followed suit as Azriel dismounted as well. "Get in the grass and lay down. I'm going to see what's going on. Don't move."

"But . . ."

"Now!" Azriel disappeared up the hill, as Cole took his sister's hand and led her toward a patch of tall grass.

"It sounds like battle," the girl squeaked.

"It sounds like war," Zek answered, standing in the road.

"Zek, get in the grass," Cole ordered.

"No way, I want to see what is going on."

"Are you crazy?" Lily demanded. "Azriel told us to . . ."

"I don't care what he says," Zek fired back as he disappeared after the Lamean.

A silence settled between Cole and Lily as they hid in the swaying weeds. He could hear their hearts pounding. Flies buzzed around a dead animal not too far away from them, as birds squawked and frogs croaked. Odessa sat down in the road, still harnessed to the cart. They continued to hear the noise of battle, as it grew louder and louder. Screams and curses came from beyond the hill, metal clanging against metal and the duller thud of metal on wood.

I wonder if the bridge is under attack.

"Lily, stay here."

"You're leaving me?" she panicked.

"Just *stay* here!" He stood up. "Watch Odessa. Be brave." Cole felt his legs shaking, and he could hear her begging him to come back. His hand brushed against Odessa's furry face and wet nose as he passed her. Then, when he reached the top of the hill, his heart caught in this throat. Stretched below him, the road led to a massive bridge, and upon the bridge an intense battle raged.

Nearest him the wind whipped the emerald banners with the Oldaem crest. Beyond them he noticed the purple flags of Leoj. *The war is here now?* He had no idea the fighting would have already reached the shores of Oldaem. Soldiers of both sides lie sprawled across the bridge, and more dead bodies lined the road leading up to it. Cole couldn't tell which side had the upper hand. Smoke billowed from the burning guard towers at both ends of the bridge, and Cole couldn't even tell where each country had set up their main bases. It was as if both sides were fighting from both sides, the bridge trembling under the weight of all the men. Zek and Azriel were nowhere to be seen. Cole's gaze shifted to the channel. Rocky cliffs stretched along both sides of it, making a water crossing difficult. More soldiers were spilling out from the Leojian ships pulled up along the western shore. Brandishing their weapons, screams in their throats, they scrambled up toward the bridge. Oldaem's forces rolled boulders down on them and bombarded them with fire arrows. But the Leojian troops managed to maneuver around behind them. Where they were coming from, Cole could not tell. A couple ships erupted in flames. Blood had spilled all over the bridge and the cliffs and on the grass and the road. Bile rose in his throat. *What do I do?*

"Hey, you!"

243

Cole turned quickly to see a soldier in purple armor running at him to his left, the Leoj crest upon his breastplate.

"Are you an Oldaem spy or scout?" He held a sword to Cole, blood dripping down from his helmet.

"No . . . I." Cole could barely speak.

"Is that your cart?" The Leojian pointed at it and Odessa still sitting in the middle of the road.

"I don't know."

"Either way you're dead." Just as the soldier swung his sword, Cole bolted. He ran right straight into an Oldaem archer who shot an arrow into the face of the Leojian soldier.

"Get out of here, kid," the archer said, racing toward the bridge, five more following behind him, a couple favoring injured legs.

His heart racing, Cole looked around frantically, unsure of where to go. He ran back to where he had left Lily in the grass. She was gone. "Lily!" he whispered hoarsely. Then he dropped to the ground and hid as more soldiers emerged from his left and collided with opposing forces. They killed each other in front of him. Tears ran down his face. *Someone help.*

A firm grip pulled him up. "This way!" Glancing over his shoulder, he met Azriel's urgent gaze. Relief washed over him as he looked and saw Zek and Lily waving him down toward the slope leading to the cliff bottom. Azriel grabbed the cart, and they all hurried, as fast as Odessa could trot, away from the bridge and south along the cliff front.

As they fled from the battle down the steep slope, Cole heard himself cry out, "The war has reached our shores?"

"It looks that way," Azriel answered calmly, his fist firmly gripping the reins.

"Why? How? I thought Oldaem was too powerful to let other ships even get near."

"The fact that Leoj is attacking from the south means they sailed all the way around Oldaem's eastern edge," Zek added. "Shouldn't Kaya be protecting our borders? What is going on?"

"I'm not sure." Still Azriel seemed unperturbed while Lily stared at them in fear.

"Where are we going?" she asked.

"I have an idea," the Lamean replied as they continued to push south. Eventually the sounds of battle faded. Their speed decreased as well as the slope began leveling out. By now they were all panting and trying to catch their breath.

"We can't stop," Azriel continued. "We *have* to get to the bottom of the cliff near the shore."

"Why?" Cole questioned.

"There is a small fishing village, if it still stands. A ferry may be able to take us across from there."

"Across the water?" Lily said nervously.

"Yes."

"That was crazy!" Zek exclaimed.

"They almost got me!" Cole sighed with relief.

"Have you never seen a battle before?" Zek's eyes blazed.

"Never."

"I have." He glared at Azriel who ignored him. Lily dropped back a bit.

"Keep up, Lily, there still may be soldiers nearby," Azriel said.

A narrow slope now seemed to appear out of nowhere. Such a path wouldn't have even existed further north, as the cliff there dropped sharply from top to bottom. The passage wound back and forth down the cliff and along the rock face. Cole noticed a few buildings at the bottom, seemingly undisturbed, seagulls flying over them. Finally, they reached the bottom and spotted a ferry bobbing beside a wooden dock, next to an old shack. By now they could barely see to the other side of the channel.

"Are you gonna knock?" Zek asked, scanning the area.

Cole also looked around, but no one seemed to be anywhere.

"They are probably all hiding inside their houses," Azriel said. "I'm sure they saw the Leojian ships sailing up the channel." But he approached the door and did knock. Zek gave Odessa a much-needed drink from the water bag. No one had answered Azriel's knock.

"Maybe no one is home. Let's try another bridge," Lily suggested nervously.

"Little Lily, I'm afraid any bridge we find may be under siege." Again the Lamean knocked.

"Who is it?" a voice hesitantly came from behind the door.

"Farmers, looking for safe passage across the channel."

A face appeared in the window and then disappeared quickly. "Don't you know there's a war?"

"Yes, we tried to cross the bridge, but it was under attack. If we don't cross now, I fear we may never be able to." Azriel leaned against the door from fatigue. "Please?" Silence. Cole wondered if the person would never answer.

Finally, the voice replied, "Are you . . . a Lamean?"

The question surprised Cole, as he watched from behind the cart.

"Yes." Azriel answered. The door opened to reveal a short man not much older than Azriel, his clothes dirty and stubble covering his chin. His hair was mud-colored.

"So am I. Are you crazy trying to cross at a time like this?" His frightened eyes darted back and forth from one of them to the other.

"I need to get these kids at least to Azmar."

Realizing that he had been holding his breath, Cole now inhaled deeply and waited for the man's response.

"Fine," the man said not too happily, "but only because we Lameans need to stick together. If this war gets worse I can see the New Order government drafting Old Order citizens to man the front lines."

"I need to get my cart across too."

"It'll fit. Let's go. I'll take you and turn around immediately, although I advise we don't go at all."

"Thank you." Azriel shook his hand and gave him ten golden coins. The ferry operator shut the door behind him and headed to the dock.

Quickly the man prepared the ferry, tying and untying ropes, moving boxes out of the way, and finally lowering a ramp from the dock to the deck. Cole wondered if the vessel was even big enough to carry all of them, Odessa and the cart included, but the ferryman seemed to have no doubt about its capacity. Azriel led an unsure Odessa onto the deck, Zek pushing from behind. Cole was the next to board, then turned to see his sister standing on the deck, her hands tightly clasped in front of her.

"Come on, Lily, we need to go," Azriel called out, the ferryman untying the mooring ropes.

"I think . . . I think I'm going to go back," she said faintly.

"What?" Azriel asked in surprise.

She looked down and kicked a small rock. "I'm going to go back home."

Shock hit Cole. "Lily, there is no way you'll make it alone. What are you talking about?"

"I don't want to go, okay? Leave me alone!" she screamed. He hadn't heard her yell like that before.

"Shut up and get on!" Zek ordered.

"Hey!" Azriel reprimanded. "Easy, Zek."

"I can't do it, *okay*?" Tears started welling up in the girl's eyes.

Azriel stepped off the deck and approached Lily. "What do you mean, little one?"

"I can't do it. I'm . . . I'm afraid."

"Afraid of what?" he asked gently, kneeling in front of her. Cole watched him as he gently brushed a strand of hair away from her eyes.

"It's now or never!" the ferryman shouted. The sounds of battle caught Cole's attention. It seemed the fighting was swiftly moving their way. The hair on the back of his neck stood up.

"Afraid of what?" Azriel asked again, calm as a quiet lake.

"Afraid of drowning" she said with little emotion.

A vision flashed in Cole's mind of villagers dragging his mother's lifeless body onto the shore. A tear trickled down his cheek. He watched as Azriel grabbed his sister and hugged her closely as she cried. Unable to hear what the man said to her, he only knew that she placed her hand in his and stepped slowly onto the ferry as it cast out across the water, the sounds of battle raging behind them, a tear trickling down Azriel's cheek as well.

Hours later, after crossing the channel and climbing up the other side of the cliff, hiding in tall grass and evading guards and fleeing into the woods until all sound of battle had died away, they approached the looming Avasete Mountain Range, stretching all the way from the southwestern tip of Oldaem toward Aramoor in Central Oldaem. They camped in a rocky cave at the base of a small mountain. Azriel told them Azmar lay south now. The ocean would be to their east and the mountains to their west. Tensions were high. Cole, Azriel, and Zek sat toward the back of the cave, a fire warming them. Lily remained at the entrance, staring off in to the night sky. Azriel had been with her for a while, though Cole still hadn't spoken to her. After the Lamean returned to tend to the fire and sat down, he gave Cole a knowing glance that suggested he should go check on her.

Cole's legs felt wobbly as he walked slowly to his little sister. A breeze stirred through his fiery hair as he glanced back to see Zek and Azriel engaged in a conversation or argument of some sort. Then he gently approached Lily and sat beside her. "Are you doing okay?"

"No," she answered distantly.

Cole felt the all too familiar feeling of numbness. "Me neither."

"Sorry I froze back there."

"Don't be. It was a scary day."

"Yeah, but, you need me to be brave."

"I just need you to be *you.*" *I don't know what I need.*

As they sat in silence, he noticed that she sniffled a couple of times, but whether that was because she was crying or because the air had gotten cooler, he couldn't tell.

"Cole, if I tell you something, will you promise never to make me talk about it again?"

Butterflies entered his stomach as he waited for what would come next. "Yes, Lily."

Her breathing became rapid, and she took a moment to calm down a bit. She took two or three breaths, and swallowed. "I have to tell you, because I can't keep it inside anymore."

"It's okay, Lily"

"No, it's not."

"Yes, it is."

"You don't even know what I'm going to say."

But it didn't really matter to him. Nothing she could say would change how much he loved her or how much he needed her or how much he relied on her.

"I saw it happen, Cole. I saw Mom leave the house. I saw her go into the water. I saw her sink beneath the waves. I saw Mom never come up again. I saw it happen, Cole." Tears flowed down her cheeks. "There was nothing I could do. I shouted for her to stop. I even ran after her. I tried to pull her back. She pushed me away. I stood on the shore crying for her to stop. She wouldn't listen. So I ran. I ran far away. She *wanted* to die. She wanted to leave us. She *hated* us. She *hated* me." Sobs shook her little frame.

Cole didn't touch her or offer her comfort. He had no idea what to say or do. Tears washed his cheeks. A part of him felt strangely relieved, and he didn't know why.

"I'm never going swimming again," she breathed.

That night Cole dreamt of the split in the path again. Waves crashed behind him, surging toward him. He had to make a choice or die. When he glanced behind him, he saw Lily watching his mother drown. He hated his sister. And he hated his mother. Mom terrified him. He hated the Old Order. As he followed Zek down the path, it turned into a bloody bridge. As he crossed it he heard his mother shouting, then somehow knew she was drowning. Cole was powerless to stop it.

But at the same time he loved Lily, loved his Mom, loved the Old Order.

Once more he stood before the fork in the road.

It's safer in the shadows.

It's safer in the light.

As he stood there, he didn't feel drawn to either path. A familiar numbness washed over him.

It's safest to stay at the fork.

A shadow from the mouth of the cave watched as he slept.

CHAPTER 32: SAYLA

"No! Absolutely not! For the last time, Sayla, you are to stay here for the duration of the summer." Her mother practically dragged her by the elbow into the fabric shop. The door slammed behind them. When Sayla tried to resist, her mother was bigger and stronger and determined.

"I wasn't doing anything wrong! I hate this place!" she exploded as her mother shoved her into a chair near the workshop at the back of the store. Sayla couldn't imagine a worse way to spend the summer, trapped with racks of different types of cloth and buttons. She knew it would slowly kill her.

From where she sat she could see her friends standing awkwardly by the window, unsure whether she would be able to come back out or not. She tried to mime them a message, but her mother stood in front of her and blocked her view. "You'd think you would have learned by now. That something would have gotten through that thick skull of yours." For emphasis, her mother flicked Sayla's forehead.

"Ow! I just wanted to play with my friends! It's wrong to keep me captive here!"

Her mother turned to the back room where her sisters were pretending to stitch something, but were really listening bemused as Sayla got in trouble yet again. "Raesa, go tell those boys out front to go away and find something better to do than corrupt my little girl!"

Raesa jumped out of her seat and flounced to the door. Although older than Sayla by several years, they shared many physical similarities. The main difference was that Raesa's hair was lighter in color than Sayla's. But as for personalities, Raesa, and their oldest sister, Nikala, were much more alike. Sayla thought their obsession with boys and fashion was ridiculous and stupid. Nikala had one boy that she had been with for several years, but Raesa would jump from boy to boy as if there was no tomorrow. It made Sayla want to gag. She knew Raesa thought Sayla's oldest friend was cute.

"They're not corrupting me, they're my friends, and I like playing with them!"

"Sayla"–her mother leaned forward onto the desk in front of her– "you have to find other friends. At first I thought it was just a phase, that you would grow out of it. But you're getting older, now. You're almost 9. You cannot keep running around with a group of ruffian boys."

"They aren't bad people. You just don't understand."

Raesa bounded back from the front door. "I told them to go away."

Sayla was tired of having no one take her side. She knew her sisters would jump at the chance to get her more in trouble, and if she called to her father who was in the back room, he would just side with her mother.

"Thank you," her mother replied. She turned back to Sayla. "Why can't you be more like your sisters? They're kind, responsible …"

"Annoying," Sayla muttered under her breath.

"You said I didn't understand. Make me understand, Sayla. I want to understand."

Sayla twirled her fingers in her lap. Perhaps she would try being honest. Maybe then her mother would see it from her viewpoint for once. "They're my family," she said quietly.

But it was as if they spoke two different languages. Sayla's mother threw her hands up in the air. "They're not your family, Sayla. We are. You can't expect me to believe they have your best interests in mind after what happened last month."

Sayla had been waiting for her to bring that up. *Why can't she just get over that? We didn't mean any harm by it.* "Nothing bad happened!"

"And how am I supposed to know that? You had us worried sick!"

Sayla rolled her eyes. "You were probably glad I was gone!"

Her mother ground her teeth and her eyebrows knit together. Sayla saw her mother's emerald eyes reflect the anger she felt in her own gut. "You will work here for the rest of the summer. End of story."

When Sayla was about to argue, her mother held up her hand. "Don't you talk back to me, or you'll be lucky if I let you ever speak to those boys again."

Though she wanted to defend herself, Sayla remained silent. She hunched back into the chair, determined to give her family the worst summer they had ever experienced. *If I have to suffer, I'll make sure they do too.* Silently she consoled herself by vowing that someday she would get out of there forever.

Sayla groaned as she slowly regained consciousness, feeling something soft beneath her. She had been dreaming about her family, something that she rarely did. *At least it was a normal dream.*

The memory of the recent events rushed back to her, and she opened her eyes, not sure what she expected to see. Maybe carnage and bodies. Or the inside of a prison cell. It surprised her a bit that she had awakened at all. Dusk had fallen, and she was on the ground, surrounded by blankets. *What happened?* Movement out of the corner of her eye caught her attention. To her relief, she saw only the members of her group, safe and not in danger. Shale and Aveline were leaning over Oghren who was also resting on blankets. Although he looked pale and in pain, he appeared awake and lucid. Shale was rewrapping a bandage around Oghren's shoulder while Aveline wiped a cloth over his forehead. Zayeed and Grunt were trying to assemble some sort of meal together. Trees now surrounded them. Apparently they had moved into the forest. *What happened to those men who attacked us?*

Tali, who was just returning with firewood, dumped them and ran toward her. "Sayla! You're alive!" The girl dove onto Sayla, knocking the breath out of her, and enveloping her in an embrace.

The rest of the group sprang up as soon as they heard Tali's voice. "We knew she was alive, Tali," Aveline said, rolling her eyes. She knelt next to Sayla. "But I'm glad you're awake. You took quite a tumble there."

Cautiously Sayla sat up and rubbed her head. "What happened? All I remember is falling off my horse."

251

"We were attacked by hoodlums!" Tali's eyes lit up. She had a cut just above her left eye. Although it had now scabbed over, it had bled long enough to leave a red stain down her cheek. It made her look much more fierce than usual.

"Not hoodlums," Shale corrected as he settled on the grass with the rest of the group. Oghren looked on from his spot on his blankets. "They were free Lameans."

Sayla nodded her head. "I remember them saying, 'For the Creator.' But why did they attack us?"

"Because they were stupid," Zayeed smirked. He had an impressive welt forming on the right side of his jaw. "They didn't know we were Defense trainees for one thing."

Shale shook his head, "The fallen tree was a trap. We should have suspected an ambush … I should have seen it. They wanted money, retribution ,… they weren't waiting specifically for us, just whatever unsuspecting Oldaemites happened to pass by on this road."

"It's more dangerous out here than I thought," Grunt said, shivering as he leaned up against a tree.

"They didn't know what hit them!" Tali jumped up and pretended to sword fight.

"They weren't very organized," Aveline explained to Sayla who was looking confused. "That's what made the difference. Once we joined formation, we defeated them pretty quickly. They scattered."

"Not quick enough," Oghren groaned.

"I still can't believe we beat them," Grunt sighed.

He doesn't look too much worse for wear.

They all looked shaken up, though. "Who would have thought our training would actually kick in in a time of crisis?" Grunt seemed deep in thought.

Sayla's training hadn't had opportunity to go into action, however. *It never got the chance to.* The first real fight any of them had ever seen, and Sayla had been immediately knocked out. She didn't even have a good reason like Oghren, who had been struck by an arrow. *What would I have been like in battle?* Even Tali and Grunt, the two newest Shepherd trainees, had apparently proven their worth. Sayla did not like feeling inferior to anyone. It reminded her too much of her childhood.

"Yeah! Tali surprisingly held her own!" Aveline patted her on the back.

"Held my own? I was on fire!"

"Well, I can at least see why you're a Defense student now," Aveline laughed. *What is going on?* Sayla glanced around the group. Not very long ago, they had been bickering and making fun of each other. Now everyone was acting like old pals. *It's because they've fought together.* Sayla had missed out on something important. But from the way the others were looking at her, it didn't seem as if they were trying to exclude her from the group or the sense of togetherness. *They don't feel it. It's just me.* It was because she was so different from them. Once again she was the outsider. *Maybe even Grunt belongs here more than I do.*

After assuring themselves that Sayla was going to be fine, everyone eventually returned to their tasks, except for Shale who settled onto the blanket next to her.

She took a moment to size up his battle wounds. He had the beginnings of a black eye and his nose was red and puffy. Was it broken? A cut also ran down his calf, but it did not look as if it pained him much. The others had told her how he had been the leader they all needed. During the initial panic, he had kept his self-control. Sayla remembered those brief moments where everything had sped up and she had become unnerved. If she hadn't fallen off her horse, would she have recovered herself and remained calm as well? Normally, she would have been positive that the answer was yes. But now, she had been so shaken up the past few weeks that she wasn't so sure anymore.

"How did you get that cut on your leg?"

"Oh, this?" Shale poked at the cut proudly through the hole in his pants. "I'm not really sure. So much was going on at once, ya know?"

Sayla nodded.

"I do know that it happened at some point when I was trying to get to you."

Had she just heard right? Maybe the fall had jostled her brain a bit. "You tried to get to me?"

"Well, yeah." Shale punched her arm playfully. It reminded her of the last time he had done that, when they were sitting on the hill overlooking Sea Fort. She had felt scared and vulnerable after that first dream, even before it had started to come true. But his touch had calmed her down. Now, when she was feeling scared and vulnerable again, his touch had the same welcome effect. Suddenly she felt accepted and loved in a way she had been longing for. *He said he saw me in his future.* "When you got thrown off your horse," he continued, "we didn't really know why. We thought maybe it was you who had been hit by that arrow. I mean we figured it out later, when we stitched up Valor, but at first we didn't know if you were hurt or ... or ..."

She tentatively patted his huge bicep. "I'm okay."

"I know. And I'm glad. I ran over to you as fast as I could, but it wasn't easy. I threw my body over you and was a human shield while those men were trying to shoot at you. It was pretty epic and heroic." Then he shook his head sadly. "I only wish you had been conscious to see it all."

Oh, I wish I had been conscious for that as well. It did sound quite magnificent. Sayla chided herself for having remained unconscious for so long.

"Thank you for saving me." Those words felt strange coming from her mouth. Usually other people were thanking her. *If Galen saw me now he would wonder who I am.* She certainly had changed from the gangly little brat who used to sneak away from her family as often as she could.

"Of course! I would do it again." Shale leaned up close to her. She could smell his musty, manly scent. "And I just might have to once we get to that village tomorrow."

"How close are we?"

"After the attack, we decided to head deeper into the forest. I mean, not too far, the road is just a little ways over that way." He pointed in front of them. "But this way there will be no surprises. We should reach the village early tomorrow."

"And there we pick up the slaves or whatever?"

"I don't know if it's that simple."

How could it get more complicated? They had encountered enough excitement for one journey. "What does that mean?"

He hesitated. "Did you see that smoke coming up from the trees this morning?"

She nodded. It was not uncommon for the Oldeam army to raid some rebellious Lamean village. Sometimes their homes had to go up in flames for them to remember their place. It was a common practice.

"I'm pretty sure that's where we're going."

"Wait." Sayla sat up. "These aren't already slaves? They're ... uh ... new?" Moving slaves who knew their place was one thing, but if what Shale suspected was true, then the people they would be taking to the Limestone Cliffs to mine would have spent the majority of their lives in relative freedom and would be more defiant. They really had their work cut out for them.

"Oh … that's a little different."

"Sure is! Should be really exciting. You up for it, champ?"

"Definitely!" But she sounded more confident than she felt. She was tired of being so shaken up all the time. But if Shale believed in her, then she could believe in herself. It was nice to have someone on her side again. Sayla had almost forgotten what it felt like to be part of a team. When she was little she had had her group of friends. They had felt unstoppable. *Maybe we were.* However, they had never had the chance to find out since they had gone their separate ways so many years ago.

In the Shepherd academy she had found friendship and acceptance, but she was still on her own technically. Her closest friend, Aveline, was also her competition so that they could never completely open up to each other and expose their weaknesses. But now, finally, there was someone who accepted, maybe even loved her, for who she was. *Well, for what I let him see at least.* Perhaps that was good enough for now.

CHAPTER 33: GALEN

We're going to die, Galen thought for the hundredth time as he and Gadiel crept along the shore. They had made it to the beach without any incident other than a few snide comments to each other. Galen was willing to live with that. *So far, so good.* But the closer they approached the palace, the more doubt he was beginning to feel. What exactly were they doing, anyway? They had no real plan. Slip into the palace, creep into the dungeon, and then hope that maybe Gadiel's father was being held in there? Their plan was full of "ifs" and "maybes," and Galen wondered if this was going to be his last night alive.

On top of all that, nobody had told him that once you've been aboard a ship long enough to get used to it, more or less, then stepping onto land is just as bad as the first time onto the vessel. His beloved solid ground had betrayed him, and he found himself a bit disoriented and stumbling along. It was ridiculous. *Maybe I should just stay here and join the fighting troops. It can't be worse than getting back in that boat.*

They were now edging along a rock formation just inland from the beach. Galen had seen no sign of the other rescue canoe, but Gadiel insisted they were in the right place. "Are you absolutely, positively sure the drainage tunnel is around here?"

"For the last time, yes! I got a good look at the map."

They walked on for a few more minutes. But Galen couldn't help himself. He wasn't leaving his fate in the hands of this naïve brat. "But are you sure?"

"Yes!"

"But what if you read it wrong?"

Whipping around, Gadiel threw his hands up in the air. "I know how to read a map, Galen!"

Galen shrugged. "Then where is it, oh smart one?"

Gadiel put his hands to his forehead and strained to see in the moonlight. Then his face lit up. "There," he whispered.

Sure enough, Galen thought he saw a small opening in the rock formation. It looked slightly unnatural, even artificial. Clearly it was a manmade tunnel, alright, but only visible if someone knew to look for it. Probably it had a guard posted somewhere inside. With any luck, Shepherd Seff's team would have already rescued Shepherd Demas by the time Galen and Gadiel arrived.

For now, though, they were trekking along in the dark, too afraid to even light a match. Even though dawn would soon come, it didn't help them any in the dark tunnel. Galen didn't even want to think about the sludge that he was stepping in. Maybe they were better off not being able to see anything. The stench was bad enough.

Galen took the lead, trying to stay quiet as he felt his way along the tunnel wall. *It can't be too much further. We've been walking for a while now.* Then he stopped abruptly when he felt a turn in the tunnel, and Gadiel slammed into his back. "Gadiel!" Galen hissed.

"Sorry! I can't see you."

Galen started to give him a piece of his mind about paying attention and staying quiet, but before he could get the words out, a hand closed over his mouth, yanking him farther into the darkness of the turn in the tunnel. Galen grunted in surprise, but forced himself to stop when he felt the cold metal of a sword against his throat. *This is it. Death in a sewage tunnel.* Hearing a similar groan in front of him, he wondered if Gadiel had been caught as well. Or maybe killed. The person who had grabbed Galen wasn't even breathing hard. *I guess he was chosen to guard this entrance for a reason.*

256

Someone struck a match and held it up against his face. The tiny flame was bright enough to make him squint. The person with the match sucked in their breath and turned to the left where Galen saw Gadiel being held in a similar fashion. Although Galen strained to see the person standing behind Gadiel, the light was dim and full of shadows. Then Galen flinched in recognition.

"Let them go," a low feminine voice came from the person holding the match. Veroma blew out the first and lit a second match. The hand and sword disappeared from around him as Galen found himself pushed against Gadiel. They both leaned up against the wall, surrounded by Veroma, Fyn, and the other woman of Seff's select team.

"Let me explain," Gadiel began.

"What in the One's name are you doing here?" Veroma stepped forward and got uncomfortably close to them. "You're lucky I took the time to see who you were, otherwise you would be lying dead on the ground right now." Galen did not doubt that. He was starting to wonder if it wouldn't have been safer to be captured by Leojian guards after all.

"How did you find us?" Galen asked.

He couldn't see her face very well, but he thought he heard sarcasm in her voice. "You're lucky the entire palace didn't hear you clomping around. For all we know they are on their way here right how."

"I didn't mean to give away your position," Gadiel said. "I just wanted to … you have to understand …"

"You're a fool for coming here, soldier. This is no place for an inexperienced novice. You could have gotten us all killed," Fyn spoke as if he were more than just a few years older than them. "And you're an idiot for coming along," he said, jabbing Galen.

Already inclined to agree, Galen didn't have an answer for that.

"He's my father," Gadiel insisted, using the same tactic he had pulled on Galen. "I can't just leave him here to die."

"And we are his best chance for survival," the other woman insisted.

"Liar!" Gadiel turned in her direction, for a moment forgetting to keep his voice at a whisper. "You're not even here to look for him. You're here to capture the royal family!"

Veroma's face hardened. "You were eavesdropping on our *private* meeting."

"Well, how else do you think we got this far into the tunnel?" Galen folded his arms. *That's what they get for thinking we're some stupid cabin boys.*

"We'll see how amused your commanding officer is about you two directly disobeying orders once we get back to the ship." She grabbed Gadiel's shoulder. "*You* have to understand that there are more priorities than just your father that we have to think about," Veroma said harshly. After a pause, perhaps realizing that she had gone too far, she said more softly, "Look, soldier. I knew your father. He was a good man."

"Is," Gadiel hissed.

"I'm sorry?"

"Is," Gadiel responded, louder this time. "He *is* a good man. You see? You've written him off already." Pushing away from the tunnel wall, he stood his full height, a darker shadow in the dim light of the lanterns the special forces had now lit. *Not that I'm scared of him or anything, but I definitely wouldn't want to be Veroma right now.* "That's why I had to come. Sure, maybe you think he's a good person. Doesn't stop you from turning him into a *battle tactic.* A strategy. Well, you forget … that he's a person. And I am *not* leaving here without at least looking for him."

Veroma held her ground. "You will do no such thing. Or Alyson will tie you up and leave you right here until we accomplish our task." *That's her name: Alyson.*

"Right," Gadiel said bitingly, "because he's not the top priority."

"Because we don't even know if he's still alive."

It was as if she had punched him in the gut. He didn't have an answer for that. *It's like he didn't even consider the possibility.* At least, with all Galen's painful memories, he had been spared the feeling of being so sure of something only to be knocked down so far. Galen had been at the bottom right from the beginning. And there was some safety in that.

"Wait," Galen pointed, "were you implying that we will all be going back to the ship … together?" *And also implying that you're not going to just slit our throats here and now?*

She looked at her two companions reluctantly. "We cannot lose time turning around now, or risk you being caught on your way back and giving up our plan. You will have to continue with us. The other two are waiting for us farther up ahead. But"--she held her sword up menacingly--"you will *not* do anything stupid. You will *not* do anything more than sit in the shadows while we accomplish the mission, and you will *not* speak unless spoken to. Am I clear?"

There was an awkward silence. "Oh," Galen acted confused, "do I get to talk now? I wasn't clear on the signal."

Veroma gave a frustrated sigh and turned away from them. "Just shut up and walk."

"Now, I can do that."

After extinguishing their lanterns, they quickly met up with Endcer and the other soldier who was waiting at the entrance to the palace. Fortunately, that end of the tunnel was lighted. The bodies of two guards stationed there had been shoved into a corner, and Endcer and the other man had put on their uniforms.

"Do we get uniforms, too?" Galen asked.

"I told you not to talk." *So I guess that's a no.*

"Here's the plan," Endcer began softly. "The Oldaem army has already begun the attack on the gates. They will distract the guards as we slip inside from behind. The royal family will have retreated to the back dining hall. That is where we will take them. It will be heavily guarded, but it is our best chance."

Veroma turned to Galen and Gadiel. "You will follow closely behind us. Stay out of sight as much as possible and do not engage in any fighting unless it is absolutely necessary. Don't be stupid. I would hate to bring your dead bodies back to Zevran." Her gaze lingered for a moment on Gadiel, as if she expected him to bolt at any moment. Instead, he nodded in assent.

Galen felt a surge of adrenaline, even kind of excited, albeit it was mingled with fear. He had never seen a real battle before, let alone been in the middle of one. It gave him a kind of helpless feeling, but that was something he was familiar with and it did not bother him very much. Long ago he had learned to move past it and concentrate on the task at hand. True, he was mainly supposed just to observe and not participate, but it was still exhilarating.

As they broke into the Leoj palace, Galen quietly looked around. Of course, they were still in its dark recesses and not the main part yet. But Gadiel had told him earlier how long-standing palaces such as this one and the one in Oldaem had many hidden passages that led all over. The one they were in now would lead them to the dining hall where the royal family had supposedly retreated to.

"How do you know all this stuff about palaces?" Galen had asked Gadiel as they had paddled the canoe to shore.

"Because I played in them." *Of course you did.*

After a series of twists and turns, they came to a set of stone stairs. "This is it," Fyn whispered to Galen.

Veroma stood against the door and listened, then mouthed to Galen, "You stay here." He got the message. Gadiel and Galen stepped back as the five elite soldiers counted to three and then rushed into the room beyond, shutting the door firmly behind them. The two settled into the shadows, neither saying a word. Galen's heart raced at the thought of what must be going on above. How long would it be before the Special Forces team came back with the members of the Royal Leojian family?

The wait felt like an eternity. Galen itched to be part of the fight, to be part of the excitement. *I'm always the one who has to sit it out.* He had done that while his friends had gone on big adventures and left him alone in Aramoor. And he was doing it yet again. At that moment Galen wanted nothing more than to bust through that door and get in on the action.

Gadiel tensed beside him. "Did you hear that?"

"Hear what?"

"I think it was a scream."

Now that Gadiel had mentioned it, he could hear a distant clanking sound. *It must be the fighting.* What was taking them so long anyway?

"Maybe they need our help."

"You're kidding, right? They're specially trained for this sort of thing."

"Then where are they? What's taking them so long?"

Gadiel had a point. Galen had been under the impression that the extraction would be a quick one. "Maybe we could just … ya know … peak through the door. Just a little bit."

"Yeah," Gadiel nodded nonchalantly. "Just to make sure everything is going okay."

They nodded in agreement. Technically, peeking through the door didn't count as leaving the passageway.

Careful not to make noise, they climbed the steps. Galen reached it first and grabbed the heavy door handle. Pulling it open, he encountered the most horrific scene he had ever seen in his life. The room had once been beautiful. A long table sat off to one side, but was now split in half. A forgotten fire smoldered in a large fireplace. Blood covered the ornate white stone along the walls, and the drapes that had hung on them were torn. Bodies of men in the purple and black colors of Leoj sprawled all over the floor. The most disturbing part, however, were the ones who were still alive and fighting.

Galen could only see three of the five Oldaemite soldiers. Veroma, Alyson, and the man whose name Galen did not know were fighting desperately for their lives. Each of them was taking on three or four guards at a time. Seeing Veroma go down, he instinctively he ran to aid her. Alyson, who was fighting closest to the door, noticed him out of the corner of her eye and screamed, "Run!" before being cut down.

Galen didn't have a chance to react. Pain exploded in the back of his head and suddenly he was not in a castle surrounded by screaming and fighting.

He was back in Aramoor, back in that terrible alleyway that haunted his nightmares.

Wrapping his arms around his head, he had attempted to protect it from the constant blows raining down on him. Galen had tried to avoid the boys, sought to run home or at least into a store once he saw them walking toward him. But it had been too late. They had backed him into the alley behind the trash pile. Where no one would hear him or even care if they did. "Stupid beggar!" they screamed. "You think you're better than us because you're not Lamean?"

"Stop!" Galen had shouted. "Please, I didn't do anything to you!"

"Aww, he's begging now," one of them taunted as a kick landed in Galen's gut. He wheezed for breath.

Eventually, Galen gave up trying to make them stop and focused on trying to not pass out. By now he was used to it, having been in this situation so many times, and he had learned that sometimes it was best just to shut up and endure it.

Galen sucked in his breath as another fist landed against his cheek. He tried not to let them know how much pain he was in. *Maybe if I act like I fainted, they'll go away.*

Just as he was contemplating this, he heard someone yell, "Stop!" and, surprisingly, his tormentors did.

"What are you doing?" the voice screamed at them. The bullies looked around guiltily. Galen's vision was blurry, but he saw an older boy holding one of his attackers by the hair. The boy was bigger than those who had been hitting him, even the leader. He had to be at least a head taller than Galen. *Why did he stop?* People had walked by while he was being beat up before, but they had all just hurriedly continued on their way. This person was different.

"Get out of here," the tall boy ordered, shoving the gang leader to the ground. "And if I *ever* see you hurting this kid again, you better watch out."

And just like that, they scattered. Galen fell back against the trash pile in surprised relief. His head hurt most of all. But he had one last thought before he blacked out. *He saved my life, and he didn't even know me. Someday I want to be just like him.*

Just like him. Just like who, again? Galen's head pounded. *Why does my head hurt so much?* Opening his eyes, he immediately pressed his hand against his mouth to suppress a shriek. Lying next to him was a Leojian soldier, eyes staring and not moving. Shuddering, Galen looked around in horror. Bodies were everywhere. The worst was when he made out the still forms of Veroma and Endcer. *The Leojians knew we were coming.*

A flash of movement jerked his attention to the right where he saw Gadiel bloody and on his knees. Above him stood a beautiful young woman in a blue dress and with a gold circlet around her head. She held a sword, about to drive it straight through Gadiel's heart.

CHAPTER 34: GALEN

Gadiel looked terrified. He was a soldier cowering beneath a young woman in an expensive light blue dress, but in that moment Galen did not blame him one bit.

Galen was feeling pretty fearful himself, but with the memory of the boy who had stopped the beating, he knew what he had to do. In reality it was probably a few seconds at most, but to Galen it felt like an eternity. As he watched the sword swing back for the fatal strike, three things happened at once. The woman turned with her back completely to Galen's side of the room. Gadiel yelled a guttural, "Creator save me!" and held his hands up in weak defense. And Galen, in one swift motion, leapt up, grabbed a sword from the dead soldier beside him, flew across the room, and slammed the handle of the sword against the woman's head. She immediately collapsed with a choked sigh, the sword dropping harmlessly beside her with a clink on the tile floor.

Rasping for breath, Gadiel collapsed forward as well. Then he looked up at Galen. "Thank you."

People didn't usually tell him that. Of course, he didn't usually deserve it. "I still hate your guts."

Gadiel nodded. "I can live with that."

"You okay?"

"I'm fine." He glanced down at the blood that covered him. "It's, uh, not mine."

Galen pointed his sword at the fallen woman. Her long auburn hair had draped itself all around her. *She's the enemy,* he reminded himself. "She alive?"

Gadiel leaned cautiously toward as if he feared she would spring up at any moment. "Yeah. Yeah, I can see her breathing."

"So I'm guessing that's the princess, then."

Slowly, Gadiel stood and looked around the room. "I think so." He pointed to the door they had entered through. "I'm guessing she was cornered in here. I think she was trying to get out that door at the same time we were trying to get in. Which is why she knocked you on the head."

Apparently the rush of the moment had temporarily blocked the pain, but as soon as Gadiel reminded him, Galen's head began to throb again. "Argh, I forgot about that!" He clutched the back of his skull angrily. *Yep, there's a welt there.* "That was her?"

"I tried to warn you," Gadiel sighed, "but she swung that fire poker too fast."

Galen turned his head a bit too quickly and started seeing stars. "Fire poker? She hit me with a fire poker?"

"Solid hit, too."

"Well then how in Esis did she get a sword?"

"Same as you. Took it off a dead guy."

The room was no longer a dining hall. It was a graveyard.

A shudder went through Galen as he looked around it. Although he didn't want to, he couldn't stop himself. One by one, he identified every one of the five soldiers who had come on the mission. He had not thought highly of them, but they did not deserve to die like this. *How did I survive if they didn't?*

"Everyone thought you were dead," Gadiel said, as if reading his thoughts. "I did too," he admitted. "Although, about one second before she started to skewer me, I was really glad to find out you weren't."

"Well, that makes two of us."

When the princess stirred, they both jumped then looked awkwardly at each other when she did not wake up.

"We've gotta get her out of here before anyone notices she's missing." Somebody had to carry out the mission, and it certainly wouldn't be Seff's elite team. But when he motioned to lift her up, Gadiel stopped him.

"What? No. We're not leaving." His eyes were full of foolish determination, and Galen guessed immediately what he was thinking.

"Oh, you can't be serious!" He raised his hands in exasperation. "Could you be any more stupid? We are *not* going to look for your father right now."

"I'm not asking *you* to. You take her back to the ship. I'm going to search the palace."

His hopeless naiveté was going to get him killed. Even worse, it might cause Galen's death. "Gadiel, don't you see? The longer you stay here, the shorter your lifespan. And at this point, that's not doing anyone any good." *Although at this point I'd like to kill you myself.*

Gadiel bit his lip in grim determination. "I have to try. I can do this."

"No, you can't. Look at me." Gadiel did, his lip quivering. *He knows what I'm saying is true.* "You go out into that palace, you will die. Veroma, Endcer, they had more years of experience than you've been alive, and you see how they ended up? The information was wrong, Gadiel. Don't you see that? Which means we have absolutely *no idea* what is going on there."

"But ..." Gadiel protested weakly. "He's my father. I can't leave him out there all alone. How could I ever ... how could I ever forgive myself?"

Galen couldn't understand it. Did Royal Shepherd Demas really mean that much to Gadiel? That he would immediately, thoughtlessly, throw his own life away at the chance of saving his father's? *I have no right to tell him he can't.* For all he knew, that's what normal people did. But Galen refused to let him squander his life now. Not after Galen had so recently saved it.

"And how do you think your father would feel if he finally came home and found out his son was killed trying to rescue him on some foolhardy mission? But help me take the princess, and she'll be your way of finding him."

Gadiel's eyes dulled and looked down for a moment. After a few seconds he finally said, "We can use a tapestry."

"For what?"

"To carry her out in. I know it will still look suspicious, but if you and I dress up as guards the way the others did and carry her out in a tapestry ... well if we get spotted, maybe it will give us a few extra seconds to get away."

Galen nodded. "Let's do that." *Maybe Gadiel hadn't lost all of his brain cells. I only hope we can get her out of here before she wakes up. Or before someone comes in here and finds us.*

They paddled the canoe back to the boat as rapidly as possible, all the while looking over their shoulders to make sure no one was following them. As Galen sat in the back of the canoe, steering, he became increasingly worried. It was getting too light outside. Under the veil of night they could have slipped away without a worry, but the fact that it was daylight made him feel exposed out in the open water. *Literally anyone on the shore who happens to look in this direction will be able to see us.*

Galen picked at his guard uniform. The person he had taken it off of had been a bit rounder in the belly so the uniform hung loosely around him. He shuddered as he remembered having to remove it from the dead man. *I never wanna do that again.* The purple and black colors of the stiff overcoat felt unnatural on him after two straight years of wearing Oldaem's army green. *How does anyone fight in this?* He was a bit remorseful that he had to leave his fatigues behind, stashed in a corner of the dining hall.

The whole situation bothered him, but he couldn't put his finger on it. *Something happened during the battle.* Galen looked down at the still form of the princess lying in the bottom of the boat. *If she hadn't whacked me in the head so hard, maybe I could remember.* Though she had stirred a few times, her eyes never fluttered open. They had tied her hands and gagged her with a strip of cloth just in case. Galen hoped the massive headache she would have when she woke up would be greater than the one she had given him. Another sharp surge of pain made him groan quietly.

"How's your head?" Gadiel glanced back at him from the front where he was rowing.

"I've been hit harder," Galen answered. And he had. Several times. If he knew how to do anything, it was how to take a beating.

Gadiel frowned at the water. "Me, too."

Right, that one time when your father disappeared. Big deal.
Galen started to say something, but decided it wasn't the time.
Instead, he let his mind drift.

Today he had saved a life. That had never happened before.
Granted, the life was Gadiel's and that took a lot of the pleasure out
of it. But still, a life was a life. He wondered if the person who had
saved him would be proud of him if he knew. Too bad he had no
idea how to contact him. Nor did he really want to anyway. It had
been much too long since they had spoken. *He's a different person
now.* Would his mother and Sayla be proud if they knew? Maybe his
father, too? *Hey, Dad, turns out your son grew up to be a hero even
without you showing him how.* Fleetingly he wished he could find
those Lamean kids who had made his life so miserable for so long
and show them who was boss.

And then it hit him.

He remembered the thing that had bothered him back in the
palace dining hall.

"You're Old Order," Galen spat out. *Just let him try to deny it.*

Gadiel's paddling faltered. "What?"

"I heard you." Galen leaned forward, anger rising to the surface.
"When the princess was raising the sword and you thought you were
gonna die, you screamed, 'Creator save me' plain as day."

"I ..."

"Nobody says that. Nobody but Old Order."

Gadiel paused for a second and turned back to face Galen. His
eyes showed of fear as strongly as when he had been afraid for his life.
"Please, don't tell anybody," he whispered.

Galen almost shook with rage. "Keep paddling," he said through
gritted teeth.

"Galen, please, my father could get into a lot of trouble."

"Your father's already in a lot of trouble."

"You know what I mean." Gadiel began to paddle again. "In
trouble with other kinds of people."

"Unbelievable. You're from the Capital! Everyone in the Capital
follows the New Order."

"Not everyone," Gadiel muttered. "Old Order just isn't a very
popular point of view."

He couldn't believe this. A Royal Shepherd believed in the Old
Order? Galen had thought of Demas as a man to be respected, but
all along he had been carrying around a terrible secret. Maybe it
would be better off if he never returned from Leoj.

266

"Your father is the Royal Shepherd of Defense! How could he possibly ..."

"My father has always believed in the Old Order," Gadiel interrupted. "After he married my mother, it took a few years, but eventually she started following it as well. And my little sister and I, we have grown up with the faith. We just have an understanding not to talk about it in public."

"Wow, great way to stand up for your deity there." All religious nuts were such hypocrites.

Gadiel stopped paddling and completely shifted around in his seat. "You don't understand, Galen. It's hard to believe what we do anywhere in Oldaem, but especially in the Capital. I'm not saying I pretend to follow the New Order or anything like that. If anyone asked, I'd tell them the truth, like I told you. I keep the faith of the Old Order. I just don't advertise it."

Waiting for a response, Gadiel took a deep breath. Galen just stared at him as he kept on paddling. *At least one of us has to stay on task.* "Seems like a lot of work just to fit in."

"Well, it's better than the alternative." Gadiel pursed his lips.

"That supposed to be a shot at me?"

"At least I believe in something. We lived in the same barracks for a long time, Galen. I never once saw you leave for the temple. Or attend a religious ceremony. Or pray."

Galen didn't like how the conversation had suddenly turned on him. "So what if I don't follow an Order? I don't have to explain myself to you."

"How can you not believe in them, Galen? The Creator, the Comforter, and the Liberator are real." His voice seemed to become stronger as he talked of them. "And they have a plan to save their people. Those who believe ..."

"I never said I didn't believe in them," Galen interrupted darkly. "I know there are things we can't explain. I know the old stories are true. I said I don't follow them."

"How do you know?" Gadiel demanded, staring at him in shock.

"I just do." Galen refused to explain. He had never told anyone and especially not Gadiel.

"Then that's even worse."

And Galen exploded. At this point, he didn't even care if someone all the way on the shore could hear him. "I have no interest in following some ... celestial being ... who could care less what happens to me and probably gets amusement from my suffering."

267

When Galen had been younger, his mother had urged him to be open to people from all beliefs, including the young Lamean slaves who had picked on him. So he had tried. Tried praying, tried being nice to them even when they were mean to him. All it had earned him was another beating.

"Your suffering hurts them." Gadiel shook his head as if he felt pity for Galen. "They don't enjoy it. They care about their people. They listen when we call to them."

"How could you possibly know that?"

"I've seen them working in my life." Gadiel spoke with such intensity that he almost dropped his paddle in the water.

He doesn't know anything. He grew up in a sheltered home with two parents, Galen thought. *He has no idea what real life is like.* "Oh, really? Where was the Creator when your father disappeared, huh?" Gadiel averted his gaze as he tried to push back the tears flooding his eyes. "Where was he when that Shepherd of Spirit was murdered last year in Leoj? You call that protecting His people?"

Gadiel continued to look down, quietly listening, but shaking his head the whole time. It just gave Galen more incentive. "And where was he tonight, Gadiel? Where was he when everyone, *everyone* we came with, died? And you … you even called out to him by name, and did the Creator come? Did the Hosts of Aael rescue you? Did the Order save you when you called to them?"

"Yes," Gadiel whispered so quietly that Galen was unsure if he heard him correctly. "They did."

Galen grimaced. The kid was nuts. "No. *I* saved you. I was there, remember? It was just me. No lightning bolts, no miracles."

Finally, Gadiel looked up. His eyes were still misty, but they glowed with a strength Galen had never seen in him before. "They saved me … by using you." Then, as Galen's mouth dropped open, he slowly turned and resumed paddling in rhythm with Galen.

CHAPTER 35: SAYLA

"Okay, my turn. I've thought of an item. Guess." Shale and Sayla were in the lead of their little traveling party. It was early, but the sun was up.

"Um, is it an animal?" Sayla patted Valor's soft mane as they rode along. She was glad he was alright after yesterday's scare. In a little

268

pain, perhaps, but he was a fighter, worthy of being the horse of a Shepherd trainee. Besides, Sayla suspected he was a little embarrassed after his panic yesterday. *You and me both, buddy.*

"No, not an animal." Shale shook his tanned head. "Actually, well, sort of. Okay, yes, an animal. But only kind of." He looked into her eyes for a moment before smiling and facing forward. Sayla figured that he intended to be ready this time in case they ran into another ambush. Perhaps he was feeling some doubt after what had happened the day before. She glanced back at the other four. Oghren looked pretty miserable with his bandaged shoulder, the others just shaken. Or maybe not. Maybe Sayla was just projecting her own feelings onto them.

"A person then?" At least there was Shale. Either he didn't see her insecurities or he chose to ignore them. Sayla didn't care which it was. When she looked into his eyes she saw herself as valuable. It was something worth holding on to.

Right now, even when they were playing some silly game together, it just felt right. It had the double value of keeping them occupied and making her heart leap every time he stole a glance at her.

"Wow, good guess!" He seemed genuinely proud. "Yes. Keep going."

"Um, is it a woman?"

"No!"

"Is he well-known?"

Shale's eyes twinkled. "I'd say so."

"King Orcino?"

"Good guess, but ..." His voice trailed off as the lingering smell of smoke filled Sayla's nostrils. They were approaching a burned-over patch. Something terrible had apparently happened here. Before them spread the ashes and charred timbers of a destroyed village. "We're here." The guessing game was over for now.

Halting at the entrance to what remained of the village, Shale pulled out his map. "This has to be the place."

"So you were right, then." Aveline edged her horse alongside him so that she could also look at the map. "This is the source of the smoke we saw yesterday."

"Correct."

"So these slaves ... haven't been slaves ... ever."

"Well, they are now," Oghren snickered through his discomfort.

Sayla glanced back at Grunt. Just as she suspected, he looked practically green with the realization. The main thing she worried about was the possibility of an uprising or something on the way to the Limestone Cliffs. *Are we really equipped to deal with a mob of angry men who just had their freedom taken away from them?* No doubt they would be as hostile as those who had waylaid them yesterday. And there would likely be more of them.

For a few moments Shale studied his companions. Sayla thought they seemed a little less confident than when they had started out. "Let's go," he said finally.

Riding through this village was somehow more disturbing than the others they had trekked through. Possibly it was because this one was actually empty and didn't just seem to be without inhabitants. Sayla had a feeling it was because of what she knew they had to do there. They couldn't just ride on and pretend they hadn't seen anything. The Defense trainees had a mission to fulfill. *Maybe it will be my second chance to prove myself.*

"What exactly are we looking for?" Zayeed asked.

"Shepherd Albright said someone was going to meet us when we arrived. I guess we just keep going until we find them."

So they did. They went all the way through the village, but no one stopped them. As they came to the clearing at the end of the village Sayla was beginning to wonder if Shale had misread the map.

"You're late," a voice came from somewhere to the left and near the trees. She jumped in surprise.

A man with thick, dark hair and a matching full, dark beard stepped into view. If he hadn't been wearing green army fatigues, Sayla still would have recognized him as a soldier just by the way he carried himself. She hadn't seen another one since they had left Sea Fort. Suddenly feeling a pang in her heart, she pushed aside the memory of herself sitting alone on the pier. *You don't need him anymore.* She reminded herself that everyone she needed was right there with her.

No one answered. For all they knew, the man could be a Lamean in disguise.

The man seemed uncertain for a moment. "You are the Defense students from Woodlands, aren't you?"

"Yes," Shale nodded. "And who are you?"

The man extended his hand. "I am Tryndamere of the Oldaem army. My men and I are to assist you with your mission."

Shale took a longer look at Tryndamere. Apparently deciding that he believed him, he quickly dismounted and accepted the soldier's hand.

"Shale. Fifth-year Shepherd student and the leader of this group." Then he pointed to each of the others. "Aveline, Sayla, Oghren, Zayeed, Grunt, Tali." They nodded in turn and followed Shale's lead and dismounted as well.

"Welcome," Tryndamere nodded. "Follow me. Our camp is this way."

"Thank you, sir," Shale nodded. Although they barely even knew him, yet the man was a person who naturally seemed to command respect. *Like Shepherd Demas,* Sayla thought for a moment. *Stop. Don't think about him.*

Hopefully someday she would radiate that same kind of authority. At least their rank as Shepherd trainees seemed to earn automatic respect from Tryndamere.

They followed the tall soldier on foot, leading their horses.

"I trust your journey was uneventful?"

An uncomfortable pause.

"Uneventful is not the word I would have chosen," Oghren finally commented, rubbing his shoulder.

Tryndamere sighed. "I was afraid of that. Was it the Lameans?"

"Yes, they attacked us." Shale shook his head. "We were lucky to survive."

"I had hoped that we had contained everyone in the village, but a few of them must have escaped. Were you able to eliminate them?" Something about the way Tryndamere spoke bothered Sayla. He said it so casually. As if it was nothing to kill people. *Not really people. Just Lameans.* It still made her a bit uncomfortable.

"So you did this?" A voice came from behind Sayla. *Stop it, Grunt. Leave it alone.*

"Did what?" the military leader questioned, still casually.

"The ... the village." Grunt swallowed.

"Well of course," Tryndamere replied as they walked through the forest. "The village was insubordinate. A common problem these days, I assure you. We were sent in to take care of it."

"So you killed them all. Everyone in the village." By now Grunt looked rather green.

"Well, not all of them," the man winked. "We saved some workers for the mines."

As he was speaking, they entered a clearing that contained a camp of sorts. A few army issue tents formed a circle. At the center of the camp smoldered the remains of a cooking fire. "Ah, here we are."

Several soldiers occupied the clearing. Some were standing guard and nodded to the Shepherd students as they passed. Others appeared to be playing a card game, and still others were just sitting about. A large group of them had gathered outside the biggest tent. Five soldiers appeared and led the group's horses away for food and rest. Sayla hoped that there would be food and rest in her near future as well.

"Excuse me, sir," Aveline said as Tryndamere began leading them toward the main tent.

"Please call me Tryndamere."

"Okay then. Tryndamere. Um, I was wondering something."

"Ask." When he smiled warmly, it bothered Sayla, but she wasn't sure why.

"Well, we're supposed to take all these slaves to the Limestone Cliffs, right? But there are only seven of us, and we're still trainees. I mean, won't they resist? Especially since they only became slaves as of yesterday."

Aveline said what Sayla had been thinking for some time now. How was a small group of not-yet Shepherds supposed to keep charge of perhaps 10 or 20 men? What would happen if they were attacked again? Surely what they were doing would seem obvious to anyone who passed them on the road.

Tryndamere, however, did not seem concerned in any way. In fact, he chuckled a bit as he said, "Oh, I doubt they'll give you much trouble."

He led them inside the tent, Shale and Sayla right behind him, but when Shale abruptly halted, she bumped into his back. *He is so muscular,* she thought as she took a step back. But why had he stopped so suddenly?

As Sayla looked past his broad shoulders, she understood. Sitting in a long row, side-by-side and chained together, were their prisoners. The oldest one couldn't have been more than 12. And the youngest one ... she shuddered. The child had to be around 5. *Children. We're taking children to the mines.*

"Oh," Shale muttered. Nausea welled up in Sayla's stomach. It was not what she expected. Maybe she should have seen it coming, but she hadn't. Behind her, Grunt made heaving noises, and the others tried to muffle their gasps.

"Oh, my," Tali whispered. No one had warned them. Sayla wondered if Shepherd Albright had even known when he had sent them on this mission. *It probably wouldn't have made a difference.* A slave was a slave.

"There are 12 of them," Tryndamere said. Sayla couldn't decide if he was oblivious to their surprise or if he was relishing it. "One through six will go west to Dorhaven, and seven through twelve north to the Limestone Cliffs."

Shale recovered himself to ask the obvious question. "So we're only taking six of them, then?"

Tryndamere's lips tightened. "Actually, I need some of you to take them to Dorhaven as well."

"What?" Zayeed exclaimed. "No, we're not separating."

"Yeah, we're supposed to remain together," Tali added.

"Nobody said anything about Dorhaven or splitting up or … or anything," Shale explained.

"Allow me to clarify." Tryndamere folded his hands. "Please, let us step outside." He glanced toward the slaves. "It's rather stuffy in here."

As they exited the tent, Sayla took one final glance at the group of children. Her eyes met those of a little girl with brown stringy hair that had fallen down her face. Sayla looked away quickly, not liking the feeling that swept through her. She had to be a strong Shepherd of Defense.

"I understand it is highly unusual to ask this of you. But you see, I am in a bit of a situation," Tryndamere began. "The Defense students from Westpoint Academy were originally tasked with taking half of the merchandise to Dorhaven."

"Do you mean they couldn't make it?" Sayla asked.

"In a manner of speaking. They … ah … they ran into the same kind of trouble that you did. But they didn't fare as well."

Sayla knew that their experience could have ended much differently. *If just one thing had gone wrong …*

"Did they die?" Tali uttered, eyes wide.

"Thankfully, no," Tryndamere sighed. "But several of them were gravely injured. They had to turn back to seek medical attention. The roads in this part of the country are dangerous."

That's what happens when you let Lameans be free. Sayla did not know much about free Lameans. Back in Aramoor, there had been several Lamean slaves, but rarely any free ones. She knew the enslaved Lameans could even be trouble if given too much rein.

Galen had told her that before Sayla met him, he would get beat up by them all the time. It was something that had scarred him deeply, though he would never admit it.

But comparing that situation with the scared children in the tent seemed wrong. They did not look as if they could hurt anybody.

"I see." Shale frowned. "But wouldn't it be risky to travel in a group of three or four? I don't feel comfortable with so few."

"I agree," Tryndamere replied. "Which is why a few of my men and I will gladly accompany both of your groups."

"So then why can't your men just take them?" Aveline questioned.

"We would, but we must stay here and keep the other villages in line. I really can't spare anyone, but to ensure your safety I would be willing to." *Oh, how kind of him.*

"What do you think, Shale?" Sayla asked quietly. She knew he would say no. Maybe he would even tell Tryndamere to do his own dirty work, and they could head straight back to Woodlands Academy.

Finally, Shale nodded. "I'll lead half of us to Dorhaven."

"What!" everyone else gasped.

"You can't be serious." Oghren walked up to Shale. "I'm already injured!"

"This is unheard of!" Anger filled Aveline's face. "We're a team. We don't separate."

Shale held up his hands, and the arguments quieted. "I am the fifth-year, and I have decided." He turned to Aveline, whose arms were crossed. "I realize it is unusual, but we are at war. Things are different now. We need to do our part."

Sayla didn't want to admit it, but he had a point. Times had changed. They had to make exceptions for the greater good. She guessed the slaves going to Dorhaven would serve aboard ships and boats sailing to Leoj. And the ones sent to the Limestone Cliffs would work at mining. *I guess it won't be so bad.* They would be able to meet back up soon enough.

Glancing back to Tryndamere, Shale said, "Shall we leave at first light?"

Tryndamere smiled and patted him on the back. "Certainly. I'll leave you all to make camp. You may stay anywhere you like. Now if you'll excuse me." Then he walked back into the tent.

The Shepherd trainees headed off in different directions. Sayla started to follow Aveline to see if she could calm her down. But Shale called after her, "Sayla, wait."

She tried to act as casual as Tryndamere had. Inside she screamed, *I love it when he says my name.* "Yes, Shale?"

As he leaned in close to her, Sayla got goose bumps. "I need you to go to the Limestone Cliffs."

"What?" Hadn't he said he was going to Dorhaven? "But I want to be with you." There. She had said it. A brief wave of relief washed over her and then was replaced by the nervousness that only came when she showed part of herself to someone.

"I know." He touched her cheek. "But you're strong, Sayla. And you're a good leader. The rest of them will need you."

While she wasn't sure she believed him, at least it was nice to hear. *He trusts me.* It had been so often lately that she hadn't even believed in herself.

Reluctantly, she nodded. "Who else is going to the Limestone Cliffs?"

"I was thinking you, Aveline, and Grunt. The rest will accompany me," he answered as he brought his head even closer to hers.

"Our game," Sayla suddenly realized. "The person I was supposed to guess. It was you, wasn't it?"

"Of course." *His eyes are so beautiful.*

"I'll miss you," she admitted.

"I'll think of you every day." Her breathing slowed. Shale's hand was still on her cheek. She placed her own gently on his shoulder. There, in plain sight in the middle of the camp, with who knew how many soldiers nearby, Shale and Sayla kissed. It was quick, but passionate. Sayla felt as if her heart flew clear out of her body and exploded in the air. This kind of kiss was much different than the one she had experienced all those years ago with that terrible kid, Bryce.

Suddenly she was more clear-headed than she had been earlier. It didn't matter that those slaves inside the tent were kids. While it was unfortunate for the slaves, leading the group in charge of them would be her opportunity to prove to everyone--but mostly to herself--what kind of a person she was. That she wouldn't back down. That those dreams were stupid and wouldn't get the best of her. That falling off her horse would never have to happen again. *This is just one more step.* It would take her that much closer to becoming a Shepherd.

CHAPTER 36: DAKU

A roof of trees stretched out above him. Owls hooted and insects chirped. Although it was still day, the darkness of the forest was dense enough to fool the mind into sleepiness. Daku's horse trotted behind the priestess and her favored Warden. She seemed to exude a golden aura in her wake. It had been like this since Seafort. Now they rode straight south--he could only imagine to one of the river cities in Efil, though he couldn't be sure. She wouldn't share where they were headed, at least not with him. But he asked no questions, only followed. That's all she seemed to want from him. Thick green ferns lined the forest path. The center of Efil was dense woods with the Woodlands Academy farther west. The forest seemed bare of animals. Different shades of dark emerald surrounded them. *There is no straying from the path,* he thought to himself, only what lay ahead and behind them were options. The other two weren't speaking to him. Eventually Daku realized they weren't even paying any attention to him. He even wondered if he was still needed, or if they were planning on eliminating him at the next village.

I can't trust anyone.

It wasn't that Daku hadn't been trying. Since they had departed from Sea Fort, he had made it his personal goal to return to Malvina's good graces. He had provided her with food and water, complimented her, and focused all of his thoughts on bettering her journey, but nothing seemed to work. Still she leaned close to Jorn, whispered to *him*, let *him* assist her in whatever she needed. Now Daku brought up the rear, glowering at them as they pushed through the underbrush. The forest path smothered the sound of the horses' hooves. Malvina was special. It ate away at him that his previous failures and misgivings might have led to her losing interest in him. Out of all the priestesses in the Tower, she was one of the most beautiful, intelligent, respected, and admired. She could have selected anyone, but she had chosen him. And he had ruined it all by putting his hope and trust in *Aelwynne*--who hadn't even trusted him back. She hadn't loved him enough to wait for him. Instead, she had deserted him.

After leaving Sea Fort, they avoided other travelers and headed deep into the forest and remained on the obscure path for several days. Their pace depended on Malvina. But hidden in the shadow of the trees, their progress had slowed. They set up their camps deep in the thickets, clearing away just enough space for three to sleep around tiny fires. She wouldn't even look him in the eyes. Daku had never felt so unsettled since his journeys with her had begun. Now he spent most of his time contemplating what to do. Although, he knew, he really didn't have any choice in the matter.

Jorn glanced toward him out of the corner of his dark eyes. Hate flushed through Daku as he noticed the man smirk before looking away. Daku sighed heavily. Something needed to change — and that meant Jorn. If something happened to him, Malvina would have no choice but to rely on Daku, especially mid-mission. Was contemplating Jorn's demise considered a betrayal to her? He hoped not. Keeping himself under constant mental self-control was exhausting. But he wouldn't have it any other way.

"Stop lagging behind." It was the first words she had spoken to him in days.

"Yes, Malvina."

"Are we being followed?"

"No, Mistress."

"How can you tell? Your mind has been wandering." She didn't turn as she spoke but kept looking straight ahead. Quickly, Daku wondered if perhaps she had placed him to guard their rear because she trusted him *more* than Jorn. However, there was that kiss to consider. As disgust swept through him again, he realized that his mind *had indeed* been wandering.

"It won't happen again, Malvina."

"Don't make vows you don't intend to keep."

"Never, Mistress."

"Water, Jorn."

The other Warden quickly handed her the water bag. Daku saw water drip down her chin before she wiped it away with a golden glove. Three birds flew overhead and disappeared into the cover of the branches. Was it getting darker? He couldn't tell.

Suddenly the path split. The main one continued farther up ahead, and a smaller, less worn one broke off to their right. Silently they took the smaller path. As they made their way along the narrow trail, Daku began to feel claustrophobic. It was getting darker, but a sour yellow light now illuminated their way. He wasn't sure how Malvina made it appear without any lantern, but it continued before them. They came to a tiny cottage. A single ray of light escaped from its one front window, although a curtain blocked any view within. Vines and ferns almost completely engulfed the rock walls of the cottage. Malvina dismounted her horse, handing her reins to Jorn, who still sat atop his. Carefully she made her way to the small wooden door of the cottage and knocked three times. Then she smoothed her skirts while waiting for a response. Daku wondered if anyone was even there and if she knew whoever might live there. But then he wondered a lot of things he knew would never get answered.

The door slowly opened, and a bald little old man stood in the entrance. He wore spectacles close to his weary eyes and a tattered brown tunic and stood at least a foot shorter than Malvina. Their eyes met, he nodded, and the door closed behind her as she entered.

An awkward silence stretched between Daku and Jorn as they waited. Dismounting to give his back a rest, Daku started pacing up and down the tiny path. Jorn just stared at him.

Where are we? What are we doing here? He knew better than to knock on the door and ask Malvina. And questioning Jorn would find out nothing. Growing restless, he wanted nothing more than to run up to her, beg forgiveness, and ask to start over. There had been only a few cases he was aware of where a priestess had executed her Warden. It was only in the most extreme situations, and details of such events never got shared or discussed. *She wouldn't do that to me—would she?*

"She's disappointed in you."

Daku turned and looked at Jorn who continued to stare at him. "She doesn't tell you *everything*."

"Perhaps not. But she tells me enough. For example, I know why we're here. Do you?"

Jorn knew that he didn't. But Daku wondered if Jorn actually knew, or if he was only toying with him.

"I had a woman once."

The statement shocked Daku. It was the first and only time Jorn had shared *any* of his personal life with him. Although he questioned the truth in it and its motives, he figured he would go along with it. "What happened?"

"She had light brown hair, short and straight, and hazel eyes. She was beautiful."

Daku saw a shadow pass over Jorn's eyes. *Despair?*

"She's dead now."

Daku swallowed. "How?"

Jorn looked him straight in the face. "I killed her—for Malvina."

Glancing down, Daku imagined himself killing Aelwynne. Surely she deserved to experience at least half of the pain he felt. Then guilt washed over him.

"We were to be married. It was what I had to do to prove my loyalty. I would do it again and again and again. Malvina is the best thing in my life. I was smart enough not to let myself fall for a wife. I never made the mistake you did," he sniffed, his voice cold. "It's why she prefers me to you. It's why you'll never be me. You're too far gone."

Anger struck him. "You don't know anything about me, Jorn, just the little bit I let show. The rest–the rest is what I hold back until needed to destroy you."

His threat didn't seem to affect Jorn at all. "You don't know yourself at all. You don't know what memories are real, and what ones Malvina placed into you to transform you into a fighter." His eyes glowed. "Does Aelwynne even exist? Or did Malvina put her in your memory as a means for you to prove your loyalty?"

The door opened as Daku's heart dropped to his knees. The old man waved the two of them in. Jorn jumped off his horse, tied both animals to a post, and swiftly entered the house. The old man stood there staring at Daku whose world was spinning. The pits of his eyes were golden. Daku couldn't interpret the man's emotion. Then Daku turned and walked away, leaving him standing there by the doorway, door still ajar, his eyes glued to him.

Heading back onto the main path, he searched the canopy of trees above him for a break in the darkness--just a tiny gap for him to see the sky. Daku pinched himself until he broke skin and bled. He needed to feel something. *Do I even exist?* The wind blew an overhead branch back and forth, allowing fragments of light to shine through. A beam of light struck his eye, as he remembered the first time he had spoken with Malvina.

"Please be seated."

Daku sat in a golden chamber on the fifth floor of the Tower. He had waited outside the door in the hallway for several minutes, staring at pictures of vast deserts he realized must have been the nation of Sther, until a tall dark man opened the door to her chambers. She had said, "Thank you, Jorn," as he shut the door, leaving the two of them alone. It was the first time he had ever been alone with a priestess, and she was beautiful.

Now he sat before her while she brushed her hair with a comb, the golden waves falling down across her shoulder. She sat on a small wooden bench adjacent to a vanity with a mirror. The room was light and bright, richly adorned with white seats and furnishings. The golden pools that were her eyes seemed so kind and understanding that Daku wanted to jump into them and swim forever. Not a word passed between them. Knowing that it wasn't his place to initiate conversation with her, he waited.

As he did he remembered standing in the line in the grand chamber with all the Wardens who had passed their training. The High Priestess of Vertloch sat upon her chair, surrounded by neophytes. Daku had already known that Malvina would claim him, after seeing her while training with Van. But being officially selected by her had been the greatest feeling he had ever experienced, second only to his wedding with Aelwynne.

"Tell me your name, Warden." Malvina's voice was like gentle music.

"Daku."

She smiled and honey seemed to drip from her perfect mouth as she spoke. "Daku. I like it. It suits you."

"Thank you."

"Do you know why I selected you?"

"No." His heart beat. She made him nervous.

"After my previous precious Warden fell to the sleep of death"–he noticed pure sadness wash over her eyes–"I never thought I would be able to trust someone again. But as I watched you train, and yes, Daku, I watched you more than just that day, I saw what kind of character you had. You are a *good* man. I *know* I can trust you. I hope you can learn to trust me."

"I will, Priestess."

"Please, call me Malvina."

"Malvina." *She's so kind.*

"Very good." She continued to brush her hair, a playful smile forming on her lips. "Are you nervous, Daku?"

"Yes, Malvina."

"Why?"

I must always be honest with my priestess. He remembered his training. "You are very beautiful."

She laughed in a way that made Daku think of a spring day in Aramoor, birds flying and flower petals floating in the breeze. "Don't be nervous."

"I will do my best, Malvina."

"You make me nervous too." She looked down and smiled again.

280

He felt a smile forming on his own lips. *You're married, Daku. Remember why you're doing this.*

"Your wife is Vorran's daughter, Aelwynne, correct?"

How did she know I was thinking of her? Nervously he swallowed. "Yes."

"She's very beautiful. You're a very lucky man."

"Thank you, Malvina."

"Vorran is a very honored man in the Tower. He does much for our High Priestess. It takes a strong woman to have a Warden for a husband. I hope we can become friends, Aelwynne and I."

"I'm sure she would love that, Malvina."

"I hope so. I hope not to come between you two. I'm sure she understands the nature of the relationship between a priestess and her Warden."

"I will make sure of it, Malvina."

"I'm sure you will." Pausing a moment, she stared into his eyes. "You're a good man, Daku. We work for the betterment of The Three. What we do is important."

"I understand."

"We will have many long years together. I hope I can prove myself to you. While a priestess must take great care in choosing a Warden, a Warden must grow to admire his priestess. I hope I do not disappoint you."

You could never disappoint me. Daku didn't answer--he only nodded. He could feel her great power flowing through his mind. A part of him wanted to resist it while another longed to embrace it. Probably, he realized, it would become a familiar feeling.

"I hope you and Jorn can become great friends. Strong and quiet, he's been through a lot, but his motives are pure."

"I look forward to getting to know more about him."

Standing, she swept toward him, wearing a simple white tunic with a golden thread woven through it. Then she kneeled before him and placed his hand in between hers. They were soft and gentle. She smelled of lilacs.

"Who are you?" Her question thundered sweetly in his mind.

"Daku."

"Where will you go?

"Wherever you go."

"Whom will you serve?"

"Only you, Mistress."

"Whom will you obey?"

281

"You, Mistress."

"I am everything. I am forever. I am your tomorrow."

Not sure how to feel about her words, he still let them seep into his being as once again he nodded. He trusted her--how could he not? She meant no harm toward him or Aelwynne. Malvina had been the perfect priestess to join up with. Had it been a Crimson Priestess, things could have been much more difficult and much worse. Aelwynne would understand. She *had* to. One day he would explain everything to her.

"Come. We have our first mission briefing. I look forward to our travels." As he watched her stand, he wanted more than anything to protect her, to be with her. He did it for Aelwynne.

You're doing it for you, a voice rang in his head. Perhaps the voice was right. Perhaps he did it for him too. He shook the thought away.

I do this for Aelwynne.

When they woke up the next morning, the old man had already left for the day. Daku wasn't sure what he and Malvina had talked about. Nor had Daku spoken to Jorn the rest of the night. He spent the majority of it sitting before the hearth, staring at the golden flames as they danced. It was a dance he wondered if he would ever quit. Not only didn't he remember falling asleep, he didn't dream that night at all. Daku stirred when the door to Malvina's chamber opened and she emerged completely dressed and ready for their departure. Jorn followed her out of the room.

As he watched her that day he realized that she had changed much since their first conversation. It had happened so gradually that he hadn't even been aware of it. Sometimes it seemed as if one can go through most of life asleep, then awaken to discover how much it had altered. But now he could do nothing about it. She looked right through him as she passed by. And he let her. There was nothing in him she didn't know, nothing in him that she hadn't created. Daku loved her. He hated her. *I am yours.*

They made their way back toward the forest path and continued along it. For hours they followed the overgrown trail until the trees started to clear out and rolling hills stretched before them once again. Daku wondered when the last time he had eaten was. But he was used to the hunger. Still, after several hours, he could sense

Malvina's weariness in traveling. Slightly off to the east there appeared to be a small village. It seemed almost lifeless as they stopped and listened. Malvina reined her mare toward the sleepy township, as once again Daku brought up the rear.

As they neared the cluster of shacks and houses, he could tell it had already been raided. None of the houses had been set on fire, but doors were smashed in, carts overturned, and several dead bodies lay strewn across the street. Whoever had raided and sacked the village hadn't left much behind. They approached a tall manor, which Daku figured was the Village Elder's residence, its door broken open. Malvina sat atop her mare and eyed him and Jorn.

"Well, what are you waiting for?" she breathed.

He knew what her question meant: she wanted them to search the house for food or valuables. He knew they had money, so it confused him as to why she asked them to do it. But as always, he didn't argue or question. Dismounting, he entered the house, noticing that Jorn still sat atop his horse. A staircase led up to the second floor, its railing shattered. Broken dishes and pots and furniture littered the floor of the once elegant house. Stepping into the kitchen, he saw its table smashed in too. A stain of red trailed across the floor and out the back door. Momentarily he wondered if it was blood, then realized he didn't care one way or the other. So far he had found nothing of value. *Why is she asking me to do this?*

Carefully climbing the stairs, he found himself in a hallway on the second floor. From the toys everywhere and the small broken bed, he guessed one room had belonged to a child. Two more rooms were similar. A fourth contained some official village documents and parchment that seemed of little importance. At the end of the hallway he encountered a door. When he tried the handle, he realized it was locked. After kicking the door as hard as he could until it burst open, he stepped into what must have been the master bedroom. Everything seemed to be in place, it was the only room untouched by the raiders or pillagers. As he sat on the bed, for the first time in days he exhaled deeply. *Why am I here?* He knew Malvina always had a reason for everything, and it wasn't his job to question it. As he sat on his bed, he thought about his own bedroom, his own bed, and his own wife. It was the first time he had truly let himself think about her since he had left Vertloch. Although memories had flashed through his mind, now for the first time he thought of her in the present. Tears almost welled up in his eyes, but he stopped himself as he saw Jorn standing in the doorway.

"What are you doing?"

Daku stood quickly. "Just looking around."

Jorn held up three bags of gold. "This is what she was hoping you'd find. Of course she would have to send me in—failed her again." He walked away.

Defeated, Daku sat back down on the bed. He wanted to lie down and close his eyes for the rest of his life. *Probably she knew there would be one room untouched in this manor and that it would test whether or not I would give in to thinking of Aelwynne. I failed once again. Stay out of my head, Aelwynne. It's what you want anyway . . . if you even exist.*

As they continued through the village, Daku wondered if Jorn was right. His memories of Aelwynne seemed hazy, and he couldn't clearly remember a time that she was in his life when Malvina was not. Did the priestess have such power? Could she have planted all memories of his wife in his brain? Daku knew that a Golden Priestess specialized in everything psychological. Did she have access to his memory? Could she sift through it while he slept at night? Why had he never considered this before? Had his memories of Aelwynne been so crystal clear before? Had time spent with Malvina clouded his past? Or was there one that even existed before Malvina entered his life? Maybe nothing mattered anymore.

Beyond the manor, in the center of the village, stood a well. The three travelers approached it, and Jorn pulled up a bucket from its depths. Malvina splashed the cool water on her face and drank deeply. Daku did the same from across the other side of the well. Their eyes almost met when he heard Jorn call for her. The other Warden had entered a small nearby house. After glancing in his direction, she followed him into it. *Probably found more gold.*

"Sir?" a tiny voice said behind him.

Daku whirled around to see a little dark-complexioned boy with darker circles under his eyes look up at him as he approached. "Stay back," Daku warned.

"Sir?"

Instinctively Daku pulled out his sword. *I can't trust anyone.*

As the small boy neared him, Daku could tell he was a Lamean, and suddenly realized the entire village had been a Lamean one. Also he noticed that the boy had his hand pressed against a bloody wound, festering on his side. The child gasped for breath and walked painfully. Sliding his sword back into its scabbard, Daku eyed him carefully. "Are you alone?"

"Yes. They're all dead."

"Who did this?"

"I don't know." Then he collapsed against the well.

Daku swallowed nervously as he stared at the bleeding child who continued to struggle for breath. The boy must be near death, and Daku wondered what he should do. He felt nothing, not even pity. But, for the first time in he did not know how long, he thought perhaps he *should* be feeling something.

"May I please . . ." The boy started coughing, and then continued, "may I please have some water? Just a little?"

"Who are you talking to?" Jorn's voice rang out from the entrance to the house.

He can't see the boy behind the well. "No one."

"Malvina asks for you."

Leaving the boy to lie by the well, Daku hurried to the house. He brushed past Jorn as he entered the dark room, Malvina stood there among the broken rubble while the other Warden remained outside.

"Another Lamean village."

"Yes, Mistress."

"What do you feel for them?"

"Nothing, Mistress."

"What do you feel for me?"

His heart started racing. *How could she doubt my feelings? It was she who has been keeping me at bay.* "I love you, Malvina."

"What should we do for this village?"

"There is nothing we *can* do."

"I see." Opening her palm, she revealed several golden coins and dropped them in the empty house. "For the dead." Then she came toward him and placed her hand gently on his cheek. "Are you a good man, Daku?" she asked without looking at him.

I don't know what to say. I don't know who or what I am anymore. "I am yours."

Exiting the house, she climbed back on to her mare. Jorn was already sitting on top of his mount, sheathing his sword. Daku stepped outside and headed toward the well for one more last drink. A dead boy lay beside the well, a fresh wound on his side. Jorn smiled.

As their journey continued, Daku realized that it seemed as if they were heading toward Merrowhaven, a floating river city adjacent to Evodotar and northeast of Aramoor. The breeze from the ocean and the approaching river cooled the air, but it didn't ease the heaviness that now seemed to be weighing Malvina down. The horses clopped up and over the bluffs that led south. Tall grass waved in the wind, and several clusters of small unnamed villages stretched all around them. They didn't stop. Malvina seemed determined not to halt unless absolutely necessary.

A gentle rain fell as they entered the river village of Merrowhaven, and they left their horses at the village stables. As Jorn dealt with the stable owner, Malvina stood silently in the rain. Almost every structure in the village rested upon pontoons, and small boats floated back and forth, transporting people and supplies from one place to another. Even at night the village was alive. Lamplights reflected off the water. These people were used to life on the river. Fish being their primary export, several fishing vendors lined the streets, even in the rain. Water didn't stop business or foot traffic. The place was busy in spite of the thunder rolling above them. It wasn't a rich village, though, mostly small wooden shanties.

The most interesting thing about Merrowhaven was that everyone stared at them as they passed. He noticed some almost looked with a sense of recognition at Malvina. Keeping her gaze down, she didn't speak or look at anyone. Jorn's fierce glare kept most away. Daku noticed a lot of pointing and whispering. He wondered where they were headed. Unlike other villages, Malvina seemed to go through this one with a definite purpose. After crossing several floating platforms, and weaving their way in and out of throngs of shoppers and villagers, they made their way off of another platform and up a small hill. Larger houses lined the roads, and short, stubby trees and tall rocks jutted between each dwelling.

Malvina approached a large softly lit two-story residence and opened the front door. Jorn and Daku followed as she swept inside. For the first time since leaving Vertloch, she removed her gloves and veil and placed them on a small table. Daku had the feeling she knew whose house it was, and that it was familiar.

A tall sad-looking woman stood in the doorway of the kitchen. She once had surely been beautiful, though now her golden hair had faded to mostly white. He watched as Malvina nodded at her, the woman nodding hesitantly back, then, shaking her head, she disappeared back into the kitchen. Malvina made her up way the staircase and motioned for the Wardens to follow.

"In case you're wondering . . . she's my mother," she breathed as she ascended the stairs. "Do not speak to her. Do not speak to anyone here about me."

"Yes, Mistress," they chanted.

"There are four rooms in this hallway. You each get a separate one. Pick one and stay there until I wake you in the morning. Get good rest. We will be on the river tomorrow, and remember, sleeping on a riverboat does not rejuvenate like resting on solid ground. Rest. You'll need it to face what's to come."

They walked down a long hallway. Jorn tried a door to his right, and entered it. Malvina opened the door across from Jorn's and disappeared into it, which left two rooms at the end of the hallway. "The one on the left," Daku heard Malvina say behind her door, and then silence.

As he stood in the empty hallway, he was aware of her mother in the kitchen. A part of him wanted to run down the steps and question her about her daughter. *What made Malvina the way she is? How did she become a priestess? Did she grow up here? Do you know whom she loves? Does she stay in contact? Where is her father?*

Instead he continued down the hall and opened the bedroom door. It was neatly kept, a yellow blanket rolled out over a wooden bed with a feather mattress. A small desk and chair sat by a window overlooking the river town down the hill. Daku placed his pouch on the desk and the weapons on the floor underneath. Then sitting on the hard chair, he tried to think, but nothing came to mind. It puzzled him how sometimes questions would fly back and forth in his mind, and other times it would as be still as the surface of a pond. He was tired of it all. After pulling his shirt over his head, he unlaced his boots and kicked them off. When he sat on his bed, it found it incredibly soft. If Malvina didn't wake him up in the morning, he might sleep for days. Eyeing his chest, stomach, and arms, he began to finger all the cuts and scratches and bruises from years of fighting and killing and defending himself. He wasn't sure where he had even gotten them all from. In fact, he couldn't remember much of anything at the moment. *What is happening to me?*

The door creaked open, and Daku glanced behind him to see a freshly cleaned Malvina, dressed in a loose fitting white nightgown. Her hair, pulled tightly in a bun, emphasized her perfect face, a few strands of golden ringlets framing it. Not a defect, not a blemish. What her intentions or mood were was a mystery, as always. She held a single candle and poked her head in the door. Their shadows danced on the ceiling above them. Daku stopped breathing. *She is stunning. She is here.*

"May I come in?"

287

She never asks my permission for anything. "Of course!" He couldn't move.

She stepped in with her bare feet, shut the door behind her, and locked it. Then looked at him as he sat on his bed. "May I sit down?"

"Yes, please do!" he exclaimed, about to get up.

"Don't rise. Stay where you are."

Daku watched her carefully as she pulled the chair to face him as he perched on the bed. She scooted in closer as their knees touched. He could feel her breath upon him.

"Can I do something for you?" he asked. And he meant it. He would do anything for her.

"We need to talk--priestess to Warden, Malvina to Daku."

"Yes, Mistress.

Her face relaxed. It was as if she took another veil off, one he hadn't noticed she had on before. Daku could *finally* read an emotion on her face: concern.

"You've been angry with me." She looked down.

"No! I haven't!"

"I've disappointed you." Her tone was almost unrecognizable.

"You could *never* disappoint me, Mistress."

"Malvina."

"Malvina."

"The missions keep being handed out . . . the traveling never ends . . . it gets to be so, exhausting," She rubbed her temples with her fingers.

He hurt for her. "I wish I could take your fatigue."

"It's sweet of you to say, Daku."

Her eyes continued to be closed, as he stared at her. *What should I do? What should I be doing? How can I show her I'm loyal to the end?*

"I know things have been difficult. I know we've seen things and had to do things that will never make us the same again"--her eyes met his--"but we've done them *together.*"

"Yes, Malvina. I wouldn't have it any other way."

"Wouldn't you?" Her expression became fierce. "And Aelwynne?" Now she sounded hurt. "What if she had been home? What if she had waited for you? What then?"

She's jealous--she actually cares for me. Suddenly speechless, he couldn't find his voice. Nor could he meet her gaze.

Her eyes looked hollow. "This is the first time I've returned to Merrowhaven since I left to begin priestess training." Then she paused. She sounded different than she ever had before, almost unrecognizable, vulnerable . . . human. Flawed. She spoke slowly. "I never fit in here. I never made a difference. No one ever took me seriously. I was just the fisherman's daughter"—she glanced up—"look at me now."

Daku couldn't keep his eyes off her.

Swallowing, she continued, "My father told me to trust you."

Her father?

"He told me you only had the best intentions for me. He can read people just by watching them. I had some serious doubts about you, after you went home to find Aelwynne, after watching your mind drift away from me . . . day after day . . . further and further . . . it's as if I had lost you."

Your father?

"In the cottage in the woods, Daku." She sighed. "They've lived apart since I was 15." Moving closer, she took his hands in hers. He started to tremble. "Can I trust you, Daku? Are you mine? Fully? Completely? Before we do what is asked of us, one of the most challenging, dangerous, nearly impossible missions asked of a priestess, I need to know I have a piece of myself accompanying me. A third." She whispered so close to his face that their noses were almost touching. "My favored third. I *can't* lose another Warden, Daku."

Emotions rose and swelled so much that they almost overflowed out of him. "You won't lose me."

As she tightened her grip, her voice cracked like a whip, golden tears in her eyes. "Prove it."

Her gaze burned into him. "I'll prove it."

"Prove it."

"I am yours!"

"What's your name?"

"Daku."

"What do you do?"

"I'm a Warden."

"What do you believe in?"

"The Three."

"Whom do you love?"

Malvina. "Malvina."

She kissed him.

A heavy fog settled over them the next morning as they made their way down the hill. Daku watched Malvina whisper with a couple of riverboat captains, trying to agree upon a price for transportation. He wasn't sure where they were heading, and she couldn't seem to settle on an appropriate price. Finally, a bald man with a painted head shook hands with Malvina, after they had sold the horses to a vendor, and the three of them walked up the gangplank of a small riverboat. The four members of the crew eyed them wearily as they boarded, and the captain showed them to a small cabin that Malvina would take as her own for the journey. It contained only a tiny bed in the corner, and a small table with three short chairs around it. They sat, the river rocking them back and forth, as they could hear the captain barking orders to his crew about setting sail on the winding river to the south. The vessel slipped away from the dock.

Malvina eyed them silently, both Wardens anxiously awaiting her orders.

"We are headed to Aramoor."

My home!

"But it is only the first stop we take," she began, speaking slowly and distinctly. "Once there, we find a large merchant ship for us to embark upon a further voyage." Her eyes met Daku's.

After our conversation last night, I finally feel at peace with her. We are one.

"Once we arrive, we will no longer be traveling as a priestess and her two Wardens. In order to travel legitimately with merchants, we must *become* merchants. That will be our cover."

Their eyes met again. Daku swallowed.

"Our final destination will be the Capital City. The Palace itself."

What could we be doing in the palace? He decided not to think about it. She would tell them when she wanted to. Her timing was always perfect.

"One final word about our cover. We will be in Aramoor for many days and nights. We must become established within the city as merchants. Our names will change, our attitudes, our voices, everything about us must be different." She looked down at her hands. "That will be all."

Immediately they stood, the chairs scraping across the wooden floor. As Daku and Jorn headed to the door, her words stopped them in their tracks.

"I will be the merchant."

"Yes, Mistress," they replied.

"As for you two"--her voice became soft and melodic, almost a hypnotic whisper--"your roles are very important." She lifted her gaze to meet both of theirs.

Daku couldn't figure out how she was able to look them both in the eye at the same time, but hearing Jorn's heart almost beat out of his chest assured him that was happening.

"One of you will play the roll of my brother."

The room was still and silent as they waited for the rest.

"The other will play my lover."

Daku bounded up the steps for fresh air, leaving Malvina and Jorn in the room together. She had asked him to give them the room. He didn't know why, nor want to know. At one moment he felt completely loved by her, trusted by her, needed by her. Then seconds later, he felt vulnerable, confused, exposed, stupid, deceived . . . *Is this what love is supposed to be? Is this who I am?*

The riverboat sailed across the murky, roiling water. A deep chill filled him. *Whom will she ask me to be?* He wished he knew with full certainty that all that happened had been worth it. In a way Daku realized that he was also a vessel, his life the river, the waves each choice he made and would make. Perhaps he could sum up the journey of his life in one word: regret. It had become the only constant in his life . . . at least at this moment. Every moment brought a new realization. Sometimes things were clear, and sometimes they were clouded with a golden haze. Perhaps existing was the problem. Perhaps it would be easier to throw himself off the ship and sink beneath the water. But he couldn't even gather up the resolution to make even that decision. Nothing was in his hands, not even his existence. It all belonged to Malvina. He had given it to her. The part that disgusted him the most was that a part of him was glad he had done it. Regret and relief both sat side by side within him. *I am a Warden. I am Daku. I am human. I am failure.*

"I knew you'd be here."

Chills ran up and down his spine at the sound of Aelwynne's voice. Leaning against the railing, he took a deep breath, then slowly turned and saw her standing on the deck of the small vessel. No one else was around, and nobody even manned the tiller. He wondered where the crew had disappeared to. The fog seemed to billow around her. Her hands folded in front of her, she wore amethyst robes, her face unreadable. Aelwynne's dark hair fell gently down behind her, her silver eyes poring into his being. She was stunning.

"Aelwynne," he breathed.

She approached slowly, nearly floating before him, eyes unflinching. "I figured you would head to Aramoor. You loved it there."

How is she here? What is she doing? How did she know? Daku was speechless.

Now she stood beside him, also leaning against the railing. The breeze from the river didn't even ruffle her hair. It remained perfectly still.

Daku turned to face the water as she was doing.

"I miss you," she whispered.

Tears nearly spilled down his cheeks, but he forced them back. It was the Warden's way. "You left *me*," he said with a bite in his voice.

"I could *never* leave you."

"You walked out on me!"

"You left *me* screaming your name in the rain, remember?"

He could still hear the crash of the lightning, the rumbling of the thunder, the watchful eyes from second-story windows, the sound of her cries . . . the pain of goodbye.

"I did it for you, Aelwynne." His throat constricting, he looked away.

"Did you?"

"Yes." He swallowed. "I swear."

A purple tear fell down her cheek. "I think you did it for *you.*"

Maybe she was right. Or maybe she was wrong. It didn't matter. Daku had done it, and he was who he was. He couldn't possibly turn back now. Nothing could bring him back.

"Do you love her?" she asked, silver eyes sparkling, knowing the answer.

"Not like I loved you."

She sighed. Her questions came quickly. "Who are you, Daku?"

Emptiness. "I don't know."

"Where are you going?"

"I don't know."

"Who are you becoming?"

Slowly and sadly he answered, "I . . . don't know."

She looked up at him. "Are you okay with this?"

"I think I have to be." It was the saddest he had ever felt in his life. The realization hit him like a crashing wave. There was no coming back from what he had become, no rescue on the horizon. It was the reality of humanity, the inevitability of imperfection, the devastating certainty of constant failure. And at that moment he realized Aelwynne had left because he could never give her what he promised.

"When you were a child, Daku, you wanted to be a hero. You protected your friends. What happened?"

"Life . . . or something like it."

"You're not too far gone. You told someone that once."

He shook his head. "What if I was wrong?"

She started to walk away from him. "Then Esis is doomed."

"Aelwynne, don't leave." Her image started to fade into the fog, into the mist of his mind and imagination.

"You're the one who needs to remain. I'm not the one fading. Daku is the one vanishing."

Now he was crying, as fragments of her face disintegrated into silver vapor and drifted away in the breeze, wafting around him. Her mouth was gone, her nose was fading, her eyes the only thing remaining.

"I'm sorry. I'm sorry, Aelwynne." His tears stained his face.

"I'm *sorry* I couldn't protect you from this," her voice replied. "I'm sorry I couldn't be enough."

"You *were* enough," he pleaded, "I choose darkness. I chose me."

"Someday soon, Daku."

"Don't leave!" He ran across the deck, the last traces of her eyes scattering with the wind. "Wait! Someday what?"

"Someday Esis will be made whole. Someday we can change. Someday we can be forgiven. Someday we can be together in Najoh."

"Najoh? Aelwynne," he sobbed.

"Someday . . . soon, Daku. Someday soon."

Daku stood on the deck with four crewmembers: one steering the tiller at the helm, another securing a rope here or there, the other two eyeing him. Ignoring them, he walked to the railing and sat at the gangway and hung his legs over the side of the boat. Jorn stood opposite him. While he wasn't sure, Daku almost thought he saw the man wipe a tear away as he then walked by him.

I don't know, Aelwynne, if you're real or not. I don't know if Malvina created you. He sighed deeply. *But if she did . . . it was the best thing she's done in my life.*

You belong to me, Malvina's voice rang through his core.

I don't know if you're real.

Malvina's voice grew stronger. *Forsake them.*

"Aelwynne . . ."

Forsake them all.

"My love."

You serve me.

He couldn't speak. Couldn't think. Couldn't remember.

Golden eyes.

"Someday soon . . . Aelwynne . . . someday soon."

Whom do you love, Daku? Malvina asked.

You, Malvina. Only you.

"Najoh. Someday soon . . . I'll meet you there . . ."

The lights of the boat flickered across the water as it sailed to Aramoor.

CHAPTER 37: GALEN

Galen's stomach was upset, and this time it wasn't from the constant rocking of the boat. He was sitting on the floor outside of the captain's quarters, waiting for Zevran to summon him. Gadiel sat on the other side of the doorway. They didn't speak--hadn't since that night, two days ago now, when so much had gone wrong. That did not really bother him. Yes, he had saved Gadiel's life, sure, but that didn't make them friends.

At least now Galen was able to pinpoint exactly what he hated so much about Gadiel. It went down to his core beliefs. He was Old Order. Galen still couldn't believe it. *I guess it makes some sense if his father raised him in it.* But after Shepherd Demas disappeared? How had that not shaken his son's views? *Because he's too stupid to see what's right in front of him.* The Order didn't care. Galen didn't doubt they existed. In fact, they could even be watching Esis right now. But that didn't mean they ever planned on stepping off their thrones and helping anybody. Of that Galen was absolutely sure.

He stole a glance at Gadiel who now wore his other pair of green fatigues. Luckily, they both had a replacement and could discard that stuffy Leojian uniform. Gadiel stared unseeingly out to the sea and looked as exhausted as Galen felt.

For the past two days they had had little rest. Just as they had come into sight of the Oldeam vessel, two Leojian boats had left the shore in pursuit of their small canoe. They paddled as fast as they could, but the other crafts were making faster progress. Zevran and Adar had run out to meet them as they hurriedly paddled up. The officer looked furious. "How dare you leave!" he had screamed.

"We need help! Hurry!" Galen screamed back as he and Gadiel tried to steady the canoe and lift the princess aboard the ship at the same time.

"Who is that? Where are the others?" Adar asked, confused.

"No time!" Gadiel answered. "Leojians are right behind us!"

"I'm not just leaving them there!" Zevran shouted.

"They're not coming back! We have to go!" To Galen's surprise, Zevran listened to him.

With Zevran and Adar's help, they made it quickly into the vessel, but had to abandon the canoe as the general rushed to the helm while Adar ran to hoist more sail. Gadiel and Galen collapsed onto the deck, out of breath and full of fear.

Their rest didn't last long. Lying where she had been placed on the deck, the princess suddenly jerked awake. Galen and Gadiel lunged toward her before she could make any sudden movements. Even with her hands tied, she fought them with surprising strength, and it took both of them to hold her down. *I guess it's true what they say about the royal Leojian family being trained to fight.*

As they attempted to make their escape from the vessels tailing them, the clouds that had been just blocking the stars before now became a storm. Almost without warning, thunder rolled across the sky, and it started pouring rain. Although Galen figured it would aid in their getaway, the same storm that distracted their enemy could also destroy them.

The past couple of days had been an endless fight with nature. They had eventually lost the crafts that were chasing them. Galen wondered if they had capsized, or just turned around. A childhood friend of his had once told him about the time his own boat had capsized, stranding him for a time on a foreign island. The problem in Galen's case was that if it came down to that, Leoj was the closest land mass.

Finally, though, after a couple sleepless nights, the storm had subsided. Now the sun was out, but they still had no time to rest. Unfinished business needed to be attended to. Galen and Gadiel had explained what had happened as best as they could. Zevran still could not get over the fact that they had failed to obey a direct order and entered a war zone. They were waiting now outside his quarters for him to tell them what their punishment would be.

The door creaked open, and they wearily stood up, ready to face their fate. Zevran admitted them without a word.

The furnishings in the captain's quarters were sparse. It contained only a bunk in the corner and a wobbly looking table with one stool next to it. Despite that, it was clean and well kept.

Zevran gestured for them to take a seat on the bunk. They sat at opposite ends. Pulling the stool away from the table, he perched on it in front of them. His face was unreadable. "Do either of you have anything to say to me?"

Galen shook his head. Nothing he might say would change Zevran's mind about whatever he had decided.

Gadiel apparently thought differently. "I'm sorry, sir. Truly, I am. I know I shouldn't have disobeyed orders, but I really had no choice. I had to go …"

"You don't sound very sorry to me, soldier."

Gadiel looked up at Zevran with his determined, steely blue eyes. "Maybe I was unclear. I am sorry that I had to go against your orders. But I don't regret what I did."

Zevran raised an eyebrow. So did Galen. *The kid has determination, I'll give him that.* "You're not helping your case." Their commanding officer looked from one to the other. Galen hid behind a mask of indifference.

"Now I understand why Gadiel snuck away. It was reckless, but I understand. And Galen was probably just there out of stupidity."

"I'm not gonna argue that," Galen acknowledged.

"But I don't think you realize exactly what you've done here."

"Oh, you mean save the day? I'm pretty sure we got that," Galen muttered.

"Don't you dare get cocky when you have their blood on your hands."

"Excuse me?" *He couldn't possibly be inferring that …*

"Did you ever stop and think that it was *your* stupidity that got the five of them killed?"

"We already told you what happened. There were too many soldiers, there was no way out ..." Gadiel tried to explain.

Zevran cut him off. "You slowed them down. You distracted them, making them lose their concentration."

"You can't pin that on us!" Galen protested. "There were other factors. If anything, we helped them."

"We got the princess," Gadiel added.

"You should never have been there!"

Galen shook his head and looked away. *Some thanks we get. We should be heroes for coming back alive and completing the mission.* Perhaps they hadn't fully completed it yet, but once they got back to Oldaem he wanted some kind of recognition.

Gadiel was not so ready to give up either. "I had to try! My father could be in that palace somewhere!"

Zevran folded his arms. "And did you find him there? I don't see him with you."

"I didn't get the chance to look because Galen told me we had to bring your stupid prisoner back!"

"You're welcome for that," Galen added.

Zevran sighed. "Well, we're all in trouble if Galen is the one making the smart decisions."

"Hey!"

"You should never have been there. But ... you were. And you did capture the princess. And for the time being I'm stuck with you on this ship." The man seemed quite upset about that last part. "So, for now we'll have to make do with what we have. Although, after we deliver her to the Capital, do not expect to return to the army. It's quite easy to kick out someone who's already officially been kicked out, *Galen.*"

"Yeah, yeah, I get it. May I go now?" Galen asked, rising to his feet. As far as he was concerned, he was through with the whole mess. Zevran did not understand. Nobody seemed to. Maybe Gadiel did, but Galen couldn't have cared less what he thought. Especially after what he had told him as they returned. *The Creator used me? That's the stupidest thing I've ever heard.* The Creator never used anyone. That would imply that he actually cared, and Galen knew for a fact that he didn't. Probably the deity took some sort of sick satisfaction from groveling little humans like Gadiel or the Lameans who earnestly, but wrongfully asked for his help.

"Sit. Down." Galen did.

"As I was saying," Zevran continued, "there is nothing to be done about it now. We lost five people. Five good people. And we need every hand on deck. But we also have a prisoner to guard, and a pretty shoddy place to keep her. Which is why she is now the responsibility of the two of you."

Galen's ears perked up. "Excuse me?" Zevran could not be serious.

"You directly disobeyed orders," the general explained. "This is your penance."

"What do you mean?" Gadiel asked.

"I mean that until we safely deliver the princess to the Capital City, you two are personally responsible for her protection and well-being. And if she escapes, or any harm comes to her, you are responsible for that too."

Oh, I see what's going on here. We're the scapegoats.

"The five soldiers who died in Leoj would have been responsible for her if they had made it back. It is only reasonable that her actual captors do the same."

Galen wasn't buying it. Zevran was clearly just trying to protect himself from any blame. "I think what we did back in that palace should be enough to get us off the hook. Now you're just using us."

"That's your problem, Galen. You want the glory without the responsibility," he barked. Zevran's face was red and furious. "I'm giving you a chance to earn my respect back. I suggest you take it."

Too tired to put up any more of a fight, Galen decided to back off. "Fine," he said quietly, though with a tinge of bitterness that he hoped Zevran heard.

"Thank you. Now relieve Adar from watching the princess and tell him to meet me at the helm in a few minutes. He is to take Baduk's place."

"Who?"

"He's one of the Lamean slaves," Gadiel answered quietly. *Great, now we're letting them steer.*

Walking stiffly to show his discomfort, Galen headed toward the exit. "Close the door behind you," Zevran called after him. "Gadiel and I are going to have a talk." *That sounds unpleasant.* Galen was glad that for once he was not the one in the hot seat, although he was already dreading his assigned duty.

At least it was sunny now as he made his way across the deck to the "brig." Of course, the ship was much too small to contain a real prison. That meant that the cabin which Galen, Gadiel, and Adar had shared needed to be converted into a makeshift holding cell. Adar had placed some sort of lock system on the door, but it only worked from the outside, so whoever was guarding her in the room was basically stuck there until someone else let him out. Galen had suggested they just guard from the outside, but Zevran's instructions were clear: they were not to let the princess out of their sight for a moment. Her ransom was much too valuable.

"Excuse me, Galen?" a voice said from somewhere behind him, and Galen turned in confusion. It was the young Lamean girl in the pink dress he vaguely remembered from the kitchen. *She's the one that talks too much.* How did she know his name?

"Are you speaking to me?"

She nodded, nervous.

He sighed. "What do you want?"

"How's your seasickness?"

So far he had been trying not to think about it. If he ignored it, maybe the warning pangs in his stomach would go away. "What's it to you?"

"Well … I …" the girl's face was turning as pink as her dress and she self-consciously tucked a strand of hair behind her ear.

"Spit it out."

Finally she gathered her courage. "I made you a tea. For seasickness. It has ginger in it, and it's supposed to help." Then she quickly added, "I'm not sure if it will work, but if it does, maybe the trip back won't be so miserable for you."

For the first time, Galen noticed the cup in her left hand. He could feel the summer breeze on the ocean cooling his skin, and part of him wanted to accept while another part wanted to smack the drink out of her hands. Still, though, it was the second time the slave had done something nice for him. Although he hated her people and everything they stood for … but maybe, like the surprisingly strong princess, this girl was more than what she appeared to be.

Almost reluctantly, he held his hand out and she shyly handed him the tea.

"What's your name?"

"Leilani," the slave answered timidly.

"Leilani," Galen said carefully. His mouth was like cotton when he said it, but he repeated it anyway. "Thank you." Almost everything about it felt wrong. But the little sliver of his conscience that felt good about it was apparently in control.

Carefully carrying the tea, Galen arrived at the "brig." He undid the chain and rope that secured the door and opened it. Just as he did, the boat took one particularly abrupt dip, and Galen's stomach took a leap. *That's what we get for letting a Lamean be at the helm.* Frantically he took a swig of the warm tea. It was delicious. While it did not offer complete relief, he quickly could feel its soothing effect.

Pushing open the door, he entered. Adar was sitting by the entrance and the princess on one of the bunks. Galen had forgotten how beautiful she was. Although she was now wearing an Oldaem Army uniform and her long auburn hair was braided down her back, she still looked regal.

Adar squinted at the sunlight pouring in through the open door. "Hey, Galen."

"Zevran wants you to take over for the Lamean guy at the helm."

"Okay." The soldier stood and stretched a bit. Before leaving, he turned to the princess. "Thank you. I'll try what you said." She smiled and nodded. Galen followed him out the door.

"Adar."

"Yeah?"

"Any advice?"

"About what?"

"Ya know… guarding her." *Like should I pull out my dagger now, just for good measure?*

The man's face lightened. "Oh! Not really. Just … be prepared to talk, I guess. Her name is Princess Allora."

That wasn't really the kind of advice he had been aiming for. But as Adar strolled off whistling, Galen wondered exactly what had happened while he had been in the cabin.

Turning to face her, he tried to look his full height. Galen wanted her to know that she could not pull any tricks on him. He was a soldier of the Oldaem army. At least for now, anyway.

The princess yawned and leaned back onto the bunk. "Oh, am I really that nonthreatening that they send *you* in to guard me? Must be losing my touch."

"How's your head feeling?" he retorted.

"How's yours?" came the quick answer.

Galen briefly closed his eyes and took a deep breath. He was not in the mood for getting angry. Taking another sip of the ginger tea, he sat down on the floor where Adar had been previously. As he breathed in the steam he tried to imagine he was in the room alone.

"Where'd you get the drink?"

300

Galen's eyes shot open. "None of your business."

Princess Allora started twirling her fingers on the wood of the bunk. "Fine, I was just making conversation."

"Well, stop."

She raised her eyebrows. Tying to ignore her, he stared at the wall across from him.

"Got any books?"

"I said no conversations!"

"Why do you think I asked for a book?"

"We don't have books in the middle of the ocean!"

"That doesn't mean there aren't any on the ship."

"Well, there aren't. So drop it."

"Leojian ships have books ..." she mumbled.

He chose not to respond.

"When's Adar coming back? I like him better."

Galen slammed the cup down on the floor. "He isn't coming back. You're stuck here, and I'm stuck here. Deal with it." As he looked into her eyes, he saw that they were a lavender color. He had never seen eyes like them before. Quickly he glanced away.

"So ... if we're both stuck here, why won't you at least talk to me?"

Galen could not believe it. First Leilani, and now the prisoner. "Um, do I really need to spell it out for you? You're our *captive.* I'm *guarding* you, so that you don't get away. It's not the most fun thing in the world."

"Well, I'm not exactly thrilled to be here either." Her voice had a tinge of sorrow in it.

"You deserve worse for what you did to our people."

This seemed to surprise her. "I had nothing to do with that! Your *people* fought their way into my home! I was just defending myself. Not to mention, I did not set a hand on anyone but the soldier who came in with you. And even then, it was out of self defense."

She's the enemy. Of course she tells the story differently. "Call it what you want, I know what I saw."

Her face hardened. "You Oldaemites. You're all the same. So narrow-minded. You're noses are stuck so high in the air, you're unable to see anything past them." She rolled over on the bunk and faced the wall.

Finally some peace and quiet. Galen took another sip of his tea, but it did not taste the same anymore. It had gone cold.

CHAPTER 38: SAYLA

The terrain was changing. Sayla noticed it one afternoon after they had been trudging along for hours. The forest had begun to thin out a little, and there were more hills and valleys around them. It was similar to what Sayla was used to seeing at Woodlands Academy, but with less of a dense forest. It made their journey all the more difficult. She had brought along her horse, as had the other Defense trainees, but the children had no choice but to walk, so the going was slow.

Most of the time she just went on foot beside Valor instead of riding him just to keep herself from falling asleep from boredom. *I miss Shale.*

Grunt was busying himself by playing games with the slaves. Sayla could hear him behind her now. There were only six of them, but they were all crowded around him. With every low giggle coming from the children, she knew he was playing with fire, because it was frowned upon to talk very much with the slaves.

It was easy to see the looks of disapproval on the faces of Tryndamere and his two men who had come along with them. Sayla tried to mask how embarrassed she felt for Grunt. She didn't know where he was from or what customs he was used to, but playing with those children--really any contact with them at all other than what was necessary--seemed like a very bad idea.

Grunt clearly disliked the whole mission. That had been abundantly obvious from the start. But then he had even been upset when he thought the slaves would be adults.

At first, Sayla had shot some warning glances at him, but either he didn't understand what she was trying to signal him or he was ignoring it. So, now she just kept walking next to Aveline, trying to tune out the little voices.

It's better just not to think about it. Sayla had made up her mind when they were on the outskirts of Westervale that she would remain as aloof from the whole situation as possible. That meant little to no contact at all with the children. She could not think of them as anything more than the numbers, 7-12 that identified them.

"He needs to stop," Aveline said in a low voice so that Tryndamere and the others would not overhear.

"Grunt?" Sayla was thinking the same thing.

"Yes! He's making us look bad. Like we're Lamean sympathizers or something."

Sayla nodded. "Which is ironic since Lameans attacked us less than a week ago."

"It's completely unprofessional and unbecoming of a Defense Shepherd."

"Do you think he'll make it to year two?"

Sayla didn't think so. Not if he kept doing such stupid things.

"Well, he's got guts," Aveline acknowledged. "I mean what he's doing is unwise, but it's taking some sort of misguided bravery. And, Sayla, you should have seen him when we were ambushed. He didn't back down at all."

With a sigh, Sayla glanced back at Grunt. He wasn't that much taller than the oldest girl, number 11, who was walking next to him. "I just don't get him."

"You know who I don't get? Tryndamere." Aveline nodded in his diretion. Sayla looked over at him. He and one of his men were talking quietly to themselves. The soldier looked intimidating, and it wasn't even because of the uniform. It was everything about the man--his intense gaze, his broad shoulders, his slicked-back dark hair. Even Shale could not match it. "I mean I'm a fourth year Shepherd student, but he kind of scares me."

Something about Tryndamere disturbed Sayla, but she could not put a finger on it. Aveline was right. Yes, his very appearance demanded respect. But that was something admirable, not something to dislike. Sayla herself hoped to command respect one day just by walking into a room.

"Excuse me, Tryndamere?" Grunt said from the back of the group.

Aveline and Sayla exchanged apprehensive glances. What was he doing?

Tryndamere looked back over his shoulder, his dark eyes alert and piercing. "Yes, Grunt?"

"We need to stop for lunch," the trainee said matter-of-factly.

Tryndamere smiled disarmingly and slowed his pace. "We are making slower progress than I had hoped. We cannot stop for a few more hours at least."

"It's the kids. I mean the slaves," Grunt corrected himself. "They're getting tired and hungry. They can't keep up this pace for much longer."

"And I thank you for your concern, but we really must keep going," Tryndamere answered calmly.

But Grunt would not give up. "But it won't do anybody any good if one of them collapses. There's nothing preventing us from stopping right now."

"Well, I am. I have traveled this road for many years, and I know the exact location we need to be at before we will stop." His voice grew softer, which made it seem menacing in Sayla's opinion. "And as for you," he added as he turned towards the slaves. "If I see any of you slowing down our pace any more than you already have, I'll have you wishing you died with the rest of your families." And he said it all so pleasantly.

Grunt was speechless. Sayla examined his face. His expression looked as if he wanted to say more, but was physically unable to. He glanced at Sayla for help.

"Grunt, just listen to him. He's just trying to keep us safe." By this point Sayla felt that she needed to step in to protect Grunt from himself. *It also wouldn't hurt to improve Tryndamere's opinion of me.*

At Sayla's words, Grunt lowered his eyes. The fight drained out of him. *Maybe he realizes how dumb he's being.* Wordlessly he nodded in assent. Their journey continued, but no longer did Sayla hear giggles coming from behind her. Grunt apparently didn't feel like playing with the children anymore. *Good. I fixed two problems with just a few words.* She was becoming a diplomat after all.

A few minutes later Sayla heard a tiny voice behind say, "Thanks for trying." She peeked at Aveline, but the girl did not appear to have heard it, too. Instead, she seemed lost in thought about something else.

Carefully Sayla glanced out of the corner of her eye and saw one of the little boys staring wide-eyed at Grunt. *That's number eight, I think.* Then she mentally scolded herself for even knowing that much. *Stay emotionally detached. It's easier that way.*

Regret filled Grunt's voice. "I'm sorry I couldn't do more."

"It's okay. I know you meant well."

"Sometimes just meaning well is not enough."

Again Sayla glanced back just in time to see the child timidly give Grunt a quick pat. "Well, this time it is." They shared a sad smile. Sayla's breath caught in her throat. Something about that little kid's smile reminded her of Galen when he was about that age, maybe 8 or 9. He had smiled so little back then, when they had first met. But every so often, Sayla or someone else would crack a hilarious joke, and she could catch a glimpse of his sweet smile. Of course, as the years went by and their little group became tightly knit, and Sayla's sense of humor improved, Galen smiled much more often. She wondered if he still smiled now. And she also wondered how much longer number eight had before he lost his smile forever.

Sayla decided to avoid such thoughts. It was much too dangerous. Instead, she decided to think about something else in order to shake off the heavy feeling she was starting to sense creeping up her spine. "Aveline, can I tell you a secret?" She tried to say it as calmly as possible, but Aveline caught the excitement in Sayla's deep green eyes.

"Um, sure. Tell me your secret. Should I prepare my own gossip and giggles as well?" Aveline smirked.

Sayla acknowledged that might have sounded a little silly coming from her, but she had already said it. "Something like that. And then, if you're up for it, we can braid each other's hair."

"Oh, for the One's sake, just tell me your big secret," Aveline laughed.

Well, it wasn't Sayla's greatest secret, but it was the one she was willing to tell. *You don't want to know my real secrets.*

Sayla leaned in closely. She didn't want Grunt or anyone else to overhear. "Well, the day before we left, back at the camp, Shale and I … we kissed."

Aveline's jaw dropped. "You're kidding."

Finally, she had been able to tell someone! Sayla had been carrying the memory of the kiss with her the entire trip from Westervale, going over it in her mind every once in a while. She broke into a grin. "No, really!"

"Wait, did he kiss you, or did you kiss him?"

"Does it matter?"

"So you kissed him then." Aveline snickered.

"We kissed each other!" Sayla answered defensively.

"Sure. I guess I'll just have to ask Shale when we get back."

Sayla gasped. "Don't you dare!"

Aveline winked. Sayla didn't know what that meant, but she hoped it meant she was kidding. She would just die if Shale found out she was blabbing about their moment of intimacy. But talking about it somehow brought a sense of normalcy to the mission at hand.

"Oh, come on, Sayla. You know this can only be a temporary thing anyway."

"What are you implying?" But Sayla knew what Aveline meant. She had already thought about it.

"I mean that he's almost a full-blown Shepherd. And Shepherds don't have families. They have to choose their country first. Always."

"I know." Sayla grew serious. She knew that the vows he would take in the near future said something about serving the country and region to his best ability. That included giving up the idea of a family. True, some Shepherds had families anyway, if they were not immediately selected to serve in a region. But those situations almost always ended in disaster, and it impeded the Shepherd's judgment. That was why it was heavily frowned upon even to try. It was like spending five years in training for nothing to come of it. And there were plenty of unemployed Shepherds out there. "But I can't just squash what I feel for him. It's too real."

Aveline rolled her eyes. "If you say so. But are you sure he feels that strongly about you? After all, it's his future you would be putting on the line."

"I think he does," Sayla smiled. That kiss had meant something. She was sure of it.

A little while later, they did stop for lunch in a little grove of trees just off the road. After Tryndamere made the announcement that they would pause for a meal, the six slaves practically crumpled onto the cool, shaded grass.

Maybe we did work them a little too hard. Sayla was exhausted as well. *But they're going to have to get used to it if they're going to be in the mines every day.* So really, they were probably doing them a favor in teaching them how to push themselves.

Sayla and Grunt were assigned to watch the prisoners while the others scouted ahead. She knew it was really a job for one person, but clearly Tryndamere didn't trust Grunt enough to leave him alone with the prisoners or to let him accompany them. *But he trusts me. He knows I won't let any of them try anything.*

Settling down in the grass, she leaned her back against an oak tree. They were lucky to be able to rest in this spot. Tryndamere was right. Rocky outcroppings shielded them from the view of anyone else on the road and also provided additional shade.

Sayla took out her simple lunch. It was only bread and meat, but her stomach growled as loudly as if it was a feast. She began eating, keeping a subtle watch over the rest of the group. They were eating as well and talking to Grunt.

306

"You didn't pray first." The tallest girl, number 11, sat closest to her. Sayla tried to ignore her. *I don't want to talk to you.*

The girl persisted. "Why didn't you pray first?"

Sayla frowned. "What are you talking about?"

"I mean before your meal. I always pray before my meal. Why don't you?"

Sayla sighed and looked over at Grunt for a little help, but he was engaged in a different conversation and not paying the least bit of attention. "Because my God isn't so pushy that he needs to hear from me every five minutes."

Eleven studied her with interest. "So, are you New Order, then?"

Sayla stared back. "Of course I am."

The girl looked down at her bread. "It's just that I've never met a Shepherd before. I mean I know you three aren't Shepherds yet, but it's the closest I've been. No one ever came around to our village." Her voice trailed off.

Until it was burnt down, Sayla finished the girl's thought in her mind. The child seemed nice. Although Sayla didn't want to think about it, it was a pity that she was a Lamean. It meant her days had been numbered from the start.

"It's just ... I thought you'd be different." Eleven shook her head.

"Different how?" Sayla was intrigued.

"I thought you would believe like us. I thought you would defend us. Given your history and all." The girl shrugged.

"Well, I think you're mistaken on our history then." Sayla turned back to her food, hoping the conversation had ended. It was making her lose her appetite.

"No, I think you are." Eleven shook her head firmly. "My God, the Creator, he's your God too. At least he should be since you're training to be a Shepherd."

"My God is the One. Not the Creator, Liberator, or Comforter. He is the one that guides us and protects us and allows us to become Shepherds."

"Did the One create you? Did he create the original four Shepherds? Did *he* task them to care for mind, spirit, protection, and guidance?" The girl's voice was growing in intensity. Sayla's angered flared. How dare she question her religion?

"I know the story just as well as you do. The Creator formed the first four Shepherds to protect the Tower, the connection to Aael, and to guide future generations. But you're forgetting the part in which the Liberator betrayed the other two and killed them, creating

307

chaos. The One saved all of humanity by casting the 'Liberator' down from Aael and into Esis. He is the Liberator no longer, but the Betrayer. It is written that the One shall prevail against the Betrayer and free Esis once and for all." Sayla took a deep breath. Proud to call the New Order her own, she would defend it against this Lamean slave.

"The Betrayer and the One are one and the same," Eleven spoke forcefully. "He tricked the four Shepherds into falling, and he tricked you and so many other people into believing he is the rightful ruler. But he *isn't.*" She scooted closer to Sayla who was too absorbed in thought to back away. "The Creator, the Liberator, and the Comforter never betrayed each other. They were the ones betrayed. By the One and the people of Esis."

"You're wrong," Sayla shook her head. "Your beliefs are outdated."

"Then how do you explain the Wall?"

Involuntarily Sayla gasped. "What Wall?"

"If you know your scriptures as well as you claim to, you know which Wall I'm talking about. The Wall the Betrayer tricked the four original Shepherds into building around the Tower. He told them it was to protect the Tower, but really, it broke the connection to Aael, and Esis has been in trouble ever since." Eleven looked so serious. *She actually buys into that nonsense.*

Sayla shook her head. "You don't know what you're talking about. They've filled your head up with that crazy story. I get the basis, trust me, but it's not accurate any longer. That's why your people have gotten into so much trouble. You're resistant to change."

"That's because nothing *has* changed." As hungry as the girl looked, she placed her bread on her lap. "There is no New and Old because there is only The Order. They will prevail when the Liberator saves us and the Wall will be destroyed."

"You have absolutely no idea what you're talking about. Have you ever even seen a copy of the scriptures?" After the war with Lamea, all of the original scriptures had disappeared.

"That doesn't mean I don't know what it says. No one has ever seen the Tower either, and yet even you New Order followers believe that it exists."

Sayla stopped chewing. She had finally caught the girl in a lie. "What are you talking about? That's not the same at all. All kinds of people saw the Tower in the early days."

308

"Yes, but no one has seen it since. So it requires the same amount of faith."

"Plenty of people have seen it!" Sayla wiped her hand across her forehead. It was like explaining something to a 2-year-old. "Sure, it's hard to get to because it's somewhere deep in the Woodlands Forest, but that doesn't in any way mean that it's impossible."

The girl just kept shaking her head. "You're the one who doesn't know your scriptures." She leaned forward, animatedly gesturing with her hands. "Not long after the fall of the Shepherds, the Order shielded the Tower and the Wall in light so that humanity could no longer access it. No one has been able to find it since, and no one ever will until the time of the Liberator's coming is close at hand. It will be revealed to a select few individuals first so that they may believe and lead the people. And then, at the end, all will be able to see the glory of the Order as the Wall is destroyed and the connection between Aael and Esis reestablished." She sat back and took a breath, expectantly waiting for her response.

Sayla laughed. "That's a load of nonsense. Where did they spoon-feed this stuff to you anyway?"

Number eleven held her head high. "Just because you don't believe it, or have never heard of it, doesn't make it untrue."

"Well, if you're so concerned, why don't you go look for the Tower, then? Speed up the process a little," Sayla smirked.

"Didn't you hear what I said? Looking for it doesn't just make you find it. We're asked to believe in it regardless. The only way to see the Tower is if the Creator wants you to." She glanced over at the other prisoners. "I have a feeling He has other plans for me." Then number eleven looked back regretfully at Sayla. "I guess I really was wrong about you Shepherds."

Sayla stared back down at her lunch. Though she continued eating it, she no longer tasted it, because her mind was somewhere else. Somewhere she rarely allowed herself to go.

That girl was fed all the wrong information. Was that what all Lameans believed? It was ridiculous to think that the Creator would hide the Tower from the sight of all humanity. The Liberator had killed the Creator and the Comforter long ago. It was what had started the war in Aael in the first place. *It's just a myth,* Sayla decided. Probably some ancient explorers had gotten the Tower's location wrong on a map and thought they had lost it forever. *Someone needs just to go looking in the right direction, and the Lamean's whole theory can be disproved.*

309

In fact, she could do it herself if she wanted. But it had been so long …

Sayla, at least, knew once and for all that the Old Order was based on the wrong facts. Although her New Order professors had always told her that this was so, now she was sure of it. She had become assured the moment the young Lamean girl had told her that no one could locate the Tower except for someone specifically ordained by the Creator. The whole idea was ludicrous. *If that were true, then how could three nonbelievers just stumble upon it by accident?* They had nearly gotten lost that day, but she knew it had not been a dream. It was not her imagination. Sayla had seen the fabled Tower with her own eyes. Somewhere along the strong, endless perimeter of the Wall were three names etched in the stone. And one of them was hers.

CHAPTER 39: GALEN

The wind howled as the ship swayed back and forth, deck boards creaking, the mast struggling to stay upright. For the hundredth time in the past week or so Galen felt as if he was going to die. And there was literally nothing he could do to about it.

After the initial storm the crew had encountered leaving Leoj, they had exactly two calm days during which the sun came out and, for a moment, everything was right with the world. Galen had begun to believe they would make it to the Capital City without incident. But while Galen had been taking his shift watching Princess Allora, ominous clouds had darkened the skies. Within minutes, the small vessel was hurled into another storm, this one even worse than the first.

And it had never stopped. Galen was not sure how much time had passed, but he was pretty sure it had been at least a full day that he had been trapped inside the small cabin with the princess, wondering if he would ever get out. His initial reaction had been to want to rush up to the deck and see how he could help there, but he was locked inside and no one had come to let him out. With such a small crew, Galen worried for his safety.

The storm had flung him and Allora about the cabin like ragdolls. Every muscle in Galen's body ached. Adar had rushed in a few hours ago to see if they were alright and to bring them some food, but the intensity of the storm would not let up, and he had to leave them soon after.

Before he left, Adar whispered to him that, at Zevran's orders, he would remove the lock on the door for the duration of the storm. But Galen was not to tell Princess Allora. He knew that by removing the lock, Zevran was trying to ensure Galen and Allora their best chance at survival in case the ship capsized. *Things must be pretty bad up there.*

So far, they had spent the time in uncomfortable silence, both Galen and the captive reluctant to start a conversation after the failure of their first one.

At the moment they were both clinging to the wooden frame of the bunk that was, thankfully, nailed to the wall. Another loud clap of thunder and the ship heaved once again. Galen tensed his muscles again for the blow, but Allora's arms slipped, and she rolled across the room and into the wall. "Are you okay?" Galen shouted above the wail of the wind.

Princess Allora nodded. "I'm fine." Her long hair was still braided behind her back, but little strands had begun falling in circlets around her face. She really did appear to be alright considering the circumstances, and he sensed that she was terrified by the storm. She was certainly rattled, but so was he. Anyone would be in the circumstances. From what he could see of her, Princess Allora looked as tired as he felt.

"Me too." While he still didn't trust her, during the past day that they had spent being thrown around in the storm, he felt that he had at least developed an unspoken understanding with her. Galen reached out his arm in her direction.

Princess Allora took his hand, and he pulled her back to the corner of the bunk. She then exhaled in relief, rewrapped her arms around the post, and leaned back against the frame. "Don't get me wrong, I'm all for adventure, but this is getting kind of old."

Galen agreed with her. "When this storm is over, I'm requesting a whole day of sleep."

"I guess it takes a couple shared near-death experiences to get you to warm up, huh."

Now that they were closer together, he no longer had to shout over the noise outside, though he still had to speak loudly. "Well, the number of people available for conversation has seriously decreased." He had to do something to distract himself from the constant danger outside.

311

Princess Allora pried her right arm away from the post and offered her hand. "Temporary truce?"

"Just for now." They shook hands. Her hand was cold, but soft and smooth. *She probably never worked a day in her life.*

"So have you ever been in a storm like this?" she asked as she returned to her former position. As if on cue, the ship swung hard to starboard. Loose objects rolled across the room. This time, instead of being pulled away from the bunk post, Allora smacked right into it. Unable to stop the momentum, Galen crashed on top of her.

"Oof," she grunted.

"Sorry," he murmured, as he struggled off her. She, in turn, pushed herself away from the frame of the bunk. Galen returned to their previous conversation as if nothing had happened. "What were you asking?"

"About the storm," she reminded him. "I was asking if you've ever been in one like this."

"Oh, no, not really." *Not at all.* "Honestly, I've never been out at sea this long in my life."

That seemed to surprise her. "But I thought you were navy."

"What? I'm army. Where did you get that idea?"

Princess Allora stared at him. "Um, maybe because you sailed all the way to Leoj *on a ship.*"

Galen supposed that made sense. "Well, yeah, but it was a last minute mission. All army sanctioned. Our Captain is really a General."

"The bald guy?" Princess Allora perked up. "He was very respectful. Seemed like a good person."

"He is. When he wants to be." *Not when it comes to being understanding about people who've made a few mistakes.*

"The mission then ... was to ..." She raised her voice when Galen pointed to his ear, indicating that he couldn't hear her over the howling wind and the beating rain. "The mission was to capture me? Or one of my family members?"

Galen shook his head. "No. Not originally. You were the contingency."

"Well, that makes me feel special. What was the first plan, then?"

Of course, Galen was reluctant to tell their prisoner anything, but he supposed she already knew the purpose of the mission from her father or brother. "What do you think? We were sent to rescue Royal Shepherd Demas."

In the dim light he could see her shaking head as if she didn't understand. "Who?"

"Shepherd Demas," Galen said more loudly. When she continued to shake her head and point at her ear, he added, "The Royal Shepherd your father ordered to have kidnapped from Oldaem."

A flash of lightning revealed Princess Allora staring at him with the strangest expression. He was about to try again to shout over the clamor, but he didn't get the chance.

The door swung open and Gadiel rushed in, bringing with him a gust of wind and rain. Soaked from head to toe, he looked as if he was about to fall over from exhaustion. His clothes clung to him, and his thick brown hair dripped with moisture. "Galen, we need to talk." Something in Gadiel's tone meant it was serious, and Galen scrambled to his feet. "Cover your ears with your hands for a minute," he said, looking contemptuously at the princess.

Instead, she defiantly crossed her arms. "I will not."

Angrily Gadiel whipped out his knife, which was more dangerous than he anticipated since the ship pitched forward, violently throwing him to his knees, and he came very close to stabbing himself. Instead, the knife dropped harmlessly to the floor, and he managed to pick it up again.

"Gadiel, put that away before you kill one of us!" Galen made a move to take it from him, but Gadiel pushed him away.

"Hands over your ears. Now." He directed his knife at Princess Allora.

Galen saw a flash of resistance in her lavender eyes, but she eyed the knife wearily and did as Gadiel commanded. But not without sticking her tongue out at him first.

After he sheathed his weapon, Gadiel turned back to Galen and gestured to the far corner of the room. *If there's another big wave, we'll fly across the entire room.* When they sat, they both had a clear view of the princess. Gadiel leaned in closely so Galen could hear him. "We're going to dock in Kaya. If Zevran is correct, its western port is just a few leagues away, and we can wait out the storm there."

That was news to Galen. "Wait, I thought we weren't stopping until we got to Windrip. That can't be much farther."

Gadiel shook his head. "We all thought so. But this storm … it's not letting up. We have to find shelter."

Galen paled as he realized what that meant. "Gadiel, we have a prisoner …"

"I know," Gadiel interrupted. Something about his posture irked Galen. "A very valuable prisoner who probably has people looking for her. We can't just wander into some random country and expect to keep her hidden."

"Kaya is technically Oldaem ..."

Galen raised an eyebrow in exasperation. "Only sort of! A territory is not exactly the same thing. Windrip would be so much safer." A small port city on the southern edge of Oldaem, it would have been the perfect stopping point midway between Leoj and Capital city.

"It's not safer if our boat capsizes before we can reach it," Gadiel explained. He paused for a clap of thunder. "But, trust me, I don't like it either. Not with our necks on the lines." They both looked over at the princess who still had her hands over her ears, one arm wrapped around the post and leaning back against the bunk. "That's why Zevran sent me in here. I can't stay long, I'm needed back on deck. But we have to figure out what to do with her once we dock."

Grimly Galen nodded as he realized the difficulty of the situation. Princess Allora just looked as if like she would bolt at the first opportunity. They would have to keep a close watch on her. "Somehow we have to hide her in plain sight."

"What? No way. We can't risk letting her out in public for one second. She's dangerous!" Stubbornly Gadiel folded his arms.

"Okay, oh Shepherd of Mind, what do you propose then? Sticking her in a crate?"

When Gadiel's face lit up for a second. Galen put his hand out. "We are not doing that!"

"Well, if we disguise her as a soldier, she could easily get away!"

"Then you and I will just have to watch her carefully." It really was the best plan, even if Gadiel refused to see it.

Gadiel obstinately stood as the deck rocked beneath him. *He doesn't look as dignified as he's trying to.* The constant struggle to stay balanced didn't help much. Galen felt that he should warn Gadiel to sit down, but he decided against it. "We are hiding her in some sort of box, and that's final."

Not wanting to risk flying across the room as he had several times already, Galen remained sitting on the floor. "That is, without a doubt, the second stupidest plan you've ever had. And I say that meaning that your original idea to sneak into Leoj was the first stupidest plan since it got us into this mess in the first place."

Gadiel looked as if he was about to say something, but at another clap of thunder, he fell backward and rolled away. Galen slid a few feet, but he grabbed onto something. The princess was safely clinging to the bunk post.

Although Galen tried very hard not to burst into laughter, part of him felt as if Gadiel definitely deserved that. Despite the after rumbles of the thunder, Galen heard the princess not even trying to contain her own amusement. Her laughter reminded him of the sound of a bell. She turned to Galen. "I'm uncovering my ears now."

Galen nodded. Across the cabin, Gadiel angrily stood. "We'll talk about this later with Zevran. I have to go back up." Wearily he exited, leaving Galen alone with the princess once more. He slid back over to the bunk where she was sitting.

"You listened to that whole thing, didn't you?"

Allora cleared her throat. "I did not."

Galen sighed. Gadiel needed to be more careful around her. From what he had seen, Demas's son acted like a loose canon around the prisoner. Although he could understand the anger that had built up in Gadiel, he knew that he needed to rein it in if they wanted to make it successfully to the Capital.

Even though he suspected she already knew what their plan was, Galen instructed Princess Allora to tie her hair up so she would look like a soldier. She did so calmly and without complaint, not even arguing when he explained how she would not speak unless directly addressed by someone, and how her hands would be tied in front of her at all times but covered with a jacket or blanket or something. As she quietly acquiesced, a pit formed in Galen's stomach. *She's going to try to escape.*

Zevran agreed with Galen's plan. Although not thrilled with the idea, Gadiel was reluctant to argue with Zevran again. *Whatever they spoke about must have really gotten to him.* Even when they finally docked in the western port in Kaya, the storm did not let up. As Galen pulled Allora onto the deck, a sheet of wind and rain immediately slammed them. It was difficult even to walk. Adar told them it was mid-afternoon, but it might as well have been midnight for all the visibility they had.

With Gadiel holding Princess Allora's left arm, and Galen gripping her right, they hurried down the gangplank. Adar was in the lead as they searched the streets for an inn and Leilani, the Lamean girl, followed behind. Galen hoped they would find shelter soon.

Zevran and the Lamean slave, Baduk, would be along later as soon as they could see someone about the damage to the ship.

They tried to hurry, but it was difficult even to keep upright, so that they were forced to go slowly through the street. Galen caught a few glimpses of broken-down buildings with weather-worn walls. Unsurprisingly, nobody was outside.

Suddenly, Adar pointed to the right. To Galen's relief, there appeared to be an inn. Through the pouring rain, Galen could just make out the lights flickering inside the windows, and the sign on the door that said "Vacancy."

The drenched group rushed through the door. A little bell jingled above them, announcing their arrival.

The lobby consisted of a tavern full of tables and chairs occupied with motley groups of people. Galen figured that lots of other ships had sought shelter or were marooned in the port because of the storm. While Adar located the front desk and went over to inquire about rooms, Galen looked around. *My first time in Kaya, and I haven't even seen anything.* So far it didn't look much different than Sea Fort.

Beside him, Allora adjusted her position. He could feel her shiver in the dripping uniform, her hair hanging in damp ringlets around her face. Galen didn't feel much better. His dark brown hair kept falling in his eyes, and he had constantly to brush it away. At least it was warm inside the lobby.

Silently he studied the other people in the room. A few of them had glanced toward the door when they had entered, but most had returned back to their own business or individual conversations. One particularly rowdy group of young people pointed in their direction. *Must be from Oldaem, too.* They probably recognized the uniforms.

Momentarily Galen wondered how much of the crowd consisted of merchants. His childhood friend had been on a merchant ship once when he was marooned because of a storm. His craft had actually begun to sink, and the crew had to be rescued from the ocean in the middle of the storm. Galen couldn't remember if Kaya was the country his friend had ended up in, but he suspected it was one of the others located in the near vicinity of Oldaem. Either way, it had been a miracle that Galen's friend had not perished. *He could survive anything.*

Galen shook the cobwebs of his thoughts away. It did no good to focus on the past. He had way too much going on in the present to deal with.

His mouth set in a tight line, Adar returned.

"What?" Gadiel asked.

"They have a couple rooms, but they aren't ready yet. We have to wait down here in the tavern for a few hours."

"Oh, great." Galen sighed. A few hours sitting in public with their prisoner? That did not sound like a good idea.

Allora did not react at all. She just watched the soldiers surrounding her discuss the situation. All the while, Galen and Gadiel made sure never to let go of her arms. Galen even checked to make sure the green jacket hid the ropes around her wrists. For a second, Galen did a double take. With her hair up in a bun like that, Allora sort of resembled Sayla. They did not look anything alike, but he saw the resemblance in how she carried herself. Like Sayla, Allora could look confident in even the worst of circumstances. Galen had never been able to master that ability.

After much discussion, they decided that it would be a waste of time to go back out into the storm in search of another inn, and even if they did, there was no guarantee they would find one. Adar sent Leilani with the money to pay for two adjoining rooms and then ran back to the boat to find Zevran and Baduk. That left Galen and Gadiel awkwardly standing in the entryway with Princess Allora. Finally, she seemed to grow bored and asked, "So, can we sit down now? Preferably as close to the fire as possible."

Gadiel hissed, "You don't get to talk! Just do as we say."

"You aren't *saying* anything," she retorted. "But we're blocking the entrance and looking really conspicuous at the same time. I'm just trying to help you out here."

"Shut up!" Gadiel snarled.

Galen spotted a table near the back and relatively close to the fire. "Let's just go over there. Seems safe enough."

"That's what she wants you to think," Gadiel frowned, but he reluctantly allowed them to proceed to the table. The three of them sank onto the wooden chairs. Galen felt his shoulder and back muscles begin to relax. It sure was nice to not have to worry about being jostled as people came and went through the door.

Then he realized something, "I didn't get seasick!"

Allora didn't say anything, and Gadiel muttered a half-hearted, "Congrats."

Galen glared at them. "Well, I think it's wonderful."

Allora looked at Galen tiredly and lifted her bound wrists onto the table. "Can you at least untie me for right now? If we're gonna be stuck here for hours …"

Gadiel shoved her arms back into her lap. "Absolutely not! You're lucky you're not in a box right now!"

Leaning forward, Galen snapped, "Gadiel, shut up or people will hear you." Already, an old woman to their left had stared at them in curiosity. Giving her what he hoped was a disarming smile, he turned back to the problem at hand. To Allora he said, "We can't untie you. No way."

She shrugged, "Fine. You will have fun explaining to the lovely inquiring people of this room why your 'fellow soldier' is tied up. Way to play the part there. Besides"--she pointed to the downpour outside--"where would I go?"

"She has a point," Galen frowned. He didn't like the idea, but if it would only be a few hours until the room was ready, he thought maybe it would be wise to look as inconspicuous as possible.

Gadiel stared at him with exhausted eyes. For the first time, Galen noticed the large, dark circles around Gadiel's blue eyes. He looked pale and exhausted. *We probably all do.*

Halfheartedly Gadiel looked over at Allora, who had slumped back into her chair. The fight was draining out of him. Slowly he stood up. "I'm going to get something warm." To Galen he said, "Do whatever. Just … don't get me in any more trouble." Then he stalked away.

"I should be telling you that!" Galen called after him.

Allora smirked at him, "Why do you always have to have the last word?"

"Because I always have the best words." He was surprised to find himself grinning.

She did not smile back. "Really, that's all you've got?"

"Do you want me to untie you, or not?"

At that, she perked up and held her hands forward under the table. Hesitantly, he removed the rope around her hands and put it in his pocket. "Don't try anything," he warned.

"Wouldn't dream of it," she answered, rubbing her wrists, then settling back against the chair. Galen couldn't relax with her free. *If she gets away …* he didn't want to think about it. His life would probably be forfeited. Or at least any chance at a better one.

"Wow, the rain gods really had it out for us tonight, huh?"

"You believe in … rain gods? What, are you from Beelz?"

She rolled her eyes. "It's just an expression! Leoj doesn't have all that complicated religious stuff like Oldaem does. I swear, it just gets you into trouble."

"Your religion is probably just as ridiculous as ours," Galen said.

"We don't have one. Not really," Allora answered matter-of-factly.

"That's impossible," he scoffed.

"You're just ignorant. In Leoj we believe that we are in control of our own destiny. There is no higher being to make decisions for us. It makes us accountable for our own actions, ya know?"

Galen knew exactly what she meant. "So you're all atheists?"

"We believe what makes sense, yes."

Maybe I was born in the wrong country. "Don't expect me to argue."

That seemed to surprise her. "Really? I thought all you Oldaemites were religious nuts."

He shook his head adamantly. "No way. Maybe you're not as educated as you thought. In Oldaem we can believe whatever we want. And I choose to believe in things I can see." *None of that faith mumbo jumbo.* He saw Leilani sit down at a table a few rows away. She looked so small and alone.

Allora laughed that beautiful bell-like laugh again. "People in Oldaem can believe whatever they want? That's ridiculous."

"It is not," he protested, somewhat offended.

"Then how do you explain the Lameans? You enslaved your own people."

"That's different …"

"Is it? Look around you, Galen. Look what your people have done to this country."

Without really thinking about it, Galen began to study the people in the room. Most sat at the counter, drinking heavily, their eyes sunken. *That doesn't mean anything. These are probably the scum of Kaya.*

"You can't justify destroying an entire culture and their way of life just because they disagreed with you."

"Relax!" Galen answered defensively. "It's not like I was there." About 20 years earlier Oldaem, like most of the countries around it, including Leoj, had established a small colony to share the New Order. Consisting of one of each of the four different kinds of Shepherds and various attendants and residents, it served as a safe place for any visiting Oldaemite who needed help. The colony should have represented peace between the two nations. But in Kaya something had gone wrong. The people had refused to be open to Oldaem's religion and had attacked the colony, breaking the peace treaty and instigating war between Oldaem and Kaya. Of course, in just a few short months, Oldaem, the larger and stronger country, had obliterated Kaya's forces. Now, Kaya was a territory of Oldaem, completely under the domination of the stronger nation. "Besides it ended well for them anyway. We take care of them now."

Allora stared into the distance. "Is that what you're trying to do to my country?"

Oh, right. That. He had almost forgotten she was Leojian. "It will be good for you too."

"Will it?" she asked sadly. "A future where my people are forced to submit to your country's law does not sound like a good one to me. I've already seen what you do to your own." Galen glanced over at Leilani. She was shivering because she was so far away from the fire, but she knew her place without even asking. The girl would not join them.

"Maybe with you in our custody, your father will be willing to make a deal. Stop all the fighting."

She frowned. "This never would have happened if our allies had helped us."

Galen knew she was talking of Hemia and Remia, the two small nations to the west of Oldaem. "They're too busy fighting their own war to focus on anything else."

Princess Allora smiled sadly. "I guess we all have our own wars to fight."

Reluctantly he nodded. *She's right. We do. But what's mine?*

CHAPTER 40: IAN

Thunder boomed as rain beat against the windowpane. Ian couldn't remember the last time he had seen the sun. The door of the inn frequently opened and shut as guests came in and out, voices raised to be heard above the wail of the wind. As he looked around the room in boredom he drummed his fingers against the wooden table. Although he was tired of sitting there, he couldn't leave . . . he had to stay. It was difficult to remain positive in the current state of things. But he would try . . . he would try. There were so many different people from all kinds of places all crammed in one place to escape the weather. At times Ian felt as if he was still rocking back and forth on the ship.

As laughter erupted at a table behind him, he turned to look. Bumo was practically on top of the table laughing, a leg of chicken in his fist. Helen and Jessica sat beside him, along with Captain Cid and a few of his men. All were chanting Bumo's name. For an instant Ian caught Liarra's eye across from Bumo, then turned away.

Surprised she's not chanting his name, too.

After Ian had seen Liarra and Bumo walking hand in hand on the deck, he had done his best to stay away from both of them. Once the vast storm started pummeling the ship, it became much more difficult to avoid Bumo, as Helmswoman Terra ordered all the tournament kids back to their cabins to wait out the storm. During that time Bumo had done little more than pushups and pull-ups and sit-ups. Ian had scribbled some of his thoughts down on some scraps of parchment he had received from Celes. He wasn't much of a writer--never had been. But he needed something to pass the time. Most of his thoughts included such phrases as "always alone," "someday soon," "Shepherds are strong," and "don't give up," as he attempted to steady himself by grabbing the side of the bunk beds. Bumo was so self-absorbed that he didn't even seem to notice Ian's annoyance toward him. If he did at all, Ian figured Bumo would have equated it to the bad weather. But it was so much more than that. Swallowing painfully, Ian realized he had a sore throat and a stuffy nose. It had been a rough few days for him. But he would try to look at the bright side of things.

The thing that disappointed him the most had been Liarra. She had seemed different, not like the others. Had even appeared to like him. But then she had been with Bumo, hand in hand, laughing and walking together. Ian could think of no explanation that would satisfy him.

I'm surprised she's not chanting his name too.

Their journey had been a long one. Having never traveled on a ship before, he wasn't sure how much time it was supposed to take, but he wondered if Captain Cid's crew had gotten lost. For a while he debated with himself whether they were sailing to The Capital or to Beelz. After arriving in Kaya, Ian questioned how long they would stay as well. He initially thought it was to wait out the storm and to make repairs to the boat. However, learning that Celes had caught some sort of illness and was attempting to sleep it off upstairs and the fact that he hadn't seen Terra or the majority of the crew for several days, made him curious as to how long exactly they planned to stay and where they had gone.

Thunder crashed again, as a few people nervously looked up at the rafters. As Ian held the warm cup of tea in front of him, he realized that he hadn't done anything useful or really entertaining the past several days. They spent their time at the inn mostly playing games, singing, sleeping, and studying the Tournament Reading Guide Celes had given each of them. *Maybe I should take another nap.* Laughter erupted again at Bumo's table, as he watched Cid regale the group with more tales of his chivalry. It startled him to see Liarra stand and start to approach him. Suddenly his mug became even more fascinating as he stared into it. He could sense her standing behind him.

"Hey, Ian, may I ask you a question?"

His heart was beating as fast as it could. *Just go away.* "Sure. Oh, hey Liarra, I didn't see you there."

She looked confusedly at him. "You were just staring at me."

"What? No I wasn't."

"It's fine if you were. Bumo was being obnoxious."

Oh yeah, I know how much Bumo annoys you. So much you can't keep your hands off him. He smiled. "You all sound as if you're having fun."

"Cid and Bumo are starting to repeat their stories. Jessica nearly spits up her milk from laughing so hard every time Bumo speaks. It's getting old."

Her eyes carefully studied him. *Stop being fake, Ian.* "Well, gotta do something to pass the time. So what's your question?"

"I was just wondering if you'd heard from or seen Celes?"

"No, I know she's been pretty sick."

"Maybe I should take her some soup?"

Do whatever you want. Maybe Bumo can hold your hand while you go up the stairs. "I'm sure she'd like that." Ian did *not* like feeling like this inside.

"Okay, I'll go and . . . see if she needs anything."

His forced smile began to hurt his cheeks. "Sounds good!"

"Okay." She looked at him again, then finally shook her head and stepped away. "Okay, Ian."

322

He watched her head up the stairs, thinking that girls were even more confusing than Baby Talo trying to talk, and realized he might never figure them out. He didn't know what she wanted from him. After all, he hadn't forced her to hold hands with Bumo, he had only been Ian, and it clearly hadn't been interesting enough for her. For the first time he realized how Quiana must have felt. *I'm sorry, Quiana.*

The door opened suddenly as more people entered the inn, completely soaked from head to toe. As he looked around he wondered if the inn would even be able to hold them all. It seemed to be bursting at the seams. Those who had just arrived were about his own age, including an auburn-haired girl. She had lavender eyes, the most beautiful eyes he had ever seen in his life. *Another one I need to keep away from Bumo.* Noticing the muscular boys walking closely beside her, he concluded that she must two boyfriends. Ian returned attention to his tea.

His mind drifted to the night when he had seen Bumo and Liarra holding hands. Until that moment he had been standing there looking up at the stars, feeling content and full of life. Then it was as if the wind had been sucked out of his sails. Both Bumo and Liarra made eye contact with him as they passed by, and neither pulled away from each other. Ian stood there speechless, and remained in the dark for a good two hours afterward. He had tried to rationalize why Esis was full of some guys who had it all together, and why others were like him. Then he realized that once he had become a Shepherd it didn't matter who was holding hands with whom, all that was important was who was stronger or smarter or more dependable. But it just made him even more insecure about himself. *If Liarra won't choose me, what makes me think that the tournament will?*

He remembered one time when he was little, before the birth of Baby Talo. It had been a rough day that had stood out in his memory for years to come. Ian had gone with his mother shopping in the marketplace, and she had gotten so caught up in browsing the different wares that somehow he had become separated from her. Even now he could remember looking up at the sea of faces, not being able to find his mother. After calling and asking around and searching for a long time without any luck whatsoever, he had climbed on top of a crate to look for her. Suddenly the crate had collapsed from his weight, and he had fallen on his butt. The other little kids had all started laughing at him and pointing. Bumo had been one of those kids, he now remembered. Ian had sat there in the broken crate, blood dripping down his knee, feeling very much alone, vulnerable, and very, very different. Now he again felt that same way. Being fat, Beelzian, and single made him different. It seemed as if Oldaem was a place set up to just make people like Ian stand out and stand alone. And still he was attempting to represent it as a Shepherd. It seemed impossible now.

His mom had finally found him and had wiped him off and took him home. But there would be no mommy rescue from this. No one would stand him up, rip the fat off of him, give him a more confident personality, make him stronger, and help him win the tournament. He was on his own. And that reality left him feeling like once again he was sitting in a broken crate with everyone laughing at him.

I need some fresh air. Even though the rain was pounding against the window, he decided torrential weather was better than sitting in here feeling sorry for himself. As he stood up, he heard shouting. To his surprise two large figures began pushing at each other as hard as they could. Suddenly one of the figures shoved even harder, and the other flew against a table, smashing it to the ground, plates and cups scattering as people starting shrieking and screaming. Then he realized that person who had been shoved had been none other than an angry Helen. Slowly she picked herself up as Wrexa loomed before her, looking very confident and clearly in attack mode. He recognized members of his ship's crew and some of the tournament girls trying to restrain the two of them. Captain Cid and Bumo were laughing, but Wrexa and Helen were not as they shrugged everyone off of them, then plowed into each other like two giant beasts. The innkeeper began to shout as he attempted to regain control of his establishment. It didn't work. Suddenly everyone around them seemed to have lost their minds as fighting broke out everywhere. People started swinging and tackling and shouting and laughing and groaning, and Ian realized that it was the perfect time for him to make his escape. Quickly he pushed his way past what looked like two tussling Oldaem Army recruits and made his way to the door. Pushing it open, he hurried outside into the pouring rain.

Ian raced down the street until he was a good distance from the inn. Kaya was a rundown shantytown. Although he knew it was under the control of Oldaem, that didn't mean the nation spent a coin on its upkeep. Houses and buildings looked as if they were falling into each other, and the poorly paved streets had turned into giant mud pits. While Ian doubted the rain would help the cold he felt coming on him, anything had to be better than sitting in that dreadful room for one second longer.

"Mind if I join you on an adventure?"

Ian whisked around to see the auburn-haired girl standing behind him, a cowl wrapped around her head, her wet braid hanging down her right shoulder.

"I . . . uh . . . how did you . . ."

She cut him off, a lavender twinkle in her eye. "I used that bar brawl for my escape too. If you want to be alone, I understand. I've wanted to be alone for the past several days."

Ian, what are you doing? "No! Sure! I'd love the company!" He smiled broadly and swallowed again, as she looked up at him with an expression of amusement.

"You're a cute kid. What's your name?"

She thinks I'm cute? "Ian."

"You don't look Oldaemite."

"Well, my parents are from Beelz."

"Ah, I've never been to Beelz."

"Neither have I."

"You're really tall."

"You're really pretty." *Really, Ian?*

"Ah, I use it as a disguise, I'm actually really old and ugly and wrinkled."

He laughed. "I doubt that."

"Wanna get out of the rain?" She looked up as thunder boomed again.

"Where?"

"There." She pointed up a hill along an alleyway. "Ready to run?"

I hate running. "Sure."

She grabbed his hand and they took off through the muddy streets, water splashing up and around as they raced along. For the first time in weeks Ian felt free and happy, and he held the hand of this mysterious and beautiful girl. The slope steepened as they hurried along the alleyway. Ian realized if he didn't pay close attention to their steps, he could very well get lost. Then they would have to replace him in the tournament. Finally they

325

stopped as they reached the crumbling stone wall of the city. People huddled along it under crude tents. Ian watched as the girl stood there quietly studying them. It was almost as if she had never seen homeless people before. Ian had seen some who lived in Lion's Landing, but these looked desolate. Their eyes were sunken, they were shivering, and they looked hungry--very hungry. It was the children that seemed to catch her eye. Ian felt in his coat pocket and realized he had tucked some bread away. Approaching a reddish make-shift tent with about four or five little children huddled beside a tiny mother, he knelt down and offered them his bread, the girl standing behind him. The woman's frail hands took the bread from him, then the children quickly devoured it.

I can't believe people live like this. Ian watched as sadness washed over the girl's lavender eyes and was surprised to see her remove her cowl, revealing an Oldaem Soldier's uniform beneath it. She handed it to the woman and watched her quickly drape the wet, dripping cloak around the youngest child. It was better than nothing. The mother said not a word, but her eyes spoke for her, as a tear seemed to trickle down her cheek. Maybe it was just a raindrop--Ian couldn't tell. Suddenly he saw the girl dart off along the wall, her braid flapping behind her. Ian followed, trying to keep up.

Eventually after running for a while, they came to a corner of the wall, where it angled toward the eastern part of the city. A ladder sat against the corner. It led to a platform with a wooden roof, perhaps for scouts or archers to keep watch. Before he could say anything, the girl started climbing the ladder. Following her, he reached the top to find her staring out across the ocean, seemingly lost in deep thought. Having had a lot of time for self-reflection cooped up on the ship and then in the inn, Ian didn't really feel like thinking alone anymore. He honestly wanted to have a conversation with someone who genuinely cared about him. But he couldn't remember the last time he had had that. Maybe it was on the beach with his father before he started this crazy adventure. Ian couldn't believe how far he had come and how much had happened. Was he the same person who jumped aboard the ferry? Did he need to change even more? Would he be loved if he didn't? Maybe it wasn't okay to love who he really was. Perhaps there was a reason he was always alone. Leaning over the wall beside the girl, he also stared out at the ocean. Finally he broke the silence.

"A really bad storm."

"The worst."

"Look at those waves."

"I'm glad we're not on them."

"Yeah. Me too."

"That . . . was really nice of you, Ian. Giving them your food. I wish all Oldaemites were nice like you." A faraway expression crept into her eyes. As if she was far across the sea.

"Aren't you an Oldaemite? I mean, are you a soldier?"

"Do you think there is a higher power, or do you think we're responsible for our own fates and destinies?"

Startled at the question, Ian thought about it. She clearly was not going to tell anything about herself, so he decided to indulge her. "I've always been taught in the Tide and the Rock. Like today, the Rain says it's time for renewal and rebirth. No matter what we've done, after today we have a second chance."

"Do you believe in all that stuff?"

"I do. With all of my heart."

"But why?"

"I guess . . . because I've seen what belief does for people. My Aupaipaupy was a huge believer. My father always told me about how strong his faith was. It was his faith that kept our family strong. It was faith that got them through the Beelzian civil wars. It was faith that brought my family to Oldaem to make a new and safe home for us. And it's faith that has gotten me where I am today. We have to believe in *something*. People are too mean to rely on. I sure hope we're not responsible for our own fates. If we are, Esis is doomed. Fate can't be left to human beings. They suck."

"I guess you're right."

"But you don't suck. You gave that kid your cloak. That was really nice."

"I wish I could have done more."

"You can! We can *always* help people. No matter how we're feeling about things. I've been going through some rough stuff lately, and all this has led me to see how selfish I've been acting. Things are always going to go wrong. It doesn't mean we have to only focus on our pain. There is a lot of joy in Esis. It's our job to

327

remind people about it, and to share it. Especially with people who need some."

She looked over at him. "You're a good guy, Ian. Esis needs more men like you in it."

"And I've been spending all week wishing I was someone else." He looked down, feeling a little guilty.

She rested her head on his shoulder. They stood there in silence for a while, until finally she said, "Don't wish to be someone else. Be the best you, you can be. It'll be enough someday."

He sighed. "Someday soon."

"Someday soon."

Ian watched as a tear trickled down her cheek but didn't say anything. He knew she didn't want to talk about whatever was bothering her. She shivered for a second and lifted her head up and stared out once again. "I miss my family."

He paused and followed her gaze. "I do too." After he said it, it seemed as if her family was much farther away than his was, and perhaps that she would never see them again. Suddenly he felt very blessed.

"Thanks for the adventure, Ian."

He watched her back away from the wall and toward the ladder.

"Does this mean goodbye?"

"It does." She paused for a second. "I wish we would have met in a different time and a different place."

"Maybe we will someday," he said with a smile.

"Maybe we will." She smiled back, then stepped back toward him and leaned up and kissed him on the cheek. "Be proud of who you are, Ian. I wouldn't mind living in an Esis with a bunch of Ians."

"Thanks," he whispered, barely able to speak. Suddenly his throat didn't hurt anymore. He watched her get on the ladder to head back down. "I don't even know your name."

She looked up at him, those lavender eyes twinkling once again. "Allora, but don't tell anyone."

"Okay, Allora."

"Someday soon?"

"Someday soon."

By the time he found his way back to the inn, the rain had begun to taper off slightly. As he had gone along he couldn't but help look for Allora and wondered if he ever would see her again. The Rain had worked in a mysterious way today. He felt better--restored. There was more to life, he realized, than the Bumos and the Liarras. He would be okay. After all, he had been before, and he would be again. As he neared the front door, he saw Terra heading out of the inn.

"They've been looking for you."

"Who has?" Ian asked as he approached her. Her hair was pulled back tightly into a bun.

"Your friends."

"Oh, I didn't know if anyone had even noticed I was gone."

She laughed. "You're everyone's favorite."

"I am?" he asked in surprise.

"My whole crew loves you. I hear the other recruits talking about you. A lot of us are putting our money on you to go all the way. Oldaem needs a Shepherd like you."

Terra stepped past him. "Where are you going?"

"To check on the ship. We should be sailing out tomorrow morning. Get some good rest. It will be your last on dry land for quite some time."

As he watched her leave, he realized that just because he felt a certain way about himself, didn't make it true, or mean others felt the same. *No more self pity. It's a lie. Believe in yourself, Ian. You're here for a reason. And you're Ian for a reason.*

Opening the door, he nearly ran into Liarra.

"Oh! Where have you been? I've been looking for you."

"Sorry. I went for a walk." He smiled.

"Celes is feeling better. She was asking for you too."

"Good! I'll go see her." When he went past her into the inn, Liarra remained outside, staring into nothing. Realizing that she hadn't moved, he paused in the doorway. "What are you going to do?"

"I was . . . going to see if Terra needed any help. I'm tired of watching Bumo tickle Jessica," she explained with a hint of embarrassment in her voice.

He sighed. "Bumo is just Bumo. While he has good intentions, he just . . ." Realization hit him. "He doesn't know how to be the best Bumo he can be. Give him time."

"You're so nice, Ian." She looked down and kicked a pebble. "I'm . . . I'm sorry . . . for . . ."

He smiled again. "Thanks! Don't be! Keep your chin up! The sun is shining!"

Pulling the door closed behind him, he looked around the room for lavender eyes as he headed up the stairs.

CHAPTER 41: KAYT

"Come in and sit down, Kayt."

Kayt eyed Melnora wearily as she took her place across from her in the circular glass room in the mansion belonging to Silas' family. The woman's expression was unreadable. Things weren't going well, and she knew this conversation would be unpleasant. She was sure Melnora would make it her mission to insure that it would be so. *Go against me, Melnora, I dare you. I'll destroy you.*

Clearing her throat, the woman gently folded her hands in her lap. The silk green gloves matched the rest of her outfit. "Well, I know things have been . . . awkward."

"Whatever are you talking about?" Kayt asked sweetly.

"Kayt, there is no need to continue with the pretense of kindness and gentility." She glanced around. "There is no one else here."

"I've upset you somehow." Kayt didn't flinch. "I don't see what I've done."

"You may be able to fool the people of Highdale. And you may fool Silas. But you will *never* fool me, Kayt. I've spoken with Arnand."

You didn't. Suddenly Kayt sat up straighter in her chair.

"I had a very interesting conversation with him about you."

"You had no right to go near my family."

"I see. So you still view them as your family? What of Silas, then? What exactly does he mean to you?"

"Stay away from my family."

"Do you love him?"

"That is none of your . . ."

"Do you *love* him?" Her voice cracked like a whip. Kayt had

330

never seen such shrewdness from this woman in green before her. It only heightened Kayt's resolve to stand up to her.

"It doesn't matter one way or the other. You know that. Silas may be useful." She stopped and eyed Melnora. "And if I find he is *not* useful, if you think I'm going to be stupid enough to let him take me down . . . you are even more stupid than Arnand. Let me tell you something, Melnora."

"Please do." She leaned back in her chair.

"There are two types of women in this world."

"Is that so?"

"Let me finish. I let you speak. Now, let me." Kayt reclined back, matching Melnora's posture. "There are two types of women in this world. First, there are those who wait around for things to happen and then react to them. Sometimes even with power and influence." She leaned slightly forward. "That may even be the type of woman you are. However, know this, there is another type of woman." A sly smile touched her lips. "The type who makes things happen—who bends the will of Esis in her favor. Such women create events while others struggle to keep up with the wake she leaves behind. My wake is large, Melnora." She stood. "I hope you're a good swimmer."

"Kayt, I'm going to tell Silas the truth about you."

Kayt paused in the doorway. "Go ahead." Then she smiled. "He'll never believe you."

"Yes he will!" Melnora snapped, also standing. "I'm his sister."

"Lust is a powerful force."

"Not as powerful as love."

"We'll see."

"You're not unstoppable, Kayt. Someday your actions will come back to haunt you."

For a moment Kayt drummed her fingers on the doorpost. "Know this, Melnora, if Silas can't keep up the momentum . . . if he starts to lose the election . . . if he loses his importance or role in my life . . . I'll bury him deeper than I'll bury you."

"You're a monster." Melnora was breathing heavily.

A shrug. "No. I'm a survivor."

Memories continued to flood Kayt's mind as she sat upon the swing in the royal gardens. Servants wearing green continued to scurry about the grounds, some weeding, others planting, those assigned to the palace carrying linens or other fabrics. Kayt swung back and forth, carefully watching everyone around her, the breeze gently stirring her hair. She didn't know how many days she had done the same thing again and again. It was nice to see Gragor. Unable to stay away from her, he seemed to laugh at everything she said and had apparently become fixated on her. He had thrown her many parties and dances and functions, honoring his dear childhood friend, returning not only from her studies in Westervale, but also from the horrific events she had endured in Highdale. She didn't mind the pity, not if it came with the luxuries of the Capital.

Prince Gragor was nice enough, though a little foolish and a bit petulant. His conversation skills were somewhat lacking, and he was occasionally awkward in public situations, but he was the Prince of Oldaem, and more important than that, with Prince Gragor came access to King Orcino, who had become a huge fan of Kayt's. Often Orcino would call on her for her advice on foreign policy and dealings with Leoj. She had been known for having one of the best strategic minds in Oldaem in her younger days in school. Not that he ever really heeded her advice, or even took it into consideration. She was aware that he probably considered her just a pretty face to have around, and she also recognized that he knew she wasn't an acting Shepherd anymore.

Gragor had given her access to the finest wardrobe in the Capital and her own private chambers in the eastern guest wing of the palace. She had people waiting on her hand and foot. And all she had done was walk into the palace. *Lust is a powerful force.*

Even now Gragor was staring at her as she swung. He was sitting in a shallow pool, letting the sun beat down on his extremely pale body. Kayt smiled coyly as she swung higher and higher. *I wish King Orcino would just make me the Royal Shepherd of State.* Currently that honor belonged to Shepherd Garrus, one of the most powerful political masterminds in the history of Oldaem Realm. She had great respect for him, and he had been polite enough to indulge King Orcino in sometimes including her in political discussions. Nothing too top secret or important, but enough for Kayt to at least pretend what she had to say made an impact. Although deep inside, she knew that another pretty face could waltz into the palace, and Gragor would have a new prize to be won. Kayt realized that she needed to speed up her game. Stepping from the swing, she approached the small pool. Gragor smiled a huge pasty smile. He had lackluster brown hair and skinny white arms that for a long hadn't lifted anything more heavy than a biscuit. True, he wasn't ugly--he had an attractive countenance--but it was not strong nor extremely masculine. But it honestly didn't matter what he looked like. What he represented was enough to get her down on her knees behind him and begin rubbing his shoulders.

"Thank you, Kayt. Are you enjoying your time here?"

"Yes, Gragor. So much," she answered sweetly.

"I do hope . . . I do hope you plan to stay."

Make me your Royal Shepherd of State. "Oh. I hadn't thought about it."

Disappointment filled his voice. "You hadn't . . . thought about it?"

"Well, it's just, I've spent so much time doing practically nothing the past few days, I would like to get out and see some of the Capital as it's prepping for tournament. You know, just to get some fresh air."

"Let me come with you!"

"Your highness! It would be so improper!"

"Oh, phooey. I never get to have fun!"

He's like a 35-year-old child. "You have *so* many other important things to do, Prince Gragor. You practically run Oldaem. And during the war! The people need your focus."

He sunk down into the water so that only his head bobbed above the surface. "That's what the Shepherds are for." He disappeared under the waters. Somehow she managed to keep a straight face as he kept blowing bubbles. She smiled at a passing servant. It was almost as if she was invisible to them.

"Kayt! Having a pleasant day in the gardens?"

Glancing up, she saw Royal Shepherd Garrus approaching her. Standing, she rubbed her hands together.

"Garrus, good to see you again. I see you've returned from the tournament grounds."

"Things are under way." He looked down at the pool. "Is the . . . prince . . ."

Kayt smiled coyly. "He's swimming."

"I see." Garrus chuckled and gave her a knowing smile. *He can see right through me.*

She had grown up knowing Garrus and the influence he had wielded. He had been friends with her father. Well aware of her personality and drive, he probably also knew exactly why she was there playing the dutiful girlfriend. "How are things in the nation?" she asked.

"Shaky. War has caused unrest. Attacks near the bridges have people scared."

"Leoj has directly attacked Oldaem?"

"Just skirmishes here and there. Knowledge of Demas' capture, and the fact that we don't as of yet have a Royal Shepherd of Defense within the country has spread fear among the people."

"Any nominations for replacement?"

"Yes." Then he ushered her to a bench under a tree.

Gragor sprung up from the water, gasping. "Kayt! I must have held my breath for a good four minutes! I'm amazing!"

Kayt and Garrus clapped for him from the bench. "Marvelous, your Highness!"

"Garrus! Did you see?"

"I did, Majesty! Have another go at it?" he beamed. *Garrus is good.*

"Okay! You both count this time!" the prince exclaimed.

"Okay! Ready, set, go!" Garrus replied as Gragor disappeared beneath the water. "Poor simple Gragor. You're good for him, Kayt."

"For now. Until he actually nominates his Shepherds."

"The royal family needs someone like you. I know Orcino has plans for you. You have a good chance."

"Do I?" she asked with interest.

"I think so. He hasn't said out right. But I know he enjoys your company and ideas."

"Oh come on, Garrus. I doubt he cares for my ideas in the slightest."

"Maybe not yet. But he recognizes how simple Gragor is, and I know he wants a political mind to held guide the prince. Orcino isn't getting any younger."

"*If* Gragor asks me. Will he be allowed to select his own Royal Shepherds?"

"Yes. But you never know with him. I'll help put in a good word." They both eyed the pool again.

"You seem, worried, Garrus."

"Shepherd Seff from Efil . . . it seems he's coming here to take Demas' place . . . for now at least."

"You don't like him?"

Garrus' gray eyes looked old and tired. "I don't trust him."

"Why?"

"Seff is very much about Esis unification. I don't know if allying too closely with Sther is the best idea . . . but I feel that's where Seff wants to take us."

"Do you think Orcino will go for it?"

"Time will tell. He should be arriving today."

"How many minutes?" Gragor exclaimed, gasping for breath as he burst from the shallow pool.

"Seven!" Kayt replied.

"Oh, I am a wonder!"

"Yes, you are." Garrus said, looking away.

Kayt watched as Gragor clapped his hands wildly and servants rushed to him with warm towels. After they dried him off, he approached her and Garrus.

"I think it's time for my nap."

"You've had a busy day," Kayt commented sweetly.

"Do you want to have desert with me tonight?"

"I would love to."

"Very good. Now, don't work too hard, Garrus. You're aging too quickly. You need to spend some time relaxing."

"I'll remember that. Thanks."

"I'm full of good advice!" Then he leaned down and kissed Kayt on the cheek. "I'll see you soon, beautiful creature."

"Your highness." She bowed slightly as she watched him walk off into the palace, his slippers squishing. Then she turned and looked at Garrus who smiled.

"What does the rest of your day entail, Kayt?"

"I think I will go off into the city for a bit. I need to take care of some things."

"All right. Take care. I'll keep my ears and eyes open. Be careful. I have a hunch Stherian spies infest Oldaem."

"You fear Sther more than Leoj?"

"Yes. And so should you."

"I'll be careful. And I'll be mindful as well."

"Blessings," Garrus said as he stood and walked away. Kayt watched him depart and wondered what being Royal Shepherd of State for Oldaem must be like. All the pressure he must endure, all the decisions and choices he had to make, and the enemies he must have. *Sometimes I think Garrus is too soft. I could handle it. One day I will.*

Kayt left the palace, wearing soft blue linens and a silver circlet on her golden hair. The Capital was bustling today with tournament preparations, and she noticed several Shepherd Candidates training and meeting and studying their guides and packets. She couldn't help but remember her own tournament and how she had completely dominated it. Garrus had observed from the stands, smiling down at her with approval. In those days she had been the one to watch, the one to beat. Somehow she wished that she could have gotten high acclaim from her brainpower instead of her looks. Recently she had begun to feel like nothing but a piece of meat. No one valued her for her mind, just her appearance. People regarded her as a bouquet of flowers when she wanted to be an axe. *Soon, I'll rise again. And when I do, I'll dunk you in the water myself, Gragor. Simple fool.*

Without thinking, she started out on the same path she took every time she left the palace to explore. Soon she found herself in the same neighborhood, with the same buildings and the same parks, and the same schools. Finally she stood outside a fence of a familiar elementary school and peeped through the cracks at it. Kayt could see children playing and laughing inside. The children looked happy and carefree playing behind the fence. They had no idea what was happening in Oldaem, of the war and death it brought. As she watched, her children, Lei and Balyn, laughed and ran and swung and jumped. A part of her wanted to leap over the fence and hold them both with all of her might. To teach Lei how to sew and to tuck Balyn in at night. Kayt would warn Lei about dangerous boys and how to protect herself, and how to get back up again when people knocked her down. If only she could impart to her children all the knowledge she had had to figure out on her own. What was left of the mother in her longed to laugh with them and feed them and take care of them. But instead she did nothing, just watching from outside the fence, realizing that she never would know them. It would be better for them if she didn't taint them with her cynical outlook. They were laughing now, safe and innocent. Something that she wasn't. No longer innocent, she was guilty. More than just a survivor, she *had* become a monster, destroying those who came in contact with her. Those she left in her wake could never recover. But she wouldn't allow herself to destroy her children. Instead, she just watched from the fence. Laughing when Lei did, cheering inside when Balyn scored a point in his games. Imagining a life in which she could be a simple mother: simple and safe. Those were two things she would never be again.

"Come in."

"You called for me, King Orcino?" Kayt hesitantly stood in the entrance to the throne room. After watching her children for some time, she had done some light shopping and returned to her chambers to find a notice that the king requested her presence.

"Yes, I wanted to speak to you about something." The king of Oldaem was of medium height and build with white hair and no beard or mustache. Today he wore deep blue robes and had a friendly smile on his face. But he wasn't easy to interpret, which probably added to the power he wielded. Unlike Gragor, he was actually interested in the well-being of his people, and took an active role in the events of their lives. The people admired him, and she knew that Garrus respected him. The queen had died years ago, and she felt as if Orcino had never recovered from his wife's death. The spark she remembered seeing in his eyes when she had been a child was all but gone. They had only Prince Gragor for an heir. And he was very useless and very spoiled.

"What did you need to speak to me about?"

"It might need to wait. The Royal Council is about to convene."

"Oh. I'll wait in my chambers until you're ready for me."

"How is Gragor?"

Annoying. "He's had a relaxing day."

"I invited him to sit in on this meeting. I hope he decides to come." As she watched him rub his temples she thought he seemed stressed.

"I'm sure he will. I know he's eager to emulate the wonderful leadership you've provided for so many years."

Orcino laughed heavily. "Oh, don't make up things for him. He needs to become a man. He's more than 30 and acts like a spoiled child."

"Your Highness!" she feigned surprise.

"Your Majesty, Seff is in the palace." Royal Shepherd Zorah stood in the doorway. A tall old man, Zorah wore a long white beard and a long robe. He was the Royal Spirit Shepherd. Kayt had only seen him a handful of times. She couldn't read his face at all, though she thought he had kind eyes. If not kind, then at least good at getting others to trust them.

"He's arrived! Excellent. Zorah, you're familiar with Kayt."

"How could I forget one of the most famous tournament victors of all time? Kayt, what brings you to the palace?"

"Oh, I'm just passing through." She smiled.

"She's become a very good friend to Prince Gragor," Orcino exclaimed.

"Ah good, the young prince needs good friends." Zorah replied. Kayt assumed anyone was young next to Zorah. "Your Majesty, Royal Shepherd Udina is bringing him in."

"And Garrus?"

"I've brought the prince," he replied, entering the room, his arm on Gragor's shoulder.

"Why do I have to come to this?" Gragor pouted.

"Because, Son, it's time you saw the innerworkings of the Royal Council."

"Why? I was to play a game of dice with the garden staff."

"Dice can wait."

Kayt watched as Garrus shook Zorah's hand. She sensed friendship between the two men. But then they had worked together for years, after all.

"Kayt! What are you doing here?" Gragor questioned.

"I sent for her," Orcino interjected.

"Do you want to play dice?"

"I need to be returning to my chambers," she replied.

"No! Please stay! Don't make me sit through this alone!"

"Highness, it would be improper."

Gragor turned to his father, the king. "Dad! Let her stay! You're just going to make me sit in the corner. I'd like her to sit with me."

"Very well, Gragor. But do pay attention. Kayt, make sure he does." Suddenly she realized that Orcino now depended on her to keep Gragor in line. Perhaps even to make something of him. It would be a difficult task. But if it meant staying in the palace of Oldaem Realm, she would be up to it.

"Yes, your majesty." She nodded as Orcino gave her a knowing smile. She and Gragor took their places down at a small table by a marble column. The Royal Shepherds Garrus and Zorah sat at a round table off to the side of the throne. Orcino occupied a larger chair at the table. After a bit of small talk, Royal Mind Shepherd Udina, a bit younger than Garrus, escorted the man who had to be Interim Royal Defense Shepherd Seff to the table. She saw Garrus and Seff shake hands, hesitancy in Garrus' eyes as the two men took their places. Kayt noticed that the Royal Council did not have a single woman. She planned to change that soon.

She observed them as they talked, first about minor issues of state. Garrus gave a report on Capital finances and tournament preparation. Udina spoke slowly about the state of the three academies and how all students would soon be heading to the Capital to observe the tournament. They discussed the dismissal of a headmaster at Middle Lake Academy, and Udina also spoke about needing more funding in the refurbishment of Woodlands Academy. Zorah, in his report on the state of religious affairs, described the widespread surge in popularity of New Order theological books. Unrest in the city among Lameans was also causing some problems. He mentioned how he had mobilized the Oldaem Army to crack down harder on Lamean dissenters. Vertloch City had seen an increase in population, and Seff noted that the Order of the Three was gaining popularity in Oldaem, and how useful the priestesses had become in helping maintain order in the country. Kayt could tell Garrus wasn't exactly pleased that Orcino seemed receptive to Stherian involement in Oldaem affairs.

Seff was a round man who seemed to have his glory days as a fighter long behind him. His dark hair was thinning on the top of his head, but he had a thick mustache. His quite demanding persona seemed to dominate a lot of the conversation, even though he was just presently standing in for Demas. Finally the topic of Demas came up.

"The rescue mission was partially successful," Seff stated with confidence.

"How so?" Orcino questioned.

"Have you located Demas?" Zorah asked slowly.

"No. We haven't. Spies have placed him within Leoj custody, however we don't know where exactly they are holding him."

"You know with full confidence Leoj has taken him?" Garrus asked suspiciously.

"Who else, Garrus, would be to blame? We are at war with Leoj," Seff snapped.

"No one is questioning who is at war, Seff," Zorah calmly replied. "I only wonder if we are 100 percent certain Leoj is responsible for his abduction. You say you can confirm he is in Leoj custody?"

"Yes, Zorah. We can. We have to trust in the Oldaem Military. They have been trained at the highest level. It's their report."

"How can we confirm the report?" Garrus persisted.

Seff paused and smiled. Udina came to his defense. "Now, Garrus, Zorah, I know that losing Demas has been difficult. However, it must be stated that Seff is very good at what he does. And he has this nation's best interest at heart. We have to trust that his people know what they are doing. Seff, tell them about the successful mission."

"What has happened?" Orcino interrupted.

Kayt felt a bony elbow dig into her side. She turned and saw Gragor smiling. He leaned over to her. "Isn't this boring? Just a bunch of old men talking about old men things. I'd much rather play dice."

"Oh, your highness, you're so silly." She smiled back, then returned her attention to the conversation at the table. *Idiot.*

Seff stood and started walking around the table. "My men have been successful in infiltrating the royal stronghold of Leoj and abducting the Leojian Princess Allora. We should be able to break her once we have her here in the palace, and see where exactly Demas is located, and not only that, but perhaps use her as a leverage for his return."

"A good plan," Udina, the Mind Shepherd, exclaimed. Orcino seemed to nod in agreement.

"I would just hate to think we have wrongly accused Leoj," Garrus mused. Zorah nodded.

Seff glared in Zorah's direction. "I tire of your bigoted outlook on the Stherians. They are not the enemy!"

"We just need to be careful," Zorah replied. "Their religious fervor for the Order of the Three makes them dangerous. They don't have Oldaem's New Order vision in mind."

"Oldaem is built on more than just religion," Seff insisted.

"New Stherian Towers are built every day on foreign soil," Garrus responded. "Their priestesses roam Oldaem freely. We need to be careful, your Majesty."

"Your Majesty," Seff interjected, "I know I just arrived, but I must say that Oldaem needs to be united, not further separated by religious intolerance. Sther could be a very resourceful ally, and I know that High Priestess A'delath holds Oldaem in high regard, and would love to offer her protection, financial assistance, and support in these dangerous times of war. We don't know where Hemia and Remia will stand, and word is that Kaya is looking to rebel once again. We can't fight every nation at the same time. It might be wise to consider an alliance with Sther at some point in the future."

"I disagree," Zorah protested as Garrus nodded sadly. Udina stared at the floor. "I appreciate you trying to help, Seff," Zorah continued, "I know that times have been difficult, and tensions are high, but I've been monitoring the Stherian situation closely, and the priestesses' presence in Oldaem is actually causing distrust and unrest. I agree we need to be unified, but we need to be a unified religious front. If the Stherians and the Lameans were to team up, Oldaem could be completely overthrown."

"Zorah, that is not going to happen." Udina shook his head.

"Once Princess Allora arrives we will question her," King Orcino finally spoke, "and then see what our next step will be."

"Allow me to handle the questioning." Seff responded. "I lost a lot of good people during the rescue mission. She has a lot to answer for."

"Very well. In the meantime, I feel good about allowing Shepherd Seff to be Interim Royal Shepherd of Defense until we have more information and can insure Demas' release. This is what I've decided."

Kayt could sense increased tension in the room after Orcino made his decision. Zorah and Garrus eyed each other uneasily, as Seff seemed to exude more confidence and Udina kept his face impassive. Kayt found the entire interchange absolutely fascinating. She agreed with Zorah and Garrus that Sther needed to be watched. Seff seemed incredibly too eager to enter into alliance with a mysterious pagan nation. The One needed to be respected, not pushed aside for a false trio of goddesses.

The conversation lasted for an hour or so longer, until finally Orcino dismissed them all, whispering quietly to Shepherd Seff as Zorah and Udina left arguing together. Garrus nodded politely to Kayt as he departed, and she looked over at Gragor who had fallen asleep on the table. After servants had carried the prince out of the room, Kayt found herself standing alone before the Royal King of Oldaem.

"What are your thoughts?"

I can't believe he's asking me. "With respect, your Majesty, I would pay heed to the words of your royal Shepherd of State. I think Garrus and Zorah are right. I would be hesitant to trust Sther."

"No. I mean about my son."

There it is. "Oh. I enjoy his company."

"I fear he isn't fit to be king after I die. I've never told that to anyone outside of my Royal Shepherds."

341

"Your Majesty, he will grow into it."

He looked pensively at her. "Perhaps . . . perhaps with the right guidance."

"Your Majesty?"

"Gragor needs someone like you. Someone who is knowledgeable about politics and who can protect him from usurpers and threats to the throne. He must have someone with a good head on her shoulders, someone who will guide him away from ruin and embarrassment. I've been waiting a long time for someone like you."

"What kind words." *Is he saying he wants me to be the Prince's Royal Shepherd of State?*

"I do hope you're up for the challenge."

"What are you asking me to do?"

"I'm asking you to marry Gragor."

CHAPTER 42: GALEN

"Argh! Get off me!" Galen shouted above the roar of the crowd. Gadiel was on top of him, fingers in his face and elbows in his neck. Galen was not sure what had happened in the past few minutes. One second he had been sitting at the table peacefully enjoying the warmth coming from the fire, and the next he had been crashed into by a very tall and solid-looking girl who was then pummeled by another rather large Beelzian woman. Then the room had erupted into chaos.

Plates flew, tables collapsed, and Galen was slowly being trampled by the people around him. "I'm trying, too!" Gadiel barked from above Galen. People were everywhere with no room even to move around in. *Stupid storm. People have probably been cooped up in here all day.* Strangely, many seemed to be actually enjoying the mayhem. Except Galen who was still trying to shove Gadiel off of him.

Finally, Galen freed his right arm from under Gadiel's knee and jabbed him hard in the stomach.

"Oof!" Gadiel grunted and collapsed to the side. Shoving him all the way off him, Galen grabbed onto a chair to pull himself to a standing position. Gadiel managed to get to his feet as well and turned accusingly to Galen. "You hit me again, I'm hitting back."

"Oh, please, that was a freebie. I still owed you from that one time on the ship *and* I saved your life."

Gadiel gritted his teeth. "*Stop* bringing that up."

"I'll bring it up whenever I want!"

Gadiel's eyes flared and he looked as if he was going to start a fight then and there. Suddenly, something behind Galen made Gadiel's entire face pale with horror. "Where is she?" he whispered.

About to ask whom he meant, he then realized there could only be one possibility. He whirled around to examine the table he and Princess Allora had been sitting at just minutes ago. But now she was gone.

With that one realization, Galen felt as if the rest of his life had just vanished with the princess. *She was just waiting for the right opportunity.* "She was right there ..."

"Well, she's not there anymore, genius! You untied her, didn't you?"

"I was watching her." He didn't like Gadiel's self-righteous attitude.

"Oh, you were watching her! That makes me feel *so* much better," Gadiel feigned relief. "Where did she go then? To the ladies room?" he asked sarcastically.

"You know what, Gadiel? It's a little hard to keep a close watch on someone while being trampled by you."

Gadiel threw up his hands. "I was coming back here and got hit by a plate or something. Look." Gadiel turned to reveal a big purple stain on the back of his uniform jacket.

"Looks like pie."

"We have more important things to worry about here!"

He was right. "Okay, she can't have gone far. At most she's been gone, like, five to ten minutes."

"Do you think she left the inn?" Gadiel wondered as he looked out the window at the continuing storm.

"I don't know. It's raining pretty hard out there." The tavern was crowded with people. "Let's ask around. Someone may have seen her."

The room was beginning to calm down now. Some walked toward the stairs, heading to their rooms exhausted and happy. Others were still angry and had to be pulled apart. The two girls who had started the whole thing had been separated by the other people at their table and were cooling off on opposite sides of the room.

Galen made his way down one side of the tavern while Gadiel questioned people on the other side.

Those whom Galen asked did not seem to remember the female Oldaemite soldier that he had been sitting with earlier. A few people recalled seeing them walk in, or sit down, but nothing after Galen had lost sight of Allora. *How could I have been so thoughtless?* He never should have untied her. Galen hated to admit that he had fallen right into the trap that her beautiful lavender eyes had set. *Gadiel was right.*

"Galen!" Gadiel beckoned him toward the window where he was standing. "I spoke to a woman who remembers her."

Thank goodness. "What did she say exactly?"

"The lady remembers Allora because in the midst of everything, she came up to her and asked to borrow her cowl, because she was going outside and didn't have her jacket. The woman thought it was strange, but wasn't about to say no to an Oldaemite soldier, and she gave it to her."

"So she left." Galen sighed.

"So she left," Gadiel echoed, staring out at the storm.

"Great."

"Perfect."

Galen looked out at the rain and then remorsefully back at the fire he had been sitting near just moments ago. "We have to clean this up before Zevran finds out."

"Let's go, then."

They decided not to split up. While they would have covered more ground separately, there was no way to communicate if one of them somehow found the missing princess, nor would either have any backup if one of them got into trouble. Like it or not, they were in it together.

Quickly they made their way along the main road leading away from the inn. Their assumption was that maybe Princess Allora was heading back toward the docks. After a while Galen pulled Gadiel into an overhang for some relief from the constant, battering rain. It was starting to get darker, and it had been hard to see much even during the day. Quite possibly Zevran and Adar had returned to the inn and discovered them gone. Kaya was a big place with a lot of people in it. How were they ever supposed to find someone who was trying hard not to be found?

"I think we need to rethink this."

344

"Which part?" Gadiel sullenly wrung moisture from the sleeve of his jacket though it didn't really do any good. He would be drenched again the moment they stepped back onto the street.

"What if she didn't go toward the docks?"

"Why wouldn't she? It's the fastest way out of the country."

"Because it's too obvious." Galen had been doing some thinking, trying to figure out what he would do if he was trying to evade his captors. "Because she would know that was the first place we'd look."

Gadiel began to realize what Galen was saying. "So you think she went inland?"

He shrugged. "That's what I'd do."

The two soldiers doubled back toward the inn, but this time took the street leading toward the eastern side of the city.

After knocking on a few doors, it became apparent that nobody wanted to talk to them. *Maybe it's the uniform.* And it was no wonder they seemed distrustful of people from Oldaem. The city was not at all how Galen had pictured it in his mind. Everything was deteriorated and crumbling. While it was a port, just like Sea Fort, it showed no sign of the latter city's prosperity. Galen wondered if the rest of Kaya looked like this. *Maybe Princess Allora had a point.* Perhaps Oldaem wasn't taking very good care of the territory after all. As they hurried along, the buildings grew more and more ramshackle. Few people answered the door when Galen or Gadiel knocked, and of those who did, none admitted to seeing an Oldaemite soldier dressed like they were. It was if she had vanished into thin air.

It wasn't long before they had nearly reached the city wall. A small shantytown spread along the wall with people huddled underneath soaked tents, trying to find shelter from the storm. *Yeah, at least you have some sort of protection.* Galen didn't even have that at the moment. And if they didn't find the princess tonight ... if he survived he'd probably be in worse shape than these people.

They slowed as they reached the wall. "We just walked, like, all the way across the city. Maybe she's down one of those countless streets that we didn't investigate." Gadiel slicked his soaked hair back in exasperation.

Galen was getting tired. *How could I have been so thoughtless? This is all my fault.* How would they ever find the princess? She could have slipped into any of those houses that had refused to open their doors to them. Or she could have actually gone to the docks. In fact, she could be anywhere. And it was dark now. *What are we even doing out here?* "Maybe we should call it a day."

Gadiel shook his head. "We can't go back without her."

"She could have left the city, Gadiel," Galen said, staring at the city wall. "We've been searching for hours. There's no way we're going to find her tonight."

"We have too. Besides, the gates were probably already closed by the time she got here. She's probably still inside the city, waiting till morning to get out." Gadiel jogged over to the nearest tent, a flimsy red cloth propped up against the wall. "Hey, when does the gate close?"

Galen ran to catch up. Huddled under the tent were a woman, her children, and another person facing the back of the tent. The woman looked up at Gadiel, fear draining her already pale features. She shook so much, she couldn't even answer. Galen approached the family. "He's talking to you, lady. When does the gate close?"

"Before sunset," she whispered as she shook. "Before sunset."

Without a word, the two soldiers turned away from the tent. Gadiel led the way as they stared at the city wall. "See? So that means there's a good chance ... what?"

Galen had held up his hand. He hadn't paid much attention to the family under the tent, but something had caught his attention, and he just now realized what it was. "The littlest kid. Did you see what she was wearing?"

"I don't know. A hood?"

"No one else had one. That family had nothing. So where would they get their hands on something that ... nice?" Bits and pieces began to fall into place. The woman at the inn who said that Princess Allora "borrowed" her cowl. The child in the shantytown wearing one ... The person in the back of the tent!

Gadiel realized it at the same time.

They bolted back to the tent just in time to see a figure dart into the shadows of the alleyway. As Galen passed by the tent, he saw the mother and her children huddling closely together. But of course, Princess Allora was no longer hiding in the back.

There was no time to think, just act. Galen followed down the alleyway, hoping to catch up with her. Gadiel darted down another street. *He's trying to cut her off.*

When he reached a bend in the shoddy street, he just caught a glimpse of her braid flying behind her as she turned to the left.

"Stop!" he screamed. She didn't. Where was Gadiel? He should have caught up by now.

Galen turned left as well and found himself in a deserted alley. The street didn't go through–instead it was a dead end. Silently he started down the narrow street, listening for any sign of movement. It was so quiet that the only thing Galen could here was the crunch of his boots on broken glass and the rain beating down on the dirt. Trash piles littered the street, and she could be hiding in any one of them. "Allora," he whispered, "I know you're here. There's nowhere to run."

His boots crunched again as he stopped in the middle of the street and listened. Nothing. And then Galen heard a *whoosh* just in time to turn to the right and feel the full brunt of a big rock slamming into his shoulder. The blow momentarily knocked him to his knees and gave Princess Allora just enough time to shove him out of the way and run past Galen into the night.

But as she crossed the intersection, Gadiel suddenly appeared and tackled her to the ground. Galen rushed toward the two who were entangled in a vicious fight on the ground. Much to Galen's dismay, Princess Allora kicked Gadiel hard in the stomach and rolled away as he curled up. "Oh, no you don't!" Galen cried as he dove forward and grabbed onto her legs. Instantly she sat up and delivered a stinging slap to his face. Galen's grip loosened, but Gadiel had gotten enough time to whip out his knife. Pulling her backward, he held the knife to her throat.

Princess Allora bit her lip and reluctantly held up her hands in surrender. Although she was breathing heavily, her face red, resistance still gleamed in her eyes. Galen stood, pulled out the rope that was still in his pocket, and began to tie her hands behind her back. "I hope this doesn't ruin our budding relationship," she said winking at him over her shoulder.

Sighing, he helped her to her feet and looked at her in exhaustion. She shrugged back. Gadiel grabbed one arm and Galen the other as the trio marched back toward the inn.

"There." Gadiel finished securing Princess Allora's right arm to the chair they had placed in the center of the room. "Try and get out of that." When they had arrived back at the inn, they had encountered Adar who had given the wonderful news that Zevran had not returned yet. *Well, that's one storm we'll get to avoid.* Adar had come back alone, but found Leilani who had told him of the chaos in the lobby and that she hadn't seen Galen or Gadiel since. When he was about to set out to look for them, they had appeared on the street in front of the inn, drenched. He had then helped them slip in through a back entrance that led up the stairs and to the rented room.

They were there now, taking precautions to make sure their prisoner remained that way this time. Allora was sitting grumpily in the chair, her hands secured to the wooden arms and her ankles tied to the legs. "Is this really necessary?"

"You had us chasing you all over the city!" Galen exclaimed in exasperation. "After I untied your hands on good faith and everything."

"I hate to say I told you so," Gadiel smirked.

"Oh, shut up," Galen snapped.

Allora leaned forward in the chair. "Well, what did you think I was going to do? Just sit there and see my only chance slip away? That fight was a prime opportunity."

"Yeah, well welcome to the rest of your stay in Kaya. Hope you got all your sight-seeing done tonight." Gadiel leaned against the door of the room.

"Relax, Gadiel. I doubt I'll get another chance like that one." Allora stared off into the distance as if she was thinking about something or someone else. Despite the fact that it was her fault he had stumbled around in the rain all evening and gotten slapped in the face, Galen felt a little sorry for her. Could he really blame her for trying to escape? Would he have done anything different in her place?

Just because she's our prisoner doesn't mean she's not a person. "Look at it this way," he offered. "The closer we get to Oldaem, the closer you technically get to going back home." He sat on the bed.

"How do you figure?" She raised an eyebrow.

"We just need you so that we can trade you for Royal Shepherd Demas. So once we get to Oldaem, it will just be a little while until you get shipped back to Leoj."

Allora scoffed. "Is that really what you think is going to happen to me once I get to Oldaem?" Her voice shook. "Try torture or public humiliation, or maybe even execution. That's what I have to look forward to. So excuse me for trying to avoid that."

348

"We don't even want you! We want to make a deal with your father!"

"They're going to think I know things," Allora insisted. "They're going to think I know where your Royal Shepherd is."

"Do you?" Gadiel pushed away from the door, suddenly interested in the conversation. "Do you know where my father is?" His voice was a low growl.

Allora appeared surprised. "Your father? The man you're looking for ... he's your father?"

Gadiel's face was stony. Galen nodded at her. She leaned back in the chair. "Oh. That makes sense," she said quietly. It was as if she suddenly understood why Gadiel had been so rude to her. "I'm sorry for your loss," she said.

Gadiel ignored her comment. "Do you know where he is?" he pressed.

"I don't even know where my father is, let alone yours." Allora stared at the floor. "I wish I could help you."

"You have to know something. Your father is the king!"

"Does your father tell you everything he does?" she snapped. "I didn't even know he had captured your Royal Shepherd." She looked at Galen, as if pleading for him to understand. "I don't even know how he could have accomplished it. Or where they took him. Honestly."

Although Galen didn't know why, he believed her. Maybe it was the sorrowful expression that he sensed she was not feigning, or perhaps it was because she had been generally so positive, even in the face of danger, and now her eyes uncharacteristically betrayed the real feelings inside. Clearly, she was scared. Galen didn't want to believe what Allora feared would happen when she arrived in the Capital of Oldaem. His country was better than that. She would be a political prisoner, basically just an unwilling guest of the palace. Nothing more. But he felt a small inkling of doubt as he looked at her, tied to a chair with two guards. Suddenly the room felt too small. He got off the bed and opened the door. "I'm going downstairs."

"Don't be gone too long," Gadiel called after him.

As he went down the stairs he decided that he would be gone as long as he wanted. He had some thinking to do. Soon he found himself sitting in the tavern downstairs, staring into a mug of warm tea. The lobby had almost emptied by now. It was late. Everyone was probably asleep. Galen felt as if it would take years for the chill to leave his body. At least he had been able to change out of his wet clothes, but the cold was still there. Maybe it had always been there and would never go away.

"You look like you've had a rough day." Galen looked up to see the owner of the voice, a tall chubby kid with a silly grin. He was also holding a mug with steam rising out of it.

"Guess so," Galen answered reluctantly. He didn't feel like talking, especially to a Beelzian.

"Mine has been … interesting, too."

Why is he here?

The guy nodded politely, then asked, "Mind if I join you?" He pulled out the chair across from him.

Galen sat up, "Uh, yes, actually, I …"

"Oh, I won't be long." He plopped his large mass down onto the chair. *It's a miracle that chair didn't break,* Galen mused. There was still time. "So you're a soldier." The kid took a sip out of his mug.

"Did the uniform give it away?" *What kind of person just sits at another individual's table?*

"Why are you in such a bad mood?" *Wow, and straightforward, too.* Somehow he reminded Galen of Allora.

"Why are you in such a good one?"

"Because I'm going to be a Shepherd." The kid smiled from ear to ear. "Name's Ian, by the way."

Galen stopped sipping his tea. "Wait, what? You're from Oldaem?"

"Born and raised in Lion's Landing." Ian swelled with pride.

"And you're on your way to the tournament." Galen realized Ian was probably with that group of Oldaemites he had seen when they had first entered the inn.

"Well, we were until the storm damaged our ship."

Galen exhaled. "Yeah, same for us. And I'm Galen."

"Storms get in the way of all kinds of plans, huh, Galen?"

"Why do you want to be a Shepherd?" Galen blurted out without thinking.

Ian did not even react with surprise. "Because I want to help people. I want to make a difference. I want to be someone whom people can look up to. I want to be …" His voice trailed off.

"Important?" Galen offered quietly.

"Yeah." Ian smiled, staring out the window at the rain that had resumed. "I want to find out whom I'm supposed to be."

"What if who you're supposed to be … is someone you don't like?"

350

"Then maybe that's not who you're supposed to be." Ian stared at Galen. "I think we all have a purpose, you know? A crab isn't meant to be a fish. A crab can try all it wants to be a fish, but in the end it won't work out."

"That's a stupid metaphor. Crabs can't be fish, because they suck at swimming. They don't have anything useful that fish have. No gills, no fins." *No talent.*

Ian shook his head. "But you're forgetting something. I mean, you're right. Crabs would be terrible at trying to be a fish. But that's because they were meant for something else. They have pincers and little legs and sometimes a shell, which would all make for a pretty terrible fish. But it makes them really good at being a crab."

Is that what I am? A crab trying to be a fish? In his 21 years of life, Galen had tried so hard at every turn, but he had nothing to show for it. Sayla got to be the Shepherd. Someone else always got to be the hero when Galen was playing victim. If it hadn't been for Gadiel, they probably would have lost Allora. It seemed that he could never do anything right. Or, if he could, there was always someone who could do it better. Galen pushed his chair away from the table. "Good luck in your tournament."

Ian nodded and smiled that goofy grin again. "Good luck with whatever you're doing, too."

Galen thought about the girl upstairs whose life rested in his hands. Was he making the wrong decision all over again? "Thanks," he replied. "I'm going to need it."

CHAPTER 43: SAYLA

Sayla was getting restless. The original plan had been to drop off the slaves at the cliffs and let the local mine workers handle it from there. But now it had been two weeks, and they were still at the Limestone Cliffs. The slaves had become acquainted with their routine. The military officers in charge seemed to have everything under control. *So then why are we still here?*

Apparently Tryndamere had received word that the roads were becoming more and more unsafe. Skirmishes had broken out all over the place, and there were even rumors that some Leojian troops had managed to land in Oldaem and were hiding out, attacking bridges and destroying trade among the regions. Sayla understood about the

351

roads becoming treacherous. But wasn't that enough incentive to leave sooner rather than later? She was eager to meet up with Shale and the rest of the group.

The tournament was close at hand. Probably the Candidates were already training at the Capital City. The other Shepherd students from Woodlands Academy, and probably the other trainees from Westpoint and Middle Lake, should already be there. But not Sayla, Aveline, and Grunt. *No, we're stuck here, way up in the north with a bunch of slaves.*

They had been passing the time helping out as guards. Grunt and Aveline were currently inside the caves watching the slaves. Sayla had gone into the caves for the first few days, but it reminded her too much of the collapsing chamber in her dream, and she was not eager to make that become a reality. Instead she had volunteered to serve outside.

But that was really unnecessary. The Limestone Cliffs actually were cliffs, and looking down from them made Sayla feel as if she were somehow at the edge of the world. But, more importantly, scattered along the cliffs were deep ore mines. They had people inside extracting ore that others brought out in wheelbarrows. More laborers processed the ore in temporary buildings set up all along the cliff front. It was a booming operation.

The children Sayla's group had brought mainly helped inside the caves so that she didn't see them very much. From Aveline, she had learned that they ran errands and held torches for the adult workers.

It made sense to her. If the adults from the destroyed village had been captured they would have been much more rebellious and difficult to transport, especially with pockets of free Lameans all along the route to Westervale. She knew Grunt was upset about it. Although too intimidated by Tryndamere actually to say anything about it out loud, his face clearly revealed his true feelings. He did not like the fact that they were children. For that matter, he probably didn't like that the adults were working in the mines too. *But somebody has to do it.*

She knew the mining was important for the military. They needed all the weapons they could get in the war with Leoj. But Sayla was tired of viewing the smelting and manufacturing day in and day out. She would much rather be using the weapons than watch them be made.

Sayla now sat on the ground a few yards away from the cave site of the day, distracting herself by tossing pebbles at a spider crawling along the ground in front of her. Covered with dust and dripping with sweat, slave number eleven helped haul out another wheelbarrow of rock. Uncomfortable with the sight, Sayla looked away.

It had been a mistake to talk with the girl. That had humanized her too much, and their conversation kept distracting Sayla at the most inopportune times. Already she had enough trouble sleeping as it was, but now it seemed that just as she would finally be about to fall asleep each night, a mental image of the Tower made her sit up, wide awake.

It's just a stupid story. Eleven didn't know what she was talking about, because she had never seen the Tower. Sayla had, and even though she and her friends had decided long ago never to tell their secret, it did not mean that they had imagined it. It had always seemed too serious a subject to talk about. Something about the Wall had given Sayla a strange feeling, and she knew that the others had sensed it too. It was not the kind of experience one discussed.

In fact, until that first disturbing dream, she had not even thought about it in ages. And after she had dreamed of the little redheaded boy and the rainbow river and Galen all at the Tower, she had tried to push it all to the furthest recesses of her mind. *But then that girl had to go and bring it up again.* Sayla had enough problems as it was.

She didn't need the distraction of something that had happened when she was just a little kid. It no longer had any significance to her life except to confirm her beliefs in the New Order. Better to leave all those memories in the past. *I don't need them anymore.* She had grown up since then and had a new family.

Glancing up from her rock throwing, she noticed Aveline jog out of the caves and head in her direction. Grunt followed behind more slowly, dragging his heels. "Sayla, can you trade off with Grunt now? I think he needs to stay out here for a while."

Sayla's heartbeat quickened. "Uh, I'd rather stay out here." She didn't mention that if she went inside she feared she would cause a cave-in. Aveline wouldn't have understood that.

"Well, *he* can't handle it in there." Aveline pointed an accusing finger at Grunt, who had just caught up with her.

"I'm fine in there. You're the one that's being a jerk!" he snapped.

Sayla had never heard him talk like that, and it caught her off guard. "What happened?"

"He's fraternizing with the slaves," Aveline complained.

"I'm just helping," he protested. "And you could stand to help a little too."

"That's not our job, Grunt. Our responsibility is to make sure they don't try to escape or stop working, not to take over for them!" Aveline turned to Sayla and explained, "He keeps trying to do their work even though the guards and I keep telling him to cut it out. It's embarrassing!"

"What's embarrassing is the way you keep treating those poor people. They *are* people, Aveline. You keep forgetting that!" Grunt's face had begun to redden. Perhaps the strongest opinion than Sayla had ever seen him present, it might have been a good thing if he had directed it at something more appropriate.

"Sure they're people," she interjected, attempting to help him understand. "But they're slaves first. You're making us look bad. What you don't realize is that your actions reflect upon the whole of Woodlands Academy."

"Thank you!" Aveline nodded at her. "That's what I've been trying to tell him."

Grunt looked at Sayla in disbelief. "Good. I hope my actions do reflect on Woodlands Academy. Because it seems that I'm the only one who's acting with any decency around here." He advanced toward Sayla until he was standing directly in front of her. "I know you see them as more than just slaves. I saw you talking to Eleven that day on the way here. I just don't get why you're hiding it. Being a Shepherd of Defense is about protecting those people who need it. Well, we have to protect them. They can't defend themselves!"

Suddenly Galen's voice from both of Sayla's dreams slammed into her head. "Protect them," he had said. "They can't protect themselves." Clearly he could not have meant the Lameans. It hadn't even been the real Galen who had said it, just a figment of her imagination when she had eaten something too late before going to bed. The real Galen would never stand up for a race of slaves. The real Galen hated Lameans more than anyone else Sayla knew, and he did not hide that fact.

It had to be just a coincidence. Those dreams were upsetting her even more than she had realized. She needed to get herself together if she wanted to obtain that spot as the fifth-year Shepherd. Her mind had become a jumble of confusion, and she had to push through the fog every day just to function. But one thing was clear. Whatever had happened in her dream, it did not apply to the reality she was living at the moment. "They're past protection, Grunt. They're slaves. You

354

have to get that into that thick skull of yours. This isn't what I meant when I told you just get the job done."

Aveline smirked, but Grunt made a pained expression and shook his head sadly. "I don't understand why you're lying to yourself. Is being popular that important to you? That you would put someone else's life on the line? I thought you were different," he said sullenly as he headed back inside the cave.

"Maybe he just needs time." Sayla stood up and dusted off her black leggings. "He'll get over it in time." But she couldn't shake Grunt's comment as easily. Sure, she had changed from the person she used to be. But that didn't mean it had to be a bad thing. Grunt was wrong. She wasn't lying to herself. Like the rest of them, she was here on a mission, and that was the end of it. Who cared about senseless prophecies or confusing dreams? What mattered was what was right in front of her. And that was all she would focus on.

CHAPTER 44: DAKU

The storm continued to rage as the vessel struggled against the strong current toward the village of Aramoor. It pushed them close to the rocks along the shore. The wind roared and at times whipped them about almost in a complete circle. The small crew did their best to keep the boat intact, but with minimal success. Because of the damage the vessel had already suffered, Daku wondered if they would have to disembark earlier than planned.

His mind had seemed at times to freeze. He would be overhearing a conversation between two crewmembers, when all of a sudden, their speech would slur and their movements slow down, and he would feel heavy and extremely fatigued. Sometime it seemed as if the light around him began flashing. During such moments he would see her golden eyes and feel her arms around him. The light flashes alternating with the intervals when the world seemed to creep at a snail's pace left him with intense headaches. At the moment he had one, and the crashing storm surrounding him wasn't helping anything. He saw Jorn assisting the crew, at Malvina's request, but for some reason she had begun ignoring him again. He figured it was because of his conversation with Aelwynne several days ago. At one point he had thought it reality--had actually wished it had been. However, after the blinding flashes, excruciating headaches, sleepless nights alternating with ferocious nightmares, and remembering how she had abandoned him, Daku felt as if he would be happy never to see her again. He knew there was a fine line between love and hatred, and at the moment, he felt deep hatred for his once-wife, and had no idea what could possibly reverse that. Daku tried to express that to Malvina just by the way he looked at her, but she seemed uninterested or distracted. He never could tell. Daku wanted to do *something* for her that would let her know of his deep devotion and loyalty to her. But he couldn't think of anything. So he stood upon the deck in the storm, almost hoping the boat would capsize and trap him underneath it. Then he would float out to sea and be forgotten forever. A chill seized him as he realized that, as far as Aelwynne was concerned, he already had been forgotten.

And then he saw it--Aramoor, stretched off in the distance. The river swept past a hill to the east and into the bayside village of Aramoor. Presently, through the haze of the storm, during the flashes of lightning (and when those flashes in his mind weren't blinding him), he could see the village clock tower, the one tall structure sitting right in the center of the township. The sight triggered memories of his boyhood: running through the streets with Bug, sailing away with his father, attempting to climb the clock tower, being a hero . . .

Golden eyes. You belong to me. You are mine. Lightning. Screaming. Death. Blood. Golden Blood. A floating city. Leoj. A dead Shepherd. A war. A lie. A betrayal. Malvina. Malvina. Malvina.

"There is only one thing required of you in this forsaken dump."

"Yes, Malvina." He wasn't sure when she had joined him on deck, rain soaking both of them.

"A ship. You must find us a ship that will take us south through the channel that cuts across Oldaem, west around the tip of Oldaem, and then north to the Capital, our final destination."

"Yes, Malvina."

"I don't want to stay here long." Rain dripped off the tip of her nose. Her eyes then met him, golden circles glowing in the midst of them.

"Neither do I." Daku meant it. He had no desire to face his past, a wonderful past that he could never reclaim. And he especially didn't want to meet his father.

As she turned from him, he could see Jorn facing her on the other side of the deck, a smile spreading across his face. "Actions have consequences, Daku. You seem to keep forgetting that."

"I . . ."

"Don't speak," she hissed as thunder echoed around her. She seemed to glow a sickly yellow hue as she kept her back to him, a dark cloak wrapped around her. "All I need from you here is a ship. Don't think. Don't remember. Don't get nostalgic. And never forget that you're a merchant." Then she turned back to him and smiled. "You're my brother."

As he walked around Aramoor the next day, the sun shining brightly, he realized that it was nearly impossible for him to do as Malvina requested. At every turn he had a memory, at every older face, he could place a name. Each footstep brought with them scenes from his childhood. Daku passed the alleyway where his dreams of being a hero first came true. He saw the bench he had sat on with Bug for so many conversations, the school he had attended, the market he used to run through, and then he came to the clock tower.

Once he had brought Aelwynne to Aramoor after their marriage, as they were heading to Vertloch. And he remembered it had been her favorite place in the entire city. But then it had been his, too. As a boy he had looked up at the tower and watched the hands of the clock mark the passage of time. Back then he had wondered what time would to do him. Now he knew, and how he wished he could climb up that tower to reverse the clock. He would change so much. *Golden eyes.* Perhaps he would change nothing. *Aelwynne.* Or he would change everything. His head pounding again, he sat down on the bench under the tower and stared at the people as they passed by.

That morning Jorn had gone shopping for clothing for all three of them, and now Daku wore a brown merchant cloak. He had scrubbed off all the filth from their travels. It had felt cleansing to do so, though some damage could never be washed away. Now, he was Varic the merchant, brother to Vivienne, the merchant, who was lover to Cullen the merchant. *Of course I'm the brother.*

As he looked around Aramoor, a pleasant breeze drifted in from the bay. Behind him and beyond the clock tower was the coast and the town front with the inn that Vivienne and Cullen were resting in. To the east flowed the river they had sailed in from as well as the wealthier part of town. North of him lie more shops and vendors and the dense forests in which he used to play. And to the west was his father's home. A place he hadn't visited since he and Aelwynne had said goodbye and he now planned to avoid at all costs.

A group of children ran in front of him, laughing and screaming joyfully. The youngest girl fell down, and the other kids kept going, leaving her behind. Intense sadness filled her eyes until the oldest boy stopped, walked back to her, and helped her up. He dusted off her knees and knelt down and looked into her eyes to make sure she was okay. She nodded happily, took his hand, and the two of them raced off to join the others. *Bug.* Then he wasn't sure if what he saw actually happened, or if he had just witnessed a memory. Daku sighed.

The clock tower struck the hour, and his memories took flight again . . . to a different time . . . a different place . . . a forbidden place . . . but he couldn't resist it . . . he wanted to go there. He *had* to go there. Back . . . back . . .

The waves were crashing on the rocky shores of Najoh. Daku sat staring out into the blue water. His head was clear, his mind was fresh, and the salty breeze made him long for more adventure. Adventure, which would lead him to becoming a hero. Birds soared high above, and the chatter of the crowds in the busy trading nation of Najoh surrounded him. He was happy. Even though he had been waiting a long time for his father, he didn't mind. There wasn't really anything he could do anyway. Adventure was something he had just experienced. Danger. Excitement. And still he had wanted more. His father's merchant ship had capsized in the recent storm, and they had found themselves in a strange land with strange people and strange food. Daku loved it. The past few days his father had spent each and every day attempting to find passage home. It was, however, a busy time of year in Najoh, and merchants from all over had arrived for a Harvest Festival. No one would be departing for several days, and those ships would have little or no room, not even for a merchant and his young adult son.

The clock tower chimed behind him. *Was it really so late in the day?* When he glanced behind to find the time, he saw her for the first time. *Beautiful.* The material of her light-blue gown was so weightless that it fluttered in the wind. She stood staring across the sea, her silver eyes reflecting the play of light on the water. Stretching her slim arms far above her head, she yawned. Captivated, he felt himself walking toward her. Now she had her eyes closed, as the sounds of the crashing waves must have drowned out his footsteps across the rocky embankment.

"Are you here for the festival?" he asked.

Her eyes fluttered open and she smiled, taken aback by his sudden appearance.

"Actually no. Are you?"

"Shipwreck." He smiled.

"Sounds exciting."

"It was. I nearly died."

"Did you? I've never nearly died."

"You should try it. It was a rush."

"You want me to die?" She smirked as she took a step closer.

"What? No. That's not what I'm saying."

"What are you saying, then?"

"I'm saying . . ." *Real smooth, Daku.* "Let me start over." He extended his hand to her. "Hi. I'm Daku."

"Aelwynne." She took his hand in hers, and they shook.

Time seemed to slow as they did. Her hand felt soft and warm in his, and he didn't want to let go. "So, why are you here?" he asked.

"My father is here on business. The nature of his work makes him travel a lot."

"Me, too. My father is a merchant. What does your father do?"

"He's a religious agent for Sther."

"Big country! My father hates going there."

"I've never been. He's stationed in Vertloch Tower in Oldaem."

"I'm from Oldaem, too. Aramoor. It's really small."

"I'd love to see it someday." She smiled.

"Maybe someday you will."

"I hope so." She studied him for a second.

While he couldn't read her face, he could tell she was thinking about something. She seemed curious or intrigued. The breeze made a couple of the ringlets of her dark hair drop down over her eyes and blow back and forth.

"There's something about you, Daku."

Smiling slightly, he stared back at her. "What do you mean?"

"What is it? I can't put my finger on it." Pausing, she looked up into his eyes. Daku felt that he could stare into her silver eyes for days. "Tell me, what makes you special?"

Daku thought long and hard but couldn't really think of anything. He was just a merchant's kid. Then he knew: "I want to be a hero."

She smiled, as if it perfectly fit what she expected. "And why is that?"

"Because it would mean people would love me." He was surprised he said it, having never really spoken the thought out loud before. Daku realized that it made him sound effeminate, maybe even weak. But by the look in her eyes it was the perfect response to her question.

"I know I just met you, Daku the hero. But I'm sure there are many people who love you. You know . . . it's not because you're a hero that people love you, I'm sure."

The sun was setting as silence settled among them. Orange and purple seemed to be battling it out in the sky. Purple was winning, although pink and some shades of pale blue were also taking a stand. The sun was dim enough as it dropped into the ocean that one could look almost directly into it and not have to squint. The dusk more clearly accentuated the planes of Aelwynne's face. She had such clear skin, not a blemish or mark on it, and she looked so kind and vulnerable, yet strong and wise. He couldn't have explained the appearance of her face if he had tried. Nor did he desire to. At that moment, staring at her, he wanted her all for himself. And at that moment he decided that even not being a hero would be okay, if it meant spending just a few more days with her. But the idea of an unknown future scared him. He wanted the clock tower in Najoh to stop at that instant, for time to freeze, while they existed there together in the sunset.

But as always the sun vanished below the horizon. Yet not before she said one more thing, which would stick with him for

360

the rest of his days. "People will love you for being *you*. Daku, who you are, is the most important thing that you will ever have. Protect it. Nurture it. Love it. *Then* you'll become a hero."

"Aelwynne!" They turned and saw a tall man with straight black hair standing on the road behind them, a giant tome in his arms. His face had a darker countenance to it, but Daku could see the family resemblance.

"Coming, Father!" she replied, and then turned back to face Daku. "When will I see you again?" Her smile revealed a row of perfect white teeth.

"Someday soon."

Then he watched her walk back toward her father, take his arm, and disappear into the dusk as the events of the festival began. He hadn't sat there for long, before his own father appeared on the road, standing there smiling at him, shaking his head.

"It seems you've had a productive day, Daku."

"Any luck, Father, getting a ship?"

His eyes twinkled. "Yes. But it will be at least two or three months. I found work in the city. I hope you don't mind."

"I don't mind at all."

His father was shorter than him. Not fat in the slightest, but stocky and bald. A hard worker, he was the get-the-job-done type of man that Daku greatly respected. It had just been the two of them, since Daku's mother had died giving birth to him. Although he had never known a mother, having a father was enough. "I met someone, Dad."

"Did you?" His father took his place beside him, sitting on the rock, watching the stars come out.

"Her name is Aelwynne."

"Is she pretty?"

"Beautiful."

"I hope more than that."

"So much more than that. I can't explain it. I've never met anyone like her before."

"Pursue it then. Stars don't shine brightly forever. The mornings always come, and they disappear."

"But they'll come back out again the next night!"

"But only for a time. And I believe they're different stars. It's possible that one night you may see a certain star you're fond of, but then never see it again in your lifetime."

For a few moments he thought about it, then glanced over at his father, who seemed to be in somewhat of a pensive mood. "Dad, what makes a hero?"

"Everyone needs a hero, Son. Sometimes it seems, though, that they are few and far between."

"Have you ever had a hero?"

"Your mom."

"Really?"

"Really. I could never be her hero, though."

"Why not?"

He turned and looked at Daku. "Because she thought of you as her hero."

Daku found himself standing before his childhood home, not knowing what had led him there. Perhaps it had been memories of joy and laughter and safety. Strangely, he felt guilty for allowing them to surface. Yet, still he paused before the townhouse, much like the other ones on the street beside it. It looked just as he remembered it, perhaps a bit smaller than he recalled. *I was supposed to get a ship today. And I've done nothing.* Should he head toward the harbor? Instead, he sat down on his front steps as he had so many times in the past. Like he had when he had conversations with Bug, with his father, and even with Aelwynne.

Recently he had begun to question whether he could ever do anything right. He couldn't seem to do things that were *good,* and he couldn't do whatever would please Malvina. At times he wondered if she set him up for failure just so she could punish him. Could the whole purpose of her coming here to Aramoor and sending him out into its streets be just to torture him? If so, was she succeeding? Either way, as he sat there, it felt better than anything he had done since he had left for Leoj months ago. A sudden resolve hit him as he fought back another one of those golden flashes that threatened to take over his mind. Tomorrow he would find a ship. Today, he would see his father. Rising to his feet, he walked up toward his house, took a deep breath, and knocked on the door.

CHAPTER 45: IAN

Ian leaned against the ship's railing, studying the massive palace that stretched along the shoreline. While he was happy to see land, he was even more excited at the thought of what awaited him in the Capital. As he looked around, he saw all the other tournament Candidates watching the approaching city. A cheer erupted from their throats as the same thoughts must have hit them all at the same time: no more ships, no more storms, no more oceans, no more being unimportant. Soon all of them would take center stage in the various arenas, in front of all of Oldaem, as the main spectacles of the most famous tournament the nation would ever see. And Ian was determined to be one of the victors. He was a fish who was meant to swim, and he finally *knew* it.

The thought of his conversation with the Oldaemite soldier made him smile to himself. The sadness he had recognized in the young man's eyes was why he had approached him. Ian realized that he could start changing Esis one person at a time. Taking Allora's advice, he would seek to be the best version of himself he could be, and, he hoped, someday soon would be sooner than expected.

The nervousness of those around him was almost palpable. Even Bumo was showing a sickly greenish hue. It gave Ian all the more confidence. If he failed in the tournament, it meant that he should be a crab instead, and then he would be the best crab he could be. The relief that came with that understanding now motivated him to do his best in absolutely everything he might ever face in his future. And that would start with having the best attitude he could about the whole tournament experience. *How proud my Aupaipaupy would be.* While he missed his family, at the same time they were with him--and always would be. *I'll make you proud, Quiana. And I'll find you a boyfriend in this tournament.*

As Terra began barking orders to the crew, Ian noticed Cid asleep at the helm, a Lamean sitting beside him and steering the ship toward the docks of the gigantic Capital spread out before them. Ian had never seen such a massive place before in his life. However, he could not wait to start exploring, meeting new people, and trying all the different foods. Still, he remembered Celes telling everyone the night before that they would be facing the most grueling training any of them had ever experienced, and to say goodbye to such luxuries as eating whatever they wanted and doing whatever they desired.

363

Nervousness threatened to cloud his thoughts, but he batted it away. *Love every second, Ian.*

I wonder how Bumo is doing. Glancing again at his friend, he saw that he still had his arm around Jessica, but the sparkle behind his eyes seemed to have dimmed. Perhaps for the first time, Bumo realized that he was truly just one of many vying for the prize, instead of being the obvious victor. When he caught Ian's gaze, he winked at him. Ian smiled back and shook his head. They had mended their friendship, as much as one ever could with someone like Bumo.

It had been the first night back on the ship after leaving the city of Kaya. The evening air was cool, the storm having brought a massive temperature change with it, and the stars were out. The rest of the tournament Candidates strolled the deck as well, just excited to finally be heading toward the tournament. Wrexa and Helen had found a new respect for each other and were at the moment sparring on the deck while Cid played referee. Liarra had her nose in a book, and the blondes were braiding each other's hair. Celes was engaged in a conversation with Terra, one that seemed as though it should not be disturbed, while the crew silently did their jobs above and below deck.

Ian had been standing by the starboard railing, daydreaming about lavender eyes, when he sensed Bumo beside him.

"Sometimes, I just wanna be away from girls, you know?" he said, as if they were continuing a conversation.

"No, Bumo. I really don't." *Does he seriously not realize what he did?*

"Really?"

"Really."

"Well, yeah, like Jessica and Alala just won't stop touching me. My hair, my face, my arms, it just gets to be exhausting."

"I thought you liked that kind of thing."

"Sometimes . . . I guess."

Silence settled between them. Ian returned his gaze to the ocean. *Just go away, Bumo. Go back to your girls.*

"So . . . I've kind of . . ." Bumo mumbled something that Ian didn't catch.

"Come again?"

"I . . ."

Ian shook his head. "Bumo, I can't understand what you're saying."

"I miss you," Bumo blurted out.

It took a moment for Ian to realize what he meant. Perhaps it had at last dawned on Bumo that a friendship was built upon more than just physical proximity, but actually might need some intentional interaction and a little effort to maintain. Since Bumo had found his "girls," Ian had pretty much ceased to exist in his friend's mind. However, Ian wasn't ready to let Bumo have his forgiveness that easily. He decided to play dumb. "What do you mean? We've been together this whole time."

"Yeah, I know but . . ." Bumo sighed. "I guess I've been a bit distracted."

"Bumo, you're *always* the same. You're always obsessed with girls."

"Yeah, but this time, maybe I went a bit . . . overboard."

"Really?"

"Yeah, I mean with Jessica . . . and Alala . . . and Erina . . . and Liarra . . . and two of the Lamean crew girls . . ."–he swallowed–"and Helen."

Helen? Really, Bumo!

"What happened to our friendship?" He sighed heavily.

As Ian finally looked at Bumo, it dawned on him how disappointed he had been with him. Not because he was girl-crazy–Bumo had always been like that–but because he was so inconsiderate as not to notice or care that the *one* girl Ian could possibly like or have a shot at, he had swooped up carelessly, and then dropped. Ian had learned to speak his mind more since the voyage began through watching Celes, his encounter with Allora, and even by talking to the brooding Oldaemite soldier. Now he found himself saying things he never would have done just a few months before. "Bumo, I really liked her."

"Who?"

His voice rose. "Oh, come on, Bumo. *Liarra.* I liked her. She seemed different, even possibly interested in me, and then you just come along and hold her hand, and flex your abs, and sweep her away, and then throw her overboard. It's not right, Bumo. The way you treat girls isn't right, or respectful, or ... it's just . . . wrong." Ian realized his voice was louder than he had intended it to be. Bumo looked ashamed, maybe for the first time in his life.

"I know," he said timidly.

"And the way you ignore me any time a pretty girl walks by isn't right either. That isn't *friendship.*"

Bumo just stared at the water.

"Man, I have been there for you through *everything.* I know you can't take it back, and I know you are who you are, I guess . . ." Ian swallowed. "All I can ask is if you should happen upon a reddish-haired girl with lavender eyes who goes by a name that I *promised* I wouldn't tell . . . just *please* don't talk to her."

That made Bumo smirk as he looked up. "Wait. You *met* someone?"

"I met someone!" Ian snapped back. "DOES THAT MAKE YOU JEALOUS?"

Bumo immediately began hugging Ian, chuckling. "Let's gooooo, Lover Boy!"

"Get off me!"

But Bumo held him tighter. And after resisting for a bit, Ian hugged him back. It felt good just to hug someone. Bumo may have been selfish, and girl-crazed, and overconfident, but he was Ian's friend. And he would love all of Bumo, not just the nice parts. "I'm sorry," Bumo whispered.

Ian had never once heard those words come from him.

Bumo kept hugging him and speaking, and Ian realized maybe the hug was more for Bumo's benefit than his own. "The truth is, Ian, I don't think I'm a very good person. I don't even think I'm that good-looking. Like, I know I have muscles and such and I look like a sun god, but like . . . I *wish* I had *your* personality. I wish I could have a conversation like you have with people. You're everyone's *favorite.*"

Ian was stunned. It had been the second time he'd heard that from someone.

Then Bumo pulled away. "And if you ever tell anyone I said this, I'll deny it forever and drown you in the ocean."

Ian smiled and looked at him. They were more alike than Ian realized. And they were both just trying to figure out who they were on Esis. What their purposes were. Who was the crab and who was the fish? Ian's heart swelled with love for Bumo, and he realized he would never look at him the same way again. "I love you, Bumo."

"Why are you being so mushy?" he said, pushing Ian away, and Ian accepted it as the most loving shove he'd ever gotten from anyone.

Bumo winked at him, as they leaned against the railing. Ian winked back as Bumo kissed Jessica quickly on the cheek. *Oh, Bumo!*

Celes had appeared on deck and begun gathering all of the tournament recruits around her. Taking a position in front of the helm, she asked them all to sit on the deck. The crew moved aside to give them room. Ian saw Liarra eyeing him but pretended not to notice.

"We will be arriving at the southern-most pier of the Capital. Once we do, I will escort you through the city and to the northern arena. Your quarters are below it, as well as the training grounds where the majority of your work will begin. Since it's the busiest time of year in the city, make sure you don't lag behind. You don't want to get lost. Stay together and try not to speak to anyone. I believe that because of the storm we are the last of the regions to arrive." She looked at all of them with pride in her eyes. "I believe in all of you. I have watched you all since the moment we all met. I *know* that you have it in you. Make me proud."

They all crowded at the railing as *The Dolphin* docked. Ian could hear the buzz from the crowds in the port. For a moment he felt as if he was home in Lion's Landing, except fthe sheer mass of people far overshadowed what he was used to. Before he knew it, he found himself pushed down the gangplank by the others, all eager to get to the arena. He wished he had been able to say goodbye to Terra and some of the Lamean crewmembers.

Vendors and merchants, all intent on getting their gold from the new arrivals in the Capital, crowded the streets. Tournament announcements hung from every building. Ian noticed children battling each other in the streets with wooden swords. Priestesses and their Wardens wound their way through the crowds as well. New Order priests preached their beliefs, and he even observed some homeless Lameans begging. Still they continued to walk.

High on a hill in the center of the Capital loomed the Palace. It seemed to shimmer in the sun. Ian wondered what it must be like inside. The architecture of the Capital was intimidating to say the least. High, gray, towering walls surrounded the city, and shorter walls divided it into individual districts. The Capital had six districts, just as there were six regions in Oldaem, and each district seemed to have a distinct style reflecting a particular region. Seeing as Ian hadn't traveled through Oldaem before, he wasn't sure which district was like which region. As they went along Celes' voice droned on, describing certain buildings and libraries and historical structures. Not extremely interested in the history of the Capital's architecture, he figured it wouldn't play a big role in the tournament. Then it struck him–*The TOURNAMENT!* For the first time it really hit him as to what would be expected of him. Who would he be facing? What would he have to do exactly? Would he even physically be able to do it? Surely, he would. The STC wouldn't select someone who would be physically incapable of performing . . . would they? Carriages and carts rattled past them, different languages struck the ear, and the smell of all kinds of food wafted through the air. So much of this place reminded him of Lion's Landing, while at the same time much was also completely foreign to him.

He wasn't sure how long they walked, but it seemed they passed gate after gate until they finally entered the arts district of the Capital. Nestled among the giant buildings were four massive arenas. Each about the same size, they were open to the sky and circular in structure.

"The dormitories are beneath Arena 3. This is where I'm taking you first. The arena attendants will take over from here, after I check you in. Women's quarters are in the east wing, and the men will reside in the west wing. I'll see you at orientation. I'll be sitting at the long table at the front with the rest of the region representatives. Good luck! Be brave! And don't die!" she chuckled as she led them into the arena. Gulping, Ian wondered if death was indeed a possibility.

That night he sat on his bunk, studying the room around him. Including him and Bumo, it housed 28 guys. Some of them seemed to be friends and were laughing boisterously, while others stuck to themselves, clearly not interested in bonding with potential competition. Bumo and Ian mostly spoke only to each other, although they really didn't have much to say. After they had arrived, tournament officials had immediately separated them by gender. Robin, a stocky, muscular steward who looked about their age, had taken charge of the men. He hadn't said much to them, only inquiring about how their voyage had gone and then announcing what time orientation began the next morning. After walking through long corridors, they arrived at their quarters. It wasn't the most luxurious of settings, but Ian realized guys didn't need much. He wondered what the girl's living quarters were like. Probably identical. After lights out, Ian laid there in the darkness, wishing he could throw open his bedroom window, feel the ocean breeze, smell his mother's cooking, and hear the barking dog down below him. Gradually he realized that everyone in the room were barking dogs, waiting to be noticed. *Fighting* to be noticed. Ian decided he would notice them, regardless whether he won or lost. He would do his best to befriend all of the tournament competitors, including the massive guy three bunks down that made Wrexa look like a tiny school girl. After whispering a prayer to whatever deity might exist, he fell asleep.

The next morning, after dressing like everyone else in gray shorts and a tunic that fit a bit too snugly, Ian shuffled through the corridors again to an all-male mess hall, and then outside to the arena itself, where he sat with all the rest of the guys, the girls on the other half of the aisle. They all wore gray, and he noticed Jessica had manufactured some sort of gray bow that now adorned her hair. Toward the front a long table had a large sign that announced, "WELCOME TOURNAMENT PLAYERS, WE'RE GLAD YOU'RE HERE." Sitting at the table was Celes and six other older people, who must have been the region representatives. He also recognized the STC sitting high above the arena, and a host of other adults standing with them. He knew he was among Oldaem's leading Shepherds, and he felt honored to be there. A previously unseen woman took the stand, and began to address them. She was short, and every feature about her was rounded. The fact that she was rather hefty gave him hope once again. Her voice was high-pitched, and he could tell she considered herself to be very important. He decided to sit up straighter. If she considered herself important, he decided he would do the same.

"Welcome, Candidates!" she began as everyone around him erupted into applause and cheers.

He joined in, noticing Bumo, who was seated two rows ahead of him, looking back at him, his eyes sparkling. It seemed surreal to actually be here.

"Some of you came from nearby. Others have traveled far. But you have all arrived! All fifty-six of you! Thirty-two of you, unfortunately, will leave here failures . . ."

369

He felt the tension grow in the arena. He was aware of the numbers, but as he looked around he tried to imagine thirty-two of them gone. It was more than half.

"Twenty-four of you will continue on and join the pool of fully realized Shepherds!"

Once again a cheer erupted, but she quieted them.

"Now, I know you all have dreams of becoming a certain *type* of Shepherd, but that will be left up to the tournament facilitators once the victors are crowned." Her expression changed. "Oh my goodness, how embarrassing, I didn't introduce myself."

Ian could see a bead of sweat trickle down her head and she dabbled at it with a cloth.

"My name is Delia, and I am the Tournament Mistress."

She paused for applause, and received a smattering. *What is a Tournament Mistress?*

"I will be giving all instructions, awarding all prizes, and mediating all events. You should get use to my lovely face." When she laughed, Ian imagined she was the type of woman who made herself laugh often. "There will be four main events, but before I get to that, let me introduce you to two *wonderful* individuals."

Ian watched as she guided a tall, handsome, muscular man, and a beautiful, fit, slim woman to the front. They stood confidently next to her, towering over her.

"This is Daphne and Orion, they will be your Tournament Trainers. For the rest of the day, and the weeks to come, they will be getting you fit for the various events. They are both well-rounded in Defense, Spirit, Mind, and State. Listen to their advice, and you'll all do well." Applause followed the introductions as they both smiled broadly.

He figured Bumo would love to be Orion one day. But, honestly, so would he.

"As I was saying, there will be four events, one for each area of Shepherdhood. Two events will happen simultaneously in each of the four arenas, and for each event, you will be split into four equal groups of fourteen picked at random. The first events will be Mind and State. That means that twenty-eight of you will be divided in half between Arena's 1 and 2, battling each other in the Mind Competition. The other twenty-eight will be divided into two groups of fourteen in Arena's 3 and 4 to participate in the State Competition. While I can't tell you intimate details as far as what awaits you in the competitions, I can give you some generalizations.

As far as the Mind Competition goes, you will be involved in some sort of scavenger hunt in groups of two, which will stretch you further mentally than you've ever been before. The State Competition will be a debate over Oldaem issues. I'm sure Orion and Daphne will have you very prepared." She reached for a glass of water and sipped it slowly.

This is a lot of information to take in. So far, a scavenger hunt and a debate. Nothing that involves running super fast or overcoming fat boy problems. That's a relief. And I'll only have to face thirteen people at a time, instead of fifty-five.

"After the State and Mind Competitions are complete, the groups will stay intact and switch arenas, so the Mind competitors will face the State challenge, and visa versa." She spoke as if she had come up with the challenges and structure herself, and was very pleased with it. When she paused once again for applause, they indulged her.

"Defense and Spirit will go next. Once again, everyone's names will enter the pool of names to be drawn at random, and twenty-eight of you will be split between 1 and 2 for the Defense Competition, and the rest of the twenty-eight will be divided into two groups of fourteen between Arenas 3 and 4 for the Spirit Competition. The Defense Competition will be extremely physical, as expected. I can't reveal exactly what to expect, but I can tell you in each arena you will form two teams of seven."

I hope we're not fighting to the death. Ian reluctantly remembered signing his waiver. *Killed . . . mangled . . . exploded . . . was it?*

"The Spirit Competition I'm most excited about, and I must tell you details so that you can be prepared for it . . . drum roll please."

The crowd mimicked the sound of drums, and Ian noticed Celes had nodded off. *Well, she's had quite the journey for her age.* Then he wondered what Terra and Cid were up to now, and what had become of those lavender eyes.

"A talent show!"

Ian's heart dropped. Out of everything he would face he was most nervous about the talent show. While pretty sure that during the physical defense challenge he could use his weight as an advantage, he had *no* idea what he could do as a talent. *Why not a pie eating competition?*

"We all look forward to seeing all of your skills. At the end of the events, final scores will be tallied and the top twenty-four people will be the winners, no matter where they are from. I hope you understand that this means that a person may get the highest score among their specific group of fourteen in an event, and still not become one of the top twenty-four. A 10 is the perfect score for each event. The total amount of points at the end of the competition can be 40. So, you see, the goal is to be really well-rounded. Usually, if one scores a 36-40 total amount of points, they will have a good chance of becoming one of the final twenty-four. After the final competition, all will return here, to this arena, where the Shepherds will be crowned!" She paused for effect, expecting a large cheer, but Ian suspected everyone was feeling what he did: confusion, fear, nervousness, fatigue, and frustration at the amount of information that had just been dumped on them.

Then she continued with what Ian hoped to be her final statement. "The judges will be a group of twenty-four Shepherd professors from each of our three esteemed academies. Each academy has brought eight professors, two from each area of study. These judges will be split among our four arenas, and will be judging you *individually*, not as groups. They will decide the victors. We wish you the best of luck!"

Now the regional representatives stood and clapped, and Ian looked up and realized the group of older adults high above in the stands must be the judges. Ian tried to smile at them, but the sun blinded his eyes. Suddenly a trumpet flourished, and a fanfare wafted through the arena. Noticing that the people on the stage began to bow, as well as everyone around him, Ian did the same, like a respectful tournament applicant, until the music finished. Because he had bowed so deeply, he couldn't see the stage. *Royalty? The King?* He couldn't imagine whom everyone was showing such respect for. Then a voice broke into his thoughts.

"Welcome all, and rise."

Ian slid back into his chair to see a finely dressed but somewhat effeminate man with a crown, bowing as if he had performed some kind of difficult trick. *The King?*

His voice had a whine to it. "I am Prince Gragor of Oldaem, and I wanted to wish you the best of luck! As you know, my father is aging, and soon, I will be crowned king, I guess . . . after he . . .I mean . . . *if* he . . . and I hope he doesn't . . . like *ever* . . ." Pausing, he looked slightly confused.

This Prince doesn't seem very . . . royal . . . he seems . . . awkward. Ian suddenly felt badly for him.

"What I'm trying to say is, some of you may become Royal Shepherds someday. That would be wonderful!" The crowd cheered again. Ian noticed that Prince Gragor looked behind him to his right, apparently for what seemed to be affirmation from a golden-haired woman in a blue tunic and a golden circlet on her head. She nodded to the prince, and her mouth smiled, but not her eyes. The prince didn't seem to notice.

People clapped, and guards escorted him off the stage with the golden-haired woman, the prince taking her hand as they walked. *I guess that's his girlfriend.*

After further inane explanations from Mistress Delia, more applause and scheduling information, all the region representatives left the stage, the chairs were cleared away, and Orion and Daphne stood before them.

"I hope you're ready for pain." Orion said sharply.

"I hope you're ready to start," Daphne added.

"I hope you can stay sane."

"I hope you have the heart."

"Let's begin!" they exclaimed together.

They rhyme. How cute.

But Ian immediately regretted thinking it. They were anything but cute. Pushups, sit-ups, running laps, pull-ups, or attempted pull-ups in his case, were followed by drill sergeant type shouting, physical pushing, vomiting--much of it coming from Ian--collapsing, aching, and crying. People like Bumo and Wrexa and Helen seemed to love it. Even Liarra appeared to be doing fine. But Jessica and Erina and several other girls had to be carried back to their dormitories.

Such activity continued day after day. The Candidates also participated in grueling mental memory challenges, history of Oldaem lectures, and religious mini debates, the content most of which Ian had never heard of. It interested him that Daphne, the Spirit expert, seemed to promote New Order teachings as the only acceptable theology. Ian had never considered it appropriate to have one religion pushed upon everyone else as law. It made him uncomfortable.

Day after day the excruciating program continued. Ian almost seemed to lose track of time and rarely had opportunity to talk to anyone. He only saw the girls during training sessions. But he did start to notice, however, his stomach shrinking, and Bumo's body

373

getting even stronger. Still Ian never found himself complaining, just wondering if the point of this was to turn all potential crabs into fish.

Even during extremely rainy days their training continued, and they never had personal time with either Orion or Daphne. Each day was similar, consisting of silent breakfasts, which they must use for meditation, then training, lunch, which was social time--in reality, most were too exhausted actually to talk to each other--more training, a sack supper, which turned into nap time for Ian, night training, and then bed. Each day echoed the previous one. Ian felt his arms and back strengthening and his gut shrinking. His Aupainana would be so disappointed. He could still hear her pleading with him not to lose weight, and to hoard food to maintain his Beelzian physique.

After several weeks the Tournament Facilitators seemed to notice everyone's fatigue and gave them a "Good Job-With-Your-Training-Party" in Arena 3. Everyone was actually allowed to wear their own clothing, as he saw Jessica and Erina in their heels and low cut blouses and Bumo in a tight-fitting tunic that showed off his body. However, Ian still wore his gray standard tournament outfit. As he sat by himself high on the risers in the arena, just enjoying the time alone, he realized that it had been a while since he had had that opportunity. Looking at his hands, he curled them into fists and noticed never before seen veins on them that ran up his arms. He sighed deeply. *If Allora could see me now.* He wondered what had become of her, what she was doing, if she was happy, and then chastised himself for being so caught up with someone he had spent only a couple hours with and was way out of his league.

The tournament was still a few weeks out, and Ian wondered what would become of him. Hearing huffing and puffing, he noticed Wrexa climbing the stairs toward him. As he watched her stumble and smash into a few bleachers, he remembered her sight wasn't the best. Before he knew it, she had engulfed him in a hug.

"Wrexa so proud of Cuz-Cuz."

"I haven't seen much of you? Are you surviving okay?" he managed to gasp.

"Wrexa tired." She put him down and plopped next to him, nearly breaking the bleachers with their weight.

"Ian's tired, too." *Great, now I'm talking about myself in the third person too.*

"You look different!" she said and smiled, revealing something green between her teeth. Ian decided to let it be.

"How so?"

"More like Bumo, less like Ian."

"Losing weight?"

"Gaining muscle. Gaining confidence. Gaining handsome."

He smiled. "Thanks, Wrexa."

"That not a compliment. Do you miss family?"

"Yes. Sometimes. But I'm glad I'm here. How about you?"

"Only if I lose. Then I'll miss family. If I win, I won't."

Ian looked at her confused. "That doesn't make sense. What about *now?*"

"Huh?" She returned his gaze with genuine bewilderment.

He chuckled. "Never mind."

"So, Shepherds *must* be New Order?"

"It sure seems that way, doesn't it?"

"Yes. I'm not New Order. Are you the New Order, Cuz-Cuz?"

As he thought about it he wasn't sure he was. And he didn't even know the name of their Beelzian religion. "I guess I still need to see. But so far, I'm not very impressed. I don't like the whole force-people-to-believe-what-you-believe concept."

"I don't like Capital food. I miss honey-roasted Sea Bass."

"Me too." *We have such deep discussions.* When she paused, he followed her gaze. Liarra was standing not too far down the steps, her expression suggesting a need to speak with him.

"I'll let you speak to you and Bumo's girl." Wrexa said, hugging him again. "I love you, Cuz-Cuz. I hope you win. But I hope I win more." Then she put him down again and walked past Liarra, fist bumping her and nearly knocking her back down the stairs. But Wrexa didn't seem to notice as she disappeared down the many steps leading to the floor of the arena, singing a Beelzian hymn at the top of her lungs, off-tune of course.

Ian stared at Liarra and then looked down, not really sure what to say to her at this point. Their relationship had been rather awkward ever since Kaya. He had seen her and occasionally watched her during training, and she seemed to hold her own against the other girls. Sometimes their eyes met, and then he would glance away, aware of her lingering gaze. It was always as if she wanted to say something to him. *I guess now's her chance.*

"Hey, Ian," she said as she approached.

"Hey, Liarra."

Quietly she took a place beside him, not too close, but not too far away. Her green dress, which went to about her knees, made her blue eyes seem almost green as well. The eyes weren't lavender, but

375

they were stunning. Having grown out a bit, her straight black hair almost reached her shoulders. Liarra really was beautiful.

She seemed as if she was struggling to find her words, and he let her think in silence. The night was cloudy but warm. It had rained the past two days, but had finally cleared up. "There is so much I've been wanting to say to you." The seriousness of her tone caught him off guard.

"Oh, really?"

"Yeah. I tried to in Kaya . . . but you seemed . . . distracted."

"Yeah, it had been a crazy day." *I miss you, Allora. Do you even remember me?*

"Yeah, I know. It's been a few crazy weeks."

When she sighed deeply, he almost felt sorry for her. Then he remembered her hand in hand with Bumo, and he didn't feel *that* sorry. "So, what's up?" he asked casually.

After a little more thoughtful silence, she turned to him and the words began to burst from her lips like a wave crashing upon the shore. "I'm sorry, okay? I'm sorry! I didn't think I'd ever be *that* girl! I mean, after I told you I wasn't interested in Bumo, I went and did *that!* I was so *foolish!* I can't believe I did it! That I was stupid enough to think that a guy like him could ever want a girl like me! But I did! I believed it, fell for it. And I looked like an idiot doing it! And then I hurt *you!* And I never wanted to hurt you. You're different! You're so sweet and kind to everyone. You're funny and genuine and real and smart, and I wanted to be with someone like you. And then I threw it all away for a dumb guy that doesn't even look my way anymore. I just . . . I am so sorry! And I know you're clearly done with me and that I can't take it back! And now I'm blubbering. Ugh, I'm so annoying. And I know that I hurt you, and I never wanted to hurt someone like you! We were supposed to be the different ones, but I messed up!" She swallowed as tears filled eyes. "I don't know what came over me. A guy like *him,* with a girl like *me?* Ridiculous!"

For a moment she paused. But Ian's thoughts were elsewhere. For reasons he could not quite understand, perhaps because Liarra touched similar fears in him, Allora now filled his mind. Again he wondered if the girl even remembered him. That their encounter had been no more than a fleeting moment during the rain in a distant city neither of them would never see again. As Liarra carefully studied him, waiting for a response, he sat in silence, staring back, a torrent of conflicting emotions raging inside him.

Finally she stood and began to pace the top row of seats in the arena. "I never fit in at the orphanage, Ian, and I still *never* do. Anywhere. I'm starting to wonder if I ever will. Back home, I was the weird girl, the odd-girl-out, the one without a boyfriend, the one who pretended not to want one. I thought if I could be like Jessica or Erina or Alala, maybe, a guy like *Bumo* would notice me. I thought I could be like them. But they don't even *talk* to me. Why is life so hard?"

"It's the hardest thing in the world." For a moment he forgot Allora and thought only of Liarra. Suddenly he had so much he wanted to say to her. He remembered she was the girl he had assumed didn't care what people thought of her. *We're so alike, Liarra. You have no idea how much alike. I've never fit in either. Never have. And I've wondered if I ever will. You think you were the weird one. Well, I was the weird boy, the odd one out, the one without a girlfriend. I couldn't ever measure up to Bumo. I wondered if it was okay to be Ian after all.* Although he wanted to tell her all this, he also realized that he had discovered that it would have to be something she figured out on her own.

"You know, you're changing, Ian. You look stronger now--healthier." She smiled. "But you haven't let it affect your personality at all."

"I think this is going to change all of us."

"Maybe it will."

A gust of wind whipped around them, and Ian could tell she was cold. Goose bumps raced up and down her arms.

"I really am sorry, Ian. I tried to tell you in Kaya . . . but . . ."

"I know." He averted his face. "And I'm sorry too--for pulling away, and for shutting you out, and for treating you badly."

"Don't apologize. You have *no* reason to apologize."

Her eyes were blue again--a brilliant blue—and he thought of when she had entered the room at that first orientation meeting. His heart was beating like that again. *What is wrong with me?*

"I'm not going to become a Shepherd. I know that."

"Why do you say that?"

"I'm not cut out for it."

"I think you've been doing well!"

"Thanks for saying it, Ian, but let's be realistic."

"No! Don't give up! Remember, you wanted to *help* people! You still can!"

"I hope you're right."

Perhaps it had been his fault from the start. Everything. He had placed Liarra on a pedestal, believing her to be *different.* But it dawned on him that she wasn't different in the way he had hoped. Rather, she was normal--human. It was dangerous to put people in positions in which they could fail you. Pedestals were dangerous. But if *people* didn't belong on a pedestal, what did? Then, he thought of something--a higher power.

"So . . . New Order or Old Order?" he asked.

She looked at him in surprise, smiled, then spoke with resolution. "Old Order."

"Really? You finished the book?"

"Yes. A couple weeks ago. I realized it may be problematic for to-be-Shepherds, but New Order seems . . . off. Haven't you felt it?"

"Yes," he admitted.

"I would love to tell you all about it." Her smile seemed genuine for maybe the first time in weeks.

"I would love to hear about it."

She told him, and he listened. But besides listening to her, he watched her blue eyes dance and glisten. Ian noticed that they weren't as spectacular as he had once thought. They weren't lavender--just standard blue. Normal. And maybe that was okay. Perhaps even better-and *safer.* She was *normal. He* was *normal.* He watched the pedestal Allora had been sitting on crumble before his eyes. After the rubble cleared he saw Liarra's eyes--standard blue ones--and decided he was okay looking at normal eyes after all. Besides, *she* was okay with looking at his, and that was the best part of all.

CHAPTER 46: SAYLA

It had happened again. Just when Sayla had been lulling herself into a false sense of security, the dreams returned--with a vengeance. This time it was a combination of both of her previous dreams, but something was different. Everything seemed too bright and too colorful. Just seeing things of a normal hue seemed blinding. And everything was sharper, yet somehow distorted.

Shepherd Demas was still chained in a cell, but now the bruises on his face were darker, the strangely colored golden blood flowing even more brightly. Again she fell through the floor and found

378

herself outside the large Tower with the massive wall surrounding it, all playing out like a bad memory. The little redheaded boy asked, "What do I do?" and she still had no response. Galen appeared in the rainbow river, but instead of telling her to "protect them" he screamed, "What are you doing? You're running out of time!"

And then the river swept her into the next dream. A man covered in gold murdered the mysterious old man. Even despite the intense colors, their faces were still distorted. Then the richly adorned room spun around her, and she found herself once again being smothered by falling boulders.

That was when she woke up.

Sayla jerked against the wall of rock she had been leaning up against. It was mid-afternoon. She had dozed off while she was supposed to be watching the slaves during their lunch break. As she twisted her head around, she fully expected them all to have already disappeared. But, breathing a sigh of relief, she saw them all sitting tiredly, still eating their meager meal. A guard standing nearby watched with disapproval. She, in turn, returned the look, though she didn't have as good a reason. *It was an accident!* she wanted to scream at him.

"Don't worry, we didn't go anywhere," the little boy, Grunt's friend, number eight, said to her. He had such a young voice.

Sayla wiped the sleep out of her eyes and became fully alert. "How long was I out?" Her conscience reminded her that it wasn't proper to engage the slaves in conversation any more than necessary. *Well, this is definitely necessary.*

"Not long. Maybe five minutes." He had such bright little brown eyes. *How does he look so full of life when his life is worth so little?*

Still, it was good that she hadn't been out long. It had felt as if she had been trapped in her dream for days, but apparently it had only been a few minutes.

"You must be tired."

"I haven't gotten a lot of sleep lately," she reluctantly replied.

"Well, you should try working instead of throwing rocks at bugs! Ever since we came here . . . well, I'm so tired at the end of the day, I've never slept better!" The boy smiled through a gap in his teeth. He had little freckles like ... like the boy in Sayla's dream.

In one heart-stopping moment of panic, Sayla looked more closely at number eight. *Is he ...?* But his hair was brown, not red, and his face was longer. Relieved, she wiped a bead of sweat from her brow. *It's not him. It's not that boy.* He was just some slave who was talking to her.

Sayla looked around. Aveline and Grunt were not in sight, and the guard was not watching her closely. She turned back to number eight.

"Maybe I like throwing rocks at bugs," she said solemnly.

"You're not killing them, are you?" the little slave asked suspiciously.

"Nope. Just toughening them up a little. Sometimes that's the only way to get their attention."

"What do you do when you get their attention?"

"You help them out. Maybe they're stuck in some high grass, or about to walk out in front of a bird that will eat them. But at least now they know you're there. So you throw the rocks to coax them away from the real trouble." Picking up a pebble, she twirled it with her thumb.

"Really?" He stared at her.

She looked back at him, her face impassive. Then she broke into a smile. "Nah, I was just bored."

He giggled, the gap in his teeth creating a low whistle. "You're funny. I don't care what the others say about you. I like you!"

Her smile faded as reality hit her once more. Hastily she rose to her feet and walked over to stand by the guard.

A few minutes later, he whistled and said gruffly, "Time to get back to work." Some of the slaves yawned, others staggered to their feet. Sayla pulled the dark fabric of her Shepherd student tunic away from her skin. Her loose light brown curls fell limply out of the bun. It was the heat of the day, not the most ideal time to be working in a humid cave. She did not envy the jobs of the slaves, even if they did get a full night's sleep.

It was late afternoon by the time Grunt and Aveline caught up with her at the cave site. Tryndamere had assigned them to assist with some cleanup at one of their previous work sites. Grunt set his pack down and sat in the shade, looking toward the cave, while Aveline stood next to Sayla.

Aveline elbowed her. "How's it been here today?"

Sayla rolled her neck. "I'm ready to get out of here."

"Me, too!" She sighed. "But we received some good news while we were with Tryndamere today. The rest of our group is almost here! They're only about a day's journey away."

Although it was surprising news, Sayla couldn't help but feel a leap of excitement at the prospect of seeing Shale soon. "That's great! But I thought we were supposed to meet back near Westervale."

"The plans changed when we were detained here," Tryndamere said as he walked up and joined them. "Your group finished at Westpoint and headed this way. I just received word this morning. They should be here early tomorrow, and you will be able to leave with them. It will be safer for you three to travel with the rest of your party."

I hope we have enough time to get to the tournament. They had been delayed so long, and it had been totally unnecessary. *We'll be lucky if we get there in time for the main event to start.*

"Then can we leave by tomorrow afternoon?" Sayla questioned.

Before he could answer, they heard an unusual, deep popping noise. It was loud, but had an almost hollowness to it.

"What was that?" Aveline asked.

"Probably just a ..." Tryndamere began, but he stopped short.

Another low rumble, like thunder this time, but it wasn't coming from the sky. Sayla listened carefully. Warning bells went off in her mind. It sounded as if it was coming from the ...

"Cave-in!" a man yelled as he ran out of the mine shaft. Instantly, screams and shrieks erupted everywhere.

"No," Sayla mumbled to herself, "this isn't like my dream. I'm not inside."

"What?" Aveline shouted over the commotion.

"Nothing." Sayla shook her head. She had to stay outside of the cave. Although she knew it was silly, she still had a nagging sensation of fear crawling up her spine.

Men and women began hysterically fleeing the mine opening. Many of them were bleeding, and dirt and dust covered all of them. Grunt rushed toward them, pulling the children away from the entrance as soon as they stumbled out. He wiped some dirt off Eleven's face and hugged her while she cried.

Tryndamere sighed disapprovingly. Embarrassed, Sayla looked away. Grunt was making a mockery of the title of Shepherd in front of the Oldaem military. Instead, she looked back at the cave. The rumbling had stopped and the injured were being attended to.

"Regroup at the campsite!" Tryndamere ordered. "Nobody go back inside. It's unstable. We will return to work as soon as we can determine another safe working zone. This is going to set us behind schedule," he said with a grimace to Aveline who shook her head sadly.

"Where's Eight?" Grunt looked up suddenly from his place beside the children. Sayla studied the faces of the dusty children who had escaped the collapse. She counted five altogether. None of them had the bright-eyed face of the little boy she had been talking to earlier.

"He was behind me," number ten cried. "I fell, and he helped me up. I didn't see him come out." Hot tears made a path down her dirt-stained face.

Aveline was standing with her arms crossed and an uncaring expression on her face. Sayla mirrored it.

"We have to help him!" Grunt screamed at Tryndamere, at anyone who would listen.

"It's too dangerous," Aveline said gruffly, grabbing his arm. "It's a cave-in."

He shoved her away. "There's a kid still in there!"

"There's a slave still in there," Aveline corrected.

"Yeah, and five surviving out of six is pretty good," Tryndamere added.

"We're running out of time!" Grunt made an exasperated grumble and turned to Sayla, who was standing a few feet away, watching the whole thing. "And *you*. How can you go along with this? How can you just stay silent?" He looked at her imploringly.

Sayla fought back the concern she was worried would show on her face. "Grunt," she explained, her voice lowered so that only he would hear, "I've told you a million times you just do what you have to do."

"But this ... this is evil. This is *disgusting*."

"You just do it, Grunt." Sayla tried to remain calm. "Sometimes you just have to ..."

"To what?" he interrupted. "Push your conscience away so that you can be accepted? Ignore what's right so that you can win?"

Sayla stole a glance at Aveline. The girl was so strong, so smart. Not only was she her competition, Aveline was apparently not plagued with unexpected doubts. "If that's what it takes," she answered faintly.

"So, even though it's wrong, I'm supposed to just stand there and let it happen?"

All her life people had never trusted Sayla's judgment. *Why are you hanging out with stupid boys? Why do you want to be a*

Shepherd? Why are you leaving Aramoor? Why are you New Order?
"You do what you have to do to get ahead!" she screamed. "To *win!*"

Grunt just stared at her. Behind them she could hear groans as people frantically raced around, trying to determine if anyone else had been left behind in the cave.

"Thanks," he said finally. It was not sarcastic or accusing.

"What are you talking about?" She did not like the look in his eye.

"I'm listening to your advice," he replied sadly. "You go ahead and win your race, Sayla. But I'm running the one that matters."

He touched her shoulder lightly, and then bolted into the cave. Everyone was so surprised that nobody tried to stop him. Except Sayla.

"Grunt! Grunt come back! You can't go in there!" She raced after him, but Aveline tackled her to the ground.

"Sayla, stop!"

"Let me go, I *have* to get him!" she screamed as she tried to break free of her arms.

Before Aveline could respond, the low rumble began again, but more intense this time. It was as if the earth was splitting apart from deep inside the cave, sending shockwaves through the ground under Sayla's boots. Then the entire cave opening vanished.

"No!" Sayla shrieked. "No, no, no!" She fought desperately against Aveline, who held her tightly. Dust and pebbles flew through the air as rubble sealed the entrance to the cave.

Flashes of her dream mingled with the sight before her. The world was too bright, too sharp, too painful. The cave collapsing not on her ... but on Grunt. Galen telling her, "You're running out of time! We're running out of time!" Everything slowed down until she heard nothing but her own heartbeat. The rumbling ceased.

Sayla beat the ground with her fists. She cried and screamed and fought Aveline.

"He made his choice!" Aveline yelled at her.

Soon there were other arms around Sayla, pulling her back, trying to comfort her.

But she heard none of it. Instead she just kept repeating, "It was supposed to be me. It was supposed to be me."

But it wasn't. It was Grunt who would never come out of that cave. He and the little kid whose only fault was being born into the wrong race. She could have protected those who couldn't protect themselves--could have done something before Grunt ran out of time. But she hadn't. She had just stood there.

383

"It should have been me ..."

CHAPTER 47: DAKU

"May I help you?" the small blonde woman behind the door asked, opening it slightly.

"Oh . . . I." Daku swallowed in confusion. Had his father moved away?

"Yes?" she continued, opening it wider. Three little heads poked out from underneath her large, almost dirty skirt. An apron covered the front of it.

She clapped her hands together to get the flour off of them. He noticed a golden bangle with three rubies encircling her wrist. *For someone with a skirt so dirty, that bangle sure looks expensive.* "I am looking for a man who used to live here with his son . . . years ago, well . . . not so long ago I thought. His name was Sten . . . he had a son . . . whose name was . . ."

"Daku." she sighed. "Yes, I remember the family and him as a boy. I was only a little older. He was always running around town with his two friends." She smiled.

Daku kept his face stolid.

"Are you a friend of the family?"

He swallowed again. "Yes. My name is Varic. I'm a merchant. I'm traveling with my sister and her husband. We're seeking a ship, and I was hoping Sten could help me." Tears nearly came to his eyes. "He's helped me so much in the past."

"Sten is dead and buried for three years. Daku is off and married to the sweetest thing, living their lives together on the coast." Her smile faded. "I'm sorry you didn't know."

"Daddy, how big is Oldaem?"

"Quite big, Daku."

"Like, bigger than our house?"

"Much bigger, Little One."

"Bigger than Aramoor?"

"Bigger than Aramoor." His smile broadened and his eyes sparkled.

"Can I see it all someday?"

"I sure hope so! There are a lot of people out there who will need your help, Little Hero."

"I'm a hero?" Daku asked while picking his nose.

Sten bounced him on his knee as they overlooked the port of Aramoor. The hill that sat behind their house had a perfect view of the village, the clock tower, but mostly the bay that housed all of the ships.

"Yes, Little One, you are. You see, you rescued Mommy and Daddy's marriage."

"What was Mommy like?"

Sten fought back tears, just as he did every time he spoke of his late wife. "She was just a lady, Daku. She wouldn't want to be remembered as anything special or extraordinary." He smiled. "I can hear her now, saying, 'Sten don't go exaggerating about me to your crew.'" Then he looked at his little boy. "She hated when I did that."

"But . . . you thought she was something special, right?"

His father leaned close and whispered, "I *knew* she was. She was the most special woman there ever was. She was beautiful, and kind, and loving, and compassionate, and strong, and stubborn. Oh, Daku. How you'd have loved her."

"I *do* love her, Daddy."

"She loved you, Son."

Daku laid his head against his father's chest. "Thank you, Daddy."

"For what, Little One?"

"For loving me."

"Always."

"Let's live here forever, Daddy. I don't need to see Oldaem after all."

Sten chuckled. "What made you change your mind?"

"This is enough. I think this is enough."

Sten squeezed him a little bit tighter. "I do too, Son."

Daku sat on the hill alone behind his house. The woman with the golden bangle must have thought Varic the merchant had been great friends with Sten. She allowed him to come through the house and see it one last time before letting him sit outside on the hill for as long as Varic wanted. Then she even wrapped him in a blanket and gave him something warm to sip on. Returning to the house, the woman ushered away the three children who had been watching him from the back windows.

So much had changed for Daku. A part of him wished that all the woman had said about him was true. *Happily married and living on the coast.* Being a hero had been impossible. He should have stayed in Aramoor. Then he realized that life was always a confusing thing. If he had remained in Aramoor, he *never* would have met Aelwynne. She had been the best thing in his life. But leaving Aramoor had led him to Malvina—and the death of his father. The woman had said he died of "natural causes." There was nothing natural about death. Maybe he could have done something to prevent it. There were so many "what-if's" that it became impossible to consider all the possibilities. Then he wondered what had become of Bug and his friend. He hadn't seen or heard from them since he had introduced them to Aelwynne before moving to Vertloch. They had been so sad when he first sailed away to get married. Especially Bug. He practically broke her heart, but he had never really seen her in that way. His little Bug, he could never imagine having romantic feelings for her. Yet, in leaving, he made Aelwynne the happiest she had ever been in her life. Then it dawned on Daku that no matter what he did, he wound up hurting someone. Was this the essence of life? And if it was, how could *any* hero exist? He rose. *They couldn't.*

You've chosen your path. You know what is ahead of you. There is no point in turning back now, because there is nothing to turn back to. Too far gone. Too far gone. Too far gone. Golden whispers plagued him. *Get a ship. Get a ship. Get a ship.*

"Malvina, I've obtained us a ship."

"Vivienne," she hissed. "And it's about time," she answered without looking at him. Her back was to him, and she sat facing the window, staring out of the highest room of the inn.

Aramore had only one inn, and he knew his friend's mother had run it back when they were younger. He did his best not to show his face to the innkeeper, but had just headed up the stairs and straight to her room. He was glad he had not been there when Malvina had rented it.

"I'm sorry for the delay."

"Your father is dead. Was that your delay?"

Don't ever mention my father again. "Um, no. There didn't seem to be any ships available. But I found one that departs for the Capital the day after tomorrow. I was able to bring him down quite a bit from his asking price. I hope this pleases you, *Vivienne.*"

"I should be able to mention your father to you, if I choose, Varic. *This* pleases me." Finally she turned to look at him and rose from her chair. She had put on the outfit Jorn had bought for her. It was a short skirt with a merchant's jacket, both yellow in appearance, with a white blouse, and a hat with a golden veil adorning her face. She looked breathtaking. "Do I please you, Varic?"

"Yes . . ."

Stepping incredibly close to him, she kissed him on the cheek. "But I am your sister, Varic."

"Yes." He averted his face.

She giggled, as she seldom did, and took both of his hands in hers. Then she whispered, "Come with me," and led him out of the room and down the stairs and out of the inn.

Daku had no idea where they were going or what they were doing. All he could think about was his father. He wondered where he was buried and when exactly he had died. Had he been angry with him for not staying in touch? Yet at the same time he was entranced with Vivienne. With her touch, her smell, her looks, her words. It was as if a battle was taking place in his mind. But she was winning—as she usually did.

Soon he found himself in the Aramoor gardens. It had a whole section of sunflowers, something he hadn't remembered before. Vivienne took a seat on a bench and patted the place beside her. When he sat down, she rested her head on his shoulder.

They sat there, and strangely enough, Varic felt at peace. He wondered what would have happened had he met Vivienne in Merrowhaven when she was a young girl, before her training. Would they have fallen in love? He hoped they would have. She was breathtakingly beautiful, and at the end of the day, just a girl.

"What a lovely hat!"

"Oh, this old thing?" Vivienne asked as she sat up and smiled.

A brunette-haired gardener came toward her, wiping the dirt off of her hands and onto her already filthy skirt. She held a tiny shovel in her right hand. "Yes, wherever did you get it?"

"My husband purchased it for me at your general store. He said there was some lovely merchandise here. We've never been to Aramoor. My brother and I were just admiring your lovely flowers."

"They are *beautiful,* aren't they? I tend to them early every morning, usually before the sun rises. I only moved here last spring, but it's been such a friendly place to live. Where are you all from?"

Varic looked at Vivienne and saw how calmly she lied to this woman, how easily it came to her, and how friendly she could seem to be.

"We're from the Trade Nation of Najoh. My brother, husband, and I are all merchants. We're heading to the Capital like everyone else for the tournament. I'm so excited, I've never been!"

She would choose Najoh just to torture me.

"Ah, my sweet nephew is competing in it."

"How exciting!" Vivienne exclaimed with a golden smile.

"Yes!"

"What a lovely silver necklace you have!"

The farmer reached up to feel it. "It's a family heirloom, been with us for generations."

"I *love* the golden detail surrounding the emerald stones. It really glistens in the sun."

"I love it too! That's my favorite part about it!"

"Well," she rose, Varic with her, "we really must be off to find my husband. He's been trying to get us a ship. It's such a busy place for such a small village. Everyone has been *so* nice!"

"Best of luck to you! And may the Creator, Comforter, and Liberator be with you! It's nice to see a brother and sister still so close as adults." Then she returned to her flowers, fingering her necklace.

Vivienne and Varic walked among the gardens and out toward the northern gate of the city, the one that led into the forest Daku had frequented as a child. Nobody was around, and Vivienne's whole persona changed, aware that no one could possibly be listening. She seemed annoyed or disappointed.

"I've been contemplating how to spend our day together tomorrow, since we don't leave until the day after. I had sent Jorn away on business, and I had planned just to spend time with *you.* But I can't help but feel your loyalty to me continues to waiver."

"Never!" Daku burst out.

"Silence," she hissed again. "No matter what I do . . . no matter where we go . . . you *always* consider your past, and that pitiful, weak, poor excuse of a woman, Aelwynne. She plagues you more than I."

"I am only human."

"I don't want excuses. I want devotion. I *need* devotion. Or perhaps I need another Warden."

"No. Please. Give me a chance. I'll do *anything!*" He could feel golden waves of air surrounding them, drawing him in, closer, closer, closer. *Golden eyes.*

"I will spend the day alone. I had hoped we could be together . . . but . . . it doesn't seem that will happen. I must have time to think." She walked away from him, back toward the town. "You don't love me."

He followed her in desperation. "I *do* love you! Please, tell me what I can do to prove my devotion to you!"

She stopped, turned, and smiled. "The necklace."

"The . . . necklace?"

"Yes. The necklace. Remember the gardener? I want her necklace."

"I shall . . . check the general store?"

"No, you *fool.*" she growled. "I want *that* necklace." Then she resumed walking away.

"It shall be done."

A golden aura seemed to radiate from her as she departed, and Aramoor started to disappear. The golden light blinded him and pounded in his head. Suddenly, he felt her arms surround him, even though he wasn't sure how she had returned to him so quickly, as she whispered in his ear.

"I want *her* necklace . . . covered in *her* blood . . . *do* what Wardens do best . . . that is . . . *if* you actually love me. My love for *her* blood . . . and the necklace."

The next morning Daku woke before dawn. The night before, he had purchased some dark clothing, something unassuming that wouldn't make him stand out. He was no longer Daku or Varic–he was a shadow. He knew that farmers and gardeners got up before the sun did, which meant he would have to be awake that much earlier. Slipping on his dark clothing and masking his face with some black fabric, just below his eyes, he pulled up the black cowl around his head, grabbed his knife, and slipped out of the door. Jorn was nowhere to be found. Malvina was asleep in the next room, and hopefully no one else in Aramoor would be up yet. The last thing he needed would be to run into the innkeeper.

As he quietly crept down the hallway his mind raced with how he would accomplish his mission. He had killed before, but this felt different--purposeless. He knew she was testing him, and yet, perhaps he *needed* to be tested. Recently he had been weak and soft and forgetful of everything he had been trained to do. And he had to remember there was nothing to go home to. Everything was gone. Everyone was gone. If he didn't do this, she would probably kill him. He did this now for *his* life, for his future. *Could she possibly love me?* That thought was what excited him and motivated him the most. Although it was dark, everything around him seemed to be illuminated by a golden hue, though he wasn't sure how or why it was. Perhaps she had finally nestled herself into his brain permanently so that he wouldn't be able to escape her. What he would do now would make her a part of himself forever. No turning back.

Daku slipped down the stairs and past the front desk. An older woman slept in the chair behind it. When he glanced at her face, it was the spitting image of his friend. Quickly he left the inn.

As he stalked through the empty dark streets as silent as a whisper, he passed familiar buildings and landmarks, but he did not pause at any of them. He headed to the gardens, to the golden sunflowers, and it would be there he would wait. When he came to the clock tower, he refused to look at it, walked by Bug's old house and pretended he didn't see it. Reaching the turn toward his house and his hill, he proceeded as if neither existed.

Once at the gardens, he slipped behind a tree. Discovering that it was still deserted, he started toward the patch of sunflowers. Then his Warden's intuition starting screaming, and he dropped behind some rose bushes. Someone was approaching. If he didn't find a hiding spot, the person would discover him. But to move too soon could be just as risky. The timing had to be *perfect*. His senses became more alert. He waited and counted to five, and then as the figure started toward where he hid, he flung himself to the other side of the bush and crawled to the cover of some trees, the beginnings of the northern forest. There he cautiously stood and peered from behind a tree to see an Aramoor guard doing his rounds. *There's no need for you to die today too, sir. You best be on your way.* The guard went around a building. Once again, no one seemed to be in sight.

He had a couple options of how he could do this. First, he could wait for the woman to come to the gardens, watch her all day, and then follow her home and do it there tonight. However, if he did that, he would waste the entire day, and Malvina might be disappointed that it took him so long. The best way to accomplish this would be to wait among the sunflowers and strike from there, pulling her down to where he was. Daku just had to hope she would be the first to arrive, as she said she usually did. Bolting toward the patch of sunflowers, he crouched behind them.

It seemed as if he waited for hours, though he really had no sense of the actual passage of time. Wherever he looked, a golden hue would illuminate the garden. That had never happened to him before. Perhaps the golden power had started to become imbedded within him, in order to aid whatever new missions he might have to fulfill. Daku felt powerful, unstoppable, immune to defeat . . . or pain. *Feeling nothing is better than feeling pain.* The guard made his rounds five to six times. The tower clock struck the fourth hour but the sun was still below the horizon. As he crouched there he thought of nothing but what must happen next. How he would pull her down. How he would cover her mouth with his strong hand, how he would take the life from her—quickly, effortlessly, and efficiently. It's what he was trained to do.

If you love me ... her necklace ... her blood.

He would prove it to her. He had nothing to lose.

Memories flashed through his mind. Golden-hued visions of previous kills. Daku remembered his first kill, an old Stherian advisor who had turned traitor. Next a Shepherd in Leoj. Like an unending nightmare, he relived swordfights and explosions. Then he saw a gardener with her basket and spade and silver necklace heading toward a golden patch of sunflowers. Malvina's kiss caressed him, to be replaced by his father's face. The gardener bent down and began weeding the patch. Najoh with its white stony shores filled his mind. His father's face returned. The woman hummed what seemed to be an Old Order hymn. Bug smiled at him, and he raced through the forest with his friends. More explosions and murder and Jorn killing a child by a well. Then he could hear the gardener's breath near him, hear her footsteps. Golden light bathed everything while golden stars and a golden moon circled overhead. As he felt himself leap on the woman, Aelwynne's face filled his vision. When he pulled the gardener down, Malvina's face smiled at him. Gripping the blade, he saw the sadness on his father's face, then as the knife plunged into her, Aelwynne's kiss stirred old passions while the gardener pled, "Liberator, save me." Little Daku happily made himself comfortable on his father's knee as Sten said, "Because she thought of you as her hero." Golden blood stained his hand while Jorn laughed. A floating village mingled with others on fire. Fingering the silver necklace, he ran through the woods with his friends as fast as he could, Bug, the little girl, bouncing behind him, his other friend speeding ahead of him. When he climbed the clock tower and looked below at his past, his present, and his future, all he saw was a blaze of gold.

An exhausted Varic returned to the inn. It had been a long, early, morning for the merchant, and he was looking forward to presenting his sister with a lovely necklace he had purchased from the general store. He had taken the time to wrap it lovingly and intentionally. On the card he had written,

"To my beloved sister, Vivienne,
I hope this necklace proves my devotion to you and our cause.
I apologize for the red stains upon the silver chain.
I'm sure you'll find a way to remove them.
All my love,
Varic."

Caressing the box in his hands, he took the stairs calmly and slowly. The sun had risen, and their ship would depart the next morning. As he walked down the hallway toward her room, her door shut, then banged open again. Varic stopped in the hallway when he heard Vivienne and Cullen speaking.

Daku crept up to the door and glanced back down the hallway. No one was there. Sliding as close to the door as possible, he stretched out on the floor and peered through the crack between the door and its frame. He could see Malvina and Jorn kissing. Then she pulled away and examined something that sparkled in her hand.

"Jorn. It's beautiful."

"I hope this proves my love for you."

"Nothing could be better."

Daku watched as they hugged. Suddenly his heart sank to his knees. For in her hand, she clutched a golden bangle with three red rubies on it, covered in blood.

My house. My hill. The blonde woman. Her bangle. Her children. Her orphans. Her blood. Golden eyes.

CHAPTER 48: KAYT

A bird sang outside her widow. Kayt hated it. Perched on a nearby tree, its incessant twittering was shrill and irritating. It reminded her Gragor. *He wants me to marry him.*

She couldn't be respected for her mind, for her ideas. No. Because she was a woman she had to be relegated to the role of *wife*. Not Shepherd of State. Not Advisor. *Wife*. It made her boil inside.

A knock at the door admitted two servants who started making up her bed and fluffing her pillows. She still sat in her nightgown, even though it was past noon. There was nothing for her to do. She knew the Royal Council had been meeting every day, but she hadn't seen Garrus in more than a week. He was her only window into the inner workings of the Capital. Gragor had become a huge fan of playing at dice, and he spent the majority of his days below her window in the gardens dueling with servants and nobles and himself.

Should I agree to this? Kayt had to weigh the pros and cons. If she said yes, she would have full access and insight into the happenings of the nation, but without any influence whatsoever. Although she would live a life of luxury, she would really have nothing of substance to keep her occupied. While one day she might be queen, she couldn't remember the last time a queen of Oldaem was known for anything other than her beauty, her charity work, and her figure. *No thank you. There has to be another way.*

Still, it might be better than nothing. In essence she had no family, no Shepherd employment prospects. It might be her best bet. The door shut, as the servants left her alone once again. Slowly she crossed the room to the looking glass against the wall. Her green eyes pierced back at her. Even unkempt, she knew she was attractive. Her blonde hair was braided into a single braid that hung loosely over her shoulder. *What should I do?*

"Kayt?"

Recognizing Garrus' voice, she immediately draped a robe over herself, and opened the door.

"I thought you'd forgotten me," she said, walking away from him.

"Things have been . . ."

She cut him off. "Busy?"

"Seff has been preparing everyone for Allora's arrival. He wants everyone to know he will be taking over all questioning of the prisoner."

"How many meetings does that take?"

They both sat a small table in her room, surrounded on three sides by the glass walls that overlooked the gardens.

Garrus studied her and smiled, although she could tell there was much going on in his mind. "Too many. Seff's just throwing his weight around, testing the water, seeing how much leeway Orcino will give him."

"And?"

"Orcino is captivated by him. There is a power struggle going on between Seff and Zorah. It's almost as if there's a line drawn in the sand."

"Udina and Seff versus you and Zorah?"

Again Garrus smiled. Kayt knew he wouldn't reveal his hand that easily. A good Shepherd of State was a friend to all.

"I am just doing my best to serve His Majesty."

"Of course."

"And you? How have you served his Majesty lately?"

"I accompanied him to the Tournament Orientation," she sighed.

"I heard the prince made a great impression." Garrus' eyes flashed with mischief.

"His Majesty always does." Kayt shuddered, remembering how they had held hands the entire time as they left the arena. It seemed so juvenile to her.

"So are you going to agree to the King's terms?"

"You mean?"

"Becoming the Princess of Oldaem." Another smile. He truly did know everything.

"What do you think I should do?"

"As if you care what my opinion is."

The man knew her all too well. But Kayt would do what *she* wanted. Still, she also realized that he had a better reading of the pulse of the Kingdom than anyone else. That fact alone warranted his opinion.

"I do care," she sighed.

"I think you would bring a whole new meaning to 'Princess of Oldaem.' The question is, can you swallow your pride long enough to don an outrageous dress with satin gloves and a seemingly humble demeanor. Submissive at times, coy, and possibly shy?" That knowing smiled continued. She hated that he recognized that it would be a challenge for her. "You've almost mastered the doe-eyed look."

"You're no help, Garrus. Do not mock me."

He rose. "You're right. I've overstayed my welcome as it is." Pushing back his chair, he headed toward the door.

She quickly stood as well, rushing to catch up. "Wait, what about the war with Leoj?"

Garrus turned and grinned patronizingly. "Now, that's nothing to worry *your* pretty little head over, sweet *Princess.*"

As she watched the door close behind him she wondered how she exactly fit into the schemes Garrus had planned for her. Kayt *knew* he had plans. Garrus always did. But she needed one of her own.

The next few days passed lazily as those before them. Continuing to indulge Gragor with her presence, she laughed when required, kissed when she had no other choice. She put on the makeup and did her hair and attended the parties. And she giggled and blushed and feigned disinterest in the politics of Oldaem when it pleased Gragor to be distracted. Always she felt Garrus' amused eyes every time she saw him, and noticed that Seff seemed completely oblivious to her. Perhaps that was a good thing. Orcino hadn't called for her in weeks, and she hadn't seen Udina at all. He was whom she wanted to speak with. The Shepherd of Mind was a conundrum to her. Kayt didn't understand his motivations or what drove his loyalties. Before she could ever deal with the Royal Council she would need to understand what motivated its members.

Still she frequented the school playground as often as she could, although she was unable to get there every day. Soon it started becoming three times a week at most, though even then she didn't stay for long. Every time she went it was as if Balyn and Lei grew faster and faster. They never noticed her, and even if they did, they wouldn't know who she was. By now it had become difficult to leave the palace without people recognizing her. She was quickly becoming the talk of the Capital, second only to the approaching tournament. People wondered who the prince's new woman friend was. Some knew who she was. Many of the nobles would also definitely know, as word of the scandal in Highdale had certainly reached the palace. The looks of pity she received from many nobles testified to that. She wondered if Garrus had something to do with it spreading so quickly.

A couple evenings later she was dressing herself for another party Gragor had thrown in her honor. Her head was already pounding from the events of the day. The prince had wanted to go on a tour of the Capital with her. She sat with him in his royal carriage for five or six hours as they bounced and bumped through the streets. The people of the Capital were thrilled to see the Royal Prince and his mysterious blonde companion. But it was a nightmare to her. The jolting continuously hit her head on the roof of the carriage, as she was a bit taller than he. Because Gragor slept the majority of the time, Kayt, bored out of her mind, just watched the buildings pass by. At one point, when he had slumped against her shoulder, she had wanted to throw him out of the carriage.

Now she was pulling on her pale silk gloves as someone knocked. Expecting that it was Garrus or Gragor, ready to escort her to the dinner, she was surprised to find Zorah, the Royal Shepherd of Spirit, outside her door.

"I hope I'm not bothering you."

"Not at all, Shepherd Zorah." *What could he possibly want?* Despite the curiosity that instantly filled her, she tried to make herself inscrutable. Based on the amused look on his face, she figured she was failing. *Why do all of these Royal Shepherds put me to shame so easily?*

"I know you're wondering why I'm here, and at this hour."

"Not at all Shepherd. I am honored by your presence."

"Yes. I've seen you out and about with His Majesty, and I believe you had the joy of attending a Royal Council meeting a few weeks back."

"Yes, Shepherd."

"That's why I'm here." His eyes suddenly became veiled. *What's he after?*

"Perhaps, I may accompany you to the party. The halls are long and these legs don't support themselves as they once did."

Kayt had noticed Zorah seemed to struggle to get around.

"Of course, I would be honored." She adjusted her gloves, put the finishing touches to her hair, and, taking Zorah's arm, they left her quarters.

The first few steps were in silence, except for his labored breathing as they plodded slowly down the corridor. Kayt wasn't sure if the man was just trying to catch his breath or if he was searching for finding the right words to say to her. She had heard and seen him here and there around the Capital. Everyone seemed to greatly respect the official. Even as a girl, she remembered Zorah seeming to be the most widely revered Shepherd of all. A Shepherd of Spirit must be kind above all else, tolerant, judicious, and extremely faithful. He was devoutly religious to the New Order. Kayt was as well, in theory, though not as fiercely devoted in practice, which she planned to be . . . someday. However, sometimes life got in the way. Guilt washed over her as she walked next to this holy man who had done so much good for Oldaem in the name of the New Order. Quite possibly she might learn quite a bit from him. Even if he did plan on using her like everyone else in the palace had been doing. But she didn't really mind if she could somehow swing it to her advantage.

"Are you enjoying your stay here?"

Small talk first? Fine. "Yes, Shepherd. Everyone has been so friendly to me."

"If only nice and good were the same."

"If only." *What does he mean?*

"I get the feeling you'll be staying with us for quite some time."

He didn't look at her as they walked but kept his gaze straight ahead.

"I only want to serve the crown as best as possible."

"What a political answer." He smiled. "You truly are a Shepherd of State."

"Well, what I mean is . . ."

"This war with Leoj has me concerned."

Now she decided just to let him do the talking.

"Human beings can be devious sorts. Bending wills to their way, twisting words to align with their stories, changing characters to gain something undeserved." Zorah shook his head. "Yes, they can be devious sorts." They continued to walk as he continued slowly to shake his head. Portraits of royalty from the past hung along the corridors. Kayt looked at them. Most of them she had never heard of. The majority of the paintings were of men. "We attack and murder and capture," he continued, "because we assume a nation is responsible for the loss of our Royal Shepherd of Defense. But nothing is ever as it seems. Nothing is as clean and tidy as that. There is always something beneath the surface." He met her gaze. "Always."

Somehow Kayt wanted to trust him--figured that Garrus did also. She wanted to be able to remember this conversation word for word later.

"Some may have a lot to gain from an alliance with Sther. A lot to gain," he mumbled.

Kayt could only assume he met Udina and Seff, although what the Royal Shepherd of Mind and the Interim Royal Shepherd of Defense would have to gain by aligning with the largest, most powerful, most unknown country on Esis was beyond her understanding. So much, in fact, that it seemed ludicrous. None of the Royal Shepherds hurt for money, so it couldn't be motivated by wealth or greed. They had access to whatever they wanted. Oldaem had always stood on its own two feet. Why bow to another nation? It would only weaken the country. The Royal Shepherds were supposed to support and protect Oldaem, not compromise and sell out to someone potentially deadly. The thought of the Priestesses of the Three roaming freely across Oldaem made her shudder. Besides, why now? Why, after years of faithful service to the crown, would they betray everything now? What would Seff or Udina possibly have to gain? It made absolutely no sense. Perhaps Zorah was finally cracking under the pressure. She glanced at him as he slowly walked, his body nearly buckling beneath him. Zorah seemed to be relying on her for each step.

"Some may have a lot to gain," he continued, "but most have a lot to lose."

"Yes, Shepherd," she heard herself whisper.

"I believe Sther to be behind the murder of our Shepherds in Leoj. I believe they set up Leoj to take the fall for everything, and they used it as a spark to ignite Oldaem and Leoj into a deadly war, including the capture of Demas. For what purpose, I'm not sure."

Why would be telling me this, a complete stranger? For whatever reason, he trusts me.

"Seff, for some reason, blindly trusts the Stherians so much that he is pushing for religious diversity and inclusion in Oldaem. Do you understand how dangerous this could be? More priestesses? More free Lameans? It could literally cripple our entire social structure." Starting to cough, he held a handkerchief over his mouth.

"Do you need to sit down?" she asked as they approached a bench.

"No, don't be ridiculous," he said after finally catching his breath. Zorah seemed to suppress an undercurrent of agitation. "I don't trust A'delath, I *never* will. None of us should ever trust her." After glancing away for a moment, he looked at Kayt intensely. "I've known for years something like this would cross our borders . . . dark days are upon Oldaem. I think there is only one solution . . ." His words began to come faster, as if he was short on time. "We need to bring in someone we can watch, someone we could monitor, someone we could follow . . . someone we should *not* trust, but let into the inner circle and trail . . . if we were to bring in a Stherian Ambassador . . ."

398

"Kayt?" Gragor's voice rang out from down the hall.

Zorah's voice strengthened. "I tell you this, because I *know* you will be with us for quite some time. Gragor will need guidance from someone who is devoted to the *New Order,* like I know *you* are. It's the main reason I pushed Orcino to suggest *you* for Gragor's bride."

"I . . . what?" *It was Zorah?*

"Don't let Oldaem fall into pagan hands, pagan leadership, pagan beliefs. Inclusion is *dangerous.* The New Order is truth! We need to protect it! The people . . ."

"Kayt! Where are you?" the prince bellowed once again. The sounds of the party drifted down the hall.

"Promise me, Kayt, you'll do your best to protect the New Order."

"I promise." A sense of pride swelled up inside her. *Finally* she had a reason to *be* whom she needed to be. She believed wholeheartedly in the New Order, but she wasn't sure how to act as a devoted New Order follower. "Could you teach me? Teach me everything there is to know about the New Order?"

Relief washed over the man's eyes. "Of course, daughter of the light. The One preserve you." Quickly kissing her hands, he then disappeared down a side corridor as Gragor approached.

"There you are, my love! What has kept you?"

She smiled innocently. "I was praying to the One."

After a little too much dancing, and a little too much sweet punch, Kayt's head continued to pound. She couldn't help but remember similar parties as she slipped away to the balcony to get some fresh air. In those days, however, she was dancing with a different prince–Silas, the to-be-Regent of Highdale. She thought of one of her last nights with him, at a political party thrown at his manor. Melnora had glared at her from across the room, possibly remembering their previous conversation, as Kayt continued to entertain some of Silas' supporters, both monetary and political. Silas had constantly winked at her from across the room, and often she would pull him into hallways for sweet kisses of affirmation, but on that particular night, the mood seemed to be changing a bit at the campaign party. It appeared as if his supporters were dwindling, and he was losing momentum, while his opponent and his Shepherds were growing stronger. Kayt began to feel a bit uneasy about the future, how humiliating it would be to lose. The worst part of all was that Melnora seemed to almost accept the possibility. Was the woman sabotaging the campaign just to malign her? Half of the guest list hadn't shown up, and a servant/spy had returned from the opponent's party to report those individuals had been present there. While Silas still seemed to have hope, it was then that Kayt decided not to remain aboard a sinking ship. At that moment she had concocted her plan, and it was not long after she executed it.

Now a new plan began to form in Kayt's mind on this night. As she looked down from the balcony over the Capital, she could see all the buildings and houses and shops and inns spreading below the palace. Observing the four arenas, she thought of all the kids who were training to be like her. Formulating a prayer to the One for guidance, she decided to try to mean it, much as she had done on her way after leaving Highdale. Prayer had been a confusing thing to her before. She would have to ask Zorah about that as well.

"It's stuffy in there."

Kayt whipped around to find a short balding man who seemed to radiate strength in spite of his stature. *Seff.*

Play the role. "I enjoy the dancing," she said with the most innocent voice she could muster.

"Then why are you out here?" the Interim Defense Shepherd asked, a smile in return. A guarded one, she could tell.

She giggled. *I've mastered the giggle.* "I must have spun myself out here." Playfully she patted his arm. "I came to see the stars. Aren't they lovely?"

"The brightest in Oldaem can be found from this palace, I assure you."

"It must be nice to be here, instead of in military bases like Lion's Landing or Sea Fort. I would *never* want to be cooped up in a stuffy fort."

"Ah, yes, the luxuries of the Capital are to be envied."

"Oh! Is that why you came to visit?"

He chuckled in reply. Either she had lulled him into a false sense of security, or he had mastered the chuckle. "My dear, I'm not visiting. I'm the Interim Royal Shepherd of Defense now, until we retrieve Demas from the Leojians."

"Oh! I hadn't heard." She smiled beautifully.

"You were in the meeting with Prince Gragor a few weeks back, were you not? We were introduced." His smile broadened.

"All this political intrigue has been lost to me since I left Highdale."

"I see. I thought maybe it was effects from all that dancing."

They both laughed together under the stars. She thought that perhaps one started to twinkle. Or maybe it was her nerves making her eyes twitch. In her mind Kayt could still hear the urgency in Zorah's voice. *Now, what is Seff after?*

"People are funny, aren't they?" he said as they looked down from the balcony at a pair of young lovers holding hands in the gardens. They were probably servants from the castle, engaged in a forbidden rendezvous while the party preoccupied everyone else.

"What do you mean?"

"Some people are completely blind to what is going on around them. They go through life, seemingly uninterested in the impossible or the fantastic happenings of all that surrounds them. While others are more aware."

"Oh?" Uncomfortably she smoothed her skirts.

"Which are you?" he asked innocently.

"I beg your pardon."

"Kayt, you were the top of your class. You ran an incredible campaign for Silas, you outmaneuvered him again by destroying his character to escape a loss, you are well-studied, you are intelligent, you are going to be *chosen* for a reason. Knowing all of that about you, my question still stands. Which ... one ... are ... you?" His gaze bore into her.

Still, she did not flinch but giggled again. "Oh, Seff. I'm so different now than what I was before. Life changes you. Sometimes, after you take a beating, you just decide to bow out. Highdale was my curtain call. I've decided to live a less complicated life. Gragor fascinates me, amuses me, makes me laugh." She almost believed herself what she had just said. "I don't want to be a part of those other things anymore." Her eyes were those of a young, excited, naive girl. They were exactly how she wanted them to look.

"I give you this warning then," he said, starting to turn away from her. "You can take it or leave it."

"A warning?" Kayt giggled again. "Is it about the pastries, because I already made that mistake." With a grin she rubbed her flat stomach.

"Zorah is a New Order radical, who is close-minded, manipulative, and very, *very* dangerous. Watch your back with him. He's not what he seems to be, and he *always* has an agenda."

"Which one is Zorah again?" she teased.

He stared at her. "I know you will have sway with Gragor in the near future. Please keep him from the tyrannical rule Zorah wants to put in place." Seff appeared genuinely concerned, and for a moment, he seemed to revert to the possibly fat, helpless, bullied boy he might have been as a child. "Perhaps Oldaem needs more protection than we realize. More support and open-mindedness to get us through these approaching dark times."

"Lady Kayt, Prince Gragor and King Orcino request your presence in the Royal Hall," announced a timid servant who had appeared out of nowhere.

The servant disappeared behind a curtain, as the sounds of dancing and music and laughter had ceased. It was as if the entire party was waiting for her.

"I'm sorry to cut this short, Shepherd, but they *are* waiting for me."

"Yes, I know. Please, just . . . *think* about what I said to you."

Once again she looked up at the night sky. "You're right about those stars. They shine the brightest in the palace." Then she disappeared back into the party.

She walked in silence, all eyes upon her, toward the royal thrones of Gragor and Orcino. Udina and Garrus whispered intensely to each other off in a corner. Seff was still on the balcony and Zorah nowhere to be seen. Her mind was buzzing. Whom could she trust? Both had made valid points. How could they trust a foreign nation like Sther, and at the same time, Zorah did seem like a tyrannical religious radical, possibly wanting to control *everything* on his own. She began to wonder if she could even trust Garrus.

As Kayt continued toward the thrones she could hear the whispers about her. How beautiful she looked, how sorry for her they felt, how terribly she had been wronged in Highdale, how amazing for her to be given a new purpose, how elegant her dress was, and how lucky Oldaem was to have such a fine lady in their palace. The hushed sighs silenced as she knelt before the king and prince. Gragor rose, and approaching her, placed both hands in hers and stared into her eyes.

Although aware that he was saying something to her, her mind kept wandering. Out of the corners of her eyes she noticed that everyone seemed to be hanging on his every word. As Kayt met his gaze and maintained her perfect smile, she wondered, *What should I do? Whom should I trust?* Gragar droned on while her thoughts raced. For some reason she thought about the large family she had grown up in, how she had had to struggle for every scrap of attention she ever received. Her whole life had been like that. She had had to demand respect at school and to get a Shepherd interview. Everything had been a constant battle. After the defeat of Silas' political campaign and the tears she had shed at the library, she had fought to rise again. Suddenly it dawned on her that she didn't need Zorah or Seff. She didn't need *anyone*. The only person she could count on was herself, as long as she had *fight* in her. Kayt was a survivor. Now, at last she was *finally* in the perfect place to make some changes to the Royal Council.

Gragor knelt before her. "Kayt of Dagonfell, will you be my wife?"

CHAPTER 49: SAYLA

In front of her was the wall of the tent, but Sayla didn't see it. Nor did she feel anything. If only she could not think anything either--but her mind was racing.

I could have stopped it. The thought wouldn't leave her alone. *His death was my fault. Their deaths were my fault.* The first time she had actually taken one of her dreams seriously, and she had gotten it all wrong. She had never been the one in danger of losing her life. Instead, she had been the one who was supposed to be the hero--not Grunt.

The all-consuming knot in her stomach assured her that she had been given the dream for a reason. Somehow she had always known that her dreams were meant for a purpose, though she had never let herself admit it before. But after seeing Grunt die, watching as the cave collapsed around him, she couldn't ignore it anymore.

Sayla lie on her bedroll and let her thoughts swirl around her. Unable to eat or sleep, she had stared at nothing, her mind wandering, ever since the disaster at the cave.

It was as if nothing mattered anymore. She had failed. Sayla had followed the rules, was well liked, and was on her way to becoming everything a Shepherd was meant to be. But Grunt was dead. That innocent kid who had shown nothing but kindness to her, had perished, because she had followed the rules. *Maybe the rules are wrong.*

Allowing herself to think that way was dangerous. All her life, Sayla's ambition had been her driving force. Always she had believed that she was meant for something greater, and when she had gotten into the Shepherd Academy, it had just felt right.

Who cared if she had to sacrifice a few ideals, lose a couple friends, or join a new religion? She was on her way to the top. But a life was different. Her devotion had cost a life. And Sayla wasn't sure if that was something she could live with.

So, for the time being, she had chosen not to live at all. *At least if I had died in that cave in I wouldn't have to feel what I do right now.*

Out of the corner of her eye, she saw the tent flap open. She didn't care who it was. Aveline had been in and out every few hours checking on her, trying to get her to eat or sleep. But Sayla had refused to even acknowledge Aveline's presence.

This time, however, a much deeper voice broke into her thoughts.

"Sayla?"

Although she immediately recognized Shale's voice, it wasn't enough to make her react. She continued to stare at the tent wall. *You're just like the rest of them.*

"See? She's been ignoring me like that ever since yesterday." Aveline entered behind him and crossed her arms. "I don't know what's up with her. She hasn't eaten or slept. She's just been lying there, screaming that it should have been her instead of Grunt. I think maybe she's in shock. Maybe you can knock some sense into her." Aveline shrugged, but there was concern in her voice. After glancing once more at the bedroll where Sayla was lying, she turned on her heels and exited the tent.

Shale knelt beside her. "Sayla." He shook her shoulder. She didn't respond. "Sayla, we just got here, and I gotta say, as my current lady love I was very concerned that you weren't there to greet me and call me a brave champion and stuff. Sayla." Again he shook. But she only rolled on her side, her back to him.

"Tryndamere and Aveline filled us in on what happened. I mean it's sad and all." His voice denied his words. "But ... come on Sayla, it's not worth being all dramatic about. I mean, you're usually attractive, but you look pretty terrible right now." She still wore the same rumpled, dust-covered trainee uniform that she had been in yesterday. Sayla hadn't even taken her boots off. Her light brown hair was tangled all around her face and dark circles shadowed her eyes.

"I know that you think Grunt was trying to be a hero or something," he continued. "But what he did was dumb. He gave away his life for some slave. That was his fault, not yours. I mean, if you're looking for someone to admire, I'm right here."

Shale's voice had always been so soothing, but now it began to grate on her nerves. She didn't know if she could trust him anymore. For that matter, she didn't know if she could trust anyone. And she certainly couldn't trust her own judgment.

Behind her, Sayla heard someone enter the tent. "Here," Aveline's voice said, "she needs to drink something." The tent flap closed again.

"Hey, it's a long way to the Capital, and we have to leave soon in order to make it in time for the tournament. Don't you want to go to the tournament?"

Did she? Nothing seemed to matter anymore. Who cared about some kids competing for a spot in one of the Shepherd academies? It was all a lie anyway. Those young people didn't know what they were getting themselves into. They were as naïve as Sayla had been when she was sixteen, full of ideals and grand plans.

But she couldn't stay here, either. Unable to bear the thought of having to look at those caves again, she had no choice but to go with her group. Sayla had planned to be whatever she needed to be to get ahead, but now she was tired of faking it as a strong, unbeatable fighter.

No longer did she want to be that person. Doing that, she now realized, would destroy everything she valued. She had already given up so much. Too much. Once it had seemed to be worth it. But now, when the lie was removed, she had nothing left. She didn't know who she was anymore. Everything she had believed in so strongly had crumbled with Grunt's death.

Rolling over to face Shale, she slowly nodded. "I'll go," she said softly. It was all she could bring herself to say.

"Yes!" He grabbed her hand. "Aveline was all worried that I couldn't get you to talk, but I just have this incredible way with people. I knew I could get through to you." He beamed at her.

As Sayla studied Shale's eyes, she wasn't sure what she saw there. Ambition, maybe. It was what had attracted her to him in the first place. *Maybe I was looking for the wrong things.* But she couldn't just shut off her feelings. Even the mood she was in right now did not instantly turn her away from him. Maybe Sayla could trust him at least a little. She would have to wait and see.

405

"Now, then. You drink this. You're probably dehydrated, and if we want to get a move on by this evening, we need you strong and ready to go." Shale eagerly handed her a canteen.

Sayla accepted it. Her stomach was too knotted to be hungry, but the lack of water and the summer heat even in the shade was starting to get to her. "Thanks." After drinking the whole thing, she licked her lips. It had tasted like water, but had a sweet aftertaste that she did not recognize.

"What was that?" she asked.

"Oh, water," Shale smirked. "And some sleeping herb."

"What?" She sat up. *No, no, no, I can't fall asleep. I can't.*

"You didn't sleep all night," he explained happily, ignoring her reaction. "This will help you."

"No! It makes everything worse!" Leaping to her feet, she rushed at him. Surprised, he backed away as she grabbed the collar of his black shirt. "You don't understand! I can't go back there! I can't go back there!"

Shale tried to push her away, but she shoved him back first. "It's going to happen again!"

Finally he succeeded in grabbing her arms, but still she fought against him, screaming as she had at the caves. She couldn't let it happen again—must not fall asleep. Everything that had gone wrong had happened after she had that first dream. It was the catalyst.

But already Sayla could feel the drug taking affect. Her limbs became sluggish, her eyes felt heavy. Although she battled it with all she had, eventually she fell limply into Shale's arms.

This dream was different, because immediately Sayla was aware that she was dreaming. "Come on, Sayla, wake up," she commanded. Nothing happened. She pinched her arm, slapped herself in the face. Nothing.

With a sigh she took stock of her surroundings. She was still in her Shepherd's uniform, but it was clean now and her hair was in a bun. Sayla stood in a dense forest. It was beautiful and green. Although she had never seen any greenery quite like it before, still, something about the forest felt oddly familiar. Just looking at the trees calmed her a bit, even though she knew it was a dream and just minutes ago she had been screaming and fighting against it.

Hearing a noise behind her, she dodged behind a thick tree and looked around its massive trunk. The trunk was not straight as she would have expected. Instead, it leaned forward as if bowing. Then she realized the other trees in the forest were also all inclined in the

406

same direction. "Like they're keeping a secret," she whispered. Even before Sayla looked in the direction the trees indicated, she already knew what they were pointing at. What she saw explained the odd familiarity she felt. In front of her was the colossal Tower that she had seen once in person so many years ago. But something was different.

It no longer had a wall around it. The massive stone wall that she had carved her name into had vanished. Instead, the Tower was easily visible in all its glory. As if drawn by an invisible cord she walked toward it. It was beautiful.

The Tower was made of black opal. From a distance it appeared a solid dark, but as Sayla approached, she could see the hint of other colors in it as well. She continued until she came close enough to touch it. Inlaid within the black stone of the Tower was every color imaginable, some that she couldn't even put a name to. It was the most beautiful thing she had ever seen.

Gingerly she placed her fingers on the smooth stone in front of her. It buzzed with energy. Instantly she withdrew her hand and looked up. Sayla could not even see the top of the Tower. It seemed to go on forever, enshrouded in light. The little slave girl had called it a link between Esis and Aael. Standing here now, for the first time Sayla wondered if that could be true.

Suddenly she heard footsteps behind her and turned to see four people walking toward the Tower. They were unlike anyone Sayla had ever met before. Each wore robes of bright colors like the ones that shimmered in the material of the Tower.

The first was a woman, beautiful with ivory skin and long brown hair. Standing next to her was a man with blonde hair and eyes even bluer than Galen's. Beside him was another man with skin and hair as dark as the Tower. The last person was a woman with curly red hair that hung all the way to her feet. All of them were tall. And all of them wore Shepherd medallions around their necks. "The first Shepherds," she gasped. Both New Order and Old Order agreed that the first humans created in Esis were the original four Shepherds, tasked with protecting the Tower.

Sayla thought about running to hide behind the tree trunk again, but somehow she knew they couldn't see her. Instead she sat down in the grass and watched as they approached.

"It is a good idea," the blonde man insisted. "It is the only sure way to protect the Tower."

407

"I do not believe it would be wise," the dark-skinned man protested, shaking his head. "We were instructed not to build anything around it."

"Instructed by whom? The Creator?" The blonde man pointed toward the Tower. "He is concealing something from us. He wants to see us fail."

"He wants what is best for us," the woman with red hair insisted. "And if he chooses to conceal something from us, so be it. I trust him regardless."

"I do as well," the other woman agreed. "The Order has given us ample supplies to watch over this Tower. Why would we need to add anything to it when it is perfection already?"

"We cannot expect to watch over this Tower with only the supplies he has given us. Do you not want to know the secrets that are hidden beyond?" The blonde man separated himself from the other three. "I am the Shepherd of Spirit. I can feel that this is right. And think how impressed The Order will be once they see how innovative we are on our own."

The redheaded woman shook her head sadly. "It was the one thing he asked us not to do."

"He has a point," the brunette woman relented. "The being that spoke to us yesterday made it sound as if the Creator may be concealing all of his knowledge from us. What if he wants us to figure it out on our own?"

"But building a wall?" The dark-skinned man sounded doubtful. "What if it is not his will?"

Sayla did not get a chance to hear the answer. The voices of the Shepherds drifted away as they walked farther from the Tower. *I'm seeing the beginning,* she realized. The original Shepherds were the ones that built the wall. *And broke the connection.* Her attention shifted back to the Tower.

She had never gotten a good look at the Tower years before, but it was clearly the same one. Just the sight of it brought her thoughts back to a memory so cherished that she rarely let herself remember it.

The scenery changed with her thoughts. It was no longer midday, but dark outside. Sayla flew through the air until she landed hard on her back against a rocky hill. Startled, she tumbled a few feet before coming to a stop. Groggily she sat up, her legs tangled in the pink fabric beneath her. *I can't believe Mother always makes me wear these awful dresses.* Then Sayla looked up, expecting nothing but

408

trees, but instead, in the moonlight, she caught a glimpse of the outline of the biggest Tower she had ever seen.

"Are you okay?" a voice asked behind her. But she barely heard it, being too busy looking in awe at the sight before her. After sitting there for a few moments to regain her wits, she turned to face her companions.

Galen reached out his hand and pulled her to her feet. "Do you see it?" he whispered.

Sayla nodded enthusiastically. "What is it? Do you think it's ..." Then she squealed.

"It's the Tower," announced the voice behind Galen and Sayla. Sayla thought he should know what he was talking about. After all, he was the oldest.

"What do you mean *the* Tower?" Galen asked suspiciously. He looked so small compared to the tall boy behind him. But Galen was strong, though. Sayla knew it even if Galen didn't yet.

"The one from the legend, silly!" she said, jumping up and down in her excitement. "And we've seen it! I thought it wasn't true, but look it's right there in front of us plain as day even though it's nighttime!"

"My mom always said it was real, but I never believed her," Galen whispered.

"It's ... I don't know how to explain it," the oldest boy said reverently. His dark hair ruffled in the light breeze. *He's perfect,* Sayla thought to herself. "But being here--I like the way it makes me feel," he said innocently. "My mind is so clear. It's as if everything makes sense."

Sayla agreed. A calming sensation spread through her body unlike anything she had ever experienced before. And being there with her two best friends just felt right. Nothing could be the same after this. It was a day she would remember for the rest of her life.

Then Sayla looked up at the moon. As she did, it faded as the sun came out. The sky grew brighter, but smoke obscured it. The sound of screaming came from behind her. "Galen!" she called. But he was no longer there. Neither of her two friends were. She was alone.

Then she heard the clang of metal against metal, shouts and barked commands. *A battle.* The sky was red as if the sun was bleeding.

A deafening *boom* shook the ground, knocking her off her feet and tumbling her the rest of the way down the steep, rocky hill. She stopped at the base of the Wall.

Once more, Sayla woozily rose to her feet. Her pulse quickened when she recognized this part of the Wall. Tentatively, she brushed away some ivy growing along it until she saw them--the names. She ran her fingers along the bottom one—hers—then delicately traced Galen's name in the middle and finally the one above it. A snapping caused her to look up.

A crack had formed at the top of the Wall. Fragments started popping out of it, just as they had done in the cave. Frightened, Sayla backed away. The crack along the Wall spread, quickly crawling all the way down, splitting the three names in half before coming to a stop at the ground. There followed a few seconds of uneasy silence.

Then the entire Wall came crashing down. Sayla dove to avoid the falling debries, but one piece struck her in the back, and stars exploded in her vision.

Breathing heavily and crying once more, she woke up in her bedroll. She did not feel rested at all.

Wearily, Sayla stumbled to her feet and exited the tent to find nobody around. *I have to look one last time.* For the few minutes it took her to reach the cave site she walked alone with her thoughts. It sat untouched, the boulders still blocking the entrance. She approached it, braver this time. Her dream had reminded her of what she had once been, and she wondered if she could ever regain that lost innocence.

Spotting a patch of yellow flowers growing near the cave entrance, Sayla picked one and placed it on one of the boulders. "I'll make this right," she promised Grunt. "I'll make this right."

CHAPTER 50: GALEN

According to Zevran's map, their ship and its important cargo were just passing the southern Oldaem port city of Tan-Um. They should arrive at the Capital within a few days. Galen guessed they might miss the opening ceremonies of the tournament, but that was about it. They had been stuck in Kaya for way too long. It turned out their vessel had suffered great damage from the storm. If they had been out on the open ocean much longer the craft would have sunk.

Galen heaved a sigh as he headed back to where they had again confined the princess. It was his turn to watch her. Gadiel had been with her all day, and he was supposed to take the next 12-hour shift.

That was how they had done it back at the inn on Kaya, and that was how they continued to do it once their ship was ready to take to sea once more.

At least one good thing had come from their delay in Kaya. Zevran had hired a few men whose silence could be bought with gold, and they were now the new crew. That left Gadiel and Galen free to guard Princess Allora. They had never told the general about her attempted escape, but every time Galen talked to him, he got the inexplicable feeling that Zevran had figured it out anyway. *Or maybe Adar or Leilani told him.*

Either way, Galen had felt uneasy since the whole ordeal had happened. However, it surprisingly had nothing to do with Princess Allora herself. After placing himself in her shoes the night she had tried to escape, Galen had begun to understand her a little bit more. He had decided that maybe he did not need to be so rude to her. While he had never quite been able to accept that he could choose to be a likable person, what that tournament kid, Ian, had said, had really made him think. Regardless of the fact that Princess Allora came from Leoj and was, in fact, very clearly the enemy, she was still a human being.

Now their time together was much more pleasant, and he was even starting to look forward to seeing her, although he was hesitant to admit it to anyone. In reality, though, nothing had changed. She was still the prisoner and he the guard. Her attitude never wavered. It was his that was changing. His step developed a spring to it as he got closer to the cabin.

When Galen arrived, he unhooked the latch locking the princess and Gadiel inside. Just as he started to open the door, Gadiel yanked it from the inside and angrily stormed out of the room. Instantly Galen closed the door from the outside again. "What's the matter with you?"

Gadiel turned on his heels. "That girl knows something, Galen. She *knows* something." He pointed at the door. "I can feel it. But she won't talk."

It was the same conversation they had had multiple times. Galen was tired of it. "It's not your job to make her talk. All you have to do is get her to the Capital in one piece."

"You're starting to agree with her!" Gadiel's face turned beet red. "Don't fall under her spell again, Galen. Remember what happened last time you did that? She *nearly got away.*"

411

"That's not what happened," Galen sighed. Then he stared at the door suspiciously. "You tied her up again, didn't you?"

"I don't have to defend my actions to you! She's dangerous!"

"Because she kicked you in the stomach? Real scary." Galen smirked.

"Apparently her beauty has clouded your memory. She tried to kill me. Remember?" Dumfounded, Gadiel stared at him.

Galen tried a calmer tactic. He had learned to pick his battles, and this one was not worth getting upset over. "Listen, man, I don't think she knows what you believe she does. You're just trying to find someone to blame for what happened to your father, and she's the easiest target."

Gadiel scoffed, "Well, you would know about that, wouldn't you?"

The humor left Galen's tone. "Excuse me?"

"I don't know what some Lamean ever did to you, but I know that it couldn't be worth taking it out on every single one that you meet."

Galen felt his fist clenching as he edged toward him. "You little ..."

"Gadiel, the captain requests your presence on deck," one of the new deckhands said as he approached.

Gadiel saluted sarcastically at Galen and departed. The deckhand stayed behind to lock Galen into the cabin. Grinding his teeth, Galen stepped inside.

Princess Allora sat on the bunk, one wrist tied skillfully to the support post, the other trying to yank the ropes off. She was still dressed in her Oldaem warrior garb with her thick braid running down her back. When Galen entered, Allora looked over at him and grumpily asked, "Well, it's about time. Little help here?"

"Sorry," he muttered as he loosened the rope. Allora pulled her right hand free and massaged her wrist.

"I thought you were going to talk to him!" Her lavender eyes stared imploringly. "Don't tell me you forgot again."

"I did talk to him!" Galen sat down on the bunk beside her. It had become a normal routine to sit across from each other and talk for hours during his shift guarding her. It had started slowly at first—a little conversation here or there. But to their surprise, Allora and Galen had found they had a lot to discuss. Now, instead of dreading it, guarding Princess Allora had become his favorite part of the day.

On the other hand, Gadiel was apparently nothing but rude. At first, Allora had been sympathetic. She said she understood how it

412

felt to be missing her father and if she was in his situation, she probably would react the same. Galen had informed her that losing a father was not nearly as bad as not ever having one at all and then he had accidentally let out more personal information than he had planned.

It was just that Allora was so easy to talk to. He had never expected to get along so well with a Leojian. Yes, she was the enemy. But she wasn't.

Allora didn't look as if she believed Galen. "I talked to him. But it's not like I'm his favorite person," he continued.

"What does he expect me to do?" she exclaimed exasperatedly. "Jump into the ocean and swim away? We aren't even close to land yet!" Then she paused as she saw Galen's face change. "Are we?"

"We just passed Tan-Um a couple hours ago," he said, his voice strained. He knew how she was dreading the completion of their journey to Oldaem. Part of him was looking forward to finally being back on solid ground, and maybe even being recognized as a hero, but he would be sorry to lose Allora's company. She was quirky and interesting in a way that intrigued him. Princess Allora had lost so much and faced an uncertain future, yet she still had such an optimistic attitude. *I don't understand it.*

"I don't know what that means."

"It's one of Oldaem's southern ports. The Capital is just a couple days northwest after that."

"Oh," she said in a faint voice.

"It's not gonna be what you think. You'll see." Galen wasn't completely convinced of that himself, but he had to hold on to the belief that he was working for the good people. What would he do if he lost even that? It wasn't as if he had that much to begin with. For a fleeting moment, he imagined Sayla in his position. *What would Sayla do if she found out that something she valued was based on a lie?* Galen didn't know why he thought of her at that instant. She was probably off at the tournament with her Shepherd friends having the time of her life. She had everything she had ever wanted. Then he frowned. No, their situations were very different. Still, he hoped she was doing well. *I miss you, Sayla. I miss our conversations.* He sent a silent thought in her direction.

"I think you're the one who is going to be surprised," the princess sighed.

"You're wrong." It was all he could think of to say. He wasn't sure himself about what lay ahead anymore. If Leojians could be friendly,

413

if enemies could become friends … then maybe Oldaemites weren't always good, and maybe friends could become enemies. Galen supposed anything was possible.

"Have you ever been to the Capital?"

"A few times." Galen thought back. "For the tournament. The one that's going on right now. It's an annual thing. Last time I was there was about five years ago." *Exactly five years ago.*

Allora giggled.

"What?" Galen asked.

"Oh, nothing. I was just trying to imagine you being in that Shepherd Tournament thing." She continued to smile although the giggling stopped.

"And why would that make you laugh?"

"Well, you're so clumsy," she said matter-of-factly with no hint of sarcasm.

"I am not clumsy!"

"Really? Because every time I've fought you you've found some way to fall over."

"All your fault!"

"Hmm, bested by a girl. Just as bad." Her eyes twinkled.

Galen leaned back against the rough wooden wall of the cabin. "Anyway, it wasn't me competing. I had a couple of friends that did, and I went to see them."

"Did any of them win?"

"One did. A girl actually. Sayla." He remembered the look of sheer joy on her face as she stood among the winners. Galen had been proud of her. It had always been her greatest wish to become a Shepherd, and now she was still on her way to being one. *I hope it's all you've ever dreamed of.* "You remind me of her," he added as an afterthought.

"How so?"

"I don't really know. I mean you look nothing alike. That comment about me losing to a girl is something she would tell me. I guess it's more …"--he tried to put his finger on it--"it's more the way you see things."

"And how do I see things, Galen?" she teased.

"You're strong-willed. Aggressive. You have an adventurous spirit. And you don't let circumstances get in the way of your attitude or how you live. Sayla is like that too. At least, she was."

"What do you mean she *was?*"

Galen shrugged halfheartedly. "People change. She might not be that person anymore. I haven't seen her in two, three years." *Exactly three years.*

The princess looked thoughtfully toward the door. Galen wondered if she was imagining what lie beyond it. The ocean? Leoj? "You know, I'm almost 18."

"I didn't."

"It's late summer now. I turn 18 this fall." She pulled her knees to her chest and wrapped her arms around them. "My mother always told me that the leaves changing colors were a present for me."

"Is orange your favorite color?"

"Red."

Me too, Galen thought.

"We were going to have a big celebration," she continued, but more slowly, as if she chose every word carefully. "Turning 18 is a big deal in Leoj. At first, we were going to invite all the lords and governors. That all changed when the war started. Despite the war going on, my father promised to make my day special, even if it was just spent with the four of us." Allora gazed at him with a pained expression that he rarely saw her make. "Now, we can't have even that. And I know it's a silly thing to think about. Birthday celebrations are so inconsequential. But the truth is, I would give up every birthday celebration for the rest of my life if I could just spend a little more time with my brother, my mother, and my father." It was not the first time Galen had started to feel guilty about tearing her family apart, but hearing it from her side made him feel even worse. *What wouldn't I give for a chance to meet my father?*

Tears filled her eyes but she quickly wiped them away with the back of her hand. "But I'm here. And I'm going to be okay. You're right. People leave. Sometimes they don't choose to, but it happens anyway. The thing that matters is how we react to it. And that's where you could use some work." Her eyes smiled through the tears.

Galen couldn't argue with that. He tried to think back to a time when he had been happy—really happy. Not on his recent travels, and certainly not in Sea Fort. Even Aramoor had had its dark alleys. But one memory stuck out, and once it surfaced in his mind, he could not stop thinking about it. For the first time in a long time, Galen allowed himself to remember the day they had found the Tower.

415

CHAPTER 51: KAYT

Kayt walked the streets of Highdale in disguise to get a pulse on the election, pulling her lavender shawl around her shoulders. Posters and flyers everywhere promoted the current Regent and his inner circle. She noticed and heard many conversations about how people already trusted what they had, about how they questioned whether or not Silas could *actually* lead, how Kayt's role as his Shepherd of State wouldn't be enough to pull Silas' inability to impress other leaders.

As part of her plan to sway opinion, she had divided the region into three areas: the southern portion, which included the major city of Azmar and other surrounding villages; the Channel People; and the northern portion, covering everything east of the Barisan Mountain range to Highdale, the Capital in the west. Isprig was basically divided in half as a result of the Barisan Mountain range. The Channel People, as they were formally known, went about life in a very different way, residing on the rocky shores of the natural channel that split Oldaem in two. She had sent out the to-be-Shepherd of Mind to campaign in the south, the would-be Shepherd of Defense to sway the Channel people, and Melnora, as Shepherd of Spirit, to the northeast. She would personally handle Highdale. The reports coming back had been dismal, except among the Channel People. The people of Isprig mostly fished along the channel and did some ore mining in the mountain range. Highdale nestled on a lofty hilltop, and extensive deposits of gold and metal ore existed beneath the city. The area produced the majority of the country's wealth and why the region of Isprig had been so important to the Capital.

People all across Isprig seemed to be under the impression that if something wasn't broke, it didn't need to be fixed, which was why the current Regent of Isprig had ruled for so many years. The inhabitants of Isprig were New Order believers, set in their ways, resistant to change, and quite content with the ways things were going. The challenge of changing such minds had excited Kayt. However, she had also expected that she wouldn't be working alongside fools. And fools they were! The Defense Shepherd Silas had picked was hotheaded and lazy and incredibly unlikeable. However, Silas and he had been friends in school, and he wouldn't budge on the choice. Kayt detested the man. The Mind Shepherd she had met during her tournament. He was very unmemorable and had bad hygiene. And she didn't even want to think about her dislike for Melnora. Silas had been more stubborn than she had originally realized. The campaign was crumbling, and fast. While people in Highdale at first seemed to be the most open to her campaign, it was travelers from other areas that kept changing voters' minds. It was literally like the tide at sea. And currently, Highdale favored the current Regent.

As Kayt sat on a bench and watched two children playing, she fought back memories of her own children and Arnand. She hadn't left her family for this. *Something has to change.* Kayt had begun concocting her plan the previous night at the party, when she had noticed so many "supporters" had defected to the opposing side. But she wasn't going to wait until election night to lose and be embarrassed, smile and wave, and take it like a good soldier. No way. She was getting out before then. Everything was ready in her mind, and she even knew where she was going to go next. It had been her desire to learn more about the New Order from the original sources themselves. Instead of returning home, she decided that she would spend several months at the library in Westervale, up in Rahvil. There she could "heal" and then decide what to do next. Election Day was tomorrow. Things would have to commence tonight.

For a moment she stood and looked around Highdale. It really was a beautiful city, and a shame that things had turned out the way they did. People always seemed to disappoint her--they just couldn't ever meet her standards. They seemed content to wallow in their mediocre lives, and it made her sick. That had been one reason she had left Arnand. He was content with just "existing." But she wanted more--demanded more. And tonight, she would get more--by running. She knew that destruction would follow in her wake, and maybe there needed to be.

Silas had lied to her, telling her that she would have full control of his campaign and that they would win. He claimed the people hated their current Regent. And he had said a lot of things to convince her to leave her family, including his promise to love her forever. While she didn't necessarily care about the "love" part, perhaps it would been an added bonus if things had turned out the way as planned. They could have ruled together. Maybe then she would have finally been able to stop having to fight for everything in life.

In a family with so many "extraordinary," or "beautiful," or "talented," daughters, Kayt had no choice but to figure out how to survive. She wasn't the most beautiful, talented, or smartest, but she could *fight* the hardest. Now Silas would pay—heavily--for the great disappointment he had caused for her. Kayt was tired of being disappointed.

That night they were to have dinner in his quarters. He had invited just her, as he usually did about once a week. His servants would bring them a romantic meal, and they would talk, mostly about things unrelated to the campaign--at his request to her chagrin.

Returning to his manor, she entered and carefully placed her warmest lavender shawl in the corner of the entrance hall, under a table, and headed up the stairs, past Melnora, giving her a glare. Once inside her chambers, she bathed, put on the best perfumes Highdale could offer, dressed in a low-cut light pink gown, and let her hair hang loosely around her shoulders.

Then she walked down the halls of the corridor of the manor for what she knew would be the last time. Opening the door to his room, she found him sitting at a small candle-lit table for two. He rose and smiled and walked toward her.

"You look stunning."

"Thank you, Silas." she breathed as he kissed her on the cheek.

He held her in his arms. "Tomorrow is the big day."

"Yes." She looked away.

He turned her face towards his. "Is something wrong, my love?"

"How I wish things would have turned out differently."

"What do you mean?"

At that moment she knew that she still could make a choice. She could stop all of this, sit down, enjoy her meal with the man she claimed to love, and lose with dignity beside him tomorrow. Or she could ask him to leave the room and initiate her plan. Kayt looked into his blue eyes. Once she had thought him so handsome, so intriguing, so possibly powerful. He would be able to grant her everything she wanted: status, power, intrigue, excitement, and more. But now, he was just pitiful, weak, and ignorant--a disappointment. And she was done with disappointments. "Silas, do you think you could do something for me? It's frightfully cold in here . . . could you . . ."

"Would you like a blanket?" he interrupted.

"No," she snapped, then smiled, regaining her composure. "I would like my lavender shawl. I think I accidently left it on the table in the entrance hall when I came in this afternoon." She looked at him with doe-eyes. "Would you retrieve it for me?"

Confused, he replied, "Of course my love." And stepped outside of the room, shutting the door behind him.

Kayt stared at the closed door. No one would be close by. On their intimate evenings, he always sent the servants and guards far away. But she didn't have much time. Slowly and methodically she overturned the two chairs. Blowing out the candles, she broke one in half. Then she took a plate and threw it against the wall. It shattered, and she impassively watched the food slide down the wall to the floor. Next she overturned the table. The spilled wine pooled amongst the shattered glass on the marble floor. Going over to the bed, she rolled around on it, ripped some of the sheets, shredded the contents of a pillow, and yanked down the fabric canopy over the bed. Now for herself. First she slammed her face against the wooden bedpost until the skin around her eye began to show bruising. After tearing the front of her pink gown down the middle to expose her undergarments, she punched herself in the arms until they also were bruised. She roughed up her hair. And when she was done, she walked to the room's mirror and calmly studied her reflection. Nearly unrecognizable, she looked the victim of a violent attack. *You're a fighter.* Slowly she picked up a jagged fragment of a plate and sliced her cheek with it. Blood trickled down her face. First came the tears, and then the screaming.

Collapsing into a heap on the floor, she wailed at the top of her lungs. Footsteps raced toward the room, the door swung open, and a servant girl stared at her with terrified eyes.

"Please!" Kayt shrieked. "Help me!"

The girl ran to her side. "What . . . what happened to you?"

"Get the city guards! Quickly! He'll come back! He'll come back! " Kayt screamed louder, tears streaming down her face. "QUICKLY!"

The girl ran off, as another taller servant woman stood, lurking in the doorway, taking in the destruction around the room. As Kayt continued to sob on the floor, the taller girl nervously approached her. Kayt began to shake. The servant knelt down beside her. "It will be alright, Miss."

Clinging to the servant, Kayt sobbed, "He'll come back. Help me!"

"Don't worry, help is coming."

As she wept in the servant's arms, Kayt could feel the girl's fear. "Miss . . . what happened here?"

"They'll never believe me . . ." she whispered and shuddered. "They'll never believe me. How could he?" Then she broke down again.

"I'll believe you. Tell me what happened?"

"He . . . Silas . . . he . . ." Abruptly she pulled the servant down to eyelevel. "You have to get me out of here! He'll come back! He'll come back!"

The door swung open, and Silas entered. His eyes widened in shock as they darted about the room, viewing the destruction around him.

Kayt screamed at the top of her lungs and backed away as fast as she could toward the corner of the room. "Not again! Please! No! Not again!"

The servant dashed to the room's fireplace, grabbed the fire poker, and stood in front of Kayt. "Step back! Don't come any closer!"

"What? I . . ." Bewildered, Silas put his hands up and edged away from them both. Because Kayt continued to scream as loudly as she could, he couldn't get a word out.

City guards burst into the room behind the smaller servant girl, Melnora on their heels. The sister stared around the room in horror. The girl with the poker screamed to the guards, "Get Silas, he attacked her, he *forced* himself on her! Look at her! She's terrified."

"Get away from me, Silas!" Kayt shouted. Then to the guards, "Please help me!"

"What are you talking about?" Silas asked in astonishment.

Immediately the guards surrounded and restrained him.

"What is the meaning of this?" Melnora demanded.

The soldier in charge gently approached Kayt, who was now weeping bitterly in a corner of the room. Kneeling beside her, he said, "Shepherd Kayt, please tell us what happened."

"I came in to find her laying beaten on the floor," the younger servant girl interjected. "The room was destroyed, she was bleeding, her clothes torn, the bed a mess. She was terrified *he* would come back." She shot Silas a deadly look.

"This is ridiculous!" he exploded.

Melnora was about to shout the same when the officer in charge gave them both warning glances. "Sir, you'd be wise to say nothing right now without legal counsel." Then he returned his attention to Kayt. "Please, Shepherd, it's okay, you're safe now. What happened?"

Slowly she told them of how it had just been a simple dinner at first, like every other time, then how he had become drunk, started getting angry and belligerent, and began yelling and breaking things. When she had asked for him to stop, he wouldn't. Then he started roughly kissing her, and she begged him to stop, and he wouldn't . . . and how he . . . she wasn't able to get out the worst part of it, but she knew everyone in the room believed her, except for Melnora.

The younger servant who had discovered her, nodded in agreement. "She's right. I heard the scuffle. I heard the screams, but Silas had asked me not to disturb them. I was afraid to disobey."

"Afraid?" Silas said incredulously.

Then Kayt's gaze shifted to Melnora. "And *her* . . ."–she held up a shaking finger toward Melnora–"she knew it was happening the whole time, and did *nothing*."

"This is absurd!" the woman exclaimed.

The servant once again came to Kayt's defense. "No, she's right! Shepherd Melnora was seen exiting the hall during the scuffle, but once again, there was nothing I could do."

"You're lying!" Melnora shouted.

Another guard spoke up. "No, the servant is telling the truth. I saw her too."

"What?" Melnora whipped around, flabbergasted.

"As did I," a second guard added.

"Silas, you are under arrest for this brutal attack. Anything you say can be used against you. Come with us."

The guards led the befuddled man away, confusion and tears in his eyes, as he dropped a lavender shawl and a red flower on the floor. Melnora watched in horror, then followed them out, but not before turning and looking directly at Kayt. Kayt stared back unwaveringly. *I'll bury him deeper than I'll bury you,* she thought. Melnora glared at her as though she was a monster.

That night a servant and two city guards had drinks at a tavern together with nearly acquired gold. *I always survive, no matter who is left in my wake. Now to Westervale. I always survive. That I do.*

"I do," Kayt breathed.

Gragor kissed her before the entire royal court. All the nobles of Oldaem were there. They had been married in the palace chapel to the One. Flowers bedecked her hair, and she wore an extravagant white gown, laced with crimson flowers. She held his hands and looked into his eyes. For a moment she saw Silas in him, and then she saw Arnand, but staring back at her was only the clueless prince. *At least this time love is not involved. Without love, hurt cannot exist. Love brings pain and disappointment. When people love, people leave. Now I'm in control.* She felt the eyes of the Royal Shepherds upon her. Garrus and Zorah, Udina and Seff all stood around the king. Soon she would be among them, though she trusted none of them, expect perhaps Garrus. But none should trust her.

That night, after the wedding festivities, after the dancing and the drinking and the laughing and giggling and kissing and mouthing pleasantries and playing the role of Princess of Oldaem and wife to the handsome prince, after being handed an envelope by a servant, which she pocketed and forgot about, after Gragor had *finally* fallen asleep, Kayt found herself in her nightgown staring at a letter on her balcony beneath a full moon. Recognizing the handwriting, she could not bring herself to read it. After all, she had gone to school with him as a boy. What could Arnand possibly want to say to her now? Word of her marriage must have reached him. The letter couldn't possibly be to wish her good luck. The king had granted a royal divorce between the two of them. The envelope merely said "Kayt" and was sealed with his family's crest.

It was a cool night, the leaves of the trees rustling in the early morning breeze. Midnight had come and gone, and dawn was still hours away. She could hear Gragor's snores, and she couldn't bring herself to fall asleep beside him. Now it was just she and her letter and her memories. All three would bring pain. *There cannot be pain without love.* Maybe it was true, and maybe it wasn't. At the moment she wished for the numbness she had felt in Westervale. Then, as if watching from a great distance, she felt herself break the seal, open the letter, and scan the words. To her shock she saw the handwriting of a little child.

"Mom,

"I no I nevar met you. I no you had to go a way. I hear yor the prinsess now. I hope yor hapy. The kassel is prettyful. Dad said you wer 2. I hope you get to have new kids. If you do luv them o k ? We have Dad and he luvs us. We go on a boat tomorow a way from oldam. we r moving kuz dad says its too hard to live here. Lei says hi and she wishes she culd luv you.

"Be a nice prinsess k?

"Yor son Balyn."

When people love, people leave. Her mind drifted to a conversation with Brulis, a Shepherd of Mind she had spoken with in Westervale on a cliff overlooking the library . . . it seemed so long ago.

His voice had sadly echoed. "Ussa . . . Fenris . . . Arissa . . . Lily . . . Belen . . . Cole . . . their names are engraved on my heart. I miss them every day. But I do it for Oldaem. Keep the Faith, Kayt." And he was gone. She realized then, possibly for the first time, how different they truly were. For her, her country never came first, but neither did her family. It was always her. She always came first.

A single tear trickled down Kayt's cheek. She didn't know why. Perhaps it was the wind, the cold, or possibly just sheer exhaustion. Balyn . . . Lei . . . Arnand . . . she missed them too.

CHAPTER 52: GALEN

It was the middle of the night when they finally docked. They had made it, had brought the princess to the Capital. Galen had succeeded and would be recognized, maybe even receive a promotion in the military. But his heart wasn't in it anymore.

The glow from their torches cast distorted shadows across the dark brick of the passageway they were now making their way through. They were somewhere in the underbelly of the palace. It didn't appear so magnificent from underneath. Instead, it seemed dark and intimidating. *I guess that's what it is supposed to look like to the people that pass through here.*

As soon as the ship had neared the city, they had dispatched a courier bird to the palace to announce their soon arrival. In no time, two larger vessels bearing the seal of the royal palace joined them and guided them past the regular port to what Zevran had identified as the private harbor of the king. The castle itself was not terribly close to the water, but enough business went on between the Royal Shepherds and the royal family that they had their own dock.

Once Galen and the rest of the crew had disembarked, everything just went in a whirlwind. An escort of five guards had appeared to take the princess into custody. Galen did not get a chance to talk with her or give her any encouraging words, but he gave her arm a squeeze as he and Gadiel handed her over to them.

It had been a long time since Galen had seen the Capital, but he didn't get much of a view as they flew by in the carriage. They avoided most busy streets altogether since they were headed straight to the stronghold where King Orcino and Prince Gragor resided. Regardless, Galen could hear laughter and music drifting from the alleys. *The tournament has begun.*

Gadiel kept uneasily watching through the window of the carriage until they reached the lower sector of the palace. Now, as they were trudging through its depths, Galen finally realized why Gadiel now kept rushing ahead of him. *This is his home.* He had almost forgotten that Gadiel had grown up in a palace.

The group finally came to a set of twisting stone steps that led to a thick door. It sickeningly reminded him of his short time in the Leoj palace. Galen wondered if Princess Allora was thinking the same. He could barely see her up ahead surrounded by the guards. *She probably has other things on her mind.*

After Galen followed the others through the large door, he found himself in an open room. Intricate patterns climbed up the various pillars and reappeared on the black and white floor tiles. He could not see how far back the room went. Only a few torches on the pillars illuminated the chamber, and he had to depend on the light from the torches held by the guards in front of him.

Princess Allora vanished into the darkness. Galen could faintly hear their footsteps as they marched away. A portly man in red robes greeted Zevran, "Welcome. You have no idea how relieved I am to see you here, and better yet, successful." They shook hands. The balding man turned to Galen, Gadiel, and Adar. "You have served your country well this day. Your bravery will not be ..."

Impatiently, Gadiel broke in, "Where are the Royal Shepherds?"

"I think he is one," Adar leaned toward Galen and whispered quietly. The man did have a Shepherd's medallion hanging around his neck. Galen thought he had seen the individual before somewhere, but he was having trouble placing his face.

"I am one of them," the man assured them.

"No, you're not," Gadiel scoffed. "Now where are they? I want to speak to them."

"Gadiel," Zevran growled in warning. But Gadiel appeared to be getting even more distressed.

"Where is Royal Shepherd Garrus?"

"I would be glad to answer any questions you may have," the Shepherd tried one more time. His voice was steely calm, but Galen could make out a vein beginning to pop out of his large neck. But then he couldn't really blame him. Gadiel made Galen frustrated all the time.

"Except apparently for the only one I've asked you!" Gadiel's voice echoed through the room.

"Gadiel, stand down!" Zevran commanded once more.

The large man was short, but reeked of authority. Rising to his full height, he snapped, "Do you know whom you're talking to, boy?"

"Do you know who *you're* talking to?" Gadiel spat back. Galen figured Gadiel was just embarrassing himself now.

"What is the meaning of all this yelling?" A new voice came from the shadows. It belonged to a thin old man with a long white beard.

"Shepherd Zorah!" Gadiel burst forward.

The Royal Shepherd of Spirit turned in surprise. "Gadiel, is that you?" He looked closer.

"It is," Gadiel answered, bowing in respectful greeting. Zevran motioned for Galen and Adar to do the same. "And he ..." Gadiel began as he turned toward the larger man.

"Is the Interim Royal Shepherd of Defense," Royal Shepherd Zorah clarified quietly. He looked like a gentle old man, but Galen felt wary of anyone in such a high position. Shepherds of Spirit always made him uncomfortable.

But Gadiel seemed to trust him, though, and lowered his voice. "Oh."

"Shepherd Seff," Zorah gestured, "I don't believe you've ever been introduced to Royal Shepherd Demas' son."

"Ah, yes. You were stationed in Sea Fort," Seff looked Gadiel over. "And why, might I ask, are you not there now?" His tone reeked with condescension. Gadiel had certainly not made a friend this evening.

Not everyone just puts up with your disrespect, Galen grinned inwardly. Maybe he and Shepherd Seff would get along, he thought as he leaned against the nearest pillar. This was getting interesting.

"I selected him for the mission," Zevran explained. "He saw the men who took the Royal Shepherd. If we had been able to overtake them at sea, he would have been able to identify them."

"I was not aware of this," Shepherd Seff stated. "I told you specifically to select a few recruits who were unimportant and would not be missed."

"Well, ouch. We're right here." Galen gestured at himself and Adar.

"Nothing can be done about it now," Zorah acknowledged. "But if I had known, I would have advised against it as well." The Shepherd of Spirit leaned toward Zevran and whispered a bit too loudly, "He's got a bit of his father's impulsiveness in him."

Galen snorted.

"I did just fine!" Gadiel countered. "Captain Zevran failed to mention how I saved the whole operation! It would have been a complete failure without me!"

Galen stiffened. "Uh, excuse me? You don't get all that credit, buddy."

Gadiel ignored him and turned again to Shepherd Seff. "That information you sent us in with? All wrong. Your specially trained people? All dead. Without me, there would have been no captive to bring back. So you should be thanking me, not insulting me."

Two men approached from a door off to the far right. "Then it seems you deserve a hero's welcome," the older one said.

At the sound of the voice, a wave of relief appeared to wash over Gadiel's face. The first thing Galen noticed about the two newcomers was that they also each had Shepherd medallions hanging around their necks.

Without a word, Gadiel rushed over to them. He bowed as he had previously done to Royal Shepherd Zorah. "Royal Shepherds Udina and Garrus," Shepherd Seff announced.

"I am pleased to see you, though I wish it was under different circumstances," Royal Shepherd Garrus said as he placed his arm on Gadiel's shoulder. "Is it true what you said just now? Did you singlehandedly capture the princess of Leoj?"

"Yeah, we're all dying to know," Galen added.

Gadiel gave a halfhearted glance toward Galen. "I had some help."

"And by help he means I saved his life," Galen emphasized.

"Then you both will be properly rewarded," Royal Shepherd Udina declared. That was what Galen had been hoping to hear the entire time. Capturing an enemy princess from a foreign land in a time of war had to count for something.

Then Gadiel surprised the whole room by declaring, "I don't want a reward. Just a favor."

The Royal Shepherds glanced at each other. "Ask," Zorah said.

Gadiel took a deep breath. "I want to be present for the interviews with the princess."

So that's what this was all about. It explained Gadiel's uneasiness, his urgency to speak to the Royal Shepherds. Gadiel must have taken Galen's words to heart. If Gadiel couldn't be the one to get information out of Princess Allora, he wanted to be there when someone else did.

"Absolutely not," Shepherd Seff quickly replied.

"Why not? It is not an unreasonable request."

"Because I will be conducting her interview, and I do not want you interfering with it."

"It's customary for a prisoner to be interviewed by all Royal Shepherds separately. You are not conducting all four interrogations," Gadiel argued.

"In fact, I am the sole questioner," the Shepherd of Defense answered proudly. "And I exercise my authority to deny you access. I don't care whose son you are."

Royal Shepherd Garrus stepped between them. "There is no need for discord. We're all on the same side. And he has a point, Seff."

Shepherd Seff eyed Shepherd Garrus. Galen didn't know much about politics, but he could sense some tension in this room. "I was given full permission by King Orcino to be the sole interrogator. We agreed there would be faster results that way."

"I disagree," Shepherd Garrus replied. "Which is why Udina and I have just come from an audience with the king."

"You what?" Shepherd Seff turned to Udina, surprised. "We discussed this!"

"And I agreed with you when we spoke last," the Shepherd of Mind explained. "But we each have a specific responsibility as Shepherds of Mind, State, Defense, and Spirit, and it is our differences that make us stronger."

"Princess Allora will be interviewed by each of us separately," Royal Shepherd Garrus concluded, much to Shepherd Seff's dismay. He held up a paper with the royal seal on it. It appeared as if Seff did not want to say anything more about it until after he had left the company of the soldiers. "And I motion to grant Gadiel's request."

427

"I concur," Zorah answered. Udina nodded in agreement.

Seff looked at the others in dismay. Finally, he sighed, "Fine. But we will discuss this again tomorrow with the king." Then he left the room.

"Thank you," Gadiel told the Royal Shepherd of State.

"Are you sure you want to do this?" Shepherd Garrus asked. "You need to go home. Your family does not even know you're here."

"I have to do this first. I'll see them after I have news of my father."

Royal Shepherd Garrus nodded, then stepped closer to Galen. It made him uneasy. He had never met someone so powerful, let alone talked to them. "I suppose you'll be wanting in on this favor as well."

"No," Gadiel answered for him. Galen had been about to answer no, that he was perfectly content with the deed to an island off the coast. But it irked him that Gadiel answered for him, and it gave him pause to stop and think. He had been worried he was leaving Allora in unknown hands. But the Royal Shepherds he had just met did not seem bad at all. And while he was unsure about Shepherd Seff, it was most likely that Gadiel had simply rubbed him the wrong way as he was apt to do others. Galen remembered once seeing Seff at some sort of rally. He did not seem like a bad person either. Still, it couldn't hurt to make sure. If he could be by Allora's side during the interviews, it might even comfort her a little to have him there.

"Yes," Galen, replied confidently. "I want to be there, too."

They sat in a cold, bare room with no windows. A small table in the middle had a chair on either side. Princess Allora sat in one, Royal Shepherd Udina in the other. After the meeting the previous night, the Royal Shepherd of Mind had elected to be the first to interview to the princess. From his position at the back of the room, Galen could see Allora's face clearly. She did not look afraid. In fact, she appeared somewhat bored. Galen wondered if she was hiding her true feelings.

Gadiel shifted restlessly beside Galen. So far, not much had happened at all. Shepherd Udina just stared at Allora. No movement, no talking, just his gaze fixed on her. She stared back. An unspoken battle went on between them. Finally, Shepherd Udina leaned back in his chair and asked simply, "Where is Royal Shepherd Demas?"

"I don't know," she replied simply.

428

"I think you do."

"Well, for being a Shepherd of Mind, you're not all that bright."

"You're pretending to be some naïve ..."

"I'm not pretending to be anything ..."

"... But I can see right through it."

"And what is it you think you see, Shepherd?"

"That you're hiding something. I find it difficult to believe your father would tell you nothing of such a significant plan." Shepherd Udina crossed his arms. Galen was starting to feel uncomfortable. *It's just part of the process,* he reassured himself. Udina was not being uncivil, he was just asking questions.

"Well, he didn't. He had no cause to. I was not even aware of a plan to kidnap that Royal Shepherd, much less the execution of it. I am just as in the dark as you." Galen could see the dignified poise that came from her royal blood. He wanted to believe her.

"You will make things infinitely easier on yourself if you just tell the truth."

"I am telling the truth." Next to Galen, Gadiel shook his head.

"We can use you either way, here, princess." Shepherd Udina leaned forward and smiled. "Word is on its way to your father that you are here. And I can assure you that he will be very eager to trade Shepherd Demas for his heir."

Allora smirked, "My father would not give up a war just for me. He's smarter than that. I'm not his heir, you imbecile. If you wanted to capture someone as valuable to him as your Royal Shepherd of Defense is to you, you should have taken my brother."

"Well, that would have been rather difficult considering that he's dead," Udina replied.

Galen's eyes widened. Allora's face instantly paled but she continued just to stare at the man sitting across from her. She did not even appear to breath. "Killed in the siege on your castle," Udina continued. "Your mother, too. Such a shame. That means no more potential for more heirs, either. Which leaves us with just ... you."

"You lie," Allora whispered.

"Not at all." The Royal Shepherd of Mind walked around the table until he stood right in front of her, then leaned forward on the armrest of her chair. "But it doesn't matter whether you believe me or not. Your father knows the truth. You see, now, how very valuable you are." As Galen's heart now began to beat rapidly, he could only imagine how Allora was feeling. The Royal Shepherd of Mind had known what to say to instantly put a crack in her armor. "In fact, you're even more important than you were when we first captured you. At the time, we had no knowledge of their deaths. Isn't it funny how things work out sometimes?" Shepherd Udina smiled at Galen and Gadiel. "And we have you two to thank for that." Galen wanted to melt into the floor.

"Your father will give us whatever we want to ensure your passage home." Udina rose to his full height and headed toward the door. "And if you tell us where Royal Shepherd Demas is being held, we might just let you arrive there safely. Think about it." The Shepherd gestured for Galen and Gadiel to follow him out.

Galen did not look at Allora as he left. He was too ashamed. This was his fault. *To find out about her family like this …* Galen placed his head in his hands. *And still three more interviews to go.*

"So sorry to keep you waiting, my dear." Royal Shepherd Zorah settled into his seat across from Princess Allora. It was early evening. The Royal Shepherd of Spirit had decided to speak with Princess Allora next, but he had been unable to make it to the palace until the evening after Udina's visit.

Galen had not seen her since the previous meeting. She had been given a beautiful black and green dress befitting of her station. But although she looked composed, the circles around her eyes and the tangles in her braid hinted at how she was really feeling.

"Prince Gragor has recently wed and there were many celebrations to attend. I must admit, I'm not as young as I used to be, and now it takes longer for me to recover from such events." Zorah chuckled.

"Who in the world did they convince to marry him?" Gadiel whispered.

Zorah swung around to face Gadiel. "I believe you were instructed to observe without speaking, young man."

In fact, Shepherd Garrus had warned them before the first interview, that if they interfered at all, they would be in serious trouble.

"I imagine you've been to your share of balls and celebrations," Shepherd Zorah commented, again facing Allora. "Tell me, what are they like in Leoj?"

She glared at him. But the Royal Shepherd of Spirit did not seem offended. "I visited Leoj once. It was long ago, before the war. I knew

430

those Shepherds that were murdered in the colony." He adjusted his position. "I do not blame you or your family for their deaths."

This time, she looked at him in surprise. "And can you keep a secret?" he asked confidentially.

"Everyone here seems to think so."

"I do not think we should place blame on your country for Demas' disappearance either."

"What? That's preposterous!" Gadiel blurted out.

Shepherd Zorah glared at him. "You will leave next time I hear a word from you."

Grunting angrily, Gadiel leaned against the wall.

"What do you mean?" Allora reluctantly asked.

"Whether they actually took him or not, I do not know. But it was certainly Oldaem's fault for ever leaving open the opportunity, for allowing the war in the first place. Tell me, Princess Allora, are you familiar with the New Order?"

"Only a little." She watched Shepherd Zorah curiously. Galen wondered if she had noticed the differences between the Shepherd of Mind and the Shepherd of Spirit. Their tactics were so dissimilar. He wondered if their goals differed as well.

"The One teaches us that if we are not unified, we will fall apart. Oldaem is not unified as it was in the days of the early kings. We seem to have lost our purpose. I know that Leoj is not the true enemy," Zorah spoke fervently. "Oldaem is. We are a poison growing from the inside. Ending the war with Leoj would be treating the symptom, not the disease. But at least it is a start," he reluctantly added. "Help me fix my country, Princess Allora. And in turn, I will help restore yours."

He's good, Galen thought to himself. *If I were her, I'd spill everything right now.* And she looked as if she wanted to. But Galen genuinely believed she did not have the knowledge the Royal Shepherds were seeking.

She's the heir to the throne. Princess Allora now had so much more responsibility than she had expected to have just a couple days ago. And even sitting in this room, listening to the honeyed words coming from Shepherd Zorah's mouth, Galen was not reassured that he had made the right decision. *Maybe I should have just let her go in Kaya.*

But it was too late now, anyway. Nothing to be done about it but wait through the next few days. *And still two more interviews to go.*

CHAPTER 53: SAYLA

Just a little while longer. Sayla meandered aimlessly through the town of Azmar. It was midday, and the rest of the little squad of Defense students had gone off in search of a place to eat and rest the horses. The town was normally large and busy, but today it was bursting at the seams with overflow from the tournament visitors. Oldaem Realm was, at most, three or four day's journey away. During the course of her time as a student of Woodlands Academy, she had passed through Azmar every year on the way to the tournament. They had always spent the night there. This year was slightly different, though, since they were traveling through so late in the season.

"Let's just keep going," Sayla had insisted to the rest of the group as they dismounted in the square after first arriving. "It's too crowded here, which means that everything will be overpriced … and that's assuming we can even find a decent place to stay."

"Oh, stop being a worry wart!" Tali exclaimed as she bounded along. "We'll find something. We're Shepherd trainees. People have to give us stuff!"

As Oghren and Zayeed snickered, Sayla cringed.

"So you wanna just kick some poor old lady into the streets so we can take her room? Because you think we're more important than her?" Sayla furiously wiped some dust off her black leather boots.

"Wait, which old lady are we talking about?" Shale asked, having missed part of the discussionn.

"There's an old lady?" Zayeed asked.

"Is it that one?" Oghren pointed at an elderly woman crossing the street.

"There is not actually an old lady!" Aveline shouted to rein the conversation in.

"I'm just trying to make the point that maybe we could stop thinking all about ourselves for a change," Sayla continued. "We are future Shepherds after all."

Tali stared at her blankly. "I just wanted to buy some food."

Sayla looked at her. *Maybe I overreacted a little.* The truth was that she had not said very much at all to her traveling companions the past couple weeks. She had spent most of her time either having nightmares, avoiding them, or trying not to think about the nightmares.

Looks of concern and confusion continually passed among her friends. Although aware of what was going on, Sayla chose to ignore it. They wouldn't understand. No one could have. She desperately wished she could talk to someone who would.

"Then let's just get lunch somewhere and head out. It won't hurt us to sleep on the road again."

Sayla's suggestion immediately met with groans from everyone.

"Are you kidding me? I want a nice fluffy bed in a cool room away from mosquitoes!" Zayeed protested.

"It's too crowded here," Sayla insisted.

"But we always stay in Azmar." When Shale tried to put his hand on Sayla's shoulder, she jerked away from his touch. How could she have ever found him attractive? The man she saw before her now was arrogant and selfish. She needed someone who would understand what she was going through. *Maybe Galen would understand.*

"Just because we've always done something doesn't make it right!" she shrieked. Throwing the reins of her horse to the ground, Sayla angrily grabbed a brown knapsack off the saddle. "Go get your lunch without me. You people make me sick." While she was aware of the puzzled looks at her back, she just kept walking.

Even as her boots crunched determinedly on the white gravel, she had no idea where she was going. Nor was she really looking for anything. *Except some answers.* Her frustration was not about her friends or their sleeping preferences. She just needed to be alone for a little while. Lately it seemed as if she was riding a sea of emotions. At one moment she felt terrified, the next she was depressed, and sometimes she exploded in a fit of anger. She hated being around people, but was terrified of the thoughts that surfaced when she was alone.

Blindly, Sayla meandered down street after street. People were everywhere, but no one paid her any mind. *One of the advantages of being in a crowd.*

"I don't know how much longer I can do this," she mumbled. Not sure who she was any more, she feared she had lost her purpose in life. It was hard to cling to a sinking ship. And it didn't help that she still had no idea what her dreams could mean or where they were even coming from. What she really wanted to know was why she was the one having them at all.

Pausing in the middle of the street, Sayla threw her hands into the air and screamed at the blue sky, "What do you want from me?" It didn't matter who saw her. Nobody was looking in her direction anyway.

The sky chose not to respond. Just beyond the edge of the street stood a stucco wall with an iron gate. The gate opened on a little courtyard. It was a small oasis in a bustling city. Sayla couldn't tell if it was privately owned or attached to one of the buildings that contained the stores on either side of the courtyard.

After a quick glance to see if anyone was around, Sayla deftly climbed over the closed gate and into the grassy courtyard. A fountain gurgled in the middle. She started toward it, but stopped when she heard something rustle. *I'm not alone.*

All of her instincts kicked in as she prepared either to explain what she was doing in the enclosure, or to bolt away.

But what she saw—rather whom she saw—was nowhere near what she expected.

Sitting atop the tiled roof of the building to her left was a young boy with bright red hair, freckles, and a sullen expression.

"No way," Sayla whispered to herself. "No. Oh, no."

Instantly she recognized him as the lad from her dreams. He had been at the Tower, had asked her, "What do I do?" and muttered, "Maybe today will be the day." The red, yellow, and purple current had then swept him away. For a while Sayla had scanned every young face she passed in mortal fear of recognizing one of them as his. But here he was. He was real, and he was sitting right in front of her.

Strangely, he didn't seem to notice her as he stared off into the distance. The boy had not even moved when she entered the courtyard. The little kid's lack of reaction to her arrival gave her a few seconds to ponder what to do. On reflex alone, she wanted to get as far away from him as quickly as possible. But the memory of Grunt's face as he said his final words to her kept her rooted to the ground.

Get out of here, Sayla, part of her mind screamed. *You don't even know him. Just don't get involved.*

But another portion of her brain begged for her not to make the same mistake twice. *There's a reason he was in your dream. Maybe if you try this time, you can actually help him. You didn't help Grunt. Or Royal Shepherd Demas. Don't waste another chance.*

Sayla closed her eyes. She really shouldn't have invoked that unseen deity by asking it a direct question. By now she should have known better.

"Hey," Sayla's voice cracked.

The redheaded kid did not react.

"Hey," she called, louder this time. This time, his face turned in her direction. It sent a chill up her spine. "Um, hi. I was just, uh, passing by, and I saw you ... up there ... and ... I was just wondering ... if you possibly needed help ... with something?"

The boy's brow furrowed, but he did not answer.

Sayla gestured awkwardly. "It's totally, *totally* fine if you say no. Just thought I'd offer." She could think of few times she had ever felt so uncomfortable. *I'm just making a fool of myself. I shouldn't ...*

"Do you know where my dad is?" His voice broke into her thoughts.

"Oh, wow, you actually do need help with something," Sayla said faintly. *Now what?* "Um, what's your name?"

"Cole." Finally, she had a name to put to the face. "My dad is a Shepherd of Mind. Brulis. I'm looking for him."

Sayla did a double take. "Shepherd Brulis? From Rahvil?"

"Yes!" Cole perked up. "Do you know him? Do you know where he is?"

In fact, Sayla had met him at an event a couple years before. She didn't remember a whole lot about him except that he had been very clearly Old Order. After Sayla had discovered that, she hadn't been interested in talking to him further. "No." She shook her head. "Sorry." At that moment, she genuinely wished she had more to offer the kid.

"Figures." Cole looked away.

"If I were you, I'd look in the Capital. He is probably there for the tournament."

"Where do you think I'm headed, lady?"

Sayla shifted awkwardly. *I'm off the hook. At least I tried.* She really wanted to leave now.

But there was no way she could.

"Is there ... anything else I can help you with?"

Cole skeptically looked Sayla up and down. "Got any food?" She could not read his face. What was he thinking? For one so young he seemed as if he had experienced much pain. She recognized the look–had seen it in Galen's young eyes when she had first met him. Yet, Cole's seemed as if they were still struggling to find hope. That he longed for something to believe in. And at the moment he wanted her to be able to help him.

"Why are you looking for him?" she blurted out.

A shadow passed over his face. "My mom's dead," he said, fighting back tears.

Instantly her heart swelled with compassion. The Sayla of just a few weeks ago would have scoffed and told him to get over it or something equally as harsh. But now all she felt was a kindred spirit. "Stay there," she told him, then swiftly climbed the fence and onto the roof. After dusting off her black leggings, she settled down next to the boy from her dream. She took a deep breath. "You know, I have a friend who never even knew his father. And for a while that really bothered him. He used to hunt everywhere for something about him, but he never got anything. And in the end, the endless search just hurt him." Then Sayla hesitantly added, "It actually made him kind of bitter. I don't think he's ever completely gotten over it."

The thought of Galen gave her heart a pang. She remembered having talks like this with him. Once he had even told Sayla that he needed her. Maybe he felt the same kind of loss that Cole was experiencing now.

Cole closed his eyes. "But I do know my father. I just lost him for a little while. When I find him, he'll fix everything."

Even as he said it, Sayla wasn't sure if the boy believed it himself. She did not know any details of his situation, but she knew that nothing was ever that simple. Obviously he was hurting from the loss of his mother and was probably all alone now. Maybe he felt lost, the way she did.

"I'm sorry for your loss. I … I know how it feels to lose somebody."

Cole turned his intense gaze toward her. "Your mom died, too?" he asked in a voice reminding Sayla of slave number eight. She pushed the memory away.

"No. A friend."

"That's not the same," Cole snapped back so quickly it made her jump. A strange intensity about him kept her a bit on edge.

But at the same time, she felt as if she had to explain everything to him. At least she knew they had some supernatural connection. Maybe, here was someone who could empathize with her to some degree. "He died because of me. It was my fault." She had never said it out loud before. Her green eyes filled with tears. Sayla had Cole's full attention. And now that she had started talking, it all came out in a flood. "I could have stopped it. But I didn't. Because I was stupid and ignored all the warning signs. His blood is on my hands. I know that. But no one else sees it, and that makes it so much worse. And

… and now I don't know what to do. Everything I thought I knew … everyone I thought I knew … I was so wrong. I don't know who I am. I don't know what to believe in."

Sayla tucked back a loose strand from her hair. Since she had spent so much time out in the sun the past summer, the ends of her hair were turning blonde. "But you know … there's something kind of freeing in that. I tried so hard to shape everyone's views and expectations of me that I got into this huge tangle. I guess I even fooled myself. But I suppose now I'm free to make my own decisions. The choice is mine." And for the first time, she really believed it. "It's up to me."

"But then, how do you know what to choose?" Cole broke in. "What if there are two sides, and you kind of want to agree with both? How do you know which one is right?"

Sayla thought about it. "I don't know," she answered finally. "I guess we just try to be one of the good guys." But in order to do that, Sayla realized, she would have to be very intentional with her decisions. Taking credit for her own actions was a lot of responsibility. It allowed no room for knee-jerk reactions. She could not let her emotions get the better of her any longer. Then looking decisively at him, she declared, "You can make the change. You can make the right choice. Who knows, maybe today will be the day?"

Cole looked at her a bit strangely. Sayla had only repeated that last sentence that he had spoken in her dream, because she thought, in some way, that it might comfort him. But now she was worried it had sparked something in his mind. *That's what I get for talking with people who should only be figments of my imagination.* "I'm gonna go now." She stood abruptly. As she climbed back down the fence, she turned toward him one last time. "I hope you find your dad."

"Thanks," she heard coming from behind her as she hastily left the courtyard.

Sayla hurried around to the front of the store where she found a vender selling fruit. "What would you like, dear?" the woman asked. Distracted with her own thoughts, Sayla didn't respond. Her apprehension had returned. For a few moments on that roof she had forgotten that the boy she was talking to was someone she had dreamed of with startling accuracy months before. *Something is seriously wrong with me.* All she wanted was to be normal.

"It's okay to be different, you know." Startled, Sayla whipped around to see a man with short brown hair standing in line behind her.

"What?" How had he known what she was thinking?

He seemed to be about her age, and a farmer from the appearance of his clothes. But as she looked into his brown eyes, she wondered if he was older than she thought. He gave the impression that he had seen many things in life.

"The fruit," he explained, gesturing to the display on the cart before her. "Everybody always chooses apples during this time of year." He picked a shiny apple from the selection for emphasis. "And true, apples are delicious."

Sayla breathed a sigh of relief. He was just a farmer talking about fruit. Nothing to be on edge about. Instead, she played along. "Then why wouldn't you take the apples? Apples are safe. You know what you're getting."

"Because if you sample something different, you might find something that you like even more. A pomegranate, for instance." The man set down the apple and picked up a round, pink-colored fruit that Sayla had never paid much attention to. "They're kind of weird, and not very popular, but sample one right now, during late summer, and it will change your life." His eyes twinkled as he spoke.

"Really?" She looked at the odd fruit skeptically.

The farmer nodded. "Sometimes not being normal is a risk worth taking."

At a loss for words, she just stared at him.

"It was nice talking with you," he smiled. "Now if you'll excuse me, I'm looking for someone I came here with. I thought I saw him around this area ..." The man walked off toward the street Sayla had just come from.

Sayla turned back to the vendor, a slow calm making its way through her muscles. "I'll take a pomegranate, please."

CHAPTER 54: COLE

"There are always two paths, Cole. It's always your choice."

Cole looked into Azriel's eyes as the man knelt down before him. Cole could see tears starting to form.

"Please know that you are never alone. That you won't be stuck in the middle forever. And please know, that no matter where you go, the Creator, Comforter, and Liberator are watching out for you."

As the boy studied Azriel's eyes, he sensed such kindness there. Such understanding. He had grown to love and greatly respect the man, while at the same time remaining incredibly wary of him. It was a difficult thing to explain. During the past several months, throughout all of their travels, he had never once seen Azriel mistreat anyone or display disrespect to someone. Azriel had always shown such kindness and love to everyone they had encountered. Could he really be so nice? And now their paths must end.

He knew Lily was devastated, having already witnessed their goodbye. And now she had turned away, her back to them, looking into Azmar, the surprisingly large city that stretched behind his back. Zek stood with her. His parting with Azriel had been less touching. They had never seemed to hit it off, but that wasn't due to Azriel's attempts. Zek never opened up to him, and he seemed to always be unhappy with Cole whenever he and Azriel had heart-to-heart talks. Azriel just seemed to grasp things more. There was no one he enjoyed reminiscing about his parents with more than the man. Azriel would listen and nod and smile and respond at the *perfect* moment. Lily had begged Azriel to take them all the way to the Capital, but he explained that he was needed elsewhere, and that he had commitments back in Soma.

Cole felt a lump form in his throat. He hadn't cried since his mother's death, but the thought of Azriel leaving them alone saddened him. He could feel Zek's eyes on him as he continued to listen to Azriel.

"I know you've felt stuck in the middle all of your life. That being stuck there has almost seemed *safe* to you. It's where you go to retreat now." A shadow began to cover his face as he spoke. "Being in the middle isn't safe. It's dangerous." He paused. "Cole, you *have* to take a stand. By choosing the middle, you haven't chosen at all. There really is no middle ground. It's light . . . or it's darkness. The shade is darkness." Azriel smiled. He looked up in the cloudy sky, and for a moment, the clouds almost seemed to part, bathing them in golden sunlight. "I love you very much, Cole. And I've enjoyed the time we've spent together. Take care of Lily. She needs you." Glancing beyond the boy, he added, "And take care of Zek. He needs you too."

With that, Azriel enveloped Cole in a gigantic hug, and the boy clung to him. A single tear fell down Cole's cheek, and he quickly wiped it away. Azriel's hug reminded him of Fenris' hugs, which was why Cole loved hugging the man.

"It's going to feel sometimes as if Esis is against you," Azriel said finally. "Like everyone has abandoned you, and you're the smallest and most unimportant thing in Oldaem. That you don't matter and that there's no point in trying anymore."

Those were Fenris' words.

"It's a lie. Cole. You are *loved. You matter. You have a purpose.* Don't blame them."

And with that, a Lamean farmer and his cow wheeled his cart away from Azmar, back over the bridge to Aerion, and on to Soma. As Cole stood there, watching them go, he thought of all the times he had stood on the roof seeing Fenris leave him. He remembered the sight of his father departing, and his mother's body being dragged to shore. *People always leave.* He felt a tiny hand slip into his, as Lily slipped beside him. She was crying softly, but not Cole. The boy was trying to process everything he had learned from Azriel, all they had done on their journey together.

The truth was that Azriel was supposed to have gone long ago. They should have arrived in Azmar at least two months earlier. That had been the plan. But plans always change. And after they left the cave after the Leojian attack, they began to travel slower and more cautiously. Zek took rear guard. Cole always looked toward his right, and Lily had "left patrol," while Azriel drove the cart and Odessa only had to walk. Zek and Azriel had spent a lot of time arguing Old Order mythology, which surprised Cole, since he thought Zek had finally resigned himself to let the farmer believe whatever he wanted. Cole had to admit that both sides presented very logical arguments. However Azriel's position always came from one of passion and understanding, whereas Zek's side seemed motivated by hatred and hurt. Although Cole could honestly relate more to Zek's position than Azriel's, something in Azriel's eyes made Cole realize that perhaps the man had also faced challenges and pain in his life. Azriel had just decided to deal with it differently. And that necessity continued to loom over Cole's head: *whom should I become?*

While riding down the hill from the cave, overlooking the channel, Azriel mentioned it might be a good idea not to head straight to Azmar, out of concern that was where the next attack may take place. Instead, he asked them if they would be okay with going with him along the coast of the channel, delivering grain to the region of Isprig. Most farmers and Channel People would have by now sold the majority of their personal grain and wares to Azmar for delivery to the Capital. Azriel thought that perhaps these people

440

would need his cargo of grain more. Lily loved the idea, as the more of Oldaem she could see, the better, while Cole wished they could just keep heading to Azmar. Leojian invasion or not, he just wanted to find his father. As for Zek, he only desired to get to Azmar so that Azriel would leave them. However, because of the state of Lily's mind and mood, Cole agreed to go along with the suggestion, and so they became grain delivery people.

Cole became increasingly irritated as the days passed. Each one seemed more of the same. Every day was Azriel engaging the Channel-People in conversation and listening to every old woman's tale of her days as a Shepherd. The passing days were a meal at this hut, a conversation by that fence, or he and Zek lugging sacks of grain on their backs to the little community the cart wouldn't be able to reach because of the condition of the roads.

Once a week Azriel would stop and make them all take a day of rest. A day in which they would sit in a rocky field and stare up at the clouds, and Azriel would tell them all tales of the Old Order. Lily *loved* them, and Cole had to admit that they were interesting. Zek would mostly sleep, or at least he would keep his eyes closed, unresponsive. Sometimes, the Channel People sat in the fields with them and listened to Azriel's stories. He became almost royalty to them. Every week more and more Channel People started to join them in the fields during Azriel's-story-time-day-of-rest. After a while they would bring food, and it became a community event. The same people would travel down to whatever field along the coast he stopped at next. When they spent more and more time at each succeeding community, Cole wondered if they would *ever* reach Azmar.

It also surprised him to see a new Lily emerge. She almost had a transformation from the bratty little sister, to Azriel's right-hand woman. The way she interacted with the Channel People, the maturity she showed, how well-spoken she now seemed to be, rightly shocked Cole. Sometimes, of course, when she started throwing rocks at birds, then Azriel would ask her to stop, or if she began endlessly singing a song at the top of her lungs, he would kindly ask to cease. Although occasional moments still revealed her age, for the most part Lily had grown up. He thought how proud Arissa would be. And then he would wonder how she and Belen were doing. But he would shake the thought from his mind. There was nothing he could do for them, even if they weren't doing very well. Lily also no longer allowed Zek to annoy her. Having mastered putting him in his place,

441

she won every argument he tried to start. So much, in fact, that Zek mostly kept to himself, except for the few conversations and wrestling matches he would begin with Cole.

The goodbye to the Channel People would forever stay in Cole's mind. After huddling around Azriel and praying to the Creator for his safety, they gave gifts and money, which he refused to accept, and Cole noticed Azriel had tears in his eyes as they pulled away and headed toward Azmar. He remembered Lily had asked the man why he had spent so much time with them, and why he did what he did for them, leaving them a lot of the grain for next to nothing.

"Because people need love," he had answered.

Once they had arrived in Azmar, Zek pushed for the three of them to continue on to the Capital quickly, but once again, Lily asked Cole if they could stay and help Azriel for a few weeks. He agreed, and so more of the same continued in Azmar. They had their one-day-a-week where they would pick a field on the outskirts of Azmar, and Azriel would tell them stories. It seemed as if he could never run out of stories. People started coming out to hear them, too.

Cole always kept an eye out for his father. While Zek was hauling grain, or if Lily was talking to someone about Azriel's stories, or while the man was engaged in listening to a sad story from a villager, Cole would climb up to a higher elevation, and peer over the rooftops and stables and towers for his father. There was always a slight chance he *could* be in Azmar, on his way to the Capital. While they remained in the city, travelers filled the inns on their way to the tournament. The natural city to stop at, it sat right outside of the mountain pass that cut through the Barisan Mountain range. If one didn't use that pass, one would have to climb the mountain or head farther north to another pass.

As he remembered the curly-haired-green-eyed girl and their conversation on the roof, something about it wouldn't leave his mind. The tears in her eyes had left him confused. Somehow he had the impression that he had seen her before, but he couldn't place where. But the main thing that stuck with him was what she said about the issue of blame. Everything had always been someone else's fault to Cole. What if some of what happened to them had been *his* responsibility. Or even if all of it had been because of his own failure? His choices, he now realized, did matter. And that terrified him.

That night, after another unsuccessful day of searching for his father, Cole sat in the room of the inn that Azriel had paid for, lying on his bed, staring at the ceiling. Tomorrow they were to head for the mountain pass. Cole wondered how they would be able to make it over the pass without the man's guidance. They were simply three tiny specks on a very large Esis. And he knew Esis to be a cruel and uncaring place. If only there were more people like Azriel in it. Deep down Cole knew he could never be the type of person that the man was, or even that of his brother Fenris. It just wasn't who he was. He simply didn't know how to "love" someone that much. Cole had felt numb inside for so many years that the closest he had come to loving anyone had been through Azriel. But now that he too had left him, he figured his influence would probably wear off, unless Cole held true to those stories and messages Azriel had loved to preach about. But in a place like Oldaem, there were too many other things to distract you. Cole had to save his family, find his father, and protect Lily. The condition of his character would have to wait until other things got settled first.

The door opened slowly to reveal a sweaty Zek returning to the room.

"Where's Lily?" Cole asked without looking at him.

"She's buying some supplies for tomorrow, and saying goodbye to everyone we met. She's crazy. We met *so* many people," Zek said, kicking off his shoes.

Rolling over, Cole pointed at the bag in Zek's hand. "What did you get?"

"Goodies," Zek smiled mischievously. "Enough to get us to the Capital, that's for sure." Throwing the bag on the floor, he jumped on the bed and lay down beside Cole. "I'm exhausted. I could sleep for years."

"Yeah, me, too." Cole returned to staring at the ceiling.

Zek reached his arm over and tussled Cole's hair. "How was your day, Little Boy?"

"Don't!" Cole said, pushing him away. "It was fine." Sadness washed over the boy. "I wonder if I'll ever find him."

Zek grabbed Cole by the arm and dragged him up from the bed. "Well, let's look."

"I've looked all day," Cole muttered wearily, watching Zek head toward the window and shove it open.

"You coming?" Zek asked, a twinkle in his eye.

"Out the window?"

"On the roof. I know how you *love* roofs." The older boy smiled kindly as Cole studied his face. He looked at Zek not as his equal, but as someone to look up to, as someone to respect and who could protect him. However rude or indifferent Zek continued to be, a part of Cole still yearned for his approval, for Zek to like him. Cole wanted to be like Zek, because unlike Azriel, the boy didn't seem vulnerable to hurt or pain. Strong, Zek didn't need the protection of any unseen beings from up in the sky—he could take care of himself. Cole hadn't recently seen any beings come to his aid. And they sure hadn't saved his mom. Yes, he wanted to be like Zek. With a smile, he grabbed Zek's strong arm and allowed him to lift him through the window and on top of one of the rooftops of Azmar.

The sun was setting as they found a place to sit. They both scanned the streets for a redheaded man. While they saw a couple, none of them were Brulis. Eventually it became too dark to see anyone, yet they remained on the roof, talking and laughing, letting the cool evening breeze drift over them.

"I'm glad he's gone," Zek declared after a period of silence had settled between them.

"Azriel?"

"Yeah."

Cole still could not understand why Zek didn't like Azriel, except that they were polar opposites. "Why?"

"Because now we can face reality."

"What do you mean?"

"Azriel gave people false hope," Zek said, his face looking pained. "He gave people these unseen deities who could wave their hands and make pain go away, or at least the hope of them. But people like us, Cole, we know differently." He looked at him. "When was the last time anything removed your pain?"

"Never," Cole answered sadly.

"Exactly. *Never.* Azriel was a liar. Either that, or he never had to face any bad things in his life. Nothing is ever as neat and tidy as he would make people believe. You just have to do whatever you have to do to survive."

"They definitely aren't." Zek made a lot of sense.

Zek scooted closer to him. "Cole, what do you believe? I want to know? What do you plan to do?"

"Plan to do about what?"

"Just like, in life! After you find your dad, what are you going to do?" Zek seemed passionate and interested, two things he rarely appeared to be.

The questions puzzled Cole, yet it seemed as if Zek was showing signs of some depth, which Lily swore he didn't have. "The truth is Zek, I really don't know."

"Well, what do you *want* to do?"

Cole sighed and thought about it. He hadn't had any time to really think about himself. For the first time he saw a similarity between Zek and Azriel. They were both concerned about who he was, or who he was becoming, and he couldn't figure out why. Azriel always spoke about *love,* but Zek had no interest in that. None of it made sense. "I guess . . . I want normal. Whatever that means."

"Normal for who?"

"Normal for me. My family. We used to be . . . happy." Cole almost smiled as he remembered happy winter nights together with his family in their tiny cottage before the birth of Belen. While there hadn't been many, still there had been a few. But, sadly, he also recalled darker nights before his dad left, nights when he would hear screaming between his parents while he was up in his room with his siblings. Things smashing, too, but Fenris would always tell them stories to make them laugh. Afterward, they would go back downstairs and everything would be all right, a smile on both his parents' faces. Still, there was always a look in his mom's eyes he couldn't explain--one that terrified him and made Cole avoid her. It was why he never entered her dark room. He feared her. And he wasn't sure why. Things definitely weren't neat and tidy.

"What about everyone else?"

"Who?"

"The people of Esis. What do you want for them?"

Why is he asking me all of this? Since when has he cared? "I guess, in a perfect Esis, everyone would have normal lives too, where no one had death or pain or people leaving them." He studied Zek's face. "Where parents didn't die. They would have a savior." When he put his arm around the older boy's shoulders, Zek let him.

Zek's voice remained soft and controlled. "And if you could give people all those things . . . would you?"

Cole knew the answer to that question. "Yes." Although he realized that he could never be that person.

"How?"

"Hey, you two stinky heads! Time for bed! We have to get up early!" Lily's voice snapped them back to reality as she poked her head out the window.

445

Cole removed his arm from Zek's shoulder, and they both returned to the room. Lily stood there scowling, holding Zek's bag.

"Where did you get all this gold?"

"Give me that!" Zek growled, reaching for it. She pulled it away.

"Where did you get this gold?"

"None of your business!"

"Please, let's keep it down. People are probably sleeping," Cole said. He stared at Zek and Lily, both of whom looked furious.

It only made Lily shout louder. "WHERE DID YOU GET THIS GOLD?"

"Shut up!" Zek lunged toward her and ripped the bag out of her arms, Lily then bolted toward him and wrapped her arms around it, pulling with all of her might.

Cole ran to them both. "Stop it!"

"Give it back!" Lily shrieked.

"It's mine!" Zek pulled in turn.

Cole could tell Zek was restraining himself a little bit, that if he had wanted to, he could have thrown Lily clear across the room. Grabbing his sister, Cole wrestled her away from Zek. "Lily stop! It's *his* stuff!"

"No it's not! There is no way he could have *earned* all this money. He stole it! We aren't supposed to steal. That's *not* who we are!"

"*You* don't know who I am!" Zek yelled back "All you did was talk to *Azriel!*"

"Azriel wouldn't want this, Cole!" She looked at him with tears in her eyes. "Don't you care anymore about his teachings?"

"He's gone!" Zek shouted. "He left us, Lily! Now we have to do what we can to make it."

"This *isn't* the way! Have you already forgotten *everything?*" She stared at Cole in shock, pleading with her eyes.

Cole stood there frozen. Now that Azriel was gone, all that mattered was finding their father. "Zek is right, Lily."

"What?"

"We need the money, Lily."

She started yelling again. "You lied to him, Cole! You told him you would look out for me *and* for Zek! He trusted you, and you lied to him!"

"He abandoned us!" Cole fired back. "Don't you see that?"

"After *all* he's taught us. After all he's done for us, the *second* he leaves us, you go back to your stupid little boy ways with your dumb friend. I *hate* you, Zek!"

446

"You're just a stupid little girl," he said quietly.

"Hey!" Cole protested. "Don't call her stupid."

"I'm sorry, Cole. But he filled her head with nonsense." Zek sat on the bed, holding the bag of gold in his hands.

Lily jumped on her bed and rolled over, turning her back to them both. They could barely hear her say, "I won't eat anything you buy with it. I won't touch that money. You broke my heart, Cole."

With that, she said not another word that night. Cole felt badly, but he didn't know what else to do. Lily had it in her head that some magical invisible being would lead them to their father without any trouble. Zek was just being realistic. Pulling off his shirt, Zek tucked the bag under his pillow, blew out the candle, and got into bed.

For a moment Cole stood there in darkness. Usually he slept next to his sister, but he could tell she didn't want him anywhere near her. Instead, he crawled into bed beside Zek who was already drifting off to sleep. Cole lay on his side with his back toward him. For the first time in a while, he had a clear plan of action. *Zek was smart to steal that money.* With it they could buy protection and food and even possibly passage through the mountain pass tomorrow. Lily would just have to get over it. *We have to do what we have to do to survive. No matter what it takes.* As he drifted off to sleep beside Zek, he felt safe for one of the first times since they had left Middle Lake. Azriel had protected them before. Now he would have to trust Zek. Different method of protection. Different course of action. Same result. Choice made. Consequences would be dealt with. But like Azriel, Zek *must* care for him too. There would be no other reason he would have asked him all those questions on the roof. After scooting a little closer to the older boy, he fell asleep.

That night Cole dreamed of the curly-haired girl. She was walking away from him as he stood on a sea of glass. As usual, the glass was cloudy, blocking any sight of what lurked beneath. She cried as she walked away from him and into a bright light.

Then, as he turned from her, he found himself face to face with his mother. Terror struck him again, as once more she stretched out her hands to him. As her fingers brushed his neck, he fled from her. But no matter how fast he ran, his mother was always right behind him.

Suddenly he lay face down on the glass sea, attempting to get a glimpse of what was beneath. Horror then struck him as the mist dissolved beneath the glass, and he saw a reflection of himself, pounding up against the undersurface of the sea. Struggling to breathe, he desperately tried to smash the barrier. But he couldn't. And he knew he was going to die.

Cole jerked awoke, shivering and confused, the blankets in a tangled mess. As he looked around the dark room, he saw nothing to fear. He heard light breathing from Lily in the adjacent bed, and from Zek beside him. Then, trembling uncontrollably, he lay back down, pulled the blankets around him, slid closer to Zek for warmth, and fell back to sleep. A crimson shadow stood on the darkened streets, staring up at the window of the inn.

CHAPTER 55: IAN

Ian flexed his fingers nervously from his seat in the center of Arena 1 and watched the stands. They were filling up quickly with people from all over Oldaem. The very first event of the tournament was about to begin.

After his weeks of extensive training, Ian had hoped to feel a little bit more prepared. The truth was, that while his gut had shrunk more than he had expected, he was nowhere near Bumo's physique, and his self-confidence hadn't grown at all. All the other Candidates looked so much stronger and much more intimidating.

Despite all that, Ian still couldn't help but be excited. The tournament would commence in just a few minutes! The Opening Ceremonies at the start of the week had been a lot of fun. First came a parade during which everyone had cheered for the future Shepherds. Ian had felt honored to be a part of this great tradition. The Shepherd System was what made Oldaem so unique, so powerful. *I still can't believe I'm here.*

At the Opening Ceremonies the officials had randomly selected four groups of fourteen Candidates. Ian's name had been drawn for Arena 1, which meant his first competition would be Mind. Arena 2 also would have a different Mind competition, and Arenas 3 and 4 were holding competitions for State. Ian knew that after this arena, he would be sent to one of the State games and would have to prepare a debate. The thought of speaking by himself in front of so many people terrified him. But then he mentally scolded himself. *One problem at a time.*

First, he had to survive the Mind competition. Sitting to the left of Ian was Liarra, and next to her was Bumo. The three of them were the only Candidates representing the region of Soma. The other eleven were people Ian had seen during training, but had never really spoken to.

That fact made him a little bit nervous. Sitting on his right was a youth whom Ian had discovered was to be his partner for the competition. The names had been selected at random as they entered the arena. Ian looked apprehensively at his teammate. All he knew about him was that his name was Joel. But he also one of the only Shepherd Candidates in the arena, probably in any of them, who was more massive. Ian figured his mom would probably be upset that he wasn't the biggest.

Ian glanced over jealously at Bumo and Liarra. *Of course, they would be partners.* But he wasn't upset with either of them anymore. That didn't mean he could resist being a little jealous, though. Liarra smiled at him apologetically. *She's so pretty.* Ian smiled back to let her know that he was okay with the situation. It wasn't as if she could help it.

Joel slouched in his seat, his arms crossed over his chest, a frown on his face resembling that of an angry bulldog. But Ian didn't want to make any snap judgments. *Maybe as a team we'll surprise everyone and be amazing.*

They weren't.

Try as he might, Ian, even with his usual sunny personality, had trouble keeping calm. They had been given a series of riddles that were clues to the objects they had to find. Each team would have one full day to obtain all the items. The first team to locate everything would get the most points, and every team after that would receive points according to the time it took to solve the riddles.

Since it was the game focusing on Mind, Ian carefully tried to strategize and interpret the riddles. But he had never been good at riddles.

Ian held up the paper. "What is bright like a diamond, hard like a rock, but destroyed by too much pressure?" He and his teammate

449

were standing at the edge of the arena. They had the entire arena at their disposal. Inside were bins of items, people with stalls of goods, and signs indicating where certain categories were located. The clues could lead anywhere, and there was a treasure trove of stuff, some valuable, and some junk for them to choose from.

"I don't know, a diamond?"

"It can't be a diamond, Joel, diamond is part of the clue."

"Well, what do you think it is?"

Ian had to consider that one. He knew the Shepherds wouldn't make it something easy or obvious. This was the Mind game anyway. The item had to be something obscure, abstract. He glanced at the Shepherd assigned to accompany them. Of course he could offer no help. He was just supposed to be a silent observer, able to report Ian and Joel's actions to the judges. And then there was the audience watching their every move as well.

"What is something that can be destroyed with too much pressure?" he wondered aloud. With a sigh Ian looked down at the paper again. "I don't know, let's just skip it and move on to the next one."

"I guess so," Joel said with a tone of resignation.

Ian glanced at him before looking back at the list. It was like working with an angry sloth. "How about, 'Something you need to see yourself clearly?'"

"A shoe."

Ian looked impatiently at Joel who had sat down in the dirt and was staring at his own shoe. "Are you trying to make us lose? Of course it's not a shoe!"

The youth's eyes widened above his chubby cheeks. "You don't know me, Ian! Just leave me alone!" Then he proceeded to curl up into a ball on the ground. The silent Shepherd pulled out a booklet and started writing in it.

Baffled, Ian stared at his partner. *Of all the times to have a mental breakdown.* It seemed as if Ian could never catch a break. "I'm sorry if I said something to upset you. I really don't know anything about you except that your name is Joel and you're a Candidate like me."

"Well, I'm from Highdale. In Isprig," Joel said as if Ian was supposed to understand the implication.

"Is that … bad?"

"It is when my father is the Shepherd of State there! He's been there for years. Everybody loves him. He's beaten every potential replacement every election since I can remember. And he wants me to follow in his footsteps."

"That sounds like a lot of pressure," Ian nodded. He wondered what it was like to have such a background. Ian had always felt free to make his own decisions with the support of his parents. He felt a pang of longing for his home back on the shores of Lion's Landing.

"The worst part is"–Joel glanced suspiciously at the Shepherd near them and spoke quietly–"the worst part is that I don't want to be a Shepherd. I want to be a farmer!"

This surprised Ian. He thought everyone wanted to be a Shepherd. But maybe Joel felt the longing in his heart to be a farmer the way Ian did about being a Shepherd. *No two fish in the ocean are the same. If they were, the ocean would be a very boring place.* "Well, then I hope you lose horribly to the competition."

Joel sighed. "It's a mirror."

"What is?"

"The answer to the riddle you just said. It's something you need to see yourself clearly."

Ian gasped, "Wow, I was going to say it was introspection, but I like your answer better."

As they searched the numerous stalls for a mirror, Ian finally had an idea. "It's potential!" he blurted a bit too loudly. He hoped the other teams had not overheard him.

"What are you talking about?" Joel asked.

"Just like you. You have so much potential. I can tell you're smart, maybe just like your father. But with too much pressure you're not living up to it. It's the answer to the first riddle!"

"That doesn't make any sense, Ian. We have to find something *tangible* to bring back. Not a theory!"

Ian shook his head. "We just have to figure out something that fits with it. It's potential."

"Well, I think its ice," Joel breathed.

"Ice?"

"Yeah, it's bright as a diamond, hard as a rock, and it melts under the sun."

Ian shook his head. "That's too easy. It can't be ice."

Later, Ian found out that it was, in fact, just that. Joel turned out to be a good teammate once Ian had a few conversations with him. And even though Joel had no desire to win, Ian was able to convince him to persevere through the competition anyway.

As they located their last item, Ian noticed that no one seemed to have finished already. Did they actually have a chance of winning the whole thing? Although he wanted to make a break for the finish line, he held himself back. Joel looked miserable, realizing that they were about to be first. Instead, they calmly walked toward the platform.

Out of the corner of his eye, Ian spotted Liarra and Bumo break into a run. They had found all the items as well! Ian shot a glance at Joel, who sullenly nodded, and they began to run. The crowd went wild.

Based on their location in the arena, Ian and Joel had the lead and would likely make it to the finish line first even if they were slower runners. Ian pushed ahead, but his mind was racing even faster. His partner didn't want to win. Bumo and Liarra desperately did. Without thinking any further, Ian threw himself onto the ground. Joel stopped beside him, "What are you doing?" he asked breathlessly.

"A cramp!" Ian shouted over the gasp of the audience. "I have a cramp!" Hastily he grabbed his left knee for dramatic effect.

Meanwhile, Liarra and Bumo were gaining. As they caught up, both were inclined to stop and see if Ian was okay, but Ian gestured for them to keep running. With perplexed expressions on their faces, they did.

"You don't have to do this," Joel whispered as he knelt down to help Ian up.

"Don't worry about it. Second place gets almost as many points anyway." Ian limped to the finish line, joyful for for the look of glee on Bumo and Liarra's faces. Feeling not one bit of regret, he knew that he could have won. Surely he would win one of the other three competitions.

Next, was the event for State. They would have a couple days in between each one, Ian learned, so that the Candidates could rest and the arenas be reset, but he was suspicious, suspecting that it was really to get more money out of the crowds staying in the Capital for the tournament. Either way, it was nice to have some time to train, recuperate, and think. The days had gone by too slowly for him. He enjoyed the break, but like a restless wave, Ian was eager to return to the competition. *One step closer to becoming a Shepherd.*

It was time for the debate. Having never been much of a public speaker, Ian was even more nervous than he had been in the first arena. The new arena was arranged with a very large stage in the middle and two podiums on top of it. This competition would take a little longer than the last, because it would require some preparation by the Candidates.

Within a short time, Delia, the Tournament Mistress, took the stage. As the crowd applauded, she turned toward a canopied section of the arena and bowed. *The royal family must be in attendance today.* They were too far away to see clearly, though.

"This competition will consist of a debate. There are seven categories: religion, art, government, foreign affairs, military, agriculture, and history. Each of the fourteen Shepherd Candidates will be given information regarding one side of one of the topics. They will defend their position tomorrow."

An official handed Ian a large book as he heard Delia say that he would be defending the New Order in the religion section of the debate. *Great,* he thought, *I know next to nothing of the Order.*

That evening, Ian sought out Liarra. Maybe she could give him some advice from that book she had been reading. But he really just wanted to get a chance to talk with her again.

He found her sitting on the steps of the mess hall, nose buried in the book she had received for the debate.

"What are you reading?"

She looked up and grinned when she saw who it was. "It's about the history of Oldaem's military. Military tactics and stuff," she shrugged. "I would have killed for the category you got."

"Well, I would trade you if I could," Ian sat down next to her. "Can you tell me about your book?"

She held up the thick one she had been reading. "This one? I don't think it will help you ..."

"No, the other! Maybe it will help me."

When Liarra stared into his dark eyes it left butterflies in his stomach. Or maybe he was just hungry again. "Sure. It's the least I can do after you let Bumo and I win the scavenger hunt."

"It wasn't because of you," he said, shaking his head.

Liarra gave him a funny look.

"I mean it was *just* because of you," he added quickly. She laughed. He loved hearing her laugh. Then he explained why he had gotten that fake cramp.

"That was really nice of you, Ian." Liarra leaned in closer. "You're a good guy." His palms grew sweaty, and he rubbed them on his pants.

"So the Order," he said nervously. And she told him all she knew.

The next morning, armed with the knowledge he had gained from Liarra and from his history of the beliefs of the New Order, Ian felt more or less prepared. He was pitted against a skinny blonde girl whom he had never spoken to. Aware that she was supposed to defend atheism, he doubted she really believed it, just as he did not follow the Order. But the important thing for this competition was their skills in debating.

When it was his turn, Ian took the podium. Despite his preparation, his hands shook. Briefly he glanced at the skinny girl. She had a pointed nose and eyes set too close together. As she studied him skeptically, he felt as if she regarded him as little more than a pest to be disposed of.

Delia took the stage once more. "This debate will be between Ian and Natalia. Ian will take the position of the New Order, and Natalia will defend the position of atheism. Let the debate begin."

Ian cleared his throat to say something, but Natalia cut him off. "First of all, I'd just like to say that you're ignorant for believing in something as primitive as a higher being. It's outdated."

"I disagree ..." Ian began.

"Well, you shouldn't. Religion may have been relevant in the old days when it was invented, but Oldaem has moved beyond that now. We don't need a crutch like that anymore."

"What I was going to say was ..."

"Anything you have to say is irrelevant, because you allow yourself to be weakened by your religion."

The one-sided discourse went on for several more minutes, Ian getting increasingly frustrated. The girl wouldn't let him get a word in edgewise. The judges just watched and kept writing things in their notes.

"May I speak, please?" Ian finally got out.

"It's not my fault you're too weak from dependence on some unseen deity to get your point across," the blonde girl replied, folding her arms.

"Believing in something does not make you weak," he responded. "It makes you be the greatest person you can be."

"How can you be the greatest person you can be when you don't take responsibility for your own actions?" And that was when he knew he had her.

Ian recalled that rainy night in Kaya when Allora, his mysterious friend, had said something similar. Quietly he thanked the Rain for preparing him for this moment. When, it came down to it, nothing in that boring book he had been given would be useful. Instead, he decided to rely on personal experience. "So, you're saying that fate should be left up to human beings."

"Are you saying that we are not good enough?" She pointed toward the stands. "Is our king not worthy of making his own decisions? Do you think he is not smart enough?" The crowd collectively inhaled. Here was the excitement they had been waiting for.

"The king is smart enough to believe in a higher being," Ian said. "His advisors, the Royal Shepherds, are smart enough as well. They know that fate cannot be left up to human beings, because we would just make a mess of it."

"But ..." Natalia began, but this time Ian interrupted.

"It's not like we can rely on people. Could we rely on Leoj to protect our colony, even though we had a peace treaty with them? Could we even trust our leaders if we didn't think they had a higher purpose in mind? Even at the beginning of time the original four Shepherds took matters into their own hands, and *that* was when everything fell apart. There has to be a greater purpose for all that we do. All those men who have died fighting for our freedom can't have perished in vain. The Order is real, and there is someone up in Aael who takes care of us and wants the best for us. There is no alternative. There is only the Order." Ian took a deep breath. Natalia just stared at him. The audience erupted in loud cheers.

Ian won his debate against Natalia. At the end of the day, he learned that he had been victor in the day's competition. That did not mean he would beat the scores of the other Candidates yet to compete, but he had the lead over 13 others, and that was a start. It had all seemed to happen in a whirlwind.

That night as he lay in bed he went over the day's events. Some of the things he had said had not seemed to come from his own mouth. He wondered what his mother would say if she heard him speaking so adamantly about a religion he did not follow. But now Ian was confused. Did he now ahere to it? He had never called them the Order per se, but how different really was his belief in the Tide and

455

the Rock? All of the philosophical answers he had given had come from his own heart. Just replace the names, and he could have been speaking of a Beelzian religion. But the idea of actual supernatural beings intrigued him. It felt strange, yet comforting, to think that maybe, just maybe, there were real people up there somewhere watching Ian and orchestrating events that would change him and make him grow. Ian closed his eyes. It was something to think about anyway.

CHAPTER 56: COLE

The mountain path seemed endless, as a cool breeze alternated with hot dusty blasts of air. The wind was relentless as they pushed through the pass. They almost had to shout at each other to be heard, not that they had a lot to say. Lily was still furious with Zek for stealing the gold, and he had stopped pretending to even put up with her. Now taking the lead, he pushed them for long hours, waking them up early to start out again, and forcing them to press deep into the night. Cole was surprised that not many other travelers were on the road. Perhaps most had already arrived to the Capital, and there would be no reason few others to attempt the exhausting and unforgiving Barisan Mountain Path.

When they stopped for meals, Lily would go off by herself and eat what she had bought, while Zek ate the rich food he purchased with his stolen gold. Usually Cole would sit beside Zek, sharing Zek's food, feeling Lily's glares from the distance, while he would try to keep a conversation going with the older boy to pass the time. Zek would usually answer with one or two-word responses, and then once he was finished, they would continue on their way, regardless whether Cole or Lily had completed their meal or not. Sleeping was the same. Lily would be on one side of the fire Zek built, while he and Cole would be on the other, Cole usually huddled next to him for warmth. He would hear his sister shivering by herself. *It's her own fault. She wants to be judgmental, and that's what she gets.* Although in those rare moments when he and Lily actually made eye contact, he could tell what she was thinking: *Things were much easier when Azriel was here.* Perhaps she was right. But as Zek had revealed to him, it wasn't reality. *This* was reality--traveling alone through a dangerous mountain pass with so many things ready to devour you.

That was how Oldaem worked. It wasn't picnics and loving conversations and lazy days resting in fields listening to stories. No, this was the reality of Oldaem. *Might as well get used to it now. Azriel was right about one thing. There's no way to be stuck in the middle. I guess Oldaem made that choice for me.*

Soon Cole realized that his face wore a constant scowl, and he now began to snap at Zek. The older boy almost seemed to approve of Cole's attitude. Whenever they would reach a rocky incline in the pass, Zek would extend his hand to help Cole, and Cole would accept. However, they left Lily to fend for herself, carrying all of her own belongings. In reality it was almost as if they were traveling in separate parties.

Reaching the pass, they saw huge mountains stretching on both sides of them. Tufts of grass spouted out here and there. Jagged rocks and short, stunted trees ran along the trail. Because the path had been so traveled, one would have thought it would have been worn smooth. But it wasn't. Stones littered the path, and it seemed as if a rockslide could happen at any moment. The group found themselves often stopping and looking up at the hillside nervously. The wind was so strong that sometimes Cole feared it would send giant boulders raining down on them. Occasionally they passed small torrents, run-offs from the snow-capped mountains. Even at the end of summer many of the mountains still had snow on top of them, and once in a while a snow shower would obscure a distant peak.

The streams were where they would pass random travelers, though Zek rarely stopped for water. He had his own supply. Lily had drank all hers, and she would hurry to one of the streams and refill her waterbag, while the other two continued on their way. Then she would have to race to catch up. Zek never slowed down for her.

Cole grew tired of walking. His legs ached, his back hurt, his head pounded, and he wanted to stop. But the thought of being so close to his dad drove him on. Once they arrived, he realized, his sister would have bad things to say to their father about recent choices Cole had made. But he figured he would deal with that when it happened. He had to do *whatever* it took to get there as *fast* as they could. *Dad will fix everything.*

Zek seemed different. Harder. Stronger. Travel had put more muscle on his arms and legs. His scowl seemed permanently etched into his face. Because he rarely washed himself, dirt caked his skin. Now he walked with a large staff, a red piece of fabric tied to it that whipped in the wind. It was as if he was a leader of some group of people, steering them into an unknown land. Because of all the dirt and the effects of the sun, Zek was starting to almost look Beelzian or perhaps like a native of the mountains, a wild savage that if Cole had encountered alone he'd have run from. Cole wondered what *he* looked like. But the sun didn't have the same affect on him. Instead of turning brown, his white freckled skin just burned red like his hair.

Lily seemed uninterested in anything Zek did, and at times Cole wondered if she cared about *him* at all. Yet still she followed behind them, silently, doing whatever Zek asked the group to do. While she no longer fought back, Cole knew that she would never give up her beliefs or her opinions easily. In that way, she was more like Fenris than he was.

One night they had finally reached a large lake surrounded on three sides by mountains. Zek decided to rest there and get a full night's sleep. He claimed it was because there would be no point in dragging two little kid's dead bodies down the mountain and that *they* needed the rest, but Cole noticed that as soon as Zek said it, he fell asleep without even unrolling his sleeping sack or setting up camp.

Silently Cole and Lily prepared their camp on top of a little ledge overlooking the lake. Cole eyed his sister as he built a fire. She had her back to him, laying out her bedroll. Although he had a lot he wanted to say to her, he didn't even know where to begin. While he agreed with Zek's methods, it didn't mean he wanted to lose his sister. She had been there with him through everything, and he loved her very much. He wanted them to be a family together. But his pride kept him silent as he watched her lie down quietly.

As he sat by the fire he studied her. *How did we get here?* It seemed so long ago he was bouncing off to school with Lily and Belen. Now, he was clear across Oldaem and nearly to the Capital. Since leaving home he had learned a lot--and occasionally wished he hadn't. Sometimes he thought it might have been better to have stayed like little Belen who looked at his parents as perfect people who never made mistakes. He wished he wouldn't have had to fear his mother or regard his dad as a quitter. If only they could have remained the perfect parents they had been in his mind as a younger child. But he had to grow up and face reality. There was something incredibly sad in growing up that Cole wished he could have never experienced. And at the same time, there was something very liberating and exciting being out here on his own. Once again, freezing time would be like staying in the middle of both worlds--

completely impossible. Oldaem had propelled him into the decision without asking him his opinion. *I thought the Old Order always gave a choice.*

Suddenly, he saw Lily sit up, slide to the end of her bedroll, and stand. Then she walked off into the darkness to the edge of the cliff front and sat down, her legs hanging into space. Although he didn't know why, he headed toward her. While he had no idea what he was going to say, he knew they needed to talk. He sat beside her, and she continued staring across the mountain range.

"I know you're mad at me."

She didn't respond.

"I know you're disappointed and think I'm just trying to be cool like Zek."

"Zek isn't cool."

"I know, but *he* thinks he is."

"So do you."

"Lily, he's gotten us this far."

She turned to him, her eyes full of spite. "*No,* he hasn't. He's only made things worse. Azriel–he got us this far."

"Azriel left us!" Cole felt himself getting emotional.

"No, he didn't!"

"Yes, he did!"

"*No, he didn't!*"

Cole motioned around him. "Then where is he, Lily? Do you see him? 'Oh, Azriel? Can you come here?' Oh, that's right, he's *gone!* And he's *never* coming back!"

"You're *mean.*" She stood and her outline against the stars towered over him. "You've turned into a mean little boy. You've become so rude and selfish and awful. I don't even recognize you!"

Cole stared at her. "You're crazy."

"No! *You're* crazy!" She had tears in her voice. "Do you want to know why Azriel left us? Do you want to know why?"

Cole couldn't turn away. He knew the words she was saying were true, but they stung, like slaps to the face.

"Because he thought we were *ready!*"

"Ready for what?"

"Life! After *all* he taught us! After all the good he did for everyone--for *me,* for *you,* even for terrible *Zek!* He thought we were now prepared to face Oldaem!" Her words radiated power and resolution." And *I* am prepared! I've changed so much! And even though you've let Zek's darkness creep into your heart and your face,

459

Azriel *still* saw hope in you! I don't know why! I guess he wasn't right about *everything!* You *aren't* ready! I'm afraid you *never* will be!" And with that, she stomped off to her bedroll, grabbed it, and started down the path to the lake. Then she spread her bedroll among some shrubs. Even in the darkness he could tell she was shivering.

Cole couldn't think through what all she had said. Not tonight. He was too angry and exhausted and disappointed in himself and in Zek and in Azriel. Returning to his own bedroll, he pulled it away from Zek's and closer to the fire. *Just let me sleep. Just let me leave this terrible mountain pass. I'm done. I give up.*

He woke up to the sounds of screaming. Bolting from his bed, he instantly looked around. When he noticed Zek's empty bedroll he began frantically searching for his sister. *Where are they?* Then he remembered she had moved down toward the lake for the night. More shouts broke his concentration. *Someone is fighting.* After he hurried over to get a better look at the pass below him, he spotted a cart rattling quickly away toward Azmar. After scanning the the shore of the lake, he saw Lily and Zek screaming at each other by a tall rock face, his sister shoving the older boy with all of her might. Zek would regain his balance, thrust himself in front of her, and yell at her again. She continually pushed him away from her, shouting back. While he couldn't make out their exact words, based on the sheer volume of the argument he could tell it had gotten to a dangererous point. Clearly Zek had lost patience with her. It would only be a matter of time before the argument exploded into possible physical violence. Cole raced toward them, heedless of the danger of hurtling boulders.

"How could you?" Zek screamed, eyes bulging. He loomed over Lily who was refusing to back down.

"It wasn't yours," she said, suddenly calm as she noticed Cole flying toward them.

"What's going on?" Cole asked out of breath both from exertion and the thin mountain air.

Whirling to face him, Zek shouted, "Your *stupid* sister gave away all my gold! *All of my supplies!*" The boy looked almost unrecognizable.

He's losing it.

"Calm down, Zek. It's okay. We can go after them."

"No, we can't, you idiot! They already drove off!" Returning his attention to Lily, he edged toward her. "I am *sick of you!*"

"It wasn't yours in the first place! *You* stole it! They needed it more!"

"*Don't ever touch my stuff again!*" Zek shrieked as he shoved Lily with great force. She flew backward, although she managed to maintain her balance.

Cole ran in between them. "Hey! Zek! Calm down! Don't touch her!" *No one touches my family.*

"Get out of my way!" Cole felt himself hurled backward, hitting the rock wall behind him. For a moment he was dazed. But once he regained his vision, he saw Zek on top of Lily, holding her down and screaming into her face.

Rage blinded Cole as he barreled toward them. Wrapping his arms around Zek's neck, he screamed "Get off her!" and lunged his weight backward. The older boy lost his grip on Lily, and he and Cole rolled around on the ground. Sharp rocks slashed Cole's arms and back as Zek's fist smashed his face. Pinned underneath Zek, he couldn't move. Then suddenly Zek was gone.

Staggering to his feet, his vision again a bit blurry, Cole saw his sister fleeing from Zek. The girl screamed as Cole stumbled toward them. Zek had caught up with her, and Cole forced himself into a crippled run. Before he knew it he felt himself crashing into Zek. But the older boy was stronger than Cole. Before Cole could get his wits about him, Zek had already punched him two more times and had thrown him to the ground. Blood dripped from his forehead into his eyes, blinding him.

As he struggled to stand, the world spinning around him, he could still hear screaming, mostly coming from Zek. His vision cleared enough for him to see Zek gripping Lily by the shoulders, cursing and slamming her up against the rock wall. Noticing Zek's staff with the red scrap of fabric tied to it lying on the ground a few paces away, Cole raced toward it. He gripped the staff firmly and charged toward them. Adrenaline soared through him as he raised the staff and cracked against Zek's back. The boy crumpled, face first, dragging Lily down with him.

Cole rushed to her side, turning her over, and putting his hand underneath the back of her head.

"Lily, are you okay?" Feeling a warm substance on his fingers, he pulled his hand out. Blood stained it. "Lily!" he screamed. The world was still spinning and everything seemed red. Then he realized it was

461

his own blood. Ignoring it, he ripped off his shirt and tied it around her head to try to stop the bleeding. Her eyes now closed, she was unresponsive. Cole couldn't tell if she was breathing. "Lily! Wake up! Lily!" He hugged her closely to his chest, holding the shirt tightly against her wound. "Lily, please!" His tears mixed with the blood staining his face.

Suddenly he felt himself seized by the throat. Instinctively he fought the hands imprisoning him, heaving and gasping as he tried to break free. But he couldn't. It was impossible. He saw Lily's tiny frame lying on the ground, blood starting to pool around her head as Zek dragged him farther and farther away. Helpless, he tried to scream, but the grip was too tight, and he could make no sound. Cole flailed his arms and kicked as Zek pulled him across the ground, but to no avail. Rocks and thorns scratched his flesh. Before he knew it he felt himself surrounded by water.

He splashed, back-first, into the lake. Spewing water and gasping for breath, he forced himself above its surface. Zek's angry face loomed above him. The older boy gripped his shoulders and dunked him again. Cole felt his eyes start to bulge as the frigid water covered his face. Through the rippling surface of the lake he could see Zek straining to hold him down, murder in his eyes. Cole's lungs started to burn. Then as panic filled him, he started to cough and swallow water. *Why? Why Zek? I thought we were friends? What are you doing?*

Suddenly everything seemed to slow down. The hands that held him under the water weren't as powerful as before, but they were still strong, still determined. But they weren't Zek's hands. Confusion now mingled with his sense of panic. Also, the sun was no longer shining down upon them. Instead it was raining. Cole could hear thunder booming overhead and lightning striking, though muted by the water he was submerged in. His gaze slowly drifted up to the face above him. It was different, no longer Zek's murderous eyes. No longer in a lake in the middle of the Barisan Mountain Pass. Cole was now in Middle Lake, near his home. He was just a little helpless boy, no older than 4, his chubby hands fighting off hands that used to love and protect him. In shock he stared at his mother's face as she held him beneath the water. *Mom? Why?*

How could he have forgotten the time the one he loved tried to drown him? How could he have blanked out of his mind how his dad tore her away and dragged him into the house, as he coughed and spewed up water? This was why Cole had feared his mother. She had

462

never been normal. Suddenly he wondered if the good memories he had of his mother had ever ever existed. Anger surged through him as he wondered how his father could have dared to leave his children alone with her. Had Fenris, Arissa, Lily, and Belen ever known what she was capable of?

Terror struck him once more as things now sped up. He was drowning under Zek's unrelenting grasp. *I'm going to die.* The one he loved was killing him again. The one he trusted, had put his hope in. When he screamed, no sound came out. In a blur of images and memories he remembered the talks and laughs he and Zek had shared. They had swam in the lake and rode in the cart and slept under the stars, and he had felt safe. Then flashed memories of his mother's face and of her tucking him in at night and singing to him, and the swing, and picnics, and fireflies, and her smile. But she had tried to kill him . . . Then came the image of her drowned body being dragged to shore. *I've become my mother* . . . Finally he saw only darkness.

CHAPTER 57: DAKU

The palace loomed in the distance as the ship neared the Capital. Varic had never seen it though he had often heard about it. He had imagined what the tall spires and domes would look like. But his imagination never did the reality justice. Only Vertloch Tower was greater in mass, and he imagined the nation of Sther liked it that way. But he couldn't be sure, though, being unfamiliar with the ways of the Stherians.

Two massive fortresses, one to the north and the other to the south, protected the bay. They made the Capital nearly impregnable. The ship's crew began to shout orders to each other as the ship drifted to a pier. Cullen and Vivienne were down below deck. They had spent the majority of the voyage out of sight, and Varic decided not to bother his sister. He wanted to give the lovebirds as much time together as possible. Grateful for their gifts, she wore both of them now every second of every day.

Daku tried to shake the cobwebs from his mind. He had started losing grasp of what was pretend and what was reality. Visions of bloody sunflowers filled his mind. Then a face started to materialize

463

before his eyes. He thought her name was Aelwynne. *She's not real anyway, is she?*

Realizing that he had forgotten much of what had taken place during the voyage after leaving Aramoor, he wasn't sure what was happening to his mind. Perhaps Malvina had been successful in erasing all positive memories and had replaced them with fear, doubt, uncertainty, and a golden commitment, as well as false memories of Varic's made-up life. No longer did Varic struggle with morality. When he had handed over that silver necklace, he had also given away the memory of those silver eyes. Yet at the same time . . . *Daku hated* Malvina. The fact that a part of his mind was still able to conceptualize that thought terrified and confused him.

At times Daku felt during his sleep that he would wake in a haze to find Malvina peering over him. He wasn't sure if was reality or if it was fragments of his nightmares becoming reality. Most of his nightmares involved him in literally chasing after his memories. Instead of running through the forest with his friends, he now ran in darkness after the memory of that forest and friends. And instead of strolling along the beaches of Leoj with a silver-eyed-girl, he now desperately searched for a beach with a silver-eyed girl. But he could never reach them. Thunder always boomed above, and golden flashes of lightning struck the ground and split it open to reveal golden pits of terror and death. Then he would jerk awake, feeling resentment and revulsion for the Golden Priestess. Perhaps his mind was fighting back. But it seemed a losing battle. His headaches no longer came and went. Now they were constant, so much so that he barely was aware of them anymore. They had become a part of his being.

Golden eyes.

Varic was aware the tournament had begun. Vivienne loved its events. She had been talking about them for months. They excited and fascinated her and gave a thrill to the normal monotony of a merchant's life. Varic found himself walking behind her and Cullen after the ship had docked. Tournament banners and posters hung everywhere. Most of the vendors sold brochures presenting pictures, statistics, and facts about each participant. Vivienne insisted upon stopping and looking at each one. She and Cullen laughed together and gently kissed. An elderly couple passed by and looked at them fondly. Varic smiled back. He really did love his life.

"Cullen, whom do you think is favored to win?"

"Look darling, Bumo from Lion's Landing has great odds. Shall we bet on him?" Cullen asked.

"He is handsome, isn't he?" Vivienne giggled as she studied the drawing in the brochure.

"I put my money on the one from Dagonfell," Varic interjected. "He looks like he could beat any competition!"

They all smiled and chatted and enjoyed each other's company. Vivienne was determined to see every inch of the Capital before they decided where to stay. So they toured each district, looking at all the buildings and architecture. Varic was in awe. The Capital was truly beautiful. They stopped and chatted with passersby about which inn had the best accommodations. Then they walked in parks and gardens. Vivienne paused at a cluster of lovely sunflowers.

Daku's head was pounding. He glowered at Malvina as she stroked the golden flower and eyed him. *She made me do it. It wasn't my choice. Nothing is my choice. I have to get away from her.* It disgusted him when Jorn put his arm around her, not out of jealousy, but because her manipulation somehow involved the heart itself. Somehow the mind was powerful enough to affect the heart. How could the Golden Power be so strong? As he watched her examine the sunflower, he could have sworn blood started to drip from its petals.

Golden eyes.

"Varic, shall we go to the northern cliffs? I hear the view of the Western Ocean is magnificent, especially during the sunset."

"Vivienne, I would love to. But aren't you tired? Shouldn't we retire for the night?"

"Varic, you are too gentle with your sister," Cullen said, swinging an arm around them both. "She isn't porcelain. If she wants to see the sunset, let her see the sunset. Besides, we still have important business to discuss tonight, right, Viv?"

"That's right, my love."

Varic looked at her. His sister was incredibly beautiful. He was so happy for them, Cullen and she finding each other. As a girl, Vivienne had been so shy and lonely, and sometimes afraid she wouldn't find anyone. Although Cullen was an older man, he had swept her off her feet. Vivienne assured Varic that before long it would be his turn. Soon he would find a fantastic woman to love--she would make sure of it.

Varic finally agreed, and they headed off toward the northern cliffs. The sun was setting in the west, and it seemed so huge that they could almost touch it. Varic had never been this far west before, and it was as if the sun was closer to them.

They stood upon the cliffs, Vivienne and Cullen hand in hand, Varic by himself yet content. *Someday it will be my turn.* He watched them kiss and smiled.

But Daku was disgusted. Things seemed hazy and he felt nauseous. Malvina had her revolting lips on Jorn's. As Daku scanned the northern cliffs outside of the northwestern gate of the Capital, he noticed a young family laughing and playing together. Other than them, no one else was around. No path went down from the gigantic cliffs, only a sharp drop to the rocky shoreline below. *A tumble from here would end in instant death.* Slowly he shifted his gaze to Malvina and Jorn. They were so caught up in kissing . . . if he could get behind them, and shove them to their . . .

Golden eyes.

"Varic, you're right. Enough sightseeing. Which inn would you prefer?"

Feeling such great peace, Varic smiled at them both as they eyed him pleasantly. The sun had set, leaving a tapestry of colors behind. "District 3 had some nice inns. I really thought *The Maiden's Harp* had lovely accommodations."

"*The Maiden's Harp* it is!" Cullen announced.

They all walked together through the night-time streets of the Capital. Lanterns lined the roads, creating a safe enviroment. Tournament festivities continued as billboards displayed scores from previous events, and people filled the streets, playing games, eating, dancing, and laughing joyously. This was what Varic loved about Oldaem. Even in times of war, the people of Oldaem could band together and let life continue. Life could go on.

They entered the inn, and Cullen made the room arrangements. Vivienne told them to take a couple hours for themselves, as she knew they were exhausted from their travels, and she still wanted to enjoy tournament festivities. Also she mentioned it would mean a lot if they would stay at the inn. She didn't want them to get separated from each other. It was such a large city, and they had a lot of work they needed to get started with the next day. Both happily agreed, and Varic lay down on his bed. He was happy to have his own room. As he stared at the ceiling he noticed a small insect crawling across it.

Bug.

As Daku spread out across the bed in the dark room he could hear people celebrating out in the streets, but he felt no joy. For a few moments he contemplated the idea of escape, but where would he go? What would he do? There was nothing left. No one left. His head pounding once again, he sat up and headed to the window. The room was on the fifth floor of the inn. Its window didn't face the main street the inn sat upon, but rather looked out over the rooftops and spires of the Capital. The fresh air did him good. Grabbing a chair, he placed it near the window, then sat and stared out at the stars.

Something had changed for him after he killed that innocent gardener. It had intensified when he saw the bloodied jewelry Jorn had taken from the mother who had been residing in his childhood home. He had had enough of Malvina's golden games of torture. Yet, he knew, the moment she returned, he would be Varic once again. And Varic was stronger than Daku. *How do I kill Varic?*

Malvina had such incredible power. Power enough to make him unsure if the greatest thing in his life had even existed–*Aelwynne*. Just saying her name brought terrifying peace to him. He wanted to forgive her, to understand why she had left him. Yes, he had become a monster instead of the hero she had once looked up to. She was the true hero. But she hadn't saved him. Instead, she had given up on him, had abandoned him. That thought nearly brought a tear to his cheeks. But he hadn't cried since he had learned of his father's death, and before that, he couldn't even remember.

Since he didn't know when Malvina would return, he would have to hurry and do this before she did. Daku *wanted* to remember– *wanted* to reach down into the forbidden places to pull up memories of Aelwynne. He needed to see if she was real or not. As he stared into the sky a shooting star suddenly streaked light across the black expanse. Closing his eyes, he remembered.

"That's the Tower, off in the distance." Aelwynne said hesitantly, as her horse trotted up beside him.

They had ridden from Aramoor several days before. After the introductions, after the goodbyes, after the somewhat awkward conversations, it had been good to say hello and goodbye to his friends once and for all. They had to know he had grown up, that he had his own life now. He wouldn't make excuses for that. And he would never make excuses for Aelwynne.

He looked at her lovingly. She wore a gray riding coat, the skirt of her pale blue dress split down the middle to allow her to mount her ivory mare. Her hair fell loosely around her back, and her beautiful silver eyes showed concern as she reined alongside him. When she stretched out her smooth hand for him to take, he kissed it.

"It's big." He smiled.

She laughed. "Yes. And it's not even the biggest in Esis."

"Is your father to meet us there?"

"No," she said heavily.

He knew she hadn't wanted to return to Vertloch and would have preferred to live in Najoh, to raise their family there. Vertloch held negative memories for her as a child. While Vorran shielded her from the details of what he did for the High Priestess of Vertloch, she still distrusted the Tower and his service for it. But out of respect for her father, she let him work in the shadows and hoped for the light. Now Daku was to take up employment in the Tower.

"He is to meet us in our *cottage*." Suddenly her eyes had a sparkle in them.

"Our cottage?"

"Yes." She smiled. "The Tower has provided us with our own lovely cottage in the most beautiful section of Vertloch. I can't wait to see it."

Daku reined his horse closely beside her so he could lean over and kiss her, wrapping his arm around her. "I love you, my wife."

"I like the sound of that," she said happily.

"Well, get used to it."

They continued to approach the Tower. Daku was amazed how it stretched up high above the city. He wondered what it held inside. He knew priestesses followed the Order of the Three, and he wasn't sure what that meant. As a child he and his father weren't extremely religious. His father always said he believed in the Order, like his mother had, but he never really taught him anything. He remembered hugging his dad as they left Aramoor, and thought he would have to bring him to Vertloch to visit soon. Then he wondered how many rooms the cottage had.

Aelwynne rode in front of him, as he watched her from behind. She would never understand why Daku made her leave Najoh and why he agreed to work for her father. She would have to just go along with it. *I do this for you, Aelwynne.* His devotion and love for her motivated his every action. It was why he had signed up for this in the first place.

468

To his surprise, she dismounted and tied her horse to a small wooden fence that now stretched the length of the road toward the city. He had hoped they would reach the city by nightfall, to get set up in their cottage before it got too late, but clearly she had other intentions for them.

Tying his horse next to hers, he took her hand and followed her away from the city gate. Pausing at the top of a hill, she looked south across Oldaem. Then she raised her hand and pointed.

"Beyond those hills, Daku, past the forests and mountains, and even beyond the seas, is a very special place." Her voice sounded as if she had tears in it.

"Najoh," he whispered.

"I'll always be there waiting for you, my love. Even if I'm stuck in the cottage while you're working, even if you're far across the seas on some sort of mission, or when you're lost and confused and don't know where to go . . . think of Najoh, and I'll meet you there on that white, sandy beach."

He turned her to him, and she rested her face against his chest. "I'll think of Najoh, my love."

"I'll be there. Always."

"I'll meet you there."

"You will never go back there, Daku."

Malvina stood behind him, her golden eyes shining and boring into him. He didn't know when she had returned or how much she knew. Nor did he have any idea what she would do next. Stepping past him, she closed the window.

"Luckily, for *you,* I don't need Daku's loyalty and devotion anymore. Not for *now.* I'll get it back later. But for now, *Varic,* is enough."

Golden eyes.

His sister stood before him. Varic wondered how she had enjoyed the festival. Instantly he stood and embraced her. He was glad Vivienne was in his life. "I love you, Vivienne."

"I love you, too, Varic."

"Malvina." Jorn stood at the open door to his room for a moment, then closed it quietly.

Daku wanted to grab him by the throat and throw him out the window. Instead, he stood there listening.

"Jorn, what news?"

"The plans are set. The path is clear. All we have to do now is prepare," he said, exposing his teeth in a snarl.

"Sther will take its place . . ."

"Yes, Malvina."

Daku wondered what exactly they were talking about and what Varic would have to do next. "Malvina," he whispered, but she turned away from him, heading toward the door. "Malvina!" he shouted.

She stopped dead in her tracks, fists clenching. Jorn reached for the hilt of his sword as she slowly turned to face him. Golden light almost shot out of her eyes, blinding him. But he didn't look away. He met her gaze unwaveringly. Malvina didn't scare him. He would escape her somehow. Someday. *I'll meet you there. Aelwynne is in Najoh!*

"We're here to murder King Orcino," Malvina said with a sneer, Jorn matching her stare.

No. Daku thought. *I won't do it. I'll never do it.*

Golden eyes.

"*Varic*, you should get some sleep. We have a very busy week coming up. You'll need all the rest you can get. It seems we will be selling our best wares to the Royal Family. We've been invited to the palace!" Vivienne said with a lovely smile.

"How exciting!" Varic replied. Having never met royalty before, he knew an exciting week was in store for them. As he crawled into bed and pulled the covers over his head, he knew he would need every bit of strength for what was to come. *Oh, the blessed life of a merchant!* Then he fell asleep, a smile lining his loyal face.

CHAPTER 58: KAYT

Kayt stared up at the vaulted ceilings, the hours crawling by. The furnishings in the royal chambers were much more lavish than her previous apartment. Everything seemed covered with gold. It should have been enough to satisfy her boredom, just basking in her newly acquired wealth and name . . . but it wasn't. Princess of Oldaem had never been a political title before. And no one saw it as one now. Yes, she had a high profile at the tournament competition. People studied her reactions, seeing how she would swoon and laugh and cheer for those competing. They eyed her when she sighed sadly and sat down when the fat underdogs came in second during the Mind competition. She played the role expected of her, waving at villagers, kissing babies, gracefully taking Gragor's arm and walking with him wherever he wanted to go. But now she was growing bored.

She watched as Belinda, her personal maid, scrubbed the floor, removing a stain of red where Kayt had spilled juice. She doubted it would ever come out, but a part of her enjoyed watching the plump lady's maid break into a sweat putting her all into the removal of the blemish. *Some stains can never be removed.*

Her family was gone. She was still incredibly frustrated and disappointed about that reality. Still, she found herself walking outside of her children's school, peering through the fence to see if they had returned for some reason. Balyn and Lei were nowhere to be found. But she couldn't blame them. Armand had probably grown tired of constantly hearing her name spoken in the city squares. *No use dwelling on it now. They are gone.*

Most of her frustration boiled down to how useless she felt. She knew the Royal Princess Allora of Leoj had arrived, but she was locked away somewhere in the palace prison. The Shepherd within her wanted to find some way to get to the interrogation room and find out what was going on, but Gragor had kept her busy with ceremonial duties. He never wanted to go anywhere alone. She realized Royal Princess equated to Royal Adult Baby-sitter. This morning he had plans to go swimming in the ocean, beneath the northern cliffs. Kayt was to accompany him on the shores, but was not supposed to swim with him. It would seem improper. That meant she had to sit in the blazing hot sun on the sand for hours and hours while Gragor went wave- hopping. She was not looking forward to it.

Kayt hadn't seen Garrus in quite some time. In fact, since Allora's arrival all of the Royal Shepherds seemed to have dropped out of sight. The situation was chilling. Being in the know gave her power while being ignorant of what was going on put her in danger. She thought about all the people she had outmaneuvered or taken down in her wake. All of their downfalls had one consistent thread: ignorance. She *had* to know what was happening in Oldaem. Someway. Somehow.

Suddenly, her door burst open and a beach-dressed Gragor entered the room, giant floatation devices in his arms. She watched him as he tumbled over Belinda as the inflated whales and ducks fell to the floor.

"Royal Prince, forgive me!" the woman exclaimed.

"Ooomph! What a tumble! What a tumble!"

"Are you alright?" she asked as she helped him up.

"Yes, yes, tubby serving girl." He whipped around and met Kayt's eyes. "Kayt! Ready to soak up some sun?"

She coughed. "My prince."

"My love!" Suddenly he was on the bed next to her. "What is wrong? You sound . . ."

"Sick."

"Sick!"

"Yes. I believe"--she coughed again--"I've come down with . . . something."

"Where is it?"

"Where is what?"

"The thing you've come with? Is it a gift?" His eyes were wide with excitement.

She looked at him. At that moment she imagined herself grabbing the water pot beside her and smashing his face with it. Instead, she giggled. "Your Highness jokes."

He bellowed a giant laugh. She noticed Belinda struggling to keep her face impassive.

"Come on!"

Now he began to pull her. Knowing that she was stronger than he was, she didn't budge. "Please, sweet husband, my body aches, and I feel fatigued."

"What is fatigued?"

"Tired," she said with an annoyed smile.

"You can sleep on the beach."

"I'd rather sleep here."

"We can build sandcastles."

"I'd rather sleep here."

"You can watch me swim."

Idiot. "As amazing as that sounds, I don't know if I can bear it. I'm too weak."

He continued to tug at her, and she continued to resist. He had little strength in his spindly arms. Beads of sweat began to materialize on his forehead.

"You . . . don't . . . seem"--he puffed as he struggled to move her--"weak."

472

"I'm sorry, Husband. You'll have to go without me today." As she laid back down and closed her eyes she could hear sniffling as his slippers scuffed away from their bed. *Is he crying?*

"Fine," he said like a petulant child. "You're acting just like Allora. Won't do or say anything helpful."

That caught her ear as she jolted up. "What did you say?"

"I said 'helpful.'"

"No, about . . . Allora."

"Who?"

She watched as he studied Belinda's cap while she continued to scrub. Sliding to the side of the bed, she let her legs hang down over the sides. "You've heard of the results of the questioning of Princess Allora?"

Gragor grabbed Belinda's hat and brought it closely to his eyes. "What fine stitchery."

"Gragor." Kayt tried to keep her voice controlled. It was the first time she had even heard Allora's name mentioned since the captive's arrival.

"Did you make this?" he asked the maid.

Kayt found herself standing before her husband now. "Has your father told you about Allora?"

Gragor looked bored and ready to leave. He started scooping up his swim gear as he mumbled, "Yeah, something like how she won't talk or do anything, blah blah blah, I don't care. All I know is, you and her are the same. Both *useless!*"

"Sweet husband. I'm sick. It's not my fault!"

"Yeah, yeah."

The door slammed in her face. She turned and saw Belinda looking at her, hatless, it now being in Gragor's possession. "Stop staring, Workhorse." Kayt heard herself snap, as Belinda continued her scrubbing.

Orcino has spoken to Gragor about Allora and not me. Why am I left out of everything? What is going on? I have some words for Garrus.

The Royal Shepherd seemed deep in study, his eyes scanning the documents in his hands. As she continued waiting for Garrus' response she grew increasingly restless. It hadn't taken her long to slip on a low cut crimson gown, have Belinda braid her hair into a delicate weave, and step into some shoes that elevated her height. Figuring that Gragor would be out of the castle for the day, she determined to get to the bottom of what was happening. *The Princess of Oldaem is going to have some clout.*

"Garrus?"

"Just wait, Kayt," he snapped.

She swallowed. He had never raised his voice with her before. *I better tread lightly--I need him on my side. I hope he doesn't think I'm trying to push my way in . . . or push him out.*

"War expenses. Tournament expenses. The Capital's lavish ways aren't suitable during times of war," she heard him mumble under his breath. His eyes finally met hers. "Now, what's your question?"

"Allora."

"Classified."

"Even for me? Princess of Oldaem?"

"Yes. King's orders."

"Come on, Garrus," she urged with a smile. "What could I possibly do to harm things?"

His eyes almost seemed amused, and then dangerous. "I know exactly how dangerous you can be, Kayt. Besides, it's not up to me." He smiled broadly. "I'm a loyal Shepherd to the King. If you want access to Allora, you go through Orcino." His eyes returned to his documents as his voice seemed finished with the conversation. "But believe me, he's not going to want *another* opinion about how to handle her. And he's not going to want *another* Shepherd's input."

She looked at him as he ignored her. Never before had he been so reserved or distant toward her. She realized at that moment how calculating and effective Garrus must be as a Royal Shepherd of State. Maybe she was just a pawn in *his* grand scheme of manipulation. Now that she was where he needed her to be . . . she would be kept in the dark until Garrus could figure out how to use her.

Don't underestimate me, Garrus. As she stood there she realized that as far as he was concerned she had already left the room. She was invisible to him. But being invisible could also mean being deadly. Her mind raced. *The King doesn't want another Shepherd's input . . . maybe not a Shepherd . . . she smiled . . . but perhaps, a Princess . . .*

"Cookies?" she asked, sweetly. "I made them myself."

"Princess Kayt!" Orcino beamed. "Come! Of course I would love to try your cookies," he chuckled and shook his head. "How like a woman."

She giggled as she approached the golden throne, her mind visualizing Belinda as she returned from market with the most freshly baked cookies Oldaem could muster. The maid had sweat running down her face as she handed the basket over. "Thank you, Workhorse," Kayt had said.

She watched as Orcino bit into the chewy cookies. "Oldaem at war," he said, his mouth full. "Shepherd Tournament in full swing of things, and the Princess of Oldaem is going around the palace delivering cookies. Living up to your name!" His eyes glistened as he laughed.

Kayt could tell that he was truly pleased with her. She had done everything he had wanted her to do as far as the marital union was involved. Orcino expected her to babysit Gragor and wave and smile in public, and she was doing all that. As for political matters, he expected her to care about them *only* if they directly involved Gragor. And in that she had also complied--as far as Orcino was concerned.

"What tasty treats!"

"Family recipe." She winked.

"Have you delivered them to all the Royal Shepherds? I'm sure they would love them!"

"I have! They were so grateful." She had actually only sent Belinda to place four baskets outside of four Royal Shepherd office doors. *Workhorse is useful.* "I even gave some to the captain of your royal guard, the stable master, lords, ladies, and the gardeners. You know, I just love brightening up people's days."

He laughed again. "How like a woman."

Ignoring the comment, she shrugged and smiled playfully.

"Where next, little Princess? What exciting Princess duties await you now?"

As she looked at his grin she wondered why the image of women doing ignorant girl things amused him so much. *It must give him a rush of power, or a feeling that his work is important by undermining everyone around him.* Orcino had always seemed much more levelheaded than Gragor. Her whole opinion of him changed in that moment. *He doesn't take women seriously. It will be his downfall.*

"I thought I might take some to the chambers of the Leojian Princess. I hear she's here?"

He laughed. "What purpose would that serve?"

"Well, she *is* our guest, right? Or is she our prisoner? I'm not really sure what's been going on."

Kayt eyed him carefully. She knew the public had little knowledge of the Leojian captive and that public opinion was important to Orcino. He couldn't be so unaware as to know what people said. Guards, servants, lords and ladies . . . even Shepherds whispered about the crown in hallways and alleyways.

"What have you heard?" he asked slowly.

She stuffed a cookie in her mouth. "While I was at market I heard some speaking of the Leojian within our custody. Some were saying she was our guest, but the majority were saying she was being held prisoner and tortured." Kayt looked down sadly and meekly. "It worried me, especially during tournament time. There are so many foreigners here and delegates from other countries and ambassadors. I would *hate* to have our fair nation stained by lies of torture and abuse of a poor helpless Leojian girl." With a smile she held up her basket. "The name of the crown is what I want to protect, it's all I've wanted to protect. Maybe, cookies . . . will help smooth things over with our guest." She swung it back and forth. "*Everyone* can know."

Two guards walked beside her as they made their way down the narrow chamber. She had never been in this wing of the castle. The carpets were a deep blue, and several cream-colored doors remained shut as they continued through it. Kayt firmly gripped the basket of cookies in her hands as they walked. Her red dress seemed a bit tighter than it had before, and she regretted eating the cookies. "I thank you for accompanying me to the foreigner's room. But really, if you direct me to which one it is, I can manage on my own."

"King's orders, Princess. We escort you," the one on her left replied.

"How kind," she said heavily.

They turned a corner to find more doors and a hallway. Kayt imagined this was not where they questioned her. She also assumed that it might not have even been where they originally held Allora. But if rumors of foreign abuse circulated about the King of Oldaem, there would be repercussions to pay, and all its colonies could find themselves in jeopardy. Perception was reality. It was something that she had learned from her destruction of Silas. Suddenly they stopped at a door at the end of a hallway. Two guards stood outside of it. The four guards eyed each other as Kayt stepped up to the door.

"Is our guest in there?" she asked.

"Yes, the prisoner is in there."

This must be Seff's man.

The guard to her right cleared his throat.

"I mean, the guest," the first guard corrected himself, a bit confused.

"The King has allowed the princess access to the Leojian to give her some cookies."

"Cookies, sir?" Seff's man asked.

"You heard right. Let her in."

"Do we go in with her?"

"In case she tries to cut my head off with my cookies?" Kayt laughed. "I'll be fine. Besides, you'll be right out here, I'll scream really loud if something happens. The king agreed it would seem . . . forward of us to accompany treats with swords. I'll be fine."

The guards eyed each other nervously, and one of them opened the door with a key. Kayt stepped into the room, as the door closed behind her. A bit of a foyer or an entrance hallway blocked off the rest of the room toward the left. She heard her heels tap on the tiles as she stepped the few paces to the rest of the brightly lit room. As she entered and looked around, she saw more blues and lavenders, a giant window with an ocean-side view, two couches that looked incredibly soft, and a young, beautiful, auburn-haired girl sitting facing the window. Kayt approached her.

"Princess?"

"Yes," she said calmly.

"Mind if I join you?"

"Did they give me a maid now?" she asked without looking at her. Kayt could only see her profile.

A maid? Careful child. It's a long fall out that window. Kayt laughed lightly. "No, your highness. It is I, Kayt, Royal Princess of Oldaem, wife to Crowned Prince Gragor, Daughter-in-Law to King Orcino of Oldaem Realm."

"Nice to meet you. Welcome to my purple prison," Allora answered, eyes flitting to her, then back to the window.

Attitude. I like her.

"I brought cookies."

477

"Poisoned?"

"Now, what sense would that make?" Kayt asked, setting the basket down on a small table as she sat before her.

They eyed each other. The Leojian couldn't have been yet 20. Kayt had at least seven to eight years on her. But they had at least one thing in common. They were both trapped in purple prisons.

"I don't know. Oldaemites enjoy killing Royal Leojians," Allora said.

"And Leojians enjoy abducting Oldaem Shepherds."

"Yes. I know all about that. I'm hiding all these secrets within me! Because of course, royal strategists *always* tell their daughters their plans and all government information and military secrets."

Kayt studied her. *She's telling the truth. She really doesn't know anything.* "So, you don't know where Demas is?"

"I didn't even know who Demas was."

"And you don't like cookies?"

"I don't like manipulation."

"Oh, but you should. You'll find that we women need certain tools with which to survive."

"Your's is that dress?"

Although Kayt laughed, Allora remained stone-faced. "Among other things." After the silence between them intensified, Kayt rose to her feet. "Well, this has been pleasant . . ."

"I don't know what you hoped for. People continually parade in and out of here expecting different results. I don't know anything. I didn't see anything. My family was attacked before my eyes. I was taken from everything and everyone I love and was imprisoned without being guilty of any crime. I'm sorry for not turning this into a gossipy tea party between two fun-loving girls."

Kayt returned to her seat. *She's fascinating.* "You're just a child."

"What's your point?"

"Don't you understand your position?"

"Why don't you explain it to me?"

She has clout—could make demands. She could have great power here. How sad to be so naïve. "If only you had had the proper training."

"Oldaem training? So, I could be a close-minded power-hungry bigot?"

"So you could be invulnerable."

"There are more important things than power."

"Power protects."

"Until someone with more power comes along. It seems like a cycle never to be broken."

"It's why you have to keep getting more power."

"Or perhaps something else will break the cycle."

"What, naive little Princess?" *I'm sounding like the king.*

She sighed. "Being the best versions of ourselves we can be . . . something different . . . someday soon . . ." Her eyes seemed far away.

"How hopeful and senseless. I see the pain you've faced hasn't strengthened you yet."

"Or maybe it's pushed me to wisdom you'll never understand."

"What wisdom?"

"Wisdom of love and compassion. On our travels to the Capital we stopped by Kaya, and the devastating reality *your* country had left in its wake was not prosperity. It was not success or justice. It was destruction. If Oldaem had its way, the country would be a burning heap of rubble. It's what power leads to."

Love isn't strong enough. Compassion is useless. "So what do *you* suggest?"

"I don't even know the answer. It's why I don't seek power. I'm *wise* enough not to."

As Kayt looked at her, she wondered what she would have been like if she had had Allora's upbringing. She seldom thought about morals and the state of her character, but this Leojian Princess brought up thoughts and questions she hadn't considered since her conversation with Brulis above the library at Westervale. And what kind of woman would she have raised Lei to be? After a few moments she found herself reaching for a cookie and biting into it. Allora eyed it. "You sure you don't want one?" she asked, chewing.

"Fine." Allora extended her arm, and Kayt tossed one to her. She caught it and popped it into her mouth. "Where did you buy them from?"

"I don't know. My maid bought them."

"Figures. What's your maid's name?"

"Belinda." *Workhorse.*

"Surprised you know it."

"I know things that are useful to me."

"So, how am I useful to you? Clearly I fit into your schemes somehow, or you wouldn't be here. You seem the scheming type."

Kayt smiled warmly. "I just wanted to bring you some peace. I know this castle can be maddening."

479

"You're a good liar. Probably why they crowned you princess. Seems like something your country would do."

"I'm glad hurling insults at Oldaem is making you feel better. You've been speaking out a lot the past few minutes. I heard you weren't much for talking." She smiled.

Allora looked away, then sighed heavily. "Look . . . Princess Kayt, was it? I don't know you at all nor why you're here. I don't know what motivates you, but I sense that you've had pain in your life like I have. Maybe you've lost people too."

My children.

"I can tell that just by the mask you're hiding behind to protect yourself. My mom did that too. It made things difficult between her and my dad." She sighed.

Why is she telling me all this?

"I guess I just want to say that Leoj was planning a jubilee celebration before war struck out. My dad was figuring out how to prosper his people, my brother was courting this girl, and my mother was busy getting ready to redecorate the palace. As far as I knew, war was the last thing on our minds. Suddenly we get attacked . . . and I don't know what else to say, except that we didn't start it. I don't believe my dad captured Demas, because he had nothing against Oldaem. Why? Because we didn't kill those Shepherds stationed in Leoj to begin with."

"What?"

"Not that you'd believe me anyway. But Leoj had nothing to do with it. I remember my dad was shocked to find out they had died. He had good relations with them." Allora glanced up at her. "Sometimes I wonder if Oldaem did it themselves."

If Leoj didn't capture Demas . . . if Leoj didn't attack our colony and kill our Shepherds . . . than who did? Kayt's mind started spinning. She could sense genuine truth and honesty in the girl. And for the first time in a long time, Kayt felt compassion for someone—compassion for someone helpless. Although she had no idea why, she saw Allora completely differently now than she had when she first entered the room. Perhaps they had more things in common than she had first realized. Alone, vulnerable, without a family—she and Kayt could easily exchange places.

"Of course, you'll probably use everything I just said against me."

"I . . . won't."

"What?"

Kayt cleared her throat. "I won't . . . I won't say a word."

"So you're not going to help me either?"

I have to get to the bottom of this. "Actually . . . I *am* going to help you." Rising quickly and grabbing the plate of cookies from the basket, Kayt handed them to her. Allora took them and ate another one.

"Really?" Allora also stood. "How? Why?"

Finally a true purpose: protect Oldaem Realm. Help out this girl. Rise to the top. Do something different. Best version of myself? A girl without a mother? "Let me see what I can do. For now . . . don't say much. I'm guessing the Shepherds have been interrogating you. Don't trust them."

"Trust who, then? *You?*" Allora asked incredulously.

Yes. Kayt stopped and turned to her, then approached and placed her hands on her face. "Sweet princess, and I say this truly, not condescendingly . . . life is going to be *so* hard–harder than this. Something will have to change in you if you're going to survive. Esis will devour and spit you out in the process. Young and innocent and sweet won't get you far in a battle. Let me tell you from experience: existence is an endless struggle. I say this to you, because I know you've lost a mother . . ." she swallowed, and felt tears rise to her face, "and I've lost a daughter . . . I *will* get to the bottom of this . . . and I *do* believe you."

Allora stood there dumbfounded as Kayt withdrew. As she hurried to the door, she could hear behind her, "You know, Princess Kayt, you're unlike any Princess I've ever met in my life."

Kayt turned around and smiled—perhaps the first real smile in months. "I'm a relatively *new* princess."

Allora's smile twisted slightly. "You're a very scary, confusing, and strange person."

You have no idea.

Chapter 59: Galen

"So you're saying you knew absolutely nothing about the attacks, about the kidnapping, or about any aspect of the war whatsoever?'

"What do you want me to do, here, Shepherd Garrus?" Allora threw up her hands. "Lie? Would you feel better if I made something up?"

Galen's back ached from sitting against the wall for so long. They had been in the interrogation room for hours already. Royal Shepherd Garrus would not give up. He had already employed every approach he could think of, and it seemed as if he was trying them again.

"I won't feel better until Royal Shepherd Demas is home safely."

"So he can tell you how to win the war and destroy my country? Yeah, because I want that to happen …" Allora was tired and exasperated. Galen thought she might be exhausted from the constant questioning. However, she had looked more thoughtful this morning than she had previously. *Maybe she got a break from anyone talking to her yesterday.* There had been no interviews, and when Princess Allora was confined to her room, no one was allowed to enter.

"Because Demas is my personal friend," the Shepherd spoke honestly. Galen stole a sideways glance at Gadiel. That explained the unsettling camaraderie between the Royal Shepherd of State and Gadiel. The two Oldaem soldiers had been staying in a lower wing of the palace while Zevran and Adar had been released and ordered back to Sea Fort. But Galen had overheard Shepherd Garrus insisting that Gadiel go home to his father's estate and stay with his family. Gadiel always emphatically said no. He did not even want them to know he was in Oldaem Realm, much less in the palace. "And right now his children are without a father and his wife is without a husband."

Allora answered Shepherd Garrus, but she looked straight at Gadiel when she spoke. "I wish I could do something to change that. I do. Because I know how it feels. But I'm not the person to ask, and that's all I can tell you." Galen wondered if it was worse to lose the love of a father the way Gadiel and Allora had, or to never be able to feel it at all.

"Then whom do you think I should ask?"

"I'm sorry?"

Galen glanced to Shepherd Garrus. Nobody had raised that question yet. Royal Shepherd Zorah had not really accused her of being guilty, but he had not asked her who she thought was responsible.

"Do you believe it was your father who kidnapped Royal Shepherd Demas?" Shepherd Garrus asked slowly.

Allora hesitated. Galen didn't think she was sure how much she should say. She clearly didn't trust him. Regardless, she stared him in the eye as she told him quietly, "No."

Garrus took a deep breath. When Gadiel tensed beside him, Galen discreetly shook his head. *Don't make a scene now. I don't want to get kicked out.*

"Then who did?"

Allora leaned forward. "Have you questioned the people within your own government?"

"You think it was an inside job."

"She's lying," Gadiel interrupted, rushing over to the table. "You can't be falling for this."

Oh, here we go. "Gadiel, sit down," Shepherd Garrus commanded.

"She's tricking you all! It was clearly Leoj!"

"Not necessarily," Galen said, surprising everyone in the room, including himself. He stood. "We knew already there was someone involved in Oldaem, right? That's the whole reason we left so secretly."

The Royal Shepherd of State nodded. "Precisely. There's more to this than meets the eye."

"You think I don't know that?" Gadiel said harshly. "I was *there*, remember. I was there when they ... I saw their faces." Galen recognized the look on Gadiel's face as the same one he had had when Galen and Adar had first learned of the mission. It was a mixture of pain and fear.

"Were they Leojian?" The question came from the Princess of Leoj.

Gadiel spun in her direction. "Yes."

"How do you know?" Shepherd Garrus leaned forward with interest.

"Because they had eyes like hers," Gadiel pointed accusingly at Princess Allora. *Lavender eyes,* Galen thought. Only people from Leoj had eyes that color. "I already told this to Zevran, and he told Shepherd Seff," Gadiel continued. "They were dressed like Lameans so that I didn't think anything of it at first. Until it was too late ..."

Allora stared in amazement at the three Oldaemites before her. "Wait, so this whole time you've thought that my people disguised themselves *in your territory* and kidnapped your Shepherd right from under your noses?"

"We are at war," Shepherd Garrus sighed. "And Sea Fort is the closest military base to Leoj."

"So they were smart enough to infiltrate your base without anyone noticing, but not smart enough to send people who would actually blend in?"

"I know what I saw!" Gadiel insisted.

"Why didn't they kill you?" Galen blurted out.

"What?" Gadiel asked.

"If they were worried about being found out, why didn't they kill you? You saw their faces." Galen's heart started beating quicker. Something was wrong with all this. He had never really thought about it before.

"I ..." Gadiel's voice trailed off.

"Perhaps they wanted the credit," Shepherd Garrus said carefully.

"This incident has brought my country nothing but pain," Allora snapped. "So, if Leoj is responsible, and I'm not saying we are, the plan was certainly not well thought out."

"I'm not *certain* about anything at this moment," Garrus mumbled. He rose to his feet. "You would do well to keep your opinions to yourself, your highness," he said to Allora. "Especially in your next interview. If you'll excuse me." He motioned for Galen and Gadiel to follow.

As they exited the room he turned to them. "Do not speak of this to anyone," he warned. Galen was glad he was not in Princess Allora's position. He did not want to trifle with this man.

Shepherd Seff was the last of the Royal Shepherds to interview the princess. Galen had not seen him around the palace since their first meeting. He wondered what the Shepherd had been doing. Seff was very reluctant to let the two soldiers remain for the interrogation. As they sat behind him, he seemed to try to ignore them, but he kept glancing back. Gadiel, who had been more relaxed with Garrus in the room, was completely tense around Seff. Something felt different this time.

Allora could feel it too, especially with the warning from Shepherd Garrus. She eyed Shepherd Seff suspiciously. "So I hear you're not really a Royal Shepherd."

"Well, I have your father to thank for my promotion," Seff smiled menacingly.

"Seems like *you* had a lot to gain from making Gadiel's father disappear," Allora retorted.

Gadiel's jaw clenched, but he didn't say anything. *Maybe he's already thought of that.*

"You've got quite a mouth on you, girl," Seff grinned.

"Princess." Allora corrected.

"Well, tell me *princess,* how exactly did Royal Shepherd Demas disappear? But more importantly, where is he now?"

"Why don't you talk to your Shepherd buddies? I've already told them that I know nothing."

"See, I don't believe that." Seff walked around the table to Allora's chair and leaned forward. His close proximity seemed to unnerve her a bit. "I just don't think they were asking in the right way." Then he slapped her hard across the face.

Allora's head snapped back and she gasped in surprise. "Hey!" Galen shouted as he immediately began to rush to her aid.

"What are you doing?" Gadiel demanded. Galen wasn't sure if Gadiel was talking to him or Seff.

Seff whirled around. "You want results?" He snarled at Gadiel. "This is how you get results." When he turned back to face Allora, Galen stepped in front of him.

"You can't do that. She's a princess."

"She's a prisoner," Shepherd Seff shot back. "And *you* brought her here. Now, she knows things. She's the only lead we have. So you step back and let me handle this, or you get out of this room." His voice was steely calm.

"Get out of here, Galen. I can handle him." Princess Allora glared at the man, but she did not seem frightened. More than anything, she looked angry.

"I'll tell the Royal Shepherds," Gadiel's voice shook with emotion behind Galen. "You lay another hand on her, and you'll never see the inside of the palace again."

"Then your father's blood will be on your hands," Seff sneered.

"There are other ways to get the information we want," Gadiel pressed.

"You are ignorant!" Seff shouted. Pushing Galen out of the way, he threw his meaty hand around Allora's neck. She was a trained fighter, Galen knew, but from her position in the chair she didn't have much leverage. "People who think like you are the reason Oldaem has not won this war!" he spat at Gadiel.

Gadiel and Galen dashed toward Seff, but before they could pull his hand away, Allora swiftly kicked him in the knee. Seff roared back, but she knocked his hand away. "Guards!" he shouted as Galen and Gadiel tackled him.

He'll pay for this, Galen thought as he swung his arm back for a punch. But suddenly in a flash of green, the palace guards were on top of him, pulling him away from Shepherd Seff on the floor. "They attacked me!" Seff shouted.

Galen tried to fight off the guards, but he had two of them holding him down. "He attacked her!" Galen shouted back.

But the guards did not listen to him. Instead they followed Seff's orders to remove Galen and Gadiel, not just from the room, but also completely out of the palace. They were marched down the back halls and thrown out into the street.

"This is wrong," Gadiel pounded on the door. "We have to find Garrus. We have to tell him."

"Garrus is inside the palace," Galen reminded him. "How are we supposed to get to him? The guards are under orders not to let us in." He was just as furious as Gadiel. Allora's suspicions had been correct. He had promised nothing bad would happen, and his heart sank as he realized what he had said had been an unintentional lie. *I brought her here. What have I done?*

Gadiel sighed wearily, covering his face with his hands. "My mother can get us in," he said through his fingers.

It was the first time he had heard Gadiel speak of his family without being prodded by Royal Shepherd Garrus. All Galen knew was that, as a Royal Shepherd, Demas would have his own estate somewhere near the palace. That was where Gadiel's family resided. He also knew Gadiel was reluctant to face them without news of his father. "How?"

"I can … I can go … home and explain. She'll help us," Gadiel said quietly.

"Is it very far away?"

"No. But I need to go there alone. I haven't seen them in a while."

Galen nodded. He hadn't seen his mother in a while either. "You talk to her, and we'll meet up later."

"Go watch the tournament or something. There's a fountain on the east side of Arena 2. I'll meet you there around sunset."

And then Galen found himself alone in the alley.

He wasn't sure where to go. Galen hated waiting and hated feeling useless. And most of all, he disliked leaving Allora's fate up to the incompetent Gadiel.

But he was on my side in the interrogation room.

Although Gadiel was annoying and with a ridiculous temper, maybe Galen had been wrong about his true character. Probably Gadiel was a better person than he was. *Wouldn't take much.*

He wandered around for a while, eventually watching the tournament from the stands. It was the Defense competition today, something involving flags and running. But he was unable to concentrate on what was happening.

As the sun began to set, Galen found the fountain and sat to wait for Gadiel. As he looked around sullenly, he absent-mindedly ran his finger along the jagged scar that ran down his torso. It was something he used to think about every night, but now he had almost forgotten it was there. What had he become since then? He had changed so much.

It was in Aramoor where he had thought he finally understood himself and where he belonged in the universe. While he did not have a father, he did have friends who accepted him for who he was. Not only that, they made him better than who he thought he was. Sayla and …

Galen traced the carving along the edge of the fountain. *If only I could talk to them now.* Or if only he had been able to meet Sayla on that pier. He had tried to convince himself that he didn't need his friends anymore, but at that moment, sitting on the fountain, Galen recalled how much he missed them. A painful loneliness fell upon him, and he wondered if Allora felt it sitting in that interrogation room, or if Gadiel did as he went to face his grieving family.

And that was when he saw him.

At first Galen thought his eyes were playing tricks on him, projecting his memories onto someone just passing by. But as he stood and looked again he knew he was not mistaken. The man was older now, but then it had been years since Galen had seen him.

As Galen stood, frozen with surprise, more thoughts of his childhood flashed before his eyes. His heart beat faster. An indescribable joy replaced the loneliness he had just felt. It was unwarranted, and somewhere in his mind he knew it, but in an instant it felt as if his problems were over, suddenly solved by the presence of the young man walking just a few yards away. Someone he had not expected to see. Galen saw his face and thought of that alley in Aramoor—and of the Wall.

He called his name. The cloaked figure kept walking.

Galen repeated it. "Daku!"

And his hero turned around.

CHAPTER 60: VARIC

"Sometimes merchants have to do *anything* to survive."

Lately, that's what Vivienne had been telling him. A couple nights ago, Vivienne and Cullen pulled Varic into their room and sat him down. His world would changed forever. He had never known of the treachery of the Oldaem Crown, had never heard of their tyranny. Always a faithful and ignorant Oldaem civilian, he had respected the royalty, thinking that Oldaem had lived in peace and prosperity. However, after he listened to the tales of the greed and destruction and . . . murder, he realized that the nation needed to be . . . *liberated.* It was why they had come to the palace in the first place.

After their first initial business sessions with the palace merchants and harbormaster, Varic thought perhaps they would move north or even west to Remia. But clearly, Vivienne and Cullen had other plans in mind. What Varic discovered that night in the room with Vivienne and Cullen was that King Orcino had been responsible for the death of his and Vivienne's parents. Vivienne had brought them here for revenge.

At first, the news brought him to tears--not only for the loss of trust in his nation, but also at the memory of losing his parents . . . especially his father. But beyond that, he wept for Orcino. He had never taken a life that he could remember. And now, they were to assassinate the King. He understood why. Every inch of him wanted to feel the King's lifeblood flow out of him. But deep inside he heard a voice or felt a whisper that perhaps, *all of this was wrong.* He didn't know what it was, or why it spoke to him. Whenever he told Vivienne about it, she would tell him his reaction was natural, but not to dwell on it--that it was fear speaking. And fear would only get them killed. What they did was for the greater good. Orcino had been responsible for many tyrannies, including the war with Leoj, which took Cullen's brother at the siege of the royal fortress. They would do what needed to be done. *Sometimes merchants have to do anything to survive.*

The plan was set. They had worked tirelessly at arranging the details of the assasination. Now, they were heading back toward the inn. It would be the last night before the liberation of Oldaem. Tomorrow at dawn, they would strike.

The sun was setting as they made their way through the Capital streets. Merchants hawked their wares at them, and people were bartering and trading and eating and laughing. They could hear music, and children ran with sunset-colored streamers. He smiled. Vivienne and Cullen walked hand in hand in front of him. They were in love. He adored them together. Still, a pang stung within Varic's heart. He hoped one day he would find someone for himself. Deep within him he felt that he had had someone . . . a long time ago . . . but his work had gotten so chaotic and busy . . . he almost couldn't remember her name anymore. Maybe she had silver eyes . . . or maybe they were golden ones.

Several events of the tournament had ended, and the competitors were having a celebration in Arena 3. He could hear laughter and music and joyful cries. They had no idea they were living under an oppressive regime. He would save them. After all, he was a hero.

"Daku?!"

Swinging around, he saw Galen racing toward him, a large smile across his face, arms outstretched for a hug. Then to Daku's horror, Malvina also whipped around to face them, Jorn with a snarl spread across his face.

He and Malvina made eye contact. *Fix this. Take care of him. Do not return to the inn afterward. Someone may see. Meet us at the palace gates at dawn.*

"Daku! Is that really you?" he could hear Galen's voice, almost a laugh in it. Tears stung Daku's eyes. *Galen.*

"Fix this, Varic." Vivienne smiled sweetly, taking Cullen's hand. "The palace gates at dawn."

Varic watched them disappear into the crowd.

Fix this boomed into his mind.

What does she want me to do?

Suddenly, Varic felt himself engulfed in a hug from behind by a young man. Strong arms encircled him. Varic turned to see someone several years younger than him. He was well-built, lean, with brown hair that seemed in need of a trim--perhaps previously military cut-- and with a confused smile on his face.

"Daku, aren't you going to *say* anything?"

Who is Daku?

"I think you have the wrong person," Varic replied.

He felt a punch in his arm. The guy smirked. "Don't be ridiculous, man, it's me, *Galen!* It's been years, but I'd know that ugly face anywhere. Where have you *been? How* have you been? Why are you in the Capital?"

"I'm . . ." Varic stuttered, "I'm a merchant."

"Like your dad?"

Varic felt tears welling up in his mind. *My father is dead. Killed by Orcino.*

Take care of this boomed in his mind. *Golden eyes.* As Varic gripped a small knife in his pocket, he felt himself being hugged again.

"You have no idea how much I've missed you. I . . . I've been through a lot." Sadness filled his voice. "Have you heard from Sayla?" He pulled away and looked at him.

Bug. Daku swallowed.

"No." Daku answered. *I need to run. I need to get away from Malvina. I need to get Galen out of the city.*

Take care of this, Varic.

"Are you . . . alright?" Galen asked.

"I . . . I need to go," Varic replied, slowly pulling the knife out of his pocket. His feet started moving away from Galen.

"Wait! Daku!"

His legs attempted to move, but in slow motion, and his head was pounding. *Take care of this.* Then he paused, slowly turned around until Galen stood face to face with him, and golden rage swept through him.

"We have so much to talk about. Where is Aelwynne?"

Driving the knife into Galen's side, he pulled it out quickly, scarlet staining the blade. Suddenly a blow struck him from behind, and he tumbled forward over Galen.

Varic ran.

He was disoriented, everything hazy around him. People screamed as he careened forward. Racing as fast as he could, he knocked people down as he gained speed. Golden fog trailed behind him, and when he looked up, the golden clouds spread over the golden sun. Golden people stared at him with fear. Glancing at his hands, he saw bright red staining them, a crimson hue covering golden fingers. Galen's face hovered before him.

490

Dead. I've killed him. I've killed Galen.

As he ran, all he could see were golden Galens. Every little child, every old woman, every merchant or shopkeeper or soldier was Galen. They were all golden Galens.

I have to leave. I have to leave the city. I have to get away from Malvina. The gates. I'll run toward the city gates. Aelwynne, I'm coming . . . please forgive me. Please . . . forgive me.

Golden tears trickled down his cheeks as he hurtled along. Suddenly the streets before him turned into a forest path of tall, brown-trunked trees with a high canopy of emerald leaves arching overhead. No. Golden leaves were there. Daku felt much shorter suddenly, and much younger.

"Are you sure you know where you're going?" he heard Galen ask behind him. Momentarily he glanced over his shoulder to see his young friend, the one he loved and looked after, who regarded him as his hero, standing on the forest path. A concerned smile spread across his face.

"Yep," Daku answered without slowing his pace. "Forward."

Somehow that didn't seem very reassuring to the young Galen. He tried again. "It's just–I think it's getting dark--and your dad will probably start wondering where we are ..."

Little Sayla jumped in front of him before he could finish. "It's not getting dark yet, silly! Well at least not because the sun is going down." She looked up. "It's more as if the trees are getting closer and closer together the farther we go into the forest and are blocking out more sunlight. In a few more minutes, we probably won't be able to even see each other!" she exclaimed happily and skipped ahead.

"Is that supposed to sound better? It doesn't to me," Galen mumbled to himself.

Bug had caught up to him and asked him a question, her bright-green eyes full of wonder and excitement. "You do see how the trees are getting thicker, don't you? It almost looks as if they're all leaning in to tell each other a secret. Or keep a secret. Do you think they're keeping a secret?"

Daku smiled down at little Bug. As he held her hand while they continued walking, he heard himself speak: "Of course they are. There are all kinds of secrets in the world. And it's up to us to find them. Out here, who knows? There's probably a secret treasure chest buried in the ground, or the ruins of a lost city, or ..." And that's when they ran face-first into the wall.

Pulling out his knife, he carved three names upon its ancient surface . . . *Daku. Galen. Sayla. Friends Forever.* His two best friends looked at him with pride as he finished. Galen and Sayla stretched out their arms for a hug. Daku took the knife and rammed it first into Galen . . . and then Sayla. He watched both of their tiny figures fall into a pool of golden blood.

Suddenly he stood in a patch of golden sunflowers, holding an innocent gardner in his arms . . . golden blood spilling around her . . . then he was in a Leojian fortress . . . holding an Oldaem Spirit Shepherd's body in his arms . . . her golden blood oozing out of her . . . *war* . . .

He gripped his sword with all of his might as he danced blades with Jorn in the square at Vertloch. Malvina sat before them smiling. Blood dripped down his face. Jorn's eye was black and swollen. She loved watching them fight for a kiss—had made them do it so many times. Daku raised his sword high above his head as he brought it down with a crashing blow. Jorn deflected it, and then rolled behind him, and struck him from behind with the hilt of his weapon. His head throbbed and he fell on his face. By the time he looked up, Jorn and Malvina were holding each other in a passionate embrace.

Daku raced through the streets of the Capital, crashing into carts, knocking people down. His feet pounded. His heart trembled. *I have to leave the city. I have to leave the city.*

Behind him, he heard something. It sounded like a rumble, perhaps an earthquake. Looking over his shoulder, he saw a golden wave rise up high into the golden sky. It moved slowly at first, but then it began to gain speed, sweeping up everything it encountered. It was after him. As it touched every surface it turned it into solid gold. As he ran, he could see things transforming into golden statues behind him. He mustn't get stuck here--he couldn't go back.

I have to get to the front gates.

Falling to the ground, he then looked up to see a boy being attacked by a pack of Lamean boys. As he charged toward them, the Lameans shoved the small kid into an alleyway and then to the ground. They punched him in the face and kicked him in the side. Helpless and defenseless, he was in need of a hero.

Young Daku swooped in and rammed two of the kids into the wall. Then he grabbed the boy on top of the fallen kid and threw him to the ground before kicking him twice in the ribs. After punching another in the face, he put a third kid into a chokehold.

492

"Get out of here, you jerks! And never come back! Or I'll kill you all!"

The children looked up at him with fear. His knuckles were swollen and he was out of breath. As they took off, he released the boy he was holding, and threw him to the ground. "Get out of here. And if I ever see you on the streets of Aramoor again . . . I'll kill you."

Bursting into tears, the Lamean disappeared around the corner. Daku quietly approached the boy who had curled into a ball on a pile of trash heaped against the dirty side of the corner of a building. Daku knelt down beside him.

"Are you okay, kid?"

The boy didn't respond, only quietly cried.

"Hey," Daku whispered gently. Softly rolling the lad onto his back, he then cradled his head in his arms and tried to sit him up. "It's okay . . . they're gone now. You're safe. No one will hurt you. Not while I'm around."

"Who . . . who are you?"

"Daku." He smiled. "Who are you?"

"Galen," the boy said, wiping the blood away from his face.

"Don't worry about those stupid kids anymore. I killed them."

"You did?"

The older boy's eyes twinkled. "Well . . . almost." He sat down beside Galen. "You going to be okay?"

"Yeah." He sniffled. "Thanks for saving me. What are you, a hero or something?"

"Someday," Daku said proudly.

"I want to be just like you," Galen said with wonder.

"I'll teach ya everything I know." Daku flexed his muscles.

"You're pretty strong for just a kid. How old are you?"

"Ten."

"I'm eight."

"And I'm six," the girl said, jumping in.

"Who are you?" Galen asked.

"Sayla!"

"Bug! I told you to wait until I came back!" Daku scolded.

"You were amazing, Daku! You almost killed those bullies! It was incredible! You smashed his head, and choked that other one, and kicked and . . . woooow!"

Daku watched as Bug repeated on several pieces of trash littered around the alley all the moves he had just used against the Lameans. He and Galen laughed. Then she knelt down to face Galen.

"You okay, little kid?"

"Little kid? I'm older than you!"

"Yeah, but I'm stronger than you!"

"No, you're not!"

"Yes I am! Wanna fight!" she asked, holding up her fists.

"Okay . . . okay, Bug. Enough of that. We've had enough fighting to last us a while." Daku sighed. Standing, he studied the two kids. Somehow he had a feeling they would be his friends forever.

The rumble of the golden wave again caught his attention, and he glanced over his shoulder to see it crashing into the alleyway. As he raced away, Sayla and Galen vanished beneath its golden onslaught. He darted through what he thought was Aramoor, and then realized it was the Capital. The gates appeared off in the distance. The exit was within sight, promising freedom from Malvina. But no matter how hard he drove himself, the golden wave was faster. As he sped past a clock tower in a square, it began to chime.

Aelwynne stood in front of him, holding her bags, waiting for him. He smiled at her. The birds lazily flew over them, dreamily cawing above the crash of the waves of the ocean upon the shore. The clock in the tower struck the hour, and he knew it was nearly time for them to leave Aramoor and sail off to Vertloch Tower, where they would live their lives. She nodded at him, as he grinned, filled with love for her. Beyond her he saw Sayla waiting despondently. It was time to say goodbye. Aelwynne nodded again, and disappeared toward their vessel in the nearby harbor. When she waved gently at Sayla, the girl waved back, watching her leave.

Daku stood before Sayla. His little Bug came up to him and wrapped her arms around him. He held her for a long time as she cried. She had grown into such a beautiful young woman, and he cared greatly for her. Although he had protected her for years, that was no longer his job now. His responsibility was to protect Aelwynne. Life had changed. People came and went, he grew up. He had grown up, and it was time to leave Aramoor behind. But they would always have the Wall.

"I'll miss you so much, Daku."

"I know."

"Please take good care of Aelwynne. She seems . . . so wonderful." The girl looked up at him with her green eyes. "Don't ever hurt her," she smiled weakly.

"I won't. I promise."

"Thank you for saving me, Daku--from my house, from my family, from my life. You . . . you became my family."

"And you became mine."

They hugged again, and Daku fought back some tears himself. "Take care of Galen. He needs you."

"I know he does."

Daku pulled away and looked down at her. She and Galen had been all he had known until he sailed away with his father and was shipwrecked in Najoh. They would always be apart of him. He would come back soon and would visit them as often as he could. "You'll be the one, Bug. You'll be the one to become a Shepherd. I just know it."

"I know it too," she said confidently.

"Be brave, okay?"

"I will."

"And be good. It's . . . easy not to be in this world."

"I'll try to remember. You be good too. You promise?"

"I promise." And he meant it.

There was a pause as they eyed each other sadly. "Don't worry about me, Daku. I can take care of myself."

"I know you can," he said, picking up his bag from the ground. After smiling sorrowfully one last time at Bug, he turned toward his ship and his wife and his future. Behind him he could hear Bug's voice.

"Daku . . . I love you . . . I think I always will."

"I know, Sayla." Unable to face her, he knew he was breaking her heart. But he realized that with time came healing and that she would find someone else. Hopefully Galen would overcome his anger and become the man Daku knew he could be, and finally take care of the girl as she deserved.

Malvina's eyes met his. He swallowed uncomfortably. Gray water surrounded them. She shook her head slowly, her eyes unwavering. He was unable to look away from the golden pools of eternity before him. At the same time he didn't want to look away. Jorn smirked a half smile as he watched her gaze drift downward toward the approaching, tiny, perfect, innocent--bug. She crushed it beneath her heel. Golden blood oozed out of it and stained the wooden deck of the vessel heading toward the Tower of hopelessness.

Daku was aware of a golden wave behind him. Perhaps it swept up Sayla once again, or even froze her to the ground. But he knew he couldn't let it do the same to him. He ran as fast as he could–away from Aramoor. Away from Bug. Away from the boat, from his wife, from his future. Desperately racing for his life, he fled from Malvina.

Seeing the city gate clearly before him now, he knew that if he was strong enough he could be free, could escape the darkness and the evil and the pain and the regret--if he truly *was* the hero. If he was truly the person he challenged Bug to be, the man his father had been.

"Do you, Daku, take Aelwynne to be your be beloved wife, to have and to hold from this day forward, for better or for worse, for richer or poorer, in sickness and in health, to love and to cherish-- from this day forward, as long as you both shall live?"

He looked at his beautiful fiancé, her silver eyes reflecting the perfect Najoh sunset on the white sandy shores. Her ivory gown draped down around her, billowing in the winds. His father stood there watching, standing next to her father. No one else was around. A part of him wished Galen and Bug could have made it to Najoh, but they would meet Aelwynne soon enough.

He had full confidence in his answer, meant it with every fiber of his being. Daku wanted her forever--only her. They would stay together until death parted them. And then even beyond the darkness of death, he would find her again.

"I do."

"You are now man and wife. You may kiss your bride."

Daku took Aelwynne in his arms and kissed her. And as he did, he remembered the first time he had seen her. And the first time he kissed her, their cottage, sitting beneath the clock tower. He remembered Najoh and knew she was there. He would run as fast as he could to her.

You are mine.
You belong to me.
You love me.
You serve me.
It's the way.
Forsake them.
Forsake them all.

As he stood before the gates of the city, he turned and looked at the entire Capital. Every single building, every single person, every single thing was covered completely in gold. The golden tidal wave rose high into the sky like a Tower above him. At any second it would crash down upon him and take him away with it forever. But beyond the gate was Najoh, and Aelwynne waited there. As did

496

freedom and light and forgiveness and redemption. The Wall with their names inscribed upon it waited there. And their friendship.

But he couldn't do it, couldn't step through that archway. Daku didn't deserve what waited for him. He deserved only death. He just . . . wasn't . . . good enough, wasn't strong enough. Daku the Hero was dead--had died with every crime he committed. Every lie he told. Every dark choice he made. Every life he took. Only Varic the murderer still lived.

He had a choice. Silver or gold. Gold or silver.

Everyone has a choice, he realized. He had no one to blame anymore, no excuses to make. For years he had lied to himself. Nothing he had done had been for Aelwynne, to protect her. The truth was, he liked being powerful. He liked being a Warden. He liked gold.

Daku made every choice he had for himself . . . there was no denying it anymore. Saying a sad goodbye to the land of light beyond the archway, he watched as the golden tidal wave consumed him.

Varic stood before the palace gates at dawn of the next day. Vivienne and Cullen had waited for him.

"I knew you'd come," she whispered as she kissed him on the cheek.

"I did too." he replied.

"Now come . . . today is the day we liberate Oldaem, Varic."

"Let it be done," he said as the three assassins entered the underground tunnels of the Oldaem Palace.

CHAPTER 61: COLE

"Cole."

His head was pounding, his lips chapped, his lungs aching.

"Cole. Please."

Where am I?

Unable to sit up, he couldn't think or even open his eyes.

Just let me sleep.

"Come on, Cole, wake up for me."

Just . . . let . . . me . . . sleep.

He had been aware of nothing. Only water. Water turned into darkness. Darkness was comfortable ... safe. *Lily is dead.*

"Come on, Cole. You're strong. You've always been strong."

When Cole opened his eyes, the light blinded him and his head pounded even more intensely. Quickly he shut them again. *I'm alive? How am I alive? Maybe I'm dead. Just let me sleep.*

"He opened his eyes."

Cole could faintly hear voices, but he couldn't recognize any of them. Nor did he know where he was. The last he had been aware of was Zek holding him beneath the water. And the last he remembered was his mother trying to kill him. Tears welled up in his again closed eyes.

"Cole? Can you hear me?"

Azriel?

"Cole, come on, open your eyes again."

Azriel? Did you save me?

"Cole, please . . ."

Finally he opened his eyes to the fuzzy outline of someone standing above him. He was aware that he was lying on something soft beneath him and that he was inside somewhere. The room was relatively dark, but now any light seemed extremely bright. Breathing was difficult, and he wasn't strong enough to raise or lift his head. Slowly his eyes adjusted to reveal what he thought was Azriel gazing down at him. But when Cole opened his mouth to try to speak to him, nothing came out.

"What, Cole?"

He tried again. Still nothing.

"Don't worry about speaking, Cole. It's okay. You're safe now."

Finally, sound emerged. "Azriel?" he said weakly.

"Who?"

Cole started coughing and could not stop. The coughing brought up water from his lungs. A hand with a towel wiped it away from his mouth.

"Take it easy, Cole."

The fuzzy outline became clearer, and he saw clear blue eyes and red hair. *Fenris.*

"Cole, you scared me back there."

"Fenris . . . you . . . saved me."

"Yeah. That kid took off. I don't know where he went."

"Zek . . . got away?"

"Yeah, whoever he is. Don't worry about him. You're safe now. I'm not going to let anything happen to you."

As Cole felt his big brother's lips press against his forehead, relief washed over him and the tears wouldn't stop flowing. He began shaking as Fenris held him closely. Then the boy felt Fenris get into the bed beside him and hold him even tighter. Eventually, the trembling turned into shivers, the shivers into chills, and the chills into sleep.

Cole woke to see Fenris sitting in a chair next to his bed. His head felt much clearer and the pain had lessened.

"Good morning." Fenris smiled.

"Where am I?"

"In an inn by the road, outside of the Capital."

"You took me all the way to the Capital?"

"Yeah. Wasn't easy. I'll tell you the whole story once you're feeling better. I don't want to fill your tiny brain with too much," he smirked. "You need your rest."

"How long was I asleep?"

"A few days."

"I'm thirsty."

"I thought you'd have had your fill of water."

Cole frowned at him.

"Too soon? Sorry." Fenris grinned as he handed him a cup of water that Cole drank slowly.

"I'm so glad you're okay, Cole."

"What happened?"

"Well, while that psychopath was drowning you, I came upon the three of you and ran straight into the lake and tackled that monster. He's a fast swimmer, and an even faster runner. I was more concerned with you than catching him. But I wish I could have."

"And Lily?" Cole asked sadly.

Fenris smiled and pointed to the other side of the room. There, Cole saw a bandaged Lily snoring on a tattered couch. Drool spilled down from her swollen lip. It was the most beautiful sight he had ever seen.

"She's alive," Cole breathed.

"Praise the Creator," Fenris replied. "You guys got lucky. Seems someone was watching out for you. I know I wasn't led to you both on my own. Oldaem is too big for all that. The Order saved you both. I truly believe that."

"You followed us all the way from Windrip?"

"Arissa sent word to me that you both had left looking for dad. Now that you're feeling a bit better ..." Cole watched his brother rise and walk toward him, then flick him on the side of the head. "What the heck were you thinking? You both could have been killed! Are you crazy? You're both insane! You *really* thought you could travel across Esis alone? You're just kids! Babies, really! What were you thinking?"

"I had to find Dad," Cole said sadly.

Fenris threw his arms around the boy's neck and hugged him closely. "I love you both so much. You scared me to death. I can't even believe I found you. Praise the Creator."

While Cole could tell that his brother really believed the Creator responsible for their reunion, he really didn't know what to think.

"Can't a girl get any sleep around here?" Lily complained from the couch. Fenris released Cole and laughed. When Cole turned over he saw his sister standing beside him.

"Lily."

"I told you Zek was a meanie."

Cole laughed as she hugged him.

"I'm glad you didn't die," she whispered into his ear.

"Me, too, Lily."

"Even though you're a stupid babyface," she whispered again.

"I'm so . . . so sorry, Lily." And he meant it.

"Yeah, yeah . . . just get up already so that we can find Dad. I wanna watch the tournament!"

Sitting up, Cole looked at Fenris. "How far away from the Capital are we?"

"Can't be too far," Lily answered. "Fenris carried you all the way here. You owe him big time."

Sighing, Fenris shook his head. "Maybe an hour or so. Not far. We'll go tomorrow morning. I want to stay here one more night. A doctor is coming to look at Lily's head injury again."

"Her head is so hard, nothing could crush it," Cole chuckled.

"Shut up, Cole," she snapped and stuck her tongue out.

When a knock sounded on the door, Fenris let in the innkeeper with a tray full of food.

The three of them sat on the bed, eating and drinking, and laughing and talking. It was the happiest Cole had felt in months as well as the safest and the most content. Having Fenris meant they would survive. Maybe the Order did care about them after all.

That night, after Lily had already gone to sleep and after she had been cleared by the doctor to continue traveling the next day, Cole and Fenris climbed out the window and sat on the roof of the inn. Off in the distance they could see the lights of the Capital, and if they were really quiet, they thought that they could hear cheers erupting in the distance. They imagined it was the tournament. And their hope was that their dad was an hour away, watching it.

"How are Arissa and Belen?" Cole inquired as a shooting star raced overhead.

"Worried about you. Arissa is strong." He paused. "They will be okay."

"Yeah. She is strong."

"How are *you?*" Fenris asked with concern.

"Tired." Cole sighed as chills raced down his body.

Fenris immediately scooted closer and wrapped his arm around Cole's shoulders. "Me, too."

"Thank you for saving us."

"Don't even say that, Cole. I never should have gone back to Windrip. I should have figured out how to make it work at home."

"You did what you had to do. And so did I."

"Yeah . . . I know."

Cole looked in the direction of the Capital again and wondered where Zek had run off to. It still shocked him that the boy had attacked them after Cole had trusted him so much. He had loved and felt safe with him. If he had learned anything from the whole ordeal, it was not to trust anyone that wasn't family. Embarrassed that he had put Lily and himself in danger, he didn't want to talk to Fenris about Zek. Instead, he hoped he would never see Zek again.

Now he focused his thoughts on what the next day would hold. Fenris agreed to go with them to the Capital to look for their father, but only with the assurance that if they couldn't find him in three days, they would return home. Cole and Lily agreed, and hoped they wouldn't have to walk, but maybe take a ship home. Fenris had agreed, and now they were all waiting for tomorrow.

One thing continued to bother Cole, one question that he wanted to ask Fenris, but didn't know how to bring up: the truth about their mother. "Fenris."

"Yeah?"

"I need to ask you something."

"Okay."

"But I don't know how."

"You can ask me *anything,* little brother," Fenris replied gently.

Cole sighed deeply and shook his head, battling back memories of his mother's violent grip.

"What is it, Cole?" he asked, his deep blue eyes filling the boy with a sense of peace.

"I . . ." Cole swallowed. "I think Mom tried to drown me when I was little."

His brother looked away sadly.

Cole knew the truth before Fenris even spoke.

"I know."

"Why . . . why didn't anyone say anything? Why did Dad leave us alone with her? Why . . ."

"He didn't, Cole. After it happened, Dad sent Mom away for a good two years for help."

Cole was shocked. "He . . . he did?"

"Yes."

"Why . . . why don't I remember that?"

"Probably the same reason you didn't remember it happened in the first place. You blocked out the pain."

"Did . . . Arissa know?"

"Yes."

"What happened when Mom came back?"

"Dad watched her closely. We all did. She seemed much better, completely different. That's probably the Mom you remember."

"And then Dad left."

Fenris looked away. "He had to. It was his duty."

"As a Shepherd?"

"Yes."

Cole scowled. "He didn't *have* to."

"I guess not." Gently he turned Cole's face to his. "But don't be too angry with Dad. He did it for his faith. He put his faith before his family. He always has. He felt that Oldaem needed him, that it needed Old Order representatives in the government." A look of resolution crossed Fenris' face. "And he was right." Again staring in

502

the direction of the Capital, he said quietly, "I fear what will happen to Old Order believers in the future if things continue to go the way they have been."

"What do you mean? Could Dad be in danger?"

"We all could. There are very powerful men that don't think people should have the right to believe whatever they want. Dad left to fight individuals like them." He poked Cole in the stomach. "We should too, in our own way."

"So . . . you don't think Dad should come home?"

"Of *course* I want him to . . . but I understand that life is more than about what happens to *us*. There are other people to consider."

Suddenly Cole realized how brave and strong his brother really was. He was smart, too, more than Cole had ever realized before.

"I'll come home with you and Lily, Cole, so that Dad can stay and fight. I'll figure out how to make our family be okay, and I'll teach you all everything I know, until Belen is grown up and has moved out."

"But that's not fair! You should be able to live your life! You should meet someone and marry them and grow a family and be happy!"

"But why, though? Why do you think that? Why does life have to be about what makes us *happy?* There are so many people out there, Cole, that are struggling and that don't know the truth. They live lies every day. Life isn't about *us!*"

"Then, who is it about?" Cole grumbled.

Fenris smiled and looked up. "Them." Another shooting star.

Cole breathed deeply. *Back on the Order again.* He realized just how similar Azriel and Fenris were.

"You blame them, don't you?" Fenris asked with disappointment.

"How could I not?"

"It's not their fault."

"How isn't it?" Cole's voice began rising. "They did this! They took mom! They gave me a mom who wanted me dead! They sent Zek to attack us! They took Dad away! They created a world in which people hate each other and attack each other and destroy each other! They control everything! Why can't they just save us?" Sobs shook him.

Fenris silently shook his head, then hugged him tighter. "Or . . . perhaps . . . they *have* saved us. Perhaps the *Betrayer* did all those things you blame them for. Perhaps it was his plan. Perhaps the

Liberator will come and set things right . . . perhaps he's waiting for us to *believe*."

"Believing is scary, Fenris."

"Yes. It is."

"Trusting someone got me attacked."

"But trusting saved you."

"*You* saved me."

"Because I trusted in them. They led me to you."

"But how do you *know?*"

"I don't."

"Then how do you *believe?*"

"Because of faith."

"I don't have enough!"

"All you need is a little."

"What if I lose it?"

"They'll send you more."

"What if I choose the wrong thing?"

"They'll give you another choice."

"Why?" Cole cried in confusion.

Fenris paused. "Because they love you."

They entered the Capital city the next day, Fenris leading the way, Lily right behind, and Cole brought up the rear. They constantly scanned the crowds, searching for an older man with reddish hair. Fenris got directions to the arenas, as they heard the Defense and Spirit Competitions were taking place that day.

Excitement filled the air as they walked through the crowded streets. Cole couldn't believe they had made it there. Lily's head still had a bandage wrapped around it, and Cole still had bruises on his neck. But Fenris walked confidently through the streets, as if he had been there before and knew exactly where they were going.

Once they approached the arenas, they found long lines of people waiting to file in. They had no idea which of the four arenas their dad could be in. Suddenly they felt overwhelmed.

"What should we do?" Lily asked, looking up at Fenris, who continued to scan the crowd.

"I'm not sure."

"Maybe we should split up?" Cole asked.

"No! That's not happening."

"Should we check out each one?"

"We only have enough money to enter one," Fenris said, searching through his bag.

Zek would steal money. Cole shuddered at his memory.

"Let's pray." Lily said.

A big smile crossed Fenris' face. Bending down, he kissed Lily on the forehead. "What an excellent idea."

Cole felt Fenris' hand slip into his, and Lily reached for his other one. Cole took it in his, and the tiny circle started praying.

Cole had a hard time paying attention to the prayers. He watched Fenris' mouth sound out words and could tell they were full of passion and belief. Lily's eyes were also closed reverently, and the prayer made him think and remember all of the prayers Azriel would pray. Suddenly he missed Azriel a lot. *Fenris and he would be best friends.* Cole looked around, wondering if their prayer could possibly accomplish anything.

Their whole trip had been crazy and dangerous. While he had learned so much during it, yet another part of him felt as if he had learned nothing. Both his brother and sister gripped his hands tighter as the prayer continued.

Maybe I should pray too. But what's the point? Do prayers work if I don't believe? Maybe prayers will help my belief. I learned I couldn't do it on my own, that I needed help. I need help now.

Cole didn't know why, but suddenly a vision of him in a dark forest filled his mind. He saw Azriel and Fenris and Lily standing on the right fork of a forest path, standing in light and love and hope. Zek waited on the left fork, surrounded with water and his mother scowling at him. Both paths urged him forward. With a deep sigh, he put one foot in front of the other and stepped out of the shadows and on to the right path . . . and into the light. He started to pray.

After they opened their eyes, they saw a redheaded man standing before them, a shocked expression on his face.

Dad.

CHAPTER 62: SAYLA

The room was empty. Gingerly Sayla knelt on the hard wooden floor beneath her. The boards creaked under her weight, but it was the only sound in the room. The silence of the New Order Temple left her alone with her thoughts, a place she did not often like to be.

She had gone there seeking comfort, clarity ... she didn't exactly know what. When she had finally arrived in the Capital the day before, the tournament was well under way. Hoards of people clogged the streets, but apparently none of them were eager to visit a small Temple of the New Order. Sayla had occasionally gone to the one on the grounds of Woodlands Academy, but that one was peaceful and nestled in the forest. Birds would always sing outside it.

This temple was lavish with strange ornaments that Sayla did not understand the meanings of and nearly every surface was gilded with gold.

Gold.

Her mind flashed back to her second dream, the one that had haunted her the most: the dream that had warned her that someone would die in a cave and she had ignorantly thought it would be her. But right now it was the first part of that dream that bothered her.

Even as dusk approached and the shadows grew around her, Sayla could see the glint of the gold throughout the room. An uneasy sensation formed in the pit of her stomach.

"You're beautiful, Sayla. Don't ever let your sisters tell you differently," Daku had said. He had told her that her several times. Whenever he said something like that, she had felt so at ease, so comforted by his presence. She would always think that maybe he meant it differently this time—that he could fix all her problems. Daku was all she needed.

But then her dream had twisted reality. As he was telling her stories of his travels, the golden color had covered him until he was frozen solid. The look in his unmoving golden eyes ... Sayla preferred to think about them as the warm brown she knew they really were. Then as she began to wonder where he was, the knot in her stomach tightened.

Desperately, Sayla tried to push the dream images away as a feeling of unexplainable panic rose within her. *I have to get out of this temple.* So much for receiving comfort. Entering the temple had made her more uneasy than if she just hadn't gone in at all. *I don't understand. If the One is giving me these dreams, why won't he answer me when I seek his help?*

Something was wrong. What it might be she didn't know, but she couldn't get the feeling out of her gut or the horrifying images of Daku covered in gold out of her mind. Never had she experienced such a vivid recollection of a dream when she was awake.

Stumbling out of the New Order Temple, glad for the first time that no one was there to see her, she hugged the iron railing of the front steps and let herself slide down its post, clutching it to steady herself.

After her encounter with the boy sitting on the roof in Azmar, her relentless dreams had ceased, and for the first time in a long time, Sayla had been able to sleep well. Although she still went to bed every night in fear of another nightmare, her outlook was starting to change about the whole thing. Maybe having these dreams was okay. Perhaps one day she would even be able to call them a blessing.

But not yet. It was easy to think better of those cursed dreams when she wasn't actually having them. As Sayla sat in the grass in front of the temple, confronted once more by the reality of her nightmares, she felt as if she couldn't breathe.

Finally, as the sun dipped out of sight, she began to breathe easier, her racing heart slowed, and she regained control of herself.

What in Esis was that? She looked back into the temple. *Well, I'm not going back in there again.* She had hoped to replicate the seed of peace that had begun growing in Azmar, but apparently that temple was not the place to do it. *Where then?* Sayla felt as if she didn't know anything anymore.

More than anything right now she wished that just for one miraculous moment she could be with her friends again. Not her Shepherd Trainee partners, but her real friends. *Family.*

Sayla had called Daku and Galen that on the day her mother had refused to let her see them all summer all those years ago. She had meant it then and … and she meant it now. *I still need them.* Although she had tried to convince herself that she had moved past all that, she knew that their names would be inscribed forever on that Wall. Theirs was an unbreakable friendship. *But I haven't seen Daku in years. He's married now. And Galen didn't meet me on the pier.*

Galen had always needed her and Daku. And there had been a time when all three needed each other, but Galen was always the last to admit it. Sayla did not consider her early life to be particularly easy or enjoyable, but she realized his had been harder. While he

507

acknowledged it, she knew he had always been terrified they would leave him. And then Daku did just that. And Sayla the same not long after.

Galen had always acted so cocky and arrogant, but Sayla was one of the few people who knew that it was a front. When he let his defenses down, Galen could be sweet, and caring, and genuine. He was so much more than ...

"Hey, babe, wanna sit by me at the tournament tomorrow?" Shale bounded up to her.

She eyed him wearily. "How did you find me?"

"Um, cause I'm amazing," he laughed. *And that's as genuine as he gets.*

"Shale, do you think it's okay to be different?"

"What do you mean? Like, is it okay to be better than other people? I say, if you got it, flaunt it, ya know?" He grinned in that way that she had once loved so much. Today, she just frowned.

"No, I mean weird different. Unpopular different."

His expression was as if she spoke in a foreign language.

"Like ... Grunt was."

Shale burst into laughter. "You mean, like a freak?" Sayla winced at his choice of words. As he put his arm around her, she tensed. "Sayla, why are you still troubled by that? It was *weeks* ago. I mean, he never really fit in as a Defense Shepherd anyway ... who knows how he even got in ..."

Unable to stand his attitude anymore and cringing at the feeling of his breath on her cheek, she shoved him away with the strength of a Shepherd of Defense. "You know what? I see why he was picked. I see exactly why. He deserved to be in the academy more than anyone else." Taking a breath, she added, "Especially you. Especially me. All we do is look out for ourselves. It's not *us* we're supposed to be defending! It's the weak–the helpless. Someone saw potential in him. I don't know if it was the STC, or the One or ... or ... someone else. Someone sees potential in me, too." Her eyes brimmed with tears. "It's our job to protect them. Because they can't protect themselves."

She could sense Shale's confused look at her back as she stalked off into the night.

With a gasp, Galen bolted upright. Then, he immediately fell back onto the pillows. *Bad idea.* He groaned. Everywhere hurt. No, not everywhere. Just his left side. Gingerly he pulled up the blanket covering his bare chest and patted the bandage. He would be okay.

But nothing was really okay.

"Wanna talk about it?"

Galen's head jerked toward the door in surprise. He had thought he was alone in his room in the palace.

Gadiel leaned the chair on its back two legs, his arms crossed over his army uniform, and smugly looked at Galen.

He was pretty much the last person Galen wanted to see. "Not with you," he snapped.

"Oh, well in that case, let me go get one of the dozens of people lining up outside the door to see you." Getting out of the chair, he opened the door wide to reveal the empty hallway beyond. "Hmm. That's weird."

"Ugh. Go away." Galen started to roll over, but his side protested.

"Not until you say thank you."

"What?"

"I know you're probably not used to saying it, so I'll give you a second." Gadiel sat back down in the chair and resumed his former position.

Galen stared at the ceiling. The light in the room told him it was morning. Not only didn't he remember coming back to the palace, he was unsure why they had even been allowed back in.

"How much do you remember, anyway?"

Galen grabbed his side. "Enough," he groaned.

He remembered seeing Daku and the utter joy it had momentarily brought. But from the instant he had started up a conversation, he had realized that something was different about his old friend. Galen hadn't known what it was, but he had been so happy to see him that he didn't think about it. This was Daku, after all. He could overcome anything.

And then Galen remembered the pain. He had not seen the knife, only felt it as it drove into his body. But what he had noticed was the look on Daku's face. It was almost unrecognizable.

"Oh, good," Gadiel's irritating voice interrupted his thoughts. "So you remember the part where I hit your attacker so that he ran away instead of killing you? You remember how I called for help and tore

509

my *own* shirt to stop the bleeding with, or how I helped the doctor bandage you and called a carriage to return us to the palace after my mom cleared it?"

Galen did, having never lost consciousness. But now all he could visualize in his mind was Daku's face. *What would he have done if Gadiel hadn't been there?*

"Because I'm pretty sure all of that counts as me saving your life," Gadiel continued. "Which means my debt to you is paid. So repeat after me: thank you, Gadiel for saving my butt."

"He wasn't going to kill me," was all Galen said.

Recognizing the hurt in Galen's voice, Gadiel dropped his humorous tone. "Hey," he asked more gently, "did you know that guy?"

Galen hesitated. "Please, just leave me alone." He didn't want to talk about it with Gadiel—or anyone else, for that matter. Nor did he wish to think about it anymore. Galen knew the stab wound would heal. But he had suffered a more frightening one. The person he had always looked to as his protector had tried to kill him.

Gadiel sighed. "It's just a flesh wound, Galen. You're not gonna die. I don't know if that guy was trying to mug you or… or what. The tournament brings a lot of crazies every year. But… if you're feeling better, the real reason I came here … we have some unfinished business to take care of."

It hit Galen as hard as when Allora had struck him with a fire poker. He had almost forgotten. *Seff.* What he had done to Allora had been wrong. Galen shoved his own problems aside for the time being.

"Allora … is she …"

Gadiel exhaled. "I don't know. When I came to get you, my mother was headed to the palace, and when I got there with you in the carriage, no one tried to stop us …" His voice trailed off.

"So what then?"

"Well, by the time I came in, the Shepherds had locked themselves in the council room. I was told to go straight to my quarters. I have no idea what happened after we left yesterday."

The news made Galen's heart sink. *Was Allora all right? How long had she been locked in a room with that madman Seff? Had the other Royal Shepherds come to her aid, or did they agree with his methods?* Galen couldn't trust anyone. The palace of Oldaem was a dangerous place.

"And then this morning a messenger came and announced that we were to have an audience with the Royal Shepherds as soon as you awakened."

At this, Galen did sit upright. "They want to speak with *us?* Specifically? About what?"

"About yesterday, I assume," Gadiel surmised. "We kind of physically attacked a Royal ... well, an Interim Royal Shepherd."

"But it will give us a chance to tell them what happened if they don't already know, right?"

Gadiel shrugged. "There's only one way to find out." But he looked nervous. And Galen felt the same way. Still, he would rather face this situation than stay in this room thinking about his encounter with Daku.

"Then what are we waiting for?" Galen shrugged on a new green shirt since his old one was ruined and splashed water from the basin onto his face. Although he felt weak, he didn't want to appear that way in front of the Shepherds. He needed to be able to defend the Princess of Leoj. *What a strange few months it's been.*

Galen had never been in a great meeting hall before. It seemed more unassuming than he expected. An empty throne was the only touch of royal splender. But he could feel the power inside the room, not radiating from the walls or tapestries, but from the men sitting at the wooden table.

Royal Shepherd Udina stood. "Please, take a seat." He gestured to two chairs at the end of the table.

Galen could feel Shepherd Seff's glare. He glared back. Each of the Royal Shepherds seemed on edge.

"I hear you had an interesting day out in the Capital, yesterday." Shepherd Garrus directed the comment at Galen. "I trust you're feeling alright now."

"I'm fine." Galen answered curtly. He debated whether to continue. *Now might be my only chance.* "At the moment I'm more concerned with Princess Allora's well-being."

"That is, in fact, the reason you are here," Zorah said quietly.

"We were kicked out of the palace yesterday," Gadiel interjected.

"You attacked a Royal Shepherd, boy." The first time Seff had spoken, his voice was a low growl. "You're lucky you didn't receive worse punishment."

"You're *not* a Royal Shepherd," Gadiel mentioned for the umpteenth time. "Am I the only one that hasn't forgotten that?"

511

"We only did that because he attacked the princess!" Galen interrupted.

"I did no such thing," Seff countered.

"Liar!" Galen gave Seff his full attention. "We saw you! Both of us! You hit her. You choked her. Who knows what you did after your men pulled us out of the room!" As Galen stood up, he saw the guards in the corners of the room inch a bit closer. *Let them come.*

"Soldier!" Shepherd Udina rose as well. "I believe you are mistaken in what you saw. Any injuries Princess Allora may have sustained during her stay here can be accounted for by a nasty fall she took down the stairs yesterday. That is all."

For a moment, Galen just stared, dumfounded. *Is that seriously the story they're going with?* At least it sounded as if the injuries she had sustained were not life threatening.

Gadiel was the first to respond. "We know what we saw." He looked at Shepherd Garrus. "What is this? Are you all lying for Seff now?"

"We are protecting the crown," Garrus said, jaws clenched.

Galen was new to palace politics, but he thought he understood this one. Shepherds Garrus, Zorah, and even Udina did not look as if they expected for a moment that Galen and Gadiel would believe their ridiculous lie. But although what Seff had done was outside of their consent, they had not been made aware in time to stop it and now had to deal with the repercussions. *They're just trying to clean up his mess.*

"I won't lie about this." Gadiel shook his head emphatically.

"We don't need you to lie, we just need you to stand there," Seff said, the oily tone back in his voice.

"What are you talking about?"

Shepherd Garrus cleared his throat. "There have been some, ah, rumors going on about the treatment of our Leojian guest. We need to put them to rest. So, per order of the king, Princess Allora will attend the final event of the tournament tomorrow."

"What does that have to do with us?" Galen asked suspiciously, although he had a feeling he already knew the answer.

"Because you're going to guard her," Udina answered.

That's what he had been afraid of. "Why us? Out of all your trusted palace guards, why would you pick us?" There had to be a catch.

"She trusts you two," Royal Shepherd Zorah stated.

512

"And if you lose her," Shepherd Seff grinned, "your lives will be forfeit."

Galen and Gadiel exchanged glances. They didn't exactly have a great record with this sort of thing.

"You can't do that." Gadiel's voice was stony. "We won't go."

Shepherd Garrus looked carefully at Gadiel. Then he said, "Either you do what we tell you, or we arrest you right now for the assault of a Royal Shepherd. Maybe even conspiracy against the king."

Galen's breathing caught. *So that's what this is. Blackmail.*

"Are we clear?" Shepherd Udina asked. The palace guards inched even closer, ready to strike if Galen or Gadiel gave the wrong answer. Galen had been wrong about all of them. The Royal Shepherds were like four heads of the same snake.

He was getting tired of being used. It had not been his choice to embark on the journey to Leoj, and now it was not his choice to help these people cover up a lie. People took advantage of him all the time because he was unimportant, because he was disposable. While he was determined to stop the cycle, he couldn't yet. For now, he had to bite back his pride. *Just one more time.* And after this, no more. Then he would take control of his own destiny.

Gadiel's voice trembled with rage. "My father would never use people like this."

"And clearly he's paying for that with his life," Shepherd Udina spat back.

With a growl Gadiel lunged across the table. But the palace guards got to him first and pulled his arms back in restraint. Galen had sat watching silently from his chair. While he was not the calculating type, at the moment his chief concern was how to keep Allora safe. If guarding her was the only way to do that, then so be it. He couldn't do a lot of protecting from behind a jail cell. "Fine," he said. "On the condition that you don't hurt her anymore."

Every Shepherd looked down except for Seff. "Fine," he echoed. It was as much an admission of guilt as Galen was likely to get.

"Gadiel?" Garrus asked.

His lips compressed in a thin line, Gadiel nodded. But his silence spoke more than words.

Before they picked up Princess Allora at her room, Galen was not sure what to expect. Finally though, she came out wearing a bright blue dress. It reminded him of the one she had been wearing when they had first met. He also saw why the official story was that she had fallen down a flight of stairs.

Most of the left side of her face was a light purple tint. Her eye was swollen, and she had a nasty cut above her eyebrow that had long since stopped bleeding, but looked as if it could break open at any time. Galen seethed when he saw Seff's workmanship. It was easy to see Allora's injuries up close, but the heavy make up and thick headband she was wearing would lessen the effect from a distance. *Because she fell down the stairs.*

Allora did seem glad to see them, though. She didn't say anything in earshot of the palace, but once they had safely left the grounds and the carriage that drove them to the arena had long since disappeared, she let out a tired groan.

"Are you alright?" Galen reached for her shoulder.

"I'm fine," she nodded. "Nothing I can't handle."

"What he did to you was wrong," Gadiel stated. "It may not mean anything to you now, but on the behalf of the real Royal Shepherd of Defense, I apologize." It was probably the nicest thing he had ever said to her.

"You know, Gadiel, you're not such a bad guy. I understand why you were mad at me when we first met. I mean, I tried to kill you. But I accept your apology."

Suddenly Galen didn't care about the consequences. She did not deserve what had happened to her. Already the majority of her family had been killed and she had been forcefully taken to a foreign land. Galen could not bear to play a role in it any longer. He hated being a pawn. "Leave," he whispered. "Just go, Allora. We won't try to stop you this time."

Allora looked at him sadly, and then to Gadiel. "Thank you, but no," she shook her head. "They told me the consequences of doing that, too. I'll find another way."

Then she lifted her head high and confidently as they stood at the entrance of the arena. Even despite the bruises, Galen thought she was the most beautiful woman he had ever seen. "Now," she looked at her guards, "let's go put on a show."

CHAPTER 64: SAYLA

Somehow she had ended up sitting next to Shale, something that did not please Sayla the way it would have a few months ago. Instead, she was willing to rip her ears off if she could avoid hearing one more self-righteous speech out of him.

They were watching the Spirit competition, a talent show. It was the last day of the tournament, warm and bright. Luckily, any Shepherd Trainees currently attending an academy received seats of honor under a covered canopy in the middle of the stands. She sat with the rest of the students from Woodlands Academy. Across the stadium she could see an identical canopy that she knew sheltered those from Westpoint, and to her left were the students of Middle Lake. Sayla could make out a few familiar faces, but most of those who had participated in her tournament were no longer in the program.

And of course, to her right was a private section reserved for the Royal family or the Royal Shepherds should they choose to attend an event. So far the box had been unusually empty, although there were a few people there today. *Probably the family of one of the Royal Shepherds.* It certainly wasn't the king.

Sayla turned her attention back to the events of the competition. Currently a strong, muscular boy was doing some pretty impressive shirtless pushups. The female judges certainly seemed to be paying full attention.

Sayla rested her elbow on the cushioned armrest and her head on her hand.

"Pshaw, I can do better than that." Shale unwittingly pushed her arm away as he leaned on the armrest. "I'd like to see him do that with one hand behind his back."

As if on cue, the contestant started doing one-armed pushups. The crowd went wild.

"His form is all wrong," Shale assured her as he attempted for the third time that day to put his arm around her. She dodged it as she had all the others.

Sayla already knew that the contestant's form was off. Clearly the youth lacked any type of professional training. It reminded Sayla of a time when she had been young and naïve, long before her tournament days.

"Push-up contest!" she had suddenly screamed at Daku and Galen, jumping off of the rope swing she had been playing on. They were by a small stream just a little ways outside of Aramoor. During springtime it was one of her favorite spots in the whole world. That day was the first time she and Daku had deemed their new friend, Galen, worthy to see it. A creek ran among the trees, just deep enough to swim in. Daku had made a little wooden swing above it so they could get a running start and jump into the stream.

"What do you mean push-up contest?" Galen asked lazily, lounging on his back in the shaded grass. "Why do we always have to be doing something? Why can't we just look at the clouds?"

Daku chuckled, his brown eyes dancing. "You just gotta get used to her. She's a whirlwind."

"A whirlwind who can beat you at push-ups!" Sayla tackled Daku to the ground.

Laughing, he gently pushed her off. "How about you challenge someone closer to your own size?"

The girl thought it was a brilliant idea. She plopped next to Galen, straightened her shoulders, and said in her most regal voice, "I challenge you, sir, to a duel of the muscles!"

"I'm taller than you!" he protested.

"Oh, so you're afraid of me."

"No, I don't want to hurt your feelings."

"I'm not some baby, I'm practically ten-years-old!"

"You're six," Daku corrected.

"I said practically!"

"That gives me two years more muscles than you," Galen said.

"Then what are you so afraid of?"

"I told you. I am too awesome. I would destroy you, and you would go crying home to your mommy, because you would be so afraid of my amazing strength." A smiled played at the corners of Galen's mouth.

"Right, and that's why we found you all afraid in that alley with like six *slaves* beating you up." Sayla laughed. But she was the only one who did.

Galen's smile disappeared.

Daku immediately sat up. "Bug, what did I tell you about saying things like that?"

Sayla realized her mistake. For the first time she began to sense something beneath his smug exterior. "I wasn't trying to be mean. I'm sorry."

Galen studied her for a moment, then, to her relief, he rolled over onto his stomach and lifted his arms. "So, push up contest, huh?"

516

Later, Sayla always told Galen that she let him win that day, because she felt sorry for him.

He had never believed her.

They had always had a unique understanding of each other. Although were quite different in many ways, circumstances had united them into a tightly knit friendship. Really, it was Daku who had brought them together. Sayla still felt a dull ache when she thought about the day he left with his wife. *What was her name?* She had seemed nice enough. That made the pain even harder to bear.

But he had told her to take care of Galen. Even though he might be older, she was much more motivated and stable. And she had taken care of him—for a while. While she had left just like everybody else, she had known what she was doing and had done it anyway. *I can't just put my life on hold for you,* she had thought. Now she wondered if it might have been the most important part of her life that she had set aside.

Shale giggled and jerked Sayla back to reality. "This girl is so dumb. I mean if it's a comedy routine she's going for... Well, mission accomplished." He tried to put his arm around Sayla again. Again, she artfully dodged him and leaned closer to Tali on the left.

The girl he was speaking of was the Candidate currently on stage. She was trying to tell a joke or something, but it was falling flat. Not only wasn't it funny, it actually was sad. Sayla looked at Shale in disgust. *How could I ever have fallen for him?* But as she watched Shale compliment himself on how great he had been during his Shepherd tournament, she saw something she hadn't realized before.

For the first time Sayla realized why he had so attracted her. *He reminds me of Galen.* Galen had always been known for having an overconfident aura about him. People that didn't know him as well as she did tended to dislike him. Terrible at creating good first impressions, he would always speak his mind and promote himself.

But there was a fundamental difference between the two. Before, Sayla had been blinded by Shale's looks and popularity. And he did have a certain charm. But now she saw something else. "You're an idiot," she told him matter of factly.

Shale tore his attention away from the talent show. "I ... what?"

Tali, who was sitting on the other side of Sayla, stared at her in surprise, then pretended not to be listening.

"You heard me. I mean, you might not understand what such complicated words mean, but you definitely heard me."

Shale didn't know what to say. "You mean idiot in, like, an attractive sort of way, right?"

It was as if Sayla had opened a door that now she could not close. "No. I mean that you can't see past your own reflection in the mirror. That you think you're the most amazing person to ever walk in Oldaem. Yeah, you have the knack for being a Shepherd of Defense, and you're really attractive. But what good is it all if you're using that for the wrong reasons? For a long time I was doing the same thing with my own talents. Or even pretending I didn't have them so that I could fit in. So *you* would accept me. But I don't need your acceptance."

His face darkened. "What are you saying?"

"Well, first of all, it's over between us. Whatever *it* was." Sayla was pretty sure all their relationship had consisted of were the two of them coming up with new ways to admire Shale. "And second, you need to realize how shallow you are. I don't know if there's anything more to you than what I can see right now, but for your sake, I really hope there is. Nobody needs to get stuck with someone as superficial as you. I like your confidence. But you're like a tree without roots." Finally she took a breath. "And, well, I'd rather be with someone who's maybe less confident, but full of perseverance."

Suddenly, Sayla felt a red blush crawling up her face. While she had spoken rather quietly, she worried the other trainees had heard her. In the heat of the moment she had forgotten where she was. Tali stared straight ahead, but with an expression of shock on her face.

"I'm gonna walk around a bit," Sayla managed to say as she hastily left.

She wandered around, just following the flow of the crowd as they strolled around the large stadium. Some kid down on the stage was making a speech or something. Before she knew it, she had gone almost a quarter of the way around the arena. Sayla glanced back to see the Woodlands Academy section a ways off into the distance. By now she was nearly at the portion of the arena reserved for members of the royal court and a sense of curiosity filled her. *I wonder which Royal Shepherd's family is here today.* She had only ever met one Royal Shepherd, and it had caused her a lot more stress than she preferred.

Sayla waded through the throngs of people, trying to catch a glimpse. As she got closer, she could make out two men and a woman.

518

Wait. Something seemed familiar about the man nearest her. She squinted, trying to see more clearly. The curled hair around the ears. The slouching posture. The shape of his face.

Galen? Impossible. He's in Sea Fort. Isn't he? She had to get closer. *Maybe there was some reason ... maybe he had been here, and that's why he hadn't met me at the pier. What is he doing in the Capital?* The closer she got, the more sure she became.

Sayla smiled. Maybe this was a sign. Maybe this was why she had felt so lost recently, because she was meant to fit in with *him*—that *he* was the person she needed most. Her pace quickened.

Then, the person next to him leaned forward.

Sayla stopped dead in her tracks. The beautiful woman leaned her head on Galen's shoulder, and he took her arm protectively. Gently. Lovingly.

Oh, was all she could think. *That's why he's here.* It almost felt like Daku leaving all over again. Although she had finally acknowledged her feelings for him, it was now too late.

She wasn't sure what she had been hoping would happen with Galen–they hadn't seen each other in two years. But she saw him smiling with the gorgeous, possibly royal, auburn-haired woman next to him, and Sayla knew it was too late. Again.

CHAPTER 65: GALEN

Galen abruptly jerked up in his seat. "Hey, that's that kid!" He pointed at the contestant currently taking the stage, pulling a girl up with him. It was getting to be a very interesting competition. For a few moments Galen could imagine that maybe he and Allora and Gadiel were just three regular people on an outing to see the tournament.

"What kid?" Allora asked rapidly. She had already been staring intently at the center of the arena.

"The guy from Kaya," Galen explained. "His group stayed in our inn?" Gadiel and Allora gave him blank expressions. "I think his name is Ian? Yeah, that sounds right. He looks skinnier now. They were headed here, too, and got stuck in the same storm as us."

"Shh, I'm trying to listen," Allora hushed him.

Galen turned back to the Spirit competition.

Ian was saying something. "Maybe it was all fun and games to you. Maybe it even meant nothing to you. Or was just a form of entertainment. But as someone who has gone through this all of his life . . . it made me . . . sad." The audience had gone still. "You see, I don't see this as how Shepherds should act. And maybe . . . maybe I don't know, because I'm not a Shepherd. But I think a Shepherd, especially a Spirit Shepherd, should build people up . . . not tear them down."

Well, clearly he hasn't met any real Shepherds. From what Galen had seen, they were probably all corrupt. If the Royal Shepherds, the heads of the whole system, were that malicious and manipulative, maybe the entire organization was worthless. Maybe even all of Oldaem.

Galen had a pretty realistic view of the world, yet even he had been surprised by the lack of morals in the palace.

Allora let out a faint gasp.

Gadiel asked, "Are you alright?"

Her face was pale. "I have a bit of a headache. The sun isn't helping." No wonder she had a headache with all those bruises on her face, Galen thought, promising himself that if he ever got the chance, he would give Shepherd Seff much more than a headache to complain about.

Without asking Allora carefully laid her head on Galen's shoulder. Goosebumps crawled up his arm where her hair touched. He hoped she didn't notice. Gently he reassuringly placed his hand over hers. Galen knew what it felt like to be alone and abandoned.

A strange sensation shot up Galen's spine. Why did he have the feeling that he was being watched? In a moment of panic he feared that maybe someone from the palace had changed his mind and sent guards to arrest him. He quickly scanned the arena around him.

At that moment the crowd burst into cheers. Several people stood up clapping. Allora was one of them, a big smile on her face. But Galen was too busy searching the crowd for any soldiers. Instead, he spotted a girl in a black Defense uniform, not clapping or cheering, but instead staring straight at him. The look of surprise on her own face must have mirrored his own.

Sayla.

How? How could the three of them be in the same city at the same time? What were the odds of Galen seeing Daku one day and Sayla the next when he hadn't encountered either of them in years?

Oldaem was huge, and they each had gone their separate ways. What a strange coincidence. *What if it's not?*

Galen didn't want to think about that possibility. That maybe there was someone pulling strings in his life, using him as a puppet the way the Lameans believed. Enough people had already manipulated him for their own purposes. He didn't need some deity doing the same. It risked toppling everything he had built for himself in his own little world.

But Galen believed in what he could see. And right now he saw Sayla. And suddenly nothing else mattered.

He charged for the aisle. "Hey! Where are you going?" he heard Gadiel shout.

"I'll be right back," he managed to reply as he left.

She hadn't moved from the spot where he had first seen her.

People milled all around them, but as Galen approached he saw only her. He stopped about three feet in front of her.

"Hey, stranger," she said.

"I'm sorry I didn't meet you at the pier," Galen said. "I wanted to. But I couldn't."

Sayla swallowed and nodded her head faintly. "I understand." Her eyes flicked to the stands where he had been sitting moments ago. "Things come up."

Galen stared into her beautiful green eyes for a moment, and she gazed back. Then they embraced. A feeling of calm and relief flooded over him as if he had been stuck in a raging storm and finally found land. A sense of rightness. A sense of home.

Finally, he pulled back. "You're taller."

"You're fatter." She punched his flat stomach.

"What are you doing here? I can't believe it. It's been so long."

"What am *I* doing here? I'm here every year! What are *you* doing here? I thought you were in Sea Fort. You must've been there if you got my letter." Again she glanced at where he had been sitting.

Realizing where she was looking, he figured she must have been wondering what he was doing in the section reserved for members of the palace. "Oh, yeah. Um, it's because ..." It occurred to him that maybe seeing Sayla created a perfect opportunity. He could tell her everything that was going on and maybe she knew someone that could do something about it. He could trust her.

But he had trusted Daku, too.

That's different, Galen reminded himself. Something was wrong with Daku. But he couldn't throw his burdens on her. Sayla was now

521

a member of the Shepherd system, the same group of people who had hurt Allora and, Galen suspected, were framing Leoj.

But he could trust her. It was Sayla.

Galen realized he had been silent for too long. "It's because I've been doing some work here. For the tournament." *Why had he lied?*

Sayla looked doubtful. "During a war?"

He shrugged. "What can I say? The tournament is a big deal."

"I guess."

"Well, what have you been up to? Enjoying your fourth year of training?"

Sayla appeared indecisive for a moment. "It's been great. I absolutely love it. It's where I belong."

Galen had always known she had what it took to become a Shepherd. But he wondered if she believed what she was saying.

"So, you're doing well, then," he pressed. Something was bothering her.

"Yep. Absolutely nothing out of the ordinary worth mentioning."

"Same."

"Great." She managed a smile.

Why is this conversation so awkward?

Galen wanted nothing more than to tell her everything. All those nights on the ship when he had longed for someone to talk to came rushing back. But he couldn't bring himself to relate to her the things he had done and experienced. The fear. The guilt. Apparently doing well, she didn't need him anymore.

"Have you heard from Daku at all?"

The question caught him off guard. Of course she would ask. Hadn't Galen asked Daku the same thing?

Galen clutched his side where the wound still burned. He had to protect Sayla. She didn't need to know. It would break her heart all over again, and she seemed to be doing all right now.

"No," he lied. "Have … have you?" Cold fear washed over him as he realized it was possible she had already encountered him in his changed state. Or maybe she would run into him while they were all still in Oldaem Realm.

"No," she shook her head. "I've wanted to write to him, too, but I don't even know where he is."

"Sometimes it's better not to think about it." Galen gently touched her shoulder. She needed to stay far away from Daku, but he couldn't explain why.

"Yeah, you've mentioned that before." Sayla smiled with her mouth, but her eyes told an entirely different story. One that he did not understand.

"Well, it's as true now as it was the first time I told you." He looked back at the royal canopy. Gadiel was glaring at him. "I better go." He wanted so badly to stay, to fix whatever had come between them.

Sayla looked at him. "Will you be around for a couple more days? It would be ... nice to see you again before I leave for Woodlands."

"I'll be heading back to Sea Fort," he said more severely than he meant it. He had no idea if that was actually true. "But if you ever need anything, you can find me there. I promise I'll come next time."

"Deal." She hugged him once more, and he hugged back, wishing he never had to let go. But he had a pressing matter to deal with here–one that didn't involve Sayla.

Sayla turned to go, then paused. "Hey, Galen."

He stopped.

"Um, I have a weird question to ask you. But it'll bother me forever if I don't ask it now."

He went back to her. She looked almost fearful. "Go ahead."

"If you were to, say, feel obligated to ... oh I don't know ... protect someone ... or maybe a group of people ... who were defenseless ... who would they be?" She awkwardly tugged at a loose strand of hair falling out of the bun on her head.

But Galen had an answer. "People who are innocent and wrongfully accused."

Sayla looked kind of green. "I thought you'd say something like that."

"Why do you ask?" There was definitely something she wasn't telling him.

"Just wondering," she sighed. "Also, watch out for fire pokers." She disappeared into the crowd before he could ask her if it was that obvious that he had been hit in the head with one just a couple months before.

As soon as she left, Galen felt her absence. Hopefully someday, after all this was over, he and Sayla and maybe even Daku would be able to sit down together and laugh and catch up. *Someday.* Galen hoped that someday was soon. But he had a sinking feeling it would never happen.

CHAPTER 66: IAN

"3 . . . 2 . . . 1 . . . Go!"

As Ian ripped off his blindfold he heard an explosion. Disoriented and confused as light blinded him, he tried to get his bearings. All around him he could hear shouting and screaming and the cheers of the crowd. His competitors were running toward something, or maybe those were his allies. He couldn't be sure. All he knew was that the Defense Competition had begun, and he was already losing it.

Hurridly glancing around the arena, he saw several large, clearly artificial mounds. Rough barriers dotted the floor of the arena. Behind him and toward the corner he saw an iron jail cell. Standing there in front of it was a competitor just like him, wearing a red feather in her hair, and red paint on her face. She also had paint smattered around her wrists. Quickly checking himself, he saw the same color around his own.

She's on my team. Suddenly a competitor in blue rushed up a mound in front of him. Immediately two red team members tackled him and hauled him to the jail behind Ian. He noticed the person in blue bleeding as he went.

Looks like it hurt.

However, he couldn't see the opposing team's jail cell, where he imagined he would wind up if he attempted to run up one of their hills. The thought of all that racing around had him already tired.

Suddenly he heard someone shouting at him. "Glet haer flug!"

The cheering was so loud around him, and he was still so disoriented he couldn't understand what they were shouting.

"What?" Ian shouted back.

The muscular guy in red rolled his eyes, ran towards Ian, placed his hands on his shoulders, shook him, and shouted, "Get their flag!" He was pointing now to the farthest mound at the opposite end of the arena. At its summit was a blue flag. And standing before the flagpole, even from this far away Ian could tell, was no one other than the massive individual who slept a few bunks away from him. Ian swallowed and imagined being tackled by him.

That would really hurt.

His teammate immediately darted to his right as Ian looked up and saw boulders tumbling right toward them. Ian jumped out of the way and rolled just in time to avoid being smashed. Ian wondered how heavy those boulders were. His fellow teammate leaped to his feet, dodging more boulders and ripping his shirt off in the process. The crowd went wild.

Of course. Another would-be Bumo.

Ian looked around. It seemed that besides him and the massive guy, everyone else in the game was slim and muscular. People were tackling each other, freeing each other from jail, picking up random weapons in the arena, and doing battle with each other. Some were bleeding, others laughing or even crying, and the crowd loved it. Ian noticed both flags were still flying high, and he also realized that except for dodging the one boulder, he himself still hadn't moved.

Come on, Ian. This is what you signed up for. You want to be a Shepherd of Defense! Show them how it's done!

He started running toward the hill with the flag, then stopped. *Wait.*

The artificial terrain created especially for the event was rough, and it seemed no matter where he ran, he had to go up some sort of slope. But he wasn't as winded as he would have been before the weeks of training. He decided to study all his teammates and their opponents before rushing into something he wasn't prepared for.

He counted seven blue team members, though he didn't know any of them personally except for the biggest one, and that was only because he had heard him snoring like a savage beast every night. Jib wasn't a huge fan of his. But then he wasn't a fan of anyone.

He looked around his own team, and started counting. Besides the shirtless wonder, there was a pretty fast and agile girl who was guarding their flag. He figured she would do a good job and remembered that she had won most of the foot races they had had during training. He was number three. At that moment he noticed two team members on the blue side collide and imagined that they would both have very bad headaches from now on. Then he resumed counting his teammates: "four . . . five . . . six . . . wait . . . is it seven to six? Where is number seven?" He could not find their seventh member, and for a while, wondered if it was an uneven match. Also he realized that if he didn't get in the game soon, he would have an incredibly low Defense score. Sucking in the much smaller gut he had now, he started toward the opponent's mound.

As his eyes scanned it, he noticed that besides Jib there were two others playing defense on the blue team. There was no way he could sneak up there. They would see him coming and would definitely outrun him. Suddenly more boulders began to rain down on them, and Ian rolled out of the way once again.

Where are those boulders coming from?

For the first time he scanned the edges of the arena. Spread in a circle, along the walls of the arena, various obstacles lined the sides, diminishing the size of the playing field.

Strange.

Ian started walking toward his left. As he did he felt the ground underneath him start to change. They had been playing on some sort of grasslike matting, but as he neared the sides of the area, he noticed the matting seemed to disappear, replaced by soft dirt. In front of him he noticed a long barrier, maybe limestone. It had no door in it, and its purpose was unclear, except for making the arena smaller. About seven or eight feet tall, it almost made a wall as it circled the arena. Its height seemed to vary. Ian leaned against it.

What is this for?

As he returned to his team's territory he heard cheers and shouts from the audience. What must the judges have thought as they watched him walk around the wall with his right hand running along the length of it?

Finally he reached an area of more barricades that almost formed a square while blocking any view of one section of the wall except when standing inside of the barrier. Noticing an opening in the square, he entered it. Once inside, he saw another opening, this one in the ground.

The hole was quite large, and he briefly wondered if it was some underground dwelling for some monster that would soon emerge and kill them all, then rejected the idea as silly. Still . . . it was suspicious. As he realized he would never run up that hill and face Jib directly, and he wasn't fast enough to chase someone down, he decided to check out whatever might be down there. Dropping into the hole, he started inching along the passage it led into.

The smell of dirt and worms filled his nostrils. It wasn't a very long passage. He could hear the muffled shouts and screams of the crowd as he crawled. The tunnel dipped down for a bit, and then as it sloped back up again, he noticed light beginning to grow in front of him. *How can there be light underground?* As he neared the light the dirt beneath him turned into something harder. *Limestone? . . . I'm inside the wall? It's not a wall! It's a tunnel! How could no one see this hole?*

Now able to stand up, he increased his pace. Lanterns hung along the wall every few paces. As he started to run through the tunnel, he realized that it must lead into the territory of the opposing team.

Would it take him directly to their flag? His heart started racing as he ran. Although his feet made clopping noises like that of a fat horse, he didn't care. He had figured out something no one else had noticed. Suddenly, as the tunnel curved to the right, he realized he must be in enemy territory. If there was an entrance on his side, there must be one for them too. Deciding that he had better be careful, he began to walk softly. He wasn't sure what he would do if he encountered someone. Perhaps he would directly charge the person and knock them unconscious. *Violent.* The thought made him uncomfortable.

Stop! You want to be a Defense Shepherd! Imagine you're defending your family, and not a flag! With that thought he sped up again.

Suddenly he came face to face with a ladder. Ian started climbing it, wondering where it could lead. *Hopefully to victory.* After going up about 10 rungs, he stepped out on a wooden platform. As he paused on the platform, he realized he was still beneath ground . . . or perhaps beneath a hill . . . and before him stood a metal pole . . . and attached to the pole was some sort of wheel. When he began to turn the wheel to the left he noticed the pole began to slide downward.

I'm lowering their flag pole!

Muffled screams and shouts filtered down the opening the flag pole had extended through. A broad smile spread across his face as he spun the wheel. Before he knew it, the blue flag was in his hands.

Now I have to get back! And fast! They'll be trying to figure out how to get down here.

Instantly he slid down the ladder, skinning his hands in the process. Then turning to the left, he raced down the corridor.

I got it! I've won for my team! I never imagined I could do it! I thought I was too fat, too useless! Just a crab trying to be a fish! Praise the Tide and the Rock! Someone is looking out for me!

Tears filled his eyes as he ran. He had never gone so fast in his life. As he ran he was racing toward that ferry, and making it . . . as he ran he was outdistancing Bumo, . . . he was running after Allora, and catching up with her, taking her hand and . . . no . . . Liarra . . . *ugh* . . . it didn't matter . . . he smiled . . . and wiped a tear away . . . he was *good* enough . . .

Now he could see the entrance to the passageway ahead of him and knew the tunnel was off to his left. In his mind he could see the finish line. It was right there.

And then he stopped dead in his tracks.

Standing before him . . . blocking the corridor was Wrexa, the seventh member of his team. She was crying.

"Wrexa . . ." He stopped, panting. "What's wrong with you? I've got the flag!"

"Cuz-Cuz . . . what you do down here?"

"I found this tunnel!"

"Me, too." She plopped down and began to cry again.

"Are you okay?" He knelt down. "Are you hurt?"

"Yes." She sniffled. "Inside."

"What do you mean?" *I need to run, anyone could be coming at any second.*

"Everyone is brave. Helen . . . you . . . Bumo . . . who is cute boy . . . even Alala . . . but Wrexa . . . Wrexa is a scardy-sea lion."

"Why do you call yourself a scardy-sea lion?"

"Because I am! *I came down here to hide because I was scared!*" she sobbed.

Ian wanted to dart past her, to win for his team. But his cousin, part of his *family,* was sad. And Ian knew what it felt like to be sad and not to be noticed. He remembered the barking dog. With a sigh he sat down beside her, the flag in his lap.

"What are you afraid of?"

"Losing. Dying. Never being loved."

I hear you there.

"Fat girls want love too," she bawled.

"Who do you like?"

"Bumo."

Of course. Ian smiled and shook his head. *Well if Helen had a chance . . .* "Have you told him?"

"No. Too scared."

"I get scared, too. Life can be really scary, can't it?"

"Yeah. DON'T TELL I CRY LIKE A SEA TURTLE STUCK IN SEA WEED! I'LL SMASH FACE WITH FIST!"

He smiled. "I won't. I promise."

"Also . . ." she sniffled, "I can't win. I can't win anything. I lose every game we play."

"You've lost everything?" He hadn't heard how she had done so far.

"Yes!" she wiped her nose. "And . . . I have family secret." She was whispering now. Ian had lean to closer.

"More . . . secrets?"

"Yes! More!"

"What is it?"

"This will shock cousin, I think . . ." She cupped her hand around her mouth and placed it against his ear. "I can't see too good."

She was crying again, as Ian put his arm around her. He didn't know what to say to her. But he realized, sometimes people just wanted someone to listen. So he listened to her . . . and he also listened to the thunder of footsteps running toward him in the corridor.

"Ian?"

"Hey, Bumo," Ian said with a smile. Bumo looked exhausted. He hadn't seen him since the blindfold had been put on his face.

"We won," Bumo smiled broadly. "I found the flag!"

"I expected nothing less of you."

"Liarra and I did."

"You were on the same team *again?*"

"I know, crazy right? Luck of the random draw."

It was another reception for the tournament Candidates. They only had one more event to go, and it would be tomorrow. Then Ian would compete in the Spirit Competition and perform his talent . . . whatever that was. Ian looked around at everybody. Although everyone else had dressed up, he continued to wear his standard uniform.

"Why don't you dress up for these things?" Bumo asked, the top four buttons of his shirt undone.

"I dunno."

"I heard Wrexa won it for your team! That's awesome! She came out of some tunnel or something waving the flag. I sure didn't use a tunnel," Bumo said, flexing his muscles.

"Yeah it was pretty wonderful to see her win it all for us."

"Can you believe it all ends tomorrow?"

"No, I really can't." Ian thought of how they had gone swimming the night he decided to gather up the courage to ask his family if he could attend the tournament. They had been friends for so long that Ian knew exactly what Bumo was thinking. Bumo was nervous. Bumo was excited. And Bumo was thinking about girls.

"Jessica is upset."

Knew it.

"Really, why?"

"I guess some of the other girls have been giving her a hard time. Like, they don't get why she's here. She hasn't done too well."

"Ah, I'm sorry to hear that."

"Yeah . . . I don't really know what to say to help her . . . I mean . . . I've been doing . . . well . . . a perfect job . . . so it's kind of awkward."

"Maybe she just wants you to listen?"

"I hear people making fun of her all the time. I know she's really nervous about the Spirit Competition . . . I guess her talent is . . . telling jokes . . . and she's pretty terrible. We're only given one minute each to impress . . . my talent is shirtless pushups . . . that *always* impresses . . . but Jessica can't do that."

"No . . . no . . . she sure can't." *I don't even know what I'm going to do yet . . .*

"She's been . . . getting kind of annoying."

"Bumo . . . that's not nice . . . you've been pretty close to her this whole time . . ."

"Yeah . . . but everything is almost over."

"So?"

"So . . . we're almost over."

Ian looked at him and realized that Jessica would be Bumo's next cast-aside, and he hurt for her already.

That night Ian had a nightmare. Before he drifted off to sleep he thought about all that he could do for his talent. Nothing came to mind. He could eat a lot, could gut fish. Maybe he could even juggle two fish at a time . . . he couldn't sing . . . he was tone deaf . . . nor could he paint or draw or dance or tell jokes or do shirtless pushups.

That night, Ian dreamed of himself doing shirtless pushups with everyone laughing at him.

Ian sat in the rows of competitors as each one got their minute of fame. Some sang beautifully, others danced. One competitor sewed together a pillow in exactly one minute. Delia the Tournament Mistress continued to host and continued to crack herself up. A panel of judges sat off to the right on the stage. After the competitors performed, they would stand before the judges to receive public scrutiny or praise. Mostly the judges were nice. One judge always had something negative to say, but nothing too harsh.

Wrexa asked for four child volunteers from the stands, and then lifted them up and down like weights. That seemed to impress the crowd.

And then it came to Jessica's turn . . .

As soon as she started walking toward the stands, Ian could hear snickering behind him. It upset him. No one deserved to be mocked. Everyone should have their chance.

"Shhhhh!" he snapped, but they only laughed louder.

As Jessica climbed the steps, he noticed her skirt was a bit too short and had ridden up her legs. The girls pointed and chortled again. Ian shook his head.

These are potential Shepherds? Ridiculous.

Ian could see fear in Jessica's face, although she tried to mask it with forced confidence. He could also tell she had been crying not too long ago. As she took the megaphone in her hands, Delia eyed her and reminded the crowd she had one minute to impress, then counted her down. Jessica stood there frozen. Finally she mustered up some courage.

"W . . . why is the . . . ocean blue?"

Ian could hear an awkward hush fall upon the crowd. As he continued to hear the mockery behind him, he balled his hand into a fist.

"Because all the little fish go blu, blu blu."

No one laughed. The judges rolled their eyes, even the nice one.

She continued. "Uhh . . . w . . . why did the skeleton go to the party alone?"

"You suck," someone shouted.

"B . . . because he had no body to go with him . . ."

"Does she have to use the whole minute?" one of the judges said clearly into her megaphone. The crowd erupted in laughter.

"*She's* the best joke of the day," another judge added.

Delia came from behind, and whispered in Jessica's ear. The girl looked horrified as she quickly adjusted her skirt.

"What makes her think she could be a Shepherd? She's a joke. She's been a joke this whole time," someone whispered behind Ian.

"How did she even make the cut?"

"She's been terrible from the beginning."

"No one takes her seriously."

"W . . . w . . . why do milking stools only h . . . have three legs?"

"Here we go," another person muttered.

"Because the . . . cow's got . . . the 'udder.'"

531

"She's the cow," a girl boomed behind Ian. And they all erupted in laughter.

The judge stood up. "Thank you! Minute is done."

"B . . . but . . . it's only been 30 seconds . . ." Jessica said nervously.

"Wait . . ." The judge stood there with a smirk on his face in silence while Jessica looked at him in confusion. He paused for several seconds. "*Now* the minute is done." Everyone cheered and laughed and Delia ushered Jessica off the stage. The girl looked horrified as she took her seat. Ian could tell that she was barely holding herself together.

"It's all in good fun, now," Delia said, trying to ease any tension there may have been. "We love all of our competitors."

But it wasn't fun . . . and it wasn't enough. He had heard the fat jokes one too many times. While he had seen people attempt to put band-aids over their words, it never stopped the bleeding. He was tired of it all. What had happened had been a disgrace to the name of Shepherd.

"Aupaiano of Lion's Landing," Delia cried out.

People started clapping, and as he rose, he heard snickering in the back again. He left behind the basket of fish he had planned to juggle. It wasn't his talent. And though he still didn't know what it was, he did know what he had to do now.

Heading toward Jessica, he grabbed her hand. He could tell she had been crying from her ruined makeup. "Come with me," he whispered and dragged her up with him.

She stumbled beside him as they took the stairs.

"Is she part of your act?" Delia asked, a bit unpleased and confused. "This wasn't in the run sheet."

"There's been a change of plans," he snapped, pushing past her and reaching for the megaphone, Jessica timidly stood behind him.

Delia followed and announced, "You have one minute to impress . . . three . . . two . . . one . . . begin."

Ian eyed the judges, who looked at him in amusement, as if because he was fat, he should be hilarious . . . or because he was far too tall, he should be a clown. Scanning the crowd, he saw his fellow competitors, the ones who were laughing, and the one who had been the guardian of the flag on his team actually sitting quietly, although with a smirk on her face.

"My name is Ian. And I'm from Lion's Landing." People seemed puzzled. He pulled Jessica by his side. "This is Jessica." Lifting her hand up in the air beside his, he said, "This is the girl you just mocked and made cry. It's . . . why her makeup looks so rough now." Mumbling began to spread through the stands now, but he continued. "Maybe it was all fun and games—entertainment–to you. Maybe it meant nothing to you. But as someone who has gone through this all of his life . . . it made me . . . sad." He looked down. One could hear a pin drop. "You see, I don't see this as how Shepherds should act. And maybe . . . maybe I don't know, because I'm not a Shepherd. But I think a Shepherd, especially a Spirit Shepherd, should build people up . . . not tear them down. So, although I barely know Jessica . . . and although she hasn't always paid attention to *me* . . . I'm going to use the few seconds I have left to build up in her . . . what you all just tore down." Sweat beaded on his forehead.

"Jessica is beautiful. Jessica is good at making hair bows. You should have seen her gray bow. Jessica is very talkative. She would be really good at talking to people as a Shepherd of State or Spirit or something. She is very loyal. She has stuck by my best friend Bumo's side, even when he cheated on her with the girl I liked . . ." He swallowed. "Okay, maybe that was too personal." Some in the crowd laughed uncomfortably. "Um . . . Jessica is really kind to animals. I saw how she interacted with a cat once back in Kaya. Her laugh makes other people laugh. And as far as laughs go . . . I'd say it's pretty cool." He looked at her.

She seemed shocked, but her confidence seemed to be returning.

What else should I say? Images of her kissing Bumo flashed through his mind.

"She's very . . . affectionate. She shows people she loves them. And she has been a very good friend to Alala and Erina. I've seen them go through a lot together . . . we *all* have gone through a lot together." Passion and pride swelled through him as he remembered all they had endured. "Through storms and interviews and sickness and conversations in inns over drinks and training and conversations in the rain and vomit and sweat and blood and mind games and debates and . . . and . . . what I mean to say is that the people of Soma stick together. That's why I'm defending her . . . and so should the people of Oldaem . . . so . . . let's not tear each other down . . . there's enough people out in Esis who already do that . . . let's build each other up . . . that's what true Shepherds should do."

After a stunned silence, some in the audience began cheering, and it began to spread. Many were on their feet . . . the judges said nothing . . . he really wasn't aware of anything . . . except that he hadn't used his minute to show a talent, which meant he would probably be disqualified . . . and that he was being hugged by the first time by a beautiful blonde girl named Jessica . . . he had just made a friend.

"It's over . . . we did it." Liarra sat beside him on the top steps of Arena 3.

It had become his favorite spot, but it wouldn't be for long. Win or lose, they would all be leaving the Capital soon. Everything had been a whirlwind. For dramatic effect, the judges would keep the scores of the final events secret until the closing ceremonies when the top 24 Shepherds would be selected and placed in their specific categories. Ian had no idea where he ranked.

It was finished: the training . . . the hours . . . the uncertainty . . . and the adventure. He couldn't believe it.

"I'm proud of you, Ian," she said, a twinkle in her eyes.

"I'm proud of you, too. You thought you couldn't make it." He grinned nervously. *She always made him feel that way.*

"So did you."

"I knew you could."

"I knew *you* could."

"Thanks for the book. It really helped during the debate."

"Thanks for being there for me. It's helped me through *everything,*" she said, leaning her head against his shoulder.

Her presence beside him made him feel safe and cared for. He wished this night would last forever.

"Ian . . . what do you think is going to happen next?"

"I have no idea."

And he meant it. He didn't know who would be selected, what they would be named as, and where they would be sent. There were three different academies. Middle Lake Academy was the closest to Lion's Landing . . . but it still wasn't home.

"Well . . ." She sat back up and looked at him, "I want you to know . . . that no matter what happens . . . or where we end up . . . that . . ." She swallowed.

His heart pounding, he waited. "Yeah?"

"I . . . I've enjoyed . . . Um . . . you mean a great . . . what I mean to say is . . ."

"Bum Bum!"

Talo?

Ian looked down and saw three beautiful faces . . . three double chins . . . three sets of arms outstretched toward him, and his heart leapt into his throat.

My family.

"You . . . you came!" he gasped.

As he raced down the steps, he could sense Liarra's grin and allowed himself to be embraced by a wave of love . . .

The stars overhead watched a Beelzian family dance around the arena. Ian recounted every event and every victory and defeat . . . every journey and person encountered . . . except for Allora . . . he kept that to himself . . . and he wondered if he always would. His family had brought with them the dog that could barely move, and it barked freely with joy and love. Everyone laughed and sang and ate some more, and Liarra joined them. Everybody talked and sang late into the night. They were a happy family, but most of all, they were family. The Tide rose and fell. The Rock stood still. Win or lose . . .

It's okay to be Ian after all.

CHAPTER 67: KAYT

Although she had dug, prodded, asked around, Kayt still had not learned anything more. The Royal Shepherds were nowhere to be found. Gragor had spent every minute at the tournament, and Orcino wasn't taking any visitors. At the moment, she sat at a small table in her royal chambers, waiting for her husband to return. She knew he had been at the tournament that day, witnessing the final events, and would be home late. Her stomach grumbled, but she didn't eat. Kayt needed to speak to him. It was the only time that she remembered actually waiting for his arrival.

Realizing that there could be no way he was the idiot he pretended to be, she had a number of questions for him. He had to know *something* from growing up in the palace watching Zorah and Garrus and Demas and Udina every day. And Gragor *had* to know something more about Seff. There was something she was missing.

Kayt believed Allora completely. She didn't think Leoj was responsible for Demas . . . and now she didn't believe the nation had even initiated the war. Someone or something else was responsible, *but who?* That was what she needed to get to the bottom of. Who would have something to gain from Oldaem and Leoj being at war? And what would they have to gain? Who would benefit from abducting Oldaem's Royal Shepherd of Defense . . . practically any rival nation? *Any rival nation . . .* her mind was spinning.

Eventually, once she had enough evidence, she would present it all before Orcino himself . . . and she would be responsible for the salvation of Oldaem. *Talk about being in the right place at the right time.* Also, a part of her worried for Allora. The girl really had gotten the worst end of everything. She had just been someone's innocent daughter . . . trying to find her way on Esis. It made her wonder how she would feel if something had happened to Lei . . .

I will help you, Allora. I'm going to get you out of this.

"It's over!" the door swung open revealing Gragor, already removing his outerwear. "Another tournament over." Poking his head back out the door, he shouted, "Someone get me the results! I don't want to wait until tomorrow to find out who won!"

Kayt rose to greet him but he swept right by her. "My Prince, I'm so glad you've returned . . . I missed you."

"'Little fish go blu, blue, blue' . . . HILARIOUS!"

"My Prince?"

"Oh, hello, Kayt. Feeling better?" he asked, looking right past her and sitting on the floor to remove his boots.

"Yes. That was a few days ago that I didn't feel well."

"Well, just take lots of fluids and getting plenty of bed rest. You'll kick it soon."

He's not listening to me. She looked at him irritably as he struggled to remove his boots.

"I'm eating with Dad today."

"The king?"

"Yes . . . yes . . . he wants to have supper with me. Says he has something very important to discuss with me. Whatever that means."

What could this be about? "Really? Is . . . everything okay?"

"I can't get this boot off!"

Kayt sat down on the floor with him and pulled on his boot as hard as she could. Eventually it slipped off, and with the boot came a strong stench.

"Have you seen my slippers?"

"I'm afraid not, Husband."

"Slippers!" he called out. "Where are you?"

"Do . . . you expect them to answer?" she asked hesitently.

"Who?"

"The slippers." She wasn't amused.

"Well, wouldn't that be ridiculous?" he chuckled as his head disappeared under his bed.

He has to know something. "So . . . you have no idea what he might want to tell you, tonight?"

"Who?" he responded, muffled by a giant bed.

"Your father," she answered a little too loudly.

"Oh, who knows? He told me to come straight away. Says it's serious. I'm sure he's just going to tell me about his rash again. Did you know that he found it on his . . ."

"Gragor," she interrupted.

"Ow!" he shrieked, bumping his head. "I found them!" He emerged from under the bed with a broad smile.

"I'm so . . . so glad."

"Me, too!" Immediately he began struggling to put them on.

I need a different approach. "Please, my love, allow me."

After he perched on the edge of the bed, she sat on the floor and took her time slipping on his footwear. "I've been . . . concerned," she said sweetly.

"About what?"

"Everything . . . do you ever . . . wonder . . . if all the Royal Shepherds are . . . oh, I don't know . . . trustworthy?"

"Like . . . if they can keep secrets?" he asked, genuinely confused.

"Well . . . more than that . . . I don't know. I just want to make sure that everyone surrounding you and your father has your best interests at heart."

"I know the servants like us!" he said excitedly.

"Yes . . . and as important as that is . . . I guess what I'm saying is . . . seeing as I don't have as much access to your father as you do . . . I want him to know that . . . he should keep his eyes open . . . he shouldn't trust everyone so easily . . . not people around Oldaem . . . and not people within Oldaem . . . not even our allies . . . and maybe we should be careful when making allies . . ." *What am I saying? Why even bother? Does he even understand anything?*

"I think I know what you're getting at," he said with his eyes closed.

"You do?" she asked, adjusting his final slipper.

537

"Yes. And now I have a very important question to ask you."

"Okay." She leaned closer.

"Why did the skeleton go to the party alone?" he asked with a mischievous twinkle in his eyes.

She sighed. "Why?"

"Because he had no *body* to go with!" And with that Gragor laughed loudly as he headed toward the door.

"Wait . . . you're leaving already? I had some questions about Shepherd Seff."

"Yeah . . . Dad's expecting me. I'll be back *very* late, so don't wait up. Whenever he invites me to his chambers it always takes such a long time."

"But . . ."

"Bye!"

The door closed in her face, leaving her in the room alone. *What is he going to tell Gragor?* But she knew one thing for certain. She wouldn't get any answers about Seff or the Royal Shepherds or Leoj by sitting in her room alone all night. Actions always revealed intentions, and she knew the Royal Shepherds were about to do something. And whatever it was, it revolved around Allora.

"I've brought goodies again," Kayt said sweetly to the guards outside of Allora's door.

"Our . . . *guest* has just returned from the tournament. She is not to be bothered."

"You would refuse the king's command?"

"The king has sent no word about this."

"You will address me as your highness."

"Yes, your highness," Seff's man said as he bowed slightly.

"Such disrespect. The last guards who disrespected me ended up on the gallows."

She noticed the guard on the left side of the door swallow uncomfortably as he eyed his comrade.

"Hey . . . maybe we should just let her in."

"No way . . . not without permission from the . . ."

"There's been a personnel change order," she heard Garrus announce behind her. Accompanied by two of his own men, he was quickly approaching.

"Royal Shepherd Garrus!" Seff's man said, a hint of surprise in his voice.

Garrus handed him a piece of parchment with the seal of the king. "It seems that Seff requires your assistance in his office. Better hurry."

"Yes, Sir," both saluted and started down the hallway.

Garrus' men took their place at Allora's door.

"What are you up to, Garrus?" Kayt asked suspiciously.

"I should ask the same of you." He smiled as he started walking away.

"Wait . . . where are you going?"

"Don't you have some *goodies* to deliver?" he asked, their eyes meeting. A silent understanding passed between them, although Kayt couldn't formulate it into a coherent thought. Nodding, she turned the knob and stepped into Allora's chambers.

The room was darker than before, probably because the sun had set and the only light that illuminated the room came from a few candles and sconces set along the walls. Not immediately seeing the princess, she stood by the door and looked around the room.

"Allora? It's me . . . Kayt. Are you in here?"

The splash of water caught her attention.

"I'm over here."

When Kayt stepped farther into the room she saw Allora sitting at a small desk in one corner, pressing a wet towel against her cheek. Even from the other end of the room, she could tell Allora was nursing a swollen cheek and a blackening eye.

"What in Esis . . ." Kayt exclaimed, horrified as she neared her.

"Yeah . . . it hurts."

"Who did this to you?" Kayt demanded, kneeling before Allora's chair.

"A Royal Shepherd. Treating his guest with a little violence. Welcome to Oldaem."

"Which one?" Kayt was shocked.

"Seff . . . he wasn't liking my answers . . . or lack of."

"So . . . he . . . beat you up?"

"Threw me around the room a little, too." She rubbed the side of her stomach. "Got a couple good kicks in while he was at it."

"And how did he think he would get away with this."

"I 'fell' down the stairs . . . that's my story, according to him."

"Ridiculous." Kayt pulled up a chair and sat on it. "Foolish too. Have all the Shepherds been rough to you during questioning?"

"No . . . actually . . . Seff was by far the worst . . . Udina was a little bit intense . . . Zorah was pretty nice . . . but Garrus . . . almost seemed to . . . believe me."

Kayt nodded. "I think maybe we can trust him . . . maybe . . . he let me in here. I'm not sure how, but he had a document with the king's stamp of approval on it. Maybe King Orcino is figuring things out too. "

"Really? Are you serious?" Hope momentarily flashed in Allora's eyes.

"Yes."

"But figuring out what? Who is responsible? Who has been framing Leoj?"

"I don't know . . . but now I have my suspicions," she said, eying Allora's swollen face.

"So do I." Allora rubbed her cheek. "But what would Seff have to gain by sending Leoj to war?"

"Well, we both know what he *has* gained by eliminating Demas. But where could Demas be?"

"He's not in Leoj . . . maybe another country? Maybe here in Oldaem?"

"Royal Shepherd Zorah seems to think Seff wants to ally with Sther . . . could Demas be in Sther?"

"It would be ludicrous for Seff to trust Priestess A'delath! I don't know much about politics, but even *I* know that she's trouble. My father always avoided negotiations with her like he would a plague!"

Kayt thought rapidly. "Maybe he's in Hemia or Remia . . . maybe the nations are posing at war, while harboring our Royal Shepherd of Defense." *Nothing makes sense.*

"I think he's *here* . . . I bet Demas is in Oldaem . . . right under your noses. You *have* to tell the King."

"I need *proof.* Just my baseless accusations against Seff will not hold up. King Orcino doesn't respect the opinions of women at all, least of all mine."

"Maybe Garrus can help?"

"Maybe . . . *if* we can trust him."

"We have to trust *someone.*"

Kayt noticed the water in the basin Allora was dipping her towel had turned a dark color. "Here, let me get you some clean water." Grabbing the basin, she emptied it out the window. "There are some treats in the basket, if you're hungry. I don't know how they're feeding you." Crossing the room to the pitcher as Allora ate, she

540

poured fresh water into basin and picked up a fresh towel from the neatly folded pile on a different desk. She returned with everything, and placed it before the young princess.

"Thanks, Kayt."

"Hey . . . I don't just do this for *you*, okay . . . there are some suspicious happenings in my country, and I plan to reverse them." She paused. "And it's *Princess* Kayt."

Allora paused. "Well, thank you just the same, Princess. But none of your reasons had to do with replacing my water."

"Well . . . I grew tired of watching you smear your blood across your face."

"Thanks," she said meekly.

"Did a healer come in and look at that."

"Yeah . . . Galen sent in someone." She blushed.

"Who is Galen?"

"My . . . bodyguard . . . I guess."

She likes him. Kayt noticed Allora's face flush at mention of him. *Girls always have weaknesses. Those weaknesses are always men. I'm glad I don't have a weakness.* "Sure." Kayt shook her head.

"So . . . what's your plan . . . what should we do?"

"I need solid evidence." She began to think again, as she noticed Allora looking pensively. "What did Seff say to you during your interrogation?"

"He mostly yelled questions at me. Honestly . . . it felt more as if he just wanted to beat me up rather than actually get information out of me . . . it was like . . . he didn't expect me to say anything . . . like he needed no answers. It's what was different between him and the others."

"The king needs to at least see what he's done to you. Were there any witnesses to your abuse?"

"Well . . . Galen and Gadiel . . . that's Demas' son . . . they saw him slap me across the face and kind of strangle me . . . but he threw them out right after. Then he questioned me alone."

"That may be enough. Do you trust these bodyguards?" Kayt carefully studied her.

She nodded. "With my life. Later tonight Galen and I are going to get some fresh air together, a walk along the rooftops of the castle . . . for some reason Seff allows me to leave my room to do things that seem . . . logical for a *guest* to do. Keeping up appearances, I guess. "

"Just in case . . . still say nothing to Galen until I get a little bit more evidence." Kayt stood.

"Where are you going?"

"To see the king . . . but I need to check out one suspicion that I have first." *I think Orcino has already reached the same conclusion we have.*

Someone at the door knocked, and Allora quickly rose. "Who is it?" she called out.

"It's Galen. Ready to walk?"

Allora quickly faced Kayt with eyes full of concern.

"It's okay, Allora . . . tell him, yes. And when he asks later who I am . . . just tell him it was the stupid princess delivering baked goods." She smiled. "I'm famous for my cookie recipe."

"The cookies you *bought*."

"Those cookies precisely." Kayt smiled again.

"Yes, Galen," Allora said more loudly. "Let me put on something warmer . . . I know how windy those ramparts get."

Quickly Allora dressed, and Kayt helped her. She wasn't sure why she did, or why she had changed her water or treated her gently. No, she wasn't sure--except that every time she looked at Allora she saw Lei's little eyes. Second chances weren't really a reality . . . but she could dream . . . after all, what was dreaming for?

They heard Galen's voice again. It sounded . . . reserved. "Oh . . . and Shepherd Seff is . . . here too . . . to escort us . . ."

Allora and Kayt looked at each other fearfully.

Great. What should I do?

"Allora . . ." Kayt whispered calmly "let *me* handle Seff. You just focus on acting afraid of him."

"That won't be hard," she said, rubbing her cheek again.

"Ready?" Kayt asked, looking into those beautiful lavender eyes.

"Ready," Allora replied firmly. "I trust you."

Dumbfounded, Kayt stared at her and nodded. Chills raced up and down her spine. For the first time in years someone trusted her that could actually *safely* put her trust in her. It felt kind of nice being . . . good . . . even if for only a moment . . . *Perhaps some monsters can be . . . good, too.*

"Let me go first," Kayt said.

"You sure?"

"Yes."

Kayt pushed past her and opened the door.

Standing outside was Seff, surrounded by the two guards who had originally manned the door, Garrus' two soldiers, and a well-built young soldier who must have been Galen. A petulant expression on his face, he seemed to Kayt to be the kind of kid who was too big for his britches. Kayt was sure that if she spoke with him, she would despise him. *What does Allora see in him?* She decided to take control of the situation and speak first.

"Shepherd Seff . . . what a pleasant surprise."

He clearly had known she was there. But still, his face radiated surprise. "Princess Kayt, always a pleasure. Delivering more tasty treats to our guest?"

"Of course." She noticed the guards bow, Galen included. But he didn't make eye contact with her, apparently watching Allora's door.

"Galen, please escort our guest to the rooftops for some fresh air. It's quite the view at this time of night. Lovely breeze too. Do dress warmly," Seff said in his most kind voice.

"Yes, sir," Galen replied and darted into Allora's room, closing the door behind him.

Kayt stood there serenely, her gaze locked with Seff's. His face was unreadable. Without looking away from her he addressed his men. "Guards, please join Garrus' men watching this door. Allow Galen and Allora to go to the rooftops and wait here for their return. The king wants heightened security on her chambers once she gets back. We never can be too careful."

"Yes, Sir," they echoed, taking positions beside Garrus' guards, one on the right, the other on the left.

"Well . . . I must return to my quarters," Kayt said calmly. "It's been quite a day."

"Allow *me* to accompany you?"

"I think I will be fine on my own."

"No . . . I insist," Seff said, taking her arm in his. "I've been meaning to speak with you anyway."

"Yes. Thank you. I would like that." *What is he doing?*

They walked awkwardly arm-in-arm through the corridors of the palace. The hour was late, and Kayt was tired. But she knew she had to see the king, had to figure out what he was telling Gragor, and she had to see if Orcino would be receptive to her, even perhaps without solid evidence. Relieved that Seff wasn't a Mind Shepherd, she didn't want him to be aware of what she was thinking right now. Kayt tried to control her breathing. Seff, a large man, was quite solid. It would be hard to get away from his grip if the necessary time arose. There was a reason he was Defense. Now she could sense his discomfort beside her as she walked. *He said he wanted to talk to me. Let him speak first. Hold your cards closely, Kayt.*

543

"Did you hear about the tournament?" Seff asked.

"I heard it was exciting as usual," she replied coolly.

"Yes. It was. Not as much excitement as last year's tournament, with the announcement of the attack of our colony in Leoj. I can't believe it's been a year."

"Neither can I." *An attack you probably planned.*

"You seem to be deep in thought."

"I'm just tired."

"I heard you've been a little under the weather."

"Yes, I have been."

"But not enough to keep you from . . . baking?"

"It . . . always makes me feel better."

"Did you bake down in our kitchens?"

Careful, Kayt. He's fishing and could easily catch you in a lie. "No, in the village."

"I see. You always do like to explore. My men tell me you go out a lot."

"Oh . . . I didn't know the Princess of Oldaem was vulnerable to constant scrutiny and observation by the *Interim* Royal Shepherd of Defense. What is it about me that fascinates you so much? And during wartime?" *Careful, Kayt.*

He smiled. "Your spirit."

They continued to walk, getting closer to her personal chambers with Gragor. The king's chambers were now in the opposite direction. *I just need to lose Seff.*

"How are Allora's injuries? Did she tell you how she got them?" he asked calmly without looking at her.

Kayt's heart caught in her throat. *What should I say?* "Yes. She did."

He turned and looked at her. She stared back at him with just as much intensity.

"She said she took *quite* the tumble."

A broad smile spread across his face. "Yes she did—down the stairs. She got quite banged up. You've seemed to have . . . taken an interest in our young Leojian guest . . . have you not?"

"It's a Princess' responsibility to host palace guests."

"You do your job . . . very well, it seems. I *knew* you'd be good for our crowned prince."

"Thank you. I think I am, too."

They arrived at Kayt and Gragor's door. Seff slipped away from her, and stood to face her.

"It will be . . . interesting to watch."

"What will be interesting, Shepherd?"

"What you do now."

"What do you mean?"

He started walking away, and then swung around. "What you will do now that you understand your role as Royal Princess of Oldaem. You are high profile, my Princess. One day you will be queen. I'm not the only one observing you." Bowing deeply, he again smiled. "By the way . . . you seem so much different than the wide-eyed-girl I spoke with out on that balcony many, many nights ago . . . it seems like so long ago now . . . interesting how things change, isn't it?"

"Yes."

"Good night, Princess. Get good rest. You'll need your strength tomorrow."

And with that, she watched him walk away.

Suddenly she felt very exposed and vulnerable standing outside of her room. She knew it would be safer to enter her chambers and go to sleep. Clearly Seff had eyes everywhere. But Kayt wasn't afraid of him. Monsters weren't afraid of monsters. She was dangerous, deadly, and someone to fear. *I will get to the king, and I will destroy you, Seff.*

Hurrying into her room, she changed into something darker and less conspicuous than the honey-colored dress she had been wearing. She cloaked a dark-blue cowl around her head and made her way toward the chamber of the king.

She knew it would be heavily guarded. It always was. If he was having an important meeting with his son, she doubted she would even get access to his room that night. But she had to try. Carefully she slipped past the grand staircase and toward the king's Royal Wing. She had actually never been in the king's bedchambers, which is where she imagined he was hosting his son. As she walked along the hallway, she looked at the deep-red carpets and the hanging tapestries of previous kings of Oldaem. What power each man had. She imagined that with such power came no fear, no uncertainty. It was that power and control she strove for. With absolute control came the need to trust no one. *Ignorance brings destruction. I will not be ignorant. Allora, I hope you will not be either.*

After she had gone a ways down the crimson-carpeted hallway, she began to wonder why it was unguarded. Since she had entered this part of the palace she had not encountered a single royal guard.

545

How strange. The present hallway had no doors along it. As she turned a corner she saw golden double doors down at the far end. *The chamber of the king.* Again she pondered the absence of guards. *Maybe he sent them all away.*

She slowed her pace as she neared the room and listened for any voices beyond the door. Hearing nothing, she glanced behind her to make sure no one was watching. The hallway was clear as she leaned her ear against the door. Still nothing. *Maybe he's already in bed. What should I do?*

Kayt knew she needed to talk to him immediately. The situation at hand demanded swift and decisive action. But she could play the stupid girl routine if she found herself in trouble. With that in mind, she tried the doors, and to her surprise found them unlocked. Quietly she stepped inside.

Everything inside was a striking red color. A giant canopy bed stood before her, golden arches hung with scarlet fabrics extending all the way down to the floor. To the right was a dressing area, surrounded by thick red curtains, and an unlit fireplace to her left. Beyond the canopy bed in front of her opened a balcony. Faint voices came through the doorway to it. She decided to hide and listen first, then figure out what to do. Silently she crept to the red curtains of the dressing area closest to the balcony window from where Gragor and Orcino were engaged in conversation. Concealing herself behind the curtain, she listened intensely to her husband and the king.

She recognized Gragor's voice immediately. "Are you sure, Father?" He sounded concerned.

"I'm afraid so."

"So . . . what do we do?"

"That's what I'm trying to figure out."

What are they talking about? I'm too late. I missed it.

"Whom can we trust?" Never had she heard Gragor so serious before.

I knew there was more to him. Why does he always play the fool?

"Until we know for sure . . . my son . . ." Their footsteps approached the room, followed by the sound of the balcony door closing behind them. With that sound came a scraping noise that seemed to come from the fireplace.

A mouse?

They stood right in front of her, and she slowed her breathing to ensure the curtains shielding her didn't move.

546

"Say nothing to anybody. I *know* we can trust Garrus . . . but he may be the *only* one . . ."

"What of Zorah?"

"I *hope* we can."

He knows! Orcino has to know the truth about Seff! Relief washed over Kayt. *You're mine, Seff. It's going to be okay, Allora.*

"Powerful men are always the most vulnerable," another voice hissed in front of her.

Who was that?

The curtains blocked her vision, but she didn't dare peek out now. Then she heard what sounded like the door to the room being locked.

"Who . . . who are you people? How did you get in here?" Orcino demanded.

"They *think* they are in control. They *think* they hold all the cards . . . and then their kingdoms fall between their fingers . . . I've seen it time and time again," the voice continued. A woman, and she sounded calm and . . . deadly.

Kayt's heart started pounding. Through a thin gap between curtains she could see the shadows of five figures standing in the room. Two of them were Orcino and Gragor . . . one woman . . . *Who are the other two?*

"Gragor . . . get behind me," Orcino said shakily. "What do you want? Money? Gold? Property? I can give you *anything!*"

"Why would I want anything when I already have everything?" the woman asked.

"Then what . . . *what* are you doing here?" Kayt noticed Orcino's voice starting to rise.

"A'delath demands your blood!" the voice said firmly.

"No! The One preserve us!" Gragor shouted!

"Help! Guards!" Orcino screamed.

Kayt listened in horror to the sounds of struggle, followed by a grunt and the sound of blows. Numb, she couldn't move or even breathe. Although she did not want to look, she knew she had to. Only the sound of weeping now broke the silence. She was sure it was coming from Gragor. Slowly and carefully she pulled aside the curtain, just enough to get a partial view.

Kneeling with their mouths gagged with golden fabric were Orcino and Gragor, bloody and beaten, arms tied behind their backs. Two men dressed in black had them at knifepoint. They both appeared physically strong. One man seemed older than the other, but the younger one had a more dangerous look in his eyes. The king and his son knelt fearfully before a stunning woman in gold who watched them calmly.

Kayt knew that she should rush out now and hurl herself against them. That she should do *something* to save them. But all she really think of was to hide. How had they gotten in there? What was going on? The only thing she knew was that the king and prince of Oldaem were about to get their throats slit by what appeared to be two Wardens and a Golden Priestess.

"Why . . . why are you doing this?" Orcino choked out, blood dripping from his mouth.

The Golden Priestess took a step closer to them. "I am Malvina, the Golden Priestess. To put your trust in the One was foolish. It is the Three who will liberate Oldaem from the clutches of death." When she stretched out her hands for the knives, Kayt watched in horror as the two Wardens obediently handed them to her.

"Please . . . please . . . mercy," Orcino sobbed.

"Even kings kneel to me."

The woman made two quick slashes, and Orcino and Gragor lay dead before her.

"Wardens . . . clean the room."

"Yes Priestess," they echoed.

Kayt looked down as blood oozed beneath the curtains and seeped toward her feet. *They are headed this way!*

CHAPTER 68: DAKU

Daku remembered a time when he was young. His father had brought home some biscuits for supper. Needing to run off to do something with work, he instructed the boy not to eat any of them. Then he made him promise to be good and to obey.

But once Daku's father had left, the boy ate a biscuit. At first he felt guilty that he had let his father down. To make himself feel better he ate another biscuit. Afterward he felt even worse. At this point, however, he realized there was nothing he could do to replace the biscuits he had eaten, so he ate two more biscuits. With each one Daku felt worse. He knew that he hadn't obeyed.

Once his father returned home, he asked Daku what had happened to the biscuits. Daku lied and said he had no idea. But his father knew the truth and looked at his son with an expression of great disappointment. That memory always stuck out in his mind though, there was nothing he could do now to placate his father. His dad was dead and gone, just like the biscuits. Once again, he had chosen not to be good and there was nothing to be done about it. Numbness replaced regret.

He saw the two corpses beneath his feet and Malvina's golden eyes watching his. Daku felt no remorse for their deaths, felt no pain--nothing. It's what he had chosen.

"Wardens, clean the room!"

"Yes, Priestess!" he heard himself say along with Jorn.

Soundlessly they cleaned everything up. It had been as if they had never entered. Malvina just stood staring at them.

Daku eyed the dressing room area and noticed that blood had seeped into it. He was aware of a person hiding there but wasn't sure if Jorn was or not. Instead, he cleaned around the feet without saying a word although he was not sure why he remained silent. Possibly it was the tiny part of him that still loathed Malvina, that hoped someday she would suffer as he had. Perhaps the choice not to kill the person behind the curtain would lead to that result. It wasn't a righteous anger that filled him ... it was a numb loathing of more of the same.

As they stood with their backs to the fireplace, the secret passageway through which they entered, Malvina silently looked pleased. She still said nothing as they closed it behind them and headed back into the dark underbelly of the castle ... the one their contact had showed them. She lit the way with a sickly yellow hue as usual. Daku brought up the rear.

Although he didn't know what was next, he didn't care. A part of him hoped she would take him back to the inn and end his life. Nothing had to be better than existing in eternal numbness.

Too far gone. Too far gone. Too far gone. The Wall is crumbled. I've killed Galen. I've killed the king and the prince. I've killed the gardener. I've killed the Shepherd. I've killed my father. I've killed Aelwynne. I've killed love. Too far gone. Too far gone. You've chosen this. One more step. I am yours. Too far gone.

Daku's mind drifted as they walked through darkness. Then he remembered something he thought he had forgotten. Something that no longer mattered.

"Come in and sit down."

Daku nervously stood in the open doorway. He could hear the busy sounds of Najoh in the background. Vorran sat before him at his desk in a small gatehouse type building adjacent to the entrance of a large Stherian Tower. It was here that Vorran, Aelwynne's father, was currently stationed. And it was here that Daku would ask for her hand.

"Thank you, sir," he said politely as he sat on the hard wooden chair.

"I think I know why you're here." Vorran said with a tint of strained politeness in his voice.

"Really, sir?"

"I know you've been spending much time with my daughter . . . more time than I wish."

Daku hung his head. "Yes, sir."

"You're fond of her."

Daku swallowed, then replied, "I love her, sir."

"Love?" Vorran spat out. His eyes dripped with fury. "How do you know?"

"I . . . feel that . . ."

"You *feel!*" he said incredulously with a laugh. "What a stupid thing to say."

It shocked Daku. "You didn't let me finish!"

"I don't *need* to. Feelings can't be trusted. They lead you astray. Daku, Daku, Daku . . . maybe it's good you came to me after all."

How could perfect Aelwynne come from this menacing man? Then he collected himself. "I feel she is my next breath. I know she is my next breath. I choose for her to be. I *understand* that love is a choice. I have chosen her. And I will choose her every day."

"How sentimental. How noble," Vorran said sarcastically. "If only it was that easy."

Daku studied him. *What is he getting at?*

"While I care greatly for my daughter . . . it is not her romantic life that motivates me and moves me into paternal defense. It is her . . . role on Esis."

"Her . . . role?"

"Yes . . . you see . . . A'delath has huge plans for her."

"The . . . High Priestess of Sther?"

550

"Yes . . ." The man bowed his head reverently. "There is power within her. It is for the good of Sther that we exist. For the furthering of the work of The Three."

Aelwynne needs protection–protection from him.

"What are you saying?" Daku breathed.

"The Three are powerful. The Three provide strength and wisdom, justice and providence. When you serve them . . . you become unstoppable."

Unstoppable?

"I sense you have a *hero* complex . . . do you not?"

"How . . . how do you know?"

"I work closely with the Golden Sect. It deals in psychological manipulation. I can read you like a book. You're here to ask for my daughter's hand in marriage."

Daku paused. "Yes. I am."

"I see." Vorran focused back on his work, studying the pages on his desk.

Daku sat there in silence. "Sir?"

"That is all."

A sudden strength filled Daku's voice. "No . . . it's not."

"Ah . . ." a twinkle filled his eyes. "So, you're ready to *fight* for her?"

"Yes, sir. I'd do . . . anything."

"Anything?"

To get her away from you, to protect her from you . . . yes.

He removed his spectacles. "Interesting that you'd say *anything.*" He cleared his throat and drummed his fingers on the wooden top of his desk. Then he continued. "Priestesses of the Three have Wardens, Daku–men who devote their lives to them, who would die for them. And with that devotion, great power is bestowed upon them."

Power to protect Aelwynne.

"If you vow to live the life of a Warden . . . I will grant you my daughter's hand in marriage."

Daku was hesitant. "Why? Why me? Why do you want *me*?"

Vorran smiled. "Because I think . . . that after a while . . . you will see that you'll make the choice to stay a Warden no longer for Aelwynne . . . but for yourself."

Anger flooded through Daku. "You're *wrong!* If I do this–if I agree to this . . . it will be to *protect* her. It will be to protect her from the likes of . . . *you.*"

551

Vorran flashed him a dangerous smile. "My boy . . . do we have a deal? The Priestesses of the Three work in the shadows for the *light*. Is that a life you want?"

I would do anything to protect her. And one day I will be powerful enough to free her from him. "We have a deal."

Vorran shook hands with Daku, then put his spectacles back on. "Excellent. You'll live in Vertloch, near *me*. It will be good to have you so close by . . . *son*. Oh . . . and Aelwynne can never know . . . *or you will never see her again."*

Fear surged through Daku. He realized that Vorran did indeed have the power to make that a reality. The Three were a mystery to him. But one he would soon decode.

As he was about to exit, thoughts of his own father's loving nature and all he had taught him flooded through Daku's mind. He thought of Bug and Galen . . . of the Wall and the Tower . . . and of the tales of his mother and what it meant to be a hero. He wondered what Vorran was like when he was younger. Pain and pity flushed through him. "You know . . . Vorran . . . you're not too far gone."

A dark shadow of sadness fell over the man's eyes. "Yes I am . . ."

A Golden Priestess and her two Wardens left the catacombs of the Palace and returned to the streets of the Capital. Since Malvina no longer needed Varic, the merchant was dead. Only Daku remained–the Daku who no longer was a Warden for Aelwynne, but for himself.

They made their way back to their inn. Tomorrow they would sail away. If she didn't kill him.

Too far gone. Too far gone.

CHAPTER 69: KAYT

"It's a girl!" the midwife announced.

Kayt's head was throbbing–in fact, her entire body. But now relief and joy surged through it.

A little girl? A little girl of my own?

Tears streamed down Kayt's face. "Let me . . . see her?"

Arnand stood beside her and squeezed her hand. "The midwife is preparing her for you." He kissed her on her perspiring forehead. "You did it. I'm proud of you."

I did it.

She had brought life into the world, something she had never planned to do. Kayt had never intended to be a mother. But then she had never expected to get married and wind up an unemployed Shepherd. But as always, life took charge and led her to places that she never dreamed she'd go.

Holding her daughter in her arms, she looked deeply into the clear blue eyes. Tears streamed down her cheeks, but not ones of joy or even pain. They were tears of fear. Kayt was afraid. She feared what this little innocent being would grow up to be while in her care.

A monster raising an angel ... I'm not good enough ...

Hearing the scraping noise from the fireplace again, she let out her breath for the first time in what felt like hours. They were gone, and she was safe. What she didn't understand was why whoever had been cleaning up the blood from around her feet didn't kill or alert her presence to the murderous Golden Priestess.

Gragor is dead. Orcino is dead. I saw her slit their ...

Bile rose up in her throat. Kayt wanted to empty herself on the floor, but she knew she couldn't. She knew she had to get out of there as quickly as she could.

As she darted from behind the curtain toward the door, she was aware of their two bodies lying silently on the floor, but she didn't look at them. She couldn't.

Suddenly she found herself walking down the empty hallway back toward her room. She never passed a servant or a guard. Before she knew it she was sitting in her bed with the covers over her legs.

What should I do? If anyone discovers I was in that room, I could be implicated for their murder. Yet only I know the truth about what happened. What should I do?

"Belinda?" she called.

Quickly, the servant poked her head in. "Yes, Highness?"

"Would you please check on Gragor in the king's Chambers? He asked me to send for him if the hour got too late."

"Um ... yes ... however, I was told not to interrupt the King this evening."

"Belinda. You don't answer to anyone but me. Now go before I throw you from the balcony."

The woman closed the door behind her.

Kayt sat there in silence and waited.

It wasn't long before she could hear the screams and shouts of the palace staff. People ran back and forth in the corridor outside her room. Still, she waited. She didn't know what she should think or whom she could trust. Nor could she even formulate her thoughts into a solid plan. She could only sit in silence. Exhaustion swept over her. *Could I have done anything differently? Should I have tried to save them? What does this mean now? Is Sther responsible for everything? How did they get into the palace? Does this mean I'm queen of Oldaem now?*

The door pounded. "Princess! Princess! Are you awake?"

She could hear Belinda's frantic voice. *It's time.* "Yes ..."

"Something ... something has happened ... and ..."

Kayt could tell Belinda was crying ... and frantic.

"What is it, Belinda?"

"The Royal Shepherds ... they are meeting in the council room ... they request you join them ..."

"Now?"

"Yes, now."

"I'll be there shortly."

Kayt entered the room as the voices speaking hushed to silence. They all watched as she approached, wrapped herself in a robe to look as if she had been sleeping. The last to arrive, she took a seat at the table ... at the spot King Orcino usually sat during council meetings. Garrus, Udina, Zorah, and Seff each had guarded or stressed expressions. She was careful not to eye Seff too closely.

"Princess ... sorry for the lateness of the hour ... but something has happened," Zorah said weakly.

Garrus reached for her hand, and she grabbed it.

"What is it?"

"This is going to be extremely difficult to hear," Udina added.

She watched them as they glanced at each other hesitantly. Finally Garrus nodded, turned to her, and broke the silence.

"Orcino and Gragor are dead."

"Murdered," Seff added.

Kayt felt tears well up in her eyes. For the first time she allowed herself to give in to the horror of what she had witnessed in the royal bedchamber. Even then she refused to completely break down, but she did let the tears flow. *It would be an appropriate response for a wife who just lost the man she loved.*

"A servant found their bodies ..." Udina slowly spoke. "They had been ..."

"She doesn't need to hear the details," Zorah quietly interrupted.

Seff looked at him incredulously. "Yes she does. She is the only member of the royal family left alive. She needs to be aware of exactly what happened."

They all looked at him in silence. Kayt continued to weep softly.

"Give her a minute," Garrus whispered as he patted her hand.

Seff turned angrily and looked directly at her. "Their throats were slit. They looked pretty beaten too. Someone cleaned up the blood. It seems as if they were taken by surprise, as nothing in the room suggested a struggle."

Kayt struggled to get her breath as she remembered watching the blade slice through their necks. An image of the golden eyes of the priestess sent chills racing up and down her spine.

"How could this have happened? How could assassins reach the royal chambers?" she demanded, looking directly at Seff.

The man looked away as Garrus said, "That is what we are trying to figure out. There is a lot ... that isn't making sense."

They sat in silence for moment. It was clear they had no idea how to proceed.

The question must be asked. "Do we ... know who did this?"

"No." Garrus answered.

Seff spat out angrily. "Oh *come on,* Garrus! Don't be ridiculous! It's obvious!"

"Not now, Seff ... not in front of the princess."

"There isn't anyone else it could be it! It *had* to be ..."

"Seff," Zorah slowly interjected, "I know you're upset ... but jumping to conclusions isn't wise ... right, Udina?"

Kayt glanced at Udina who was staring at the surface of the table. Slowly he looked up. "It's the only thing that makes sense to me."

Seff stood and started pacing. "The king *demanded* she be free to go to the tournament to keep up appearances of us treating her as our guest. He demanded she have time to walk the ramparts of the castle at night. She has no alibi! She was not accounted for! It *had* to be her!"

"We don't know that!" Garrus shouted. "We can't be so hasty to blame Leoj for *everything!*"

"But it makes sense," Udina softly stated.

"You think ... *Allora* did this?" Kayt asked Seff.

"I *know* she did," he exploded.

Suddenly a guard stepped in, the guard she knew to be loyal to Seff. "Shepherd Seff, I'm sorry to interrupt."

"What is it?" Seff snapped.

Kayt watched the guard swallow, sweat beading on his forehead. *He looks nervous.*

"Some of my men ..." He looked down and coughed, then continued, "... saw Princess Allora ... with the young soldier ... leaving the king's room ... coming from his chambers ..."

He's lying.

Seff looked vindicated, and started toward him. "Where is she now?"

"Back in her chambers with him. They are out on the balcony."

"Arrest them," Seff ordered.

"Seff!" Garrus jumped up.

"What? Are you kidding? What more proof than this do you need?" His eyes were bulging.

Her heart began to race. *He set her up ... it's Seff ... he's connected somehow ... to Sther? To the priestess? How?*

"We need ... we need to put this to ... a vote." Zorah coughed fiercely as he tried to speak.

"Why? *How?* I am the Royal Shepherd of Defense! I *failed* at protecting his majesty! The least I can do now is to ensure his murderer is brought to justice!" He eyed the guard again. "Arrest them *now*! Throw them in the dungeons!"

Kayt felt Garrus eyeing her, and she turned to him. "What do you think, your Highness?"

Her face started to flush and she wanted to spit out that she had witnessed what had happened and that Seff was lying. But she knew there was danger in exposing everything. Seff was powerful and clearly had a lot of eyes and ears around her. For that matter, she still didn't know if she could trust *any* of the Shepherds in the room. Still ... Orcino had said Garrus could be trusted, and she sensed the same in her gut. It would be more effective to take Seff out by surprise instead of meeting him on headfirst. *He can't suspect me.*

"Highness?" Zorah asked incredulously. "No," Garrus said thoughtfully. They all looked at him. "We *have* to handle this delicately. Under no circumstances are you to take the princess into custody." He looked sharply at Seff. "We need to proceed cautiously. The political ramifications are ..."

"Fine ... I'll just ..."

"Don't do *anything*, Seff ..." Garrus said firmly.

The soldier left the four of them alone, and they sat in silence for a moment.

"Tomorrow is the closing ceremonies for the tournament," Garrus continued. "I don't think we should reveal news of the king until after the tournament guests have left the city."

"I agree," Udina said.

"Who ... who is in ... charge in the mean time?" Kayt asked as carefully as possible.

"Until a new Monarch is selected ..." Zorah looked around at the others ... "the Royal Shepherds are."

"And what happens to me?" she asked again, looking at Garrus.

"Our mission now ... is to ensure *your* safety," Seff put in gently. "It might be a good idea if you stay in your quarters for now ... heavily guarded. There might be more Leojian agents within our walls. I have men already searching."

"Yes ... that sounds reasonable. But, Seff ... *stop* speaking as if Leoj is to blame," Garrus added.

"The eye witnesses!"

"Will be investigated with due process." Garrus turned away from him.

"I have a man who can watch her," Zorah offered.

A man? Who?

Seff stormed away without saying a word.

"Udina ... maybe you should join him." Garrus suggested after Seff had disappeared. "We make decisions together ... not alone."

"Yes ... I think that is a wise idea." Udina rose and faced Kayt. "I'm deeply sorry for your loss."

"Thank you, Udina." Kayt replied, watching him leave the room.

The three of them sat silently at the table.

I need to talk to Garrus ... but Zorah is here ...

"Tell me what you know?" Garrus quickly said, rising and heading to the door. After peeking through to make sure no one was around, he shut and locked it, then returned to his seat.

Kayt eyed Zorah who looked at her with surprise.

"Kayt ... we can trust Zorah ... now, tell me what you know!" Garrus quickly spit out. "Hurry before they come back. I don't think Seff will leave you alone with us for long."

I guess I have to trust someone. She swallowed. *Here we go.* "Allora didn't do it."

"How do you know?" Zorah demanded.

"Because I was there."

Shock filled both their faces.

"I wasn't supposed to be there." Emotion flooded over her again. She realized that she couldn't even remember the last time she had cried. "After speaking with Allora ... who was beaten to a pulp by Seff during their questioning ... I thought that perhaps ... Seff could somehow be involved or implicated in Demas' disappearance ... I wanted to tell the king ... but it seemed, after overhearing him speaking with Gragor ... he had the same suspicions."

"I've suspected Seff for some time now ... both of us have," Garrus said, while Zorah nodded sadly. "Did you ... see who killed them?" he asked slowly.

Golden eyes filled her memory. "It was Sther ... a Golden Priestess ... Malvina ... and her two Wardens."

"Sther ..." Garrus exclaimed in horror.

Despair flooded Zorah's eyes. "This means ..."

"How could Seff align with Sther?" Garrus asked angrily.

"We both know he's been pushing for it." Zorah shook his head.

"But we still don't know for sure ... we need to keep an eye on him ... but it won't be enough."

Kayt watched Zorah and Garrus eye each other. It seemed as if they had been suspecting the possibility for some time now. She could tell they had a plan in motion--they had just yet to fill her in on it.

"What ... are you going to do?"

Zorah sighed heavily and nodded at Garrus. He returned his nod.

"It's not what *we* are going to do that matters ... it's what *you* will do next that will make the difference."

"What do you mean, Zorah? What do you want me to do?"

"Hawke."

Kayt gasped as a man emerged from the shadows of the window. His hair was white as snow, but his face was young and strong with eyes like dark pits. Wearing all black, he took a position behind Zorah.

"Who ... who is this?"

"This is Hawke ... my man who will be 'watching you,' but you both will do far more than that."

"What do you mean?"

"From the moment you came here Kayt," Garrus said, "Zorah and I knew that you were so much more. You have many skills. We know that you are ruthless and quick thinking. *Princess* isn't enough for you ... you know it, and we know it. *Queen* isn't an option anymore either ... so this is what you will do ... should you choose to agree. And I think you will."

As she looked at the expression upon his face, she knew he was a shrewd thinker, but she had not known the depth of planning that must have taken place between him and Zorah.

"The nation will expect you to disappear for a while ... to be in mourning," Zorah said, sounding out of breath and tired. "It will provide the perfect cover for your training."

"What training?" *What do they want me to do?*

"We need more evidence that Sther was linked with Seff. In addition, we must find out whether Sther was behind the abduction of Demas ... and even possibly igniting the war between us. After that is exposed ... we will have to figure out what to do about Sther." Garrus watched her for her response.

Sther's military might was unknown to her, mostly unknown to everyone in Oldaem. But it was clearly more powerful than anyone had realized. She didn't even want to think what would happen should that nation mount an attack upon Oldaem.

"Hawke is an ex-Warden for the Three. But now he works for me. He can ... sense the power in others ... he can ... track those who have it," Zorah said with a careful smile.

"So you want me to ..."

Garrus interrupted her. "We want you to accompany Hawke. You will receive intensive training ... then, leave the Capital ... track the murderous priestess Malvina ... get the answers we need ..."–his eyes glistened–"and then kill her."

"You will be the New Order's first Priestess Hunter," Zorah explained. "We will handle matters here ... if I know Seff ... his next step will be to make an official alliance with Sther in order to eradicate Leoj completely ... there will be a Stherian Ambassador within our walls soon.

"If we charge Allora with the murder, the war with Leoj will intensify ... and she may even be executed for a crime they did not commit ... but if we play our cards right ... if we keep this information to ourselves ... we may be able to prevent a catastrophic war with Sther. Once we know the truth about Seff, and have the tangible proof we need ... and the head of Malvina ... we'll be in a much better position."

Kayt looked over at Hawke who continued to stare into seeming nothingness.

Poor Allora ... but what I can do for her?

"Why me?" Kayt asked. It was almost too much to take in and was so different than her own plans. She had dreamt of power, of becoming a Royal Shepherd someday. Every thing she had done ... every action she had performed had been toward that goal. Now everything was changing once again. A new power was stirring within her, a new drive. *A Priestess Hunter ... for the One ...*

"Did you ever stop to think, that perhaps the One placed you here for this purpose ... placed you in that royal chamber to witness what you did ... brought you here to the inner sanctum of Oldaem Realm ... for such a time as this?" Zorah asked. "Oldaem is going to need to be more unified now than ever before. These priestesses have caused so much chaos and devastation ... I believe the One sent you, ... a warrior ... *mentally* ... and soon physically ... to accomplish what he needs you to do in order to eradicate darkness from the land." Zorah spoke with such power and passion that the room almost seemed to shake beneath her. "You've been chosen, Kayt."

What an honor. What a privilege.

Not that long ago she had stood dejected on a hill overlooking a library, with an ignorant Old Order Shepherd filling her head with lies ... she had nothing ... she had lost everything ... but now ... all of Oldaem was at her fingertips. Energy surged through her. She would be the one to make the nation complete. And it started with the blood of the priestess.

"We will tell the people you have entered a period of mourning ... Seff too ... when in reality ... your training will begin immediately," Zorah said, glancing up at Hawke.

"You asked, 'Why you?'" Garrus approached her and looked into her eyes. "You *know* the answer, Kayt."

"Because I'm a monster."

"So ... let the training begin." Hawke stretched out his hand for hers.

She rose and took it. They walked out of the chamber together, darkness all around them ... behind her ... and before her.

Once, a monster raising an angel, but now, I'm a monster for the One.

CHAPTER 70: GALEN

The view from Princess Allora's balcony was beautiful. Galen leaned back against the bench he and Allora were sitting on. After their day spent in the Capital, Gadiel had received permission to go to his father's estate and be with his family. He was to report to the palace every morning until his orders changed. It did not appear that either of them would be going back to Sea Fort anytime soon as long as they were useful to the king and his Royal Shepherd puppets. Actually, Galen was starting to wonder if he had it backwards and the Royal Shepherds were the ones pulling the strings.

Either way, the palace halls had been eerily silent for the past few hours. Nobody bothered them. The whole situation was odd. First they treated Allora practically like an animal, and then as a guest. He would never understand their motivations.

"Who was it that you seemed so eager to talk to in the arena earlier?" Allora broke the peaceful silence. She had unbound her hair, and it flowed softly over her blue dress. In all appearances she looked relaxed, but Galen knew that she wasn't. She couldn't be as long as she was still a prisoner in Oldaem.

"An old friend. The one I said you reminded me of."

"And you didn't know she'd be there?"

"No, it was a total surprise." Galen shook his head.

"And the person who attacked you, did you know him, too?"

Galen looked at her abruptly. Having not told her about that, he hadn't thought she knew.

"Gadiel told me," she explained. "When you were talking with your friend."

Galen sighed. *Of course.* Even when Gadiel wasn't present he could still manage to get on his nerves. "Sounds as if you and Gadiel are best friends now."

She grinned. "It helps that he doesn't hate me anymore."

"Well, I still dislike him."

"He saved your life."

"Yeah, he keeps reminding me about that."

561

"Sounds familiar," Allora giggled. It was nice to hear her laugh. "You two are more alike than either of you realize."

Galen groaned. "Let's change the subject, please."

"Does it hurt?" Allora asked, gesturing at his side.

"Not as much as what it symbolizes," he mumbled.

Allora didn't know what he meant, but it didn't seem to matter. "Do you ever wonder ... why things happen?"

"All the time," he replied, staring at his hands.

"Ever found any answers?"

"Nothing that doesn't sound like fantasy."

Allora looked out at the trees below the balcony. By now it was growing dark, but they were still easy to make out. "I've been thinking about our conversation in the inn at Kaya lately. And I think maybe we were wrong."

"Wrong about what?"

"Thinking that no one's out there. Thinking that no one cares."

"Did you get those ideas from Gadiel?" he groaned. *Not Allora, too.* He thought she was too smart for that religious nonsense.

"No, I've just been thinking," she insisted. "Everything that's been going on. The war, the deaths. It can't all be for nothing ... it just can't."

Galen shook his head adamantly. "See, I used to think so, too. That, yeah, maybe someone out there did care for me. Maybe even the Order. And when I thought about it I felt needed and it was great. For about five seconds. And then everything got worse. I'm not saying the Order isn't out there. They might even be watching us. But they don't care what happens to us."

"That's what I'm struggling with, too," Allora admitted. "Why did my mother and brother have to die? Why do I have to be a prisoner in Oldaem?"

"And have you found an answer?"

"No." She frowned. "But I'm starting to find peace. I don't think the Order had anything to do with all the bad things that have happened. And maybe I'll never understand why. All I know is that when I gave my fear up to them, it ... it worked. I feel stronger now. I feel like I can face anything."

Galen never got the chance to respond.

But Shepherd Seff did.

"So you've found religion," he smirked. Galen and Allora jumped off the bench. Galen moved protectively in front of the princess. Seff was standing in the doorway with several armed guards, their swords drawn. "Good. You're gonna need it where you're going."

"What are you doing here?" Allora asked.

He stepped forward. "Princess Allora, you are under arrest for the murders of King Orcino and Prince Gragor."

"What?" Both Galen and Allora asked in shock. The king was dead? How could that be? But Allora could not have done it even if she had wanted to. Galen had guarded her all day. Unless …

"And you're under arrest for high treason," Seff continued, turning to Galen. "We know you helped her kill them."

Then everything erupted into chaos. Galen managed to disarm the guard closest to him, but as he grabbed for the sword, another guard kicked it off the balcony. The unarmed guard was pinned below him, but viciously resisting, and now the other guard closed in quickly. Galen felt himself lifted off the ground by the back of his shirt. The guard below him swiftly punched him in the stomach.

With a moan, he doubled over, but then jerked backward and slammed his assailant in the face. The hand on his shirt disappeared. However, the guard on the floor in front of him had not, and he jerked Galen's leg from under him and he hit the ground with a thud, knocking his breath out.

There were simply too many of them.

A well-placed boot smashing into Galen's face was all it took to subdue him. His face exploded into a wave of pain and nausea and briefly he wondered if his nose was broken.

Despite his blurry vision, Galen could just make out Allora trying desperately to fight off too many guards. A boot dug painfully into his back, while unseen hands wrenched his arms tightly behind his back and secured them in chains.

Allora went down. Someone grabbed her arms too, but they did not stop hitting her. Galen screamed for them to stop, but no one seemed to hear him. Someone yanked him up by his hair.

Before Galen knew it he and Allora were marched down to the dungeons of Oldaem. Alone. Without an ally. And framed for murder.

CHAPTER 71: DAKU

Too far gone.

The door closed behind the assassins as they entered their room at the inn. Laughter and tales of the recently concluded tournament filled the room. People had no idea their royal king and prince were dead, no idea what would happen next.

Malvina and Jorn smiled at each other as they held hands and ascended the stairs before Daku. No longer did he experience golden flashes or have a headache. It was as if Malvina had used up all she needed of him, as if he no longer had a purpose. Now it was time for him to die.

Fully aware that Malvina would kill him at any moment, he was ready for it. The burden of his life had become too much to bear, too overwhelming. No matter what he did or said, it wasn't enough to overcome the darkness around him. He realized this time it was a golden darkness. It had ruled his heart, clouded his mind, and filled him with a power that had destroyed him. Daku recognized that darkness and light could not coexist within his heart. He had tried to make it work by hanging on to both Aelwynne and Malvina. But it was impossible. Now he had to make a choice, one that he had done again and again. But in doing so he had broken the heart of the only source of light he had. And because of that, it was time for him to die.

"No. You're not too far gone."

Daku stopped on the steps.

What was that? he asked himself.

Glancing around, he saw no one near him. People continued to chatter with each other in the tavern, unaware that Daku was even there. The innkeeper laughed uproariously. Suddenly Malvina stopped and turned around and looked at him pathetically.

"Daku, stop dawdling. Come meet your fate." Then she resumed climbing the stairs, Jorn chortling in front of her.

"Who is there?" Daku whispered softly.

"You're not too far gone. There is always Najoh. There is always light."

As Daku felt peace wash over him he knew that he wasn't hearing an audible voice. But he felt words pour deeply into his hurting soul. A wave of love swept through him.

What is happening to me?

"Remember ... the Wall ..."

564

Tears filled his eyes at the memory of three innocent names carved upon stone.

No ... I'm too far gone. I gave it all up already. I chose darkness. I chose death. The wave consumed me.

"I don't care ... I choose you."

Daku didn't know what was happening as a mixture of confusion and fear and relief filled him. *Why relief?* Because for the first time in a long time ... he realized he still may have ... *hope.* Slowly he sat down on the stairs, and listened.

"Daku ... you are not too far gone ... you have hope."

But ... everything I've done ...

"I don't care ... I love you anyway."

I've stolen.

"I love you."

I've betrayed.

"I love you."

I've killed.

"I still love you."

I broke ... my vows.

"I'll keep mine."

I ... forgot how to love ...

"I'll teach you again."

I stopped believing ...

"I believe in you."

But why? I don't understand!

"It's simple, young hero ... because ... I ... love ... you. And always will."

Who are you?

"I think you know ... deep inside ... you know, your mother ... knew me."

My ... mother?

"Don't give up, Daku. Fight. Fight for light. Fight for truth. Fight for love. Don't ... give up. I love you. I need you. I remember you. Don't ... give ... up."

"The Creator ... the Comforter ... and the Liberator."

"I ... see," Sten replied, looking doubtful and shaking his head.

Daku sat on the dock, dangling his feet into the water. It was a warm sunny day in Aramoor. He looked at Galen paddling around and rolled his eyes. The waves were gentle today, so gentle that even Bug seemed to manage them. Then Daku returned his attention to his father and the conversation he was having with a Free Lamean who was helping him prepare the small fishing boat they were about to embark upon together. One thing Daku noticed about his father was that he didn't care where someone was from--he would talk to *anyone*. His dad had noticed that Galen had been glaring at the Lamean the entire morning.

Galen ... not all Lameans beat you up.

"So ... what exactly is their purpose?" Sten asked the Lamean.

A kind smile came to the fisherman's eyes. "To save Oldaem."

"From what?" Sten asked.

Daku wondered why his dad suddenly cared so much about this Old Order religion. They weren't religious at home at all. But apparently his mother had been.

He winked down at Bug who had grabbed his feet. She was becoming really pretty for a 13-year-old girl. Galen began kicking his legs, and she bobbed up and down in the water as she hung on to his feet.

"To save Oldaem from the Betrayer. But you know what the most amazing part about the Order is?"

"What?" Sten seemed incredibly interested.

"They still love him. They *still* feel remorse for the actions of the Betrayer. If he had been repentant ... if he had been truly sorry for what he did ... if he had not forgotten how to love ... Oldaem would be a very different place now."

"They still ... love him?"

"Yes." The Lamean looked up into the clouds and smiled. "And they still love us when we fail them."

"Wow ..." Sten's smile seemed put on. "That sounds like a nice bedtime story ... but *how* could it be real?"

"What would be the point of living, my friend ... if we existed only to die and be forgotten, our legacies and our actions not mattering ... everything we did ... slipping through the sands of time?" Passion now filled his voice. "I have *hope,* because I *believe* that the Liberator will come again and free us from this. And even if I die before it happens ... someday soon I'll be raised up again to meet in the streets of Aael all those I love and have lost." His eyes had misted. "It's why I know it doesn't matter what happens to me here, even if I don't know who I am or whom I should be. It doesn't matter if I'm not good enough or too far-gone. It ... does ... not ... matter, ...

because I have a Creator ... Comforter ... and Liberator ... who are enough for me ... and who are all those things for me ... it's enough, Sten, my friend. I hope someday you'll see it, too."

Sten didn't answer. Instead he turned to his son. "Daku, I'm going fishing for a while, make sure you keep your friends safe. I'll be back soon. I love you."

Daku watched the small boat sail away with his dad into the bay.

"Do you believe all that stuff, Daku?" Bug asked him.

"I don't know."

"Could there *really* be people up there in those clouds that ... *love* us ... no matter what we do? Doesn't seem very fair for them," she said, pulling herself up on the dock.

"No ... it doesn't. Maybe that's the point."

The three of them found themselves on their backs, gazing up into the cloudless sky.

"I hope it's true," Daku said after a long silence.

"Really? Why?" Bug asked him.

"So I can meet my mom. So Galen can meet his dad. So *you* can have a family who loves you ... besides us."

Hope ... is a powerful thing. We all need a little bit of hope. Heroes give hope.

Daku smiled. True or not, it was then he decided he would give hope to his two friends who depended so much on him.

The other stuff, he would figure out later. He would need more proof. Oldaem would need more proof.

"Guys ... can we just ... pretend ... for a moment ... just for a *moment* ... that it *is* true? That the Comforter, Creator, and Liberator ... *are* true ... and that they ... *love* us?"

"What?" Galen abruptly sat up. "Believe what the *Lameans* do?"

Sayla punched him in the arm. "Come on, *Galen,* just for a second? I think it's a nice idea."

"I'll put you in a choke hold if you don't," Daku smirked.

"Ugh ... *fine.*"

The three of them reclined in silence, the summer breeze blowing over them. They let themselves believe. They let themselves ... rest. Daku suddenly remembered the Wall and sighed comfortably.

"How do ... you feel?" he asked, not opening his eyes.

"*Loved,*" Bug breathed.

"*Needed,*" Galen whispered.

Daku said nothing. The others opened their eyes and looked at him. He could feel their gaze on him.

"How about *you?*" Galen asked.

"Forgiven."

"Do it," Malvina commanded, sitting on the bed.

Tied to a chair and stripped down to his undergarments, Daku eyed Jorn who held a sharp knife. He had never seen the man smile so intensely. Malvina rose and then knelt beside her Warden.

"Do you know why this is happening?" she whispered, a sour smell coming from her lips.

Because I'm too far gone.

"No you're not," the voice breathed.

"Because you are *weak*. In Sther, the weak are put out of their misery. I do you a favor today, Daku . . . Esis would eat you up and spit you out. You're not strong enough to handle what is to come. The Golden Power has no use for a mind so weak."

"I love you," the voice whispered again.

"You have failed at everything. You have failed everyone ... you have failed me. You have failed A'delath, you have failed the Three ... you failed your *father* ... "

"Fight, Daku ... please ... fight."

"You failed *Galen* ... and *Bug* ... you failed ... *Aelwynne* ..."

"Don't ... say ... her ... name."

She laughed. "I'm sorry ... did you say *something?*" She leaned closer, her golden eyes twitching.

"Don't ... say ... her ... name."

He watched her stand to her full height, Jorn nearby, gripping the knife.

"Or *what?*" she hissed.

"Or I'll *kill* you."

"I love you. I forgive you. I need you. Fight, Daku."

"Aelwynne." Then she turned away and waved her hand.

That's when the knife sliced into Daku's arm.

He screamed in pain, as Jorn twisted it and yanked it out, blood dripping down. Waves of pain and terror blasted throughout him.

"Finish him," he heard her say.

Jorn lunged at him, and Daku threw his weight toward the right, knocking the chair over and himself to the floor. As Jorn tried to slash him with the knife, Daku squirmed and fought against his bindings.

SOMEONE, HELP ME! ANYONE! CREATOR! COMFORTOR! LIBERATOR! HELP ME!

He strained against the ropes holding him. Suddenly they snapped as he rolled away from Jorn and the knife stabbed into the wooden floor.

"Kill him!" Malvina shouted.

Staggering to his feet, Daku knocked the knife out of Jorn's hands.

The Warden's dull eyes met his as the man pounced on him, his leathery hands wrapping around Daku's throat. Fighing for breath, Daku tore at Jorn's hands, but he couldn't free himself. He could faintly hear Malvina's laughter as the world around him began to fade into a golden darkness. A golden darkness he was familiar with. A part of him wanted to sink into it, to rest in it and shut out the world forever.

It was a world that never seemed to give him the peace or freedom or forgiveness he longed for. Malvina was right. He had failed, wasn't a hero. In fact, he was nothing—was worthless. His life had been one of constant loss: Bug ... Galen ... his father . . . Aelwynne. He had never let himself believe since that moment with his little family by the waters of Aramoor. Maybe if he had, life would have gone differently ... or maybe it would have been just as difficult, but he remembered now how he felt in that moment ... *forgiven.* It was the one thing he craved, but the one thing he couldn't allow himself to hope for. But the voice whispering in his head, that loving voice continued to wait for it to be allowed inside, unlike Malvina's shouts and screams. This one was different ... this one was ... full of *light.*

He embraced the voice ... embraced the light ... let it calm his nerves ... prayed again in his mind, and put all his strength in shoving Jorn backward.

Jorn's hands still clung to his neck, but Daku's legs were free. He began to run toward the Warden, the room whirling past him, Golden Darkness approaching ... and Jorn back-peddling in fear. The momentum became so great they were almost tumbling over each other. With a desperate burst of strength, Daku lunged forward, and before he knew it, Jorn's grip released as glass smashed like a broken mirror of regret, and Daku watched as Jorn crashed through the window behind him and tumbled down into the street beneath the second-story window of their room. Blood pooled beneath Jorn's body.

Daku felt breath return to him, the golden darkness diminishing as he gingerly touched his neck. Pain flared in his throat. Slowly he turned around to see Malvina standing there in shock and fear.

"Daku ... I."

"Don't ... move."

"Well done ... you proved yourself." She smiled nervously.

"Shut up," he snapped.

"I *planned* for you to do that. Killing Jorn was what I've been *wanting* you to do from the beginning!"

The desperation in her words revealed to Daku that her Golden power only worked on the mind and couldn't possibly defend her from physical harm. She wasn't a Crimson Priestess.

"You destroyed my life." Anger surged in his gut.

"I ... you were strong ... you're the strongest we've ever seen in the Tower."

"You lied to me!"

"I was only trying to make you stronger!"

"You took *everything* from me," he hissed as she backed away, terror in her eyes.

Her eyes flashed. "Varic!"

"Varic is *dead*!" Then he slapped her face, and she fell to the floor.

Daku towered above her, Malvina on her hands and knees, crawling quickly to the door. He placed his bare foot on her back, pinning her down.

"Help!" she screamed. "Someone help me!"

Turning her over, he glared into the eyes that had once entranced him ... eyes he now wanted to pluck out. "Shut up, or you die *now*."

Suddenly her screams ceased and a strange smile transformed her face. "Yes ... Daku ... of course ..." He looked at her in confusion.

"What?"

"Do it." He felt her stop struggling beneath him. "Do what you do best ... kill me. It's who you are. It's what you do. In killing me ... you'll take my power with you." The smile intensified. "Make me proud."

At the moment he wanted nothing more than to kill her, to feel her blood on his hands, to avenge all those she had caused him to murder. He *wanted* to kill her. Daku felt his hands tighten around her neck. Her golden eyes began to bulge, and he squeezed tighter.

"Daku ..."

"Leave me alone!" he shouted! That voice must not witness this.

"Daku ... I love you. I forgive you. Don't ... do ... this."

"Who ... are you talking to?" she coughed and asked as she struggled for breath.

"Shut up!"

"Daku ... don't."

"IF YOU'RE REAL, PROVE IT! SHOW ME YOURSELF! DO SOMETHING!" He continued to strangle her as tears streamed down his face. "SAVE ME FROM MYSELF!"

Silence.

As he stared at the helpless woman beneath his grip, the face of the gardener looked up at him ... the face of the Spirit Shepherd ... the king ... the prince ... Galen ... the child by the well ... his father ... Aelwynne ...

"You wanted this," Malvina painfully breathed. "From the beginning ... *this* is what you wanted ... you did this for *you.*"

"You're right." Swallowing, he released his grip. "And now I don't do this for *me* ... I don't even do this for *Aelwynne* ... I do this for *Them.*" He struck her in the head in just the right place.

Then he stood and stared at the Golden Priestess lying before him. Taking the ropes that had once bound him, he tied her to the bed. Remembering her touch, he shuddered. She continued to breathe, unconscious beneath him.

Almost in a daze, he looked around the room. Furniture had been destroyed and shattered glass had been strewn across the floor. Daku noticed shards of it in his chest, and he had almost forgotten about his stab wound. Hobbling over to the broken window, he stared down into the street. A large pool of blood stained the street, but Jorn's body was gone.

After cleaning himself up, dressing himself and his wound, Daku descended the stairs. He realized the noise from the dining hall must have been so loud that no one had heard the struggle above. People were still celebrating and laughing and dancing and *living.*

Daku pushed open the door to the streets. They were mostly emptying out for the night. Stepping away from the inn, he started down the streets of Oldaem Realm. As he walked along, candlelight twinkled in windows, and he could see families putting their children to bed for the night. People praying and smiling and laughing and talking and resting. He wanted nothing more than to be like them.

All night he wandered each district of the city, contemplating what to do next, gathering up the courage to do it. Every now and and then he eyed one of the gates exiting from the city. He wondered, as he looked at each house, what stories its residents might tell. What failings had they made? What vows had they broken? How had they faced each and every day? For the first time in a long time everything was clear before him. Taking a deep breath, he gazed up into the stars and allowed himself to think of Aelwynne without fear or guilt.

At last he understood how and why all of it had happened. Having loved Aelwynne almost too much, he had placed that love before everything else, and had used it as an excuse to perform the dark deeds he had. It had allowed him to become selfish. His sins had tainted their love, had been an excuse for him to do things for *himself* instead of for others. She had been his fatal flaw.

Now, we'll start over, Aelwynne. Let's start over believing in something ... something more powerful than golden darkness ... something more powerful than evil ... something that whispers my name ... and captivates my heart ...

"To whoever is up there ... I'm sorry ... I'm so ... sorry. Please ... *forgive* me." And he meant it.

What he had done still stained his hands. Who he had been would still plague his heart. But he would keep believing regardless. And keep fighting. *Maybe that's the best we can do ... maybe* They *will do the rest.*

Tomorrow he would take a ship to Najoh where Aelwynne was waiting ... where hope was waiting ... where love was waiting.

Daku walked the streets of the Capital hand-in-hand with silver shadows of Aelwynne and Sayla and Galen and his father. They laughed and remembered. Apologizing, they were forgiven. And they agreed to start over, to press on, and to hold true to that vow on the Wall. They looked at him as their hero ... and he would be ... forever ... no matter what he faced. No golden wave was hovering over them. They were free. When he looked around and saw no one beside him, he smiled.

I'll be okay. Someday Esis will be made whole. Someday we can change and be forgiven. Someday we can be together in Najoh.

Finally he felt loved.

Finally he felt needed.

Finally he felt *forgiven.*

"What's Your Name?"

"Daku."

"What do you do?"

"I'm a husband."

"What do you believe in?"

"I don't know yet, but something ... someday soon."

"Whom do you love?"

"Aelwynne."

CHAPTER 72: COLE

Cole sat beside his father in the stands of the arena. Still unable to believe it was true, he squeezed his dad's hand to make sure he was still there. Lily sat on the other side of his father and Fenris next to her. He wished he could be between his dad and his brother, but at the moment he was sitting next to an old woman who kept sneezing.

Cole was overwhelmed with the amount of people who thronged the arena. He had never seen so many all in one place. The tournament had ended the day before, and it was time for the closing ceremony.

After they had run into their father a lot of tears and explanations and stories had followed. He had immediately taken them into a private room only Shepherds had access to in the underbelly of the arena. There they spent the rest of the day talking. The room was lavish and had the softest couch Cole had ever sat on.

"You knew?" Cole asked with disappointment? "You knew mom was dead?"

"Yes," Brulis said, hanging his head.

"Then how could ..." Anger flamed up in the boy.

"Cole," Fenris interjected, "let him speak."

"I'm sorry." Tears filled their father's eyes as he reached for Fenris' hand, who was beside him on the couch. The three of them sat in a row as Lily, her sad eyes staring at them, occupied a chair. "I *wanted* to come home immediately, of *course* I did ... but I received word that ... well ... of things I can't talk about ... It was necessary for me to come here to the Capital ... I *need* to be here for now." He glanced over at Fenris. "I knew Fenris and Arissa would take good care of you until I was able to make it home, and I can't *believe* you came here."

"We needed you," Lily said dejectedly.

"I need you, too," he sighed back.

With that, Lily rushed over, and they hugged and cried together.

They didn't talk about him coming home again. After insisting that he needed to be in the Capital, and that they must trust him, and that they should head back home as soon as possible, they hesitantly agreed. Their father handed them quite a large sum of money to carry them through at least six months. Fenris would stay with them to protect them. After the closing ceremonies ended he would send them away safely on a ship. But he would return home when he could. And he *promised* that he would come soon. Cole determined to wait for him on the roof every day until he did. After all, he was used to that.

The crowds watched as the Tournament Mistress took the platform. Cole looked down at the stadium and saw all the competitors sitting in chairs nervously waiting to hear their fates. He chuckled at the sight of the Tournament Mistress who was already out of breath because of her weight. She reminded him a bit of Martha, the old woman who had taken them with her husband, Wilber, on the cart. Now he wondered how the couple was doing. He often thought about all they had gone through on the way to the Capital. It may have been a mistake, but he had grown up a lot during it, learning a lot more about who he was. But he still knew he had much more to discover.

"Welcome to the closing ceremonies!" The crowd cheered wildly.

Cole cheered with them, his voice mixing with his family's.

Everything will finally be okay.

"Today, we appoint twenty-four fresh new Shepherds ... the brightest future prospects Oldaem has!"

Cole watched as three older Shepherds joined her on the platform and were introduced as the three Headmasters of the academies. And Cole realized he recognized the older woman from The City of Flowers. She was the Headmistress of Middle Lake Academy. Today it would be accepting eight new first-year students each, two for each category.

The Headmaster from Woodlands Academy began first. He called out names as girls and boys excitedly made their way to the front. The Headmaster told each new Shepherd why they had scored the points they did, and what type of Shepherd they would become. Eight newly appointed Shepherd Trainees stood proudly behind the headmaster.

Next, Middle Lake Academy went, and none of the victors really stood out to Cole, except for one guy whom Lily said was really handsome. He had seen some posters of him in the streets. The crowd began chanting "Bumo! Bumo!" as he approached with a broad smile. Once he was appointed to be a Defense Shepherd Trainee he crowed like a rooster. The crowd went wild again, and Cole laughed.

The Westpoint Academy Headmaster was the last one to stand. Only eight more remained to be chosen. Cole wanted it to last forever, because he knew after it was finished, he would be heading home on a ship, away from his dad. He clung to his father's hand tighter than before. The Headmaster rattled off the names of the victors as they each came up and claimed their prizes: bright futures as Shepherds.

"Come on, let's leave so we can beat the crowd out. There's only one more to go." he heard his father say, as Cole watched him rise. He stood, too, watching Lily and Fenris follow their father up the stairs toward the exit.

"Cole, come on," Fenris said.

Cole heard the crowd cheering, but missed the name of the last winner. He stepped out of the row of seats and hurried after his family up the stairs. They disappeared through the exit door, and Cole turned around one last time to get a glimpse of the final winner. Then he laughed when he saw a tall, heavyset, dark-haired boy accept the mantel of Spirit Shepherd. He couldn't be sure, but he could have sworn he saw tears in the kid's eyes.

"Bad things are always going to happen to you, Cole." Brulis' eyes looked deeply into those of his son.

Cole looked away toward Lily and Fenris who stood hand in hand. They had already said their goodbyes to their father. Now they waited for Cole by the gangplank of the ship that would carry them home.

"Sometimes life can get out of control. There is nothing you can do about it. You have to figure out how to be okay ... even if you're not." He knelt down and put his hands on the boy's shoulders. "I've learned in my life that we can't do it alone." Then he eyed Fenris who was nodding. "I know Fenris has spoken to you of the Old

Order. It was all I asked him to do for you while I was gone. Cole ... they are *real,* and they love you. Get to know them."

As Cole felt his dad kiss his forehead, a lump formed in his throat. He didn't want to be separated from him again.

"You can't blame others for everything that happens to you, Cole. At some point in your life ... you're going to have to accept the blame for your own actions and accept the consequences. It's a part of growing up and becoming a man." Brulis smiled gently. "But because of the Order's love for us ... if we only *ask* for forgiveness and turn down a different path ... a better path ... they will always accept us ... no matter what we've done." Hugging his son tightly, he whispered, "There is no better way." Cole never wanted to let him go. "What you did to find me was very brave. I'm very proud of you, my son. Keep taking care of Lily ... and look after Belen. I'll be home soon. I promise."

"I love you, Daddy."

"I love you, son."

After one final prayer as a family, Cole stood watching his father disappear into the crowd. Maybe his dad was right--that he *was* responsible for his actions and their consequences. Perhaps it was time to stop accusing the Order for his mother's death. To stop blaming others for everything. He had been unhappy because it's what he had chosen to be. But maybe, with the help of a loving family and an Order up above who might love him ... maybe he could finally choose the right things.

Maybe today will be the day.

Then he turned to face his siblings. He loved them so much. Cole hoped someday to be half the man Fenris was. He was so good and strong and smart. Fenris would keep them safe, would be what his dad needed him to be.

Lily smiled back, a tooth recently missing. She looked so much older than she had before before their journey to the Capital. Cole felt great respect for this little sister who had braved the journey with him, and who had emerged stronger and wiser and braver than he had. She had been right all along. And Azriel. He thought how things would have gone if he had listened to them from the beginning. Maybe it would have been easier.

"Come on, Cole! It's time to go home," she said with a smile as she stepped onto the ship.

Cole stood at the bottom of the gangplank and looked up at Fenris who was busy talking to some of the crewmembers. Then he decided to take one final look at the Capital. He wondered what his father had to do ... who his father had to protect. While he didn't know when he would ever return to the city, he decided that if he did he would be a new Cole ... a better Cole. At last he started to board the ship.

A strong blow struck the back of his skull.

And then he saw only darkness.

Cole awoke with a throbbing head and a dry throat. He had no idea where he was or what had happened. Struggling to see in the darkness, he could only tell that there was bundles of straw beneath him and that the floor felt dirty. Then he realized that he was rocking back and forth.

Am ... I on a ship?

"Hello?" he called out weakly. His throat hurt. When he touched the back of his head, he felt dried blood beneath his fingers.

What happened? Where am I?

"Shhh!" someone whispered. "She'll hear you," a young voice said. "I don't want her to come in. Not again." Whoever it was sounded as if he or she had been crying.

Cole whipped around but it was too dark to see anyone. "Who are you?" he asked.

"Shut up!" the voice ordered. It sounded like a boy his own age.

Suddenly the cabin door burst open and bright light flooded the room. Blinded, Cole covered his eyes with his hand. As footsteps approached, fear seized his throat. At the same moment he realized he was shackled to the wall. Someone began snoring in the background. The boy who had been talking to him was now pretending to be asleep.

"I see you're awake," the looming figure announced. It was the voice of a woman.

As his eyes adjusted to the light, he could see standing before him a tall thin woman dressed in a red gown, a crimson veil falling before her face. Her hair was dark as it hung behind her back.

"Who ... who are you?"

She continued to stand motionless before him, her face unreadable. Cole was terrified of her.

"Cole ... it's interesting to finally meet you ... lucid. I've heard so much about you."

He couldn't be sure, but he thought she cracked a careful smile.

"Why have you taken me? Where am I? What is going on?"

"So many questions for a boy who was once so confident in what he chose."

What is happening?

She kept her back straight as she kneeled before him. "Are you afraid, child?"

"Very." He couldn't stop shivering.

"Good. You should be. Especially if you are who we think you are." Rising, she started toward the door.

"Wait! Who do you think I am? Where are we going?"

The door closed again, leaving Cole in darkness.

After struggling for a moment against his shackles and realizing it was useless, he fell to the floor in a heap ... defeated ... afraid ... alone.

Slow laughter filled the room. It seemed ... almost familiar to him.

"Hello?" he said uneasily.

"Her name is Verena," someone again whispered. "She's a Crimson Priestess of the Three."

"Who ... who are you? Why are we in here?" The cabin was black as night.

"We sail towards Sther ... towards A'delath ... the High Priestess of the Three ... it is she who will know ... the truth about you." The whispering seemed to get louder ... it was approaching him.

"What about me?" Cole demanded. He was getting frustrated, but he was even more afraid.

He heard the sound of a match striking as someone lit a small lantern. The figure holding it was still a ways across the room, but the light bobbed nearer and nearer. Cole's fear intensified.

"Who ... who are you?" Cole struggled to swallow.

"I ... am her Warden."

"Who ... does ... she think I am?"

"For months ... she ... has been following you ... she has been watching you like a crimson shadow in the night."

A shadow!

"She has been ... waiting to see what you would do ... a boy around your age ... what you would choose ... to see if you have incredible knowledge or faith in the Old Order ... if you are without blemish ... or taint ... of the darkness." The whispering figure came nearer, the light only illuminating a somewhat muscular arm.

578

"That's not me ... I'm ... not ... perfect."

"No ... but you have chosen ... light," the whisper said in disgust. "You're not special ... you are one of many being taken to Sther ... because *he* must be ... stopped."

"Who?" Cole asked, his shivering intensifying as the sickly yellow light approached. Although he strained to see, he couldn't makeout any details in the face before him.

"The Liberator. He has come."

Shock struck him. "You think *I* am the Liberator?" Confusion swept through him. *A shadow! Watching me for months? Her Warden? The Liberator? Me?*

"Perhaps time ... will ... tell. A'delath will decide." The Warden set the lantern on the floor, revealing bare feet. The person's face was still hidden in the darkness.

"What's your ... name?"

"If you are the Liberator ... you ... will die."

Horror filled Cole as the face entered the light, a face he had once loved and trusted--Zek.

EPILOGUE

A tall man watched as the funeral procession made its way through the rainy streets of the Capital. Endless throngs of people dressed in black grieved for their beloved king and prince. A small path cleared for the Royal Shepherds who sadly followed after the coffins of the deceased royal family. The princess, dressed in black lace, a black veil shielding her from the prying eyes of the people, accompanied them.

Whispers of murder and treachery spread through the crowds. No one was entirely sure what had happened on that final night of the tournament events when the king and prince were found dead in their chambers. Some whispered it was suicide, stating the responsibilities of the crown had been too much to bear for someone so gentle as King Orcino. Others said they had succumbed to the pressures of war. A few stated they had died at the hands of the princess, who was intent upon seizing Oldaem Realm for herself. Perhaps, some suggested, the Royal Shepherds had killed them, plunging the nation into a dictatorship. Some put the blame on Sther, that a Crimson Priestess had been seen fleeing the palace late that night after the murders. Others argued that it had been a Lamean plot to return Oldaem to Old Order ways. Most, however, believed that Allora, the Princess of Leoj had somehow evaded the guards, slipped into the inner chambers, and took the innocent lives of their rulers.

The man joined the procession as it led to the royal catacombs, the place all Oldaem royalty were finally laid to rest. A scaffold had been erected for the ceremony, and it was there the Royal Shepherds took their places, along with the Princess of Oldaem. The crowds watched as the coffins were lowered into their final resting place. Following the Oldaem fanfare played by trumpets and horns, the Royal Shepherds took their turns providing words of peace and comfort to the people of Oldaem Realm.

First the newly named Royal Shepherd of Defense, Seff stated that it would be his personal mission to ensure the safety of the people of Oldaem. That he would see to it personally that those responsible would meet their much-deserved justice.

Mind Shepherd Udina challenged the people of Oldaem to find ways that they could better the lives of all those around them. That each and every one of them had a role to fill in Oldaem, and he urged them to fill that role to the best of their abilities.

State Shepherd Garrus explained that the Realm was in good hands—those of the Royal Shepherds—until the people elected a new Monarch, and that Princess Kayt would be entering a period of mourning for an undetermined amount of time. Murmuring began to spread as he announced that Princess Allora of Leoj had been charged with the murder of the king and prince, and that she had been taken into custody and would be sentenced to death. He added that the war with Leoj would intensify, and that all must continue to provide resources for the war effort.

Then Garrus stepped back, and Zorah slowly approached the front.

The man hadn't intended to stay in the Capital this long. He had been planning on getting a ship several days earlier, but it had proved more challenging than he had expected. He decided at least to remain until the royal funeral ceremonies concluded. After all, as a loyal citizen of Oldaem, he felt he owed the crown at least his presence.

Finally, Spirit Shepherd Zorah offered up a closing prayer to the One, the dominant religion in Oldaem. He challenged all to give their hearts to the One during this uncertain time. Then he continued with warnings of pagan religions and false beliefs that would undermine Oldaem. He spoke of religious unity and togetherness and called for greater religious fervor.

Then, remembering that his ship would depart within the hour, the watcher's thoughts turned to figuring out how to maneuver his way through the crowd. Even as he pushed through it, he kept glancing back to Zorah, ears tuned in to his every word.

"Excuse me, ma'am," he whispered as he pushed past an older woman.

The crowd seemed to squeeze in tighter as he heard Zorah's tone change.

Blocking his way were two very large men, standing side by side. It would be difficult to get by them.

"One more thing," he heard Zorah say.

I guess I can wait until the speech is over, but it will be a mad dash back toward the city center. Eying the people around him, he realized he had no choice. *I hope I make my ship.*

"Because the war with Leoj is intensifying," Zorah continued, "and because it seems they have become bolder by attacking Oldaem bridges and villages on our mainland ... and now because they are responsible for the death of our king ..."

581

People continued to hang on his every word. The tall man turned around and listened intently.

"The Royal Shepherds have decided to ally with Sther."

Shocked gasps and whispering broke out amongst the people. The man swallowed uncomfortably.

"We believe this alliance will win us the war with Leoj and will deter any other foreign nations from allying with Leoj, until we can vanquish them."

The whispers turned into animated discussion, as the man peered up at the scaffold. It seemed someone was walking up the back steps and joining them onto the ledge. Another man suddenly blocked his view, and he had to push past a young man standing beside him.

"Excuse me, I can't see."

The man didn't answer, only leaned against the woman next to him, to get a better view himself.

"To help ease Oldaem into this new alliance, someone has arrived to join our inner council to help with decision making and to guide our nation to peace and a swift resolution to this war." He cleared his throat as a figure dressed in lavender appeared next to him.

Daku gasped in horror.

Zorah's voice rose in a flourish as he addressed the crowd: "Allow me to introduce you to the new Ambassador from Sther ... the Amethyst Priestess ... Aelwynne."

TO BE CONTINUED IN
THE SHEPHERDS OF OLDAEM
BOOK 2: PURSUIT

ABOUT THE AUTHORS

A secondary English instructor at Burton Adventist Academy in Arlington Texas, Devin was born in Punxsutawney, Pennsylvania in 1987 and raised in Keene, Texas. He graduated with his Bachelor of Arts in English from Southwestern Adventist University in 2009 and received his Masters of Divinity from Andrews University in 2012. He has been heavily involved in summer camp ministries, having worked 10 summers as Programs Director at Camp Yorktown Bay, Nameless Valley Ranch, and Lake Whitney Ranch. He has a passion for literature and ministry and loves intertwining God and prose in his classroom. He has written 13 original plays and his hobbies include playing piano, tennis, strategy board games, and hanging out with friends.

Stephanie Wilczynski was born in Orlando, Florida in 1991, but has lived in Texas for the majority of her life. She graduated with a Bachelor of Arts in English and a minor in music from Southwestern Adventist University in 2014. She is very passionate about summer camp and has been involved in the ministry for the past seven summers first as a counselor and lifeguard at Nameless Valley Ranch, then Activities Director at Lake Whitney Ranch. Stephanie has been married to her best friend, Jonny Wilczynski for just over a year. They reside in McAllen, Texas where Stephanie teaches middle school language arts and reading at South Texas Christian Academy.

43033390R00350

Made in the USA
Charleston, SC
14 June 2015